*W*hen the house lights dimmed, the magic began. As the dark velvet curtain separating the orchestra from the audience made its slow, dramatic ascent, the air seemed to lighten, cleansing itself until it was weightless, completely clear, a transparent canvas on which the glory of sound could display its colors. Excitement crackled in the atmosphere with an almost visible electricity that jolted the senses and alerted the soul that something special was about to occur.

The concertmaster stood, placing his violin beneath his chin. A halo of heightened anticipation lit the enormous stage of the Opera Ház with a burnished glow, glittering like the gold leaf that decorated the balcony balustrades and the bronze crystal of the grand chandeliers. His bow stroked the note of C. Sounds filled the hall as the musicians tuned their instruments. Strings squealed. Horns bleated. Oboes, bassoons, and basses moaned a rising dissonance until, when everyone was in accord, the cacophony ceased. The concertmaster took his seat and placed his violin on his lap. Silence descended.

Suddenly, a wild burst of applause overwhelmed the golden auditorium, signaling the appearance of the evening's maestro, Zoltán Gáspár.

As he took his place on the conductor's podium, the audience rose. Shouts of *Bravo!* and waves of raucous enthusiasm greeted him. And then, a hush, a moment of undeniable, unmistakable respect. This man had survived some of Hungary's darkest times. This man had crawled out from the hell of enforced anonymity back into the musical firmament where he belonged. To most people there, Zoltán Gáspár was a true Magyar, a true descendent of Árpád, leader of the seven tribes that swept down from the Urals and formed primitive Hungary. Gáspár had triumphed over those who had worked so hard to squash his spirit and control his soul. He had defied them. Better than that, his presence here this evening proved he had beaten them.

Zoltán acknowledged his audience with a deep, formal bow and a slight uptilt of his lips. Then he turned. His mouth widened into a generous smile as he welcomed his musicians to the performance. Just a few hours before, they had completed their daily four hours of rehearsal. The last run-through, the rehearsal known as the "general," had been flawless. Sometimes that portends a brilliant concert. Sometimes it's an omen of disaster. Tonight, everyone in that orchestra knew he had to push beyond, had to strive for that rare level of excellence that can only be described as inspired. A concert as historic as this deserved nothing less.

Katalin Gáspár paced her dressing room nervously, trying to concentrate on the concerto she was scheduled to play, but her mind was hopelessly distracted. At that very moment a small but intensely loyal coterie was already in place, ready to act. Each of them understood what was expected of him and what he could expect in return if something went wrong. After tonight, Katalin's life would never be the same. In less than two hours, all that she had known would become part of her past; all that she wanted for her future would depend on the mercy of the gods.

Quickly, Katalin turned away from the mirror, reluctant to confront the frightened woman residing there. Instead, her deep-set celadon eyes fixed on the three bouquets that graced the sideboard on the opposite wall. A crystal globe of pale pink tulips was from the man she loved. The Herend vase filled with a dozen red Bulgarian roses was from the man she had once loved but had to leave. And in a humble crockery pot stood a single wild rose, from the man whose friendship had been a lifelong secret.

Unable to contain her thoughts, Katalin opened the door of her dressing room and stepped into the hallway. Just then, the lights of the

Opera House dimmed. The orchestra had completed Zoltán Kodály's "The Peacock." They had accepted their applause and were ready to begin the next selection. The lights backstage also went black. Katalin began to tremble. Her hands grew moist, her breathing rapid and shallow. For as long as she could remember she had been terrified of the dark. Never had the suit of night felt comfortable, never had it brought her peace or solitude. Experience had taught her that bad things happened under the cover of night. Police came. Soldiers came. Death came.

Shutting her eyes against the blackness, she had a flash of unexpected memory. A dark room, suddenly softly lit, and a bright red lamp shade trimmed with plump pompons that bounced and bobbled at the slightest provocation. A smile touching her lips, she thought of him and the first time they made love.

For her, it was the first time ever. They had been sitting in the cramped, dimly lit parlor, holding hands and talking, at first with the caution that accompanies reacquaintance. They talked for hours, until words that earlier in the evening had flowed like wine from a cask slowed, falling from their lips one by one, like the last precious drops in a bottle. The air grew heavy with their intimacy. When finally he kissed her, it was as if time had quickened, telescoping years into minutes, hours into seconds. They clung to each other as if this pocket of privacy had been granted to them with the proviso that it be used then or immediately be forfeited. Soon, the rising heat of their young passion had propelled them into the other room. There, amidst a jumble of lacy throw pillows and crocheted coverlets, they moved toward consummating a relationship that had started years before.

His fingers prowled beneath her clothes, bewitching her, enticing her to surrender to the touch of his hands upon her skin. Intrigued and excited by the exquisite sensations he had awakened within her, she allowed herself to block out everything other than what she was feeling. When he began to undress her, she scurried out of her blouse, desperate to be free of whatever separated her flesh from his. His arm slipped behind her back and unhooked her brassiere. His lips followed his hands, as slowly he removed the silky piece of lingerie. She sighed as her body trembled beneath his. Warmed by the knowledge that he was pleasing her, his hands journeyed further. Suddenly, she pulled away. Startled, he switched on the lights. Assuming she had been struck by an attack of virginal shyness, he searched her face for regret, retreat, perhaps even anger. But she hadn't rushed to cover her breasts. She wasn't blushing. She hadn't moved away.

"I want you," he said quietly, certain he had hurt her, or offended her, "but if you're not ready, I'll wait."

A faint pink wash of embarrassment tinged her cheeks.

"I'm afraid of the dark," she said.

She could still feel the kindness in his touch as his hand patted her face.

"Close your eyes," he said. "The way you do when you're playing the piano." Willingly, she complied.

He took her face in his hands and kissed her, delicately, reassuringly. Then he drew her to him, caressing her body with long, sensuous strokes. He continued to kiss her as gently he laid her down on the bed, disrobing her, exploring the lush landscape of her body. All the while he whispered to her, encouraging her to enjoy the colors rainbowing the inside of her eyelids, to concentrate on nothing other than sensations of the moment. When they had finished, when his lips had reluctantly separated from her flesh, then, and only then, did he allow her to open her eyes. At some point during their lovemaking, he had extinguished the lamp. The room was black.

"I wanted to show you that beautiful things can happen in the dark," he said.

Now, as she stood in the darkened hallway of the Opera House, remembering, she nodded, as if he were there with her.

Tonight I need the darkness to be my friend, she said to herself, afraid even to whisper her thoughts for fear that someone might overhear.

The opening strains of Brahms's "Hungarian Rhapsodies" intruded on her reminiscence. For a moment the music sluiced over her, soothing her, as music always did.

The calm was short-lived. Feeling suddenly energized by a sense of purpose as well as foreboding, Katalin returned to her dressing room and stood before her mirror. As she freshened her makeup, she cleansed her mind of everything except the Liszt she would perform. Mentally, she played each note, reviewed every measure. As she did, her fingers moved up and down an imaginary keyboard while her body swayed to the rhythm of a silent, very personal theme.

Despite her personal stake in the outcome of this concert, as a musician and especially as a Hungarian, tonight's program infused her with pride. It had been designed as a national salute, featuring works by two of Hungary's greatest composers—Liszt and Kodály—as well as Brahms's famous tribute to the melodies of the Magyars.

Katalin had made her own patriotic contribution to the evening. Normally, concert pianists wore black. Their gowns were somber raiments, classic and formal. Makeup was subdued, hairstyles severe. Tonight, though, Katalin's long strawberry-blond hair draped her shoulders, caught by two wooden combs that pulled the luxurious mane from her face. Her skirt was the red of the Hungarian flag; her top, a white, puffy-sleeved peasant's blouse garnished with the boldly colored floral embroidery of the heartland. Wrapped around her hips was a glorious shawl of creamy silk, a sensuously fringed square emblazoned with hand-stitched wildflowers and birds. It had belonged to Mária Gáspár, Katalin's mother. Years ago, Mária had loaned it to Katalin for the final round of the Salzburg Competition in the hope that it would bring her daughter luck. It had. Katalin had won first prize. As she smoothed the folds of the magnificent shawl, she prayed that it still possessed the power of good fortune.

"Ten minutes, Miss Gáspár."

The stage manager had rapped lightly on her door, but the knocking rattled her nonetheless.

"*Köszönöm,*" she said, fighting to control the thunderous pounding of her heart.

With a shaky hand she rouged her lips and smoothed her hair. Drawing a deep breath, she allowed herself one last look at her flowers before taking her place at the side of the stage. As she listened to the orchestra play the last glorious strains of the "Rhapsodies" and waited for her cue, she wondered if this might be her last concert. It was possible, and the thought chilled her. She couldn't imagine a life without performing. She couldn't imagine waking up in the morning without going to the piano to practice. She couldn't imagine never again sharing something as precious as a Beethoven sonata or a Chopin étude with an audience.

But, Katalin thought as she rubbed her arms to smooth the goose bumps that had risen on her skin, she was not the young idealist anymore. She no longer believed she could bury herself in her music and ignore the rest of the world. Tonight she would walk out onto the stage of the Opera Ház an internationally acclaimed pianist, but her celebrity had not come without cost.

There had been years of loneliness and isolation, years of constant battling to lead a normal life. Yet for her, life had never been normal. She had always felt separate and apart, as if she was standing outside looking in. Although she knew she had something that few in the universe possessed, talent was small comfort to a child who'd sacrificed a childhood, to a girl who had tested her friends' loyalties once too often, or to a young woman who had kept love on the shelf so long it had spoiled.

"But," Katalin said aloud, needing to gauge her level of confidence, "you have to forget the past and concentrate on the future. You have to walk out there tonight and give the performance of your life. Because your life depends on it!"

• • •

For the first time in her life, Judit Strasser didn't envy Katalin. It felt strange, actually, anticipating her appearance without feeling a twinge of rivalry pinching her stomach. They had been friends since the cradle— best friends mostly, enemies never—and though Judit loved Katalin with a genuineness common to lifetime relationships, an insistent strain of insecurity had prompted her to challenge that love many times. As she listened to the Brahms, she tried to recall a single moment when she hadn't wished for something Katalin had—her talent, her straight hair, her slim figure, her thick eyebrows, her international fame. Yet at this moment, Judit wouldn't have traded places with Katalin for anything.

Just that afternoon, she had pleaded with Katalin to reconsider her plans. Judit feared for her friend, but more, she couldn't imagine life without Katalin; she couldn't bear the thought of not being near enough to reach out for her or to bask in the warmth of her reflected aura.

"But you don't need me anymore," Katalin had said as a way of allaying Judit's fears.

"I'll always need you," Judit had replied. "Maybe not in the same way as I once did," she added, acknowledging the changes that had taken place in their relationship over the years, the changes that had taken place in her. "But the truth is, I think we share the same heart. I think we were connected at birth and only the skill of a clever surgeon permitted us to live separate lives."

Katalin had laughed. And Judit had laughed. First, because for too long she had feared she would never hear Katalin laugh again, and also because the pure joy in Katalin's laughter had always been infectious.

"That surgeon wasn't as clever as you say," Katalin had told her. "Because your share of the heart has always been bigger and more generous than mine. And besides, if we're both really honest, we never led separate lives, even though God knows there were times when even an ocean wasn't large enough to satisfy our need for distance."

It was then, when Katalin's laughter turned to tears and she grabbed for Judit, clinging to her as they had when they were small, that Judit had admitted she would do whatever Katalin asked, despite the fact that to do so was to put her own life and the lives of her family at risk.

A tired old gelding dragged the gypsy *vardo* along the back road leading to Esztergom. A pregnant mare lumbered behind, her tail swishing flies off her back, her enlarged bottom swaying from side to side as the painted wagon made its way out of Budapest. A young man with mocha skin, licorice hair, and obsidian eyes led the gelding along the path. Bedecked in the flamboyant manner of the Rom—red pantaloons, a green shirt, a paisley vest, a blue kerchief, white socks, black shoes, and of course the thick golden hoop that dangled from his left ear—he whistled as he walked.

His wife, also clad in a cotton rainbow, also laden with chains and earrings and bracelets of gold, perched on the front bench of the *vardo*, her knees splayed, her arms resting on her thighs. Though she was young and slim, her skin was weathered and her posture stooped, making her appear older and harder than she was. As they passed a trio of Hungarian soldiers she bowed her kerchiefed head, to avoid the look of disgust she knew would be in their eyes.

"Where are you going?" one of the soldiers demanded.

"Esztergom," the gypsy answered without breaking his stride.

"What a cesspool you and your kind have made of that city," another soldier said, spitting and wrinkling his nose as he recalled the last time he had been forced to patrol the gypsy camp outside Esztergom.

"Nothing stinks worse than a gypsy," the third soldier added. "Horse shit smells better."

Inside, the gypsy bristled, but his face remained expressionless. He simply continued leading the gelding down the road. Over the years he had become less vulnerable to the stinging pain of prejudice. He believed that, often, the violent hatred of others had served to make the gypsies stronger and more defiant. They had maintained their traditions and their customs despite constant attacks of self-righteous bigotry, despite the numbers they had lost in the Holocaust, despite the general mistrust of just about everyone. There would be no change, because there could never be total assimilation. Aside from the vast dissimilarity in customs, there would always be the obvious difference of color. The others would always be white. And the gypsy would always be brown.

"What are you carrying inside that crate you call a home?"

"Things I call my belongings."

The gypsy didn't bother to disguise his sarcasm. Harassing gypsies was a recognized national sport. They would taunt him, humiliate his wife, search his caravan, and when they had finished degrading them—unless they were of the more savage persuasion who enjoyed inflicting pain—the soldiers would go on their way feeling better about themselves for having disrupted his journey.

"Is this one of your belongings?" One of the soldiers grabbed the woman's hand and pulled her toward him until her face was next to his.

He stuck his tongue out and wiggled it in front of her nose. Just as he was about to kiss her, she opened her mouth and breathed on him. The putrid smell of her breath sent him reeling. As he backed off, gagging, she spread her lips in a wide, mocking smile.

As if to cover up for the blundering of their companion, the two other soldiers walked around the back of the *vardo*. It was a square caravan with small curtained windows cut into the sides. Brightly painted shutters and gaily stenciled flowers decorated the movable home. Pots and pans hung from a rack nailed over the back door. Trunks were lashed to the roof. A guitar and a zither dangled from velvet ropes tied to a thick brass railing. Inside, when the men opened the door, they saw stacks of fat, lumpy cushions, boxes of open foodstuffs, and a pile of filthy rags they never even recognized as a wardrobe. Crumpled in a ball in a corner, partly hidden behind a curtain of glass beads, was a child.

"Who's that?"

"My daughter," the gypsy said, jumping up onto the *vardo*, positioning himself between the two soldiers and the sleeping child.

"How old is she?"

"Two. Soon I'll be able to get a bride's price for her. And it'll be a good one because she's still a virgin." The gypsy pushed aside the beads so that the soldiers could get a better look at the merchandise soon to go on sale. The child's skin was the same light brown as her father's, her hair the same shade of pitch. "Either of you interested?" he said, offering the men a lascivious smile punctuated with dark spaces.

The soldiers couldn't get away quickly enough. The gypsy returned to the front of the *vardo*, picked up the reins, nodded to his wife, and once again began to lead his grubby troupe toward Esztergom.

Had the soldiers been more interested, they might have noticed that beneath the blankets the child's hands were white; beneath the kerchief and black wig was a mane of soft chestnut brown hair; and beneath the closed eyelids slept eyes of pale translucent green.

The American Embassy at 12 Szabadság tér was an elegant yellow building facing a statue of a Russian soldier, which usually wore a floral wreath—more for the benefit of those who worked in the Embassy than as tribute to the soldier. Across the street was a radio station that had known censorship-free broadcasting only once in its history, and a lovely green park where every now and then old men shared the wooden benches with young mothers who rocked their children to sleep in hooded prams, and lovers strolled hand-in-hand beneath the trees, and life appeared normal.

Inside the Embassy that particular evening, however, life was anything but normal. The ambassador had left only moments before to attend the concert at the Opera House. Though he had been accompanied by the expected entourage of assistants and consuls, most of his staff remained behind, following up on an undercover operation that had begun months before.

The wind of change had been blowing through Hungary for some time. In the beginning, it was as gentle as a zephyr, teasing those who had stubbornly held on to the dream of freedom. Then, the little breeze began to gather strength. As more and more people began to believe in the possibility of change, the notion had begun to gust and bellow. Slowly, people began to trust one another and reach out to one another for help. Underground networks were established for exchanging information. Political splinter groups formed, determined to challenge the status quo.

For almost two years the ambassador's staff had been establishing contacts, cultivating relationships, listening to shifts in the wind. Tonight, if all went well, one man, the leader of a reform group, would be hailed as a hero, while another, a man who would stop at nothing to maintain the status quo, would be exposed as a traitor.

They hid in the bowels of the Opera Ház, more than a hundred of them. Walachian gypsies from Esztergom. Lovari gypsies from Pécs. The nomadic Rom from across the Romanian border in Transylvania. They had been there since the night before, when a friend had unlocked a secret door to let them in. They camped there as they camped anywhere, squatting on blankets that covered the cold floor, sitting in groups, peeling fruit, eating clumps of bread and cheese, sipping wine from goatskins. They were patient because they were there by choice. They had been asked to help a tribesman and they had agreed.

Now, they waited for the signal to move. When it came they would invade the auditorium. They would infiltrate the musical temple so sacred to the *gorgio*. They would sneak up into the boxes, out onto the floor. They would appear from every door, every opening. And then they would extract their revenge. They would disgrace completely one who had brought disgrace to them. They would do the worst thing a gypsy could do to a non-gypsy. They would claim her as one of their own.

The Brahms was over. The maestro was about to introduce the evening's soloist, but in the dress circle someone who had lingered too long over a glass of champagne in the salon during intermission was creating a disturbance. Zoltán looked up and glared with disapproval. Such disrespect! Behavior like this was not simply rude—it was intolerable. No Hungarian would ever dream of disrupting a musical performance. But then, Zoltán thought as he realized who the laggard was, she was not a Hungarian.

All eyes turned toward the tall, sleek brunette who was the object of Zoltán's scorn. Without apology she slipped into one of the boxes reserved for distinguished guests. For an instant she met Zoltán's gaze. A corner of her lush red mouth twisted into an arrogant sneer. Then she took her seat. Playing to her audience like a diva, she tossed back her mane of thick brown hair, allowing the light from the chandeliers to capture the brilliance of the diamond clusters that adorned her ears. Inwardly, she smiled at the gasp emitted when the light touched her diamond collar and blazed with the fire only perfect stones produce.

Normally, there was nothing she relished more than a grand entrance, knowing that while women were staring at the lean lines of her long black lace gown, men were eyeing the sensuous curves of her body. For a moment she indulged in a warm bath of ego satisfaction, but quickly the feeling cooled. A cloak of resentment replaced the fur that had draped her shoulders. There was too little triumph in the impression she made in her designer gown and her array of important jewels, here in this city of drab hausfraus. Here, unlike Paris or London, her stature, her unerring sense of style went unchallenged. And triumph without challenge was unsatisfying.

As if to prove her point, she peered down into the rows below her. The audience, as always, was predominantly old, mostly venerable women in ill-fitting clothes that looked as if the mothballs they had been stored in still clung to their hems, pathetic examples of faded femininity, all of them hostages to dreary, socialistic frumpery.

The men fared no better in their baggy suits tailored of inferior cloth and their shabby pointy-toed shoes. Because this concert had been declared an official occasion, there were more uniforms in attendance than usual. She liked that. At least army officers and government officials bedecked in ribbons and medals presented a more sophisticated image. They walked smartly. Their shoes were polished. Their clothes were clean and crisply ironed. The fact that no one smiled and that guns hung from holsters or nestled beneath jackets was depressing, but so was everything about this evening.

So was everything about her life.

●　　●　　●

Katalin's knees wobbled as she made her way around the orchestra to the footlights, bowed her head, and offered a deep, respectful curtsy. As she always did when she arose, she lifted her eyes first to the delicately frescoed ceiling and then slowly let her gaze descend, seeking a spot within the crowd—a piece of woodwork, a bit of curtain, an exit sign beaming above a doorway. She didn't like to look at thousands of individual faces. She preferred to think of the audience as a singular mass, as one ear, one listener, one person with whom she and her music could be intimate. Usually she focused on her spot, nodded a second time, and took her seat at the piano. But tonight, like a piece of metal caught in the pull of a magnet, her eyes were drawn to the royal box. She tried to resist, but his stare was too demanding. She fixed on him and for a long, wistful moment, she thought they returned to another time, a time when love had been the dominant emotion in their lives, not hate; a time when his arms had been her sanctuary, her arms his refuge. She tried to cling to the memories, to retrieve the sweetness of the past, but the interlude of softness was gone as quickly as it had come. His eyes hardened into steel as she continued to blaze her defiance at him. She knew he wanted her to accord him and his associates the honor of a special curtsy. Instead, she tipped her chin, set her mouth, and dismissed him with a deliberate turn of her head.

Helpless to stop herself, she felt her gaze stray to a box on a lower circle. Like a homing device connected directly to her heart, her eyes riveted on another face, drinking in the sharp planes of his cheekbones and the strong ridge of his brow. She lingered on the graceful arch of his lips. Her life with him had held moments of black emptiness and uncertainty, as well as times filled with such joy that, thinking of them, she felt a warm rush suffuse her body.

It was only a few seconds, but as she stood there, locked in the safety of his view, time dissolved. Fear and doubt disintegrated. As long as he loved her, she could do anything.

Suddenly, in the periphery of her consciousness, she realized the applause had quieted. The reverie faded as Katalin was reminded of her purpose. To cloak the awkward moment, she took another quick bow. It was then, when she tried to regroup, when she looked away, up toward that invisible spot that was her comfort zone, that she noticed it. It was nothing definite, nothing with any recognizable form. In fact, it was nothing but an odd glimmering, something that seemed out of place, yet eerily familiar.

She had seen it late that afternoon, when she had come to tune the Bösendorfer. All the while she worked on the grand piano—adjusting the sound, checking the flexibility of the keyboard, the tightness of the strings, the responsiveness of the hammers—she had not been able to shake the feeling that unfriendly eyes were trained on her. Once or twice she had scanned the empty horseshoe-shaped auditorium. She had peered through three levels of Roman arches, searching the dim interiors for movement. Apart from two security men, it appeared she was alone. Yet when she had panned the uppermost tier, the one above the royal box, she had noticed the same odd glimmer coming from the booth next to the one housing the main spotlight. It had unnerved her then. It unnerved her now, as she seated herself at the piano.

An almost imperceptible tapping intruded on her thoughts. Automatically, the soloist looked toward the conductor. Zoltán's eyes bored into Katalin's, asking if she was all right. She breathed deeply, loosened her shoulders and arms, closed her eyes, stretched her fingers, warmed her hands, and then nodded. Yes, she was fine. She was ready. Zoltán raised his baton. A hundred musicians came to attention.

The majestic notes of Franz Liszt's Concerto No. 1 for Piano and Orchestra in E-flat major began to fill the hall, coaxed into existence slowly, carefully. Then, with an authoritative thrust, Zoltán raised his hand and signaled his musicians to unleash the full power of the composition. As he heard their explosive response, a surge of exhilaration embraced his soul. He bathed in the rapture of it, washing himself with the pure ecstasy of knowing that he and his seed—his beautiful, beloved Katalin—were producing music as grand as this.

Katalin felt it too. Her entire being was absorbed in the magic of the performance, filling her with such divine pleasure that there was no room for extraneous thought or superficial feeling. There was nothing except her hands and the keys beneath them, nothing save the piano and the orchestra behind her, the conductor beside her. There was nothing except this rare and exquisite moment, when every cell felt alive and jubilant.

It was a perfect fusion of elements: composer, conductor, orchestra, and soloist. Together, they attained a level of perfection that mesmerized the hall. As the third movement raced toward its final crescendo, the music swelled into a triumphant roar. Its awesome power gripped the soul of everyone present, overwhelming the senses and obliterating all other sound—including the click of a trigger.

I

Allegro

1920–1957

1

Budapest, Hungary

Zoltán Gáspár was born on June 4, 1920, the day the Treaty of Trianon was signed. On that day, Hungary paid dearly for its participation in the Great War. Wielding a pen more devastating than the sharpest ax, the Western Allies butchered Hungary's borders. Its only access to the sea was eliminated. Its size was reduced by more than ninety thousand square miles, nearly two-thirds of its territory; its population by thirteen million. Suddenly, people who had been Hungarian for generations were Yugoslavians or Romanians or Austrians or Czechoslovakians. Suddenly, land lush with fertile soil, forests rife with much-needed lumber, and mountains rich with thick veins of coal and bauxite offered their bounty to other nations. When the diplomats left the Grand Trianon at Versailles, the children of Árpád were left with little but their pride.

In the small village outside of Debrecen where Zoltán Gáspár's family lived, there was more to worry about than boundary changes. Life had always been difficult for those who worked the Great Plain, but now, with the economy worsening, the *puszta* became a region of tremendous hardship and trial.

György Gáspár was better off than most of the peasantry. He was a smallholder with enough land to eke out a living wage. For that wage he and his family worked seven days a week to coax wheat from the fields—hiring harvesters and navvies as extra hands only during the busy season—while at the same time ranching sheep, hogs, and a sizable herd of Nonius horses. Smaller, faster, and imbued with greater stamina than most horses, the Nonius breed—a mix of Siglavy Arabian and Spanish Andalusian—recalled the wild horses the Magyars had brought with them from Asia in the ninth century. Because György, his father, uncles, and two brothers were csikós, highly skilled horsemen, the Gáspár stable was a source of tremendous pride as well as income. György bred and trained the superb, sturdy animals that strode the Plains with such powerful grace. He taught them how to control runaway herds and to steer lazy flocks. And, because everyone on the puszta loved watching the horses perform, he kept half a dozen for show.

Like all Hungarians, the Gáspárs reveled in music and food. Because workdays on the puszta were long, leisure rare, and pleasures few, it was not unusual on a Sunday or holiday to find a group of people crowded around Eva Gáspár's table, eating gulyás or pörkölt, drinking Bikavér, the famous Bull's Blood wine from Eger, and rejoicing in the merriment provided by local musicians.

György was one of those musicians. Like others for whom playing was a diversion and not one's lifework, György regarded music as the ultimate accomplishment; a musician, the supreme artist. How magical he thought it was to be able to join disparate sounds to create a melody, to be able to make an inanimate object sing. He was not schooled in the violin. He could barely read, but he had an excellent ear and a love of music that was as profound and sincere as that of any of the stars of the concert stage.

György had never told anyone, including his wife, how he felt about the violin and the frown of fortune that had left him a farmer instead of a musician, but when his youngest son, Zoltán, began to show an interest, György gleefully handed the boy a violin, a bow, and a tightly wrapped package of unfulfilled dreams. In the beginning, though György's skills were primitive by professional standards, his basic knowledge of the workings of the instrument provided a rudimentary education. He showed the small boy how to balance the violin on his shoulder and rest it under his chin, how to slide the bow gently across the strings, how to cup his tiny fingers around the neck and create harmonious sounds by pressing down on the fingerboard. Zoltán was four years old. Within a week he had mastered his first piece of music.

Zoltán was fascinated by the wooden box with the four strings stretched across it, playing it constantly, the way other children played with a favorite toy. As much as he loved running in the fields and riding his father's horses, nothing compared to the special joy he felt when he heard the violin speak. To him it sounded like the birds that awakened him in springtime or the wind that whispered to him on a winter's night. While his brothers filled their off hours grooming the horses, riding, or practicing the tricks of the *csikós*, Zoltán made friends with the violin. Within six months it was clear that he had learned as much as his father could teach. Without hesitation György rushed into Debrecen to find a suitable teacher. When the professors at the university agreed to allow Zoltán to audition and then confirmed that indeed the young boy possessed a remarkable talent, György felt as if God had answered his prayers.

From that moment on, life on the Gáspár farm centered around Zoltán and his violin. Though his four older brothers and older sister were required to tend the animals before and after school as well as to lend a hand in the fields, Zoltán was relieved of all responsibility so that he could devote himself solely to his music.

Three mornings a week, well before dawn, Eva saddled her horse, seated Zoltán in front of her, and rode with her son into the city for his lessons. With the patience of one who believed she had been chosen to do this service, she'd wait outside while Zoltán worked with his teacher. Eva didn't even dismount. She sat on her horse, her head high and proud, hoping that someone would stop and ask what she was doing there so that she could boast about being the mother of a prodigy. Occasionally, someone did. After the lesson Eva escorted her son home. He was expected to nap and then practice. She was expected to complete her chores. Though Zoltán sometimes complained to his closest brother, Miklós, and his older sister, Zsuzsanna, about the harshness of his schedule, and though sometimes it hurt him to feel the jealous anger of his other siblings, whose own burdens had been increased because of him and whose pleasures had been reduced because of the cost of his lessons, secretly he knew he would endure whatever was necessary. He had no choice. The violin was his destiny.

Several months after beginning his lessons, when it was decided that perhaps his talent warranted instruction by no less than the head of the Conservatory, he met the woman who would guide his destiny. Edit Vásáry was a thin, stiff, humorless woman. Once, she had been an acclaimed soloist. When the Great War interrupted her career and killed her husband, she quit the stage, took to wearing only black, and devoted herself to teaching. To Madame Vásáry talent was an obligation that demanded fulfillment. If one accepted that maxim—and to become one of Madame's students one had to accept that maxim—one accepted her other canons as well. She repeated them throughout her lessons, making her students recite them like a catechism, pounding them into their heads: Practicing was a privilege; resting was slacking; sleeping and eating were necessities of nature and nothing more; total commitment was essential to achieve even minimal success.

The first time Zoltán met her, he was terrified. Ushered into her office by a university official and introduced, he had been too nervous to look at her. Instead, he had stood before her like a rowdy waiting to be punished, his head bowed, his violin hanging from one hand, his bow from the other. When he heard the door close and realized they were alone, his knees shook.

"Whose violin is that?" Her voice wasn't strong, but the authority she invested in her words amplified them until they seemed to echo.

"My father's," Zoltán said, stuttering a bit, wishing he was any place other than where he was.

"Give it to me."

As Zoltán handed her the violin and the bow, he looked up, seeing her for the first time. Her hair was fleece-white, pulled into a severe bun that sat primly at the nape of her neck. Her skin was almost as white as her hair and so thin that Zoltán was certain if he looked hard enough, he could see through to her bones. Though she walked with the aid of a cane, there seemed little else about her that was frail. Her step was slow but sure, and when she handed him a smaller violin than the one he had been using, one scaled for a child, he noticed she had long, tapering fingers that seemed much younger than the rest of her hand, which was heavily veined and spotted with age.

"This," she said, nodding emphatically at the new violin, "is the proper size for a boy of your age. I'll give you five minutes to adjust. Then I'll return and the audition will begin."

She left the room, but the power of her presence remained, like a lingering perfume. Quickly, as if there were a stopwatch ticking, Zoltán lifted the violin to his shoulder and seesawed the bow across the strings, not really listening or feeling, just doing as he was told. After a few seconds, curiosity got the better of him. When he felt certain she wasn't watching through some secret peephole, he toyed with the new instrument, playing a tune he had composed for his own amusement. The sound was different. The feel was different. Actually, he decided after playing another piece, more deliberately this time, it wasn't so much that it was different as it was right.

When Madame returned, she noticed a smile on his face but chose to ignore it. She pounded her cane on the floor. The smile disappeared.

"Play," she commanded, taking a seat across from him, folding her hands in her lap, and staring at him through the round, wire-rimmed glasses perched on the end of her nose.

"What should I play?" he asked, wondering whether or not he really wanted to impress her. His father had told him she was the best tutor in the region. Some said she was the finest in Eastern Europe. His mother declared that to be accepted as one of Madame's students was a rare honor. But standing there in that small room, looking up at her steel gray eyes and hard, cold mouth, Zoltán was certain that being taught by her would be an excruciating exercise in endurance and sacrifice.

"What do you know?"

"A sonata by Corelli, two of the *Four Seasons* by Vivaldi, and a concerto by Bach." He had rehearsed each piece until his fingers had trembled from exhaustion.

"Corelli."

Naturally, she had selected the one that had given him the most difficulty. Now, to make matters worse, he was going to have to play on a strange instrument.

He raised the violin, tucked it under his chin, said a silent prayer, and commenced playing. When he had finished the Corelli she demanded the Vivaldi, and when he had finished that, the Bach. An hour and a half later he stood before her, drained and nervous. Suddenly, there was no question about how he wanted this audition to turn out. Having given her his best—and even he knew that the music he had charmed from that violin had been exquisite—he longed for her approval, her praise, her assurance that he did indeed have the gift.

"Be here Monday morning" was all he got.

For three years Zoltán trained with the formidable Madame Vásáry. Under her tutelage he learned the rigid discipline required of a musician. It didn't matter that he was young and small. She had divined that his talent was huge, and therefore his prospects great. She worked him with the same determination that György worked his horses. She gave him exercises to strengthen his fingers, scales to increase agility. She taught him how to position the violin to produce the least amount of strain on his arm and neck. She showed him how to sit and stand to relieve pressure on his back and legs during long performances. She told him what to eat, what to drink, and how long to sleep. And she demanded no less than four hours' practice a day. It was grueling, but Zoltán never complained. The harder she worked him, the more he loved the music; the more she demanded, the greater his desire to succeed. His day was long and without any of the normal childhood diversions, but Zoltán didn't care. He could hear his progress. He could feel the tools of expression forming in his fingers. He could see his repertoire enlarging and gaining in importance with each new, more complex composition she handed him.

"First the fingering. Then the melody," she told him repeatedly. "You can't sing until you know the words. You can't create the music until you've mastered the technique."

Zoltán was eight years old when he first performed in front of an audience, the youngest guest soloist ever to appear with the Prague Philharmonic Orchestra.

He expected to be frightened, overwhelmed by the size of the audience, the grandeur of the hall, the presence of critics. Instead, from the instant he walked onstage, he felt a surge of energy course through his body like an electrical current, stunning him for the moment, then charging him with an uncommon brilliance. He played as if he were possessed, as if his hands and the instrument they held had been abducted by Orpheus, the god whose music was so awesome that even the mightiest of rivers stopped flowing just to listen. And afterward, his ears rang with the unrestrained, passionate applause that greeted his performance. His soul fed on the sound of thousands of *Bravos!* that echoed throughout the Philharmonia, the sight of thousands of people standing out of respect for his musicianship.

For György Gáspár, who, along with Madame Vásáry, had accompanied the young boy to Prague, his son's triumph was a miracle. As he sat in the audience that night and watched Zoltán, listening to the golden sounds those small hands were creating, he wept and uttered a silent prayer of thanks. Somehow, he had produced a musical genius. His child, his progeny had a talent that defied description, a talent that would lift the Gáspárs out of the dim anonymity of the *puszta* and catapult them into the glorious spotlight.

The only one who did not return from Prague on the wings of exaltation was Madame Vásáry.

"The Tchaikovsky was all right. The Beethoven was flawed."

Zoltán's heart sank. He was certain she had been pleased by his performance, proud of the ovations he had received. Though he hadn't expected her to enthuse about his playing—after so many years, he knew that was hardly her style—he had expected *something:* a word, a gesture, a pat on the head. After the Tchaikovsky he had glanced up at the box where she and his father sat. Though she remained seated while György and the other guests in their box stood and applauded, Zoltán was positive he had caught a smile flirting with her lips. Looking at her now, however, in her somber black dress and thick black stockings, with her stern visage and rigid posture, he was forced to believe he had simply imagined it and to wonder if she ever smiled.

"We have work to do." She tapped her cane on a chair, indicating that he was to sit. On his music stand he found a book of scales.

"I've done enough scales," Zoltán whined, suddenly angry at her refusal to toss him so much as a crumb of praise.

"You'll never do enough scales," she said with clear disapproval. "Especially if you intend to master Paganini."

Zoltán's shock was immediate. Niccolò Paganini was regarded as the greatest of all violin virtuosos. His playing was legendary, his compositions some of the most difficult ever penned. Few tested their ability with Paganini. Of those who did, fewer survived.

That night, though he had been so tired he had excused himself immediately after supper, Zoltán couldn't sleep. He crept out of bed and tiptoed out of the house. It was warm for May, so he dropped his blanket on the ground before climbing the huge tree that was his favorite thinking place. As he leaned back and rested in a crook of the large oak, it seemed appropriate to be out under the stars, given the magnitude of his thoughts. He closed his eyes and breathed in the loamy scent of the farm at rest. He listened for the ubiquitous symphony of the animals, but it was late and the barnyard was still. He was glad. For a child whose entire life centered on the creation of sound, just then it was silence he craved.

"Zoltán."

Zsuzsanna's voice was low, but it startled him just the same.

"Up here," he whispered, watching as she shinnied up the trunk and joined him on his perch.

Zsuzsanna was five years older than Zoltán. The day he was born she had declared herself his keeper. Though she had four other brothers, he was the one she claimed—probably because she had been present at his birth, fetching water and towels for the doctor who attended her mother. Zsuzsanna had been the first to hold Zoltán. She had trembled when the doctor placed the tiny red wriggling bundle in her arms, but when Zoltán had opened his eyes and suddenly stopped squalling, she took it as a sign. She didn't know he couldn't really see. She didn't know that he had quieted because she had put her finger near enough to his mouth for him to suck. She didn't care about any of that. He had looked at her and grabbed for her and, with his first contented gurgle, had made her feel more special than anyone ever had before. From that moment on she mothered him and sistered him and befriended him in equal measure, always seeming able to divine which role he required most. Just then, she suspected, he needed a dollop of all three.

"What's the matter?" she asked.

"Madame wants me to play Paganini."

Zsuzsanna gasped with excitement. To feel part of his life and understand his dreams, she had made it her business to learn the names of the composers and musicians who peopled Zoltán's world.

"That's wonderful," she exclaimed, taking him in her arms and hugging him, mindful not to throw either of them off balance.

"I don't know if I can do it."

"Of course you can!"

He shook his head and shrugged his shoulders, suddenly looking very small and very much his age. The moonlight kissed his cheeks, touching the tears that rested there and making them sparkle like chips of finely cut glass. Zsuzsanna took his hands in hers and squeezed them gently.

"Zoltán, Madame Vásáry wouldn't give you Paganini if she didn't think you could master him. She's too proud and too vain to take a chance like that. You're her star, my little brother. She wants you to shine."

For a thirteen-year-old, Zsuzsanna's insights were extremely keen. Madame Vásáry saw in Zoltán an opportunity for immortality. She had trained some stellar violinists in her day and had established a reputation as one of Europe's finest string tutors, but she had yet to affix her signature on a protégé of irrefutable, undeniable greatness. When Zoltán had auditioned for her she had tingled inside, knowing that at last she had found the clay with which to mold her monument. Then, when he had performed so magnificently in Prague, she decided to quicken the pace of his education. Though he was only eight, in the world of music "prodigy" was not a title that lasted past the teens. Too, she was aging. Her body was beginning to defy her and though her mind was sharp and her fingers could still demonstrate technique and style, she feared that her skills would diminish before she could perfect his.

For the next two years she pushed him so hard that often he cried himself to sleep. At the end of each day his arms ached. His fingers grew stiff; his brain went numb. He was a ten-year-old trying to keep up with his schoolwork, maintain a five-hour practice schedule, please his parents, please Madame, and learn the intricacies of Paganini. He should have been laughing and playing. He should have been riding horses with his brothers or roughhousing with friends. But he was not an ordinary boy. Because of his gift—often he thought of it as a curse—he was not allowed to be young. He had to be careful not to hurt his hands, not to get overtired so that he diminished the effectiveness of his practice sessions, not to get sick and miss a lesson. At only ten, the entire focus of his life was the quest for perfection.

Zoltán became withdrawn. He rarely smiled and never laughed. Though Eva filled his plate, he merely picked at his food. He was exhausted, both physically and emotionally. His parents attributed his mood swings to genius. Imre, Sándor and Tomás were too involved in their own schoolwork and after-school chores to notice, and even if they had, they, too, would have excused their brother's despondency as artistic temperament.

Only Zsuzsanna and Miklós were alarmed. They began to guard him as if they were on a suicide watch, constantly gauging his moods, checking his spirit, evaluating his frame of mind. Whenever he looked particularly sad and silent they'd kidnap him and take him west, across the Tisza river to the Hortobágy, once a large, grassy prairie where Hungarian cowboys and herdsmen roamed, to picnic on the flat, endless plain— ever watchful for the famous Hortobágy mirage, the Fata Morgana—and engage their little brother in games and laughter.

On the day of Zoltán's eleventh birthday, he stood onstage in Vienna's venerable Opera House and electrified the world with his interpretation of the incomparable Paganini "Caprices." His performance was flawless, astounding all who heard him, dazzling them with his spirited down-bow staccato and the rapidity of his left-handed pizzicato. Critics raved about his technique, comparing his virtuosity to the master himself—the shimmering use of the glissando, the octave trills, the extraordinary extensions—but more than that, they confessed to being completely overwhelmed by the romantic lushness of his musical interpretation, amazed that "a child so young could possess so old a soul."

For Zoltán, though, the greatest pleasure was to look into the audience and see his entire family seated in the special box usually reserved for royalty. He knew what it had cost György to bring seven people to Vienna. He knew what it had cost every one of them over the years to enable him to stand on that stage. To see them clapping and wiping tears of pride and love from their eyes was, he thought, the greatest accolade he could ever hope to receive.

Then, after he completed his third encore, Madame Vásáry walked out onstage, handed him a bouquet of roses, and kissed him on the cheek. It wasn't until after she had taken his hand and the two of them had accepted the ovation of the audience that he realized her dress was a sheath of flaming red. He looked at her, wide-eyed.

"In celebration of our triumph," she said, shocking him. As she turned to go, she issued a final word of instruction. "Take one more bow and exit. Always leave them wanting more."

From that moment on, Zoltán's life held only practice and performance and more practice as he traveled throughout Europe, playing concert halls from London to Moscow, building a reputation as one of the finest violinists in the world. By the time he met Mária Toth, his stature was such that even her enormous celebrity could not outshine his star.

Since the age of fourteen, when she appeared in her first play, Mária had been hailed as one of the most expressive actresses ever to appear on a Hungarian stage. Despite the fact that in 1940 she was only nineteen years old, her unique gift, an extraordinary ability to reach inside an audience's well of feelings and draw out the softest part of them, had brought her national celebrity.

Zoltán was twenty years old the first time he saw her. He was seated toward the back of the theater, his mind still on the latest radio report of the war in Europe. The instant she appeared onstage, however, his attention was riveted, his eyes never leaving her beautiful face. Her high cheekbones, broad forehead, and full eyebrows were pure Magyar, but her auburn hair and hazel eyes displayed a tantalizing blend of East and West. She was small, no taller than five feet two, but her presence was overwhelming. Her voice, too, was a surprise, deep and resonant, totally unexpected in one so petite. Zoltán sat mesmerized, listening but not hearing, watching but not seeing. He was absorbed in absorbing her, drinking her in, digesting every movement, every nuance.

After the final curtain he found his way backstage and stationed himself outside her dressing room door. It was the first time in his life he had ever done anything so bold and capricious. But it was also the first time in his life he had ever felt the way he did.

He waited for more than an hour. Had she left by some other exit? Just as he was about to concede defeat, the door opened and the angel of the stage stood before him.

Seeing her face only inches away from his own startled him, prompting him to blurt out, "I think I love you."

"Should I be shocked or flattered?" she asked, allowing the corner of her mouth to tilt upward in the beginning of a smile.

"Actually, I'm shocked by what I said." He laughed, feeling utterly foolish. "But you should be flattered."

Mária turned, about to dismiss him, when something about this young man made her stop. Yes, he was handsome, with thick brown hair, a square chin balanced by a broad brow, and a full mouth that invited attention, but many of the Romeos who bivouacked outside her dressing room were handsome. No, she was taken by his manner, the unselfconscious, honest way he had approached her. Most young men put on airs around her, trying too hard to please. This man was not pretentious. This man was being himself, and that was charming.

"Gáspár," he said, stumbling over his own name as he held out his hand, wishing he was more experienced, more adept with women. "Gáspár Zoltán."

"The violinist?"

All his hours of practice and study and work and sacrifice had suddenly paid off. She knew who he was!

"The very same," he said, trying to sound casual, hoping she couldn't hear the whooshing sound of his blood racing through his body.

"I'm impressed. And honored."

She smiled. Zoltán blushed and then wanted to kick himself. He couldn't decide which was more embarrassing, her praise or his floundering. Of one thing he was certain. Zsuzsanna would never approve. Not after all the long hours she had spent coaching him about what to say and how to behave when in the company of young ladies. He had to get hold of himself. He had to comport himself like a gentleman.

"I would be honored if you'd let me take you for coffee and a pastry," he said. "The New York Café is across the street. Would that be all right?"

"That would be more than all right," she answered, and meant it.

Every night for a month Zoltán waited outside the stage door to take Mária for coffee. They'd sit and talk. They'd hold hands under the table. He'd walk her to her flat, kiss her hurriedly on the cheek, and leave, retreating to his small hotel room to berate himself for his awkwardness. With his need to impress Mária so strong, his desire to woo her so intense, the blanks in his upbringing loomed larger and more glaring than ever before. At last, with great effort, he worked up the nerve to invite her to spend a Sunday with him.

"I want you to meet my family," he said simply.

For Mária, the day was exceptional. She had been born in Pest, the daughter of poor factory workers. Orphaned at three when a fire devoured the plant where her parents worked, she was raised behind the high walls of a Catholic convent. The only time she had ever ventured outside the city was when she ran away from the orphanage and joined a repertory company traveling to Szeged. Years later she left Budapest for the second time to star in a short-run play in Debrecen. She had never seen a farm. And she had never experienced a family, especially one like the Gáspárs.

When Mária and Zoltán drove through the gates of the Gáspár farm, they were greeted by a throng of people garbed in gaily colored folk costumes, neighbors and friends who waved and shouted greetings. But as Zoltán helped Mária out of the car, the crowd went still, watching in respectful silence as the world-renowned violinist escorted the nationally acclaimed actress into the humble one-story farmhouse. For Zoltán's relatives and neighbors, this was a moment literally to touch the stars.

Zoltán's brothers giggled like schoolboys. Tomás was so rattled he almost forgot to introduce his wife. Zsuzsanna, trying to think of Mária as a nineteen-year-old girl and not Hungary's finest actress, summoned up as much sophisticated nonchalance as she could, but the pose crumbled when they stood face to face and she gushed like every other fan. Even György turned shy and blushed when Zoltán introduced Mária and she leaned forward to buss his cheeks. The only one who appeared immune to an attack of nerves or stammering timidity was Eva, who simply opened her arms, invited the youngsters inside, and offered them a glass of apricot brandy to welcome them to her home, in the traditional way.

After the introductions, György invited everyone outside where Sándor and Imre were tending two large pigs sizzling on a spit in the stone fire pit. Tables draped in spritely hand-loomed cotton cloths sprinkled the yard with color. Hand-picked flowers waved from crockery vases. Glass carafes filled with local red wine sat on each table. Long buffets groaned with a mouth-watering assortment of specialties: a cabbage soup known as *káposztaleves*, cucumber salad, dumplings called *galuska*, green peppers filled with minced meat and covered with a rich tomato sauce, *tokány* (a paprika-flavored stew), a dish of sour cabbage, eggs, rice, smoked sausage and pork, and baskets of freshly baked breads.

As was the custom of the Plains when one farmer was hosting so many others, each family had brought dishes and glassware and utensils. The resulting array of patterns and styles and colors created a country kaleidoscope that enchanted city-bred Mária. Enchanting, too, was the open, generous manner of the people who had accepted Eva Gáspár's invitation, their friendliness and easy laughter, their genuine affection for the Gáspárs.

As Mária mingled with Zoltán's kin and neighbors, she grew giddy with an odd sense of freedom. The stiff patina that normally held her image intact softened, allowing a person she had never met before to emerge. This person was relaxed. She laughed easily and honestly. She smiled just because, and not on cue. She asked questions without knowing the answers. And she exposed more of herself to these strangers than she had ever exposed to anyone else.

"You're so lucky," she whispered to Zoltán when they had a moment alone. "What a wonderful place to grow up!"

Zoltán nodded and looked around, seeing the old house and the flat, dusty landscape with new eyes.

"I never had a family," Mária continued, her voice growing wistful. "I never had a home. The Sisters tried, I suppose, but life in the convent was so harsh, so lonely. Everything was ordered and regimented. Everything was done on time and to a schedule."

Zoltán laughed, a sound more shadowed than mirthful.

"My life was that way, too, but it wasn't the Sisters who ruled every waking moment. She did." He pointed to Madame Vásáry, who was sitting on a wooden chair with such dignity that she made it seem like a throne. "Come. I want you to meet her."

He took Mária's hand and introduced her to Madame.

"It's an honor to meet you," Mária said with genuine respect.

"May I say the same," Madame Vásáry replied, giving the actress her due.

"I hope Zoltán's going to play today," Mária said, thinking that expressing admiration of Zoltán's talent was the quickest way to win this woman's approval.

"Fiddlers play," Madame said with undisguised scorn. "Violinists perform."

Zoltán swallowed a smile. At first the thought struck him as so ludicrous he was sure his mind had been momentarily warped by the heat of the sun, but the longer he listened to Madame Vásáry and Mária fence with each other, the more obvious it became. The old woman was jealous.

"Mária," Zoltán said, deciding he needed a moment alone with his mentor. "Would you mind getting a glass of water for Madame Vásáry? She looks flushed."

Mária flashed Zoltán a look of gratitude and hurried off, eager to escape the hostile gaze of the estimable Madame Vásáry.

"You're being naughty," Zoltán said as he pulled his chair close to his teacher's and took her delicate hands in his.

"I beg your pardon," she sniffed, lifting her chin in a gesture of great indignation.

"I brought Mária over to meet you because you're one of the most important people in my life. And what do you do? You dismiss her as if she's a bothersome gnat."

"I merely corrected her use of words."

Zoltán leaned forward and, peering into her eyes, looked behind them into the depths where her true feelings resided.

"I care about her, Madame. I want you to care about her too."

"I'm not your mother. There's no need to seek my approval."

Zoltán laughed and kissed her hands. "I've sought your approval every single day of my life since I was five years old. Why wouldn't I seek it now?"

Madame Vásáry didn't answer. Instead, she fussed with her hat, bending her head away from him, fixing the brim so that the sun couldn't possibly sneak underneath and spotlight her feelings. When finally she looked up, her face void of visible emotion, and nodded in that infuriatingly imperious way of hers, saying, "She's nice enough," Zoltán did something he had never done before. He reached out and hugged her, holding her frail body gently in his arms. When they separated, though she reverted instantly to the comfort of her monarchical manner, he noticed that she didn't bother wiping away the moisture that clung to her pale gray eyes.

Helping her to her feet, Zoltán escorted Madame Vásáry to the center table, the one positioned nearest the great oak. He seated her to his right, knowing Mária would take the seat on his left. Across from them would be Zsuzsanna, her husband, Mihai Pal, and his brother Miklós. After finding Mária, fixing a plate for her, then for himself and Madame Vásáry, and settling them all in their places, Zoltán tried to relax, but it wasn't easy. He was madly in love and desperate for everything to be perfect. The day was gorgeous, but warm. His mother's dinner was superb, but some of his relatives had swilled too much wine. Mária didn't appear flustered by any of it. Still, he remained uneasy. There seemed to be so many egos to balance, so many feelings to consider. Later, he realized he should have had more faith in his family. Miklós, the most scholarly of his siblings, drew Mária into a discussion of Hungary's alliance with Mussolini's Italy and the growing closeness of their ties to Hitler's Third Reich. When he had exhausted her on the political end, Zsuzsanna took over, regaling Mária with tales of the times when Madame Vásáry's health had kept her home and she had accompanied Zoltán on his concert tours. Though Mária laughed when she was supposed to laugh, and looked impressed when she was supposed to look impressed, Zoltán sensed that she had understood immediately that his sister's dialogue was meant to establish Zsuzsanna's place in Zoltán's galaxy.

He might have been embarrassed by all their efforts to impress if he had not felt Mária's hand reach for his under the table. Her touch told him it didn't matter how many people lived in his world. As long as there was room for her.

The instant the plates were cleared, the air reverberated with the spirit of the *puszta*. György's band had gathered. His violin, two others, a clarinet, and a cimbalom were now entertaining everyone with the lively, lilting, vaguely Oriental melodies of the Magyars, the rich, free-flowing rhythms of the gypsies. Few could sit without pounding their hands together and stomping their feet. Several, including Zsuzsanna, jumped up and began twirling about in response to the music. Even Madame Vásáry allowed her fingers to twitch in her lap. Mária stood between Zoltán and his youngest brother, Miklós, clapping and thoroughly enjoying herself.

When they were all exhausted from dancing, Eva gathered her guests and led them to the grassy field adjacent to the barn. There, chairs had been set up so everyone could witness the pride of György's stable. Mária was given the seat of honor.

Suddenly, the clear summer sky was clouded by a burst of dust. Five horses galloped into view, each bearing a rider in the dress of the Plains cowboy—billowing black pants tucked into high black boots, a colorful shirt with full sleeves and an open collar, a short vest, a woven girdle, and a black felt hat with a soup-bowl brim. György and four of his sons rode on girthless saddles, steering the horses with subtle movements of their hips and thighs. Up, over hedges and fences they jumped, in perfect unison, turning, circling, leading the horses through their paces with the uninhibited joy of those who felt at one with the animals beneath them.

Sándor, Imre, Tomás, and Miklós left the field, returning a few minutes later minus their saddles and minus their boots. On their feet were sandals with cloth straps and thick wedged bottoms that molded to the contour of the horses' naked backs. Each son straddled two horses, one foot balanced on each, the reins of both horses held with a tight hand. Slowly, the four young men paraded the eight horses before the spectators. György had dismounted and stood to the side. At the crack of his long, knot-tipped whip, his sons took off, riding with amazing speed, racing up and down the field, yet keeping their mounts exactly parallel. With the grace of an acrobat, each took a turn at astounding the audience: balancing between the horses, jumping from one to the other, facing backward—all at breakneck speed, all in perfect unison. They twirled their whips in the air. As they snapped them against the wind, the horses turned. They snapped them against the ground and the horses stopped.

When all eight horses stood in front of György's guests, four on each side, a ninth horse galloped from behind the barn, reared, and trotted into the space left by the four riders, the space directly in front of Mária. György cracked his whip. The horse that held his fifth son, Zoltán, bent both forelegs and kneeled. Zoltán, his knees pressed against the side of his steed, his eyes locked on Mária's face, lifted his violin, tucked it under his chin, and began to play. The music wafted into the air like the perfume of seduction, romancing everyone who listened, not just the one for whom the song was intended. If, as the poets claimed, a heart had strings, just then they would have numbered four, because surely the music Zoltán was creating came more from his heart than from his hands.

Mária's eyes pooled with tears. Never had she experienced such a magnificent tribute. Never had she heard such an eloquent, albeit wordless, declaration of love.

Without wasting a second, Mária leapt from her chair and ran to the handsome young man with the violin.

"Yes," she shouted, throwing her arms around his neck and kissing him. "Yes!"

As Zoltán swept her into his arms, he signaled his horse to rise. He pulled on the reins and, with his lady firmly in his arms, rode away. The gathering burst into applause, all relishing the romance of it, the beauty of it, the privilege of being able to witness such a poetic moment. All, that is, except three women. Zsuzsanna and Madame Vásáry, the two who had been the most possessive, most protective of Zoltán, the two who had grafted their egos onto his success, watched the lovers leave with a searing sense of loss.

The third woman, the one who should have felt the most displaced by Zoltán's engagement, watched with a mix of emotions—happiness, sadness, relief, anxiety—but grief was not among them. While the other women felt they had lost Zoltán to Mária Toth, Eva Gáspár knew she had lost her son years before—the day his father first handed him a violin.

2

*T*heirs was a marriage of greatness, or so the newspapers said when six months later they reported the wedding of Zoltán Gáspár and Mária Toth. Six months after that, in April 1941, Hungary assisted Hitler in an invasion of Yugoslavia, thereby marking Hungary's entrance into World War II. Though the war introduced the Gáspárs to horrors previously unimaginable—including the deaths of three of Zoltán's brothers, the passing of his father, and two miscarriages for Mária—nothing could have prepared them for the night of April 7, 1951.

At two o'clock in the morning a thunderous crash awakened Mária and Zoltán. Instantly, Mária sat up, gripping the covers and pulling them under her chin. Her eyes were wide with fear. Her heart pounded inside her chest. Zoltán, too, bolted up, squinting into the dark, trying to judge what had caused such a loud noise. Three large men dressed in the uniforms of the AVO, the Hungarian Secret Police, charged into their bedroom.

"Get him." One man, clearly the leader, pointed at Zoltán.

The two others obliged by grabbing the stunned man and dragging him out of his bed.

"What the hell are you doing?" Zoltán demanded.

"You're under arrest."

"For what?" Despite the firmness of their grip, Zoltán wrestled with his captors.

"Crimes against the state."

"Bullshit!" Zoltán exclaimed. "I've done nothing wrong and you know it. Now, let me go!"

The big man nodded his head toward the door. His cronies began to haul Zoltán, who was kicking and screaming, into the next room. Mária ran to get Katalin. Terrified that a false move would result in some unspeakable act of barbarism to Zoltán, her child, or herself, she stood by helplessly as her husband was beaten and dragged from his home. When they had gone, it took Mária an hour to calm Katalin. When finally the child was asleep, Mária ran to the telephone.

"Zoltán's gone," she said, trying to control her voice in case the phone was tapped.

"Did he go alone?" Miklós heard his sister-in-law's strangled sobs and knew exactly what had happened. Midnight arrests by the dreaded AVO were becoming all too common.

"No."

"I'll be right over."

Miklós tried, but there was no way to console Mária. She was frantic for news of Zoltán's whereabouts, but no one had seen where the AVO had taken him. No one had heard even a whisper as to what they might have done with him. After discussion with Zsuzsanna and Mihai, it was decided that Miklós would move in with Mária and Katalin. At first Mária objected. She didn't want to inconvenience Miklós or to disturb the pattern of his life.

"They've disturbed my life," Miklós said, with a tight jaw. "They took my brother, and until I find him I will care for his wife and child."

Katalin, at two years old, had only a limited understanding about what had happened. She knew that some scary men had taken her father away and he hadn't come back. She knew that her Aunt Zsuzsanna and Uncle Mihai had been visiting more often than usual. And she knew that her mama was very sad. That's why she was so happy when Uncle Miklós had said he was going to stay until Papa came home. Maybe Uncle Miklós could help make Mama's bad dreams go away. Katalin had tried. Whenever she heard Mária crying or calling out her father's name, Katalin climbed into bed with her and snuggled real close, doing just what Mária did for her whenever she had bad dreams. But nothing seemed to work. Mária remained veiled in black. Miklós, on the other hand, recycled his anger into a fierce determination to find his brother and best the bastards who had arrested him.

Growing up, there had been few signs of the man Miklós would become. Though he had always been an organizer, figuring out the most efficient way to perform most tasks, he had never been overtly defiant. Occasionally he disagreed with György, but by and large he was like all the Gáspár children—polite, deferential, and respectful of authority. The only time Miklós had challenged the word of his father was when he announced that he wanted to study at the university.

György's response had been extreme dismay. Farmers needed their sons to work the land. Having sacrificed one son already—a sacrifice György was happy to make, but a loss nonetheless—he would not suffer another easily. György refused, expecting that his decision would be accepted and the matter dropped. Instead, Miklós had stood and faced his father. In a clear, low, but powerful voice he spoke of his desire to become a teacher. He had been eloquent then, expressing his needs in a manner so convincing that even György could no longer protest.

Because he had continued to work the farm while attending classes, it had taken Miklós six years to complete his studies. Upon his graduation, the University of Debrecen offered him a job as an instructor, but Miklós responded to the pull of the larger world. He took a position at the University of Budapest, where, in addition to teaching a full schedule, he furthered his own education to become a professor of philosophy, a man of letters who, though intellectually rebellious and often verbally combative, had spent most of his life championing nonviolence. Until now.

During the day, he met with anyone he thought might have a lead as to where the AVO had hidden Zoltán. He spoke to colleagues and members of the student underground, an organization with which he was very familiar. At night he became a family man. He insisted that Mária discuss her day. He helped with dinner. He joked with Katalin and read to her and played with her. He took them for Sunday walks and visits with Zsuzsanna or Ilona and Andras Strasser, Zoltán and Mária's closest friends. He did everything he could think of to fill the void that Zoltán's absence had created.

A year passed without any word. Other families whose loved ones had been arrested and sent away were beginning to weaken and accept what appeared to be the inevitable. For Miklós, Mária, Mihai, and Zsuzsanna, the silence served only to make them stronger. The four of them had forged a tight team, bolstering each other's spirits, supporting one another through the long low periods. While others mourned, they refused to surrender to their worst thoughts.

Their unifying concern was Katalin. They all fawned over her, fussing so that maybe she wouldn't notice that something basic was missing from her life. One day, however, Zsuzsanna took Mária aside.

"She's beginning to forget her father," Zsuzsanna said gently.

Mária felt as if Zsuzsanna had struck her.

"No," she protested. "That can't be."

"She's so little," Zsuzsanna said. "She wasn't quite two years old when they took him. How much can she remember?"

Mária nodded and took her sister-in-law's hand. Through the years and the hardships, the two women had grown exceptionally close.

"I won't let that happen," Mária said reassuringly.

From that day on, no matter how painful it was for her to listen, Mária played Zoltán's recordings. She put a picture of Zoltán in Katalin's room and showed her scrapbooks filled with news articles about his various concerts. She and Miklós talked about him over dinner. Zsuzsanna and Mihai began to mention him regularly in their conversations. No one knew whether or not the AVO had killed Zoltán Gáspár, but in his own house he was still very much alive.

When Katalin was three years old, Mária was told that the theater company in which she starred was being sent to Leningrad for six weeks. To care for Katalin, since the work schedules of Miklós and Zsuzsanna and Mihai did not permit them to be at home, Mária decided to accept an offer the Strassers had made.

Ilona Strasser was a doctor. Andras Strasser taught piano at the Franz Liszt Academy. Their daughter, Judit, was Katalin's age, and the Strassers tried to schedule their work so that one of them could be at home. Whenever that proved impossible, Ilona took Judit to the hospital and prevailed upon the nurses to keep an eye on her. Andras used his office as a playpen when he was teaching a class at the Academy, and when he gave private lessons in his basement studio, Judit busied herself in a corner set up just for her.

Katalin fit right in. She and Judit chattered and played at the hospital as well as they did at the Strasser apartment or in Andras's office. The place they liked the least was the studio. There, they had to be very quiet so as not to disturb the concentration of the eager young musicians who sat beside Professor Strasser. Judit, because she was so used to it, paid little attention to what was going on at the big black piano, but Katalin, drawn to it, liked to listen, especially when she felt certain she heard melodies that her father played on his recordings. She thought it was fun to watch the player's fingers dance across the keyboard. Several times, when Judit wasn't watching and couldn't see and make fun of her, she held her hands the way the older boys and girls did and wiggled her fingers, moving her hands in front of her as if she were the one filling the dingy space with such beautiful music.

Once or twice, when Professor Strasser had left the studio to accompany a student to the door, she had climbed up onto the bench and tentatively examined the long white pieces of ivory and the shorter, thinner slices of ebony. They were smooth and cool and surprisingly soft. When she plunked a finger down, the sound was loud and quickly gone. When she pressed more gently, the sound was lighter and seemed to linger a bit longer.

"This is fun," she told Judit, who was playing dolls in the corner.

"It's okay."

"Can you do it?" Katalin asked.

"A little."

"Do you think your papa could teach me?"

"Would you like to learn?"

Katalin hadn't seen Andras reenter the room. She shrugged her shoulders, suddenly embarrassed.

Andras sat next to her, held her hand, and pressed down on the center key.

"This is middle C," he said, delighted that Katalin had expressed interest. Judit often sat with him at the piano, but he was her father. This was what he did. When she was ready—and after all, three was rather young—he would teach her to play. "Middle C is the captain of the piano. Everything starts from here. This is D." He took Katalin's finger and moved it up to the next key and then to the next, identifying each of the keys in the scale. He didn't bother explaining the difference between treble and bass or showing her sharps and flats. He assumed this was a diversion from whatever game she and Judit had been playing. He was wrong.

Katalin couldn't stay away from the huge black instrument. Frequently she begged Judit to go down to the basement with her so she could press the keys and make pretty sounds. Often the two little girls sat at the piano for hours, inventing silly duets that had no melody whatsoever. It didn't matter. Somehow, creating sound satisfied a need in each of them. For Katalin, the need began to grow.

One afternoon, a month after she had first sat with Andras, he entered his makeshift studio to hear a one-finger rendition of a Beethoven motif. He recognized it as the theme of a sonata he had been teaching one of his older students. Katalin was perched on the piano stool, completely engrossed in re-creating that melody.

"Would you like to play a game?" he asked, sliding next to her.

"Sure. What kind of game?"

"You turn around. I'm going to play a note and you see if you can tell me which one it is. How does that sound?"

"Fun." Katalin giggled, eagerly reversing herself.

Andras pressed a key.

"G," she said without a moment's thought.

Andras pressed another key.

"A."

He mixed them up. He played a few sharps and flats. He struck notes in the lower register, then high on the upper end of the scale. She identified them all. The child had perfect pitch.

Later, when Andras related the tale to Ilona, his expression alternated between immense gladness and utter desolation.

"Zoltán has passed his gift on to his daughter," Andras said, as if this were the first time he had ever confronted the miracle of heredity. "She's terribly talented, Ilona. After I tested her pitch, I worked with her for a while. She can pick up tunes and replay them perfectly. It's the most astounding thing I've ever seen."

Ilona smiled, but inside she felt the seed of conflict. Judit had shown signs of musical ability. She and Andras had accepted the fact that Judit had inherited her father's talent. They had even discussed when to start training her, how hard to train her, how far they expected her to rise. Now, suddenly, their best friend's daughter had presented Andras with the answer to a teacher's dream. Katalin was clearly more than talented. She was a prodigy.

"Are you going to start to teach her now?" Ilona asked. "She's so young."

Andras heard the unspoken question in Ilona's voice: *What about our Judit?*

"Everyone starts at his own time. Judit will start later, when she's ready. Katalin must start now." His eyes turned dark. "It will be my present to Zoltán," Andras said. "My way of repaying him for all he and Mária did for us. When he comes home, his daughter will play a special recital just for him."

"That will be lovely," Ilona said, thinking what Andras was thinking. "*If* Zoltán comes home."

Every nation, at some point in its history, harbors a secret shame, a place where the basest, vilest, most sadistic impulses of man are exercised. Recsk was Hungary's secret shame. Located fifty miles northeast of Budapest, hidden behind nine-foot-high, electrically charged walls topped with barbed wire, Recsk had been built in 1948 to house enemies of the Stalinist state. So brutal was the treatment of its prisoners that Recsk became a name rarely uttered, a name spoken in whispers, if spoken at all, for fear that giving it voice might give it life.

Zoltán's crime had been to dare to speak out against the dictatorial regime of Mátyás Rákosi, the Secretary General of the Communist Party and head of the Hungarian government, who had visited a reign of terror on the Hungarian people. Occasionally, there were protests, attempts by men like Zoltán to draw attention to the crumbling economy, to the lack of human rights and the widespread discontent. But men like Zoltán, men of prominence, seriously miscalculated the protective aura of their status. They thought their visibility and popularity would protect them. They thought they could speak out on behalf of their countrymen and command a receptive ear. They were wrong. Terribly, terribly wrong.

In the days following his imprisonment Zoltán had been denied food, forbidden any contact with the outside—no books, newspapers, radio, visitors, letters. He was beaten so often he grew accustomed to seeing his body spotted with hideous bruises.

He spent his days on the gravel detail. Each day, his crew was brought to a granite outcrop, which rose almost three hundred feet in the air. He and his fellow prisoners were expected to reduce that hill to fine gravel with small picks. When one day he failed to complete his two-hand-truck quota, he was forced to stand up to his knees in cold water for an entire night. At dawn he was ordered to shoulder a hundred-pound rock and climb up and down a ladder fifteen times for the amusement of his jailers. Within his first year Zoltán lost more than seventy pounds.

Recsk was a nightmare of solitude and pain. Whatever excruciating abuses were suffered, and there were many, they had to be suffered in silence. There could be no crying out to a friend, no quiet conversations of consolation with cellmates, no requests for help from anyone. By promising an extra piece of meat or an extra ration of water, the AVO guards had created a network of spies that made every man every other man's enemy.

Months passed in a blur of terrified exhaustion. Zoltán worked long hours on little nourishment. Somehow he managed to survive the weekly interrogations, the daily indignities. The only thing that kept him sane was the knowledge that even insanity would not release him. His jailers would simply devise new ways to torture him until his body was as mutilated and mangled as his spirit.

There were times, usually after Zoltán had witnessed something particularly brutal, when he tried to understand his jailers, when he tried to fathom what would cause anyone to hold human life in such low regard. What would warp a woman so that she would force one man to urinate in a bottle and then compel his cellmate to drink it? So sadistic that she would lure a half-mad prisoner into her room with promises of sex, undress, and then wait until two AVO cohorts burst in to accuse the poor, confused man of rape? How could they pummel another human being so unmercifully and then stand aside as the matron rammed a thin glass tube up the man's penis, instructing her aides to beat him again until it broke into a thousand pieces? What would turn a quiet country boy into a monster who would haul a man in front of a bright light, then order him to stand on one foot for hours on end, watching to see which went first, the prisoner's body or his mind? Zoltán had some of his questions answered when Ferenc Kassak was transferred to Recsk.

Kassak came from Zoltán's village. His family were dwarfholders, people who owned a piece of land too small to provide an adequate living. Kassak, his father, and his brothers often hired out to work other farms in the area. Sometimes they worked for the Gáspárs. While the two men knew each other as neighbors, never had they considered themselves friends. Ferenc had always been a homely boy, with small, ferretlike eyes, thin, unmanageable yellow hair, and a nose far too large for his face. When he became an adolescent, that face became a breeding ground for ugly red pustules. Perhaps because he knew his appearance was unpleasant, he began to cultivate an unpleasant personality. He became bitter and angry whenever his advances toward girls were repulsed or his attempts at friendships with other boys were rebuffed. He became outraged that in school he seemed to work three times harder than anyone else, and then barely passed. He became frustrated when it grew clear that finding a job that would afford him any respect was almost impossible. In other words, he became a perfect candidate for the AVO.

By the time Ferenc turned up at Recsk, he wore the green uniform of State Protecting Special Group with swashbuckling pride. He had already done service at the Russian border and at the Fő Street prison in Budapest, where he had established a reputation as a ferocious taskmaster. He had already become addicted to power and revenge. When he learned that Zoltán Gáspár was among his charges, he was elated. He demanded that the prisoner be brought before him.

At first Zoltán didn't recognize Ferenc. By that time, Zoltán had been in Recsk more than two years. He doubted he would have recognized his own wife. All he saw was the green uniform and the ubiquitous billy club that hung from Kassak's belt.

"Well, well," Ferenc said. "Fancy meeting you here."

When Zoltán narrowed his eyes and still had difficulty matching the voice and the face with a name, Ferenc poked Zoltán in the stomach with the butt of his club.

"Kassak. Remember me?"

Numbly, Zoltán nodded, suddenly more frightened than he had been since the night of his arrest.

"Gáspár comes from my home town," Ferenc told his friends, all of whom smiled on command. "He was the village celebrity," Ferenc continued, stalking Zoltán as he spoke, circling him, jabbing his chin with the club whenever Zoltán attempted to follow his path. "Everybody knew Gáspár. They said he was some kind of genius. That he played the violin better than anyone else. They said he got to travel all over Europe and the Soviet Union, playing in the big halls for all kinds of important people. Of course, I was just a humble farmer. I couldn't afford a ticket to one of his concerts. And even if I could've bought one, I don't think the great Gáspár would have considered me important enough. Too bad. I would've liked hearing him play. Wouldn't you like to hear him play?" he asked his cadre.

"A chance of a lifetime," one of them answered, his mouth spread wide in a salacious grin.

Twenty randomly selected prisoners were brought into the interrogation room and told to sit in a circle on the cold concrete floor surrounding Zoltán. Ferenc and five other AVO men sat in cushy club chairs at the far end. Zoltán was given a violin.

"Play until I tell you to stop," Kassak ordered.

"And if I can't?"

"Then *they*," he said, pointing to the frightened group on the floor, "will pay for your weakness."

Moving with a slowness tinged with angry defiance, Zoltán raised the violin under his chin and began to play.

Hours passed. Eight. Ten. Fourteen hours. Zoltán feared his fingers would snap or that his arm would fall off from the strain of maintaining the same position for so long, but whenever he wavered, all he had to do was look at the terrified faces of the prisoners around him. He couldn't be responsible for anyone's being beaten. He wouldn't be responsible for anyone's being killed. No matter how tired he was, he was determined he would survive this horrendous ordeal. And so would they.

Go back, he told himself. *Go back to the beginning. Remember Madame Vásáry, the exercises she taught you to relieve strain, the thousands of hours she made you practice. Remember what it was like when you were little, the joy you derived from performing.*

By concentrating very hard he erased his surroundings and transported himself to an imaginary concert hall. He envisioned his sister, Zsuzsanna, sitting in the wings, conducting him with her index finger, as she often did when she chaperoned him, applauding him, shouting "*Bravo!*" at the end of each of his performances. He pictured his father and his mother in Vienna. He imagined Miklós and his brothers, Imre and Sándor and Tomás in the years before their deaths, trying to understand how he was able to make that box cry and laugh when each time they tried, all it did was squawk. The two people he refused to allow into his consciousness, however, were Mária and Katalin. If he saw their faces, even for a second, he feared he would go mad.

For hours he played—every concerto, every sonata, every symphony, every scale, every drill he had ever known. He played them in sequence and then invented variations of his original order, so that each time the sequence changed. For some of the prisoners at his feet, listening to him was double torture. The music insisted on lulling their exhausted bodies to sleep, but each time anyone dozed off, a guard swatted him with a rubber hose.

"Is this what they mean by a captive audience?" Ferenc laughed when the concert had gone on for fifteen agonizing hours. "You should thank me, Gáspár, for providing such interested listeners."

Zoltán wanted to kill him. Instead, he continued to play. This had become a contest, a gladiators' battle between him and the repulsive Kassak. Zoltán knew that in the end he didn't have a chance of defeating Ferenc, but he was going to do battle the best way he could.

Sixteen. Eighteen. Twenty hours.

Zoltán began to have hallucinatory flashes. His eyes blurred and he saw strange faces floating before him. Only when consciousness returned did he realize with a shudder that they were the faces of prisoners he had known, prisoners whom he had watched die.

After twenty-four hours, Ferenc stood.

"Stop!"

Zoltán stopped, but it took him several minutes to straighten his arms and bring them down to his sides. The violin fell to the floor. Ferenc picked it up. He nodded to two of his aides, who dragged Zoltán over to a bench. As Zoltán sat down, his body crumpled, drooping over the table like a leaf thirsting for water. He was barely conscious.

"Did you like your concert?" Ferenc asked the cowed group still seated on the floor.

No one moved. No one knew the right answer.

"I hated it!" With that, he smashed the violin against the concrete wall, stomping on the larger pieces until the instrument was nothing but a pile of splinters. Twenty pairs of frightened eyes stared at him. Whatever discomfort they had endured up to now had been simply a prelude to this moment.

"You know," Kassak said as he strolled across the floor to where Zoltán was, "I don't understand why everyone always said you were so special, Gáspár."

He grabbed Zoltán's hair, lifted up his head, and then let it fall, smiling as Zoltán's cheek slammed against the wooden table. Zoltán was too weak to protest. He was too weak even to cry out in pain.

"You know what? I listened to you for twenty-four hours and you didn't sound special. I didn't hear you play one thing I liked."

Zoltán's back stiffened as he felt the searing heat of an unreasonable fury about to be unleashed.

"In fact," Kassak said, leaning down and shouting in Zoltán's ear, "your playing gave me a headache. I don't like headaches."

Before anyone could even blink, Ferenc raised his club and slammed it down on Zoltán's hands, hitting him again and again, crushing his fingers until the skin lay nearly flat against the table. Ferenc wanted to hear Zoltán scream. He wanted to hear him beg for mercy. He wanted to hear cries of fear and respect and regret and apology. But no sound came from the limp body of Zoltán Gáspár. No screams. No shouts. Not even a whimper. He might have been dead except for the tears that ran silently down his cheeks.

For six weeks Zoltán's pain was so intense, so excruciating, he prayed for death to release him from this house of the damned. His release finally came, but only because Joseph Stalin died before he did. In 1953, two years and two months after his arrest, Recsk was closed. Zoltán Gáspár was allowed to return to his family.

Mária had to fight not to faint when the door opened and Zoltán stood next to Miklós in the foyer. He was so thin, so drawn. He had lost most of his hair. What little remained was the flat, lifeless white of a hospital sheet. His eyes, which she used to think were as warm as a cup of cocoa, had turned cold and muddied, like a shallow stream after a heavy winter rain. Still, he was home. He was alive and that was all that mattered. She ran to him and flung her arms around him, unable to stem the flood of tears that coursed down her cheeks. She clung to him. At first he didn't return her embrace. She held him closer, pressing his thin frame against her body, trying to tell him that whatever they had done to him, they hadn't destroyed her love. Slowly, hesitatingly, she felt his arms encircle her.

Within seconds, Zsuzsanna grabbed for her brother, touching his face, kissing his cheeks, examining him, assessing him. She cried as she welcomed him home, standing aside only so that Mihai could add his own greeting to his wife's. The Strassers tugged at Zoltán as well, Ilona's trained eyes and hands spotting more serious remnants of his incarceration than his silence. She wouldn't say anything today, but as she squeezed his arm, she promised herself that before the end of the week she would have him in her clinic for a full examination.

Katalin hung back and watched.

"Is that him?" Judit whispered.

"I guess so." She stared at Zoltán, then nudged Judit and pointed to a photograph of her father on a nearby table. "Do you think he looks like the man there?"

Judit looked at the man talking to her parents. Then she looked at the young man in the photograph, the one standing next to Mária, smiling down at a baby Mária held in her arms.

"I don't know," Judit said, as confused as Katalin.

As relatives crowded around him, Katalin continued to search for something that would assure her of his identity. He hadn't smiled, so she couldn't compare it to the picture. He hadn't said anything, but even if he had she probably wouldn't have recognized his voice. All she knew about the man called Zoltán Gáspár was that he made the most beautiful music she had ever heard.

"Look who's here, Zoltán," Mária said, linking her arm through his and guiding him farther into the room.

Sitting on the couch, looking very old and very frail, was Madame Vásáry. A swell of emotion overcame Zoltán as he looked at her. She was in her nineties now, but nonetheless it bothered him to see her so birdlike, draped in black, her flesh as desiccated and shriveled as a neglected piece of fruit.

"The day you were arrested, she went back to wearing only black," Mária said quietly, pressing Zoltán's arm to move him toward his teacher.

Zoltán walked with a leaden step, as if postponing a dreaded moment. He sat beside her. They looked into each other's souls, reaffirming a connection that had been forged an eternity ago. Madame Vásáry began to cry. Humble tears streamed down a proud and regal face. Zoltán took her in his arms and held her. As they clung to each other, Zoltán realized he owed her his life, in more ways than one. Not only had she served as midwife to his talent, but she had taught him discipline, mental strength, and emotional fortitude. Without that stock in his spiritual arsenal, surely he would have died.

Watching the reunion between Zoltán and Madame, Mária realized Katalin had yet to say hello. Trying not to attract too much attention, she went to the corner where her daughter stood, staring at the man on the couch.

"Don't you want to welcome Papa home?" Mária asked.

Katalin wanted to tell her mother that she didn't know the man with the white hair and the black-rimmed eyes. She wanted to say that he frightened her and that she needed reassurance that he was who they said he was, but she could tell how anxious Mária was for her to go to him. And so she did.

"Welcome home, Papa," Katalin said, her face flushing as everyone turned to look at her. At the sound of her voice, Zoltán's mouth trembled. Tears as big as snowflakes fell from his eyes as he held out his hands and invited Katalin into his arms.

It was then that Madame Vásáry howled, issuing a deep cry of unspeakable pain. Katalin jumped back, alarmed and bewildered. Mária, Zsuzsanna, Miklós, and the others followed Madame's eyes, which had locked on the cruel brand of the AVO. Zoltán's fingers were gnarled and bent, twisted into odd thick shapes that seemed inappropriate on his delicate hands.

Madame Vásáry took those hands in hers, holding them as gently and respectfully as one would hold an angel's wings. This was worse than simple torture, she thought, worse than a mere atrocity against man. This was a sin against God, an attack on one of His blessings, an utter revilement of His powers. Folding his hands between hers, she lifted them to her lips with reverence, as if she were about to receive the Eucharist. And then she cried, unashamedly keening over the loss of something very precious. Zoltán cried with her, finally allowing himself to vent an ineffable sadness that had coiled around him like a serpent, squeezing the life out of him until he was left with little but a shell.

The others were too stunned to speak. The shock of what had been done to Zoltán was shattering enough, but this moment between him and Madame was too private and too searing for an audience. They busied themselves with meaningless tasks. Mária went to the kitchen to refill the coffee pot. There, she wept into a towel, muffling her grief as best she could. Miklós and Mihai pretended that chairs needed rearranging. Zsuzsanna turned her back to the room and bit her lip to keep from screaming. Ilona lowered her head so no one could see the rage she was fighting. Andras had found a corner to hide his tears. The only one who seemed to know what to do next was Katalin.

"We have a surprise for you, Papa," she announced.

Zoltán wiped his eyes and turned toward the small child who stood at his elbow, really looking at her for the first time since he had walked through the door of his home. Her eyes had changed, becoming greener than he had remembered. Her face, though still full, had lost some of the babyishness that had rounded it when he had last seen her. Her hair, held by a silky ribbon, was a burnished gold, a gleaming yellow kissed with a touch of red, a color he could only compare to the rich, polished maple of a Stradivarius violin. She was staring at him, and he knew that she had as much difficulty recognizing him as he had recognizing her.

"What is it, *kicsi szilva?*"

Katalin smiled. Only her papa called her "little plum." She wrapped her arms around his neck and kissed his cheek, her way of thanking him for divining her problem and solving it.

"Uncle Andras," Katalin said, feeling much better about everything, "show Papa our surprise."

Andras walked over to a large screen and, with the help of Mihai, lifted it and put it to the side. Behind it was a spinet piano.

"While you were away," Andras said delicately, "Katalin made a new friend." He winked at Katalin and held out his hand, signaling her to come to the piano.

Suddenly shy, she climbed onto the stool and wiped her hands on her skirt. For encouragement she looked over at Judit, who was nodding enthusiastically.

"As a welcome-home treat, Katya will play the first movement of Beethoven's 'Moonlight' Sonata."

Andras stepped aside, expecting Katalin to begin immediately. Instead, she turned on the stool and looked at Zoltán.

"Will you play with me, Papa?"

An uncomfortable silence umbrellaed the room. Zoltán, swallowing a pain so sharp he thought it had cut his heart in two, looked at his daughter and said softly, "I can't."

She stared at him in disbelief. Of course he could play. She had heard his records.

Mária, noticing the child's distress, said, "Papa's very tired."

Katalin looked at his eyes, his sagging frame. He did look tired.

"Maybe some other time," she said.

"Maybe," Zoltán said, choking back a surge of unresolved anger that threatened to overwhelm him.

Katalin began to play. As Zoltán listened to the familiar strains of the sonata and realized how magnificently this four-year-old was playing, he felt as if he had been transported back to a point in time a thousand years ago. He remembered the first time he had touched the violin, the first time he had created glorious sounds from an inanimate object. He remembered how powerful he had felt, holding an instrument capable of such beauty in his hands. He looked at Katalin's face and saw the same glow that must have shone on his own face, the glow that comes from discovering one's talent.

Tears crowded his eyes as pride in his past and regret about his future stumbled over each other. His family had been overjoyed to see him, grateful he was alive. He, too, was grateful he had survived—thousands hadn't. But Recsk had changed his life. He would never play the violin again.

He looked at his daughter's hands and thought about his own. His eyes filled once again. Mária and Miklós and Zsuzsanna and his friends the Strassers promised that someday he would find peace and come to terms with his fate. Only he and Madame Vásáry knew that would never happen.

Through the thick wall of his hatred came the lilting notes of Beethoven's sonata. In a moment of awakening, Zoltán realized that the power of music had been stronger than the power of evil. His talent hadn't died in that hellhole. It had been passed on. It lived within his child.

As he listened to her play, a phrase from that long-ago time of his youth asserted itself, whispering to him as if the ghost of his mother was trying to speak to him from beyond.

"One door closes," the spirit said, "but when it does, another door opens."

Three days later, Madame Vásáry died. For her, all the doors had closed.

3

October 21, 1956

No matter how hard she tried, Katalin couldn't keep still. Impatient by nature, she found waiting almost as torturous as having her hair plaited. As she stood in the wings of the Kossuth Recital Hall listening to another student play a Chopin étude, she toyed with her skirt, pretending it was a pretty pink cloud that had ventured down from the sky just to be with her on this special day. With a flick of her hands she puffed up the soft chiffon fabric and watched gleefully as it billowed, seemed to hang in the air for a few seconds, and then fell about her in gentle folds.

It was the most beautiful dress Katalin had ever owned. It had long sheer sleeves, a ruffled collar, and a graceful three-tiered skirt that made her feel as if she were inside the petals of a flower. And, of course, it was pink. Pink had always been Katalin's best color. It softened the red in her blond hair, deepened the green of her eyes, and cast a rosy glow on her pale, china-doll skin. But aside from the color, what made this dress even more beautiful was the fact that Mária had fashioned it from a costume she had worn in one of her plays.

From the stage, a loud fortissimo jolted Katalin out of her reverie, forcing her to remember where she was and why. She listened carefully so she would know how much longer she had to wait before taking the other girl's place. As she turned away she caught a reflection of herself in a nearby mirror. Knowing that her entire family was in the audience, she checked to see that her fidgeting hadn't unloosed her braids or scuffed her shoes or scrunched down her anklets. And, although she never liked admitting she was wrong, she conceded that her mother had been right about the feathers. Katalin had wanted to save the maribou feathers that had edged the glamorous evening gown, but Mária wouldn't hear of it. Katalin was seven years old. This was her first recital. She had to behave in a certain way. She had to look a certain way. And feathers, Mária told her disappointed daughter, were not part of the classic concert pianist's look.

"It's time, Katya. Play well." Andras Strasser kissed both her cheeks, squeezed her hand, and walked out to make the introduction.

Suddenly Katalin realized she was completely alone. Uncle Andras was onstage. Her parents were beyond her immediate reach. Because she was the last to perform, all the other students were gone. She was on her own, just as she would be when she sat down at the piano. For the next thirty minutes, whatever happened was up to her. It was a startling revelation for one so young. At that moment all she wanted to do was run away.

I hate this! she thought, wringing her hands, allowing the panic she felt in the pit of her stomach to rise and vent itself. *I don't want to do this. They didn't make Judit do this. Why me? What if I mess up? What if my head shuts off or my fingers don't work? What if I fall off the bench?*

"And now," Andras said, "it is with great pleasure that I introduce a young lady who is making her debut this afternoon playing the 'Concert Allegro' in B-flat minor by Alexander Scriabin. Ladies and gentlemen," he continued, using the formal Hungarian manner of address, surname first, "I give you Miss Gáspár Katalin."

Katalin heard her name, and a rush of excitement replaced the insecurity of moments before. She breathed deeply, wiped her hands on the seat of her dress, and made her entrance. At first she was too nervous to look at anyone other than the kind, smiling face of her mentor, but as she took her place at the piano, she turned and scanned the audience, searching for her father. She was hoping for a sign of encouragement. Afterward, she hoped for a sign of approval.

Zoltán Gáspár's face was solemn, frozen in an expressionless mask. His dark brown eyes fixed on Katalin and then blinked. His head tilted ever so slightly. Others may have missed his nod, but not Katalin. She smiled, because she understood all the feeling that had been conveyed in that tiny gesture. If he didn't applaud or shout out to her or offer her broad, enthusiastic grins, it was simply his way, and Katalin accepted that. She had come to know her father as a man who had learned through painful experience that displays of sentiment were not always wise. To protect himself, he had invented an emotional shorthand, a way of reining in his feelings and reducing them to the smallest visible sign. Those who didn't know him found him often cold and aloof. His family and close friends knew better. Because they knew why.

Before Katalin began, she allowed herself a moment to study the rest of her entourage. Her mother sat next to Zoltán, her back straight, her head high, her bearing compellingly regal. Next to her were Ilona Strasser and Judit; then Aunt Zsuzsanna and Uncle Mihai; next to him, Uncle Miklós; and the Kardos family—Béla, Margit, and their children: Mátyás, Vera, and István. The twelve of them spread across the third row, a phalanx of support, their hands linked, as if by closing ranks they could ward off anything that might threaten the success of Katalin's performance. Katalin looked from one to the other, hoping to draw strength and confidence from their presence, but when her eyes reached her father's and noted the impatience shading them, she knew that, confident or not, it was time to begin.

She took another deep breath and closed her eyes, envisioning the sheet music of the allegro. She wriggled on the bench until she was comfortable, raised her hands, opened her eyes, and began to play.

Her small fingers moved swiftly and surely over the keys, compensating for the constraints of a youthful hand span with exuberant skips and leaps. Hours of scales and drills, which had seemed to have no purpose other than to torment her, rewarded her now with an almost effortless performance. She held her hands high but with a natural elegance, not the stiff pose of students who had been taught to practice with a coin resting on the back of each hand. She lifted her hands off the keys with a balletic grace, but not so often that she looked like a swimmer out of water. But beyond technique she had an instinctive interpretive feel for the music.

Zoltán watched his daughter with such burgeoning pride he was afraid he would bolt from his seat with the joy of it. She was brilliant, indeed a startlingly talented pianistic voice. As far as he was concerned, she was unlike all the other children he had seen that day, unlike most other children he had watched at recitals over the years. Usually they performed with a fervor that resulted less from actual talent than from the wish to be hailed as a prodigy. Zoltán laughed to himself. Of all the pretenders to the coveted title—and who should know better than he exactly what that title implied—his child gave true definition to the word.

"And now, as a special treat," Andras said, "I would like to invite Gáspár Mária to join her daughter onstage."

As Mária made her way to the stage, the audience expressed their appreciation with enthusiastic applause. She bowed gracefully, offered her hand to Andras for a kiss, and then took the microphone.

"This afternoon I am honored to share the spotlight with Gáspár Katalin." She turned and gave her daughter a quick wink and a loving smile. Katalin grinned. This was the part she had been looking forward to for weeks. To perform with her mother was the most exciting thing that could ever happen to her. Except, perhaps, to perform with her father.

"With your permission," Mária said, "we would like to present a piece known as a 'melo-drama' because it's part melody, part story. In this case, the story is about Babar the elephant."

The children in the audience applauded again, the smallest ones clapping the loudest. Most of them had been brought reluctantly to the recital hall to watch a relative perform. Once their kin had finished, interest in the other performances waned. Until now.

As Mária took her place on a stool near the belly of the piano and nodded to Katalin that she was ready, the hall became absolutely silent.

Mária waited, knowing that each second she delayed only increased the level of anticipation. Then, she smiled at the audience and began.

"In the great forest, a little elephant is born. His name is Babar."

Katalin's fingers danced over the keys in response to her mother's lead. The music was light, amusing, a theme befitting a jungle that was home to animals who walked and talked and danced and sang. As Mária told the tale, Katalin underscored it with music. For everyone, it was a delight. For István Kardos, it was an awakening.

István was nine. He had known Katalin for three years, but truthfully, he had never thought much about her until now. She was just a girl, the daughter of friends of his parents. She was nice enough, he supposed, but he had more important things to think about than a seven-year-old girl. Like soccer. And swimming. And riding horses. And other boy things.

The last place he had wanted to be today was inside a recital hall. He and his older brother, Mátyás, had made a dozen excuses as to why they shouldn't have to come, but his parents had insisted. He had known they would. The Kardoses would never refuse an invitation from the Gáspárs. From the day they met, it was as if they had made a pact to became instant best friends. István had thought only kids did that. But over the past three years these two families had spent every holiday and most Sundays together. He wasn't clear as to why the connection had been so immediate and so strong. Mátyás said he thought it had something to do with their uncle József, the one who died in prison.

". . . and Babar thought: I would like some fine clothes, too!"

In spite of himself, István smiled as the music painted a picture of a baby elephant prancing about in a dark suit, a red vest, and spats. The tune was bouncy, almost funny, tickling him like a soda with too much fizz. Unconsciously, his eyes were drawn to Katalin's hands. Fascinated, he watched her fingers flutter against the ivory keys. Mária spoke of danger lurking in the enchanted jungle. Katalin's fingers stiffened. She struck the notes more deliberately, more distinctly, as if she were personally reacting to the threat.

Though István was too young to understand her uncommon talent, he marveled at it nonetheless, especially when it was so obvious that he was not alone in his feelings of awe. All around him were rapt expressions of admiration. Every member of the audience was captivated, and though he guessed that some might say it was simply the presence of the legendary Mária Gáspár, he knew that Katalin Gáspár was weaving her own lyrical spell.

Though István didn't advertise his softer side, he was appreciative of expressions of familial closeness. He had been raised by demonstrative parents who shared their feelings openly with their children. He could never remember a time that Béla or Margit shied away from a kiss or a hug. It didn't matter if they were alone or in public. "Love shouldn't have to wear disguises," Margit always said.

István thought about that as he glanced over at Zoltán Gáspár. Most of the time, the older man's feelings were heavily disguised, his emotions masked. Today was different. The mask had slipped. István watched as Zoltán knotted his crippled hands together. The boy winced, convinced that Zoltán was in pain. He had to be. His hands were so gnarled, so misshapen. Usually István avoided looking at them. They made his stomach feel loose, the way it did when Béla's car roller-coastered over hilly country roads. But today his eyes fixed on those hands, which, according to his mother, had once produced some of the most magnificent music in the world. Suddenly István felt pain, a sharp twinge of sympathy as he tried to imagine what it would be like never to be able to do something you loved doing again. What if someone broke his legs and he could never play soccer again? Or swim? István shook his head, ridding himself of the thought. It was simply too horrible to contemplate.

"King Babar and Queen Celeste are indeed very happy."

Katalin played the final chords, then bounded off the bench to accept Mária's embrace. As mother and daughter held hands and took their bows, the audience burst into applause, rising for a standing ovation.

István stood also, but as he smacked his hands together he found himself peeking over at Zoltán once again. This time he saw no pain, no regret, no thoughts of what might have been. This time he saw nothing but a broad, proud smile.

In the reorganization of Budapest after the Soviets liberated Hungary from the Germans, housing was parceled out with a stingy hand. Most apartments offered minimal space—a kitchen, a bath, and anywhere from one to four bedrooms, depending on the number of family members. There were no living rooms, no formal dining rooms, no dens, no rec rooms, no garden rooms, no gardens. Because the government provided an adequate variety of concerts, plays, movies, and lectures, there was no need to waste valuable space on entertaining areas that would be used rarely, if ever. And because there were no spare rooms, there could be no reason for people to congregate and perhaps talk about the way things used to be or, worse, the way they thought things ought to be.

By Hungarian standards, the Gáspár apartment was lavish. Due to Mária's celebrity, and despite Zoltán's imprisonment, the government had granted permission for them to keep the apartment they had occupied since their marriage, a spacious two-bedroom apartment with a third room they used as a salon.

Today, that room was being used to celebrate Katalin's recital. The women had cooked for days, filling three tables with steaming pots of hearty fare. Miklós had ferried two cases of wine from Debrecen, as defiant of the rule limiting alcohol as he was about most of the rules the Soviets had imposed on the Hungarian people. Andras commandeered the Gáspárs' piano and entertained everyone with lively folk tunes that inspired hand-clapping and foot-stomping. Occasionally, Zsuzsanna, who was blessed with a rich contralto, burst into song, insisting that the others join in. All afternoon they partied. They ate. They drank. They sang songs, and once in a while one or more of them would jump to their feet for a wild csárdás.

Life had been so difficult for so many years that although no one dared express the sentiment aloud, it felt glorious to let go, to give in to the sunnier impulses of human nature, to indulge in the luxury of laughter. Katalin's recital had provided them with an excuse to forget the repressive regime of Ernö Gerö, to forget that whether or not it was formally acknowledged, they were once again an occupied nation, to forget that although Stalin was dead, his disciples lived on.

Late in the afternoon, while the others were listening to Zsuzsanna,

István found himself alone with Katalin in the kitchen. Both of them had come in search of something sweet.

"You were good today," he said, taking a piece of pastry from a tray next to the sink. "Really good."

Katalin's eyes widened with surprise. Though she was too young to have a crush, she thought István Kardos was special nonetheless. Hearing him compliment her was almost unbelievable, especially because, like most other boys she knew, he spoke to her only when necessary.

"Thanks," she said. "I'm glad you liked it."

"I did. That melo-drama thing was fun."

Katalin nodded and blushed and nervously nibbled on her lip. She didn't know what to say, what to do. He smiled at her. It made her feel funny.

"Do you have to practice a lot?" he asked between bites.

"Uh-huh." If she didn't look at his face, talking to him was easier.

"Do you mind? I mean, not being able to do what you like?"

"But this is what I like," she said, looking up, finding it strange that someone wouldn't understand the importance of music in her life. "I like the piano better than anything."

"Why?"

"Because I can do it better than anything else." Katalin shrugged, still not understanding how he could have missed something so obvious. The piano was who she was and what she would be. It was a truth she had known from the time she was three years old. "Don't you have something you do better than anything else?"

"No," he said, somewhat embarrassed, maybe even a little disappointed that he didn't have a distinctive gift to brag about.

"You have nice eyes," Katalin said, sensing that she had made him uncomfortable. "They're a real pretty blue. Deep, like the Danube."

István laughed.

"Thanks," he said, surprised, and somewhat moved. "But you don't have to try to make me feel good. I'm not jealous or angry or anything. Hey! You're lucky. You know what you're going to do. I don't, but you know what? I'm lucky too. I have nice eyes and lots of time before I have to think about grown-up things."

Katalin knew he was teasing her, but the poke was gentle. She giggled and blushed and thought that the world had never been so wonderful as it was at that exact moment. István smiled too.

But they were both mistaken. Their world was far from wonderful. And István had less time than he anticipated to think about grown-up things.

•   •   •

As the afternoon wore on and the discussions turned to more serious matters, the children wandered off, leaving the adults to their *Bikavér* and their conversation. Voices lowered automatically. Eyes searched for intruding ears. Miklós—who trusted no one outside his immediate family, and only tolerated the Kardoses because Zoltán insisted—left his seat to check the door. No one chided him for being overly suspicious. No one told him he was being foolish. Zoltán served as a painful reminder of what happened to those who were careless about voicing criticism.

"Things are happening," Miklós said, rejecting preamble as a waste of time. "Students all over the city are reacting to those students in Poznan who are rioting against the Russians. They feel if the Poles can do it, we can do it. They're talking revolution. They want the Russians out!"

"So do we all," Zsuzsanna said.

"Talk like that is meaningless without plans," Zoltán said quietly. "Do they have a strategy?"

Miklós would know. As a professor of philosophy at the university, he was well respected for his intelligence, and well known for his involvement in underground politics. Because he believed that most civil insurgencies began with those who had never experienced defeat and therefore never expected anything but victory, Miklós kept close tabs on what his students were thinking and feeling.

"They've organized a public meeting of sympathy at Bem's statue."

"When?"

"Two days from now. October twenty-third."

"I like it," Andras said, smiling wryly at the selection. General József Bem had been a Polish volunteer who supported the Hungarian revolution against the Habsburgs in 1848.

"It's not only the students who are beginning to stir things up," Mária said. "I have friends who belong to the Petőfi Club. They said that the last few meetings have been filled with nothing but talk of dissent."

"That means a lot," Ilona Strasser said. "Though they're Marxist, they've never been a reactionary group."

The Petőfi Club was a group named for another inspirational seed from the Hungarians' fight against their Austrian rulers. Sándor Petőfi was a young poet, a hero to some because of his bravery on the battlefield, a patriot to all because of the heartfelt yearning for freedom that fired his poems. Most of the members of the Petőfi Club were older—playwrights, actors, artists, and novelists—but there were several young communist philosophers who belonged and who, Mária believed, were probably responsible for the sudden shift in outlook.

"What do the Petőfis want?" Margit Kardos asked.

"They want to keep Hungarian wealth here and keep the Soviet secret police in Russia," Mária said.

"Here! Here!" Béla Kardos couldn't hide his anger. As a scientist, it infuriated him that the Russians mined valuable Hungarian uranium for their own war machine. Worse, they took without paying, leaving Hungary weakened both economically and defensively. "I've never agreed with much that the Petőfi Club says, but this time I'm on their side."

"There is only one side," Mihai said, his fists clenched.

Mihai worked at the Rakosi Metal Works on Csepel Island, a large industrial development in the middle of the Danube that was often considered the heartland of communism. It was that island which the Soviets organized first, building factories and mills and an oil refinery. It was that island that exemplified the communist system. It employed the common man, the worker, the person for whom the Marxist philosophy was supposed to care. Mihai was one of "the Reds from Csepel." But Mihai did not care for the system.

"Russian troops have to leave Hungarian soil." Miklós said it calmly, matter-of-factly, but his voice reverberated with the zeal of a patriot, of a man who had spent most of his adult life decrying the fate of his nation.

"Easier said than done, my brother." One day, Zoltán feared, Miklós was going to speak when he shouldn't.

"It may not be easy," Miklós countered, "but it must be done."

"I can't disagree," Zoltán said, shelving his concerns, knowing that voicing them was useless anyway.

"We all agree." Béla Kardos looked from one to the other, as if asking for a secret pledge. "We've given the Soviets too much already. We've given them our brothers, our land, and our money. I refuse to give them our pride."

Zoltán heard the steely anger in his friend's voice. Their eyes met and held. They didn't need words to communicate their thoughts. Whatever was being planned, they would be a part of it. Despite what they had lost. Because of what they had lost.

Three months after Recsk had been closed, Zoltán had had a visitor.

"I hate to bother you, Mr. Gáspár, but I must talk to you."

"I'm not receiving guests."

"I'm Kardos Béla. I'm looking for my brother, József. Someone told me you might be able to help me."

"They were wrong. I can't help you."

Zoltán moved to close the door, but Béla jammed it with his foot, gently but firmly holding it open.

"I don't know where my brother is. I don't even know if he's dead or alive. After months of asking around, I was told he was in Recsk and that you were one of his cellmates. If you can't—or won't—say anything else, please just tell me if that much is true."

Béla's eyes were pleading for a response. Zoltán began to shake. For two years he had been conditioned to expect that questions were merely a prelude to torture. He wanted to slam the door, to rid himself of this inquisitor, yet the other man's anguish was too obvious to ignore. Fear and anxiety poured out of him like a bilious odor, casting a dark aura over them both. Zoltán's family had suffered not knowing where he was or what was happening to him. Clearly, this man had suffered also.

He stepped back, opened the door, and led Béla inside, offering him a chair opposite the sofa where he seated himself. He hesitated. Béla waited.

"Yes, I knew him," Zoltán said at last, prompted by the recollection of how cruel he had thought it was that he had been denied information he had wanted, unwilling to repeat the offense himself. "Yes, we were cellmates."

Tears sprang up in Béla's eyes, rilling down his face like a stream racing after a storm.

"It's taken me so long to find out anything," he cried. "I'm grateful even for that. Is there anything else you can tell me?"

As Béla wiped his eyes, Zoltán considered his request. There was a great deal he could tell this man. But should he? Was ignorance less devastating than knowledge? Was a lie kinder than the truth?

Béla seemed to sense the conflict raging within Zoltán.

"I expect the worst," he said quietly.

Zoltán poured a glass of wine for Béla and himself. He sipped his slowly, wishing it could anesthetize him to the pain he was about to recount, the hurt he was about to inflict.

"József had been in Recsk for six months when I arrived. He was physically weakened, but his spirit was strong."

A brief smile grazed his lips, a smile that said József Kardos had been very courageous. Béla nodded. He imagined his brother would have been brave. He was pleased to know that he was.

"There wasn't much camaraderie there," Zoltán continued, his voice low, his words measured, as if he needed to concentrate on containing the malevolence inherent in these memories. "If you reached out to help someone else, they beat you back. It didn't take long to get the message that it was every man for himself. Once or twice, though, József and I did reach out. I guess that's why I felt so horrible about what happened."

"Tell me about the times you spoke." Béla wanted to prolong the conversation, to allow himself time to accept what he knew was coming.

"The first time was on a Sunday. I only know that because the AVO guards made certain that Sundays were more terrifying than any other day of the week. Anyway, according to one of the guards, József had been insolent. To teach him a lesson they brought him into a room and made him face a wall that had a window in it. Shining through the window, directly into his eyes, was a bright white light. They put the pointed end of a pencil against his forehead, the other end against the window, and told him that if the pencil dropped, he would be beaten to death."

Béla groaned.

"József and I knew of men who had been forced to play this particular game. They had fainted from the glare of the light and were, in fact, beaten to death. József withstood the torture, but when he was returned to the cell, the pencil was stuck in his forehead. When I went to pull it out, he shook me off, warning me not to touch him, not to brand myself a trouble maker."

Béla didn't speak. He simply stared into space and shook his head from side to side, slowly, rhythmically, like a weighted pendulum.

"He repaid me by teaching me how to cope with some of the more disgusting aspects of our life in Recsk. Every once in a while the guards insisted that we use our food plates as toilets. For two days I refused to eat. I couldn't." Even now, Zoltán cringed from the thought. "József warned me that if I fainted during inspections or let up on my daily gravel load, they'd kill me. He tried to teach me to pick at my food so I'd get just enough to nourish myself. When I couldn't do it, he fed me from his plate."

It was hard for Béla to believe what he was hearing, but to look into Zoltán's eyes and at his hands left no doubt that every word he spoke was the truth.

"How did he die?" Béla asked suddenly. He couldn't have spared his brother the torment József endured, but he could spare this man the torture of reliving it.

Zoltán leaned toward Béla, a man who just an hour before had been a stranger. He took Béla's hands in his and began to tell him of the last days of József Kardos.

"For some reason, or no reason, the AVO became convinced that József knew the locations of secret political meetings. Naturally, József insisted he knew of no such meetings. They insisted he did. They cut his food and water to a bare subsistence level and still ordered him to

put in a full day's work. At night they interrogated him. József continued
to protest his innocence. They continued to brutalize him."

Zoltán fought to squelch the rising emotion that threatened to choke
his speech and wet his eyes. When he was able, he continued.

"He withstood unspeakable things. But then the guards told him
they were going to arrest his wife and use her for their own pleasure.
They described what they wanted to do to her, how they planned to
abuse her. It was just too much. József's mind snapped. That night he
hanged himself with his shirt. The next morning I cut him down."

A deep, throaty sob burst through Béla's lips. He collapsed into
Zoltán's grasp, keening for his brother. Zoltán cried with him, for him,
for József, for himself. For a long while, the two men comforted each
other. Then they talked. Later, when Béla went home to tell his wife
and sister-in-law what he had discovered, his only comfort was that he
had also discovered a friend.

"How'd I do?" Katalin asked Judit.

The two girls were sitting cross-legged on Katalin's bed, their shoes
tossed haphazardly on the floor, their hands sticky with poppy seeds and
slivers of parchment-thin dough the Hungarians call *rétes*.

"You did fine," Judit said impatiently, having answered the same
question five times already. "But if you ask me again, I'll scream."

"No, you won't." Katalin smiled. She knew she was being a pest,
but she didn't care. More to the point, she knew Judit didn't care.

"Okay, I won't." Judit laughed too. "Are you eating that?"

Katalin shook her head no. Judit grabbed another piece of pastry
and shoveled it into her mouth, licking her fingers and lips like a cat.

"When are you going to give a recital?" Katalin asked, undoing her
braids, letting her hair fall down her back in soft red squiggles.

"Who knows? Whenever Papa says so."

"I wanted you to give your recital when I gave mine."

"Me too." Judit understood that, since both of them did everything
else together, Katalin had assumed they would ascend the musical ladder
together as well. Judit was more realistic. She had spent years listening
to her own father extol the talents of Katalin Gáspár, while doling out
only occasional praise for Judit's abilities. "It would've been fun, but I'm
not as good as you, Katya."

"Sure you are."

"No, Katalin. You're better."

"I don't like being better than you."

"Why not?"

"I'm better than Karolyi Anna and she hates me."

Judit groaned with exasperation.

"Don't be a silly goose! I don't hate you. I could never hate you. We're best, best, best, best friends!"

"No matter what?" Katalin held up her hand.

Judit linked her pinky around her friend's. "No matter what."

"Good." Katalin smiled. The issue was settled.

Vera Kardos peeked into the room. "My brothers are annoying me. What're you two doing?"

"Nothing. Come in."

Vera Kardos was eleven years old and extremely thin. At five she had struggled valiantly against rheumatic fever. Though her doctors assured her she had won the battle, she knew she had lost the war. Her heart was frail, unable to tolerate stress, incapable of withstanding undue strain. Yet, in spite of the limitations placed on her by her condition, Vera was a happy, generous child who had somehow managed to avoid the I-am-sick-and-therefore-the-center-of-the-universe syndrome that seemed to affect so many other young victims of serious disease.

Katalin and Judit loved having Vera around, because she took them seriously. She didn't dismiss them or treat them as if they were unworthy because they were younger. She played dress-up with them and combed their hair into extravagant theatrical styles. She let them practice their hairdressing techniques on her own thick brown tresses, allowing them to braid, curl, and twist to their heart's content. She never made fun of them or appeared bored with them, even though sometimes Katalin's boundless inquisitiveness was exhausting and Judit's practical jokes unnerving. Moreover, she listened to them, encouraging them to share their worries and express their concerns. In Hungary in 1956, even small children fell victim to the tension pervading the atmosphere. Having Vera as a sounding board had proved a blessing for Katalin and Judit.

"Vera, tell us a story." Judit adored stories, especially when Vera told them. She had a sweet, melodious voice that made even the simplest tale sound like a Puccini aria.

"Please," Katalin begged—she, too, a fan.

Vera crawled between them on the bed and rested her back against one of Katalin's pillows.

"Which one would you like?"

"It's Katya's day," Judit said. "Let her choose."

" 'The Princess Who Laughed Roses.' "

"I knew you'd pick that one." Judit grimaced as she stretched out next to Vera and tucked her hands behind her head. "She thinks she's the princess in the story."

"Do not!"

"Do too!"

"Once upon a time," Vera began, raising her voice to silence theirs, "there lived a king who had a beautiful daughter. When she cried, gleaming white pearls rolled down her cheeks. When she laughed, rose petals fell from between her lips. And if she took off her shoes and walked about barefooted, she left gold coins wherever she stepped."

Vera continued the simple story, telling of the handsome prince who sent emissaries far and wide into his kingdom to find this magical princess. As in most folktales, there was a bête noire, a witch who wanted the prince to marry her daughter instead. The evil witch and her daughter kidnapped the princess, gouged out her eyes, and threw her into a deep, dark pit. A humble gardener found her and, feeling sorry for the poor blind girl, brought her home.

Meanwhile, the prince was miserable. His betrothed didn't cry pearls or laugh roses or mark her path with golden coins. She never laughed. She never cried. And she never took off her shoes. Besides all that, she was ugly.

The gardener, too, was unhappy. He wanted his young charge to smile, but he knew that until her eyesight was restored, her mood would remain as black as her world. Hearing of a witch who sold eyes, he went to the sorceress's hut, buying a pair she claimed she found in a ditch. When the gardener put them in place, he and his wife were astounded at the sudden, radiant beauty that overwhelmed the princess. She was instantly transformed into a magnificent, magical creature. She was so excited she began to laugh. Rose petals fell from her lips. She cried with joy and dazzling pearls danced down her cheeks. She ran about the room and they all watched in amazement as gold coins spotted the floor where she stepped. Out of gratitude, she gave the gardener and his wife the pearls and the coins and then set out for the prince's castle.

When she arrived, she was given a job as chambermaid for the evil queen. She served her queen as best she could, but one day, while she was dressing her employer for a ball, a pin pricked the older woman's skin. The queen was so angry she turned around and slapped the girl, making her cry. As glistening white pearls slid down her cheeks, the prince happened by. One look and he knew he had found his true love. Naturally, they lived happily ever after.

"I love that story," Katalin said with a satisfied sigh. "Don't you love that story?" she asked Vera.

"Yes, Katya, I do."

"See," Katalin said, turning to Judit, who seemed preoccupied with something on Katalin's nightstand. "It's two against one."

Suddenly Judit turned, faced the other two girls, and laughed. Rose petals popped out of her mouth. One or two stuck to her lips, causing her to sputter and spit. Vera and Katalin stared at first and then collapsed with laughter.

Within the week, some of that laughter would be stilled forever.

4

"It's happening, Zoltán. People are coming out of their houses and storming the streets demanding freedom. It's the most exciting thing I've ever seen!"

Miklós walked as he talked, pacing the perimeter of the Gáspár living room like a surveyor. His face was animated, his speech punctuated with gestures. He had rushed over to his brother's after the demonstration at the József Bem statue, eager to share the joy he felt.

"They expected a handful of students," he said, his eyes ablaze, his hand curled into a truculent fist. "Do you know what they found? Fifty thousand patriots. Fifty thousand! Can you imagine? I don't know where they came from, but they just kept coming, circling Bem, shouting 'The Russians must go!' "

Zoltán and Mária sat transfixed, listening to Miklós recount the events of the day as if he were describing a religious vision.

"Tonight they're gathering at Parliament Square. You must come. You must be part of it."

"Of course we'll go," Zoltán said, his answer spiced with indignation, as if Miklós had challenged his patriotism. "We are part of it."

Miklós, Mihai, the others—they spoke about freedom, but in truth only Zoltán knew what freedom looked like, what it felt like, in the way that only someone who has been unjustly imprisoned can. Of course he would go to Parliament Square.

They walked from their apartment in Buda, across the Chain Bridge into Pest, along the Danube to the large square in front of the Parliament building. Along the way they stopped for the Strassers and then joined the others flooding the streets. They beckoned to those who remained unsure, those who watched from open windows with curious eyes. Not everyone was ready to expose himself to the watchful, vengeful stare of the AVO and the Soviets. Those who did marched to a rhythm of hope. Though no one dared to sing its song aloud, for the moment, they felt satisfied to be able to hum it to themselves.

As they entered Kossuth tér, their eyes widened in awe. The 700,000-foot square was a sea of people. Surely, with so many voices speaking, finally they would be heard?

Instinctively, Andras and Zoltán hoisted their young daughters onto their shoulders, keeping them clear of the crush of the throng. If the adults were awed by the size of the assembly, Katalin and Judit were thunderstruck. Neither of them had ever seen so many people in one place at the same time. They were both excited and frightened by what they saw, what they heard.

Despite their youth, these two small girls understood much of what was happening. They understood that things were not right, that there were too many don'ts, too many rules. They understood that the soldiers with the red stripes running down their pant legs and the red stars on their caps were there to make them obey and to punish them if they didn't. They understood because even for seven-year-olds, it was hard to remain innocent when looking at Zoltán's hands or listening to Andras and Ilona speak of the years during the war when they had been forced into hiding in order to avoid becoming two more names on the long list of Hungarian Jews herded onto trains and sent to their deaths at Auschwitz.

"Look at the flags," Katalin said, pointing out the hundreds of flags with the red crest of Soviet communism ripped from the center.

Judit followed her friend's finger until she was distracted by the sound of her mother's voice chanting "We want Nagy Imre! We want Nagy Imre!"

Ilona and thousands of others took up the call, insisting that Imre Nagy come out and address them. Imre Nagy was a faithful communist who had been granted power and then had it snatched away from him two years before because he was considered too liberal. To many he was a hero. To those in power he was a threat. To most loyalists, however, he remained the best solution. With Nagy in power, it was believed, Hungary would have more freedom than it currently enjoyed, but could still remain a good communist nation.

When Nagy stepped out onto the balcony, the crowd went wild. Katalin and Judit reached out and clasped hands, hanging on to their fathers and each other, looking up toward the balcony as if God himself had appeared. Katalin glanced down at her mother and saw tears in Mária's eyes. Andras, too, appeared misty as Nagy began to address them.

"Dear comrades," he said.

"We're not comrades," Zoltán shouted, his words flying over the crowd like a spark in dry wood.

All around them, thousands of angry voices echoed Zoltán's sentiment. Suddenly, a violent protest flamed throughout the square.

"Dear friends," Nagy began again. This time, he was greeted with uproarious approval.

Soon, another chant rose from the crowd.

"Now or never! Now or never!"

Even Katalin recognized it as a phrase from an old Hungarian poem. She and Judit joined in, enjoying the sensation of being part of history.

Nagy held up his hands, asking for silence. In a voice trembling with emotion, he began to sing a hymn previously banned by communist edict: "God Bless Hungary."

As Zoltán scanned the scene, listening to the masses intone their precious hymn, watching their faces brighten with a light only faith can provide, he thought his heart would burst with the elation he felt. It was as if someone had clothed his dreams in reality. How many nights had he prayed for a moment like this, a moment when his people would stand up and demand change? He turned, looking for Miklós, wanting to share this triumphant time with his brother. But Miklós was gone.

Several blocks away, down past the Elizabeth Bridge, Radio Budapest was under siege. Housed in a cluster of buildings near the museum park on Bródy Sándor Street, the radio station served as a magnet for those who wanted an end to oppression. Students still charged from their experience at the Bem statue, those who had just left Kossuth tér exalted after hearing Imre Nagy speak, citizens who happened by and noticed a crowd gathering, youngsters on the scent of a fight—all drew together outside the thick wooden doors that guarded the enclave.

To many, the radio station was a symbol of their subjugation. Protected around the clock by a team of AVO sharpshooters, Radio Budapest functioned like an insistent nanny, force-feeding its children propaganda and lies even when they protested they had had enough, that they were full and couldn't stomach any more. It was the very center of communist control—run by the Council of Communist Ministers, manned by more than 1,200 people, all of whom were required to belong to the Communist Party. Before tonight, the only alternative had been Radio Free Europe.

At nine o'clock a group of university students stood outside the wooden gates, shouting that they be allowed to enter so they could broadcast their demands. Their request was denied. Enraged, the young rebels thrust toward the gates, heaving against the heavy doors, trying to push them open. In response, dozens of tear-gas bombs rained down on the crowd. Two enormous beacons clicked on, flooding the area with harsh white light, giving the AVO men inside the building and their spies out on the street a chance to identify the leaders of this insolent insurgency.

A bellow of dissent roared through the air. Stones were hurled, aimed at the spotlights. In retaliation the AVO men aimed down into the mob, but they had machine guns in their hands, not stones. When they fired, lights didn't blink. Lives were snuffed out. Bodies fell. Women screamed. Frustrated, angry men shouted obscenities. The AVO continued to fire.

Suddenly, an army officer leaped onto a truck and shouted at the gunmen, demanding that they stop the killing. From deep within the crowd, Miklós Gáspár watched in horror as a spray of bullets came from somewhere inside the building, tearing into the flesh of the well-intentioned soldier, jerking his body around until all the life within it had been spilled onto the truck in a deadly red pool.

Reaction was instantaneous. The crowd surged forward, beating on the doors. Miklós stood where he was. He was being knocked and jostled about, but still he didn't move. He couldn't. He was paralyzed by the obvious: Without weapons, their efforts were futile.

Just then, up from the southern part of the city, Miklós spotted a line of trucks driving into view. Within minutes, workmen from Csepel climbed down and began unloading arms and ammunition they must have stolen from the munitions plants in which they worked. As Miklós watched several of them erect machine-gun emplacements on top of the trucks, he noticed Mihai directing some of the activity.

"Mihai," he shouted, running toward his brother-in-law. "What are you doing?"

"Joining the fight," Mihai said as he climbed up onto one of the trucks, aimed the heavy gun mounted there, and shot out one of the beacons.

The crowd howled its approval.

From atop another truck, one of Mihai's fellow workers calmly destroyed the second spotlight.

Again, the people shouted their thanks.

Just then, an ambulance drove into the center of the square. Several of the men began waving at the driver, trying to steer him toward the wounded who had been pulled off to the side. But the driver bypassed the wounded and continued toward the door. Within seconds, the vehicle was surrounded. The driver stopped but refused to be questioned. The crowd pressed against the window. Ignoring them, he stepped on the accelerator and started toward the doors. In doing so, he ran over someone's foot. When the crowd heard the victim's cry of pain, they mobbed the driver, dragging him out of the ambulance. Miklós and several others opened the back doors and climbed inside. Instead of medical supplies, the ambulance was stocked with guns and ammunition for the AVO.

The minute the crowd realized they had an AVO man in their possession, years of pent-up fury was released. They jumped on him, beating him, pummeling him, paying him back for all those who had been abused by his organization of terrorists. Mercifully, someone stopped the carnage by shooting the helpless man.

Meanwhile, a group of young men had emptied the ambulance of its cargo, handing weapons to any man willing to take them. The men from Csepel armed themselves from their cache and joined their brethren. From the top windows a storm of bullets, from the guns Hungarians sardonically called "Russian guitars," rained down over the makeshift army. Mihai and Miklós stood their ground. They tossed grenades. They instructed youngsters barely old enough to drive how to build protective barricades. They sent a team of Csepel workers and a few young boys into a nearby building to try to make their way inside the complex via a series of tunnels built during the war. They were determined to take the radio station.

Several hours later, they did.

Béla Kardos was not a revolutionary. He was a man of science, an intellectual who never really understood the essence of religious or political fervor. He lived his life according to formulas, not illusion. But that night, on October 23, Béla Kardos did not behave like a scholar. He acted like a zealot consumed with an intense hunger.

He and Margit lived on Dózsa György út, a large boulevard that lined the southern edge of the main park in Pest. From their apartment they had a clear view of the massive metal statue of Josef Stalin. Tonight a crowd had gathered at the statue. Some were carrying torches. Others had long ropes. Others had brought their cars and were shining their headlights on the black image of the despot who had insinuated his malevolence into their lives. People were shouting slogans, decrying the Russian presence, demanding food, the end of the AVO, the beginning of freedom.

Béla was touched, but, as always, his natural restraint inhibited him. Yet the more he watched, the stranger he began to feel. It was as if the scene before him acted as a catalyst prompting the reorganization of his own molecular structure, rewiring his impulses, recircuiting his emotional system to respond to a new set of charges. Slowly, he was being drawn into the action, lured into the fray. When he saw two young men climbing to the top of the massive statue accompanied by raucous chants of encouragement from the crowd below, he found he could no longer resist the pull of rebellion.

He ran outside, followed closely by Margit and their three children. At first he stood back and watched as the climbers hoisted a huge cable and attached it to Stalin's head. As they slid down, Béla ran toward the cable, grabbing on, standing shoulder to shoulder with a group of workmen who were tugging on the line in a desperate attempt to bow the head of the heinous Stalin. Like a man possessed, he pushed his body beyond its limits. Though his hands were scraped and bloody and every muscle ached, he felt nothing but the exhilaration of the moment, welcoming the pain like a penitent.

As he and the workmen continued to pull on the cable, and hundreds of hands continued to push, still others pounded against the iron with hammers and mallets. The sound was deafening, but to most it pealed like the bells of the basilica which had once occupied this very spot.

Like so many of those standing around her, Vera Kardos's immediate reaction had been to raise her hands to cover her ears, but just as she was about to press her hands against her head she stopped. She couldn't do it. It was wrong. To muffle the sound of Stalin's demise was a sacrilege. Though her head reeled from the earsplitting clamor, she endured, just as her parents and millions of others had endured the horrors of the dead dictator's regime.

Despite Herculean efforts, the statue refused to budge. Men heaved and tugged. Women flailed at its body, beating against it with their fists. Children kicked the massive boots that held the monster in place. Finally, three young workmen arrived with acetylene torches, which they immediately applied to the back of Stalin's knees. As the hot blue flame sliced the iron flesh of the hateful structure, Béla and the men on the ropes pulled again. This time, the behemoth lurched forward, slanting like a diver poised over a cliff. The metal at the knees continued to give, but death was too slow in coming for the bloodthirsty mob.

Mátyás was young, but he was strong and able. Grasping the situation, he corraled several of his friends, rummaged about the trucks parked alongside the road, and ran to the back of the statue. Together, they jammed crowbars into one of the cracked metal joints, pumping up and down, seesawing furiously, until at last the evil giant fell head first into the square.

István screamed along with everyone else. He screamed so loud he felt as if his lungs would burst, yet when he listened for his voice, he heard only one voice made up of thousands infected with a nearly insane glee at the sight of their oppressor lying face down at their feet. Restraining his excitement, he watched as the hammers and mallets began again, this time bent on totally crushing the statue. Several people began shouting: "We want our church back!" Others shouted curses and vowed further vengeance. István's blood coursed through his body as if the fear and exaltation he was feeling just then were racing for control of his being.

Just then, he noticed his mother walking toward the statue, her face set with a look he couldn't recall ever seeing before. With the dignified calm of a loyal subject about to pay obeisance to a monarch, she neared the head of the statue, stared down at it, and spat. The hammering stopped. The banging ceased. For a second that seemed like an eternity, silence prevailed. Margit's audience was stunned. Many knew who she was—a highly respected chemist, a quiet, cerebral family woman—yet even those who didn't would never ever have cast her in this role. All activity remained suspended while people considered what she had done. Then, as if a hive had been slashed open, people converged on the statue like a mass of frenzied bees, buzzing around it, spitting at it, demanding that the hulk be turned over so they could spit in Stalin's face. They were crazed with revenge, fueled by the heady sensation of being free to release their rage.

They might have continued for hours if not for the truck that backed up and stopped at the deposed statue. A group of students jumped out and tied the truncated mass to the back of the truck.

"What are you doing?" shouted István.

"Taking the old boy for a ride," the leader shouted back as he gave the signal for the truck to start.

Before anyone could object, the driver proceeded up Stalin Square, down Stalin Street, and into the center of town, dragging the offensive idol behind. Like the Pied Piper, the sound of the iron banging through the streets enticed more and more people to join the parade. Soon the bizarre procession moved toward the main boulevard that circled Budapest. István, Mátyás, Vera, Margit, and Béla Kardos marched arm in arm, shouting, brandishing sticks and stones and anything else they could find to express their disobedience.

As they crossed Rákóczi Street, they saw they were not alone in their conversion to lawlessness. Neighbors and friends who, like them, had always been upstanding, tractable citizens were rioting alongside a band of unrestrained students, trashing the building that housed the city's propaganda press, the communist newspaper, *Szabad Nep* ("Free People"). Within minutes the offices were in shambles, ravaged by bare hands eager to destroy the place they considered the house of lies.

Like a plague of locusts, the mass moved next to the bookstore where university students were compelled to buy all their communist texts. Everyone, including the scholarly Kardoses, hurled bricks through the large windows that fronted the store, then jumped inside and began tossing the hateful tomes of propaganda and doctrine into a pile in the middle of the street. Several workmen doused the books with gasoline, creating an immense bonfire of hate. For five hours, students and children like Mátyás, István, and Vera, who had been taught to revere the written word, stood alongside their parents and pitched books into the conflagration, applauding as the communist lies burned.

As the flames of inchoate freedom rose higher and higher, the orange fingers of the blaze reaching toward the clear October sky, Béla Kardos called his family around him.

"This is a wonderful time," he said to them, raising his voice so he could be heard above the din. "But it's also a dangerous, frightening time."

István nodded, secretly grateful that his father had validated those moments when he had felt nothing but fear. Instinctively, he grabbed hold of Béla's hand. From him, he drew strength. With him, he felt safe.

"As exciting as this is," Béla said, "as exhilarating as it feels to trample the symbols of those who have trampled all over us, do not think our insubordination will go unanswered. Oppressors don't like those who speak out or rise up or challenge them. They're going to fight back. And when they do, it's going to be ugly."

"I don't care," Mátyás said, his fourteen-year-old face aglow with optimism. "I'm willing to fight to the end."

"Me too," echoed István, realigning his features so that his visage was as somber as his older brother's.

Béla patted the heads of his sons, proud of their patriotic instincts, impressed by their bravery. Suddenly, his gaze was distracted, lured to a spot beyond the crowd. There, lying on his side, still lashed to the back of a truck, the metallic despot seemed to be viewing the wreckage of his sovereignty with sightless eyes. His legs had been cut off. His body had been brutalized. But still, a terrifying aura of potency seemed to surround his image. Béla looked at his children, at his fellow citizens. Everyone was brimming with promise, bursting with faith in a favorable outcome. He tried to remember what life had been like before Stalin, but all he could remember was life under Stalin. All he could think of was the suffering of József and Zoltán and of the countless others who had died thinking they would fight to the end.

"Of course we'll fight," he said quietly. "But let's hope the end is later, rather than sooner."

That night, Mátyás and István talked of nothing but the revolution.

"What do you think is going to happen?" István asked, aware that Mátyás wasn't equipped to give a knowledgeable response, needing one anyway.

"I don't know, but the Russians aren't going to take this lying down. That's for sure."

István shivered. Old black-and-white photographs of armies on the march he had seen in schoolbooks and tattered magazines suddenly sprang to life, parading across his visual field in full, frighteningly real color.

"People are going to be killed," he whispered.

Mátyás tipped his head from side to side, as if to say "Probably."

"Do you think anyone we know will be killed?"

Mátyás didn't answer. The question hung in the air, creating an anxious silence. István felt as if he were counting the seconds between a lightning bolt and the clap of thunder.

Mátyás turned and looked at his little brother. István was a spunky kid, never one to enjoy sitting on the bench, never one to avoid a confrontation or run from a tussle. But they weren't talking about a schoolyard brawl. This was a revolution. And much as Mátyás would have liked to spare his brother by telling him not to worry, that nothing was going to happen to those he loved, even at his young age he knew there were no sidelines to a revolution, once the first gun had been fired.

"I hope not, István, but you saw what was going on in the streets today. Everybody was fighting. Old people. Kids. Women. I don't think we have any other choice. If we want the Russians out, we have to throw them out!" He said it calmly, as if it were not at all unusual for a boy of fourteen to be telling his nine-year-old brother that they had to be prepared to fight one of the most powerful armies on earth.

"That's okay for you to say. You're big and strong. What could I do?" István asked, his face washed with disappointment. "I'm too little to help."

"The only people who are too little to help are those who don't want to. Believe me, István, if you want to help, you will."

The next day, István got his chance.

While Mátyás and István slept, the Russians moved. At four o'clock on the morning of October 24, a thickly plated armored car mounted with machine guns rolled through the dark, silent streets of Budapest. Slowly, like a giant deadly armadillo, it crawled from Kálvin tér down Üllői út toward the ancient Kilian Barracks. Kilian, known in its precommunist days as the Maria Theresa Barracks, once the home of the soldiers selected to defend the honor of Budapest, now served as an administrative center. Though it was staffed by a small elite guard numbering about four hundred, it quartered no battle-sized troops, warehoused no heavy guns or tanks.

As the mighty six-wheeled Russian car lumbered into view, several weary but alert soldiers prepared to defend their camp. All night they had waited on the roof of the barracks, keeping watch, building an arsenal. They had no weapons other than those they had stolen from the AVO, yet still they stood ready, armed mainly with handmade gasoline bombs, fortified with the belief that momentum was on their side and that victory was not unthinkable.

They waited until the reconnaissance car was directly beneath them, then lit the cloth wicks sticking up through slits in the bottle caps and tossed the flaming incendiaries into the air, watching as they painted golden streaks on the dark canvas of night. The first bomb landed on the pavement of Üllői Street, crashing, splashing the ground with quick, violent bursts of heat, light, and fire. The brilliance of the flames must have blinded the driver, because suddenly the car reeled, slamming into the wall of the barracks. Three more bombs found their mark, wrapping the car in a blazing orange cloak, sending it limping down the street like a lame bull. Finally, its own gasoline tank exploded and the ugly beast was consumed.

By nine o'clock that morning, the Kilian Barracks had become the site of a major battle in the fight for Budapest. Like dozens of other young boys from all over the city who had heard of the predawn skirmish, István and Mátyás Kardos had enlisted as part of the defense team, flocking to the aid of the soldiers of Kilian. Some of the boys had brought their own gasoline bombs. Others carried old guns, knives, stones, bricks, anything they thought might serve as a weapon. All were ready to grapple with the Russian bear.

The Kilian Barracks stood at one of the major intersections in the city of Pest, on the southeast corner of Üllői Street and Ferenc Boulevard. On the northeast corner a stretch of houses hid the Corvin Cinema and an arcade fronted by a large open archway. While uniformed soldiers guarded the upper floors of the barracks itself, and the roof of the Corvin was manned by civilians, the cellars of the buildings flanking Üllői Street were fortified by zealous, wide-eyed youngsters, most of them no older than sixteen.

While Üllői Street appeared relatively secure, Ferenc Boulevard wasn't as easy to protect. There, the path was wide enough for tanks to maneuver, to shift position, to set their guns, and to fire at targets as large as rooftops or as small as children. But in that battle, on that day, it was the children who destroyed the tanks.

Several times, while sitting around the barracks, Russian commanders had confided to their Hungarian counterparts that the only way to stop a Russian tank was to slip a gasoline bomb directly under the guns. As those same Hungarian officers now explained the situation to their ragtag troops—that very soon Russian retaliation would begin in earnest, and essentially they were helpless against heavy tanks—two things became clear: Their main objective had to be the demolition of the tanks, and only someone very small and very brave could climb up under the guns.

Suddenly the lookout shouted, "Here it comes."

Together, István and the others watched as a huge tank waddled across the Petőfi Bridge, turned north, and started up the boulevard. It was still some distance from them and yet its size and potential force sent a current of intimidation rippling through the air. Orders were given for everyone to take his position. István scrambled down from the roof into the basement, finding a spot by a window so he could look through the small dirty glass at the reconnaissance car that had driven down that same path just hours before. Now, it lay crippled in the middle of the street. At first, when he heard the story of the quick demise of that car, and then when he had viewed the damage, walking around it, stalking it, studying it from every side and every angle, István had found it easy to believe those who claimed the Russians were beatable. Now, having seen the tank, even if only for a brief moment, he wondered.

All the windows in the basement were open. Though there were thirty young boys crowded in that musty cellar and dozens of others hiding behind windows up and down the street, though military men stood on alert and civilian soldiers hid behind a huge archway in the center of Üllői Street, a pregnant silence covered the neighborhood. No one spoke. No one coughed. No one moved. It seemed as if no one allowed himself even to take a breath for fear of hastening the inevitable. Ferenc Boulevard seemed deserted. There were no people on the streets. No faces poking out of curtained windows. No eyes peeking from behind barely cracked doors. Yet through the eerie hush, the ominous clatter marking the tank's progress reverberated.

While István stood transfixed at the window, Mátyás and several of the older boys busied themselves stockpiling gasoline bombs. There were six of them jammed into a space that could accommodate only three, a confined alcove tucked beneath the spine of a rickety wooden staircase. Mátyás's nose crinkled at the stinging smell that permeated the stagnant air. Every now and then his stomach lurched from an attack of nausea, but he fought it off each time, determined to stick to his task. His hands were slimy, but he worked quickly, pouring the greenish fluid into empty soda bottles and jelly jars and any other bottles with metal caps the boys had been able to scavenge. Next to him, another boy slit the caps while yet another threaded the hole with a piece of cloth that would serve as a detonator. As each bomb was completed it was carefully boxed. When the box was filled, a runner carried it to the roof or shoved it into a corner for use by the boys themselves. Though Mátyás and his cohorts were too far from the windows to hear what was happening in the street, they quickened their pace. The confrontation was imminent. The anxiety of the younger boys was palpable.

Suddenly, word filtered down from the roof that the tank was near. Next, they heard lookouts at the Corvin Cinema shout that two more tanks were coming from the north, the area where the night before the *Szabad Nep* bookstore had been torched. From the west, one of the officers in charge of the barracks spotted four more monsters pushing toward them.

Seven tanks converged on Kilian Barracks. Seven tanks outfitted with heavy machine guns and rifles. Seven tanks driven by Russian officers with only one objective—to squash any thoughts the Hungarians might have of freedom.

The tanks jockeyed into position, covering the barracks, the entrance to the boulevard, and access to Üllői Street. Though they had been waiting hours for this, once the guns began to shoot, István, Mátyás, and the others felt as if they had been taken by surprise. In a sense, they had. They were children. They were innocents. They had no idea as to the destructive force of a tank. They would never have imagined that within minutes an entire corner of the barracks would be ripped from its foundation, seventy people would be killed and more than a hundred and fifty injured. Yet they had been witness to it all.

Horrifying as it was, the scene was bewitching, luring them out from their trenches, up onto the street, where the armored death machine doled out its violence in merciless bursts of fire. Mátyás, unaware that István had shadowed him up the stairs, beckoned to his cronies, pointing across the street to the arcade archway. It appeared to be a better vantage point for attack. The three others nodded, checked to see that the street was momentarily clear, grabbed as many bombs as they could carry, and dashed out, across the street and behind the concrete arch. As István watched them go, he noticed that Mátyás had left a box of bombs behind.

While he considered his next move—if he should make a next move—a lone mechanic, who had been working for hours on an antitank gun he had detached from the wrecked Russian reconnaissance car, decided he had repaired it as best he could. The mechanic and a crew of young machine workers carted the unwieldy weapon into the street.

"Stand back!" the mechanic shouted, waving everyone away, afraid that the gun might explode.

He sighted the tank rumbling down Üllői Street and fired, keeping his finger pressed against the trigger, bracing himself so he could absorb the recoil of the powerful gun. Bullets flew through the air so rapidly it was difficult to tell how many, if any, actually hit. But then suddenly, almost miraculously, the front end of the tank reared like a startled stallion. A huge explosion followed. Flames belched out of the battered top, bursting into the air, splitting shards of hot metal and puffs of thick black smoke. A delighted roar went up as every Hungarian within view celebrated the humiliation of the monstrous machine. Even more delicious was the sight of the tank retreating to lick its wounds.

"They'll be back," someone whispered as the gun was carted off the street by a company of young men and secured inside the Corvin Cinema.

István fixed on the rear of the injured tank. Watching it hobble away, he knew his companion was right. This fight wasn't over. It was just beginning. Moreover, whether or not he had intended to be a soldier when he'd left his house this morning, he had become one now. He couldn't leave. He wouldn't desert his countrymen. Not with the smell of triumph still burning his nose, or the sight of two boys his age lying dead in the street slicing his heart. He had been there only a matter of hours, yet in the last few minutes István felt as if he had bypassed his adolescence entirely and gone from child to adult, catapulted by the scenes and sounds of war. He felt different somehow, but he was too young to recognize the sensations of commitment and duty. All he knew was that something inside him was pushing his body to do things he didn't recall his mind requesting.

When the Russians did return, advancing with more caution and more determination, István's eyes were drawn to what remained of the upper floors of the barracks. There, skilled Kilian marksmen with high-powered rifles took aim on their oppressors. Their bullets found their targets, killing several of the Russians, causing one of the tanks to crash into the one that lay idle at the head of Üllői Street. From the roof a shower of gasoline bombs splattered against the already wounded vehicle. They exploded. There were pockets of fire and signs of devastation. But still, the tanks kept coming.

István reached down and grabbed two of the bombs in the box by his side. Lighting them, he raced out into the street, oblivious to the cries of the boys with whom he had been standing, mindless of the horrified stare of his brother, who watched from across the street. He ran directly into the face of the tank, crouching, making himself even smaller, even more invisible. When he was close enough to smell the burning metal, he climbed up under the guns and tossed his bombs inside the open turret, then jumped off, rolled out of the path of the oncoming rubber tires, and waited. One. Two. Three. The tank blew, tossing sparks and flames and bits of metal into the air. The thunderous boom of destruction drowned out the anguished screams of the men burning inside. István heard nothing except the roar of his own personal victory.

He hadn't seen Mátyás, but when a pair of strong arms lifted him out of the street and dragged him into a nearby building, he didn't have to look to know whose arms held him.

"I don't know whether to punch you or hug you," Mátyás said, his voice cracking. "You scared me to death."

"Sorry," István said, although both of them knew he was not sorry at all. "I was one of the smaller ones. If I didn't do it, that tank would've rolled over those people."

"You're all right, little brother." Mátyás grinned, grabbed István and hugged him.

Outside, five Russian tanks were hammering away at the barracks and the surrounding buildings. Whole floors had collapsed. Shells and bullets continued to bombard the walls of the Kilian Barracks, punishing the building for the arrogance of the soldiers defending it. The adults did whatever they could. But again, it was the children who created one of the best maneuvers of the day.

István, Mátyás, and several others strung together a thin rope, which they stretched across Üllői Street, from the cellar of Kilian to a cellar in the middle of the Corvin Cinema block. At one end of this single string barricade, they hung five large hand grenades. When one of the tanks—satisfied that they had ruined the barracks, now intent on wreaking havoc on the surrounding area—moved onto Üllői Street, the boys took their positions, some on one side, the rest across the street. Bobbing the string up and down with extreme gentleness, they moved the grenades into positions they believed would fall beneath the tracks of the oncoming tank. They had guessed, but they had guessed right. When the grenades exploded, the tracks were blown off their cogs. The tank was rendered helpless, unable to escape the rooftop flame-throwers, who rained fire onto the enemy until there was nothing except smoke and the scent of burning gasoline.

With three tanks immobilized, the remaining four withdrew. It had taken the men of Kilian Barracks, the civilians who had come to their aid, and the boys of Budapest only ninety minutes to effect such destruction. But it had not been achieved without a price. There were hundreds of dead, hundreds more injured. The barracks was ruined. Other buildings stood on the verge of collapse.

They had not beaten the Russians. To believe that was folly. This incident was too small, too isolated, too inconsequential to be held up as a turning point. There would be more acts of defiance, more examples of David pestering Goliath. But eventually the giant would weary of the game. He would tire of the inconvenience and the humiliation. He would raise his heavy boot and crush everything in his path.

That night, broadcasting from an improvised studio, Radio Budapest spoke to the Hungarian people:

Several listeners asked us to explain under what conditions and with what task the Soviet units are stationed in Hungary in accordance with the Warsaw Pact. On Tuesday, October twenty-third, the enemies of our people turned a demonstration held by university youth into an organized counterrevolutionary provocation and with their armed attacks endangered the order of the whole country and the life of the population. The Hungarian government, conscious of its responsibility in order to restore order and security, asked that Soviet troops help in controlling the murderous attacks of counterrevolutionary bands. The Soviet soldiers are risking their lives in order to defend

*the lives of the capital's peaceful population and the peace of our
nation.*

*After order is restored, the Soviet troops will return to their
bases. Workers of Budapest! Welcome with affection our friends
and allies!*

"May God rip my tongue from my mouth before I ever welcome a
Russian soldier with affection."

Zoltán's words spewed from his lips in violent rage. He couldn't
believe what he was hearing. He knew that Radio Budapest was a mouth-
piece for the Soviet-controlled government, but to twist the facts so hor-
rendously and so audaciously was an affront to the intelligence of
everyone listening.

"How ridiculous," he continued. "Since when is freedom a danger?
Since when do people have to be protected from democracy?"

"They have to make some excuse for bringing the Russians in,"
Mária said.

"There can be no excuse for Hungarians allowing outsiders to kill
Hungarians!"

"I agree, but no one's going to believe this trash."

"How can they? All they have to do is look out their windows to
know the truth. There are bombs going off everywhere."

"Is the man on the radio telling lies, Papa?"

Katalin had been sitting on the floor in front of the radio, straining
to understand what the voice was saying and why her parents were so
upset.

"Yes, *edesem*," Zoltán said, softening, as he always did when he
spoke to his daughter, yet unable to cleanse his voice of all its venom.
"He most certainly is."

"Why?"

To Katalin it seemed totally outrageous that someone would do that.
Mária and Zoltán had taught her that lying was terrible, that even if the
truth was painful or had the potential of attracting trouble or punishment,
it was always better than an untruth. As if to make their point, if she
was caught in a lie—and once or twice she had been—she had been
punished twice: once for the offense and once for the lie.

"Because he doesn't want us to know that the Hungarians have
decided they're fed up with the Russians."

"Why don't we like them?" Katalin asked.

"Because they don't treat us right."

After Zoltán said it, he marveled at the realization that in trying to
clarify years of abuses and lists of grievances, that in trying to make

oppression understandable for a child, he had reduced the horror of Soviet domination to one simple, honest statement of fact: The Russians didn't treat the Hungarians right.

The city was at war and Margit Kardos had been frantic much of the morning with concern for her sons. When she had awakened they were gone, without any word about where they were going. Béla was dispatched to check on the boys' favorite haunts. His report had frightened her more than her imagination. He told her of coming onto streets where unarmed civilians were fighting tanks and armored cars. He told her how he had found himself caught up in the melee.

He had been running along Népszinhaz Street, watching boys his sons' ages attack a reconnaissance car with primitive gasoline bombs. He thought he had hung back, that he was outside the fray, but before he could say yes or no, two bombs had been shoved into his hands. "Get them!" someone shouted. The voice was young, but its echo was from someone older. A third voice shouted "Get them!" When he recognized it as his own, he stopped, reached back, and pitched both bombs at the menacing car. Alongside him, a man of about sixty and a boy of seventeen also launched bombs. When they hit and the car exploded, Béla told his wife, he felt exhilarated.

"I was never a soldier," he reminded her. "I spent the war in a chemical factory, serving the state with my brain and not my brawn. When I used to listen to the stories of those who fought, of those who had come face to face with the enemy, I never understood the light that came into their eyes when they talked about their exploits. Today, I understood. I felt the joy of knowing that in some small way I had fought back against someone who wanted to rule me against my will. I said no."

If Béla had not felt that joy, he might have dealt with Mátyás and István differently. He might have lectured them on safety and expediency and discretion being the better part of valor. Instead, he applauded their bravery.

"When I think what might have happened, my blood runs cold. But you stood up for what's right and that's worthy of high praise." He was still dazed by the notion that his fourteen-year-old had organized a group of his peers into a courageous fighting unit, that his nine-year-old son had singlehandedly stopped a tank. "Had you asked me, I wouldn't have let you go. I love you and I wouldn't ever put you in harm's way. But with you sitting here, safe and untouched, hearing what you did and what you accomplished, I'm beyond words."

Margit watched her husband reach out and enfold his sons, hugging them to his chest, showering them with paternal pride. She watched Vera join the circle, sitting at her father's knee, clutching the hand of her youngest brother. Margit's heart warmed at the sight, and for a moment she basked in the sunlit comfort of family.

Suddenly, her vision blurred. The picture became distorted. She shivered, trembling as if a swath of cold air had come down from the Russian steppes to invade her home. She forced herself to refocus, to drink in the image of Béla and Mátyás and István and Vera, as if by doing so she could make the icy fear disappear. But deep inside she knew. For the Kardos family, the sun had set.

5

Noontime, October 25

Thousands gathered in Kossuth tér. They came in droves, decrying the habits of oppression, chanting slogans of freedom. Two days before, this square had housed a similar throng, had heard similar exhortations. But today the tone was more strident, the attitude more confident. Those who massed in front of the Parliament building weren't the same meek, submissive populace that had stood there before. In the forty-eight hours since that last assemblage, these people had sampled triumph. They had tasted victory and had become intoxicated by it. Some were there to offer orderly petitions for change. Some were there to fight. Some were there simply to bear witness. But whatever had propelled them to come, whatever compelled them to stay, their presence represented a daring challenge.

Zoltán and Béla were the first of their entourage to notice the communist response to that challenge.

"Look there," Zoltán whispered, nodding his head in the direction of the Parliament building, where AVO men with machine guns stood sentry on the roof.

Béla motioned behind them, pointing out the string of armed AVO lining the tops of the Supreme Court building and the Agricultural Ministry. Both of them studied the intimidating line of powerful Russian tanks guarding the foot of Parliament.

"They're not playing games," Béla said, involuntarily taking a half-step backward, as if retreating in the face of such awesome weaponry.

"Neither are we," Zoltán countered, his manner unafraid, his jaw tight with purpose and commitment.

Since that first day—because Zoltán had borne his pain and tolerated his deformity with a courage that trivialized ordinary complaints or discomforts, and because he had refused to subject those around him to a single word of lamentation—Béla had thought of Zoltán as a model of control. Today, however, the anger that simmered beneath the surface of Zoltán's disciplined facade was brimming with Vesuvian heat.

"I wish I knew where István and Mátyás went," Béla said, his own concern mounting because of the rising concern he sensed in his stalwart friend. "I don't like them wandering off."

"I'm sure they didn't go far. Don't worry. They'll find us."

Zoltán tried to assure Béla that the boys were all right, but he, too, was beginning to question the wisdom of having allowed the children to accompany them to this rally. As if to reassure himself that his own offspring was safe, he reached down and took Katalin's hand. Katalin clasped it gratefully.

Though she was with her parents—and believed with all the naïveté of a young mind that nothing terrible could ever happen when she was with her parents—Katalin was scared. The aura clouding the square was dark, and everyone from the youngest child to the most senior citizen felt it. Katalin edged closer to her father, hoping to hide in the tangled forest of grown-up limbs. Usually, confidence and hope were her companions, but lately fear was constantly at her side and she didn't like it. Fear made her think awful thoughts. It made her feel funny inside. It made her do things she didn't usually do, like saying prayers other than before she went to bed; or wandering out of her room every few minutes to check on her parents' whereabouts; or staring intensely at friends like Vera and Judit, as if trying to commit their images to memory; or clinging to her father the way she was at this moment.

She didn't like the conversations she had overheard between Uncle Miklós and her father, between her mother and Mrs. Kardos or Aunt Ilona. She didn't like hearing Aunt Zsuzsanna talk about leaving Hungary "if things don't work out." She didn't even like the sound of the grown-ups' voices. There was no softness, no lilt, no sense of quiet or calm. There was only strain and tension, as if they were speaking through a distortion device. It seemed hard to believe that just a few days ago she had given her recital and everyone she cared most about in the world had been in her home, laughing and singing and eating. It seemed hard to believe because since then, there had been no music and no one had laughed.

"I'm nervous." Margit's hands wouldn't stop trembling. The cold that had barnacled her soul the night before still clung to her. Though she chided herself for surrendering to something as foolish as mere premonition, her eyes darted about the crowd continuously, frantically, as if she needed to watch everything, to see everything, to be aware of everything that was going on.

"I am, too," Mária said, putting her arm around her friend's shoulders.

Normally, Margit was subdued, even-tempered, and logical, rarely allowing an exhibition of her feelings. Mária was the one most susceptible to the tidal waves of emotion, the least embarrassed about displaying her moods. Today, however, the roles were reversed, and for Mária the change was unnerving. In spite of her wish to appear in control—if not for Margit's sake, for Katalin's—she, too, studied the crowd, trying to get a fix on the tone. One moment it felt confrontational but respectful. The next moment it was clearly provocative.

"I have this horrible feeling that I shouldn't be here," Margit said, her eyes growing wider, wilder. "That I should take Béla and the children and run as fast and as far from this place as we can."

"It's the tanks," Mária said, stating the obvious, wondering why she felt the need to justify her friend's sense of impending disaster. Margit was right to worry. She was right to be concerned about her family. Tens of thousands of people were jamming the square. While they outnumbered the enemy, without weapons they were helpless to overpower them.

Somewhere to the left a voice called for Imre Nagy. Another voice echoed the call, and then another and another. From the back, the crowd pushed forward. When they did, those in front found themselves pitted against the Soviet tanks. Quickly, they pushed in reverse, refusing to go nose to nose with such formidable opposition. The calls for Nagy subsided, and an odd silence descended on the square. There were no menacing chants, no threatening gestures. Just a pause, as if both sides were waiting to see what happened next.

Their silence had become a taunting voice shrieking into the ear of a nervous AVO man. As he watched the mass below him from atop the Supreme Court building, his finger tightened around the trigger of his gun. He had a stitch in his side from standing in one position for so long, and his bladder felt uncomfortably full. Though the air was cool, the sun was strong. He squinted, trying to follow the movement of the crowd. People moved forward and then back, blending into a sinuous blob of color, a blob that in his skittish mind began to grow and take on sinister proportions. Suddenly, senselessly, he fired into the crowd. His bullet whizzed down into the square, landing in the soft flesh of a baby napping in its mother's arms. The woman and her dead child were thrown to the ground. The silence became deeper as tremors of shock spread through the square. Slowly, the woman struggled to her feet, clutching her baby to her bosom. Then, her eyes damp with grief, she raised her child above her head and ran toward one of the Soviet tanks, shouting, "You've killed my child! Kill me! Kill me!"

No one except those closest to her heard her cries. The AVO had begun firing wildly into the crowd.

The distraught woman flung herself against the tank, crying, beating her fists against the cold, unfeeling metal. Inside that tank, a Soviet captain wiped tears from his eyes. He was a father. He couldn't bear looking at the lifeless body of the dead infant or the anguished face of the mother. Without giving a thought to any personal consequence, he gripped the handles of the huge gun in front of him, took aim at the roof of the Supreme Court building, and calmly slaughtered an entire line of AVO sharpshooters.

Margit grabbed Béla's arm. "We have to get out of here!"

"There's no place to go."

A quick look around the square confirmed what he said. There was no possible escape route. All the normal exits were blocked, either by the crowd or by Soviet artillery.

"Where are the boys? Where are my sons?"

"I don't know," Béla said, alarmed by the manic edge of Margit's hysteria, "but we must stay calm."

He slipped his arm around her waist, holding her close, trying to anchor her and make her feel as secure as he could under the circumstances.

While Béla comforted his wife, Zoltán's gaze traveled from the Ministry of Agriculture, the building directly opposite the Supreme Court, back to the tank commander who had just broken rank. His heart stopped. The mighty gun of the sympathetic Soviet had spun around and was now aimed at the Ministry. He, Mária, Katalin, the Kardoses, and the thousands of others packed into the square were trapped in the middle of a battle about to be waged between the Russians and the AVO. Zoltán's head jerked back in the direction of the Ministry. The guards were leaning forward, their machine guns at the ready. One of them must have spotted the new position of the tank gun. Within seconds, a storm of bullets rained down into the crowd. Bullets streaked past Zoltán, some coming so close he was certain he heard a whoosh as they whizzed by.

Instinctively, he turned to look for Mária—which was probably why he didn't see the two bullets that hit Béla and Margit, why he wasn't prepared to see Béla face down on the pavement, a gaping hole in his back, or to see Margit sprawled out in Katalin's lap, her chest painted with blood, her dying eyes desperately searching for the face of a loved one.

"Papa! Papa!"

Katalin's screams pierced Zoltán's soul. Had she been hit? Was the blood he saw oozing onto the pavement hers? Mad with fear, he fell to his knees.

"Are you all right, *kicsi szilva*? Tell Papa where it hurts." Frantically, but carefully, so as not to disturb Margit, he examined Katalin, poking, prodding, checking, rechecking, assuring himself as best he could that she had not been struck.

"I'm fine, Papa," Katalin said, choking back tears. "I'm fine. But Margit. She's . . ."

Quickly he turned to Margit. As he hunkered over her, wishing he could help, knowing he couldn't, knowing, too, that he didn't dare remove her from his frightened daughter's lap in case there was a chance of saving her, he wondered what was going to come of all this. Zoltán Gáspár was not a religious man. He offered no prayers, requested no absolution, subscribed to no recognized system of belief. But even he could not accept that this sort of pain and suffering was without purpose. With a gentle hand he patted Margit's cheek and whispered words of consolation, words of hope.

Suddenly Vera, who had been by Béla's side when he was hit, rushed to her mother's side, where she collapsed, her breathing dangerously shallow.

"Mama, please don't die," she sobbed. "Please! Someone will come. Someone will help. Please. Be strong. I love you. Be strong."

While Zoltán went to tend to Béla, Mária knelt beside Vera, easing her off Margit so the injured woman had room to breathe. As she embraced Vera's frail, trembling body, she wished she could infuse the child with enough strength to survive this harrowing ordeal. Mária guessed that Béla was dead. Looking at her friend, she feared that soon, if they didn't get medical assistance, Margit would be also. As she worried about what would happen to the three children, she looked lovingly at her own.

Katalin was being as brave as she could. She sat pillar still, determined not to move for fear of jostling Margit. For a while her face remained a mask of intense concentration, with not a muscle flexing or an eyelash blinking. Then Vera's agony overwhelmed her. Katalin loved Vera too much not to be affected by the sight of her bending over her mother, brushing a few stray locks off Margit's face, smoothing the collar of Margit's blouse, her hand stopping short of the stained circle that defined Margit's chest. Tears flowed from Katalin's eyes.

Inside, Katalin felt anything but quiet. She was terrified. When the bullet had hit Margit, she had fallen backward, pushing Katalin to the ground, falling on her, pinning her to the pavement. Now, Margit's blood was spilling onto her skirt, seeping through the thin cotton fabric onto her thighs. For a second it felt wet and hot against her skin. Then it turned cold, making Katalin shiver. She had heard that when people died they turned cold. Was it because their blood kept them warm? If all of Margit's blood drained out of her body would she die in Katalin's lap? Katalin thought about pressing her hand against the hole the bullet had left, but she couldn't bring herself to do it. What if she hurt Margit? Then again, what if she did nothing and Margit died? Needing some sort of answer, Katalin—for the first time since they had fallen—looked down, directly into Margit's eyes. She had never noticed how blue they were. Like István's.

"I love you," she said simply. "Please get well."

The eyes smiled up at her. Then they went dark. Katalin felt Margit's body jerk. Then she felt nothing.

"Mama." Because Katalin didn't want to upset Vera, she spoke so softly that at first Mária didn't hear her. "Mama."

Mária heard the pleading in the child's voice and immediately turned her attention away from Zoltán and Béla, back to Margit. One look and she understood why the color had completely drained from Katalin's face.

"Zoltán! Get help!" Mária moved Vera out of the way and grabbed Margit's wrist, searching for a pulse.

Zoltán covered Béla with his coat and scrambled to his feet. He looked around, reconnoitering. Above the painful cries of the hundreds of victims and the outraged howls of their families, he thought he heard an ambulance screaming into the square. Heedless of his own safety, he ran toward it, hellbent on grabbing a doctor or a nurse or a medic. The doors of the ambulance opened. Several doctors spilled out. Zoltán hastened toward them, winding his way through the chaos. All around, he heard people shouting, pleading with the doctors to come save their sisters, their fathers, their babies, their wives. But there was to be no salvation, no recovery. Zoltán was only three arms' lengths away when a barrage of AVO bullets ripped through the air, cutting the doctors down where they stood.

Zoltán felt sick. He had thought he had seen the worst of the AVO in Recsk. Certainly, he had seen enough to know that the depth of their collective sadism went beyond most human comprehension. But there were certain conventions even the most heinous adhered to, certain rules of military behavior that were never broken. To massacre those whose only crime was their willingness to save lives was unthinkable, even for the AVO.

Witnessing such senseless butchery broke Zoltán's calm. Suddenly, he was afraid. The AVO were shooting down innocent people. The Russians were shooting at the AVO. It was lunacy, but that's what made it so terrifying. There was no longer any sanity in Kossuth tér. There was only madness and death. A satanic force had been unleashed. Until it was contained, no one would be safe.

Katalin crouched low, keeping herself very small as she ran to the edge of the crowd nearest Bathori Street. While waiting for Zoltán she was certain she had spotted István. Persuading Mária to let her go hadn't been easy, but she had argued that if things got worse and they had to leave in a hurry, they'd have to have the boys with them. Trying to heed Mária's warning not to wander into open areas, she scooted in and out of pockets of people who were racing back and forth like mice in a maze, seeking a way out of the square.

When she reached the place she had pinpointed and looked around, she was disappointed and frightened. István wasn't there. Neither was Mátyás. Had something awful happened? Had she been mistaken? Or had she seen them but missed them? Had they started back while she was running here? That could be, she decided, refusing to think the worst. Just then, out of the corner of her eye, she saw them.

"István! István!" she shouted. When he didn't respond, she shouted again, stretching her voice as high as she could. "István! Mátyás!"

Both boys turned at once. Katalin couldn't understand the strange looks that passed over their faces because she couldn't see herself as they saw her. Her reddish blond hair was stringy and matted with a dark brown gook that looked suspiciously like blood. Her dress was ripped and wrinkled and blotched with the same frightening stain. Her arms were scratched. Her shins were scraped. And her eyes had a wild glint in them that scared István more than anything else.

"Katalin! What happened? Are you all right?"

István ran to her side, followed closely by Mátyás.

"It's not me," she said, suddenly upset that she had appointed herself the messenger of such tragic tidings. "Just come." She grabbed István's hand and pulled him, but he resisted.

"It's Vera, isn't it?"

"It's not Vera," she said, deliberately avoiding István's eyes, dropping his hand, tugging at Mátyás instead. "Just come," she begged.

Her urgent insistence that they follow her finally galvanized both boys. With Katalin leading the way, they elbowed a path through the crowd. It should have taken seconds, but the shelling had begun again. Thick smoke blocked their way and stung their eyes. Voices shrill with frustration mingled with the hideous crackling of artillery. Bodies that had been standing were suddenly underfoot, writhing in pain. The three youngsters clasped hands in a chain of panic, snaking in and out and around the confusion.

Several feet before their intended destination, Katalin slowed her pace. Without realizing it, she dropped their hands and hung back, unwilling actually to lead István and Mátyás to where their parents lay. They must have guessed at the truth, because as she hesitated, they sped past her.

István got there first. His eyes widened in horror as he saw his mother. Mária had closed Margit's eyes, but she had not touched her friend's body. Margit's legs were splayed. Her arms were bent, half-raised as if the idea of her own death were shocking. István threw himself at her feet, clutching at her as if he believed his touch had the power of revitalization. When she didn't respond, when reality struck, he screamed, venting the torturous pain of a child who desperately needed his mother to comfort him.

Mátyás, having witnessed the grief of his brother, spun around, knowing that Margit's death was not the final note in this dirge. He didn't see Béla. Zoltán was blocking his view. His eyes met Zoltán's. The anguish he saw there told him more than words ever could. Slowly, he allowed his gaze to move beyond Zoltán, down behind him to the ground where his father lay.

So many odd thoughts pry their way into a person's brain when first confronted with death. For Mátyás, incongruous though it might have seemed, he was most upset with the lack of dignity in Béla's pose. His father was face down. His pants had been soiled when death had loosened his bowel. Too, he was one of many lying dead in Kossuth tér, a statistic, a nameless, faceless number. Mátyás hated it. Béla Kardos was not one of many. He was unique, special, one of an exalted few. He was a renowned scientist, a man of extreme intellect, a man of unquestioned dignity. He should not have been face down anywhere, let alone in a place desecrated by the presence of the AVO and the Russians. Refusing further to humiliate his father with tears, Mátyás stiffened his back and turned to Zoltán.

"I want to bury him," he said. "Then we'll come back for my mother."

Zoltán nodded. "In the park," he said gently. "It's what others have done."

Without any further conversation, the man and the boy lifted Béla Kardos and slowly carried him out of the square to a small nearby park. There was no time for a wake or eulogies or a respectful funeral. Burial was essential. The site became inconsequential.

As Mátyás and Zoltán waited until another boy had buried his father, Mátyás realized how lucky he was to have found an available plot of earth. In the distance a mournful procession crossed the Margaret Bridge and started up, into the hills of Buda. Men bore the bodies of their loved ones on their shoulders. Women carried the children in hammocks made of shawls or coats. On the Pest side, the quay bordering the Danube was littered with families who tended their wounded, using wooden benches as makeshift stretchers, cold concrete for beds.

"I need a place for Mama," Mátyás said, fearful he would find none.

"Go," Zoltán said, patting the lad's shoulder. "I'll stay with your father."

By the time Mátyás, Mária, and István returned carrying Margit, Zoltán had dug a large grave. Katalin, who had appointed herself Vera's guardian, refused to let go of the grieving girl's hand. As they had kept pace behind the doleful cortege, Katalin had watched Vera carefully for signs of physical distress. Every now and then Vera's breathing became labored. Katalin demanded she stop, promising they would catch up, that Margit understood, that her brothers wouldn't bury their mother without Vera. Occasionally, Vera seemed to babble, talking to herself or to Margit. At first Katalin wondered if she was supposed to respond, but then she realized Vera wouldn't have heard her if she had. All she could do for her friend was to be a friend.

"I thought they might want to be together," Zoltán said as a way of explaining why there was only one grave. In truth, it was because there were more bodies in the tiny park than there was space.

He needn't have worried about the truth. The three Kardos children accepted what Zoltán said in the same numb way they appeared to have accepted the brutal slaying of their parents. Zoltán and Mária, more experienced, knew that in time their emotions, presently smothered beneath a thick, merciful blanket of shock, would erupt. They would cry and wail and mourn their loss with all the horrible intensity the circumstance deserved. For now, they were little more than wooden players in a tragedy that had begun with an ending.

While Mária fought to recall the Catholic psalms of her youth, Zoltán, Mátyás, and István gently lowered first Béla and then Margit into the earth. Mátyás had insisted that they be buried face up and that Béla's arms be wrapped around Margit.

The three Kardos children gathered beside the gaping hole that held the two who had given them life. Zoltán, Mária, and Katalin joined them. They clasped hands, forming a circle of grief, bowed their heads, and each, in whatever words or prayers they chose, silently bid Béla and Margit Kardos farewell and Godspeed.

That night, despite overwhelming exhaustion, Katalin found sleep impossible. As the minutes sluggishly ticked away she lay in her bed, her eyes wide open, her gaze fixed. Quaky, confused, she stared into the darkness searching for answers. Overhead, the ceiling became a screen on which the events of the day played over and over again—the press of the crowds, the shock of Margit's falling on her, the sight of Margit's wounds, the blueness of her eyes as they looked up and pleaded for help, the stillness that followed her passing. Katalin saw the lifeless bodies of Béla and Margit, their faces forever frozen in an expression of pain. She saw the ineffable sadness that had masked Mátyás, Vera, and István as they had filed into the Gáspár home, initially resisting Mária's offer of refuge, finally agreeing that returning to their own home just then would be too difficult. She saw the agony that had afflicted all three when Zoltán had returned from the Kardos apartment and pulled from suitcases stuffed with clothing and shoes several framed photographs of Béla and Margit.

"Why bring us those tonight?" Mátyás had asked, his tone laced with insinuation. "Couldn't you have waited?" he said, implying that perhaps Zoltán should have realized that the photographs were not a comfort but salt poured onto a newly opened wound.

"Because I don't know what will happen tomorrow," Zoltán had replied quietly.

Next to Katalin, Vera tossed and turned, mumbling in her sleep, frightening Katalin with the irregularity of her breathing.

She needs more room, Katalin thought, slithering out of bed, grabbing a blanket and her pillow and curling up in a nearby chair. Folding her legs beneath her, tucking her blanket around her, Katalin tried to get comfortable. Just as she felt some of the tension in her body ease, a noise disturbed her, an incongruous sound.

Acting on instinct, avoiding any thought of possible consequences, she moved to the door of her room and listened. Someone was fumbling with the front door lock. Carefully, quietly, she tiptoed into the living room, hugging the wall so that she melded with the shadows. As she neared the door, she saw that she had been right—someone was jiggling the lock. But it wasn't evil soldiers trying to get in. It was István trying to get out.

"Where are you going?" she whispered, not wanting to disturb Mátyás, who was asleep on the couch.

"I have to do something," István explained brusquely, his voice full of determination.

"What?"

"It doesn't matter what. I have to do it."

"It's scary out there. There are AVO and Russians and tanks and guns—"

"I know, but . . . I have to talk to my parents."

Katalin put herself in István's place. She imagined how she would feel if what had happened to him had happened to her.

"I'll go with you," she said.

"You can't. You're too young."

"You're too young to be out alone this late and you're going," she said petulantly. "So I'm going too. I just have to put clothes on."

"I don't have time to wait."

"Then I'll follow you in my nightgown."

"Okay," István said, certain that she meant it, uncertain as to whether he was relieved or resentful of her company. "But be quick."

Hoping to avoid whatever patrols might be in the area, the two youngsters skirted buildings and scooted through Buda's darkened alleyways. They spoke only when necessary, and then only in whispers. The streets were deserted. While at first István and Katalin considered that a blessing, as they neared the Chain Bridge they quickly realized it wasn't. There was no one to hide behind, no one to block them from the view of sentries posted on rooftops high up in the hills, waiting to shoot at anything suspicious.

For Katalin, the journey across the bridge was complete agony. She and István crawled the entire way on their bellies, ducking beneath the string of lights that illuminated the four-hundred-yard expanse. Each car, each truck that passed terrified them. Each sound, even the slightest creak, was suddenly magnified, momentarily paralyzing the two children with fear.

Finally, they reached the small park. Debris from the afternoon's rebellion littered the streets—cans, bottles, remnants of unused picnic baskets, remains of bloody clothing. From the direction of Kossuth tér, gusts of autumnal air whistled like the mournful song of ghosts. Clumps of sod cluttered the cobblestone path that ran alongside the quay, the earth remaining where it had been pitched by shovels digging graves. Benches that usually held lovers or old people soothed by the silent, steady flow of the Danube were littered with refuse or overturned.

As they neared the spot where they had buried Margit and Béla, István and Katalin slowed their pace. When they were only steps away, Katalin stopped and let go of István's hand.

"You go. I'll wait."

His smile of thanks was brief and wobbly. Slowly he approached the bulky mound of dirt. He didn't know where to stand, where to sit. He was surrounded by dozens of mounds of dirt beneath which he knew rested other children's parents, other parents' children. He stood off to the side, refusing to step on the souls of anyone who had died that afternoon, acknowledging that although this had once been a public park, it had suddenly become hallowed ground.

"I feel funny," he said, keeping his head bowed, his voice hushed. "I mean, I don't know if this is silly or not, or something I should be doing or something you'd disapprove of, but I had to come. I had to tell you how much I love you both and how proud I am to be your son." His hand flicked away the tears that had gathered in his eyes. "Mátyás said you were heroes today. That your names are going to be in history books." He wanted to smile, to show them that he applauded their heroism, that it was something wonderful or enviable. But being shot down like animals was neither wonderful nor enviable.

"I hate this! I hate that you're gone! That you were killed like that and . . . and . . . buried like this."

His voice strangled in his throat. He gulped several times, swallowing the lump of sadness that had pushed its way up from his heart.

"I hate how lonely I feel, and most of all I hate not knowing what to do or what to say or what to think. I guess the only thing I do know is I'll never forget you. And that Mátyás and Vera and I will always take care of each other. Even without you, we're a family."

He covered his face with his hands, allowing the flood of tears to bathe his cheeks, wetting them with the waters of innocence forever lost. Suddenly, he felt a small hand holding his. He looked up. Katalin's eyes were moist, too, but her face was oddly serene, as if somehow she had found an answer to at least one of her questions. In her free hand she held a bouquet of flowers she must have scavenged from a planting at a nearby monument and a crude cross she had constructed by twisting hairpins around two twigs.

"I know God's not supposed to live in Hungary," she said shyly, "but whenever I feel really scared and kind of lost, Mama always tells me that I can never be alone, because even though I can't see Him, God is always with me. So don't be scared for your Mama and Papa, István. God is with them."

With great solemnity she bent down, stuck the cross into the ground, rose, and handed the scraggly flowers to István, who gently laid them on Béla and Margit's grave. Then, as if completing a prescribed ritual, the two youngsters clasped hands and bowed their heads. As they did, István stole a glance at the small girl standing next to him.

Her eyes were tightly shut and her grip was so intense he could only imagine the fervor of her prayers. She was a baby, he thought as he looked at her in the moonlight, hardly the person he would have selected to share such a traumatic event in his life. Yet throughout the day, she had been there, hovering over him, looking after him, providing whatever solace and comfort she could. Tonight, though at first he had resented her insinuating herself into his plans, he was now grateful. Thanks to her, he hadn't had to make this doleful journey by himself. Thanks to her, he could leave this spot believing that his parents would rest in peace.

He was nine. She was seven. But István knew if he lived to be a hundred, he would never forget this night. Or her.

6

$\mathcal{T}$he next four days tested the mettle of every Hungarian. Buildings were bombed. Food supplies dwindled. The death toll rose. Women, children, and untrained, unarmed men were forced to take to the streets, fighting not only the sophisticated Russians but the sadistic AVO as well. The mood throughout the city was urgent, as if a cosmic clock were ticking away the last minutes of a nation.

Inside the Gáspár apartment the conversation was somber. Miklós had just returned from Tatabánya, a town west of Budapest, where he had met with the head of the coal miners.

"They're prepared to do whatever we ask," Miklós said.

"Are they prepared to strike?" From his superiors at the metalworks in Csepel, Mihai Pal knew that a last-ditch plan for a nationwide shutdown was being considered.

"Are you?" Zsuzsanna asked her husband in a tone that reminded everyone in the room that to lead such an insurgency was tantamount to laying one's head on the executioner's block.

"Yes." His voice was quiet but definite. Zsuzsanna wanted to argue, but she would never embarrass Mihai by debating his decision in public. Instead, she retreated to the corner of the couch.

Miklós returned to the discussion of his trip to Tatabánya, detailing his itinerary there as well as his hurried visits to Szeged and Debrecen.

István, huddled out of the way in a corner next to Mátyás and Vera, was completely engrossed. Though he had met Miklós at several Gáspár gatherings, István felt that tonight he was being introduced to the man's essence. Miklós was like an evangelist recruiting for God's army, voice and body quivering with an intensity born of passion, except his passion was secular; his heaven, the result of positive political change. He preached an emotional sermon centering on freedom.

The more István listened, the more enthralled he became. It was as if a window had opened and a finger of light had intruded on the darkness of his grief. For the first time since his parents had been killed, he felt hopeful. Though he suffered pangs of guilt imagining an existence without Margit and Béla—as if admitting that his life might continue without them were an act of filial disloyalty—inside, he sensed that although time had stalled with their passing, Miklós's words had lifted him out of the bog of mourning and set him on a path into tomorrow. Cautiously, István allowed himself to become entranced by the vision of a life structured around democracy. He allowed himself to consider choices, to think about options. He even permitted himself to contemplate what it might be like to be a man who set policy as opposed to a man who followed orders.

István was young. He was confused, frightened by the sound of the relentless gunfire in the streets below. Much of the conversation swirling about the room floated above his ability to comprehend. Yet he understood with complete clarity the heroic character of Miklós Gáspár. In István's mind, Miklós was a true paladin, a knightly defender of all that was good and just. Not simply because he wanted to make a difference, but because he was willing to accept the consequences of the actions required to effect such a difference. He knew the dangers of openly criticizing the government, but he did it anyway. Whether it was down in a basement shelter or outside a collective barn on the *puszta*, on the shore of Lake Balaton or on a street corner in Szeged or Miskolc or Eger, or in his brother's apartment, he spoke his mind. Independence, he said, came from courage, sacrifice, and control.

An odd bundle of sensations wrapped themselves around István's core. He glanced at Mátyás and Vera to see if they had noticed what was happening, but they, too, were listening to Miklós with rapt attention. He tried to shake it off, but it was useless. Miklós's voice had ignited a spark inside István that blazed with a strange, enticing heat. At first it frightened him, but like a moth, he was drawn to it. Eventually, he touched it. He examined it. And then, once he defined it as the light of his future, he let it burn.

Thanks to his parents and their insistence upon individual expression, István had always known who he was. Thanks to Miklós Gáspár, now he knew who he wanted to be.

"It's dangerous enough here," Zsuzsanna was saying, her sisterly pride in Miklós's accomplishments competing with her fears for his safety. "Riding around the countryside with little or no protection is suicidal."

"The people have a right to know." Miklós asserted, his voice hoarse from overuse. "And besides, this war isn't going to end here. It's going to spread. We need to be able to mobilize a militia."

"Must you conscript every single person yourself?" Zsuzsanna asked, her exasperation evident.

Miklós went to his sister. He bent down and gently kissed her forehead. A brief smile visited his face.

"I'm not doing this alone, Zsazsa."

Though Zoltán was grateful for Miklós's efforts to mollify Zsuzsanna and respected his attempt at modesty, he knew that his older brother was putting on a show. From everything Zoltán had heard, Miklós's efforts had been Herculean and singular. He had organized teams of runners, drafted volunteers, raised money, coordinated the farmers, and arranged shipments of food and supplies to help those who were without. For weeks, even before the first shot had been fired, Miklós had done nothing except eat, drink, sleep, and live the fight for freedom.

To Zoltán, Miklós's transformation from farmer's son to daring insurgent was nothing short of astounding. This man, this crusader, used to be more at home cradling a foal or tending an injured kitten, massaging Zoltan's arms when they had cramped from excessive practicing, mediating arguments among Zoltán, Sándor, Tomás, and Imre, dancing the *csárdás* in the yard outside the Gáspár farmhouse. What, Zoltán wondered again, had happened to his scholarly, meditative brother that would have caused him to replace the book with the gun?

Just that evening, before Zsuzsanna and Mihai had arrived, Zoltán and Miklós had been having a quiet coffee alone in the kitchen.

"When did you become such a diehard revolutionary?" Zoltán had asked after hearing some of Miklós's more perilous exploits. "What happened to you?"

Miklós's thick black eyebrows furrowed, drawing together in a deep, dark line.

"It's not what happened to me," he said, hesitantly, as if he were afraid to state the truth for fear of upsetting Zoltán. "It was what happened to you."

Zoltán grimaced and waved his hand as a way of letting Miklós know that he didn't wish to discuss his incarceration, but Miklós refused to be silenced.

"Ever since that night those animals dragged you out of here and carted you off to Recsk, I've had an anger boiling in my gut, eating away at me. I lived here, Zoltán. Each night, I watched your daughter toddle into your room and over to your side of the bed to pat the pillow where your head should have been. I watched your wife set a plate for you every single night you were gone. I comforted your sister and held our mother's hand when she died grief-stricken over your imprisonment. And when you returned I looked at what they had done to you and swore that one day I would pay them back."

Zoltán lowered his head so as not to meet his brother's gaze. For years he, too, had harbored thoughts of retaliation. For more nights than he cared to count, his sleep had been interrupted by violent dreams of reprisal and revenge. But he had suppressed his vindictiveness. He had buried it beneath layers of hatred for the AVO and layers of love for Mária and Katalin.

Now, as he stood off to the side watching his brother, Zoltán wondered about his own tolerance level, his own limits. He had taken up arms against the Russians and would do so again, but Miklós was willing to die rather than agree to continued repression. Mihái, too, had fought, now going further by declaring he'd prefer becoming a target than remaining a victim. Even Zsuzsanna was threatening to leave Hungary if that was the only way for her to be free. It appeared that his family had reached their limits. Yet he, Zoltán Gáspár, had not. Obviously, he had more room in his glass of poison, more space in his scrapbook of horrors. Perhaps the difference between him and them was that they accepted death as a natural consequence of revenge. He had escaped death too many times to treat it lightly. He had watched people die and, worse, had watched their murderers laugh at the sight of their pain and delight in the sound of a final human breath. No. He would not grant his enemy the pleasure of his death. Somehow, he would survive this holocaust. If Recsk had taught him anything, it was that for those intent on killing, life was the ultimate revenge.

Slowly, his eyes swept the room, taking in the sight of his sister and brother, his sister's husband, his friends' orphaned children, and, sharing a big armchair, his daughter and his wife. Katalin was snuggled in Mária's lap, her legs curled into a tight curve, her head pressed against her mother's chest. She was frightened—he could see that. Each time there was a volley of gunfire outside or she heard someone speak of another neighbor who had died or been injured, she winced, huddling closer to Mária. Zoltán wished he could spare her the horror of battle, but he knew that was impossible. Her innocence had been blown away days before, when she had watched Margit die in her arms.

"Why do you take such risks?" Zoltán heard István ask, wondering also where Miklós had found the courage to sing forbidden hymns publicly and to quote authors the Soviets had banned.

"Because I have to set an example. I have to prove that one can do the unthinkable and survive."

"Are you going to stand there and tell us that you really believe we can beat the Russians?" Mátyás couldn't control his incredulousness.

Miklós returned the young man's cynicism the only way he knew how—with optimism. "Yes. I honestly believe we can. But first, we have to believe we can."

"I'm trying," Zsuzsanna said, "but it gets harder each time I hear about another friend who's gotten in the way of one of their machine guns." As if to underline her point, her eyes drifted toward the three Kardos children.

"There's no such thing as a painless birth."

"Or a painless death," she retorted.

"I'm with you, Miklós." Mihai stepped forward and draped his muscular arm around the slight shoulders of his brother-in-law.

Miklós was moved. "Thank you," he said, in a voice muted with humility. "Your support means a lot to me, but I don't know if I'm the right man, Mihai."

"A lot of us think so. In fact, there are many who want you to lead the new Hungary."

A stunned hush descended on the room. Zoltán, Mária, Katalin, and István smiled with approval and the pride of possession, making it clear that they felt honored to be able to claim connection to this man. Zsuzsanna, Mátyás, and Vera shook their heads, skeptical about the very existence of a new Hungary, fearful for anyone who would stand in the face of such a determined and powerful force of destruction.

"That may be," Miklós said, sensing the dichotomous feelings rebounding around him, breaking the silence with a bitter laugh. "But don't forget, there are just as many who simply want me dead."

On October 29, the unthinkable happened. The Russians retreated.

For five days Hungary was a free nation. For five days people believed that the curse of perpetual domination had finally been dispelled.

Newspapers reappeared. Though they were filled with more rumor than fact, the revival of the press revived hope. Reporters from all over Europe poured into Budapest, bringing in news of the outside world, sending out word of what was happening there. Mozart's *Requiem Mass,* a piece deemed *verboten* by the communists, was played on the radio in honor of those who had died in the fight for liberation. October 23 was declared a national holiday. On street corners, boxes filled with forints donated for the care of those impoverished or made homeless by the insurrection sat unguarded, waiting for dusk, when young boys like Mátyás and István came to collect and distribute the money. Use of the word *comrade* was officially banned. The Kossuth seal—the crest of Lajos Kossuth, the leading Hungarian patriot of the revolutions of 1848—banished under Soviet rule, once again became the symbol of the land. And József Cardinal Mindszenty, Prince Primate of the Catholic Church, a prisoner of the communists for more than eight years, was freed from his jail by four officers of the Hungarian Army.

The Gáspár apartment became both meeting hall and day-care center. Zoltán and Mária opened their home to those who needed a place to gather and to gather strength. They also provided shelter for the babies of this reluctant army, often leaving Vera, Katalin, and Judit in charge.

Ilona and Andras Strasser converted the basement studio where Andras taught Katalin and Judit to play the piano into a makeshift clinic to care for those whose injuries were serious but not life-threatening enough to tax the already overcrowded hospitals.

Zsuzsanna worked in one of the many soup kitchens operating out of churches and schools.

Mihai and his fellow workers from Csepel took to the streets, to try to repair some of the damage while at the same time keeping alert for the many AVO men still at large.

For five days the people dreamed and planned and hoped. They trusted that the will of the revolution had prevailed and that a future of peace and sovereignty was finally possible.

At four o'clock in the morning on Sunday, November 4, Russian tanks squashed that future.

They rolled into Budapest with a vengeance—two thousand tanks. Not the old, stodgy ones boys like István had crippled. These were T-54's, heavily armored and practically invincible. Two thousand more waited outside the city.

The tanks were followed by 140,000 infantry. Not those garrisoned as part of the Warsaw Pact, but Mongols from the Central Asian Republics who would not be tempted by their humanity to interfere with their mission of death, as their predecessors had.

Jet planes roared overhead. Rockets whizzed through the air. Squads equipped with flamethrowers rampaged, incinerating anything or anyone in their path. This time, the Soviets had stocked their arsenals with submachine guns, armor-piercing batteries, bazookas, armed jeeps, and every other sophisticated weapon known to man. As before, the Hungarians had little more than their homemade gasoline bombs.

That first day, the Russians mutilated as much of the city as they could, thinking that a quick, devastating blitzkrieg would force immediate submission. They were wrong. Word spread quickly: Stay inside and out of the way. While most Hungarians complied, some of the braver citizens ventured out, erecting barricades to protect the vital arteries of Pest. At Móricz Zsigmond Square, a major intersection, a group of students attempted to squelch the Russian onslaught by constructing a huge barricade of overturned streetcars and timbers. Five reconnaissance cars filled with soldiers attacked. The students battled back, chasing three of the cars back to Gellért Hill, killing sixty-seven. The Russians retaliated quickly, sending in seven tanks. On the way, they splattered every building in their path with bullets. Just before reaching the square, they extracted payment for their losses. They rounded up twenty boys and executed them.

Despite the odds, for thirty-six miraculous hours the students held Móricz Zsigmond Square against an assault that would have subdued most armies. They destroyed three tanks, fended off mortar attacks and incendiary bombs, as buildings fell and people died. Still they resisted. Finally, inevitably, the square fell. But to those students who survived, there was no sense of defeat. Calmly, like veterans, they surveyed the damage and decided that while the Russians had won the contest, in the process the prize had been destroyed.

"I can't stand it," Mátyás said, squeezing his voice through gritted teeth. "There has to be a way to stop them!"

His pacing had taken on a manic edge. For hours he had been parading back and forth across the Gáspár living room. Every so often he would pause, but only long enough to peek out through a slit in the boarded-up window. The streets were empty. All he could see was smoke and wreckage.

The Russians were raining destruction from the sky with a barrage of high-explosive shells. The drumming was intense and unremitting.

"This is just an overture," Mátyás continued. "If we don't do something, and fast, they'll bring in their tanks. One shot. That's all it'll take. One shot and they'll blow up this building and we'll all be crushed. We can't just sit here and wait to die."

"Please, Mátyás," Vera said, her dark brown eyes rimmed with the shadows of her grief. "The last thing this family needs is another hero."

István turned and stared at his sister. Her tone had a sharp, poisoned edge. If he didn't know better, he might have inferred that in some odd way, she blamed their parents for their own deaths; that she felt that her being orphaned was their fault; that they had been incautious or imprudent or unaccountably stupid to be in the wrong place at the wrong time.

"The last thing anybody needs is more death."

Mátyás's retort was quick and cold. Again, István was stunned. Mátyás had never ever spoken harshly to Vera.

Suddenly, there was silence. And then a deep, tremulous rumbling invaded the room. Glasses and vases resting on tables rattled. Pictures shuddered on the walls. Even the floor trembled. The tanks had begun to climb the hill.

"See, Mátyás was right." Judit was petrified. She had felt her chair move. But instead of displaying even the slightest hint of fear, she stood— quickly, so as to avoid being in the chair if it moved again—marched to Mátyás's side, and placing her hands firmly on her hips, struck as dramatic a pose as she could summon. "If we want the Russians out, we have to push them out."

"We're supposed to stay here." Katalin regretted her words the instant they came out of her mouth. She hated sounding like a coward, especially in front of István, but obedience was a habit. Mária had told the children to remain inside, out of harm's way. The numbers of wounded were rising rapidly, so she and Zoltán had gone to help out at Ilona's clinic.

"The Russians weren't *supposed* to come back!"

"Leave her alone." István understood that his brother's sarcasm was a disguise for frustration, but still.

Katalin couldn't stop the grateful blush from rising to her cheeks. Thankfully, before the others had a chance to notice, Mátyás moved his storm toward the door. Judit trailed behind him as closely as thunder follows lightning.

"Are you coming?" he demanded of István.

"Of course I'm coming." István glowered at his brother, but then turned to his sister, patted her arm, and kissed her cheek. "We'll be careful, Vera. I promise."

Vera shook him off and looked away, her jaw quivering, her eyes hot with tears of resentment.

"Katalin?" István said gently, knowing he was asking her to make a choice, unwilling to push her either way.

Katalin's confusion was obvious. She knew she should stay with Vera—because she was supposed to, and because Vera was far too frail to be left alone—but in her gut she wanted to go with the others. She looked at Vera and feared that if she went, Vera might have a crisis and need someone. She looked at Mátyás and István and feared that if she went, she might never return.

The grumbling of tanks and the staccato of artillery fire scored the drama being played out in the Gáspár living room. The threat of extinction hovered over the apartment on Tárnok Street.

"Go if you want." Vera's voice was soft as she spoke to Katalin, minus the anger and accusation that had characterized it just moments before. "I'll be all right."

"But what if . . ."

"No matter how nervous I'll be in here, I wouldn't last five minutes out there," Vera said honestly.

Katalin hugged her, silently thanking her for permission to do what she felt she had to do. Quickly she joined the others as they ran into the hall and down the stairs.

Once alone, Vera stared at the closed door. Suddenly she was furious with herself. Her brothers and her two closest friends had descended into a war zone with her selfish outburst ringing in their ears. Was she right in thinking they were mad to jeopardize their lives this way? Was she wrong to criticize them for wanting to strike back at the people who killed her parents? Or was it that she was jealous of their bravery? Of their physical ability to go, as compared to her inability to do anything?

She didn't know what to think. Over the past few days the boundaries between right and wrong had shifted and blurred beyond simple recognition. Lifelines had been cut. Everyday patterns that had once provided comfort had been broken. Even the tight reins of repression, which in its unrelenting rigidity had afforded a perverse security, had loosened. To Vera, it seemed as if the only thing that was certain was uncertainty. That and the fact that Mátyás and István were all she had. If they were killed, she would be completely, utterly alone.

Quietly, as if the softest footstep might set off a devastating explosion, she walked to the window. Pressing her face against the boards, she peered through the skinny vee, straining to see beyond the limits of her view. Blips of color cut through the thick gray smoke that clogged the air, as people seeking cover dashed from one end of her restricted panorama to another. A burst of gunfire was followed by a chorus of pain-laden shrieks. Vera's heart raced. Her eyes teared.

"I should have wished them luck," she whispered, frightened that even now her wishes were too late.

• • •

Like most of the other houses on Tárnok Street, Katalin's building was constructed around a common courtyard. In better days the residents maintained a small garden in the center of the cobblestoned square, planting bulbs and rose bushes and bunches of annuals to insure a florescence that continued from early April into October. Usually, when the blooming ended, Adám Horvath, an elderly gentleman who lived on the ground floor, cleaned the garden, turned the earth, and blanketed it with a thin layer of hay so that it could rest over the winter and be ready for a vigorous spring.

As Katalin followed the others through the door that led from her quarter of the building into the courtyard, her eye was drawn to the garden. For her, it was a special place. Katalin loved flowers, roses in particular. She never came in or out without stopping to sniff their luxurious fragrance or admire the delicate perfection of a newly opened bud. She could spend hours sitting on the wooden bench that faced the garden watching the velvety petals of the roses spread and bask in the yellow glory of summer's sun; or peering out of her bedroom window watching the petunias and geraniums and daisies dance to the rhythm of wind. Even in the rain, she thought this private little Eden was beautiful.

But it wasn't beautiful now. Her roses were gone. The other flowers were gone. And worse, Adám Horvath was gone. He had been killed two days before, gunned down in the street while standing on a queue waiting to buy bread. She wished that this garden could have served as his memorial, but all that remained were empty branches, fallen leaves, and lifeless stems. There was no color except an odd, flat brown. Instead of the rich, loamy hue of a nurturing soil, this was a dead green, a color of rotting and decay, a color that reminded her of something Mr. Horvath had said just that past summer when she had been helping him weed the garden and had asked why her roses couldn't live forever.

"Because God gives them only a short time on earth," he had said, carefully pinching a faded geranium off its stem. "They bloom, thrill the world with their beauty, and then, when their time is finished, they leave and other flowers take their place."

Was it that way with people? she wondered. Was it that way for Mr. Horvath and the Kardoses? Was their time finished? Was that all God had given them? If so, what about her? How much time had God granted her?

"Katalin, are you all right?"

When she turned toward István, her eyes were wide and moist.

"I was just thinking about Mr. Horvath." István looked confused. "He used to take care of the garden, but they killed him."

István nodded solemnly, feeling the pocket of anger inside of him growing larger and larger. How many more names were going to be written on the list of the dead before the Russian appetite was satisfied? He didn't know, but at some undetermined moment in the past few days, he had decided that he would not volunteer for that list.

"Maybe you should go back upstairs," he said as Katalin's lower lip trembled. He remembered how young she was, how upset her parents would be if she was hurt, how upset he would be if he was in any way responsible for her being injured. "I don't want anything to happen to you."

Her mouth formed a quizzical moue as she considered what he said. Then she shook her head. Her mouth tightened. Her eyes dried and adopted a resolute cast. "I'll be fine. I don't think it's time yet."

István didn't understand, but he couldn't afford discussion. Mátyás was calling to them.

The four of them gathered at the entrance to the building. Mátyás heaved the huge wooden doors that led from the courtyard to the street, opening them just wide enough to look out and see but not be seen. Across the way they spotted others huddling in doorways.

"We've got to make contact with someone else," Mátyás said. "We've got to organize a defense."

Before anyone could stop him, István slid through the narrow aperture and scooted across the street. Katalin saw a door widen and then shut. She counted the minutes before it opened and István scurried back.

"Some of the students who fought in Móricz Zsigmond Square have come up here. They have ideas and a few weapons, but they need people. They've asked us to join them."

Seconds later, all four of them stood in another courtyard surrounded by scores of youngsters, most of them in their teens and early twenties, many of them as young as Katalin and Judit, all of them older than their years. They listened carefully as one young man outlined the basic problem:

"We have to find a way to kill their tanks. Since we don't have machine guns or bazookas, we're going to have to make them help us."

"How?" someone shouted from the back, his question echoed by several others.

"The one thing we have that they don't is territorial knowledge. These hills are steep and twisty. They run into dead ends and narrow corners. Maybe if we lure them into corners, we'll have a chance to bomb them out."

"What about making a clothesline of grenades and running it under the threads of the tanks," István said, recalling what they had done in the battle for Kilian Barracks.

A few people applauded. Then a few more. Ideas meant hope, and hope was infectious.

"Okay," the self-appointed leader said. "We've designated runners so we can keep in touch. We'll use this courtyard as a command center. And we've distributed as many gasoline bombs as we have. The rest is up to each and every one of you. Be imaginative and be careful."

Within seconds the crowd had dispersed. Mátyás and István had joined a pack of boys who were going to man the rooftops. Katalin and Judit stayed below. They, and a host of other young girls, had planned their own maneuvers.

While the tanks inched their way up Castle Hill, Katalin raced back to their apartment, assured Vera everything was all right, and hastily grabbed three jars of liquid soap. When Vera asked why she needed them and Katalin explained, Vera offered to help.

"I don't want to be left out," she said meekly.

Katalin hugged her and then dragged her into the hall. While Vera acted as sentry and supply depot, Katalin ran up and down, banging on the doors of every apartment in the building, begging, taking whatever people had—lard, cooking grease, soap, oil, shampoo, anything slippery—handing it to Vera and moving on to the next door. Once downstairs, Vera watched in amazement as little Katalin ran into the street, headed for the top of the first hill, and poured liquid soap on the cobblestones, making sure it oozed downward toward the advancing tanks. On other streets, other young girls followed suit. When their supplies were exhausted, they retreated behind the doors of the nearest building and waited.

Though it seemed like forever, it was only minutes later that the first tank nosed around the corner of Palota Street. At first, it appeared as if their efforts were going to have no effect. The lumbering, firebreathing behemoth continued coming toward them. Then, suddenly, it turned, veering sharply to the side. As the driver attempted to right his course, the tank slipped again, this time falling slightly backward. Something—a rock hurled from a window—hit the metal on the front of the tank. The driver, thinking the missile was a bomb, accelerated. The treads hit another patch of soap and within seconds the mighty T-54 had jammed into a building.

Before anyone inside had a chance to fire, a barrage of gasoline bombs fell from the rooftop, exploding on and around the tank, a few close enough to the turret to force it open. More bombs fell, a few dropping inside, blowing up everything and everyone within. From the tops of nearby buildings and from within adjacent courtyards, a cheer went up. It was only one tank from an army of thousands, but to those without any, it was one less to worry about.

Farther up the hill, Judit had invented her own way to trap the Russians. While at the command center she had overheard a few of the students talking about land mines. When she asked to see one, she noticed they looked like her mother's brown dinner plates flipped upside-down. Taking two other girls with her, sending two other pairs to scavenge whatever they could from their own apartments, she went to Ilona's kitchen, took as many dishes as the three girls could carry, and laid them out in the street. The result was a simulated minefield that could have fooled even the most seasoned soldier.

From her vantage point inside a darkened doorway at the head of the street, Judit watched as a Russian tank moved confidently up the hill. Her eyes never left the small windows on the turret. Holding her breath, she waited nervously for the punch line of her practical joke to be delivered. As the tank advanced, Judit began to have visions of giant, bearlike men bursting out from the ugly metal monster and rushing toward her, grabbing her, beating her, doing horrible, hideous, unimaginable things to her. A lump of paralyzing fear lodged in her throat, provoking a cough and then an attack of panic. They had heard her cough. She was certain of it. They knew who she was and where she was. The tank was getting closer. Any minute now, they would get her and punish her and . . .

Suddenly the tank stopped. Someone inside must have spotted the make-believe mines. Two seconds. Three seconds. Four seconds. For Judit, it was an eternity. The tank jerked backward. Instantly, several boys who had threaded a clothesline strung with live grenades across the street wiggled it and waggled it until it was positioned directly under the tank tracks. The explosions rocked the neighborhood and destroyed another tank. Judit cried from relief.

For the next two days the defense of Castle Hill remained in the hands of some workers and an army of children. A motorman set his trolley car on a downward path and jumped off just before it plowed into a tank, engulfing both machines in a ball of flame. Another man poured gasoline into a chasm in the cobblestones, waited until a tank rolled over, and then tossed a grenade into the open gas pit. A group of exceptionally brave girls and boys ran out and stuck lengths of plumber's pipe directly into the tracks of the tanks, jamming them, stopping them dead.

But for each small victory, there were terrible losses; for each minor triumph, a major catastrophe. No area of the city had been spared, no neighborhood left intact. Still, the people resisted.

At the end of the second day, Katalin and Judit found themselves holed up in a vacant apartment in a building on Donati Street. There, they and a host of other young people had been told to aim broomsticks out the windows. By tricking the Russians into thinking there were snipers all around, they hoped to tempt them into a dead-end street where the ragtag army had a chance of destroying the tank. For three hours the girls took turns holding the broomsticks.

"I have to see what's going on." Katalin's impatience was getting the better of her. It was late. Soon it would be dark. The thought of waiting for Russian tanks in the pitch of night terrified her. "Maybe everybody else left and we're the only ones here."

"Don't be silly," Judit whispered, her small arms strained from keeping the broomstick steady. "If we were supposed to leave, Mátyás and István would have come to get us."

"Maybe something happened to them and they can't get us and we're the only people alive in all of Budapest?"

"If it'll make you feel better, look. But don't let anyone see you."

Katalin moved onto her knees and then to her feet, keeping her body bent so that only the top of her head cleared the windowsill. Peeking out, she noted several other broomsticks, several other pairs of curious but frightened eyes.

"You were right. Everyone's still in place."

"I told you," Judit said, unable to keep a tinge of triumph from her voice.

At street level, Katalin noticed machine guns sticking out of doorways. They were empty but, like Judit's broomstick, had been placed there to tease the Russians. Every so often someone scurried across the street. A door opened. The person disappeared. She was about to drop down to the floor when she spotted Anna Karolyi, her music class nemesis, in a doorway down the block.

"Judit. Guess who's in front of number forty-five? Karolyi Anna."

"What's she doing?"

"I can't tell," Katalin said, leaning out a bit to get a better view. "Oh, wait. I see now. She's propping a gun onto a mount."

Suddenly, Katalin noticed something black edging around a corner. It took a second to realize it was the nose of a tank. Anna Karolyi also turned to look. The tank opened fire, riddling her young body with bullets.

"Anna!" Katalin screamed.

Judit was so startled by the sound of the gunfire and the hysteria in Katalin's voice, she dropped the broomstick. As she grabbed for it, Katalin lunged, too, teetering precariously out the window. If not for Judit pulling her back she might have fallen to her death.

"Did you see what they did?" Katalin sobbed as Judit held her. "That big gun just kept shooting. They shot her again and again and again. Oh, God! She's all bloody, Judit. Anna's all bloody."

Just moments before, the street had been silent. Now death shrieked through the air in a symphony of destruction: the whistle of bullets seeking a mark, the screams of victims, the sobs of those forced to witness the cold-blooded execution of a nation. Katalin and Judit cowered in a

"I think he's still alive, Zoltán."

"But?" Zsuzsanna asked her husband, sensing that his sentence was incomplete.

"I think there's a strong possibility he's on his way to a labor camp." Mihai knew that was the last thing his wife and his brother-in-law wanted to hear—most Hungarians considered death preferable to life in a Russian prison—but he also knew that they had no time for wishful thinking, no time for feel-good falsehoods.

A deep sob escaped Mária's lips. Ilona Strasser hugged her friend's shoulder, squeezing her gently, knowing that nothing could salve the pain of this test of faith.

Zoltán said nothing. His face remained void of expression. Only István, who was standing to his left, noticed that his misshapen hands had curled into stiff, bloodless fists.

"I wish I had something more definite, but these days nothing is sure." Mihai paused. "Nothing except that things are going to get worse."

Zoltán's eyes bored into Mihai's. Andras Strasser tightened his grip on Judit.

"Tomorrow, when the men report to work at Csepel, they're going to call for a general strike. Naturally, there are going to be reprisals. The AVO knows I was one of those who helped organize it. My name is on their list. If I don't get out of the country, I'm a dead man."

"We're all going to die of starvation if the Russians don't release some of the food they've stolen," Mátyás said.

Though everyone was suffering from hunger, Mátyás and István had noticed that Vera was growing weaker. Day after day, the two brothers roamed the streets, scavenging whatever they could rather than ask the Gáspárs to dip into their own limited larder any more than they already had. Still, Vera's skin continued to pale.

Zsuzsanna studied Mátyás. Her gaze traveled from him to Vera to the Strassers and then to István, to her brother Zoltán and his family. She proffered Mihai a quick smile and then faced the group. Her dark brown eyes and burnished auburn hair glowed in the reflected light of the candle she held. She was a handsome woman. In another place and time, given the tools and the inclination, she would have been beautiful. Standing in the dreary, blackened ruins of a church, surrounded by the remains of her family and friends, she was simply a figure consumed with rage.

"I say we take control of our own destinies. I say we all leave. And the sooner the better!"

Mihai nodded and smiled. If ever he had doubted his love for Zsuzsanna, she had just reaffirmed it.

"We can walk to the border and slip into Austria," he said. "I've spoken to others who are planning to go. I know the way."

"Then where?" István asked, needing as many answers as he could get.

"We'll go to the United States," Zsuzsanna said, trying to take the pulse of the room and get a sense of who was with her, who was not. She stared at Zoltán. "What do you say, brother? Will you join us?"

Mária looked at Zoltán, waiting to hear how he would respond to his sister's challenge.

"No." His voice was soft but his tone discouraged argument.

Zsuzsanna reeled from the shock of his refusal. When she and Mihai had discussed this earlier, she had counted on Zoltán and Mária and Katalin. Why would he volunteer to be a citizen of a state run by the AVO, she had said to Mihai. Hadn't they wreaked enough damage on Zoltán's life for him to reject them? But instead, he had rejected her. He stood there and with one word told her that if she wanted to leave she could, that she could live thousands of miles away, out of touch, out of reach, and he would not object.

Backing off for the moment, Zsuzsanna turned to the Strassers. They were Zoltán's closest friends. If they went, he might agree.

"How about you, Andras? Haven't you suffered enough here? Hiding from the Nazis? Running from the Russians? Don't you want to be free?"

"Of course I do," Andras said, reaching for Ilona's hand. "But as Jews it's not so easy. Who says it will be better for us in America?" He shrugged his shoulders. "Besides, we're needed here. The Jewish community needs Ilona's medical skills. They need teachers like me to bring the music to the children. And most of all," he said, looking at Judit, "they need the children to grow up and have children. If we all leave, the Nazis will have won."

"If you stay and the Russians kill you, no one wins!" Zsuzsanna's frustration was mounting.

"We'll come with you." Everyone turned. No one had expected Mátyás to make such an announcement. "István and Vera and I have nothing here. We don't even have a home." Two days before, a Russian tank had bombed the building the Kardoses had lived in, leveling it.

"Yes, you do! You live with us," Mária said, stunned and a little guilty that she had not made it clear to Margit's children that they had permanent shelter with her.

Mátyás shook his head. "Thank you, but no. We appreciate your hospitality, but we couldn't take advantage."

"You're not taking advantage. We want you to stay. Don't we, Zoltán?"

"Absolutely!" Zoltán said. "Besides, where will you go? What will you do? You're children. And you're alone."

"We're not alone," István said. "We have each other."

Katalin reached across her father and grabbed István's arm. "You can't go!" Her voice was shrill. Her eyes were wide with fear and sorrow as she looked from István to the others. "None of you can go!"

"I know how you feel, Katya," Vera said, trying to smile for the sake of her friend. "I don't want to leave you either, but all we have here are horrible memories. My brothers and I have discussed it. We have no choice. We have to go."

"How long will it take us to reach the border?" Zsuzsanna asked Mihai.

"Three days. Maybe four, depending on whether or not the Russians have troops searching the hills for runaways."

"We'll need food and water and warm clothing," she said, ignoring Mihai's obvious implication of the danger involved, still hoping that the Gáspárs would join them.

Mihai looked at his three young charges. "Take only what you can carry. Zsuzsanna and I will bring the food."

Katalin couldn't control herself. She ran to her aunt and threw her arms around her, crying, begging her to stay.

"I can't, Katya. You heard what Uncle Mihai said. He has to get out of the country or the Russians will kill him."

"But I love you!"

"I love you too, my darling." Biting back her emotions, Zsuzsanna clasped her niece tightly, wondering how she was ever going to live without this child. Katalin was her godchild, the daughter she had never had. With dampened eyes she pleaded with her sister-in-law: "Mária. Come with us. Please. While we still have the chance to escape. Let's keep this family together. Don't let us lose each other."

Mária's eyes were moist. Her voice quaked. "Whatever Zoltán wants."

Zsuzsanna threw herself at her brother's knees. "Why won't you come with us? What is here for you? Our parents are dead. Three of our brothers are dead. Miklós is as good as dead. And you. You have nothing here except pain, thanks to what they've done to you. How can you stay?"

"I have to stay," he said.

"Why? Do you have some masochistic desire to be a perpetual victim? Do you have some need to subject your wife and your child to the horrors the Russians or the AVO will inflict on you?" Zsuzsanna was shouting. Her hands were trembling as she grabbed Zoltán's arms and shook him. "I love you. I love Mária, and God knows I adore Katalin. Do you think I would be begging you like this if I didn't think it was for the best?"

He didn't answer.

"I know it will be hard." Her voice softened. She was willing to do almost anything to persuade him to go with her, but she couldn't humiliate him. She knew how much he had been through already, how much he missed his music, how much he hated having to work in a factory. "But you can't hide here anymore," she went on. "It's not safe. Don't you see that?"

"I'm not staying because I'm hiding or because I'm embarrassed to be a common laborer," Zoltán said, his broken pride lumped in his throat.

"Then why won't you come with us?"

He looked at his sister. Love and fear and a lifetime of closeness welled in her eyes.

"I don't want to lose you," he said, choking back his own tears, "but I can't go. Someone has to be here when Miklós comes home."

7

By noon the next day every factory in Csepel had shut down. By late afternoon, word of the strike had spread beyond the Red island. By nightfall the trains had stopped, truckers refused to bring food into the city unless they were assured that it would be distributed to their countrymen and not confiscated by the Russians, and the electricity that supplied the industrial centers of Budapest was disconnected.

As the clock ticked and hundreds walked away from their jobs, hundreds of others—like Mihai Pal, his wife, Zsuzsanna, and the three Kardos orphans—walked toward freedom. Knowing a strike was a possibility, Mihai had insisted that they leave at 4:00 A.M. That way, they would have cleared the city limits long before the Russians were confronted with mass betrayal and began hunting for scapegoats.

For the émigrés, the first few hours were terrifying. Armored cars filled with soldiers patrolled the city. Sentries peered down from rooftops or out of bomb-blasted windows. Innocent-looking trucks and broken-down cars parked on roadsides leading out of town hid trigger-happy AVO. The émigrés had to move quickly and quietly, with no attention-getting displays of nervousness, no time-consuming manifestations of fear.

Though it was difficult keeping up with the brisk pace Mihai set, especially in the tricky light of dawn, no one complained. Each of them simply kept his sights on the person in front, ears open for the person in back. At the snap of Mihai's fingers they would dive beneath garbage heaps or into piles of rubble, holding their breath until the danger passed. Several times they had to stay crouched down, smothered by other people's filth, while just inches away gunfire ripped into bodies and buildings with horrifying rapidity.

Finally they left Budapest and headed into the hills. Though it would have been easier to follow the course of the Danube, north toward the Czechoslovakian border and then west to Austria, Mihai rejected that as being too obvious a path. Embankments made perfect watchtowers. The last thing he intended to do was to put himself and his party in clear sight of a gun. Feeling more secure in the thick green cover of the forests, they spent the next hours moving through the woods, wrapped in a concentrated, exhilarated silence. Though hiking along uncharted paths was difficult, they persevered, refusing to surrender to fatigue or hunger or fear. What kept them going was the knowledge that their march was not a cowardly escape but a statement. They were fighting back, denying the power of the Soviets to control them. It was not easy to leave the country of one's birth, especially when the likelihood was one would never return, but at that moment, neither where they were headed nor where they were coming from seemed quite as important as the fact that they were going.

On a map it was nearly 110 miles to the border. On foot it was longer, but neither the distance nor the cold November temperature intimidated the travelers. What preyed on their minds and tested their nerves was their vulnerability. Every step meant exposing themselves to incalculable risk. They couldn't stop anywhere, couldn't trust anyone, couldn't even talk to one another for fear that the slightest sound would unearth a camouflaged gun. To steady themselves as they made their way, each drew inward to his private thoughts and feelings.

Mihai remained focused on the well-being of his band. Since he bore the burden of responsibility for their safety, until they reached Austria he would deny himself the luxury of digression. He thought only about which corner to take, which road to avoid, where to camp, how long they should rest, how much they should eat.

Mihai had never entertained notions of greatness or leadership. In school he had done nothing remarkable. His stint in the army had been unheralded; his job at the metalworks, unexceptional. Never, until October 23, had he done anything to attract notoriety. But then the revolution had started and something inside him had pushed him to the fore.

Suddenly, he was taking charge. What astounded him the most was that people listened and followed and agreed. Men who for years had worked side by side with him on the line at the metalworks but had rarely, if ever, asked for his advice or his thoughts on anything more pressing than the score of the last soccer game suddenly turned to him for guidance. Him! Little Mihai, the youngest of six, the runt, as his father used to call him.

His father. Though it had been ten years, Mihai's eyes still misted when he thought of him. József Pal had died in what the government had labeled an industrial accident. It had taken Mihai years to read between the lines and understand the truth: The AVO had killed József Pal for attempting to organize the workers of Csepel to demand safer working conditions and a better wage. How would the senior Pal have felt about what Mihai had done? He would be proud, Mihai decided.

Now, he reminded himself, the same group of savages that had killed his father roamed the woods looking for renegades. If the AVO caught them, he knew they wouldn't hesitate to torture his charges as a way of punishing him for helping to instigate the strike. He wouldn't allow that to happen. Though Mihai had never deliberately or knowingly killed anyone in his life, as he led his wife and the three Kardos children deeper into the forest, and as he thought about his father's unavenged murder, he knew that if he had to, he would.

While Zsuzsanna's husband occupied his mind with the harsh realities surrounding their escape from Hungary, she filled her head with fantasies about life in America. Everything she had ever heard or read about the United States came back to her in an exaggerated flurry. The longer they trekked, the more difficult the way, the grander her dreams became. She would live in New York City, she told herself, in a huge building that scraped the sky. She and Mihai would have a grand apartment, with lots of space and dozens of bathrooms. Perhaps she would open a restaurant. Yes, of course! It would be so lavish and so beautiful that it would rival the Café Hungária. She would decorate it in the same extravagant art nouveau style. There would be vaulted ceilings and gilded columns and wide staircases and marble floors. The food would be the finest Magyar cuisine. Everything, from chandeliers to china, from waiters to water goblets, would be the ultimate in elegance and luxe. Naturally there would be music, but not a loud, raucous gypsy band with tambourines and trashy women costumed in gold chains and garishly colored clothes! Only fine, classically trained musicians, like her brother, would entertain her clientele. It would be so wonderful, she thought, needing to squeeze her dream for energy as her body tired. The aristocracy would fight to get a table. They would arrive in chauffeured limousines, dressed in elegant gowns, bedecked in sparkling jewels. She and Mihai would become rich and famous. But best of all, she told herself as a wedge of reality intruded on her flight of fancy and she wiped a tear away, they would have enough money to send for Zoltán and Mária and Katalin, so that all of them could be together, so that all of them could be free to enjoy the American life of plenty.

For Vera, trailing behind her younger brother, István, this day was truly the longest of her life. She was so exhausted she couldn't recall its beginning, and no matter how far they went, it seemed never to end. She felt as if she had been running forever, hiding forever, being terrified every waking moment since the instant of her birth. After a while she was so numbed by fear and pain, she felt as if her feet were moving involuntarily, lifting up and setting down out of habit, not instruction from her brain. The hollow growl in her stomach became part of her anatomy; the constant thumping of her heart, a drummer's cadence. Yet she never complained, never asked for special consideration. Once or twice she did have to stop to catch her breath. She was embarrassed by her weakness, but that was nothing compared to the humiliation she felt when she had to relieve herself in the woods. Though no one saw her and she knew that the others had suffered the same indignity, Vera was an exceedingly modest child who placed a high value on privacy and propriety. Having to tend to such basic functions in such a primitive way seemed to intensify her growing sense of isolation.

She knew it would have been better if she had been able to concentrate on the future, on the good things that lay ahead for them in America, but because she, unlike Zsuzsanna, had no idea what to look forward to, Vera continuted to dwell on what she was leaving behind. Already she missed Katalin and Judit and her other friends. Being so shy, she had never had many, so the few she had were precious. She was frightened to leave Dr. Strasser, who took such gentle care of her. More than anything else, she worried that by distancing herself from her parents' grave, she was somehow diluting their memory. Several times during the group's harrowing exit from Budapest she had passed other primitive gravesites, other makeshift cemeteries where people had been buried near where they had fallen. Each time, she had tried to conjure up images of Margit and Béla as reassurance that she could call on them at will. When occasionally her vision proved faint or fleeting, she took it as an admonishment. Instead of understanding that she was only eleven years old and that anyone in her circumstance would have been too nervous and too preoccupied with her own survival to see the ghosts of the dead clearly, her head swam with voices chanting: *You go, you go alone; you go, you go alone.*

Just before sundown, Mihai spotted a small cave concealed beneath the ledge of a rocky cliff. There, hidden behind the few pines that obscured the entrance, they could build a fire and warm themselves without fear of attracting attention. After an early dinner of bread thick with lard and paprika, and pieces of cold pork and potato, Mihai, Zsuzsanna, and Vera bedded down inside the cave. Mátyás and István had drawn the first watch.

"Do you think we're doing the right thing?" István whispered to his brother, once he was certain everyone was asleep.

"We're doing the only thing we can," Mátyás answered.

István wanted to continue the conversation, to elicit further assurances from Mátyás that this whole Ulyssean journey was worthwhile, but Mátyás had retreated into his own thoughts. István fell silent, trying to shut out all intrusions. He had been charged with an important task, he reminded himself. Allowing himself to doubt was selfish and dangerous.

"But we don't know anyone in America," he said after a few minutes, unable to remain still. "And it's such a huge country. Where will we go? Who'll we live with?"

"Mama had a brother," Mátyás said. "His name is János and he lives somewhere in the United States. Once or twice I heard Mama reading his letters to Papa."

"Why don't I remember him?" Suddenly, István felt warmed by the possibility of family.

"Probably because she didn't talk about him a lot. He left Hungary after the war. I don't know how often he wrote, but the government censored most of his letters. After a while they stopped delivering them altogether."

"Maybe he just stopped writing," István said, hope souring into disappointment. "How do we know he's still alive? Or if he remembers us? And if he does, that he'll let us live with him?"

"We don't know anything, István. But his is the only name we've got."

Once again, both boys fell into an uneasy silence. Though Mátyás masked his anxiety better than his younger brother did, as he listened to the wind howl and attempted to keep warm by covering himself with fallen leaves, he tried to compile a list of their options. There were few. If their uncle took them in, he supposed their problems were solved. If János refused them or, as István believed, had died, they might have to go to an orphanage or, worse, go to separate foster homes. Mátyás's jaw tightened.

"No. I won't allow that," he swore to himself. "I promised Mama and Papa. I won't let us be separated!"

Yet even as he repeated that vow, he admitted that whether he was in Hungary or in America, while he considered himself the head of the Kardos family, others viewed him as a fourteen-year-old child.

István's thoughts were not completely dissimilar. He, too, was concerned about what might happen to them. It had been hard enough to lose their parents. The notion that he might be separated from his family, that he and Mátyás and Vera could be split up, was too horrible to contemplate.

As he sat next to his brother, guarding the cave, both of them hugging their bodies for warmth, straining their ears for sound and their eyes for any unusual movement in the blackened landscape, István mentally continued to debate their decision to leave. He agreed with Mátyás that the Russians were going to crush the revolution and that when they did, conditions would be worse—if that was possible—than under Stalin. He agreed that without a mother and a father to support them, they would become wards of a state that had proven its lack of caring for its citizens. And he agreed that no matter what, freedom was far more desirable than oppression.

Still, he had a hundred questions, no concrete answers, and a gnawing guilt about his ambivalence. He had no way of knowing that Mátyás was embroiled in the same struggle, the same quest for confirmation. To István, Mátyás seemed so sure, so aware, even about such grown-up concepts as governmental policy concerning refugees and relocation. But then again, Mátyás had always been more definite than István, more black-and-white in his approach to the world. To him, there was simply one way or the other, the right way and the wrong way. István was more pragmatic. He didn't accept the notion of absolutes. He believed in choices and shadings and the benefits of artful compromise. As the youngest of three, he had learned early on to barter for position and property. He had learned to listen to all sides before offering an opinion. But still, as the child of scientists, he, like his brother, had great respect for the power of fact.

The fact was that he and his siblings were orphans on the run. They were leaving their homeland without exit visas, without passports, and in the company of a man wanted by the Russians. They were headed for the United States with nothing except the name of a man they had never met. They didn't know where he lived, what he did, or how he would feel about taking in his dead sister's offspring.

The fact was that although they had made it through the first day of their odyssey, they had miles to go before their feet would touch free soil. So much could happen before they reached Austria.

The fact was that István was nine years old and just then, sitting outside a spooky cave on a hilltop far away from everything and everyone he knew, he was terrified.

Quietly, he took off his glove and reached inside his pocket. There, dangling from a safety pin attached to the lining of his pants, was a key. His fingers closed around it, feeling its warmth, absorbing a sense of security from its presence. Katalin had given it to him before he left.

"In case you change your mind and want to come back," she had said, shyly slipping Mária's key to the apartment into his hand. "This way, you know you always have a home."

His eyes grew moist and his fingers tightened around the key.

I can't come back now, Katya, he thought, looking over at his brother and then into the cave where his sister slept. *But I promise, someday I will.*

As the night grew longer and exhaustion began to claim him, he wondered what his chances were of ever being able to fulfill that promise. He clutched the key, holding on to it as if it were his only link with what his life had been before this very moment, and a thick cloak of sadness enveloped him. Hot tears flowed down his nearly frozen cheeks. Just then, he missed his parents so desperately and felt the pain of their deaths so keenly, that he doubled over, gripping his knees in a frantic attempt to squeeze the hurt from his body, all the while knowing he could never remove it from his soul. Slowly the pain ebbed, and as it did his mind cleared. Reluctantly he acknowledged that as tragic as their loss was to him, Margit and Béla were not the only victims of the uprising, that thousands of others had died, that thousands more were still being gunned down in the streets.

Though thoughts like that reaffirmed the reason for leaving, they heightened a secret fear István had been harboring every since he had heard the door to the Gáspár apartment close behind him.

"If someday I do come back, will anyone be there?"

For days Katalin waited for István and the others to return. She wished for it and prayed for it and, in her childish way, believed that simply because she wanted them to come back, they would. She worried each time she heard about a family of refugees being captured or a man the AVO had dubbed a traitor being shot. What if they were talking about Mihai? What if they had taken Aunt Zsuzsanna prisoner? What if they had hurt Vera? Much as she wanted to, she knew she couldn't ask for names. If she did, if she asked the question, she might have been alerting an AVO spy to the fact that someone she knew was escaping.

Even at seven years old, Katalin knew not to trust anyone. So, despite an obsessive curiosity, Katalin kept silent. And she kept waiting.

One night as she was sitting by her window staring out at the desolate courtyard garden, she heard the front door slam. An immediate smile brightened her face. She ran into the main room expecting to find Zoltán and Mária welcoming the travelers home. Instead, two men in green uniforms were looking behind curtains and under the couch, opening closet doors, marching in and around the kitchen. A third man in a green uniform stood watching them and watching her parents. The first thing that struck her was how hideously ugly he was. His skin was a mass of disgusting craters. His hair had been slicked back with a noxious tonic that smelled as awful and as oily as it made him look. But the features that disturbed Katalin the most were his eyes. They were small and narrow, hooded, as if caught in a perpetual squint, but they never stopped moving. They scanned the room as though he were looking through a gunsight. When the eyes landed on her, she felt her stomach turn.

"And this must be your daughter, eh, Zoltán?" He started to walk toward her. Zoltán blocked his path. Katalin retreated into the arms of her mother.

"What do you want, Kassak?" Zoltán asked in a voice Katalin had never heard before.

"I'm looking for your brother-in-law, Pal Mihai."

"He's not here."

The ugly man nodded to his two comrades, who instantly went to search the bedrooms.

"You wouldn't happen to know where he is, would you?" The man circled Zoltán, an insidious smirk outlining his mouth.

"What do you want with him?"

"I thought we'd have tea and cakes." Kassak laughed, amused at his own joke. Katalin thought it sounded like the snorting of a pig.

The other men came back into the room, shaking their heads. Their leader turned to Zoltán and narrowed his eyes even more, drawing them into menacing slits.

"Where is he, Gáspár?"

"I don't know." Zoltán's voice was quiet, but edged with just enough defiance to challenge his interrogator.

"Do you know what they're doing to those who oppose the Party? They're sentencing them to labor prisons in Siberia."

"Why would I know that?" Zoltán asked. "I'm a loyal communist."

Again, Kassak laughed.

"And I suppose that swine of a brother of yours was a loyal communist also."

"Which brother are you talking about, Ferenc? I had four."

Zoltán was deliberately harassing Kassak in front of his subordinates, knowing that for Kassak to respond would be to display unacceptable weakness.

"Three of your brothers are already dead," he said. "Give Miklós six months in Siberia and he'll wish he was lying next to the other Gáspár men."

Kassak infused the word *men* with such arrogant derision, it was all Zoltán could do not to lunge for his throat. Instead, he held his place like an obedient soldier, content because he had won this contest. Kassak had answered Zoltán's question. Miklós was alive! But Zoltán had no time to gloat over his victory. They were still jousting about Mihai.

"Look, Gáspár. We know that Pal left Budapest." He leaned forward, sticking his face only inches away from Zoltán's.

Katalin noticed that her father winced and curled his nose. The man's breath must be as foul as his manner, she decided.

"And you know he's wanted for trying to corrupt the minds of hundreds of loyal communist workers on Csepel Island and for threatening them unless they walked off their jobs."

"I don't work at Csepel. I don't know what you're talking about."

"I suppose you don't know about the strike?" Kassak said with mock incredulousness.

"Everybody knows about the strike."

"Is your factory on line?"

Zoltán shook his head.

"Then you're on strike as well?" He was so eager to catch Zoltán in a trap, his voice practically danced over his words.

"I'm just a humble machinist in a shoe factory. I want to work, but if the factory is shut down, I can't work."

"Who ordered the factory closed?" Kassak demanded, eager for another name to hand his superiors.

"I don't know. I don't think anyone ordered it closed."

"Then why isn't it producing its quota?"

"I guess the people of Hungary have more than enough shoes," Zoltán said with a shrug of his shoulders. "We can only wear one pair at a time. Why make more than we can use?"

The two AVO men chuckled, but Kassak had been pushed too far. He grabbed Zoltán's collar and twisted it until Zoltán choked. In a low, sinister growl he issued his ultimatum.

"Either you tell me where your stinking brother-in-law is or I'll let these two dogs loose on your wife and daughter."

Zoltán gasped for breath and massaged his neck.

"He's on his way to the West," he said.

Kassak's mouth widened in a triumphant grin. He loved flexing the muscles of his power. He loved watching those who thought they were better than him cowering with fear. He loved being the strongest.

"When did he leave?"

"Two days ago."

"Who's with him?"

"I don't know."

"Is your sister with him?"

"I suppose so."

Again, Kassak clutched at Zoltán's collar. Again, he blew his fetid breath into Zoltán's face.

"Don't suppose, Gáspár. Is she or isn't she with him?"

Zoltán nodded.

"Which route are they taking?"

The others couldn't see, but Kassak had tightened his grip. Zoltán was choking on his own saliva. He jerked his head to the side to loosen Kassak's hold. As he did, Kassak's other hand came up under his chin. Zoltán heard the click of a knife just seconds before he felt the cold, sharp steel of a blade scratch his flesh. Blood trickled down his neck. He made no effort to stop it or to break free of Kassak. For several minutes they stood in a deadly embrace, each waiting for the other to blink. Then Kassak snapped his knife back into his holder, pushed Zoltán away from him, and placed his hands on his hips.

"I have no more time to play with you," he barked. "Which way are they going?"

Zoltán's answer was not immediate. Beads of sweat gathered beneath the brow of Kassak's cap. His threat about Mária and the girl was a tactical blunder. He knew it. Worse, he was certain the others knew it. Mária Gáspár was a national heroine, practically an icon. While personally, he would have loved nothing more than rutting about with the queen of the Hungarian stage, especially in front of her supercilious husband, this was not Recsk. This was not one of the underground cells he had set aside as a private den for the indulgence of his insatiable satyriasis. This was too open, too public. He had no way of knowing whose ears were pressed against walls, no way of being certain whether one or both of his aides was truly loyal. Much as he would have enjoyed defiling Mária Gáspár and her daughter, Kassak backed off.

"I asked you a question," he barked again.

When Zoltán continued to defy him, Kassak signaled his associates.

The larger one grabbed Zoltán and pinned his arms behind his back while the other brutally pummeled his stomach. Only when he heard Katalin screaming at the men to stop did Zoltán comply.

"They're following the river," he croaked.

Kassak smiled. A slight nod of his head and the two men dropped Zoltán to the floor like a used tissue. A quick click of his heels and the three men in green uniforms departed.

For half an hour no one spoke. Quietly, holding back her tears, allowing only her soul to cry, Mária tended her husband's wounds while Katalin held Zoltán's hand, her eyes as dry as her mother's. Inside, however, she too was weeping. Inside, she too was angry, but rage was becoming as familiar a sensation as the pangs of hunger that had begun to afflict them all.

For most seven-year-olds, rage is not common, nor is the ability to control such intense feeling, but Katalin was not an ordinary child and these were not ordinary times. From the moment she had been able to understand, Katalin had been taught the basic tenets for living under repressive rule: suspicion and silence. In a society where betrayal was a means of survival, where children were taught to spy on their parents and to snitch on their friends, where disloyalty was rewarded and fealty punished, even the littlest ones were conditioned to question everyone while answering no one.

For many of her friends, including Judit, absolute discretion was difficult. Katalin, however, had become a master of restraint. She had a small list of names of those she trusted. Anyone not on that list who asked her for information, who tried to whisper secrets in her ear, who teased or tested her, was greeted with a blank face and an empty stare. Katalin, at seven, was a survivor.

When Zoltán thought it was safe, he checked the hall, felt around the room for possible listening devices, and then finally allowed himself to relax.

"You lied to him," Mária whispered, spoon-feeding him hot broth. "You gave him the wrong direction and the wrong departure date. What if he finds out?"

Zoltán shrugged. "He'll be back."

"How could you take such a chance?"

"I would not give Kassak Ferenc information that could kill my sister and her husband."

"But he might have killed you," Mária said, her voice edged with indignation as well as fear.

"He tried that once and failed. I don't think he wants to fail again."

Katalin looked up. In the time since the AVO men had gone, her mind had wandered into the woods where István and Vera and Mátyás were. That horrible man had never even asked about them. Katalin wasn't certain how that made her feel. On the one hand, his omission made her angry. It was as if her friends were irrelevant, not even important enough to track, let alone list as missing. It made her wonder whether or not she was irrelevant, whether anyone would notice her absence or care if they did. Yet part of her was filled with relief. If no one was looking for them, perhaps they would be safe.

"What do you mean, Papa," she said, tuning in to her parents' conversation, suddenly realizing that what her mother was saying was that they might not be safe. "When did he try to kill you?"

"When I was in Recsk." Zoltán said it quietly. He hadn't meant to tell them about Kassak. He regretted bringing it up, but he supposed, once Kassak had violated his home, his presence had required an explanation. "He's the man who broke my hands."

Katalin felt sick to her stomach. The thought of that horrible creature hurting her father was nauseating. A pool of saliva gathered in her mouth. Quickly, she swallowed, but another pool of sour water followed. Before she embarrassed herself, she ran to the bathroom, straddled the toilet, and spit the evil bile into the bowl. Her stomach lurched. Her throat tightened, but she hadn't eaten in so long there was nothing to bring up. Over and over again her body heaved, regurgitating all the sorrow and sadness and unrequited anger that had filled her soul over the past several weeks.

She hadn't realized she had been screaming until she felt Mária's arms close around her and heard her mother's lilting voice in her ear.

"It's all right, *dragam*. Don't cry. I know you're scared and afraid for your papa, and me, and afraid for yourself, but we're fine."

"What if he comes back?" Katalin sobbed. "What if he wants to hurt you? Or kill Papa?"

"He won't. He could have hurt us today and he didn't. What's more, because Papa was so brave, Aunt Zsuzsanna, Uncle Mihai, and our little friends are going to be free. Isn't that wonderful?"

Katalin nodded and then leaned against Mária, allowing herself to be soothed and petted and consoled. As her mother caressed her and her fears subsided, she reflected on the attitude of her parents and others she had seen in the past several days. Everyone became so exhilarated at the thought of relatives and friends crossing the Austrian border. They whispered about it and toasted to it and prayed for it. Despite her age, Katalin understood that many were willing to die for it. When she had been in the square or in the streets and found herself in the midst of shouting patriots, she, too, had followed suit and joined the chorus of those

demanding freedom. But then, as now, one question nagged at her:
"What does it feel like to be free?"

Vera was growing weaker. It had rained the day before. That night
Zsuzsanna tried valiantly to chase the chill that had wrapped itself around
the fragile young girl, but despite the warmth of the fire and whatever
clothing the others could spare to cover her, Vera continued to shiver
and shake.

"She needs to see a doctor," Zsuzsanna said, taking Mihai aside.

"We can't take the chance. With the miners on strike, the AVO are
everywhere. We have no way of knowing who's friend and who's foe."

They had circumambulated Tatabánya, but even on the distant outskirts of that city, the strike and its consequences were all anyone spoke
of. Men in sympathy with their brothers at Csepel simply had refused to
enter the mines. They knew that as they did, their names were being
inscribed on a list for retaliation—torture, murder, unspeakable atrocities
performed on innocent family members. Still, they continued to stand
firm. They would not go down into the heart of their land and bring up
the coal needed to fuel the communist regime.

The Russians were furious. They cut off food supplies. They kidnapped young men and shipped them to Siberia. They sent in tanks,
troops, and the savage AVO. Still, the mines remained shut. When the
Russians threatened to kill large numbers of those they found uncooperative, the men of Tatabánya countered with a threat to flood the mines if
one man was shot. It was a standoff. The air sizzled like the wick on a
stick of dynamite. Each minute the moment of explosion grew nearer.

"I know how dangerous it is," Zsuzsanna continued, her nerves
screaming with the precariousness of their situation, "but she needs help.
And she needs it now!"

While the others remained hidden, Mihai ventured into the city of
Tata. For several hours he lost himself in the everyday activities of the
town, in order to get a sense of what was going on. He stood in line to
buy bread. He attached himself to a crowd listening to a man reading a
newspaper. He walked into a pharmacy intending to buy some medicine
for Vera, looked at the customers milling about and the man behind the
counter, and decided not to risk it. He went into a beer hall and shared
a brew with several workers who were out of a job. He listened. He
commiserated. He pretended to be one of them. He asked as many questions as he could without attracting undue attention and gave as many
answers as he could without arousing suspicion. When none of his discus-

sions yielded the information he wanted, he found a telephone directory, locked himself in the stall of a public bathroom, and rifled through the pages searching for a doctor. He stared at each name, begging the letters on the page to speak to him, to tell him whether or not the person who belonged to that name could be trusted with their lives. The names were silent. Mihai grew nervous. He had been gone a long time. His instructions to Mátyás and Zsuzsanna had been that if he hadn't returned by nightfall, they were to change hiding places immediately and, the next morning, continue on toward the border.

After trashing the directory, and with it all hope of ever finding a doctor, he started out of town, back to where he had left his cadre. Though he hadn't wanted to make this side trip, one look at Vera had convinced him that Zsuzsanna was right. The child's health had deteriorated so dramatically that extra measures had to be taken to save her. There was no way he could have explained to Mátyás and István why he wouldn't do anything to help their sister. So he had come to Tata. But after almost a full day, he was leaving with a loaf of bread, a jar of lard, a blanket, a scraggly bunch of carrots, no medicine, and no doctor.

Once outside the city proper, he noticed that the houses were set farther and farther apart. Though Tata was moderately large, it appeared as if its environs were not as densely settled as the suburbs of Budapest. An idea began to take root. He quickened his pace, keeping his eyes open for the opportunity he was seeking. Suddenly, there it was: a truck, casually parked at the side of the road. Mihai scanned the area. There was no way for him to tell whether the truck belonged to the people who lived in the house a hundred yards to his left or to someone who was visiting that house, but it didn't matter. It was providence. Who was he to deny God's generosity?

He circled the truck, wondering if God's generosity had extended far enough to include a key. It hadn't, but Mihai was a master mechanic. Hot-wiring the engine would take only a few seconds. That was not the problem. The problem was how many people were in the house and what would they do when they heard the engine start up. Mihai could have tried to make his way to the house, peek in the windows and count heads, but he decided not to waste the time. The road was empty. There was no one else around. He jumped into the driver's seat and reached down under the dash.

It was an old truck, probably prewar. The upholstery was frayed. The metal on the inside of the doors was rusty. The clutch was wobbly and Mihai could imagine that on the road it would slip in and out of gear at will. Feeling around, he found the two wires he needed. Carefully splicing them together, he waited to hear the engine catch. Once. Twice.

Nothing happened. He began to think that perhaps the truck was a useless heap that had been abandoned. No, he told himself. He refused to believe that. Again, his eyes darted back to the house, checking for movement, for sounds, for any sign that someone had noticed him. Grabbing hold of the wires, he repeated the process. Silence. He repeated it again. This time the engine coughed. Then it wheezed. Then it sputtered. And then it hummed. Trying to contain the joy he felt, he put it into first gear and drove away, slowly, quietly. If no one had heard, he didn't alert them. Once he saw the house shrinking in the rearview mirror, and saw that still no one had come out to investigate, he shifted into third and headed toward his brood.

When he was half a mile away from where he had left Zsuzsanna and the others, he pulled off the road and parked in a thicket. Quickly he went deeper into the woods. He tore off branches, ripped up bushes, and collected leaves. When he had completely covered the truck, camouflaging it so no one would spot it, he returned to his band.

"You did the right thing," Zsuzsanna said after Mihai explained why he hadn't returned with a doctor. "Maybe the food will help."

"There will be doctors in Austria," Mihai said, trying to allay the fears of Mátyás and István. "With the truck, we'll get there that much faster. We just have to keep Vera warm until we do."

Wrapping the new blanket around her, Mihai swooped her up in his arms and hugged her to him, hoping to transfer his body heat to her. As he sat with her he watched his wife preparing a soup from the carrots he had brought and a rabbit Mátyás had bagged. Behind him, the two boys were trying to build a shelter to shield their sister from the cruel bite of the evening's wind.

Mihai was not a man prone to philosophizing, but he couldn't help wondering about the advisability of what he had done. Things were bad in Budapest, he knew that, but was this any better? Though food supplies had dwindled and bellies grumbled and fear had become a constant, was running and hiding and cooking broth from things foraged in a wintry wood better? Was it better to have taken three young children away from everything and everyone they had known? For this? Was it better to have uprooted his wife just to start all over again in a strange land among strange people? He didn't know, but one thing was certain: It was too late to go back.

Gradually, Vera's tremors eased and her body relaxed. Looking down, Mihai saw that she had fallen asleep. He also noticed that her face was extremely flushed. He pressed his wrist to her forehead. She was burning with fever.

"István," he called. "Get me Zsuzsanna's bag."

István looked at Mihai and then at Vera. He gasped. She was so limp, so lifeless. Her body was nestled against Mihai's, but even with the support of arms as muscular as his, she looked as if her skin were rubber, her skeleton made of fluid rather than bone.

"Go," Mihai said.

Seconds later, István returned carrying Zsuzsanna's knapsack. Mihai instructed him to rummage about for a bottle of aspirin. Though he knew Vera needed something stronger and worried that aspirin might be harmful to her heart condition, he decided that the first order of business was to break her fever. She had to be able to travel at dawn's light. If they were lucky, if the truck held out, if the roads were clear, if God was in fact looking out for them, perhaps by nightfall, or the next morning at the latest, they would be in Austria.

István located the bottle. Only seven pills remained.

Mihai saw the panic in the boy's eyes. "She'll be all right. You'll see. Just get something to wash these down."

István held the cup of soup with both hands, balancing it as if to lose even a single drop were sinful. While Mihai awakened Vera, István knelt by the big man's side, holding on to the precious pills while Mihai encouraged Vera to sip some of the soup. Drop by drop, the hot liquid found its way inside Vera's mouth. When she was able, Mihai fed her three pills and then more soup. Mátyás joined them with a hunk of bread, Zsuzsanna with a piece of meat.

For Vera, the night slipped by like a bedeviled fog. Her body hurt. Her face burned. Her eyes felt as if someone had splashed them with acid. All around her, she heard voices. If she strained, she could separate the sounds and discriminate between István and Mátyás, Mihai and Zsuzsanna. Yet even when she stretched her concentration to the limit, she heard no words, simply mutterings, meaningless noises that somehow had managed to push aside the thick gray curtain that hung over her. For a fleeting moment she felt connected to the world, but then the sounds faded and once again she plunged into a black abyss of tortured silence.

Occasionally when they woke her to feed her medicine and soup, she tried to speak, but the effort was too great and besides, she had nothing to say. She felt herself declining. She knew she was a burden on the others. For their sakes, as well as her own, she tried to rally, and for a while, when the aspirin took effect, she did. But once, during a brief moment of consciousness when she looked up and saw that in order to hold her, Mihai was sleeping propped against a tree, the guilt she bore over her dependence increased, adding extra weight to the millstone she carried. As the night wore on and the fever vanquished the aspirin, she drifted further and further away, deeper into resigned isolation.

When the first hint of dawn intruded on the blackness of night,

Zsuzsanna set to readying Vera for the day's journey. She washed her face and fed her, making certain that she swallowed two more of the aspirin.

"Come, darling. It's time to go." She signaled to Mátyás to help her. Carefully, the two of them lifted Vera onto their shoulders. István broke up the camp, packed all the supplies and, loaded like a pack mule, followed the trail Mihai had left, leading them out of the copse.

"We're going to carry you to the truck Mihai found," Zsuzsanna said to Vera when the girl turned her head and looked at Zsuzsanna with confused, frightened eyes. "You're going to be able to ride to freedom. How does that sound?"

For a minute it seemed as if Zsuzsanna's cheerfulness tickled Vera. She smiled, but then her lips went slack as she retreated into her fevered sleep.

Mihai had gone ahead to scout the place where he had hidden the truck. He stalked the entire area, making certain that no one was there, that no one had disturbed the camouflage. He had marked with arrows the rocks that held down the branches. He knew exactly which way those arrows were pointing. If one had been moved, he would have known it. Holding his breath, he checked every last one. Their luck had held.

When the others joined him, they put Vera in the cab cuddled in Zsuzsanna's lap, her feet resting on Mihai's leg. The boys piled into the back of the rickety pickup. It was difficult finding the way in the blue-gray light of that November morning, but Mihai had grown up in the nearby city of Györ and knew the roads. By blending in with the early morning traffic, they were able to make good time, until the inevitable happened. The truck was nearly out of gas. Quickly, Mihai and the boys conceived a plan. In Györ, Mihai reckoned there would be unmanned cars and trucks for them to tap. The trick was to find a can to hold the gasoline, then to find a vehicle with a full tank, and then, if necessary, to create a disturbance that would distract those who might not approve of what they were doing.

Once again, Mihai hid the truck, this time in the barn of a dilapidated deserted house three miles from the city. Assured that Zsuzsanna and Vera would be all right, he and the boys left on their mission. Mihai led them straight to the industrial sector, where, after reconnoitering the area, they found a loading dock with a gasoline pump, a jam of trucks, and a frenetic supervisor. As the beleaguered man tried to coordinate his crew and his truckers, István and Mátyás searched the perimeter of the building for anything they could use to hold gasoline. When finally they found a large metal jug, they signaled to Mihai, who had stationed himself inside the dock but out of sight of the supervisor.

Partially hidden by one of the walls used to segment the dock, Mihai motioned to one of the truckers to move back. As the driver obeyed and, by doing so, blocked everyone's view of the gas pump, István and Mátyás hurriedly filled the jug and sneaked away. When the driver jumped out of his cab and came around back looking for the other man to help him get ready for loading, Mihai was gone.

The jug held only half a tankful. It seemed like little reward for such tremendous risk, but they were growing accustomed to feeling as if every step they took was into uncharted waters. From moment to moment they were never certain whether they were going to be able to ford the pool or drown trying.

They were only five miles from the border when the truck died. They abandoned it and took cover in the thick marshes that covered much of that part of the land. Within minutes they realized they were not alone. Scattered throughout the rushes were clusters of people also headed for the border. Most, like Mihai's troupe, had been walking for days. Some had been captured by the Russians along the route, tossed into bunkers to await deportation, but were brave enough and lucky enough to escape. All were tired and hungry and cold and desperate to reach the small wooden footbridge at Andau, where they could cross over into freedom.

Mihai, having spoken to several mechanics he had known at Csepel, decided that despite their fatigue and despite Vera's worsening health, they had to continue on. There were rumors that AVO were in the area. Other rumors claimed the Russians were sweeping the swamps looking for escapees. Whether those rumors were the products of frightened imaginations or based on some reality didn't matter. His group was not going to wait around to find out.

Lifting Vera onto his shoulders, he and his wife and the Kardos boys attached themselves to the ragtag caravan headed through the bogs. Mile after mile, they tromped through reeds as high as Mihai's head, as thick as the thatch on the roofs of cottages they had passed along the way. István was choking, but he refused to complain. Often the mire rose up under his chin until the sludge licked his lips and demanded that he taste it. He trudged on, keeping his eyes centered on Mátyás's back.

Mátyás, too, was becoming strangled by the stringy plants clogging the marsh. He, too, trudged on, trying to appear brave, allowing frightened tears to fall only when he was certain that István couldn't see. The last thing Mátyás wanted was to appear weak. After all, he continued to remind himself, he was the head of the family. He had to remain strong. He had to lead. He had to survive.

The only thing that kept Zsuzsanna from screaming out in anger and discomfort and fear was her concern for Vera. Plodding along next to Mihai, she kept careful watch over her charge, reaching out now and then to feel the young girl's forehead, which continued to burn. When she realized that Vera was no longer sleeping but had slipped into unconsciousness, Zsuzsanna, too, began to cry.

It was then, when her tears froze on her cheeks, that she first noticed the frost. It was all around her, icing the thin reeds and coating the marshes with a cold white veil. The moon had risen high in the sky, glowing like a huge pearl. Stars glistened against the sable ground. A shimmering brilliance spread over the earth, dressing the swamps in silver. Zsuzsanna looked up at Mihai to see if he had noticed the descent of the fabled white night. His face was grizzled, his hair tipped with ice, his body covered with hoarfrost. She looked down at her hand. It, too, was glazed. For a moment she stopped and stared, marveling over the magnificence of a night such as this when the whole world appeared dusted with pearlescent powder.

Suddenly, she heard an intense silence. Others had stopped to look. For a long time, no one moved. There was something almost religious about the experience, something almost holy about the overwhelming whiteness, the sense of purity, the sense of innocence. But those caught in that marsh knew that in the real world innocence and purity had been crushed. Had they prevailed, there would be no caravan. There would be no one standing in the rushes in the bitter cold to witness nature's artistry.

The moment passed. The exodus began again, but this time footsteps were accompanied by the crackling of reeds. Short, staccato noises filled the air like sparks from a fireworks display. Again, people stopped. The white night had become a black trap. Each time someone moved, the ice chipped, a stalk cracked, a cattail snapped. Each sound was like a shotgun going off, alerting the enemy. Ahead were Hungarian border guards and, worse, a watchtower manned by AVO.

Quickly, word spread. Proceed slowly, in a line, not all at once. Everyone complied. Step by step they trod through the frozen bog. Mihai followed the man in front of him. Zsuzsanna followed Mihai. Mátyás followed Zsuzsanna. István followed his brother. And fear followed them all.

It took hours, but finally they reached a tiny tab of land—only as large as a football field—where the free soil of Austria intruded on the swamps of communist-occupied Hungary. To the south and east were the Hungarian marshes whence the émigrés had come. In front of them was the Einser Canal, a deep, mud-bottomed avenue into which the reed-filled swamps drained. Crossing the canal was a small wooden footbridge commonly known as the Bridge at Andau. In fact, Andau was an Austrian village several hundred yards away. Both sides of the bridge were in Hungary, but it remained the only dry way to get to Andau.

Many of the travelers were so overcome with anxiety that they defied caution and ran across the bridge, placing themselves in full view of the watchtower. Mihai and the others waited. Though most of those standing in the mire had long ago given up on the notion of miracles, there were no shots. They heard no dogs. They smelled no gunpowder. Encouraged, hysterical with the scent of freedom, a huge group followed the others over the bridge. Then, as Mihai and his troupe waited their turn in the high reeds, shots rang out. Orange flame rose into the air. Songs that had been on the lips of the freedom marchers died as their bodies fell into the icy canal. For all intents and purposes, the bridge was closed.

"What do we do?" Mátyás whispered, turning to Mihai.

"We bypass the bridge and wade through a drainage ditch that follows the border to the east."

"How's Vera?" István asked, his own legs numb with cold.

"She's fine," Zsuzsanna lied. "But the quicker we get her to Austria, the better off she'll be."

Though both boys suspected the truth, neither could deal with it. Their store of emotional energy was so sorely depleted, they had only enough to get them to safety. Keeping their eyes straight ahead, deliberately avoiding the limp body hanging over Mihai's shoulders, they followed him through the swamps, around the watchtower and up to a long, forbidding drainage ditch. Mihai waded in. When he realized how deep it was in the middle, he returned to shore.

"Can you boys swim?"

Both of them nodded and, for the first time in days, smiled.

"We're great swimmers," István said, almost boasting.

"Then go," Mihai said. "I'll ferry Vera across and then come back for Zsuzsanna."

Zsuzsanna had never learned to swim. She had never regretted it. Now she did.

István and Mátyás slipped into the icy water. Their bodies jerked from the impact of the sudden cold on their skin, but both of them were good enough swimmers to know to tread water until their body temperatures adjusted. As swiftly as they could, they sliced through the water, trying not to splash, keeping their kicks low and wide. When the light from the watchtower hit the water, both boys dived underneath, breaststroking until they had to come up for air. When finally they reached the other side, they jumped out and searched the horizon for Mihai. He was in the middle, using only one arm to pull himself through the water.

The other was tightly clasped around Vera. István and Mátyás watched with their hearts in their throats as, slowly, the man and the girl inched their way across. At the edge, Mátyás and István reached down with greedy hands and grabbed Vera, hoisting her out of the water and gently laying her on the frozen bank. When they looked back, Mihai was already on his way to get his wife.

Vera was blue. Her body was flaccid. Mátyás put his ear to her chest. He waited, curling his hands into anxious fists. Her rib cage lifted and fell. It was a strained, heavy movement, but to Mátyás and István it was glorious. She was still alive. Quickly, ignoring the fact that they, too, were half-frozen, they lifted her up and scanned the landscape until they spotted a path. Plunging into the marshland once again, they moved toward the border as fast as they could, both of them knowing that the girl they carried was on a borderline of her own.

"We have to hurry," István said, tears streaming down his face.

"I know." Mátyás, too, had surrendered to his emotions. "I just want her to be free. I just want her to be free."

"Hang on, Vera," István said, his eyes peeled in front of him, his hands gripping his sister's legs.

"Hang on, Vera," Mátyás repeated as he trailed after his little brother, his arms crooked beneath Vera's shoulders, wrapped tightly around her waist.

Over and over, like a marching song, the brothers entreated Vera to hang on. At last they cleared the swamp.

"I think I see a road," István said, hoping it wasn't a mirage.

"Over here!" someone shouted. "Over here!"

The boys saw a Red Cross truck and, outside it, several people waving them on. For an instant they didn't move.

"What if they're AVO?" Mátyás said.

"If they were, they would have shot us already," István said.

Acknowledging the truth in István's statement, Mátyás nodded and they broke into a run, tripping and stumbling the hundred or so yards to the truck.

"Are we in Austria?" István asked, looking around for some sign, some change in the landscape, some visible symbol of freedom.

"Yes."

The word was like magic. István and Mátyás grinned and cried and shivered with relief.

"Please," Mátyás said, the smile draining from his face. "This is our sister. She's awfully sick. Can anyone help us?"

Without wasting any time, two men carried Vera into the Red Cross truck, where a doctor examined her. Meanwhile, nurses wrapped the boys in warm blankets, removed their shoes, and tried to coax blood back into their frostbitten toes. When the doctor appeared, the boys jumped to their feet.

"How is she?"

"Is she going to be all right?"

"I'm sorry," the doctor said, placing an arm around each boy. "Your sister's gone."

István shook his head. "No. She can't be. We lost Mama and Papa. We can't lose Vera. No. You're wrong. She's just sick."

Mátyás, too, began mumbling his disbelief. "We were going to be free," he said. "That's why we took her away from Budapest. To be free."

"She was very ill," the doctor explained, knowing the boys were in shock and that his words were falling on deaf ears, but needing to say them anyway. "If it makes you feel any better," he continued, "she died here. She died free."

Vera had died en route from the ditch to the Red Cross truck, but these two boys didn't have to know that.

"Where's the nearest cemetery?" István asked.

The doctor looked bewildered, as did several of the others. The only one who understood was Mátyás.

"Our parents had to be buried in a park," István explained. "Their grave isn't marked. We want Vera to be buried in a cemetery. With a priest. With a stone." His voice cracked as his eyes released a torrent of tears. Mátyás stood by him, also venting his grief.

"The nearest cemetery is in Andau, four miles away."

"Is there a church in Andau?" István asked.

The doctor nodded. Mátyás and István conferred.

"Can we take Vera now?" Mátyás asked.

"Of course, but . . ."

Stopping only to put on their soaking-wet shoes, the two boys retrieved the body of their sister and started off in the direction of Andau.

"If you'd like to wait," one of the nurses said, her heart wrenched, "we have another truck which is taking women and children to Andau. It should be back any minute."

"Thank you, but no," István said. "We want this time to say good-bye."

Holding Vera, as they had when they carried her through the reeds, István and Mátyás walked the four miles to a small church in the village of Andau. Hundreds of Hungarians had camped outside the ancient stone structure. At first, the crush of people was frightening. Government officials were outside, busily preparing papers so that the refugees could be transported to Vienna for resettlement. Medical teams from Switzerland and Austria were inside tending the sick, sending emergency cases on to nearby hospitals. Local villagers were providing food and blankets and keeping large bonfires burning to provide some sort of warmth. For most, the activity and the noise were a comfort after the solitude of the road. For István and Mátyás, the confusion was unnerving.

"You stay with Vera," Mátyás said.

Fifteen minutes later he returned with the priest—a short, balding man with a kindly face—and two villagers.

"Could you help us?" Mátyás said in a voice barely above a whisper.

The priest looked at István and then at the dead girl cradled in his arms. Gently he leaned down, took the girl, and handed her to the two villagers, who carried her inside. István and Mátyás followed. The men placed Vera on the floor in front of the altar, where the priest administered the last rites.

"We want her to be buried here," Mátyás said.

"Where she'll be safe," István added, as if they needed a reason for their request.

"We'll take care of it," the priest said with a reassuring smile. "In the meanwhile, why don't you get something to eat?"

"Thank you, Father," Mátyás said. "We'll stay here with Vera."

The priest considered arguing, but simply nodded. He had officiated at too many burials in the past few days not to understand their need to hold out as long as possible. As he moved on to another group, he looked back. The two boys were flanking their dead sister. Their hands were folded and their heads were lowered. The priest sighed. The communists thought they could banish God at will. Yet look where the people escaping communism came.

Thy will be done, he thought as the next refugee family presented itself for his blessing.

By the time Mihai and Zsuzsanna arrived at the church and found the boys, Vera had been lowered into the earth. Dozens of émigrés had gathered around the open grave. Villagers, too, came to help István and Mátyás bid Vera farewell. They didn't know her, they weren't related to the mourners, but on that day, in that churchyard, they were all family, all mourners.

On December 4 a parade of women garbed in funereal black marched through the streets of Budapest, intent upon laying flowers on the grave of the unknown Hungarian soldier. Mária Gáspár and her daughter, Katalin, Ilona Strasser and her daughter, Judit, were part of the defiant procession. As they walked in the measured pace of those paying their respects to the dead, covered from head to toe in ebony cloth, they appeared like a portentous cloud warning the populace about the evil plague that had invaded their city.

As they passed, faces pressed against windows, hands waved support, heads bowed in reverence. Everyone understood the message the women were delivering. Exactly one month before, Russian tanks had stormed their homeland and raped their pride. Everyone mourned the valiant men and women and children who had resisted the invasion. Everyone knew that still, despite their losses, despite the savagery of the retaliation, people continued to fight and continued to die rather than hand themselves over to the Soviets.

Onward they walked, impervious to the gathering of Russian tanks and soldiers with machine guns aimed at their backs. Once, the soldiers approached the head of the line and ordered the women to stop. They continued walking, holding out their bunches of flowers and crying: "We have only flowers. You have guns. What are you afraid of?" One of the soldiers panicked. For no apparent reason he fired into the crowd, hitting one of the women in the leg. The women continued to walk, holding their heads high, refusing to be thwarted by the animals with red stars on their caps. Closer and closer they came to the tomb. Another soldier broke rank. At the top of his lungs he demanded that they stop. When they kept walking, he shouted again. When they continued to ignore him, he rushed at the first woman he saw and grabbed her by the arm. He screamed in her face and shook her, mindless of the fact that she had a young child hanging on to her skirts. Using every ounce of strength she possessed, Mária Gáspár broke free of his grasp and, with a dignity only someone of her talent could muster, she narrowed her eyes and glowered at him with utter loathing. Then calmly, but deliberately, she spat in his face.

That same day, Zsuzsanna and Mihai Pal and István and Mátyás Kardos arrived at Camp Kilmer in New Brunswick, New Jersey. By the middle of January, Zsuzsanna and Mihai, under the auspices of one of the many relief agencies helping to resettle Hungarian immigrants, got off the train in New York City, were brought to a three-room third-floor walk-up on 74th Street and First Avenue, where they began their new life.

It took a long time to track down János Vas, but by the end of

February he had been located and told about his nephews and their plight. On March 16, 1957, Mátyás and István Kardos arrived in Woodridge, Kentucky, and moved into a small room above the garage at the home of János and Rosza Vas. For them, too, a new life had begun.

II

Adagio

1962–1972

8

Woodridge, Kentucky, 1962

Early on, Mátyás Kardos had divined that in order to survive, one had to accommodate himself to his surroundings. At nineteen, if Mátyás was anything, he was a survivor. From the day he and István had left Camp Kilmer and arrived in Woodridge, a small town in the Cumberland Plateau region of Kentucky, Mátyás had realized that despite the good intentions of the Catholic Relief Agency that had helped relocate them, and despite the hospitality offered by János and Rosza Vas, little had changed since the day the two brothers had crossed the border into Austria. He and István were on their own.

János, whose hooded hazel eyes and thick, arched brows evidenced a haunting, yet comforting, resemblance to Margit, was tearful and effusive in his greeting, vowing to do whatever he could to help his younger sister's children. Rosza, a large woman with pale blue eyes, pink cheeks, and a high-pitched giggle that seemed inappropriate in a woman of her size, also granted the boys a warm welcome, clucking over them continuously, feeding them and hugging them, so much and so often they sometimes thought they would burst or be smothered. But their cousins, young men ranging in age from twenty-two to sixteen, were another story. Despite the language barrier, Mátyás and István couldn't miss the strong current of objection they felt emanating from the four brothers. They made little attempt to hide their displeasure at the notion of adding two more people to their already overcrowded household. As far as they were concerned, life was tough enough without taking in strangers.

János and his boys worked for Crown Collieries, the mining company that owned the three mines in the area, as well as a small preparation plant. János and the two older boys manned power shovels down in the mines. The two younger boys, each having started on the day he was old enough to get working papers, helped out in the preparation plant, sorting the coal so that it could be washed clean of impurities like ash and sulfur before being shipped. Rosza waitressed part-time at a diner in nearby Jackson.

With everyone employed, the Vas family was better off than many in the region, but *better* was a relative term. With all their wages combined, they still hovered perilously close to the poverty line. They had a car. They had food. They each had a spare pair of shoes and a winter coat, but everything they bought above and beyond basic subsistence was a stretch, a planned purchase that required weeks, often months of saving.

Woodridge was a company town, originally built by Josiah Crown in the 1800's to house the men he needed to work his mines. Generations later, descendants of the Crown family still lived in a splendid mansion high on a bluff overlooking the North Fork of the Kentucky River; the miners still lived in clapboard row houses that stood shoulder to shoulder as they followed the rise of the hills. Butted up against the street without even a small patch of green one could call a lawn or property, they had started out as basic building blocks, with no architectural flourishes, no whimsical touches. Individuality was expressed by a paint color or a flower box or the swag of a curtain viewed through a dusty windowpane. Over the years, as children married and brought their mates home, as the elderly were widowed and needed care and companionship, additions reshaped the original boxes and redesigned the aspect of the town, until Woodridge had evolved into an architectural hodgepodge, a city planner's nightmare. There were add-ons, dormered roofs, finished basements, refitted garages, and walled-in porches. None was constructed with any attempt to match or fit in. They were simply there.

The Vas house at the base of Hasen's Hill was barely adequate for their needs. The kitchen was the center of the house, boasting a large wooden table and six hand-carved chairs that János and Rosza had brought with them when they immigrated in 1939. The living room, the only other room on the main floor, was a narrow rectangle wallpapered in a busy floral print and overly furnished with a melange of chairs and tables, everything draped with lacy antimacassars and fringed shawls. In the corner closest to the front windows, Rosza had curtained off an area with a table and two chairs where she gave occasional manicures, pedicures, and facials to some of the executives' wives who thought it chic to indulge themselves with an authentic Hungarian beauty treatment.

Because there were only two bedrooms on the second floor and a third, dormitory-style bedroom in the attic, Mátyás and István were relegated to a tiny apartment above the garage which the family rented out to paying boarders whenever they could. It was a cramped space with one window, two beds, a nightstand, one chair, and a round table the boys used for everything from eating to folding laundry. It was stifling hot in the summer, cold and drafty in the winter. For storage, there was a small clothes closet but no dressers. For personal privacy, there was a lavatory with a toilet and sink, but no shower. The lighting was poor, the heating spotty. Mátyás and István loved it.

Though they would never risk hurting János and Rosza's feelings by saying so, they preferred being alone. Their pilgrimage had been a painful one. Once they had buried Vera, they had been sent to Vienna, where they had become faceless numbers in a process of expatriation. Flown to New Jersey, they had been shipped to Camp Kilmer, an old army base near New Brunswick, and quartered in spartan military barracks that did little to reassure the two boys that life in America was going to be the stuff dreams were made of. During the first few weeks, when the flow of refugees was at its peak, they were treated more like prisoners than patriots. They were preached to about freedom, interrogated about their escape, pressured about where they wanted to go, and even subtly threatened about what might happen to them if they didn't come up with the name of a relative willing to take them in. As they had throughout their odyssey, István and Mátyás had responded to this latest ordeal by clinging to each other, strengthening their bond until it was almost unbreakable.

By the time they arrived in Kentucky, they really didn't need anyone or anything except to feel safe. While it was true that János was sorely lacking in sophistication, he was not without sensitivity. When he had picked the boys up in Lexington, he had seen the fear and suspicion that clung to their eyes like the sand of sleep. During the first few weeks they were with him, he had seen them whisper to each other or glance sideways at remarks they didn't understand or suggestions they found difficult to accept or customs that appeared peculiar and, in their strangeness, threatening. János was familiar with the natural caution of the immigrant—he had experienced it himself. But their reactions went beyond the shyness of a foreigner. This was automatic mistrust, instant suspicion, a response János realized must have been conditioned by repeated exposure to danger. Though it stabbed his heart to think so, clearly his two young nephews had suffered more than their share of terror.

To assuage their fears he installed a sturdy new lock on their door, went to great lengths to point out how close they were to the main house in case of trouble, and assured them as best he could that there was very little crime in the mountains.

"No one has anything worth stealing," János had said.

Mátyás and István could understand that. The Budapest they had left behind had been economically depressed. Theft had been less of a social problem than suicide.

Once settled, they discovered another plus to living slightly removed from János and his brood—the privacy to allow memories and feelings to surface. For Mátyás and István, the past had become sacred, something only they and others who had lived it with them could discuss. It was true that János and Rosza had left Hungary during turbulent times, and certainly no immigrant ever had an easy passage from one life to another, but, the boys reasoned, the Vas family had left by choice, before the Germans had betrayed them and the Russians had "liberated" them. They had left with their family and their dreams intact, not with blood scattered along a path of escape or buried beneath the lawn of a city park.

From the beginning, Mátyás and István tried to conduct their lives the way they believed Margit and Béla would have wanted them to, but each day it became increasingly difficult to honor that commitment. Woodridge, like hundreds of small towns dotting the Appalachians, existed for the sole purpose of extracting coal from the belly of the earth. For most of the people who lived in those towns, education was not a priority. Schoolhouses were few and far between, making regular attendance an act of dedication.

Mátyás and István rose before dawn so they could walk the four miles into town. After school, István returned home to study and to do chores for Rosza. Mátyás went to the collieries, hiring on for odd jobs so he could pay room and board for himself and István. Neither brother wanted to be a burden. Neither wanted to feel beholden.

Knowing that language was the key to acceptance, they pored over their English books, struggling with new sounds, new words, and new rules of grammar. It was difficult. Many English words wouldn't translate into Hungarian, because Hungarian was a derivative language, one in which various ideas and nuances were expressed by complicated root-word modifications. English had prepositions, which in Hungarian were simply suffixes. In English, accent varied according to each word. In Hungarian the first syllable always received the greatest stress. Hungarian had diacritical marks to aid pronunciation. English did not. English had silent letters. Hungarian did not.

Alone in their room, the boys studied assiduously, testing each other, reading aloud from books and newspapers, laughing at the strange facial permutations required by the alien tongue. The one luxury they had— the radio—became not only their favorite form of entertainment, but their most effective teaching aid. They listened to it every night before they went to bed and in the morning while they dressed, mimicking the various announcers. Though they didn't understand much of what was said, at least their ears were becoming accustomed to the sound of it.

There were other adjustments as well. They had been city boys. This was pure country. At home, Mátyás and István had played soccer. No one in the hills of Kentucky played soccer. They played football and baseball. Mátyás and István had grown up listening to classical music and poetry. In Woodridge the sound was bluegrass, and the only poets of note were backwoods philosophers who glorified the land and those who worked it. Though they didn't see why, their names were a problem as well. No one could pronounce them. And everyone made fun of them, including the four Vas boys, all of whom had American names—Ernie, Pete, Fred, and Joe. Even János and Rosza were known as John and Rose outside the house. Though they were loath to give up something they considered part of their heritage, they wanted desperately to fit in. So, to the outside world, István and Mátyás gave way to Steven and Matthew.

There was another difference between life in Hungary and in the United States, but because this was more subtle, it took the boys longer to grasp. Communism, by its very nature, negated individual competition. Smothered beneath an avalanche of propaganda proclaiming the glories of a doctrine of equality, personal ambition was strongly discouraged. There were no prizes given to the ordinary man for outperforming his neighbor; no bonuses or premiums for anyone who outproduced his co-worker.

In the United States, Matthew and Steven came to learn, everything was a contest, a match, or a race. The American dream was to be number one at something, number one at anything. To be the biggest, the richest, the best, the strongest, was what mattered.

Mátyás, more cynical, was slower to accept change. After all, he told István, he wasn't certain this way was better. They weren't living any better. They were struggling to get along, straining to adjust, doing without. István countered that nothing could be worse than what they had known; here they had choices. Mátyás listened and agreed but, though he would never say this to István, even at fourteen, when they arrived he'd felt totally responsible for his brother. That sense of obligation, that need to do the right thing as a way of honoring his parents' memory had become such an obsession that it had completely colored the visions of his youth, changing them from optimistic pink to doubtful, conservative gray.

István, pragmatic by nature, approached the changes in their lives from a different angle: This is it; there's no going back; let's make the best of it. To do that, he decided he had to accelerate the pace of his education. Every day he could, he lingered after school to talk to Mrs. Mahoney, his English teacher. His appetite for knowledge about his new home was insatiable, and even though she gave him extra assignments and books she thought might help familiarize him with certain folkways and traditions, he always wanted more. He wanted to know about customs and conventions and what to do and what to expect and why this was different and if anything here was the same as it was there.

As the years went by, István and Nell Mahoney grew to be friends. He was such an eager, able student that she felt rewarded every day by his endless inquisitiveness and his unceasing desire to learn. For his part, she filled a few of the blanks left by his mother's death. Though Rosza was kind, she was not a woman István could confide in or rely upon for the wisest advice. Nell Mahoney was. She was a sympathetic ear and a gentle guide along the uncertain path of his childhood. He felt he could talk to her, not just about schoolwork, but about his dreams and his hopes for the future, his concerns about Mátyás, his uneasiness about his cousins.

"They criticize everything Matthew and I do," he said one day, hating himself for complaining about kin. "For years they were on Matthew's back because he kept up with school. *They* quit school when they were fourteen to work full-time in the mines. They didn't understand why he didn't do the same. Now that I'm fourteen, and old enough to get my papers, they want to know when I'm going to work."

"And when are you reporting for work?" Nell said, knowing it was a foregone conclusion that he would. Her father had. Her brothers had. She had been a teacher in the region for too long not to expect that every able-bodied young boy would follow the custom of beginning his apprenticeship at fourteen. From that point on, it was her job to try to keep the youngsters in school until they graduated. She had succeeded with Matthew. With most others, she failed. Rarely did she have the pleasure of sending her boys off to college. She was hoping Steven was one of that small group of precious alumni.

"I start tomorrow," István said in a voice laced with regret. "That means I won't be able to stay after school anymore."

Nell smiled and patted his arm reassuringly. "That doesn't mean we won't be friends anymore and that we won't be able to talk the way we always have," she said. "We'll just have to be more creative about finding the time."

He nodded and smiled and shuffled his feet and blushed. Nell was touched by his embarrassment, by the fact that even though he was looking more and more like a man, he was still child enough not even to think about trying to hide his feelings.

"What's going on with the Vas boys?" she asked, sensing that there was a deeper problem than a difference of opinion on the merits of education.

"They hate us."

"What makes you say that?"

"Most of the time Fred and Joe just ignore us, but Ernie and Pete never get off our backs. They resent us living with them. They keep saying if we weren't in the garage apartment they could have boarders who would pay decent rent money. They mumble under their breath whenever Rose puts a second piece of meat on one of our plates or John asks about our mom and life in Hungary. I don't know," István said, shrugging his shoulders. "It's like they feel we have an in with their parents that they don't have. You know, like we've got it easy or something." He laughed, but it wasn't his usual laugh. This one was coated with bitterness. "It's worse for Matthew. At work, they don't stop riding him. They make fun of his accent and tease him about his high school diploma and what little good it's doing him buried in the mines. They make nasty cracks about his . . . um . . . love life and things like that." Again, István blushed.

"And how is Matthew taking all this?"

"Like he always does."

Nell nodded. In the five years since she had met the Kardos boys, she had come to know them well. Matthew was more introverted than his brother, more deliberative, more intense. He was the silent one, the one who thought before he spoke, the one who tested before he trusted, the one who held on to his anger and only let it out when it suited his convenience, rather than the circumstance. Nell suspected that he filed his grievances away until the time was right to avenge them. Since she also knew him to be the self-declared head of his tiny family, she knew that if the Vas boys chose to taunt him, he would allow it until it went too far or got too outrageous. She also knew that if they ever did anything to Steven, no matter how slight, they would pay for their sins.

"Do they bother *you*?"

"It's the same stuff. You know, why bother with school? What good is it going to do? Who do I think I am? Do I think I'm special?

That I'm going to wind up different than they are? You know, that stuff."

Nell knew very well. She had taught every one of the Vas boys.

"Do you think you're different from them?"

István thought carefully before answering.

"Yes," he said, without shyness or apology. "Matthew and I started out in another place, in another world. It's not possible to see things the same way they do and so it's not possible to be the same as they are. They were born here, and though they know they have the right to do what they like, and change what they don't like, all they do is complain. They don't take advantage of what's available. They get stuck, I guess. Matthew and I learned the hard way that unless you're behind bars, no one is stuck unless he wants to be. You move. You change your life. You get things done. You just have to want to do it badly enough."

Nell Mahoney couldn't contain herself. With a burst of pride that pinked her pale skin and revitalized the blue of her eyes, she reached out and hugged Steven.

"Amen to that!" she said.

As he hugged her back and she felt the strength in his arms, she couldn't help but wonder where he would move and how his life would change and how much he would accomplish. When she released him from her embrace, she gazed deep into his eyes, trying to look through the proverbial window into his soul. Staring back at her was a young man with a strong sense of commitment and a true understanding of the difference between right and wrong. One day in the not-so-distant future, he would leave Woodridge, Kentucky. And, she told herself with supreme confidence, someday everyone who knew him would be glad to claim the acquaintance. Steven Kardos was going to make his mark. He was going to do great things.

"Because he wants to badly enough," she whispered to herself.

Ernie Vas was a twenty-seven-year-old man with no future. He wasn't stupid, yet everything he did, everything he said, projected an aura of ignorance. A schoolyard bully as a youth, Ernie claimed soldiers as his heroes. He dubbed his gang "The Hawks," nicknamed himself "The General," and tattooed a big American flag on one arm, the Marine Corps insignia on the other. He gorged himself on magazines and comic books and movies about wars and the armies that fought them.

Ernie's two greatest disapointments occurred when he enlisted in the Marines. First, there was no war for him to fight. Second, he had believed that as soon as he donned a uniform, his life would become one glorious achievement after the next; that here, among his kind, among people attuned to the peculiarities of the true military personality, great leadership potential would be recognized and acknowledged. He never rose above the rank of private.

When his tour of duty was finished, he returned to Woodridge. The simple fact was, he had no place else to go. He had acquired few skills and even fewer friends. Though he came back with a duffel full of stories about his exploits, without any wartime heroics to brag about he reverted to type.

A year after Ernie's honorable, if ignominious, discharge, Mátyás and István arrived, two young boys who had never worn a uniform, who were being hailed as heroes. The stories about how valiantly they fought during the uprising and their perilous flight from Hungary were being told at every dinner table within a fifty-mile radius, most especially at his own. Men at the mine talked about the bravery of the two Kardos boys with awe and reverence. Neighbors dropped by with old clothes and shoes, lingering so they could hear again about how a nine-year-old and a fourteen-year-old walked out of Hungary and found their way to Kentucky. Mothers mothered them. Young girls fussed over them. Everyone welcomed them. Except Ernie. Mátyás and István were the living symbols of his humiliation. They had succeeded where he had failed: They had warred and won.

In Ernie's mind, they became the enemy. Ernie, the soldier, mounted a war against them. He enlisted the aid of his brothers and the few remaining members of The Hawks. Headquarters became the back booth at O'Brian's bar, where nearly every night Ernie explained why he believed that tormenting the two illegals—as he loved to call them—was an act of patriotism.

"How do we know they're not some of Khrushchev's plants sent here to spy on us?" he'd say, playing on the fears of people confused by the growing strength of the civil rights movement and the increasing tension of the cold war. "How do we know they're not card-carrying commies sworn to destroy us?"

Other times, he'd suggest that perhaps it was cowardice that had propelled them to leave their country. "Who knows? If they and others like them had had the guts to stay and fight it out like men, maybe the Russkies would have backed off!"

At every opportunity Ernie and his disciples tormented Steven and Matthew.

The years went by and Ernie's gang dwindled. Some went into the army. Some were arrested. Some moved away. Others simply grew up and lost interest. Gradually, Ernie's influence lessened. By 1962 he had begun to feel as if he were sinking fast into a grave of oblivion. At twenty-seven, Ernie Vas was an angry young man entrapped by his own image, with nowhere to go.

On May 12, 1962, Ernie claimed his usual seat in the center of the long bar at O'Brian's. A scruffy, unpretentious place on the corner of Crown and Main, O'Brian's was more of a clubhouse than a bar. With rough-hewn wooden plank walls, a bare wooden floor that never looked clean, even after it was swept, and wide-bottomed, thickly cushioned bar stools sturdy enough to fit a big man's body, it was exactly the kind of place a workingman needed to unwind after a long, arduous day.

There were eight booths in O'Brian's—four to a side—and six round tables surrounded by barrel-backed chairs. The barstools numbered an even dozen. Ernie liked sitting in the middle so he could keep an eye on the mirror and see who was coming in the door behind him. Pete usually sat to Ernie's left, Jack Dolan to his right. The Kelly boys liked the far end of the bar. The men from Crown #2 liked the center tables; the men from Crown #3, the booths in the back. Most of the old-timers preferred the booths in the front, the ones with the best view of the TV.

That night, Walter Cronkite's big story on the national scene was a report about Secretary of Defense Robert S. McNamara. He had just returned from a place called Vietnam with assurance that U.S. military strength would not be increased above the present level.

"Bull!" Chad McDermott, a burly guy two places down from Ernie, shouted, sneering at the TV screen. "There's gonna be a war sure as my ass is settin' on this here stool. And all of us is gonna pay for it."

Ernie hoped Chad was right. If there was a war, Ernie would get a second chance at his dream. After all, he told himself, he was still young and strong, still prime soldier material. He would reenlist, only this time he would do it differently. He would control himself. He would hold back and not bash any heads until he had checked things out and knew for sure who stood with the niggers and who stood with him. He could make master sergeant in a month, maybe two.

When he returned his attention to the TV, world news was over and they were reporting on the local scene.

And from Woodridge, Kentucky, comes word that a local boy, Steven Kardos, has won first prize in a national citizenship essay contest, "What It Means to Be an American." What makes this story so heartwarming is that young Kardos isn't even a citizen yet. He and his older brother are immigrants, veterans of the tragic 1956 Hungarian uprising. They lost their parents and

their sister in that shameful episode and came here five years ago
to live with their uncle, John Vas, and his family.

The picture on the screen switched from the studio to Jackson High School auditorium, where that afternoon, flanked by Nell Mahoney, Mátyás, János, and Rosza, Caleb Crown—the man whose name was synonymous with all the wealth in the region—had presented Steven with his prize: a gold American flag pin and a check for five hundred dollars.

"Get a load of Caleb Crown, will ya," a guy from Crown #2 said, pointing to the elegant figure on the small screen. "You think if we all chipped in what we earn in a year we could afford a suit like that?"

"Put a lid on it!" Several men shushed the crowd, eager to hear the rest of the story.

The camera zoomed in on Steven's face as he read from his essay:

Americans hear the words "the home of the brave" and they
think about the battles their soldiers have fought in the name of
freedom in faraway places like Germany and Japan, Korea and
the Philippines. I hear "the home of the brave" and I think about
my parents, who died standing in a square begging for freedom.
I think of my sister, who died running from Soviet tanks, trying
desperately to hang on until she reached the Austrian border. I
think of the other two hundred thousand Hungarians who risked
their lives escaping rather than live under Russian domination.
And I think of those brave souls my brother Matthew and I left
behind, those living behind the Iron Curtain.

"The land of the free" is a phrase most Americans take for
granted. I don't. For me to be in the land of the free, I had to
walk across borders guarded by men with rifles and orders to
shoot anything that moved. I had to leave behind everything and
everyone I knew and come to a place where I knew no one and
had nothing. I had to learn a new language and make new
friends and learn new customs. And if I wanted to be a citizen,
I had to apply for it. It will take seven years for me to be an
American, but I don't care. When you've lived under Stalin and
watched Russian tanks roll through your streets, you know that
no matter how long it takes, freedom is worth the wait.

The picture shifted back to the studio. The announcer, stretching the moment as long as he could, slowly turned from the monitor he had been watching and faced the camera.

"What this country needs is more Americans like Steven Kardos."

There were about thirty men hanging out at O'Brian's that night.

Suddenly, spontaneously, all of them applauded, as if their favorite football team had just scored a touchdown. Ernie swigged the remains of his beer and demanded a scotch.

"Ain't he kin?" Liam O'Brian asked as he placed the shot glass on the bar in front of Ernie.

Ernie caught a glint of admiration in the bartender's eye and chugged the scotch as if it were water. As he sucked his lips over his teeth, his mouth puckering from the stinging taste of the liquor, he growled his displeasure.

"Yeah, but that don't mean we like the kid," Pete said, ever sensitive to the caprices of his older brother's temper.

"How can you not like him?" Dolan asked. "He's got brains and spunk."

"Don't forget his good looks." Every eye turned to the kitchen door, where Colleen O'Brian stood, her hands resting on her ample hips, her mouth spread in a smile. "So how come you're not as handsome as your cousin?" Colleen said. She didn't like Ernie and never had.

"Hey! Colleen's right. How come your face ain't as pretty as his?"

"Yeah! I thought all hunkies looked alike. What happened, Vas?"

"If you're real nice to him," a guy from the back shouted, a guy who had had more than one run-in with Ernie, "maybe the kid'll let you hang around with him and introduce you to some good-lookin' broads."

"Yeah! That way you won't have to go to the kennel to pick up the dogs we usually see you with."

The laughter was instantaneous and loud, ringing with the delight that always comes when a bully is bested. The mocking sound reverberated in Ernie's ears, crashing against his ego until he thought his head would explode. Gritting his teeth for control, he slid off the barstool.

"Go fuck yourselves!" he said to the mirthful assembly as he made an angry exit. He stood in the street, fighting to rein in his rage, but the laughter that had chased him from O'Brian's continued. Not only had they made an ass out of him, they were enjoying it.

And he had Steven Kardos to blame.

Steven had been coming down into the mines for more than a week and still couldn't get used to the interminable blackness. Matthew had told him it would be like this, that it would take awhile to adjust, but Steven was always in a rush. He always wanted to get to the next step as quickly as he could. Matthew had tried to tell his younger brother that that was all right as long as he took each step as it came, rather than taking precarious leaps, but lately Matthew worried that his words were falling on deaf ears.

Steven was beginning to formulate his own agenda, to look beyond the garage apartment and Woodridge, Kentucky. He wanted to do things on his own, to plan for himself, to care for himself. Not because he resented or disagreed with Matthew's guidance, but because he wanted to lessen Matthew's burden. The longer Matthew felt responsible for him, Steven reasoned, the less he would do for himself. Besides, he was growing impatient to participate in the larger world. That's why he had jumped when, the day of his award ceremony, Caleb Crown had offered him a summer job as a courier between surface and underground supervisors. Not only did it pay more than sorting coal at the preparation plant—it couldn't possibly have been as boring—but it afforded him an opportunity to feel part of the community.

He was a mule, ferrying everything from vital information about shuttle problems or gas buildups to a forgotten lunch bucket or telephone messages from home. The job was lowly, but Steven didn't care. He felt important. He wore a miner's cap, rode up and down in the cage, traveled back and forth between the main entries and the subentries on the mine railroad, and was beginning to find his way around the elaborate room-and-pillar system that defined the carbonized labyrinth.

One morning he was asked to relay a message to the supervisor of room D-27: *The replacement equipment requested is on its way. Proceed as usual until it arrives.* Steven left the office and rode down into the lowest part of Crown #1. It never ceased to amaze him how quickly the darkness fell upon him. Before, he had envisioned the mine as a physical form of night, a place that began in daylight and blackened gradually. Matthew and the others had warned him, they had tried to describe it for him, but none of the stories had prepared him for the actuality. Nothing was as black as the bottom of a mine. It was an endless midnight, with no dusk and no dawn, an intimidating, palpable denseness that even the brightest lights were helpless to pierce. From the instant the top of the cage entered the earth, Steven felt as if he were diving into a sea of opaque pitch and that if he wasn't very careful and alert, he would drown in its darkness.

"Where to, young man?"

"D-Twenty-seven." Steven wondered if he'd ever stop feeling grateful each time he exited the cage and felt firm ground beneath his feet.

"Hop on."

Steven climbed onto the leather bench of the single rail car they used as a quick shuttle, linking his arms around the waist of old Hiram Connelly, the shuttle engineer. Hiram was lame, having had his leg crushed five years before in a machine accident. But because he was reliable and willing to stay underground, Crown had kept him on to run the shuttle.

The small yellow car snaked its way through the narrow chamber excavated specifically for its use. Crown #1 was the largest of Crown's three mines, boasting four levels and acres of coal-rich seams. It was the only one vast enough to warrant a shuttle. In the other two, couriers relied on the cage and their feet for transportation. Knowing that D was the lowest level and 27 the room farthest from the exit, Steven used the time to review the safety precautions Matthew had drilled into him. While on the shuttle, he was supposed to keep his head down and his eyes forward to avoid errant pieces of coal or debris. He was to keep his hands tucked close to his sides to avoid bruising them against the walls. While in the various rooms where the coal was being mined, he was to stand clear of all machinery and to watch for any signs of roof or wall failure. Though the other constant hazard was the accumulation of gases like methane—a natural inhabitant of coal seams—and carbon monoxide, Matthew had told him not to worry: There were automatic methane detectors to measure how much of the harmful gas was in the air. The only way a problem could occur, Matthew explained, was if the ventilation system was faulty or if the air vents became blocked for any reason. Then, and only then, was an explosion possible.

"Here we are." Hiram stopped the trolley and waited for Steven to dismount. "I'll be back in a few," Hiram said as he waved and went on his way.

Steven took a second to get his bearings. It was supposed to be easy to find one's way in a room-and-pillar system, but just then he felt as if he were standing in the middle of a cartoonist's nightmare, a forest of gigantic black sequoias.

He knew that all tunnels intersected with one another and that the huge block in front of him was merely a pillar of coal left standing as a support for the overburden, but nonetheless he found the thickness of the pillars and the darkness of the tunnels menacing. Sucking in his nervousness, he started walking in the direction of the noise. Because he knew the internal setup of a mine, he knew that he was walking along a subentry, a tunnel built to intersect at right angles with one of the main entries, one of the original tunnels cut into the coal bed. His destination was one of the many rooms dug out of the seam at various points along each set of subentries. It was the rooms that were mined.

When he came to the entry to room 27, the clatter of the machines told him the men were down at the far end of the corridor. Keeping his head straight so that the light on the front of his hat could illuminate his way, Steven passed five thick pillars before coming upon the crew working the room.

"Anyone see Harry Wench?" Steven asked, wondering how anyone knew where anyone was down here.

Ahead of him, a cutting machine was slicing into the base of the coal face. The noise was deafening. As the teeth on the enormous saw chiseled away, Steven raised his hand to shield his eyes from flying refuse. As he did, he could hear Matthew's voice insisting that he wear goggles whenever he went down into the mine. He also heard his own voice protesting that he had enough trouble seeing in the dark as it was and besides, he was in and out, never in one place long enough to get into any trouble.

"Who you looking for, *Ishtvan?*"

Steven turned the moment he recognized Ernie's voice. He hated when his cousin mocked his own heritage by making fun of Steven's Hungarian name. But then, he disliked most things Ernie did.

"I need to deliver a message to Wench."

Nearby, several power shovels dug into the ceiling of the room. Suddenly, Steven found himself pressed up against the wall. Had Ernie knocked into him simply for the thrill of pushing him or had he tried to protect Steven from something? With Ernie, it was hard to be sure.

"Hey," Ernie said, "something's wrong with your light."

Steven tilted his head downward and held out his hand. There was no light on it except that which was reflected from Ernie's hat.

"Here," Ernie said, motioning for Steven to take off the hat, "give it to me. I know how to fix it."

Steven was so concerned about not having light to guide him back to where he would meet Hiram's tram, he didn't notice that the power shovels had stopped and that the cutting machine had retracted its saw. He never heard the rumbling. He took off his hat and handed it to Ernie.

"Watch out! It's coming down!"

All around him, men were shouting. Instinct lifted his eyes upward, toward the roof that was collapsing in front of him. Large chunks of coal rained down around him, battering his head and shoulders. Before he realized what was happening, something very sharp sliced his flesh. Something hard hit his eye and he began to scream in pain. The men closest to him rushed to his aid. One of them grabbed him, holding him against his chest until the storm of black hail subsided. Another man went for help. A third man went to find Matthew. Within minutes after the cave-in Steven was on Hiram's tram bound for the cage and the surface.

Matthew's face was white with fear as he stood waiting for his brother at the entrance to the mine.

"István! *Jézus Mária!* What happened?" Matthew leaned over Steven, pumping his hand, desperate for a response. "Talk to me, István. Tell me you're all right. Tell me what happened."

"He's fainted from the pain." It took Matthew a second to realize that the man speaking to him was a medic. Matthew stepped aside as two white-suited men lifted Steven onto a stretcher and put him in the ambulance. Before anyone could stop him, he scrambled in, alongside his brother.

Throughout the seventy-five-mile ride to Lexington, Matthew watched the medics work on Steven's face. Several times he thought he was going to be sick. The whites of both of Steven's eyes were red with blood, but his left eye was actually bleeding. His face was horribly scratched. One gash, perilously close to his left eye, was so deep, Matthew was certain he could see Steven's cheekbone.

"What's going to happen to him? He's not going to die, is he?" he knew that was the question of an hysteric, but for Matthew, that was the question he needed answered first.

"No," the young man tending Steven's wounds said. "He's not going to die."

"Then why are you taking him to Lexington? Why not Jackson?"

Waylen Cummings—that was the name on the tag pinned to his pocket—was a short man, small, with delicate fingers and skin that looked too smooth ever to sprout a beard. He was pale to begin with, but dressed in his spotless uniform, kneeling between Steven and Matthew, both of whom were drenched in soot, surrounded by the pristine interior of the ambulance, he looked too white, too frail to inspire confidence.

"We're going to Lexington because I'm concerned about his left eye."

As he spoke, his assistant handed him a small flashlight, which he shone into each of Steven's eyes, leaning over him so he could monitor even the most minute response.

"What about his left eye?" Matthew had dropped to the floor beside Cummings, afraid to sit even three feet away for fear that something terrible would happen and he would be unable to stop it.

"There's a cut on the cornea. Because he's unconscious, I can't tell how deep it is and where else he might have been cut."

"Are you talking about the optic nerve? Are you afraid the optic nerve was cut and he'll be blind?"

Cummings looked at the young man with the grimy face and the strange accent. Without knowing anything about their history, he knew that these two boys were tied to each other with strings so thick and so tight that if anything threatened the existence of one, it endangered the survival of the other. Following that assumption, Cummings knew he had two choices. He could tell Matthew the truth or he could leave that to the doctors in Lexington. As was his way, Cummings opted for the truth.

"It's a possibility," he said. "Coal is a hard substance, which makes it a strong weapon. It cuts deep. My hope is that the piece that cut his eye only grazed the surface."

"The lump that did that didn't just graze the surface." Matthew pointed to the butterfly bandage covering the gash on Steven's face. "Oh, God. What if . . ."

Matthew began to cry, soundless testimony to his pain, but he refused to wipe his eyes or to remove his gaze from his brother's battered face. As Waylen tried to comfort him, he sensed that the low, mournful sound coming from Matthew's throat rose from a place deep within his heart where he stored the memories of others for whom he had once cried.

He didn't pray much, but suddenly Waylen Cummings found himself praying that the young boy on the litter would come through this ordeal well and whole.

For more than four hours, Matthew sat in the lounge outside the operating room. Like a sooty statue, he remained stone-still, refusing to move from his chair, as if to do so would upset some cosmic balance. His hazel eyes, usually so alive with curiosity, appeared vacant and lifeless as they stared at the doors leading to where a team of specialists were working on Steven. Occasionally, a nurse came by to check on him. Each time it was the same.

"Any word on my brother?"

"Not yet. Can I offer you some coffee or a soda?"

"Thank you, no. Maybe when I hear about my brother. Maybe then."

The nurse would leave and Matthew would again retreat into his private hell of guilt and fear and anger. When he was not making bargains with God for Steven's well-being, Matthew tried to understand how this had happened. Steven was young and therefore naive and probably had been a bit careless, but he wasn't stupid. When the men had carried him out of the cage, Matthew had heard one of them say Steven hadn't been wearing his helmet. Why?

"Mr. Kardos. Your brother is out of surgery and in the recovery room."

Matthew's head snapped up as if it were on a spring.

"How is he?" he asked the surgeon, jumping to his feet, trying to anticipate the reply by searching the doctor's face for clues.

"He's going to be fine."

"Will he be blind?"

"No, but he came close. Your brother was very lucky, He must have been bombarded by huge chunks of coal."

"That's what I understand." *It's the why I still don't understand.* "Tell me what did happen."

"He suffered subconjunctival hemorrhages in both eyes." Matthew looked lost. The surgeon smiled. "Broken blood vessels. That's what's making his eyes look so red and godawful." Matthew nodded. "The cornea is scratched but that isn't too serious and will heal in a few days."

"But . . ." Matthew said, hurrying the doctor so he could hear the final bit of information.

"The lump that caused the gash on Steven's face did two things. First, it's left a permanent black scar on your brother's cheek. As you know, when coal is so deeply imbedded in the skin, it can't be completely removed."

Matthew felt his anger growing, billowing like a kite catching the wind. "What else?"

"The force of the blow caused a slight detachment of the retina. Since the retina is too delicate to be touched by surgical instruments and therefore can't be pressed back into place, we indented the choroid, pushing it up to meet the retina. If the surgery was successful—and we won't know that for several days—the retina will stay attached to the choroid."

"If not?"

"We'll have to try again."

Matthew nodded. *I have to be grateful he's alive. I have to concentrate on him getting well. Then I'll deal with how he got hurt.* "Can I see him? Can I stay with him?"

The doctor put his arm around Matthew and began to steer him down the hall. "Since Caleb Crown has insisted on paying for Steven's medical expenses, including a private room, I've asked the nurse to set up a bed so you can spend the night. Why don't I have someone find you some clean clothes? You can take a shower in the doctors' lounge and be ready when Steven comes down from the recovery room."

Matthew had a difficult time dealing with kindness from this stranger. "Thank you," he said, his voice strained from the struggle to control his surprise at Caleb Crown's generosity, his tears of relief about Steven's prognosis, and his suspicions that Steven's injuries were not as accidental as they seemed. "Thank you for everything."

•   •   •

Three days later, assured that Steven's surgery was successful, Matthew drove back to Woodridge with János. At the end of the week, he would return to take Steven home.

"So everything's okay, yes?" János had said once they were on the Interstate. He had cried when he first walked into Steven's room and looked at his face. Steven's eye was still heavily bandaged. The cut on his face also wore a thick dressing. Bruises blotched his face and neck as well as his upper body. "István will be fine. Yes?"

"That's what they say." Matthew stared straight ahead. He had no patience for small talk or detailed conversations about the state of Steven's health, but János was trying so hard to express love and concern, it was hard to deny him something so insignificant as a simple answer to a simple question.

János had called every day, as had Pete and Fred and Joe and the O'Brians and many men from the mine. Rosza had sent a package of strudel and cookies. Caleb Crown had come to the hospital to visit Steven and personally wish him well. The only person who had remained conspicuously silent was Ernie.

"Can't this heap go any faster?" Matthew didn't mean to snap at János, but he couldn't help himself.

János's car was a 1954 Chevy, which had died so many times it had surpassed the record of even the hardiest of cats. Each time it died, János had resurrected it, using whatever secondhand parts he could find—Oldsmobile fenders and Ford doors and Dodge bumpers. The car looked like a patchwork quilt on wheels. Matthew didn't mind the amused stares that greeted them as they passed the farms and stables where fancy thoroughbreds were pampered on famous Kentucky bluegrass. What he minded was the pace of the trip. The car never went over forty miles per hour. Matthew had things to do.

"I wish I could have done better for you," János said, breaking the uneasy silence that had settled between them.

Matthew turned and looked at his uncle. Even in profile, it was easy to see the lines of hardship etched on his face. His skin was wrinkled and pale from a lifetime without sun. His hairline had receded and he had begun to gray, but there were no elegant silver strands to add a touch of distinction. Instead, the color befit his life, a dull cast of ashes and cinders. His body was bent and his hands were gnarled from too many years doing young man's work, but in an odd way he wore the emblems of his poverty with pride, and for that, Matthew held him in high regard.

"I did the best I could."

"I know you did, Uncle János," Matthew said, a wave of sympathy washing over him, dampening the flames of his anger, if only for a few moments. "István and I will always be grateful to you and Aunt Rosza for taking us in."

"*Igen.* Yes," he said, lapsing into Hungarian, as he often did when he spoke to Matthew. "But my Margit and her Béla were scientists. They were schooled. They must have had wonderful dreams for you and István. I would have liked to have been able to fulfill them, for her and for you. But," he said with a resigned shrug of his shoulders, "I couldn't fulfill my own."

"It's not your fault, Uncle János. They died a long time ago and whatever dreams they had for themselves or for us died with them. It's not your fault. None of it is your fault."

He reached over and squeezed János's shoulder. The old man took his hand off the steering wheel to press Matthew's hand in response. It was the most affection they had shared in five years.

When they drove into Woodridge, Matthew asked János to drop him off at Crown #1. Without offering any explanation and despite János's protestations that he should rest and return to work the next day, Matthew grabbed a hat and goggles and took the first cage down.

He found Ernie in D-19. Without any preamble or any warning, he spun Ernie around and punched him in the face. When the smaller man fell, Matthew picked him up, punched him in the stomach, and slammed him up against a wall. Then he grabbed him by the throat.

"You set him up, you filthy pig. You're responsible for what happened to my brother."

"I don't know what you're talking about," Ernie said, jerking his neck from side to side, trying to work free of Matthew's grasp. "Get your fucking hands off me."

The machines stopped. A crowd gathered in the narrow corridor. As two dozen pairs of eyes stared at Ernie Vas, the lights from their hats attacked him with a strong white beam of accusation.

"I knew guys like you in Hungary," Matthew said, his face inches from Ernie's, his hand twisting the fabric of Ernie's shirt like a tourniquet. "They were thugs, bullies just like you, but they wore brown uniforms and called themselves the AVO. They were the scum of the earth, the lowest form of humanity. They preyed upon others just to make themselves feel powerful, to make themselves feel strong and worthwhile. But you know what? They were yellow-bellied, weak-assed pieces of shit! Just like you."

Matthew's knee shot into Ernie's groin. Vas doubled over, but Matthew yanked him up by the shirt.

"Let me go, you fucking asshole! You're out of your mind!"

"Am I?" Matthew said, his eyes wild with rage. "Then tell me why you pushed Steven against the wall just seconds before the cave-in."

Ernie turned his face away with a grunt of defiance. Matthew pulled him forward and then slammed him back against the wall.

"Stuff was beginning to fall," Ernie said quickly. "I didn't want the kid to get hurt."

"Yeah, right. You shoved him so you could disconnect his hat from the power pack. So you could con him into thinking something was wrong with his light. So you could make sure his hat was off and his face was unprotected when the roof collapsed. And when it did, you slimy bastard, you disappeared, leaving Steven alone and defenseless."

The other miners began to mumble among themselves. Many had suspected foul play in Steven's accident. Some had suspected Ernie. As each man recognized the truth, they pressed together and then forward in a threatening mass. For the first time in the memory of many, fear glistened in Ernie's eyes.

"You're lucky the doctors in Lexington know what they're doing. If Steven had been blinded, Vas, I would have come after you."

"You and what army?"

While everyone expected Matthew to react to Ernie's taunt with a punch, he simply let go of Ernie's shirt. When he spoke, his voice was calm and quiet, but there was an eerie edge to his tone that chilled the spines of his audience.

"No army. Just me." His eyes burned into Ernie's face. "I'm going to let you go this time," he said.

Ernie laughed and pushed Matthew out of his way. "I always knew you were a coward, you pink-assed commie. See," he said to the others there, believing the advantage had shifted to his side, "I always said he was a chicken. I always said—"

"But," Matthew said, his teeth gritted, his eyes locked on his enemy, "if you ever hurt my brother again, I swear on the graves of my mother and father and sister, I'll kill you."

His voice was muted, but it vibrated with a hatred that was felt by every single man there—including Ernie Vas.

9

Budapest, 1962

*K*atalin's hands tiptoed over the piano keys with great deliberation. Because it was late and she didn't want to disturb the neighbors, she had blanketed the strings, muting the piano as she often did when she wanted to work on fingering and memorization. For two hours she had been going over the same piece, studying each key as she depressed it, watching as one ivory rectangle receded and then reappeared, sinking and rising in melodic sequence.

During her afternoon practice session she had been thoroughly dissatisfied with the way she had played Schumann's *Fantasia*. To her, the second movement had lacked power; the third movement had lacked grace. Andras had suggested that perhaps it was because the piece had not yet affixed itself to the walls of her mind. To help, he had her practice the troublesome movements with alternating dynamics—playing the left hand forte while the right hand played pianissimo, then reversing it so that the right hand played more loudly than the left. When she had finished, she did feel she had conquered the passages in her right hand, but the left still needed work.

Now, as she followed the sheet music, checking to be certain that each key she touched corresponded exactly to the written score, her inner ear pressed against the silence, straining to listen to the passion of Robert Schumann. As with most great musical talents, Katalin's ability to imagine sound was exceptional. Over the years, Andras had encouraged Katalin to explore the frontiers of her sensory capacities; to elevate her tonal imagery to such a degree that the power to build musical structures in her mind would be strong enough to enable her to hear and feel all the effects of a piece before she had ever played a note.

Katalin repeated the Schumann, this time without the sheet music. When at last she had assured herself that she could play it through without any errors, she smiled. In the morning when she removed the blanket and restored sound to her piano, she was certain she would be able to give the *Fantasia* all the depth of feeling it deserved.

"Finished?" Mária spoke softly, loath to intrude. An artist herself, Mária was particularly sensitive to those first few moments after a performance when the afterglow was thick and one's insight into one's effort was keen enough to allow a fair analysis.

"For tonight," Katalin said, shooing the last notes of the composition from her mind. "I think I've mastered it, but I won't know for sure until tomorrow."

Mária walked over to Katalin and began to massage her daughter's shoulders.

"Don't overdo it," Mária said, kneading the thirteen-year-old's flesh until she felt some of the stiffness subside.

Katalin laughed. "Tell that to Andras and Papa! To them, I can never do enough."

Mária shook her head. What Katalin said was true. Andras and Zoltán had taken control of the child's life. Her talent had become their personal property, to be developed the way they wanted. Though both saw her as a star of the international concert stage, each had a slightly different vision of the means needed to achieve that end. Andras believed in practice. Zoltán believed in performing.

Andras was a teacher. He had worked with Katalin since she was three years old, showing her how to sit, how to hold her hands, how to hold her wrists and cup her fingers. He taught her flexibility through scales and exercises; phrasing and dynamics through illustrative pieces. He believed that constant repetition was required to perfect fundamentals and that only when the basics had become second nature could talent fully express itself; that in music, one had to control the body in order to grant freedom to the soul.

Zoltán agreed, to a point. Having been a student of Madame Vásáry's, he never would have denied the importance of discipline and the relevance of technique—virtuosity was nothing if not technique—but Zoltán had been a performer and it was on that point that he and Andras differed. Though Andras trained his students for recitals and competitions, he never pushed them to do too much too fast. He felt that perfection required time.

Zoltán believed that talent demanded exposure, the more the better. His own experience had convinced him that the most thrilling musical moments resulted from a mystical union of three: the composer, the performer, and the listener. He remembered his concerts. Each time he had stood before a gathering of gifted listeners, he had been inspired to move beyond the conscious level where his brain told his fingers what to do, into that subconscious level where the raw energy of talent prevailed. To him, the audience was essential to provide the wings on which the composer and the musician could fly. Without the stage and those who sat beyond, even the greatest talent lacked dimension.

"They don't mean to push," Mária said, believing that was true for Andras, knowing it wasn't true for Zoltán. "They both love you and want the best for you."

"I know," Katalin said, "and most times I don't mind."

"But . . . ?" Mária continued, waiting for Katalin to finish her sentence.

"But when I fall behind in school and I can't seem to catch up and . . ."

". . . when it seems as if other girls your age are having more fun?"

Katalin blushed and shrugged her shoulders. "Yes, that too."

Mária sat next to Katalin on the piano bench. She took her daughter's hands in hers and held them in her lap. "I know you're tired of hearing this, Katalin, but you're special. You have something very rare and very beautiful and although I know that sometimes you feel that your talent is more curse than blessing, it's a gift from God."

Katalin lowered her head, looking at the way her fingers were knitted with those of her mother.

"You have a gift," she said quietly. "You're very talented. When you were my age didn't you ever wish you were normal?"

Mária laughed.

"No, but that's probably because I didn't know what normal was. The nuns did and they thought I was quite mad. I talked to myself all the time, changing voices, making faces, pretending to have a room filled with companions when I was supposed to be silently communicating with God. I read novels and plays when I was supposed to be studying the Bible. I walked through the halls balancing books on my head and recited poetry while scrubbing the floors." Mária laughed again. "When I ran away, I think they were delighted."

An image of a group of nuns shaking their heads and expelling sighs of relief flashed before Katalin's eyes and she giggled.

"But," Mária continued, growing more serious, "don't misinterpret what I said. I didn't run *away* from acting. I ran *to* it."

"Are you happy that you did?"

"Very. Aside from you and your father, it's the most important thing in my life, *dragam*. Just as I know music is the most important thing in yours."

"Yes, yes," Katalin conceded, raising her arms in a gesture of surrender. "But for the next hour I'm going to hate it. I'm going to go into my room and grumble about how tired I am and how much I hate Schumann. I'm going to study my Russian and pretend that Ludwig van Beethoven was a butcher and that Cristofori never invented the piano."

"And in the morning?"

Katalin looked at her mother and responded with a sheepish smile. "I'll love it again."

"You won't believe what I found out!" Judit's dark brown curls bobbled as she walked, several locks dangling down her forehead. As she talked, her hand brushed them back, out of the way. "I was in the library doing my homework and I came upon a book that describes Budapest in the last century."

Katalin grabbed Judit's arm and pulled her back before she walked in the path of an oncoming trolley. When Judit was lost in a story she became so single-minded it was as if her peripheral vision narrowed and she couldn't see beyond her words.

"It must have been a book the Russians forgot to throw out because it said some wild things, things I don't think they want us to know."

"Like what?"

Judit stopped short, faced Katalin, and whispered, "Like I'm the great-granddaughter of a baron."

"And I'm a descendant of Maria Theresa," Katalin said, greeting this news as simply another of Judit's daily dramas.

"It's true," Judit said, her voice still a whisper but growing more insistent. "After I saw this in the book, I went into Mama's trunk. You know, the one where she keeps all those old pictures and letters and things?" Katalin nodded. She and Judit had spent many an afternoon rummaging around in that trunk, playing with old clothes and giggling at old photographs. "I found a paper. It was signed by Franz Josef! Can you imagine? Signed by the emperor!" Judit's dark eyes widened into saucers. "It said that from the fourteenth day of September in the year

1868, Géza Strasser was a member of the court. Then it said some other things I couldn't understand, and then it had a big scrawly signature: Baron Géza Strasser." Judit's enthusiasm was building. "I couldn't believe it, so I went back to that book I found in the library. In 1867 a law was passed that emancipated the Jews in Hungary. After that, it said, Franz Josef granted—listen to this—*noble predicate* to one hundred and twenty Jewish families. I don't know what the other titles were, but there were twenty-eight Jewish barons in Hungary. Twenty-eight! And my great-grandfather was one of them. Isn't that something?"

Katalin was impressed, but not only with Judit's news. As always, she was a bit envious of Judit's ease with scholarship. Katalin was not a good student. It wasn't that she didn't care or that she didn't put forth the effort. She spent hours at her schoolwork, but somehow, no matter how hard she tried, she simply didn't achieve the same results. Judit always explained it away with simple logic: "You can't have everything. You're a prodigy—which means you're far more talented than I am. I'm entitled to be a little smarter than you are." Nonetheless, whenever Judit displayed her intelligence, Katalin felt lacking.

"It is exciting," Katalin conceded, "but so what? What does it mean? Do you have a castle waiting for you somewhere? Do I have to call you your ladyship?"

Judit came to a complete halt, turned, stared at Katalin in amazement, and then let loose with a full belly laugh.

"I never thought about any of that," she said, between guffaws. "That would be fun. Would you like a cup of tea, your ladyship? Would you like me to draw you a bath?" she mimicked, bowing low at the waist and giving her best imitation of a humble servant.

Katalin couldn't help being drawn into Judit's fantasy. With a deep curtsy, she asked, "Please, Baroness, let me carry your books."

Judit tossed Katalin her books and stepped several paces in front of her friend.

"Come along," Judit called over her shoulder, wagging her finger at Katalin.

"Yes, Your Excellency," Katalin said.

With great ceremony the two girls paraded through the streets, Judit in front, her head held regally high, Katalin shuffling respectfully behind, both of them tittering all the way to Katalin's door.

"Maybe you're a countess," Judit said as Katalin returned her books.

"I don't think so."

"How do you know? My book said that one family in ten had a title."

"Really?" For a moment, Katalin was intrigued. But only for a moment. "No. It couldn't be. Mama and Papa never said anything about it."

"Mine didn't either, but that shouldn't surprise you. Since when do your parents tell you everything? Besides, even if they wanted to, they wouldn't. They can't. No one talks about things like that. No one talks about anything that happened before the Russians moved in. It's forbidden!" Judit said with obvious disdain.

Though Katalin had heard that same tone in Judit's voice many times before, it made her extremely nervous. Judit displayed all the symptoms of an incubating rebelliousness. She was quick to anger about conditions in Hungary—too quick, Katalin feared. One day Katalin was certain that Judit would speak without thinking and wind up in the interrogation room of the Fő Street prison.

"And we shouldn't be talking either." Force of habit had lowered Katalin's voice.

"You're right," Judit said, accommodating her friend's discomfort by changing the subject. "Where does your mother keep all her private things?"

"In that special hiding place behind my closet. Why?"

Judit's mouth broke into an impish grin. "If I were you, I'd spend my afternoon in that closet, Countess."

Judit laughed as she turned and started for home. Katalin waved her hand and clucked her tongue, as if dismissing the notion, but the instant she entered the apartment, she ran to her room. On hands and knees she crawled beneath her clothes, pushed open a secret panel, and crawled into a small cramped space stacked with boxes. By reaching up and groping around in the darkness, she found the string that controlled the light.

Katalin recognized most of the cartons immediately. They held personal props and costumes from Mária's plays. Two or three were small enough to hold papers, and so she opened those first. They seemed to contain nothing more than pictures and programs from Mária's plays and Zoltán's concerts. She went to slide the last box toward her, but it didn't move as easily as the others. It was heavy and had been taped shut. No, she decided, she wouldn't pry, even if the box did hold the papers that declared her a countess. She was about to put it aside when she noticed that the tape had begun to pull away from the cardboard. With the eager eyes of an Alice looking into Wonderland, Katalin peeked inside the box. It was filled with records. They were dusty and old and some of them had lost their labels, but she knew instantly what they were. They were her father's recordings. Gently she removed several from their container and wrapped them in a blanket she had pulled from a shelf in her closet.

Putting everything back the way it was, she took her package, closed the secret door, and headed for the practice room in the basement of Judit's building, where she knew she could be alone.

Andras was teaching a class at the Academy. Judit was doing her homework. Katalin was scheduled to use the room to practice for an upcoming concert, and she would, but first she set up the phonograph. Without even looking at the label she put the first record on the turntable. Her fingers shook as she placed the needle into the first groove. The record scratched. She held her breath. She knew she had heard these records when she was a baby, but from the day Zoltán returned, they had never been played again. Try as she might, Katalin couldn't remember how they sounded. What if she was disappointed? What if he wasn't as brilliant as everyone claimed he was?

Suddenly, the honeyed tones of a violin wafted into the air, enveloping her in a sweet veil of sound. It was the Bach "Chaconne." A shiver ran down Katalin's spine as she listened to the way the bow danced over the strings during the flightier passages, the way the more melodic phrases oozed from deep within the wood. Without being conscious of what she was doing, Katalin took her place at the piano and began to play the accompanist's part. Her eyes closed and for a brief, special moment she imagined Zoltán playing beside her. She could feel the power of his talent infusing her soul, inspiring her to play faster and better. Her fingers complied, flying over the keyboard, responding to the glory of the music and the genius creating it.

The record ended. She played the next one, and again she found herself accompanying him. She played with total commitment, throwing herself into the music as if it were the performance of her life. Perhaps it was. Certainly it was the only way she and Zoltán would ever perform a duet; the only way she and her father could ever share the blessing of their mutual gifts. By the time she had played all the records she had taken from the box in the closet, it was well after dark. Katalin knew she was expected home, but she couldn't leave. She felt compelled to stay with the ghost of her father's talent, to sit with it and mourn for it and show it the respect it deserved. And as she sat, surrounded by the specter of Zoltán's past, she wept, first for his loss, but mostly for hers.

"I want to go with you and Katalin to Moscow," Zoltán said.

"That would be wonderful," Andras said, "but it's not up to me. It's up to the minister of culture. You know that."

Zoltán's lips thinned into a determined line. "I've been thinking about this, Andras. This is Katalin's first major concert outside of Hungary. I want to be there." *As my father was there for me.*

"I know how much this means to you, and God knows I would love it if you could go, but you need approval, Zoltán. Just as I needed approval."

Zoltán nodded. He knew all about needing approval. Two years before, Mária had gone through a security check before she had been allowed to perform in Warsaw. She had gotten clearance, but only after a team of pompous bureaucrats had put her through several humiliating interviews.

As Zoltán climbed the broad stone steps to the third floor of the Ministry he fought to control the anger that flushed him whenever he found it necessary to deal with the government. He hated the men who held power in Hungary. To him, they—the Council of Ministers, the fifteen or so men who headed the various government departments, and their cohorts on the President's Council—were sellouts. They had surrendered a thousand years of history without a second glance. In exchange for better housing and a new car every five years instead of every ten, they carried out all Soviet demands, even if it meant betraying their own people.

A painfully thin young man in a starched brown uniform asked Zoltán to state his business. He did and was ushered to a wooden bench in the lobby where he was told to sit. For two hours he waited, listening to the jangle of the telephone and the annoying click of the guard's heels as he paced up and down the long hall. Who and what was he guarding? Zoltán wondered in a swelling rage. No one had gone in or out of the minister's office. No one had even come up the stairs and stopped on this floor. This was simply a tactic designed to humble him. By the time the soldier called his name, Zoltán was tempted to tell the somber-faced young man to cancel his appointment, he had changed his mind, but going to Moscow with Katalin was too important to him. With deliberate slowness he followed the young man into the presence of the minister of culture.

The room was enormous, with fifteen-foot ceilings and oversized windows. Green velvet drapes, which had begun to show their age, hung limply from brass rods bolted to the walls above the windows. A large couch and several chairs encircled a round marble-topped table horribly stained from too many spilled coffees and too many unattended cigars. Dark wood paneling gave the space an elegant air, but instead of the grand paintings the decor demanded, there were government-issue photographs of Nikita Khrushchev and János Kádár, the Hungarian Premier.

Though Andras had told him dozens of stories about the minister of culture, Zoltán had never met Tomás Kocsis before. At the sight of him Zoltán understood that this was no man of culture but a thug, a porky, blubbery bully stuffed into a fancy leather chair and parked behind a desk. Zoltán would have wagered whatever little he owned that Tomás Kocsis didn't know the difference between Franz Liszt and a shopping list.

"And what can I do for you," Kocsis asked, his thick lips spread in a false, patronizing smile.

Zoltán had to force himself not to stare at the minister's jacket. The button that held the fabric across the center of Kocsis' fleshy middle was strained almost to the breaking point.

"My daughter, Gáspár Katalin, is a pianist and is scheduled to perform with the Moscow Symphony Orchestra next month. I'd like permission to accompany her."

Kocsis' aide placed a file folder on the minister's desk and withdrew. Kocsis opened it and made a show of studying the various papers very carefully. Zoltán was certain Kocsis had been thoroughly briefed before Zoltán even entered his office.

"You know, Comrade Gáspár, travel outside of Hungary is restricted."

"Yes, I do, Minister Kocsis, but this is a special circumstance." Zoltán bowed his head and clasped his hands together, adapting as humble a pose as he could muster. "I thought that perhaps this once I might be granted dispensation so I could be with my child."

"Strasser Andras will be with your child. Not only is he her tutor, but it is my understanding that he is a close family friend."

"That is true."

"Am I to believe that you question your daughter's safety while in the custody of Professor Strasser? Is that why you want to go? To protect your daughter's innocence? Do you think the professor has perhaps too personal an interest in Gáspár Katalin?"

"Absolutely not!" Zoltán shot back, forgetting his place for a moment.

Kocsis leaned back in his chair and folded his hands across his chest. A supercilious grin insinuated itself on his mouth, angering Zoltán and making him regret his outburst. The last thing he had wanted was to allow Kocsis to think he could get the better of him. Judging from the look in his eyes, that was precisely what Kocsis thought.

"Strasser Andras is beyond reproach," Zoltán said, this time more calmly. "I have no fears for my daughter's well-being while in his care."

"Then why do you feel the need to go along?"

"Perhaps I didn't phrase it correctly. It's not a need, Comrade. It's a wish. This is Katalin's first performance with the Moscow Symphony.

My paternal pride and my sense of patriotism would like to be in the audience when she brings honor to Hungary."

Zoltán tried to appear obsequious, but his act fell short. Kocsis's fat lips withdrew their smile and curled into a jeer.

"According to these files, Gáspár, you're an extremely questionable citizen. You're considered too untrustworthy for permission to leave this country."

"Untrustworthy!" he said. "Comrade, I'm shocked by those accusations. I'm a hard worker. I've never caused any trouble. Why would I be considered untrustworthy?" Zoltán had already guessed that he was not going to be given clearance, but he had no choice except to play out this farce to its unsatisfactory conclusion.

"For one, you have traitorous relatives."

He had known that Kocsis was going to have to invent reasons why Zoltán wasn't going to be granted an exit visa, but this was unexpected. Inside, he went on alert.

"There must be some mistake. How can I have traitorous relatives when everyone in my family is dead?"

Kocsis' face reddened. He flung his neck and shoulders forward, resting his arms on his desk. His button popped, angering him even more. "Don't toy with me, Gáspár!" he roared. "We know you've been receiving letters from Pal Zsuzsanna for years. She and her husband, Mihai, are wanted for treason."

"I don't mean to disagree, but I can assure you I have received no letters from my sister." In fact, since he had never received any word from Zsuzsanna, he and Mária had feared that Zsuzsanna, Mihai, and the Kardos children had perished on their exodus into Austria.

"Are you trying to tell me there are two women named Pal Zsuzsanna living in New York City?"

"I didn't know," Zoltan said humbly, sincerely.

"And I suppose you didn't know that you have a brother in a Soviet labor camp?"

Again, Zoltán shook his head.

"I had heard he had been sent to one, but several years ago I had word that he had died."

That seemed to amuse Kocsis. He smiled and nodded, as if Zoltán had reminded him of some private joke.

"Well, he's as good as dead," the minister of culture said, sucking a lingering piece of lunch from his teeth. "He's serving a life sentence in Siberia for crimes against the state. If he's lucky, his sentence won't last too much longer."

Zoltán tried to keep his face a noncommittal void.

"With all due respect, Comrade Kocsis," he said, deciding to return to the reason for his visit, "I think it's clear that I've had no contact with these people in years. Is there no way I can persuade you to allow me to attend Katalin's concert?"

"Have you forgotten that you have a prison record of your own?"

Zoltán's fingers curled into fists. "No, sir," he said. "I haven't forgotten."

"I have a report here from Colonel Kassak." Zoltán's insides jolted from the sound of that name. "Do you remember him?"

"Kassak?" *I'll never forget him.* "No. I don't think I've ever had the pleasure."

"He was the commanding officer during your stay at Recsk and he remembers you quite clearly."

"Really?"

"Yes, really." Kocsis was growing angry at the fact that Zoltán was making no attempt to stifle the sarcasm in his voice. "He found you uncooperative."

"I can't imagine why he'd say such a thing," Zoltán said, knowing his cavalier attitude was infuriating Kocsis, but incapable now of controlling himself.

"In addition," Kocsis said, ignoring Zoltán, rattling a few papers around as if seeking confirmation for his accusation, "he felt you were a confirmed dissenter. Because of that, he has recommended that you be labeled a permanent security risk—which means you can never get an exit visa, no matter how special the circumstances. Do you understand?"

"Perfectly," Zoltán said.

As he left the room, he could feel the eyes of Kocsis following him. Nonetheless, he walked with his head high and his back straight, denying the minister the opportunity to convince himself of his triumph and Zoltán's defeat. Kocsis may have refused him the permission he had requested, but he had given him several things in return: the news that Zsuzsanna and Mihai, at least, had made it to the United States. The news that his brother Miklós, though still a prisoner, was alive. And he had given him one more reason to hate Ferenc Kassak.

Ilona Strasser had always known that medicine was her destiny. Her father had been a doctor, as had his father before him. For as long as she could remember, the Roth family's aptitude for healing had been considered a blessing, a sacred trust between themselves and God. When she was a little girl the discussions were never about whether she should enter medical school, but rather which specialty would best benefit from her unique skills.

Though she had adroit fingers and at first had appeared to be a perfect candidate for surgery, it became clear early on in her education that Ilona was a born diagnostician. Her mind was so facile and so retentive that she was able to piece together tiny bits of information and process them in such a way as to define a medical problem quickly and accurately. While other students frequently missed obscure symptoms, Ilona caught even the slightest sign of a disease. With her extraordinary compassion and her predisposition for dealing with the whole problem rather than a single side of a situation, the choice of internal medicine was clear.

For the past several years Ilona had been on staff at two hospitals, Pest Medical Center and the nearby Shalom Hospital. This day, Ilona finished her tour of the children's ward at Shalom and returned to her office an unhappy woman. One of the children, a six-year-old girl, had had a leg amputated due to bone cancer. For weeks Ilona had been trying to locate a prosthesis, but so far had been unable to find one. None of the medical facilities in the Eastern Bloc had such a small prosthesis available. The only ones they stocked, or could produce in any reasonable amount of time, were for adults, and even they were rather primitive. Having gone through her normal channels, Ilona knew she had no choice but to resort to the underground.

Closing her door, she seated herself at her desk, dialed a phone number in Paris, and waited. It took a while for the operator to go through the various checks that were required on long-distance calls. Finally she heard the familiar voice on the other end.

"*Allo.*"

"Dr. Strasser here," Ilona replied, speaking in French. If she heard a click on the line, she would switch to Yiddish. Most Hungarians and most Russians didn't understand either language. If Ilona or her contact thought there was someone listening in who did, they would resort to a prearranged code. "I need a prosthesis. Left leg. Six-year-old girl."

"Can you send me a cast of the right leg so I have the proper dimensions?"

"In the next package."

"I'll need at least a month."

"We take what we can get."

Ilona hung up the phone and sighed. It never ceased to annoy her that she had been placed in a position where she had to be so secretive. While she accepted the fact that Hungary was an occupied nation, she refused to accept isolation and retarded progress as unalterable truths. Over the years, she had tried to be a decent citizen. She tried to abide

by the letter of the law—no matter how oppressive or ridiculous she
thought the laws were—but there was no consistency. The rules kept
changing, adapting to the wishes of whichever despot was in charge at
the moment. Still, most of the time Ilona went about her business without complaint. She never challenged her superiors or did anything to
give them cause to be suspicious of her. She wouldn't, because she
wouldn't allow anything to interfere with what she regarded as her life's
mission. She had survived the Holocaust, she had survived Stalin, and
she had survived the uprising. To her mind, she had been spared for a
specific purpose: to save the lives of others. And that was what she
intended to do. In any way she could.

The year before, a dilemma and a solution had presented themselves
at the same bedside. One of her patients, an elderly Jewish man named
Martin Kornfeld, had been admitted to Shalom with a coronary. After
assessing the damage, she realized that without a pacemaker, his prognosis
was poor. Since she already knew there were no pacemakers in Hungary,
she quickly applied to the Soviet Union for one. As she expected, her
request was conveniently lost. She tried appealing to a hospital in West
Germany, but was told by her superiors that those avenues were closed.
She was without a pacemaker. Martin was without hope.

She had gone to his room to talk to him about his release and how
to care for himself at home, when he introduced her to a visitor, a
pleasant-looking middle-aged man whom Ilona judged to be an American
by the fine cut of his clothes and the quick, unguarded smile that illuminated his face.

"Ilona, I want you to meet my friend Phil King." Ilona shook the
man's hand, curious about who he was and what he was doing visiting
Kornfeld. "Dr. Strasser is doing everything she can to save me, but she's
here today to tell me she's run out of tricks. Isn't that right, Ilona?"

He looked at her, smiled, and patted her hand. That was what she
hated the most, the fact that men like Martin Kornfeld accepted the
notion that she couldn't save them. She could, if only she had the right
equipment and the proper medicine.

"You need a pacemaker, Martin. I can't get you one right away,
but I promise I'll keep trying."

"Where have you looked?"

Ilona took King's question as a challenge.

"Everywhere I could." Her words were crisp, defensive.

"How about the United States or London?"

"I have a problem importing medical supplies from the West."

King nodded. "Right. I'm sorry. I should have realized."

"We do the best we can," Ilona said, anger flashing in her eyes.
"Our resources are limited."

"Maybe I could help."

"In what way?" Ilona asked, cautious, but optimistic nevertheless.

"I know where I can get a pacemaker."

"So do I," Ilona said, her optimism dashed, her frustration mounting. "Locating a pacemaker is easy. Getting it through to me is the hard part."

"I can do that too."

"How?" Ilona was not only suspicious but loath to discuss something as delicate as this in front of a patient.

"Through a private network that's been in place since World War Two. It was started to help resettle the Jews after the Holocaust. Now, we ship food and clothing and money and whatever else is needed behind the Iron Curtain. We help any way we can."

"Not all my patients are Jewish."

King smiled. "We help any way we can," he repeated.

They arranged to meet that afternoon. King spelled out the various ways Ilona could avail herself of the network's services. He also explained that while some officials conveniently looked aside when packages from his organization were shipped in, others confiscated the goods to sell on the black market, arrested whoever was supposed to receive the package on some other trumped-up charge, and often extracted painful confessions. Since it was hard to know who was willing to cooperate and for how long, most of King's shipments were covert.

If she needed, he would ship her drugs, supplies, surgical instruments—whatever. But, he warned, she had to understand that everything he sent could be considered contraband. If caught, she would be the one her government would punish, not he. Ilona understood all too well, which was why she chose not to tell Andras about Phil King or his network or what she intended to do. She promised King she wouldn't take unnecessary risks and would call only when she truly had run out of alternatives. In the past year she had called five times. Each time, a life had been saved.

After completing this call to Paris, she decided to return to the children's ward and make the cast of the girl's right leg. As she left her office and went to lock her door, she was certain she heard a noise. She looked up. A shadow turned the corner. Footsteps ran down the hall. Had someone been listening? Or was her paranoia asserting itself? Was she going to be caught? Or was she safe . . . until the next time?

"They won't let me go." Zoltán slammed the door to Andras's office behind him so hard the windows rattled. "Not that I'm surprised. Once

178 / DORIS MORTMAN

a prisoner of the AVO, always a a prisoner of the AVO. *Jézus Mária!* When will I ever be free of them!"

Zoltán's thick eyebrows had furrowed together into an angry hedge. His body trembled with the rage he had carried with him all the way from the Ministry to the Academy.

"But," he continued, his eyes aglow with hatred, "since for some perverse reason they love to keep me informed as to the whereabouts of my family, I do have good things to report. My sister is alive and living somewhere in New York City and my brother is alive and being tortured somewhere in Siberia!" His voice reverberated with such bitterness, even Andras was surprised at its depth.

Andras approached his friend gingerly, afraid of detonating a tantrum that would attract undesirable attention.

"Come," he said as he took Zoltán's arm and steered him toward a battered armchair with frayed upholstery and a broken leg. "Sit. We'll have a coffee and talk."

Like a small child obeying a parental command, Zoltán complied, folding his exhausted body into the lopsided piece of furniture, his legs collapsed in front of him, his arms drooping over the sides of the chair.

Once Zoltán was settled, Andras went to fetch some coffee. Zoltán remained frozen to his chair. Too emotionally spent to move, he allowed his eyes to wander. He looked at the high ceilings and the large, curtainless windows. He looked at Andras's desk, a cumbersome oaken rectangle strewn with sheet music, hastily scribbled notes, telephone messages, memos, and other emblems of a busy man. He noticed the framed portraits of Mozart and Beethoven and Brahms, the phonograph on a cabinet in the corner, and the collection of recordings lined up on the two shelves underneath. An antique music stand held a signed Bartók manuscript. And then his gaze passed over the big black baby-grand piano that dominated the space. The sight of the beautifully polished instrument cut through Zoltán's soul.

Katalin should have her own grand, he thought as his eyes surveyed the lines of Andras's Bösendorfer. She shouldn't be practicing on an upright. The sound was different; the action was different. In an upright, the hammers were thrown against the strings instead of being levered up from below. Once, Zoltán had overheard Andras say that the physical sensations of the two actions were so different it was liable to confuse the reflexes of sensitive fingers. When he had questioned Andras, his friend had tried to dispel his concerns, but despite Andras's assurances that Katalin had the grand in the basement studio to practice on if she needed, and that every concert-hall green room had an upright—which didn't seem to rattle the performers who were about to take the stage and play a grand—Zoltán felt he had let his child down.

Suddenly, a gust of wind brushed his face, upsetting a pile of music stacked on a nearby shelf. The papers fluttered and then lay still. Zoltán stared at them as if they had said something he didn't like. He turned away, toward the window the breeze had come from. There, reflected in the glass, he saw a man in soiled work clothes, a man with dirt under his fingernails and holes in his socks. More symbols of inadequacy. It wasn't the lack of money that disturbed him—all Hungarians were poor unless they were on the take. It went deeper than that. It went beyond the tools hanging from his belt, beyond the soot clinging to his skin. This was a matter of the heart. Here he was in the office of a musical tutor, not as the student he once was, or the performer he once was, but as an outsider.

"It's not very good," Andras said as he placed a steaming cup of dark coffee on a table in front of Zoltán, "but it's hot."

Zoltán nodded, took the cup, and sipped from it, hoping the scalding liquid would melt the thick lump that had settled in his throat.

Andras studied his friend's sadness and saw the crack in the thick wall Zoltán had constructed around his feelings. Over the years, Zoltán had built an admirable defense system against the constant attacks on his pride, but every now and then Andras spotted a weakness in Zoltán's armor. His vulnerability was music, always the music. Whenever something underlined the completeness of his deprivation, the barriers around his soul crumbled a bit, allowing a careful observer to witness the surfacing of a pain so deep and so great that it had become part of the man's blood, part of his life force.

"I think they're going to record the concert," Andras said. "One way or another, you'll hear Katalin play in Moscow."

Zoltán nodded. Both men sipped their coffee, the silence surrounding them growing heavy with things unspoken.

"Zoltán, have you ever thought about teaching?"

Zoltán's body snapped to attention. It was as if something sharp had stuck him in the back.

"Teaching what?"

"The violin." Andras spoke carefully, aware that he was treading on shaky ground.

"How could you even ask me that?" The same pain Andras had seen moments before, the pain that Zoltán usually kept buried, reemerged. His body shook. The color drained from his face.

Outside Andras's door stood someone else deeply affected by Zoltán's pain. Katalin had come to talk to Andras about her concert program.

When she came down the hall, she had noticed that the door to Andras's office had been left ajar. She had been about to walk in when she heard her father's voice. Now she hung back, pressing closer to the wall, afraid to move for fear they might discover her.

"It's easy for me to say that." Andras refused to be put off. "You are a great talent. There are youngsters who could benefit from being taught by you."

"I *was* a great talent. But those days are over. I'm through with music." Zoltán waved his hand in a gesture of angry dismissal.

"You'll never be through with it. It's in your blood."

"What's in my blood is meaningless!" Zoltán bellowed. "I can't be a teacher because of what's missing from my hands! I can't show anyone how to coax music from a wooden box. I can't teach anyone how to use his fingers to tease emotion from tightly wound strings."

Tears stained Katalin's cheeks. She felt like a slacker, an ingrate, a thankless, callow child. Listening to Zoltán, hearing the agony in his voice, Katalin felt a wave of guilt wash over her. She had been feeling pressured about playing a difficult concerto with one of the world's finest orchestras. He would have been happy to play the simplest scale. Suddenly, like the chips inside a kaleidoscope, disparate thoughts and observations and conversations came together into a focused whole: Zoltán's records, his fanatic concern for her career, his chronic melancholy, his relentless ambition for her, his total lack of drive for himself. In a flash of recognition, she realized she had never really understood her father before. Furthermore, she supposed, she had never understood what he and everyone else seemed to want of her, which was probably why she had never determined what she wanted for herself.

"What you have in your brain is just as valuable as what you used to have in your hands," Andras insisted. "You have a sense of timing and phrasing and dynamics that could make the difference between a good violinist and a great violinist."

"I'm not a teacher, Andras," Zoltán said. "I'm not even a player. I'm a bystander. A memory. A name on a dusty recording. I can't *do* anything. I can't give anything more to your precious world of music. I haven't anything more to give."

As she continued to eavesdrop, Katalin found herself thinking about Zoltán's records. How superior his music was! How special he must have felt creating it! For most of her life she had accepted her talent as something she was born with, like her green eyes and golden hair. Talent was something she had, something Andras and Zoltán and Mária told her she should be grateful for. It was something she alternately loved and hated. But her talent was never something with direction, never something with a clearly defined future.

Listening to Zoltán changed all that. With her intimate knowledge of the fragility of a musician's soul, Katalin knew it wasn't just the music her father missed. It was the glory of it, the fame, the joy of creation, the thrill of knowing he could do something brilliantly that very few could do at all. Katalin couldn't return to him the use of his hands. She couldn't give him back the music. But, standing in that hallway, finally understanding that Zoltán's future rested within her, she vowed to do the one thing only she could do—give him back the glory.

The door opened. Andras was in the middle of a protest. He stopped. Both men turned and looked at the young girl framed within the portal. Her eyes were damp, her mouth had a downward turn, but her look was one of resolution and calm.

"What you said, Papa—it's not true." Katalin walked toward her father and took his hand. "You do have something more to give. You have me."

10

Woodridge, Kentucky, 1967

*B*luegrass Field was busy. As Matthew helped Steven drag his baggage toward the check-in counter, they were jostled so often, they were beginning to think they weren't in an airport at all, but on a bizarre ride in an amusement park.

"Lake Charles, Louisiana, please." Steven took the money for his ticket from his wallet and pushed it toward the agent.

"You'll be departing from Gate Ten in an hour and a half." The woman behind the counter handed him his boarding pass and flashed him a dazzling smile. "Y'all have a nice flight."

Steven blushed. At twenty, even though he was no longer an innocent, a beautiful blond with a honeyed voice and a movie star smile still left him flustered.

"Let's go, Romeo." Matthew chuckled as he steered Steven away from the counter toward the coffee shop. "I didn't take the early bus to Lexington so you could stand here gawking. We were supposed to have a farewell breakfast and that's exactly what I intend to do!"

When Steven's draft notice had arrived the month before, Matthew's attitude had not been this mellow. In truth, his initial reactions had been devastation and guilt. When he had come of age, he had been deferred as the single support of a household. Now, the one other person in that household was about to join the army. And unless something drastic happened within the next eight weeks, chances were that as soon as he finished basic training at Fort Polk, Steven would be shipped to Vietnam.

Aside from the obvious fear for his brother's safety, Matthew found himself struggling with other, more subtle emotions. He and Steven had lived in such close quarters for so long that Matthew couldn't imagine waking up in the morning or going to sleep at night without Steven in the next bed. He couldn't imagine not worrying about him or thinking about him, or planning for him.

Whether consciously or not, from the moment their parents had been shot, Matthew had put his life on hold. Steven became his charge, his obligation, his debt to Margit and Béla, his tribute to Vera. Everything he did—staying in Woodridge, staying in the mines, staying with the Vas family—was so that he could be a proper parent to his brother. At twenty-five, Matthew had no delusions about the future of his education. Whatever he had learned since high school, whatever he would learn, would be self-taught.

Steven's education, on the other hand, had become an obsession with Matthew and a source of tension between the two brothers. Matthew scrimped and saved, denying himself even the slightest indulgence so that he could squirrel money away for Steven's tuition. Certainly, Steven wanted to go to college—he had lofty dreams and ambitions, all of which demanded a college degree—but he refused to climb over Matthew's back in order to advance himself. He was determined to fund his own destiny.

"What do you think I've saved all this for," Matthew exclaimed, growing more and more exasperated each time he and Steven had this argument. "Mama and Papa would have wanted you to go."

"They would have wanted you to go too," Steven countered, "so don't try and make me feel as if I'm letting them down because I won't wipe out your bank account."

After his graduation from high school, Steven continued to defy Matthew. He went to work full-time in the mine. He also insisted upon contributing his fair share to their living expenses. Again, Matthew argued with him.

"I'm a supervisor now. My salary's not great, but it's enough to feed and clothe the two of us. You want to put your money away toward an education? Fine. Anything else I take as a personal insult."

The army solved the problem. Thanks to the GI Bill, Steven would get the education Matthew wanted, but it would be paid for by the United States government instead of by Matthew, which was what Steven wanted.

Matthew was also trying to come to grips with the honest fact that without Steven, he would be horribly lonely. Though there were plenty of guys to hoist a brew with at O'Brian's or to take lunch with down in the mine, Matthew had no real friends. He was admired by his co-workers and sought after for local functions like dances or church picnics, but Matthew's aura of vigilant detachment held most people at arm's length, prohibiting any serious attempts at closeness.

Though the Kardos boys still lived in the garage apartment, their relationship with János's brood had been severely damaged by the incident five years before. Matthew and Ernie barely spoke. Fred and Joe had married and now lived several towns away. Pete still lived at home but he had always grazed on the Vas side of the fence and, convinced that as long as he and Ernie shared a room it was his only recourse, continued to do so. János and Rosza, however, had decided to ignore the differences between their sons and their nephews. Rosza cooked for Matthew and Steven. She insisted that they all attend church on Sunday as a family. She expected to see them at her table on holidays. Rather than hurt her or János, they complied.

There were no women in Matthew's life. Pity the girl who sought a spiritual intimacy, the woman who attempted to touch him beyond the physical, to relate to him beyond the superficial. He wouldn't permit anyone to become involved with him, because he couldn't allow himself to become involved with anyone but Steven. Later, there would be plenty of time to think about a wife and children, later, after he had fulfilled his responsibilities.

Now, sitting over scrambled eggs, hash browns, and bacon, Matthew considered the young man who had been the sole focus of his life for so many years. With so much of himself invested, it was difficult for Matthew to view Steven objectively. Yet this morning, with his brother about to go out into the world, it seemed important for him to see what others saw.

Steven was undeniably handsome, with light brown hair and eyes so blue and clear that the intelligence and honesty that formed the corner-stones of his soul shone through. His face, still more youthful than mature, was nonetheless commanding, with sculpted cheekbones that planed down into a strong jaw, which might have appeared hard and unyielding if not for the cleft that indented the edge of his chin. The scar from his accident had healed into a thin black line that curved around his left eye. Small, cupped like a parenthesis, it added an incongruous dash of mystery to a young man who was so forthright and plain-spoken.

"Do you want your roll?"

Matthew hadn't realized how lost he was. Steven's voice startled him. "What?"

"You're not eating your roll. If you don't want it, I'll take it."

Matthew pushed his plate across the table. "You better hope Uncle Sam doesn't put you on C-rations. You'll starve to death."

"Not a chance. If I know Rosza, she'll send care packages with enough food for an entire division."

They both laughed because they knew it was true. Then Steven attacked the roll. Matthew picked at his eggs.

"I can't believe you're going," he said. "I wish I was going with you."

"Fort Polk is not exactly Paradise Island. From what I hear, Woodridge is heaven in comparison."

They both knew that Woodridge could never be defined in any lexicon as heaven and that Fort Polk had nothing to do with Matthew's comment. Neither of them was having trouble with where Steven was going or why. It was the leaving that was causing the distress.

"Can you picture me a soldier?" Steven said, changing the subject, sensitive to the fact that leavetaking was harder on the one who was staying behind.

Nostalgia chalked itself onto Matthew's face, outlining his eyes for a moment with a hard edge born of unpleasant memories. Then, remembering other things, he smiled.

"Of course I can," he said. "You forget. I saw you as a soldier. You were nine years old."

"Yeah," Steven said, he, too, traveling back in time. "I was, wasn't I?"

"How many others going through basic at Fort Polk can say they fought against the Russians?" Matthew asked, daring Steven to come up with an answer other than "none." "Why, I'll bet you're the only private who's a veteran."

Each time they laughed, each time they shared a memory, the parting became a little easier. At this moment of impending disconnection, both of them needed to relive their memories. Yet the same instincts that had helped them survive the wounds of their youth warned them to touch only the tips of their recollections, only the peaks that protruded from the dark lake that held the deepest, most painful part of their past.

"Flight Seventy-three for Lake Charles, Louisiana, will now begin boarding at Gate number Ten."

"That's me," Steven said, pushing himself away from the table with great reluctance. Matthew rose as well. As they started to leave, Steven grabbed his hand. "Mátyás, I'm scared."

"I know," Matthew said, draping his arm around his brother's shoulders, pressing against him as they proceeded toward the gate. "Me too. But everything's going to be fine. I'll write and you'll write and before you know it, you'll be home."

Steven nodded, feeling as if he were nine years old all over again, looking to Matthew to tell him what to do and where to go; believing that if Matthew said they'd be all right, they would; that if Matthew said he would watch over Steven and protect him, he would; that whatever Matthew said was right and true. But Steven wasn't nine years old and Matthew didn't have all the answers.

When they reached the gate, a thick, awkward silence closed in around them like a gray cloud before a rain. They had never before said good-bye to each other. Now, neither one could find the words. Finally, Matthew pulled Steven to him, hugged him, and whispered in Hungarian, "I love you, István. Stay safe." Then, before his heartbreak spilled onto his cheeks, he turned and walked away.

"I love you too, Mátyás," Steven said, as he watched Matthew's rugged form head back toward the terminal. "I love you too."

Matthew's original plan had been to head back to Woodridge right away, but he was so overwhelmed with emotion, so ill at ease with his new, uninvited independence, he decided to work off some nervous energy by wandering around Lexington instead. In the ten years he had lived in Kentucky, he could count the number of times he had visited here on one hand. Why was that? he wondered as he found his way into the center of town.

"Because you never have any money to spend," he reminded himself as he peeked inside several tony boutiques and read the prices on menus discreetly tucked in the lower corner of a few restaurant windows.

The more he walked, the more he realized what a mistake it had been to hibernate in Woodridge. Lexington was an interesting place. He knew it was one of the country's leading trading centers for tobacco and the chief market for racehorses, but he had never translated any of those Chamber of Commerce points of interest into anything tangible. Lexington had simply been a place with nothing to champion it except its hospital. Now, trying to put his finger on the pulse of the city, he studied the shops, the office buildings, the cars on the streets, the clothes on the women lunching in the better restaurants. He watched the people and listened to the chatter and clatter around him and found himself enjoying the sensation of discovery.

In Woodridge, life above ground was slow and lethargic. Working in an endless midnight created a nagging malaise that one carried from the mines into the streets. Except for the Crowns, people scratched the poverty line, some managing to stay on top of it, most falling hopelessly below. Here, everything felt different. The pace was hectic, the rhythm upbeat. The mood was optimistic, the general attitude more cheerful than anything Matthew had encountered at home. There was greater diversity here—more than one industry, more than one economic level, more than one opportunity to try to better one's life. There was money here. Big money. The kind that created dynasties and inherited status. The kind that bought comfort and leisure and even decadent pleasures. The kind that bought safety.

Matthew reached into his pocket and breathed a sigh of relief. There, pinned to the inside of his pants, was a sock stuffed with a fat wad of bills—his savings and Steven's. He had planned to deposit it all in the bank in Jackson, but as his fingers closed around the clump of paper, his eyes fixed on a strange arrangement of green lights parading across a store window: groupings of letters and fractions that made no sense. A crowd had gathered. Several men checked the window against figures in a newspaper. A couple of them commented on how much something or other had dropped or how much something else had gone up.

It took a few minutes before Matthew realized he was standing outside a brokerage house watching an electronic ticker tape. Matthew, trying to understand America, had read books about the stock market. He knew anyone could own a piece of a major company simply by buying a share of stock. But the possibility that he, Mátyás Kardos, could do so had never before occurred to him.

For almost an hour he stood in front of the window, transfixed. Inside, a group of men were sitting in a row of leather chairs staring up at another ticker tape, this one running across the top of the far wall. Some of the men sported broad, satisfied smiles. Others knotted their brows and gnawed on their lips. One or two appeared to be there simply to watch the show.

Behind the gallery he counted ten desks, all in full view of the tape. Each desk was manned by a frenetic creature with, it seemed, telephones attached to either side of his head. Ties loosened, shirtsleeves rolled, faces masked with a ubiquitous look of panic, the brokers all showed a frenzied exterior. Yet, beneath the manic activity, Matthew sensed a passionate, volcanic joy.

Like a seductress blandishing promises of unspeakable delights, temptation drew him in. Responding to feelings instead of thoughts, Matthew pushed open the doors and took an empty seat in the gallery. Someone had left a newspaper on a nearby chair. He picked it up and began to decipher names of companies and what was happening to them. It took a while, but by tracking two or three stocks that appeared to be exceptionally active, he noted that in general the market was up.

Whether it was a wave of emotional instability caused by Steven's leaving or an odd spurt of exhilaration caused by watching the movement of the nation's economy on a screen above his head, Matthew did something he had never done before—he surrendered to an impulse. He got up from his chair, picked a face he liked, and presented himself at the desk of Walter Perry.

"I'd like to open an account," Matthew said, hoping he had used the right words.

Walter Perry eyed him curiously through thick horn-rimmed glasses. The young man standing before him reeked of humility. His slacks, his checked shirt, his threadbare jacket, and scuffed shoes screamed penny stock. As the most junior member of the Alexander & Scott staff, Walter handled trusts. Though it was the most boring job in the house, he was accustomed to dealing with a thoroughbred clientele.

"I only manage estate portfolios," he said, allowing a trace of arrogance to creep into his voice, hoping to hand Matthew off to someone else. "Perhaps Mr. Potts could be of greater assistance."

Matthew refused to be cowed. "My name is Matthew Kardos. I have five thousand dollars to invest. I've never bought stock before, but I do have some knowledge of the way the market works. I need help and I would like you to help me."

Five thousand dollars was a decent stake, Walter admitted, but it wouldn't go very far if Mr. Kardos insisted upon blue chips or preferred. If he wanted to speculate, Walter was supposed to turn him over. *But he was being so insistent.*

"Won't you sit down, Mr. Kardos?" He offered Matthew a chair alongside his desk, ignoring the bemused stares of his fellow workers. Together, they filled out the forms required by Alexander & Scott. Then they began to discuss Matthew's goals.

"As you can see, Mr. Perry, I'm a poor man. I'm a miner from Woodridge and I've sweated every dollar I've ever earned. I don't want to be a miner for the rest of my life, and so I've decided it's time to take a few risks."

Though Walter Perry and Matthew were about the same age, Matthew's history attested to the fact that he had lived several lifetimes in his twenty-five years. Walter felt as if he were stumbling through his first. The more they talked, the more impressed Perry was. Obviously, Matthew was a man of character even if he wasn't a man of means. For Walter, that presented a problem of conscience. Much as he wanted to take Matthew's money and show him—and his superiors—how brilliantly he could play the boards, the market offered few guarantees. He had decided he liked this Hungarian émigré. What if something went wrong and he lost Matthew's savings?

"The market is very volatile. Bank notes or mutual funds would be safer."

"I've been safe for too long," Matthew said, laughing at himself for being so footloose, hearing Steven's voice in his ear telling him to dip into life's well for himself instead of drawing water for everyone else. "Suddenly I find myself with no responsibilities and no one to take care of other than myself. I'm young and, at this very moment, feeling unusually carefree." He reached into his pocket, took out the sock and then the roll of bills. Slowly—so that Walter could watch each and every bill drop onto the stack—he counted out five thousand dollars. "Mr. Perry, you have two choices," he said, leaning back in his chair, folding his arms across his chest, and offering a broad smile tinged with challenge to the startled man next to him. "Either you take this money and make me a rich man or I'm going to have to offer this golden opportunity to Mr. Potts. Now, what's it going to be?"

Matthew felt terrific. He had opened two accounts, one in his own name, one in Steven's, with the money split evenly. He had come to Lexington with $7,600. He had invested $5,000 and held onto $2,600 so that if the worst happened, he wouldn't be penniless. He had retained Steven's $1,100 as well. When he got to Jackson, he would do as he had promised and open two savings accounts.

As he stood in line for his ticket at the bus terminal he thought about the stocks he had bought. Because of Steven and because he believed the war in Vietnam had not yet run its course, he had bought defense stocks. Because he knew that the country was gobbling up its energy sources at a startling rate, he went into a few small utilities Walter said had wonderful growth potential. Because he was feeling reckless, he bought a high-flier Walter was hot on. And, because he knew that very soon Crown would have to upgrade its machinery and streamline its organization in order to insure that productivity met demand, he bought a hundred shares of Crown Coal Collieries.

"It's gone!" The young woman in front of him screeched, crashing through his reverie. "I can't find my wallet! It's gone!"

"Lady, there's people waiting. You want a ticket or not?"

The young woman glowered at the ticket agent. "I need to get to Jackson. Please," she said, softening her tone, "I'll mail you the money. Honest I will. I'm good for it—I swear I am."

"Nope. Can't do that."

"Then how do you expect me to get home?"

"Not my problem, lady."

Matthew stepped up to the window, handed the man several bills, said, "Two tickets to Jackson, please," and gave one to the distressed damsel to his left. "The bus leaves in ten minutes. If we don't hurry we'll miss it."

He smiled, expecting her to follow him, but she just stood and stared. Clearly she was suspicious and was trying to assess his intentions. While she did, he assessed her. She was young, probably about Steven's age, and quite pretty, with creamy skin, walnut brown hair pulled into a sleek ponytail, and rich chocolate brown eyes. She was small, only about five foot one, and so delicately framed he wondered how she had the strength to carry the large tote and the suitcase that stood by her feet. As was the fashion, her dress merely skimmed her thighs. Though she wore the pearl earrings and low-heeled pumps the ladies lunching in town had worn, and she had knotted a big silk square around her neck, as those stylish women had done, her face was surprisingly free of color. Her eyes weren't rimmed in Cleopatra black or lashed with paste-on Twiggy fringe. He supposed she had done something to them, but whatever it was, it had been done with a gentle hand and he liked it.

"I won't bite," he said, holding up his hands as if to prove he had no concealed weapons. "I was just trying to help."

"I know." She shook her head as if clearing it of all evil thoughts. "How unkind of me to behave so badly. Thank you."

She smiled and her whole face changed. It brightened and rounded and appeared far more beautiful than when her mouth was at rest. Her teeth were so even and so white. Though he had never thought about it before, most of the women Matthew knew had crooked teeth.

He took her suitcase in one hand, her arm in another, and led her to the bus while she explained about her visit with a school chum and the breakdown of her car, and the total lack of compassion of garage mechanics in general—the one in Lexington in particular—and the terrible inconvenience of being without a car. It wasn't until the bus pulled out of the terminal that Matthew got a chance to introduce himself.

"I'm Matthew Kardos."

"My name is Lucinda," she said, looking slightly embarrassed, as if she suddenly understood she had been monopolizing the conversation. "Do you live in Jackson or thereabouts?"

He loved the way she spoke. Her drawl made her voice sound so sweet, so lyrical. "I live in Woodridge. I work in the mines."

She blushed. He wondered why, but because he was too shy to ask, he opted to believe that shyness had prompted her flush as well.

"Do you like it? I mean the mining?"

Matthew laughed. Men who worked in the mines never thought about whether or not they liked it. They simply did it.

"It wasn't my first choice, no."

She nodded, as if she understood and agreed. "If you don't mind my saying so, you have an accent. Obviously you weren't born here."

"No. My brother and I came here in 1957 from Hungary."

She prodded him to tell her about himself. He did so willingly, losing himself in the soft brown velvet of her eyes. To him, she was the quintessential Southern belle—genteel, every inch a lady. When she waved her hands he imagined them holding a fan; when she lowered her eyes he felt certain her lashes were fluttering. Only when they reached Jackson did he realize that whatever he knew about her he had invented. She had not told him anything about herself, including her last name or where she lived.

"I live in Woodridge also," she said, answering his question with a small, guilty smile. "I'm Lucinda Crown. My daddy owns the mine."

For a moment Matthew looked stunned. Then he threw his head back and laughed.

"There must be a full moon, because so far this has been one of the strangest days of my life."

"I beg your pardon."

"Oh, I'm sorry, Lucinda—I mean, Miss Crown. I don't intend any insult. It's just I said good-bye to my brother this morning, had a highly unusual afternoon, and now, it seems, I've had the pleasure of making the acquaintance of my boss's daughter. I can't imagine what's going to happen next."

His laughter was honest and infectious. Lucinda laughed with him, noticing how his hazel eyes crinkled and his brow creased; how his hair curled when he tossed his head back and it touched his neck; how his upper lip seemed to disappear in the generous breadth of his smile. She also took note of his body. He was much taller than she—so were most people—and in incredible shape. His shoulders were broad and his muscles were firm, but there was nothing hulky about him. His waist was narrow, his hips lean, and if she had to hazard a guess, she would have said that his legs were as taut and toned as his arms. Clearly, the mines were good for something.

"What's going to happen next," she said, "is you're going to go back to calling me Lucinda and drop that silly Miss Crown stuff. Then we're going to take the bus to Woodridge, you're going to tell me how to get in touch with you, and I'm going to meet you later to give you back the money for my ticket."

"You don't have to pay me back. It was my pleasure . . . Lucinda. Really."

"What if it's my pleasure to see you again?" she asked, her eyes locked firmly on his.

"Then it would be rude of me to say no."

That night Matthew arranged to meet her at a little restaurant in Primrose, just across the county line. He couldn't remember ever feeling this nervous.

Before he got out of János's car, he must have checked himself a hundred times in the rearview mirror. All he saw reflected in it were his failings. His poverty. His lack of education. The absence of a definable future. And those were merely his obvious faults. What about the ones he was too unsophisticated even to recognize? What about his manners? The way he spoke? The things he spoke about? What did Lucinda do with men of her class? How did they treat her? How should he treat her? He was never cruel or careless with the women he dated. He always tried to be polite and show concern for their feelings, but they were ordinary women who didn't expect anything more than a drink at O'Brian's. Dinner here at the Primrose Café with its quiet, candlelit dining room would have been a rare treat—for them. But what about for the likes of Lucinda Crown?

Seated at the bar, he didn't see her walk in. She hung back for a moment, drinking in the sight of him. She had wondered if when she saw him again, she would be disappointed. She wasn't. When he turned and saw her standing in the doorway, his face lit with the most brilliant, endearing smile she had ever seen.

"Hi." He slid off the barstool and came to greet her.

As he walked toward her, she noticed again the broadness of his shoulders and the ease of his gait. During dinner she found that despite a certain reticence to discuss his private life and a hesitancy to pry beyond propriety about hers, everything about Matthew was easy and unaffected. He was basic, minus the artifice that costumed most of the young men who had been introduced to her as prospective suitors. The scent of tragedy clung to him like the dank smell of the mine. That afternoon he had given her an outline of his story, omitting the emotion that had accompanied the events, deleting the hardship that had marked his life since his arrival in the United States. Listening to him tonight, she knew it wasn't the loss of his family or the constant struggle to survive that had fashioned the man who had just taken her hand and closed it within his. It was strength of conviction and clarity of purpose that separated him from everyone else she knew.

When the check was paid and they rose to leave, Lucinda knew she was not saying good night to Matthew Kardos. At least not here and not yet.

"It's early," she said as they walked down the wooden steps of the café. Matthew thought he heard an invitation in her voice, but he dared not assume. He looked around for her car, but the only vehicle on the road was his. "I had a friend drop me off," she explained with a coy smile.

It was cool in the mountains in May. Lucinda, who was wearing a short cotton dress and an abbreviated bolero jacket, shivered slightly. Instinctively, Matthew took the lapels of the jacket and pulled them closer. Before he knew it, her lips had found his. As she moved toward him, his hands were sandwiched between their bodies. Unwittingly they pressed against the soft flesh of her breasts. He had to fight against responding too vigorously.

"My parents own a cabin near here. What if I make us a cup of coffee? We can talk some more and then you can drive me home. Okay?"

The cabin, built at the turn of the century, sat perched high on the Cumberland Plateau overlooking part of the valley surrounding the North Fork of the Kentucky River. Built of logs with rough walls and plank floors, it relied upon huge fireplaces and a coal-burning stove for heat. Rugs loomed by local weavers sprawled across the floor, spicing the tan-and-brown interior with splashes of color and texture. There were well-stuffed sofas and cozy chairs, and several hand-carved tables. Many of the furnishings—the throw pillows, the lamps, the wooden carvings, the ceramic pitchers and bowls, the quilts that served as curtains, hanging from fat brass rods—were mountain made, lending the cabin a rustic warmth that was totally irresistible.

Lucinda insisted upon building a fire in the main room. When the logs caught and the orange light suffused the generous space, she took a few pillows from a nearby couch and scattered them in front of the stone-faced hearth.

"Join me," she said, holding a glass containing two fingers of Jack Daniels's, a splash of soda, and a single ice cube, handing Matthew one with three fingers of Jack Daniels's neat.

For a while they sat in silence, the spit and crackle of the fire the only sounds other than ice clinking against glass. Matthew sipped his bourbon, enjoying the bittersweet taste of the corn mash whiskey on his tongue, the sting of it as it slid down his throat. Soon he mellowed, and the tension he had been feeling ever since he and Lucinda had entered this hideaway abated. Lucinda's perfume, a heavy lily-of-the-valley floral, mingled with the scent of the burning wood. As she moved closer, he also became conscious of the aroma of arousal and willing flesh.

He put his drink down and gently took her face in his hands, searching her eyes for approval. Her arms laced around his neck and pulled his mouth onto hers. She pressed against him immediately, as if she feared that without further encouragement he would retreat. Hungrily she nibbled at him, licking the inside of his lips and his teeth, sparring with his tongue. Within seconds they were groping at each other, fumbling with buttons and garters and zippers and stockings and shoes.

Naked, Lucinda lay before the fire, recumbent on a bed of pillows, presenting herself to him like an idol to a supplicant. Matthew knelt by her side, entranced, as strong fingers of yellow light played with her body. For the moment he allowed the firelight to do what his hands wanted desperately to do. Feeling every bit the voyeur, he followed the light as it illuminated the landscape in front of him. His eyes traveled the path of a shimmering, lambent halo, moving from the gentle turn of her calves to the flat plateau of her pelvis, the sinuous curve of her waist, the dark hollow that sheltered the source of her heat. When his gaze reached her face, he saw that she had closed her eyes, as if she, too, was responding to the exquisite eroticism of firelight upon flesh.

Matthew was glad she wasn't watching him watching her. He wanted privacy to enjoy the sight of her body, especially the wonder of her breasts. For such a small woman, they were gloriously large and lusciously full. They lay in front of him like a sacramental offering, and so he worshiped them. Lucinda felt him appreciating her, felt him wanting her. She opened her eyes and slowly cupped her breasts. With obvious pride she held them out to him, shivering as he bent down and tasted each one, savoring the sensation of each nipple hardening within his mouth. His hands quickly filled themselves with her flesh. She took hold of his. He felt his breath stick in his throat as her fingers began to work their magic.

He had slept with too many women for this to feel like the first time. Yet, miraculously, it did. Was it the softness of her skin, the seductiveness of the setting? Was it who she was and where they were? He couldn't tell, but as he felt Lucinda move beneath him, drawing him inside her, he knew he wanted to extend these moments of excruciating joy for as long as he possibly could.

• • •

For the next three months Lucinda and Matthew gorged themselves on romance. With Lucinda's parents summering in Europe, the two lovers met as often as four times a week. They ate, talked, listened to music, read poetry, and made love to each other long into the night. They never went anywhere else and never saw anyone else. The cabin became their universe; nothing beyond its walls seemed to matter.

For Matthew, life seemed bountiful. Walter's high-flier stock had paid off, giving Matthew enough money to indulge in a used car and some new clothes. Though Steven wrote often complaining that Fort Polk was an outpost of hell, and then wrote that he had volunteered to be a Green Beret and was headed for additional training at Fort Bragg, North Carolina, he was still stateside, still safe. Even the mine seemed less oppressive because at the end of the day Lucinda was always waiting for him, always ready for him.

It was the first time in Matthew's life he had ever felt anything other than burdened. Being with Lucinda was entirely joyful. Lucinda had walked into his life and flung open a window, allowing him to breathe again.

Occasionally, however, on those nights when he slept alone in his bed in the garage apartment, inner voices intruded on his sleep, confronting him with nagging questions. Lucinda was not just any girl. She was Caleb Crown's daughter. She was rich and privileged and worldly. She was also young and lusty and had not come to Matthew a virgin. Was he a fling or something more? If she did love him—he was convinced he loved her—what then? She was supposed to return to college in the fall. In December, she would make her debut into society. Reality stabbed at him. In Lucinda's world, money and image and position mattered. He wasn't someone who would impress Lucinda's college friends. He wasn't the escort Lucinda's mother wanted on her daughter's arm when she was presented at the Snowflake Cotillion. And he wasn't the sort of man Caleb Crown wanted to introduce as his son-in-law to his cronies at the club. But, he supposed, none of that was important if he was the man Lucinda wanted as a husband.

It was a question that was answered one night in late August. They were tangled in a swirl of sheets on the four-poster in the cabin bedroom, hot and sweaty from their lovemaking and the warmth of the summer evening.

"I'm pregnant," Lucinda whispered as she nibbled on Matthew's ear.

At first he wasn't certain he'd heard her right. His mind was still fogged with physical sensation.

"I said, I'm pregnant."

Matthew detached himself from her immediately, his brain reeling from the shock. "It can't be. You said you were protected."

"The IUD didn't work," she said casually, as if she were talking about a cake mix.

He sprang from the bed and struggled into his pants. This was not something he wanted to think about naked. Pacing the room as if there were an explosive in his bloodstream, he ran through a series of ideas, considering alternatives and making plans. Suddenly he became aware of Lucinda's calm. She was leaning against a stack of pillows, as contented and smug as a Persian cat. She hadn't bothered to cover herself. Matthew had to fight against being distracted by the sight of her breasts glistening with sweat and the sheet tucked between her legs in the place he had come to think of as Eden.

"We'll get married," he said, allowing a smile to dance across his lips as the thought of it became less strange and more appealing. Living with Lucinda, making love to her whenever the spirit moved them, having a child of their love to nurture and care for—he moved over to the bed and kissed her belly. "I promise I'll love and take care of you and our child."

Lucinda ran her hand through Matthew's hair. She felt his lips press against her skin. She longed to slide down and let him love her again, but she couldn't do that.

"I'm going away," she said.

"What?" Matthew sat up with a start. His heart had begun to pound inside his chest, beating like a drum.

"I'm going to Switzerland. They have a school there that accommodates young women in my . . . circumstance."

"Fine. That'll give me time to find us a house, to get everything set up for you and the baby."

"No," she said, in a tone that felt like an ice cube running down Matthew's back. "Once the baby's born, it'll be given up for adoption."

"It? Given up? What is the matter with you?" Suddenly he was on his feet, flushed with an anger that could only have come from a man who had witnessed the destruction of his own family. "You're talking about my baby. Your baby. Not it! I won't let you give our child away."

"It's not your decision." Lucinda wrapped the sheet around her nakedness.

"Why not?"

"Because I can't be sure it's your child."

Matthew's insides felt as if he were in an elevator plummeting through a thirty-story building. He grabbed the nearest chair to brace himself against the crash.

"I'm only seven weeks along. That day when I met you and I told you I had been visiting a friend, well, it was a male friend. It's very possible that this baby is his."

Matthew dropped his head into his hands, his emotions roller-coastering between anger and disappointment, rejection and betrayal—and other feelings too raw to touch.

"In a way," Lucinda said, turning her back to him as she dropped the sheet and slipped into a bathrobe, "it's a good thing that there's someone else."

"And how do you figure that?"

"When Daddy found out, he was—well, you can imagine how he was. He demanded that I tell him who the scoundrel was who had put me in a family way. He made lots of threats about what he would do to whoever was responsible. Very ugly threats."

Matthew's discomfort was growing. Lucinda's voice sounded odd. Her face had taken on a waxed aspect. Her gestures seemed rehearsed. Everything about this scene felt wrong.

"I know how much you need your job, Matthew. The very least Daddy would have done would have been to fire you. Fortunately, Daddy loathes scandal, so when I told him the other gentleman's name, he opted to drop the matter as long as I agreed to go to this school and give the baby up. It seemed like the best thing for all of us."

"The best thing . . ." Matthew muttered, his rage building. "Is that so? Because I believed you loved me and I know I love you, I would've thought the best thing would've been for us to get married and make a life for ourselves and our child. But I guess I have coal dust in my eyes, don't I, Lucinda?"

"I don't know what you're talking about." She backed away, suddenly unsure as to what he might do next.

"I'm talking about love. I'm talking about feelings. I'm talking about what we had together. What I thought we'd have together in the future."

"Future? Don't be absurd. You never really thought I'd marry you, did you? We had a good time, but that's all there was to it." Her face was hard, void of all warmth, all compassion.

Matthew laughed, but it was a hollow sound filled with pain. "No more than ten minutes ago you had your mouth all over me and I had mine all over you. Call me crazy, but I thought we had something terrific going for us. Obviously, I was wrong." He flung his shirt on, buttoned it, and stuffed it into his pants. "Well, thank you for clearing that up for me," he said as he searched for his shoes. "Now I know. I was just a summer plaything for the heiress on the hill. Is that it, Lucinda?" he asked, lacing his shoes, keeping his eyes trained on her face. "Was I an experiment? Were you comparing the sophisticated sexual technique of white-collar aristocrats to the more primitive style of black-collar peasants? Was this a kick for you, fucking one of your father's grunts? Bringing me up to this cabin night after night, playing at love while all the time you

198 / DORIS MORTMAN

were probably giggling on the telephone to your friends about what it's like to get laid by an immigrant miner." He jerked the door of the bedroom open. He took a few steps into the next room, but then he turned and bowed, bending low at the waist in a most obsequious way. "I hope you enjoyed yourself, Miss Crown. It was a pleasure to serve you."

The door slammed. She didn't move. She waited until she heard his car drive down the hill and out of her life. Only then did she allow her tears to fall.

Six weeks later Matthew received a letter from Lucinda, postmarked Lucerne, Switzerland. It was a short note simply to inform him that she had miscarried. There was no baby and no reason for them to contact each other again.

The next day he received another letter. Steven had completed his Green Beret training and was on his way to Saigon.

11

Budapest, 1968

For the Strassers and the Gáspárs it was the custom to celebrate their daughters' birthdays together. The girls had been born only weeks apart, and the two families had used the occasion not only to celebrate their love for their daughters but as a way of honoring and renewing their friendship.

The Gáspár apartment hadn't changed much over the years. Not because Mária wouldn't have liked to redecorate or refurbish, but money was scarce. If the upholstery on a chair or sofa faded or began to look threadbare, Mária simply added another throw pillow or a new hand-crocheted antimacassar. Wherever the wallpaper stained or pulled, she hung a picture or a mirror. Though the draperies, once a sumptuous Cabernet velvet, were beginning to show signs of advancing age, tied with a golden braid and gracefully swagged they seemed to defy the ravages of time, retaining more than a hint of their orginal elegance. Beneath them hung the delicate lace curtains Mária had bought to freshen the apartment for Zoltán's return from Recsk. Sadly, they had begun to yellow, but with her usual optimism Mária had declared them "antique." An ornate crystal chandelier Mária and Zoltán had bought in Vienna before the war hovered over the room, a memento of another time. Several of its diamond-shaped prisms were missing, but with its twenty lights fully illuminated, it continued to dominate the room like a dowager queen who had lost some of her glow but none of her majesty.

Wafting from Mária's kitchen this evening came the beefy smell of erőleves, a rich bouillon made of flanken and marrow bones; the more fragrant aroma of csoda csirke, a flavorful chicken fricassee drenched in mushrooms, onions, and sour cream; and the sweet fruitiness of freshly baked cherry strudel.

Bunches of wild flowers infused the room with color—in a bowl for the centerpiece, in a vase on the piano, in a glass on a lampstand. The dining table, moved from its usual spot in front of the window to the center of the room, was laid with one of Eva Gáspár's hand-embroidered cloths. Set on top of the deep red flowers and bright green leaves that emblazoned the cotton cloth were whatever pieces remained of Mária's prized Herend china and a potpourri of Austrian crystal goblets. The table was set for six. By each of the plates meant for Katalin and Judit, Mária had placed an oddly shaped package wrapped in a handkerchief and tied with a ribbon, pink for Katalin, red for Judit. Alongside those Ilona had placed an additional gift, hers wrapped in newspaper, also tied with red and pink ribbons. As always, the girls had begged to open their presents before dinner. As always, their requests had been denied.

Having tired of trying to guess the contents of the packages, the girls turned their attention to the appetizers. Judit's favorite was the herring salad. Katalin could never get enough of the goose-liver pâté, especially when she could have it with a paprika-seasoned bread finger. Andras had tried both of those and was now digging into the green peppers spread with a mixture of ewe's cheese, butter, mustard, paprika, caraway seeds, and beer. Ilona, Mária, and Zoltán were enjoying a dry Tokay.

"Egészségére!" Zoltán said to those assembled. "Cheers!"

Everyone raised a glass and joined the toast. It was so rare that they ate or drank on such a lavish scale, they wanted to enjoy every second of it.

"How is university, Judit?" Mária asked.

"I hate studying Russian, I despise listening to Soviet doctrine, but otherwise it's okay. The literature and poetry classes are the best!"

As the others talked about Judit's courses, Katalin busied herself with another hors d'oeuvre. She didn't attend the university and, in a way, regretted it. After the enormous success of her concert in Moscow, it had been decided—by her parents, Andras, and Tomás Kocsis, the minister of culture—that she should concentrate solely on her music. Enrolled in the Franz Liszt Academy, she took instruction in all aspects of classical piano literature, including biographies of the famous composers and pianists. She studied theory, interpretation, technique, and performance practices. Since there were no exceptions granted from learning Russian and doctrine, she was tutored in both of those subjects. At the behest of the government, she toured the Eastern Bloc, giving frequent recitals and concerts. And if she had time, she was permitted to read an historical novel or two.

"The one contemporary writer I'd like to study," Judit was saying with a broad stroke of awe shading her voice, "is Kovács Attila. But we can't. They've put him on the forbidden list."

"They've arrested him again," Zoltán said. He had heard about the notorious playwright's most recent imprisonment from someone who had seen Kovács being taken into Fő Street prison in chains.

"That can't be!" Judit's face was ashen. "This is the third time this year. How can they do that?" Judit lamented, her face pinched with grief. "How can they take a beautiful spirit like that and lock it up inside a cage?"

"Easily." Zoltán's mouth twisted into an ironic, knowing smile.

"Have you read any of his plays, Mária?" Ilona asked, curious about and not completely pleased with Judit's intense interest in Kovács.

Mária nodded. "He's a major talent, but it's not his writing they object to—it's his subject matter. When he was just twenty he wrote a play called The Zoo. It's a satire about the way the communist bureaucracy functions. Every character is a different animal. Each one portrays another idiosyncracy of the system. One minister, for example, is a dog who's caught its tail in its teeth and keeps running around in circles. Another is a giraffe who keeps talking over everyone else's head, giving long, boring speeches using nonsense syllables that no one can understand."

"I love it!" Judit was clapping her hands with undisguised glee. Mária was fascinated by her reaction. Ilona was displeased. "See," Judit said, poking Katalin. "Didn't I tell you he was spectacular?"

"Many times," Katalin said, nodding in agreement, keeping a smile to herself.

When the two girls had spoken about Attila Kovács—which was quite often these days—rarely was the substance of his plays the main topic of discussion. More often Judit prattled on about how handsome he was, with his long blond hair and drooping moustache; how powerful he appeared with his fiercely blue eyes and thick, Mephistophelean eyebrows; how exciting it was just to be near him and to witness him hypnotize a crowd.

She had first experienced him when she had gone to hear him read from his plays at a coffeehouse frequented by students—an underground café in a seedy section of town, its address unpublished, its door unmarked. One heard of it through word of mouth. One gained entrance via a password that changed every day.

Judit had taken Katalin once and it had frightened her. It was little more than a basement, a concrete box filled with wooden tables and chairs, smoke, and an undercurrent of rage. The students, most of them older than Judit, were not addicted to Kovács's plays because they found them amusing in the way that Molière was amusing or because his philosophy preached the searing existentialism of Kafka. They applauded his plays because they saw them as treatises of dissent—loud, bold, satirical exhortations to freedom. They heeded his message because they were revolutionaries waiting for the next time history opened a door for them, the next time they were offered an opportunity to break out of the oppressive cell in which they were living.

What had surprised Katalin most was how many people knew Judit. Obviously, her friend was a regular, like the others a revolutionary in waiting, who had, by her presence in this clandestine place, declared herself a soldier.

During dinner, while conversation swirled around her, Katalin found herself staring at Judit, measuring herself against her friend. Something Ilona said distracted her. As she turned away from Judit, her eyes were drawn to the packages alongside her plate. She had never realized before how appropriate it was that pink should be considered her color and red, Judit's. Judit was all fire and passion and zeal. She didn't simply care about something, she cared desperately. She wasn't afraid to express herself or declare herself or commit herself to a project or an ideal. She was a voracious reader, devouring books, digesting thoughts and ideas. She was playful and fun to be with. And, of course, there was Judit's music.

That was the most significant difference, Katalin thought. Judit's life didn't revolve around music. Certainly it was an important part of who she was, but it was only a part. For Katalin, it was the total essence of her being. There was not a moment in her day that wasn't devoted to some aspect of music. She thought about it, practiced it, learned about it, talked about it, even dreamed about it. She was the piano. The piano was her. There was no other way to define or describe her.

Rarely did she question it, but when she did, it disturbed her. It made her feel limited and insecure. Unless she was sitting at a keyboard, who was she? She was grateful for her talent, but had she paid too high a price for such singular ability? Though she would never have admitted it to anyone, Katalin envied Judit. Judit was involved with so many other people; she did so many different things. She reached for opportunities. She courted danger. She insisted upon biting into the juiciest part of the fruit of life. Judit's life wasn't a labor of sameness. Often, Katalin felt hers was.

"It's time to open your presents," Mária said, clapping her hands to get everyone's attention. "The smaller ones first."

As they had been instructed, Katalin and Judit each grabbed the package wrapped in a handkerchief. Carefully sliding the ribbon off, each laid her gift on the table and eagerly unfolded the damask. Inside were delicate gold filigree mirrors.

"The propmaster at the theater found these in the storage closet." Mária took pleasure in watching the girls run their fingers along the lacy gold openwork of the frames. "Since we don't use lavishly decorated sets anymore, he felt no one would miss them. When he asked me if I wanted them, I said I thought I knew of two beautiful young women who just might enjoy having something as repulsively patrician and self-indulgent as these for their dressing tables."

Katalin and Judit lifted the mirrors and held them in front of their faces. Though Katalin had no way of knowing it, this was the time when Judit went through the process of comparison and came up wanting. Peering over her glass at her friend, Judit saw a young woman with long silky hair the color of butternut and Magyar eyes tinted a pale, smoky green. She saw a heart-shaped face with soaring cheekbones, a sloping nose gently tipped, and full, ripe lips that at their peak arched like a dove in flight. When she looked into her own glass, she saw a polar opposite. Dark, wavy hair bounced disobediently about a very ordinary square face. Her eyes were a rich brown flecked with orange, wide-set and highly expressive, but because heavy lids awned them, she thought she looked drowsy or bored. To Judit, her nose seemed too broad at the bridge, her forehead too wide at the brow. While Katalin's skin made one think of pearls, hers held a trace of olive. Though her mouth was as full as Katalin's, her upper lip offered no seductive bow, no sensuous curve. As she rewrapped the mirror and thanked Mária for giving it to her, she knew that while she would indeed place it on the table nearest her bed, looking into it would never be the pleasure Mária had intended. It would simply serve as confirmation of what she already knew—she was the duckling to Katalin's swan.

"May we open the other ones?" Katalin asked, intrigued by the pancake shape of Ilona's gift.

Ilona nodded and within seconds both girls had the wrappings removed. In front of each of them was a record. They looked at Ilona, confused and curious.

"Whose shall we play first?" Andras asked, as curious as the girls.

"Let's flip a coin." Zoltán reached into his pocket and pulled out a forint.

"Heads," Judit shouted.

Zoltán rested the coin on the top of his middle finger. Using his thumb as a vault, he launched the forint into the air, caught it in his right hand, and slapped it onto the back of his left hand.

"Heads it is." He took the record from Judit and put it onto the turntable.

The sublime Romanticism of Chopin's "Fourth Ballade" filled the room. As the melody grew more intense, culminating in an exuberant coda that required a virtuoso technique of the pianist, a proud smile graced Judit's lips.

"How did you do it, Mama," she asked, staring at Ilona. "How did you make a record of me playing the Chopin?"

Ilona smiled mysteriously. "How do you know it's you?"

"Because of the rubato."

"Rubato?" Living with Zoltán and Katalin, Mária was familiar with most musical terms, but this one escaped her.

"It means robbed time," Judit explained. "It's a way of interpreting a piece by altering the tempo. You take time away from one note and pay it back several notes later. When I play the 'Fourth,' I do it the way Chopin did. I keep strict time with my left hand and add rubato with my right."

"That was my Judit?" Andras asked his wife, less interested in the how than he was in the who.

"That was our Judit," Ilona replied smugly.

"Well, *brava!*" Andras cried, leaning over to hug his daughter. "*Brava!*"

"How did you do it?" Judit repeated, still flushed by the warmth of her father's embrace.

Again, Ilona ignored the question. She handed Zoltán Katalin's record.

"Let's hear Katalin," she said.

Zoltán's heart stopped when he heard the first notes from the phonograph and recognized the "Paganini Études." A series of six études based on Paganini's breathtaking "Caprices"—the music that had crowned Zoltán king of the violin so many years before—they had been written by Franz Liszt as homage to Niccolò Paganini. At the time of their composition, the "Études" had been considered an epoch-making event in the evolution of piano virtuosity.

As Zoltán listened to the way Katalin played the études, he knew she must have spent hours studying his recordings of the "Caprices." She did with her fingers what he had done with his bow. His pizzicato became her staccato. His andante, her andante. When she played the third étude, "La Campanella," the one Liszt had taken from the rondo of Paganini's B-minor Violin Concerto, there was no doubt. Zoltán's influence was so definite and distinctive, so obvious, that even Mária glanced over at him, raising her eyebrow as if raising the perennial question about his interference with her training. He answered with a quick but convincing I'm-confused-as-well shrug of his shoulders. Clearly, Katalin hadn't told her mother about her practice sessions with his recordings either.

When the record ended, instead of the instantaneous applause that had greeted Judit's performance, there was silence. Katalin fixed on a spot near her plate. Judit, seated across from her friend, reached for Katalin's hand. There were tears in her eyes.

"You were brilliant, Katya. Absolutely brilliant."

Katalin's insecurities made it impossible for her to take a compliment easily, particularly when it was such high praise from someone who just moments before had offered her talents for approval. Katalin studied Judit carefully, looking beyond the sincerity that gazed back at her, seeking signs of jealousy or bitterness or even mockery.

"When did you decide to take on the 'Études'?" Andras asked. "I don't remember us even discussing them."

"I hope you don't mind," Katalin said quietly, wondering whether his question was a criticism. "I sort of taught them to myself."

"Mind?" Andras laughed. "How could I mind? They were extraordinary! Judit is right, Katya. You performed brilliantly!"

Katalin turned to Zoltán and Mária. "Did you like them, Mama? Papa?" Though she spoke to him, her eyes looked past his.

Mária rose from her chair, walked over to Katalin, and kissed both her daughter's cheeks. "Even God is smiling, edesem. It's not often He hears something so thrilling."

"Papa?" It concerned Katalin that he had not come over to her, that he had not moved from the phonograph. Had he guessed about the recordings? Had he buried them in the back of the closet because he had wanted to bury all the pain associated with them? Suddenly, a broad smile occupied his mouth.

"Look under your plate, kicsi szilva. Even before I heard the Liszt, I knew how great an artist you are."

Katalin lifted her dinner plate, careful not to drop any leftovers onto her grandmother's cloth. She retrieved the envelope that had been hidden there.

"Open it," Zoltán said, his smile getting brighter.

Katalin obeyed, opening the envelope, taking out the papers folded inside. As she scanned them, her face paled.

"This is an application for the Salzburg Competition."

"I know," Zoltán said.

"First prize is a scholarship to the Juilliard School of Music in New York."

"I know that too."

"Why would you want her to go to Juilliard?" Andras couldn't hide his disapproval or his feelings of betrayal. "The Academy is one of the finest music schools in the world."

Zoltán had anticipated this. He was prepared.

"That's true, Andras," he said with quiet calm. "I don't mean to take anything away from you or the Academy, but Juilliard also enjoys an international reputation."

"New York is so far away." Mária was as disturbed by Zoltán's gift as Andras was, but for different reasons. "Where will Katalin live? Who will take care of her?"

"Zsuzsanna is in New York," Zoltán said. "We will find her. She will take care of Katya."

"New York is a big city," Judit said, knowing that it was impolite for her to intrude on what appeared to be an adult conversation, but unable to control herself. The thought of Katalin's leaving Budapest and living thousands of miles away was simply too horrible to comprehend. "How will you find Zsuzsanna? And what happens if you don't?"

"There are always ways to track people," Zoltán said, looking briefly at Ilona, then returning his attention to the others.

"If we don't find Zsuzsanna, I don't want Katya going." It was so rare that Mária made absolute statements, the room silenced immediately. "She's too young! America is too far and too big. I can't send her to live among strangers."

Zoltán went to Mária, took her in his arms and kissed her. He continued to hold her as he faced the others. "Please, everyone. Why borrow trouble? The Salzburg is a great competition. Before we can worry about whether or not Katalin is going to New York, Katalin has to enter the competition. When she wins, then we can talk about New York."

Zoltán's gift cast a pall over the rest of the evening. Though Mária tried valiantly to revive the gay spirit that had preceded the opening of the envelope, it was not to be. Andras was inconsolable, but because he would never be rude in Mária's house, he reined in his anger and retreated into a somber silence.

While Mária and the girls cleared the table, Zoltán took Ilona aside.

"I need you to help me find Zsuzsanna," he said, keeping his voice low.

"How can I do that?" Ilona asked, surprise and caution registering on her face.

"By using the same source you used to get those records made."

"I don't know what you're talking about." She moved away but Zoltán caught her arm.

"Twice you were asked how you got them and twice you ignored the question. I looked at those records, Ilona. They were not made in the East. I don't know who you know or why you know them. I just want you to use them to do me a favor."

Ilona lowered her eyes, thinking, deciding what to do, what to say. How could she deny Zoltán his request? He asked so little of her. And he had given so much.

"I set up a tape recorder in the basement studio," she said, looking over at Andras to be sure he wasn't listening. "I hid in the next room and taped a practice session with each girl. Then I sent the tapes to some people who have been helping me get medical supplies from the West. They had the tapes transferred to discs."

"I take it Andras doesn't know anything about this group you're dealing with."

"No." Ilona looked directly into Zoltán's eyes. "I prefer it that way."

"I understand." He leaned forward and kissed Ilona's cheek. "And thank you. This means a lot to me."

He walked away, leaving Ilona terribly conflicted. She had watched Andras's heart break when Zoltán had suggested that Katalin study in New York with someone else. Andras had poured his soul into Katalin Gáspár. Now Zoltán wanted to take her away. Mária had said she would forbid Katalin to go if Zsuzsanna wasn't found. Zoltán had asked her to find his sister. If she followed up on his request, she would feel disloyal to Andras. If she did nothing, and therefore made certain that Katalin would stay in Hungary, she was not only being disloyal to Zoltán, she was being ungrateful and dishonest as well.

"No one ever asks what I want," Katalin said as she sat on her bed and leaned back against the headboard. "My father wants me to go to New York. Your father wants me to say here. No one even thinks to ask me what I want or how I feel."

Judit tossed her legs over the arm of a chair, folded her arms across her chest, and eyed Katalin carefully. "I'm asking you. How do you feel?"

For a few moments Katalin didn't answer. She stared at the faded floral print on her coverlet, remembering when it was new and life had seemed as rosy as the blossoms that bloomed atop her bed. Then, she had played the piano purely for the exquisite joy of if. Once she started to perform in public, the emphasis changed. The pressure took on a different feel. Katalin rarely minded the long hours of practice. She loved creating beautiful music. She was a perfectionist about her craft, and each minute devoted to that goal was time well spent. She also loved performing, forging that mystical connection between artist and audience. For her it was a blissful experience that transcended all others. Lately, though, it seemed that whenever she took the stage, she was being asked to do it to please someone other than herself. Her recitals and concerts were becoming so burdened with extraneous obligation that each time she sat down to play, she felt as if another heavy block were being placed on her back, a block with someone else's name on it.

"Angry," she said at last. "I get angry when people talk around me, as if I'm not there or I'm totally irrelevant." Her voice broke.

"You're hardly irrelevant, Katya."

"You don't think so? Do you realize that someone takes credit for everything about me? My father takes credit for my talent, my mother for my looks, your father for my training, your mother for my health. I'm sure the ghosts of my grandparents sit around heaven arguing about who gave me my posture and my skin tone and my intelligence and my sense of humor. I wonder if it's possible for me to have a single waking thought that's entirely my own."

"And I thought I was the dramatic one!" Judit had never heard Katalin speak like this. Usually she was so docile, so accepting.

"I'm not being dramatic." Katalin's voice was soft, shaky. Her eyes had pooled and for the moment, embarrassment bowed her head. "I'm telling you what I see and what I feel."

"And I'm listening, Katya. Believe me, I'm listening."

Katalin looked at Judit and nodded. She inhaled deeply, hoping to regain her normal level of control. It was unusual for Katalin to bare herself so completely, even to Judit. Yet tonight—feeling the tension between Zoltán and Andras, seeing her mother so unnerved, knowing she was the reason for all the distress—it had rattled her to the core, pushing repressed thoughts and fears forward until she couldn't hold them in.

"They discuss what I should do, where my life should go, how I should plan my future. But they never discuss it with me." She wiped her cheeks with the back of her hand. "In a way I'd love to go to New York! Then I'd have to think for myself and do for myself and be responsible for myself."

"That's true, but think of what you'd be leaving behind," Judit said pointedly.

Katalin looked at Judit. She hadn't focused on that. She had thought only about what she would be gaining if she went to New York, not what she would be losing. There, lay the prospect of independence, growth, excitement, advancement. Here, were family and familiar places and comfortable surroundings. Here, was her best friend.

"I'd have you in my heart," she said quietly, hoping she had found the words that conveyed the true depth of her love for Judit.

Judit smiled. Then her face took on a strange aspect. She swung her legs down from the arm of the chair, leaned forward, and pursed her lips. Katalin went on alert. Whenever Judit pursed her lips, she was about to say something she expected Katalin wouldn't like.

"Do you know what's funny about all this? You're feeling sorry for yourself because everyone is talking about you. How would you feel if you were I and *no* one talked about you? How would you feel if you were I and always felt invisible!" Judit looked directly into Katalin's eyes. "When you're around, I don't exist for anyone, including my parents. It's Katalin this and Katalin that and Katya's so brilliant and so beautiful and so wonderful. What about me? Did anyone give me an application for Salzburg? Did anyone ask me if I wanted to study in New York? Did anyone moon over the way I played? No. And do you know why that's so sinful? Because I'm damn good. I played that Chopin better than most. But next to you, I'm nothing. Sometimes, Katya, much as I love you, I want to scratch your eyes out."

Big, fat, sad tears rolled down Katalin's cheeks as a wave of guilt for her selfishness washed over her. Judit had always been so offhanded about the varying degrees of their talents, had seemed so indifferent to the fuss surrounding Katalin's steady rise to prominence. She appeared so sure of herself in every other way that it had never occurred to Katalin that Judit might feel insecure about anything. Yet when she thought about what Judit had said, she knew it had to be true.

How could I be so completely unaware, so completely out of touch with what's going on around me? she asked herself. *Because I'm too involved with myself. Because I'm too involved with my music. Because I'm simply too pink.*

She rose from her bed and went to her friend, wrapping her arms around Judit and holding her close.

"I love you," she said. "I would die rather than hurt you. You do know that, don't you?"

Judit returned Katalin's embrace and offered a tenuous smile of appeasement. "You can't help being who and what you are, Katya. Just as I can't help being who and what I am. Most of the time, we're good together. Every once in a while, though, it's tough."

An awkward silence fell between them like a sheer curtain, separating them with a veil of unalterable truth. They could see through it, but because they couldn't reach beyond it, neither one could heal the other's pain.

"Why don't you enter the Salzburg?" Katalin said, suddenly inspired.

Judit didn't answer right away. Katalin didn't know whether she was considering the idea or measuring her words. Judit was doing both.

"I thought about that," Judit said, "but it's a major competition and there's only one first prize. Since no one asked, I don't have to go, and frankly I'm glad. I don't want to work myself to death memorizing a complex repertoire. I don't want to compete. And," she said, verbalizing for the first time something she felt she had to say and Katalin had to hear, "I don't want to come in second to you, again."

A week later Zoltán surprised Andras with a visit to his office at the Academy.

"What can I do for you?" Andras's voice was stilted, his posture stiff. Though he motioned for Zoltán to take a seat, there was no warmth, no real hospitality in the gesture.

"I wanted to ask what you planned to include in Katalin's program," Zoltán said, hoping he had struck the right chord of deference.

"What I planned?" Andras said with high indignation. "Why ask me? I didn't plan for Katalin to enter the Salzburg Competition. This is your idea, Zoltán. You make up her program!"

For emphasis, Andras took the score he had been marking and slapped it down on his desk, rattling a sheaf of papers in its wake.

"You're her tutor," Zoltán said patiently. "She'll need your help if she's going to win."

"What if I don't want her to win? What if I think sending her away is wrong?" Andras clasped his hands in front of him and leaned forward, glowering disapproval. Zoltán responded with bemused indulgence.

"Of course you want her to win. The Salzburg is one of the most famous of all the competitions. She'll be competing against the best pianists in the world, just as you'll be competing against the best tutors. If she wins, you win."

Andras shook his head. "No. If she wins, you win, Zoltán. She'll go to New York and study at Juilliard."

Zoltán moved his chair closer to the desk. His expression grew serious, yet there was no challenge in his eyes when he leaned forward and said, "Would that really be so terrible, Andras? Would it really be such a bad move for Katalin?"

"What's wrong with the Academy?" Andras demanded, sitting back in his chair, distancing himself from Zoltán.

"Nothing. And nothing is wrong with you, my friend. I simply feel that if Katalin's ever going to reach her full potential, if she's ever going to become the international star we both know she's capable of being, she needs to leave Hungary. She needs the exposure she can get at Juilliard and the contacts she can make in America. Here, she's a prisoner of the state. She can only play in Eastern Bloc countries and only the music they allow. Is that the kind of future you want for her?"

Andras wanted desperately to protest, to mount a case for Katalin's remaining under his exclusive tutelage, but Zoltán had slashed most of his arguments, cleaving them with the sharp blade of political reality. What he said about exposure and contacts was true. What he said about Katalin's ability to tour being limited by the government was also true. The larger, more important question, however, remained: How did Andras view Katalin's future? Through her eyes or his?

"I want what's best for Katalin," Andras said firmly. "I always have."

"I don't doubt that."

"From the time she was three years old I have done everything within my power to guide her toward greatness. I was under the impression that you and Mária approved of my work. Obviously, that's no longer true."

"I never said that."

"Then what are you saying?" Andras was fighting to hold back tears. Zoltán didn't know what he would do if the battle was lost.

"What do you honestly think of Juilliard, Andras?"

Zoltán counted the seconds before Andras answered.

"It's an excellent school of music."

"Then what would be so terrible if Katalin studied there?"

Andras's sallow skin flushed red, as the resentment he had been harboring for a week sought release.

"Stop it!" he shouted, jumping up from behind his desk, flailing his arms like a windmill. "This has nothing to do with Juilliard or the Academy. This is all about you and me."

"What are you talking about?" Zoltán's facade shattered like a piece of glass as the two men faced off.

"I'm talking about you and your eternal bitterness at not being able to play the violin."

Zoltán stood so quickly, he overturned the chair he was sitting on.

"What does that have to do with anything?"

"It has everything to do with why you're taking Katalin away from me." Andras's attenuated face rounded with indignation. "You're jealous! Don't you see that? You hate what you're doing and you hate me because I'm doing what you want to do. I'm playing. I'm teaching. I'm still involved with music." Andras stopped his ranting long enough to look closely at the man opposite him. Zoltán's face was contorted with pain. Immediately, Andras's tone quieted. "As God is my witness, Zoltán, I would have done anything to have gotten you out of that cesspool before they destroyed your hands, but there was nothing I could do. What they did to you was unfair and wrong. But so is what you're doing to me."

"And what do you think I'm doing to you?"

The hollowness in Zoltán's voice alarmed Andras. His normal baritone had lowered, reverberating like an echo from deep within a cave. An uncommon chill suffused the room. Andras felt it and shivered. A space that once had been solid and impenetrable had been unlocked; the place in which Zoltán had held their friendship sacred was no longer secure. Andras knew he had trespassed where he didn't belong. He had broken the seal of Zoltán's internal crypt and demanded that he exhume a truth he preferred to keep buried. Though he regretted reopening so many old wounds, he couldn't stop himself. He, too, was angry. He, too, was hurt.

"I discovered Katalin's talent," Andras said, stating what he believed to be absolute, incontrovertible fact. "I nurtured it. I developed it. I deserve to be consulted as to how to direct it. Damn it, Zoltán, she's my protégée!"

Zoltán didn't respond. He couldn't. He was too busy grappling with ghosts. They flew in front of his face like a flock of moths, flapping, fluttering, blocking everything else from his sight. They shouted at him and haunted him with the nagging realization that Andras was right. Zoltán was jealous of Andras's ability to continue his music. He was envious of the influence Andras had on Katalin. He was tormented by no longer being able to do his life's work. And yes, he supposed he was trying to take Katalin away.

"But she's my daughter," he said to both Andras and his ghosts in a voice with no give, no room for negotiation. "I have the final say and I say she's going to Salzburg. If you don't want to train her, Andras, just say so and I'll find someone who will."

Andras wanted to scream at Zoltán, to lash out and say what was really on his mind. But he had already said too much. There were certain things that could never be said, a line that could never be crossed. Knowing that, Andras swallowed his wrath and his pride.

"I'll train her. I owe her that much."

Zoltán nodded, turned, and exited Andras's office. He offered no smile, no handshake, no comment. In his mind there was nothing more to say. Andras had a right to be angry. He had a right to feel betrayed. Zoltán had acknowledged that before he set foot in Andras's office. He had also known that in spite of his anger and his feelings of betrayal, Andras would do exactly what Zoltán wanted. Not because Andras owed Katalin anything. But because he owed Zoltán his life.

As the train from Vienna traveled through the Wachau toward Salzburg, Katalin's nose pressed against the window. As beautiful as Hungary was, its landscape lacked the startling grandeur and majesty of the Austrian countryside. Hungary was a land that rolled and swelled, but rarely peaked and soared. It had its picturesque vistas and its poetic tableaux, yet Lake Balaton, the Danube Bend, and even the mystical aura of the *puszta* paled in comparison to the glorious panorama spread before her.

The Wachau was a gorge, a segment of the Danube flanked on both sides by undulating mountains replete with vineyards. Acres of trellises laced with tangled greenery climbed the steps of the carefully terraced land.

It was an area of pure, undiluted color—vivid greens, rich browns, vibrant blues, blinding whites. Medieval villages clustered along the shore. Fortified castles perched high above the river. There was Dürnstein, where Richard the Lionhearted was imprisoned in 1193; Göttweig, an imposing Benedictine abbey; Melk, originally the seat of the Babenberg family, who preceded the Habsburgs; Maria Taferl, the two-towered pilgrimage church.

While Andras read, Katalin feasted upon the heroic beauty rushing past her. She didn't want to read or talk or even think. For a few hours, at least, she simply wanted to be. Tuning out the sounds of the train and its passengers, she closed herself into a space defined by the breadth of her vision. For a while she focused on little things—the way the style of the houses changed from medieval to Bavarian the closer they got to Salzburg; the tiny explosions of color she spotted in the distance, flowers blooming in window boxes; how many sheep were grazing in the fields, how many cows. It felt so wonderful to be silent, to be observant, to be at one with nature instead of wrestling with her music.

For months she and Andras had labored over her program. Having marveled at Katalin's unique interpretation of the Liszt études, Andras had decided to use them, as well as Busoni's Prelude and Fugue in C minor and Schumann's *Fantasia*, for the beginning rounds. Knowing that a Romantic piece was required, and knowing that most contestants relied upon Beethoven, he had selected Schubert's transcendental Sonata in B-flat major, one of the three extraordinary sonatas composed in Schubert's last year of life. For the final round—he had no doubt Katalin would be a finalist—she was to play two concertos, one of her choice, one chosen by the judges from compositions by Mozart, Chopin, and Beethoven. Katalin's choice was a composition by Brahms, the Concerto No. 2 in B-flat major. The committee's choice, given that Salzburg was the birthplace of Mozart, would probably be one of his twenty-five concerti.

Fortunately for Katalin, her ability to memorize music was exceptional. At nineteen, she had an enormous repertoire and a sense of recall that, combined with Andras's insistence upon repeated reinforcement of skills, enabled her to perform with nearly absolute accuracy. But, as her father had reminded her before she left, flawless performances alone did not win international competitions of the magnitude of the Salzburg. Interpretation was key.

It was a basic disagreement between the two men, as it often was among the judges of competitions. Some jurors positioned themselves as classicists, maintaining that the true interpretation of a piece of music was the result of a scrupulous reading of the text.

Others looked for the pianist who re-created a work every time he played it. To them, the truly great compositions were living entities, like the leaves in spring—reborn year after year, yet never precisely the same.

Though he advocated the inclusion of spirit and emotion in Katalin's playing, basically Andras was a classicist.

Katalin, however, remained true to her genes. She believed that the goal of every musician was to produce her own greatness and that imitation made talent a slave to the past. To her, to triumph, to speak like the angels, the soul had to be granted full freedom of expression. Being inspired by those who had gone before, learning technique from those who had scaled the heights, using the discoveries of others to advance one's own skills—all were vital to a serious musician's education, but she believed her father when he said, "Without emotion, music is nothing but notes."

The train slowed as it entered the station. When it came to a stop, Andras stood and reached up to retrieve their hand baggage. "Welcome to Salzburg," he said.

As they shuffled up the aisle and climbed down off the train, Katalin tried to shake the echo of Zoltán's voice and the feel of his embrace as he bid her good-bye and wished her luck. Long ago she had vowed to be his channel, to be the one who brought the magic of music back into his life. Since then she had dedicated herself to achieving the international status he wanted for her, willingly sacrificing most of her childhood on the altar of those ambitions. Now, standing in the Salzburg station, counting the other contestants who stood alongside their tutors awaiting their luggage, she felt her heart race.

The Salzburg! Held once every four years as a prelude to the famous Salzburg Festival, and considered equal in importance to the Van Cliburn and the Tchaikovsky competitions, it attracted hundreds of pianists from all over the world. Two hundred and twenty-five would begin competing early the next morning. By the end of the first week the field would have been winnowed to forty semifinalists, and eventually, five finalists. It was a grueling experience, draining body and mind, testing not only the skills but the emotional stamina of everyone who approached the keyboard. Yet there was not a person who applied who didn't come armed with the confidence to believe he could win—and the desperation that made him feel he had to win. They traveled by car or train or plane, carrying their music and their dreams, as Katalin carried hers.

Andras addressed the cab driver in German, instructing him to take them to the Gasthof Amadeus, a small, family-run guesthouse four doors in from the corner on Getreidegasse, the main street in the Old City. Getreidegasse, the heart of Salzburg, was a winding, cobbled pathway, barely wide enough for one car and always crowded with ambling pedestrians. All along its sinuous route were dozens of quaint boutiques and restaurants and doorways that opened onto idyllic courtyards with beer gardens, coffeehouses, or arcades filled with shops. The buildings, none taller than five or six stories, each connected to the other, were of a single period, their riotous Baroque architecture and fanciful facades creating the illusion that the entire street had been carved from a rainbow. Blues and yellows and lavenders washed the fronts of elegant patrician houses. Window boxes overflowed with reds and purples and pinks. Flower stalls teemed with particolored blossoms. Copper domes and brass doors and highly polished woods emblazoned the cityscape with gold.

Adding to the visual banquet were the wrought-iron signs that adorned the doorways of every shop. Crafted by local metalworkers, each sign bore the symbol of the store's specialty—a boot for a shoe store, a bunch of grapes for a liquor store, a mortar and pestle for a pharmacy—which had been interwoven with vines or flowers or birds or stags or other forms of natural imagery. Some incorporated the name of the store as part of the frame; many did not. Some were extravagantly gilded; others were brightly painted. Together, they hung like medieval pennants tatted of metallic lace.

Katalin had never seen anything like it. She could hardly wait to unpack and explore. From Getreidegasse they strolled toward Rudolfs-Kai and the Museum Bridge. They walked slowly, enjoying the scenery and the festive atmosphere that permeated the town on this warm, sunny day. As they neared the river, a summery breeze floated up from the Salzach and brushed Katalin's face with a soft warmth that felt like cashmere against her skin. She lifted her hair off her neck, braided it, and then turned her face up to the sun, letting it kiss her cheeks with its heat. Even if it was just for the duration of their walk, Katalin was determined to forget the competition and join the ranks of the vacationers she saw all around her.

At sidewalk cafés, people lingered over cold glasses of wine or iced chocolate. In the beer gardens, frosty steins promised cool refreshment. Everywhere sightseers abounded—groups of students, honeymooners, retirees, and families dragging overheated, undernapped children from one monument to another. While Katalin and Andras and most other tourists adopted a slow, meandering gait, residents moved at a quickened pace, darting to and from the outdoor markets, in and out of the riverfront stores, back and forth to their homes. For a city with a reputation for being leisurely, Salzburg was a busy place.

When Katalin and Andras reached the bridge, they paused quayside to enjoy the magnificent view from the river's edge. Andras's eyes were drawn to the silhouette of the mighty fortress-castle, Hohensalzburg, which ruled the panorama from its elevated throne of dolomite rock. Once a stronghold and sometime residence of the archbishops of Salzburg, it rose four hundred feet above the city. It was massive and impressive, but held little interest for Katalin, who was looking back at the Old City, more intrigued by the numerous steeples and belfries that poked up out of its skyline.

"Do you know what *salz* means?" Andras asked.

"Salt, I think."

"That's right. Salzburg is the city of salt. For centuries, it was the main source of economy in the region. In olden days, because salt was scarce, the more you had, the richer you were."

Katalin laughed. The thought of people putting salt in a bank instead of money or stockpiling sacks of salt instead of gold struck her as funny.

"I like that," she said, truly fascinated. As Andras pointed out Hohensalzburg and related its history, she realized she was seeing a side of Andras Strasser she had never seen before. "How do you know all this?"

"There was a time when all I did was read."

"How did you fit it in with your practicing?"

He didn't answer. His eyes went blank, as if the scene in front of him had shifted into reverse, rewinding like a spool of film, going back to that other time.

"There was no music then." His voice had changed. It was dark now, minus the buoyancy of moments before.

"When was this?"

"A long time ago." Abruptly, Andras took her arm and steered her toward the bridge. "Come. We don't have all day."

Katalin hurried along behind him. It must have been during the war. Judit said Andras refused to talk about it. It was like a non-subject in their house, something as forbidden as pork.

Once on the right bank, they turned onto Schwarzstrasse and headed for the Mozarteum, where the early rounds of the competition would take place. As quickly as the tension had arisen between them, it had dissipated, melting into a harmless pool, like ices left too long in the sun. At the music academy, a pale blue building named in honor of Salzburg's most famous son, Katalin and Andras were escorted to the various rooms where the contestants would perform. Katalin was permitted several minutes alone in each room to test the pianos. After playing a few arpeggios, running scales and some chord combinations, she jotted notes as to what, if anything, she might need done to each one to have it tuned to her liking.

Afterward, a guide took them out back into the garden. It was a lovely spot featuring a small wooden summerhouse.

"This is where Mozart finished composing his last opera, *The Magic Flute*," the guide told them, with no small amount of pride. "This pavilion was originally built for his home in Vienna. It was brought here a century ago. We call it *Zauberflötenhäuschen*, 'the little Magic Flute house.' "

"For a little house, that's a very big word," Andras whispered to Katalin as they waved farewell to the guide and cut through the gardens to Schloss Mirabell. "And people think Hungarian is difficult."

If Katalin needed additional motivation to push her beyond the opening rounds of the competition, she found it in the breathtakingly beautiful gold and marble hall where the semifinals would be performed. Situated on the second floor of the Mirabell Palace, it was a jewel of a room, small as concert halls went, but so unbelievably glorious that Katalin felt a tremor of excitement.

High-ceilinged, illuminated by imposing chandeliers that dripped hundreds of crystal teardrops, it was a glittery salon of white and gold. The walls were of gleaming, rich-looking marble, decorated with gilded moldings and towering mirrors that reflected the imperial splendor of the room. Enormous gilt-wood consoles banked beneath the mirrors held candelabra. As Katalin stood in the center of the room she closed her eyes and imagined those candelabra filled with long white candles, flickering on a night in another century when perhaps Mozart had come to entertain on the white piano that held court at the far end of the room. She wanted to sit at that piano, on the platform in the alcove from which the host and hostess of this stately palace had watched their guests as they waltzed or sat on gilded chairs listening to a musicale. She wanted to feel her hands on that keyboard, to hear her music rise from the belly of the white grand, rebound off the marble walls and fill the room with a majesty one could neither see nor touch, but could only experience through other senses.

"Uncle Andras! I've never performed anywhere this special," Katalin whispered, her eyes glistening at the thought of it.

Andras smiled. This young woman had already performed in most of the major houses in Eastern Europe. Not one of them had been plain or unimpressive, yet he understood how she felt. This room was different. Perhaps it was the romance of the Mirabell, built in 1606 by the Archbishop Wolf Dietrich for his mistress, Salome Alt, and considered by many the Taj Mahal of Salzburg.

"You will play here, Katya," Andras said, shaking his finger at her with mock severity. "But only if you practice."

Katalin groaned, but her mouth curled into a dreamy smile as she and Andras headed back to the Mozarteum, where he had reserved a practice studio.

Katalin's wish to take her place at the white Bösendorfer at the Mirabell Palace was about to be fulfilled. Despite the unmitigated heat, which became almost a hostile presence, she had breezed through the first round. Her Chopin had been masterful, her Busoni exquisite, but to those who had listened in rapt astonishment, both had paled in comparison to the power she extracted from the Schumann.

The semifinals had been going on for five days. She was the last contestant to play. As she took her bow and seated herself on the white leather bench, she drank in the scene. The chandeliers, their lights dimmed, cast a gentle yellow glow on the room. The candelabra on the consoles were lit, just as she had imagined they would be. On a pedestal next to the piano was a vase filled with white flowers. On either side of the stage were wrought-iron *torchères* with eight-branched candelabra, also lit. In the back, behind the massive assemblage of chairs, the windows were opened and sheer white curtains billowed softly in the evening breeze.

It was late. Owing to the heat and the length of the competition, the audience had lapsed into a drowsy, languorous state. Katalin breathed deeply, raised her hands, and began to play the Liszt études. Immediately the crowd was roused, startled into wakefulness by the audaciousness of her performance.

Andras stood in the back, listening, attempting to analyze what he saw written on the faces of the jurors. They were alert and eager for her to continue.

Katalin invested the Schubert with a bravura and beauty rarely experienced in competitions. For forty minutes she fused herself with Franz Schubert. She became the one dying, the one reaching for life, grasping for that last breath of inspiration before the music would be eternally silenced. As she played she paid homage to this thirty-one-year-old man—who rarely had a piano to compose on, didn't earn more than forty-three dollars throughout his lifetime from his music, and was often dismissed as merely a writer of songs—by ravishing his final burst of creativity. When she played the second movement, the *andante sostenuto*, she marveled at the genius required to pen something this heavenly, this romantic. Since she knew Schubert to be a poet, a man kissed with a sense of lyricism that made him one of the greatest melodists of all time, she allowed him to interpret himself. She let his music flow through her like a brook, bubbling without rest, moving and enchanting until the very last note. When she had finished, laid her hands in her lap, and bowed her head, she was greeted with an unprecedented ovation. Onlookers and judges alike disregarded protocol and expressed their approval with thunderous applause.

That night, Katalin and Andras celebrated at a small restaurant that sat in the shadow of the mighty Mönchsberg, the mountain ridge that dominated the Old City. Over *Tafelspitz* and *Röstkartoffeln*—boiled beef and roast potatoes—they reviewed her performance and discussed the finals.

"We've agreed upon Mozart's Concerto Number Twenty-one in C major," Andras said, sipping the froth off his beer. "Four days from tonight you will mount the stage at the Festspielhaus. Again, you're scheduled to be the last performer. Does that bother you?"

Katalin didn't have to think before answering. "I know how I play the C major and I know how I play the Brahms." She grinned at him and pinched his cheek. "It doesn't matter when I play. I'm going to win!"

Andras chuckled, but then he grew silent. After a time he sipped his beer and looked deep into Katalin's eyes.

"And when you win, you'll go to New York. How do you feel about that?"

Whether Katalin realized it or not, she had been preparing her answer to that question for a long time.

"I love you, Uncle Andras," she said. "Next to my parents, you're the most important person in my life. If not for you I wouldn't ever have had the chance even to consider whether I should go to Juilliard or stay at the Franz Liszt. I never would have learned to love the piano the way I do or be as good as I am. You've been my tutor and my friend, and for that, I'll always be grateful." She paused. Andras looked at her expectantly. "But I think Papa's right. If I can move on, I should. Not because you aren't an exceptional tutor, but because I need to grow as a performer. I need to experience new things, new ideas, new surroundings." She laughed a little, as if she had tried to envision herself wandering around New York City. "Don't get me wrong—I'm frightened to death. Judit is the adventurer, not me. The thought of going so far away from my family, being with strangers in a strange place—it's terrifying. But I think it would be good for me. What I'd like to hear is that you think it would be good for me. I'd like your blessing."

Andras was not an impulsive man. His life was measured, as if a metronome ticked in his brain, clicking back and forth in a steady, unalterable rhythm, regulating his movements and his emotions. When he reached out and offered Katalin an impromptu embrace, he was as surprised as she.

"Of course you have my blessing, Katya!" He shook his head and brushed a hand across his eyes, quickly, as if he didn't want her to see the tears he was wiping away. "God knows I want whatever is best for you. I have since the moment you sat down next to me at the piano and picked out those first few notes. But I've been selfish. I've wanted to keep you with me so I could be the only one privileged enough to act as caretaker of your enormous talent." He took her hand in his and squeezed it. "Your Papa is right. At Juilliard you will make the contacts you need to enlarge your spotlight. In no time you'll be known throughout the world. Your name will be famous. And when it is, little Katya, just remember there's a man in Budapest named Andras Strasser who always believed in you. And always will."

"Our last finalist, from Budapest, Hungary, is nineteen years old and is a student at the Franz Liszt Academy of Music. Ladies and gentlemen, Miss Katalin Gáspár."

As Katalin took the stage she was greeted by polite applause and

looks of surprise. Custom decreed that performers wore black. Katalin
had done so for the first two rounds, just as she always did for public
appearance. Tonight, however, she was dressed in white, with a glorious
hand-embroidered fringed shawl tied around her hips. That morning,
Andras had given her a package Mária had given him. If Katalin made
the finals, Andras was to give this to her for good luck. The note Mária
had included said simply, "Know that you are always wrapped in our
love." Katalin knew that Mária had intended for her to wear the shawl
as a covering going to and from the Festspielhaus, not when she was
onstage, but despite all her displays of confidence, Katalin was feeling
shaky. She felt she needed all the luck she could get. If she had to go
against tradition by wearing her luck, so be it.

Trying to ignore the audience and maintain her composure, Katalin
started for the piano. The house was full. The orchestra was waiting. But
instead of taking her place at the keyboard, Katalin broke with tradition
a second time. She reversed her step and took the microphone. Standing
before a stunned group of more than a thousand people, she turned
toward the wings and, so that everyone could understand, spoke in German to the dark-haired man with the navy blue suit and bright red bow
tie he always wore for her concerts.

"I'd like to dedicate my performance tonight to my tutor and my
friend, Herr Andras Strasser." In Hungarian, she added, "Köszönöm."
Thank you.

Having done what she wanted to do, regardless of whether it was
good form or bad, Katalin took her place at the piano and nodded to the
conductor.

Katalin had played Brahms's B-flat many times, but on this night it
was reborn with stunning energy, lush with lyricism and sensuality, as
Katalin reached deep into her own core to extract a passionate sonority
that reached beyond the stage to touch the humanity of everyone present.

Though this concerto was considered pianistically awkward and physically demanding, Katalin's fingers galloped over the keys with such technical precision and such melodic grandeur, even the least educated ears
recognized the sound of something special. Yet while the audience was
entranced, the judges listened with keen attentiveness. It was not unusual
for those performing the B-flat to try to create a virtuosic opportunity.
Brahms concerti were not vehicles for that sort of display. They were
works of great dignity, composed by a perfectionist whose highest concern
was thematic content and masterly development.

Andras had brought her recordings so that Katalin could hear the results of pianistic excess, the consequences of allowing ego to triumph over sensitive, intelligent interpretation. *When playing Brahms, restraint is power,* he said. Remembering that, Katalin reined against temptation as she strove to wrest from the work the full ardor of the composer, the searing sensitivity that was the heart of Brahms's flame.

When the final chord had been struck, waves of applause shook the concert hall. Katalin rose from the bench slowly, somewhat overwhelmed. With a graceful curtsy and a shy smile she acknowledged her audience and then made a hasty exit. She had five minutes to clear her head and prepare for the Mozart.

Andras was waiting with a glass of water and a moist towel.

"You did well, Katya," he said with typical laconism. "Very well."

Accustomed to his reserve, Katalin searched his eyes. They were smiling, even if his mouth was not. Reassured, she sat, took the glass from him, and sipped the water slowly, letting its coolness slide down her throat. She closed her eyes and tilted her head back, resting against a wall. Andras swabbed her brow and then stepped aside. They both knew she was shifting gears, calming the drama that was Brahms, summoning the delicacy that was Mozart.

"This is the harder part, isn't it, Uncle Andras?" Her eyes remained closed. Her voice trembled slightly.

Andras understood her nervousness. Because each finalist was playing a Mozart concerto, the challenge was to rise above the similarity of the material, to find a way to make Katalin's Mozart unique. He squatted alongside her chair and took her hands in his. She opened her eyes.

"Do you want to win?" he asked.

"Yes." With her decision that indeed she wanted to go to New York, winning the Salzburg had become imperative.

"How badly?"

She smiled and gave him the response she knew he wanted. "They are Clementi. I am Mozart."

As Andras nodded and returned her grin, she heard her name. She stood and faced her mentor. He kissed both her cheeks, patted her arm, and sent her back onstage.

From their first meeting until his final days, Wolfgang Amadeus Mozart hated Muzio Clementi. Mozart was considered the prince of the piano, the greatest Austrian pianist. Clementi, an Italian-born English virtuoso, was gaining in reputation and was viewed by many cognoscenti to be the greatest pianist outside of Austria. To the Austrian Emperor

Joseph II, the notion of having those two men face off against each other in his salon was simply too exhilarating to resist.

The first salvo was an improvised prelude by Clementi, followed by his own Sonata in B-flat and a toccata, one of his specialities. Mozart countered with his own prelude improvisation followed by a set of variations. Then each musician was handed a sonata of Paisiello, which they were asked to sight-read, Mozart playing the allegros, Clementi the adagios and rondos. Both were then asked to select a theme and develop it, accompanying each other, providing harmonics for each other, moving the lead back and forth until the evening ended in a two-piano explosion of sound. Alas, there was no decisive victory. Some said that Clementi, the more emotional, more dramatic pianist of the two, won. Others claimed Mozart's taste and elegance had prevailed and that he had excelled, just as the Emperor had expected.

One hundred and eighty-seven years later, Katalin Gáspár was involved in a competition every bit as challenging. What she must do now was prove—not to the audience but to the judges—that she was superior to all of them, past and present.

As she played the majestic, complex concerto, she concentrated on the legato—Mozart's most significant contribution to the development of piano technique. Before Mozart, the finger was lifted from the key just before the following note was played. There was no elision, no binding together of sounds, no blending of one moment with the next. Mozart broke with the tradition of the day by connecting consecutive notes, joining them in a seamless entity that made music "flow like oil."

Katalin moved through the piece with the spirited control of one whose soul was in harmony with the music, underlining Mozart's delicate eighteenth-century manners with her own contemporary passion. What Katalin gave the judges was classical music performed by a romantic, modern music interpreted by a classicist. What she gave the audience was a musical interlude of rare beauty. What she gave herself was the intense personal satisfaction of knowing that no matter what happened, she had played her best.

It took an hour for the judges to tally their scores. When they had reached a decision, Katalin, two young men from the Soviet Union, a Japanese girl, and a German boy took their places on the stage. Trying to stay calm during the requisite speeches and thank-yous, Katalin considered, for the millionth time, what it would mean to study in New York. The musician, the being who craved musical expression and couldn't exist without creating sound, yearned for the chance to expand her horizons. The daughter, the child whose motivation had been consistently fired by the obligation she felt toward her father, longed to complete the resurrection of Zoltán's celebrity by adding the name Gáspár to the galaxy of Salzburg winners. Like a toddler hoping to have a special wish granted, she hid her hands beneath Mária's shawl and crossed her fingers.

They called the Japanese girl to the microphone to receive the bronze medal and Katalin experienced a spasm of horrible panic, an inner hysteria that prompted thoughts like *I would've taken third . . . I'd have been happy with third . . . I would've placed . . . it would be over.* They called the name of one of the Soviet boys, placed the silver medal around his neck, and Katalin's body shook. Any second her failure would be made public. Finally they came to the winner of the gold medal. First prize at the Salzburg Piano Competition was awarded to Katalin Gáspár, who bowed her head and silently thanked God and Mária and Andras and Mozart and Franz Liszt and anyone else in the universe who might have made this moment possible.

When she took the microphone, however, she grasped the medal in her hand and thanked one person—"my greatest inspiration, my father, Zoltán Gáspár."

Zoltán read the telegram again:

KATALIN WON FIRST PRIZE AT THE SALZBURG. SHE DESERVED IT. SO DO YOU AND MÁRIA. CONGRATULATIONS. ANDRAS.

He wept as his eyes scanned the words, his emotions in turmoil. All the while she had been in Austria, Zoltán had assiduously avoided any examination of the consequences of his actions or the motivations behind them. Yet now, alone in his apartment, confronted with a *fait accompli*, he surrendered to the process of introspection.

From the start Andras had seen what Zoltán had tried to deny: Katalin's entrance in this competition was more important to Zoltán than it was to Katalin. He could protest all he wanted, but to Andras, to Mária, and probably to others, it was heartbreakingly clear that it was *his* talent he wanted judged, his skills he wanted tested. He meant it when he said that he wanted her to fulfill her potential, just as he honestly believed that studying at Juilliard was in her best interests. He was well-meaning; he loved Katalin and took great pleasure in her achievements, but there was a darker side.

Zoltán still harbored a terrible, seething resentment at the brutal cessation of his musical career. He had learned to live with his deprivation, repressing all outward signs of pain, but inside, where no one else could see, he had refused to admit this state of silence as a final and irrevocable condition. Though his hands were no longer able, his soul continued to burn with the desire; in this he was not unlike a priest who had taken his vows, willingly lived the life of a celibate, but had never fully accepted the notion that he would never again lie with a woman.

Though he hated himself for feeling this way, whenever Zoltán heard Katalin perform he became profoundly conflicted—jealous, yet proud; paternal, yet competitive. As much as he wanted for Katalin— and he wanted the world for her—he still wanted for himself. He wanted to hold a bow in his hands, to caress the strings of his violin, to make it sing and laugh and cry. He wanted to stand on a stage and electrify an audience with the power of his gift. He wanted to feel that wild exhilaration that comes only from the realization of one's life force. In his dreams he still did those things. But only in his dreams.

He stared at the telegram, letting the words blur as he envisioned Katalin onstage. He tried to hear her, to see her as she displayed the immensity of her talent. He tried to place her on a concert stage in America, in Paris, in London. This was what he had wanted, or so he had believed until it had become reality. Now that it had, Zoltán was having difficulty dealing with the fact that his daughter was going to leave him and he had initiated the leaving. She was going to fly to a foreign land where he couldn't direct her progress or measure her growth or watch the changes he knew would take place. She was still young, a girl just becoming a woman, a talent who soon would become a star.

What if she fell in love? What if she became so popular in the West, she refused to come home for fear of never being able to leave? *What if he never saw her again?*

They were all there—Zoltán, Mária, Ilona, Judit—happy, yet sad; excited, yet unsure about what was going to happen next, as Andras set down their suitcases in the Gáspár apartment and draped his arm protectively around Katalin's shoulders. Holding her next to him, staid, calm, starched Andras Strasser shouted, "Why are you all standing around looking so glum? We won! Katalin is going to New York!" His smile was so broad and so bright and so sincere, Zoltán and Ilona were too dumbstruck to react. That left Katalin to Mária and Judit. They ran to her and enveloped her in a tight circle of love and pride, feeding her with hugs and giggles and kisses.

Though Ilona was thrilled for Katalin, she kept searching her husband's face for clues. Was he as happy as he appeared? Had he resolved his conflict about Katalin's going to Juilliard? As if he had read her mind, Andras approached Zoltán and Ilona.

"Well, old friend," he said, pumping Zoltán's hand. "How does it feel to be the father of the winner of the Salzburg Competition?"

"It feels wonderful!" Zoltán said, gladly accepting Andras's embrace. "How does it feel to be the one responsible for her success?"

Andras thought for a moment and replied, "Prideful. Yes, that's it. I feel proud for all that I have been able to contribute." His smile faded and then returned, as if a cloud had passed fleetingly overhead. "Katalin competed against some major talents, and believe me, she didn't just win. She overwhelmed the other finalists. What's more, she relished the experience. You were right, Zoltán, and I was wrong. She's like a flower yearning to burst into full blossom. She needs to be in the light she'll find in New York, not in the shadows of Eastern Europe." He took his old friend's hand and squeezed it. "Now," he said before both men became more emotional than they wished, "how about a drink?"

"With pleasure!"

When everyone had an apricot brandy, Zoltán kissed his daughter and held her to him, his face a portrait of admiration and gratitude. He raised his glass to make a toast, but his heart was too full to speak. Feeling helpless, he looked to Mária, but her eyes were filled with tears.

In the end it was Judit who stepped into the center of the room and faced her friend. "As Kovács Attila says, 'Experience is not what happens to a man; it's what a man does with what happens to him.'" A broad, loving grin dominated her mouth as she raised her glass toward Katalin. "We know you'll make us proud, Katya. You always have. But because you're going so far away for such a long time, we just want you to remember one thing."

"What's that?"

"Don't forget us."

Katalin's gaze rested on Judit and then moved on to take in Andras, Ilona, Zoltán, and Mária. "That's not possible," she said, buoyed by their affection and caring. "That's simply not possible."

As Katalin moved forward to hug Judit, Ilona sidled up to Zoltán and stuffed a piece of paper into his pocket. He turned, but already her back was to him and she appeared deep in conversation with Mária. Finding an excuse, he retreated into the kitchen and hurriedly pulled the note from his pocket. It had been months since he had made his request—months, and Ilona had not given him so much as a hint as to whether she intended to do as he had asked. Though he wasn't a spiritual man, nor was he plagued by superstition, there had been times when he had felt compelled to believe that perhaps he had been cursed, that an angel with blackened wings had swooped over his cradle, damning him to a life of constant reprobation. Did this note herald yet another punishment? Would the paper be blank or, worse, hold the message that Zsuzsanna was nowhere to be found or that, God forbid, his sister and his brother-in-law were dead? His fingers shook as he unfolded the paper. It wasn't often that Zoltán Gáspár spoke to God, but as he reread Ilona's note, he offered thanks to her, and to Him.

Zsuzsanna, 352 East 74th Street, New York, New York.

12

New York, New York

*B*efore Katalin had finished with customs and immigration, she had seen enough of New York to know that it terrified her. If Kennedy Airport was any indication, this city was too big, too loud, and too confusing for someone as unsophisticated as she to manage. Throughout the long flight from Frankfurt she had tried to steel herself for her entrance into America, but, Katalin admitted now, nothing could have prepared her for the chaos that greeted her. Five planes had landed within minutes of each other, disgorging hundreds of travel-weary passengers eager to end their journeys in the least amount of time possible.

Once she had her passport and visa stamped by immigration, Katalin dragged her two suitcases into a large hall teeming with humanity. For the moment, she stood frozen in place. Before her was a frenzied mass moving at top speed. She felt as if she were watching a strange new sport in which people pulling dollies or toting suitcases fought their way toward invisible goalposts.

Hoping to avoid injury, Katalin took a deep breath and plunged headlong into the fray, sprinting toward the nearest line and holding her ground against a woman and her screaming child. While waiting for a customs agent to examine her luggage, she glanced up at the long glass wall that ran the entire length of the hall, where family and friends waited for international arrivals to conclude the tedious business of entering the country.

Her eyes scanned the faces pressed against the glass, hoping to spot her aunt and uncle. A cursory glance unnerved her. There was no one up there she recognized. Trying to calm herself, she recalled that her last view of them had been eleven years ago, that awful night in the abandoned church. Better to visualize them from a happier time, she decided. Quickly, she backtracked to the afternoon of her first recital. Then, Zsuzsanna had appeared small but statuesque, lively and spirited, with reddish hair, a smile as quick as her temper, and a bawdy laugh that made the most innocent joke sound risqué. Mihai was larger but quieter, more the observer than the participant. Katalin could hear Zsuzsanna singing and then laughing delightedly when Judit had taken Mihai's hands and embarrassed him into dancing with her in the middle of the living room. But as much as she tried to banish the image, she kept seeing that last night: Zsuzsanna looking at her through tear-filled eyes, mouthing the words *I love you* as she left the church; Mihai's strong hands on her face as he had bent down to kiss her good-bye.

Katalin searched the crowd anxiously. No one looked familiar. She searched again. A well of panic rose within her as, one by one, she eliminated people from consideration. *Where were they?*

Katalin began to wonder whether Zoltán's letter with the date and time of her arrival had reached the Pals. Though she had been granted full permission to come to New York—the Salzburg Competition was too public an event for its winner to be forced to forfeit its prize—Mihai and Zsuzsanna were still on the government's Wanted list. No letters to Zsuzsanna were sent through regular post. Those—and both Katalin and Judit were more than a little intrigued by this—were handled by Ilona. Had those letters gone astray?

"Anything to declare?" A huge man with florid skin and a bushy salt-and-pepper moustache, reminiscent of a Lewis Carroll walrus, barked at her. "Food, plants, alcohol, animals?"

She shook her head at each suggestion, waiting for him to attack her denials or to demand that she open her suitcases and empty them in front of everyone. Instead, with a wave of his thick hand, she was dismissed. She slid her bags off the bench before the official could change his mind. She felt totally at sea and unsure about where to go next.

"Through the double doors," the walrus said, his kind, sympathetic tone in opposition to his gruff visage. "And welcome to America."

She returned his smile and proceeded through the double doors, wondering who, if anyone, would be there to welcome her on the other side.

"Katya! Katya! Here. I'm here!" A blond in a too-tight red dress pushed her way through the crowd and threw her arms around Katalin.

Though the face and the body of the woman hugging her were those of a total stranger, the voice was familiar.

"You're so grown-up, so beautiful," Zsuzsanna said, speaking in rapid Hungarian, holding Katalin at arm's length so she could admire her niece. "*Jésuz Mária*. Am I happy you're here!" Her eyes puddled. She bit her heavily rouged lip to control the tears. "I've been counting the days, the minutes, the seconds!" She sighed, and because her breath crossed with her emotions, her bosom fluttered like a bird caught in the wind. "Come," she said, after she had settled herself. "You've had a long trip. Let's go home."

If Katalin thought that sounded odd at the airport, it became even more bizarre during their trip to Manhattan. *Home*. Home was not a succession of ugly brown buildings and garish billboards and dirty factories. It was not a highway jammed with big cars and angry drivers. Home was Budapest with its stately hills and its wide boulevards and the mighty Danube flowing through its center. It was a place where people rode bicycles and trolleys, and even the buildings bearing the bullet-ridden scars of war possessed an aura of grace. Katalin wasn't certain what she had expected, but she knew that what she was seeing wasn't it. Where was the America she had heard so much about? Where was the glorious New World?

"Tell me about my brother Zoltán," Zsuzsanna said, unable to take her eyes off Katalin, unwilling to let go of her hand. "And my darling Mária and the Strassers. I'm starved for information."

Katalin filled her in as best she could, attempting to encapsulate eleven years into thirty minutes, at the same time trying to deal with an onslaught of homesickness. They came to a bridge that traversed a body of water Zsuzsanna identified as the East River. Inconsequential, Katalin decided—no match for the mighty Danube. The bridge they were on? Several others she could see in the distance? Totally lacking in majesty. Spans in Budapest, Prague, even Salzburg, were elegantly built, with ferocious stone lions guarding grand entries, or graceful lanterns lighting one's way, or other cultivated architectural embellishments. These modern links were little more than metal skeletons with no soul, no heart. Even the skyline, with its titanic towers, appeared overdone.

Even more disturbing was the way Zsuzsanna had changed. Each time Katalin tried to ask about Mihai and the Kardos children, Zsuzsanna parried with another question about a long-lost friend or neighbor. Why would her aunt not answer her questions? Zsuzsanna's appearance had also changed. She had put on weight, but that didn't upset Katalin as much as the peroxide-blond hair and the overly made-up face. Katalin supposed that Zsuzsanna had always been a sensuous woman—Katalin was able to define it now, though she wouldn't have understood that word then—but now her aunt looked obvious, like one of those big advertisements that crowded the roadsides like weeds. Her dress was too low-cut, too tight, too red, too everything for Katalin's sheltered sensibility. Could it be that this was the fashion in New York?

Before Katalin realized what was happening, the taxi pulled up in front of a five-story red brick building. Most of the windows were open. Some held big electric fans. Others acted as balconies from which the apartment dwellers observed the life of the neighborhood. The instant Zsuzsanna and Katalin stepped onto the sidewalk, several of them shouted greetings.

"*Jó estét*, Zsuzsanna. Is that her?"

"*Igen*," she called in reply. "This is Katalin."

"*Szép!*"

"Of course she's beautiful," Zsuzsanna said, feigning offense. "She looks exactly like me."

The women laughed as Zsuzsanna opened the door to the building and ushered Katalin inside.

"I'm afraid we have to lug these things up three flights of stairs."

"It's okay," Katalin said, again feeling a blanket of disappointment fold around her. She had expected Zsuzsanna to be living in a better neighborhood, in a more impressive apartment. Here, the hallway was dark, the air musty with stale cooking smells. The walls, painted a sickly yellow, were cracked, lined and peeling like an old man's skin. The lighting was poor and the stairs looked as if they needed repair. Considering that Katalin had envisioned her aunt in a house only slighter smaller than the White House, 352 East 74th Street was a big letdown.

Sensing her niece's disillusionment, Zsuzsanna stopped on the second landing, turned, and faced Katalin squarely.

"I know what you're thinking," she said. "And you're right. This isn't a castle and I'm not Empress Maria Theresa. I'm sorry to break it to you so quickly, but the American dream isn't all we were led to believe. The streets are not paved with gold. Money doesn't grow on trees and every pot doesn't have a chicken stewing." She shrugged her shoulders and chuckled, exhibiting the docile acquiescence of one who long ago had come to terms with the differences between daydreams and everyday. "Life is hard here, Katya. As you can see, I'm far from rich. I have a business. I do all right. But it's not the way I thought it would be."

"Then why didn't you come home?" Katalin's voice was sharp, edged with pique. All these years she had believed that Zsuzsanna and Mihai had found the rainbow's end. That fantasy—that their lives were so much better—had made the pain of missing them less acute; the crushing void she felt from their absence, more tolerable. To learn that their reality wasn't Elysian and that still they chose to live away from their families seemed insulting.

"It wasn't the lure of money that brought me here and it's not the prospect of great wealth that keeps me here. It's the freedom, Katya, the total freedom. I come and go as I please. I say what I want, do what I want. So I don't always get everything I want. It may not be perfect, but it's a hell of a lot better than what I left behind."

Katalin was tempted to argue, to rise once again to the defense of her homeland by reminding Zsuzsanna that she and Mihai had left more than eleven years ago in the midst of an exceptionally terrible time, that things had eased a bit since then, but when Zsuzsanna continued, Katalin realized that no matter how she wanted it to be, the essence of oppression that had caused Zsuzsanna to leave remained.

"We have policemen," her aunt said, "but they're not barbarians like the AVO. They don't stand on every corner spying, hoping to catch you on some minor infraction so they can throw you into Fő Street prison and torture you just for the fun of it. They don't break into your house in the middle of the night and cart you off to some ferocious labor camp." Like a sudden fever, an anger Zsuzsanna had repressed but hadn't resolved flared and flushed her cheeks. Her body trembled and hot tears threatened her eyes. Seconds later, the storm passed. Smiling as if nothing had happened, she leaned forward and stroked Katalin's cheek. "I know how strange all of this is for you, Katya, but give it time. I have faith in New York. Soon, it will work its magic on you."

With a knowing laugh, she retrieved Katalin's suitcase and trundled up the stairs to her three-room flat.

Stepping across the threshold of Zsuzsanna's home was like stumbling onto a memory. Though the furnishings weren't the same, Zsuzsanna had replicated her apartment in Budapest. A tiny floral print papered the walls. Lacy white curtains fell in gentle folds beneath an ornate velvet cornice the color of garnets. Stretched across one wall a long, plump divan dressed in wool of a brighter red dominated the small room. Strewn with throw pillows covered with lace or edged with fringe, it looked as if it might have been more at home in a harem, but Zsuzsanna had always preferred fussy over plain, so to Katalin it looked just right. A faded chintz that must have been startling when it was new upholstered two armchairs—also overstuffed, also drowning in a sea of pillows. Lamps with fringed shades, end tables dressed with lace doilies, a coffee table laden with knickknacks, and a wooden footstool with a needlepoint seat joined the other furnishings on top of a rug that begged for repair. On the wall opposite the couch there was a fireplace that looked as if it hadn't worked in twenty years, if then. Over the mantel hung a large mirror in a wooden frame painted harlot red. Smaller mirrors, pictures in inexpensive frames, extraneous curiosities, and a collection of concert programs featuring Hungarian artists freckled the walls, while dozens of ceramic figurines crowded every available surface.

"Come, come!" Zsuzsanna opened a door and entreated Katalin to follow.

The bedroom was even smaller and fussier than the living room, a riot of pillows tossed on the bed and flowers blooming all over the walls. It took Katalin a moment to orient herself. When she did, she noticed that the double bed was pushed into a corner. Next to it was a single bed dressed in yet another floral, this coverlet conspicuous by its newness.

"You're going to sleep in here with me." Zsuzsanna said it brightly, but Katalin could see she was nervously awaiting her niece's approval. "I don't have another bedroom, so my neighbor downstairs loaned me this bed. It's okay, yes?"

It wasn't the bed or the coverlet or the cramped space that bothered Katalin. It was something else, something more important.

"Aunt Zsuzsanna, where is Uncle Mihai?"

This was not something Zsuzsanna wanted to discuss. She had hoped to avoid it a bit longer, but clearly the time had come to explain. She motioned for Katalin to sit. She cozied into the middle of her bed, clutching one of her pillows for support.

"Mihai is in Cleveland," she said matter-of-factly. "He and I have been divorced for five years."

Katalin looked stricken.

"Don't be so upset, Katya. It wasn't ugly. It was really quite simple. When we got here, we both took whatever jobs we could find. I worked as a cook. Mihai got a job working for a moving company. After two years the man who owned the restaurant where I worked died. His wife didn't have the heart to continue running the business. Her price was high, but not out of reach. I begged Mihai, and as he always did, he indulged me. Though we had to mortgage ourselves to the sky to do it, we bought the place. We fixed it up and called it Csárda. I ran the kitchen. Mihai ran the front." She laughed and shook her head, as if two opposing thoughts had just crashed into each other, one pleasant, one not. "He hated it. You know Mihai. He's a worker. He's rough. He likes doing things with his hands. Standing at a reservation desk or tending bar made him feel foolish, almost impotent, as if he had left the man he used to be back in Csepel. Without telling me, he began to ask around about jobs in metal factories. When he heard of a foreman's job in Cleveland, he applied. When he got it, he asked me to go there with him. I asked him to stay here with me. He said no. I said no. And so, we said good-bye."

"That makes me sad," Katalin said, more than a little surprised at the casual way Zsuzsanna related the breakup of her marriage. "I loved Mihai."

"I did too, *edesem*. But it's better this way. He's happy running his factory in Cleveland. I'm happy running my restaurant in New York." Suddenly she was on her feet and taking off her clothes. "Speaking of Csárda—hurry and get changed. Tonight there's a party in your honor!"

As Katalin obeyed, unpacking, burrowing through her slender wardrobe to find something to wear, she realized that Zsuzsanna had answered only one of her questions. She still hadn't told her about Mátyás, Vera, and István.

Zsuzsanna took a roundabout route to Csárda so she could give Katalin a tour of the neighborhood. She showed her her friend's bakery, her other friend's meat market. She showed her Paprikas Weiss and H. Roth & Son, the large Hungarian food emporiums. She pointed out a shoe store, a hardware store, a dress shop, and a dry cleaner, all owned by émigrés. As they passed a row of Hungarian restaurants, Zsuzsanna issued unabridged critiques on each one, sometimes praising their food and deploring their atmosphere, other times simply deploring everything. Rarely did she praise everything.

Having made a huge circle, they arrived at the corner of 74th Street and First Avenue. There, beneath a red canopy, was a hand-carved sign proclaiming this establishment to be Csárda. Zsuzsanna nudged Katalin to go ahead. As the young girl entered, a crowd of strangers shouted greetings at her in Hungarian while waving miniature red, white, and green flags. Katalin was rattled. She didn't know any of these people, yet somehow they all looked familiar. As Zsuzsanna introduced her, she realized it was because they looked just like the people she had left behind. They were Hungarians, with Magyar eyes and bushy eyebrows and straight hair and rosy cheeks. In fact, everything she had seen since her arrival had been Hungarian. Where did America begin, she wondered?

"Sophie," Zsuzsanna called to a thin blond with a square face, a large, bumped nose, an asymmetric haircut—short on one side, longer on the other—and enormous blue eyes, which were heavily lashed. Sophie's skirt barely covered her thighs and she wore black fishnet stockings. "Sophie Wisnewski, my niece, Katalin Gáspár. Sophie's Polish, but in spite of that, she's a nice girl."

Katalin smiled and shook the other girl's hand. Inside she was experiencing a flash of anxiety. If all American girls dressed like this Wisnewski person, Katalin didn't stand a chance of fitting in. Katalin's skirt was knee-length, her blouse a loose peasant style with billowy sleeves and a drawstring neck. Her hair trailed down her back in a neat braid. Her face bore no signs of makeup, her socks were parochial-school white, her shoes sensible brown oxfords.

"Sophie waitresses for me," Zsuzsanna continued. "When she's not here, she's taking some drama classes at City College or she's shopping, although where she finds her outfits is beyond me."

"Of course it's beyond you," Sophie said, with respectful irreverence. "I shop on Thirty-fourth Street. You've never been below Sixtieth."

Zsuzsanna chuckled. "Always a joke. This girl is always making jokes."

"That's why you keep me around," Sophie said. "I make you laugh."

"That you do." Zsuzsanna reached out and affectionately pinched Sophie's cheek. Katalin experienced an unexpected twinge of jealousy. "While I show Katalin the rest of the place, why don't you tell György to start dishing out the *gulyás*."

As Zsuzsanna headed toward the main dining room, Katalin was struck by the wildly exhilarating thought that perhaps Mátyás, Vera, and István were here, that Zsuzsanna hadn't mentioned them before because they were a surprise. Unable to wait for them to jump up and wave to her, she stood on her toes and peered over Zsuzsanna's shoulder, looking at every table, into every corner. She hadn't wanted to admit it, but ever since her plans to come to New York had been made definite, she had thought about what it would be like to see the three of them again. She had dreamed of little else. Often she would awaken with a blush, realizing that for most of the night the face dominating her sleep had been István's. Over the years, she had wondered what had become of them—where they lived, how they looked, what they were doing. Yet, despite the fact that after Judit, Vera had been her closest friend, and she had liked Mátyás a great deal, there was no question that the star of her nightly fantasies was István Kardos.

"Where are you going?"

Katalin had been so eager to enter the dining room, she had nearly fallen on top of Zsuzsanna.

Katalin stepped back, feeling very embarrassed. "I thought maybe the Kardoses were here. I asked you about them and when you . . . well, sort of sidestepped it, I thought maybe you were going to surprise me. Are you? Are they here?"

Zsuzsanna grabbed Katalin's hand and pulled her back into the bar, where they could be alone. Her aspect turned somber. Katalin's excitement turned to dread.

"No, they're not here. What's worse, I have no idea where they are." She paused, shoring up the courage to tell Katalin something she wasn't going to want to hear. Katalin girded herself. "Vera never made it to the United States," Zsuzsanna said, still as grief-stricken and unbelieving as she had been standing alongside Mátyás and István in that cemetery in Andau. "She tried so hard. She was so brave and so strong, but . . ." She looked at Katalin, beseeching her to understand that she had been a caring guardian, that she had done whatever was in her power to do. "Her heart was too frail. The escape was simply too strenuous."

Without realizing it, Katalin had begun to weep. Tears of lamentation filed down her cheeks in the slow, steady cadence of mourners following a casket to the grave. Blurred images of Vera asserted themselves—Vera reading stories to her and Judit, Vera collecting soap and lard, Vera sleeping in her bed, Vera closing her eyes whenever Katalin played so she could feel the music, Vera leaning over the dying form of her mother, Margit. The only scene Katalin couldn't—wouldn't—visualize, was Vera lying dead in some small town just over the Austrian border.

"At Camp Kilmer," Zsuzsanna was saying, "things were chaotic. They weren't prepared for so many refugees at one time. Because Mihai and I were adults and needed no one to sponsor us, we were processed quickly. Though I sent Mátyás our address once we had settled, I can't swear he ever got it. I called Kilmer several times to find out what had happened to him and István. The first two times, they told me the boys were still there, that the authorities were still trying to locate a relative. The last time I called, I was told the boys were gone. When I asked for an address, no one could locate their file. It was as if once they placed you, they ripped up all the paperwork and you were history. For a couple of years afterward Mihai and I tried to trace them through the church and the Hungarians we met here, but no one could come up with a thing. It was as if they vanished."

Katalin's tears continued to fall.

"My poor Katya." Zsuzsanna folded the distraught girl in her arms, cradling her as she cried. "This is not how I wanted you to begin your stay, but I guess that old adage is true. Bad news won't wait."

"I'm sorry." Sophie shuffled from one foot to the other, ill at ease to have to interrupt Zsuzsanna and her niece. "I don't mean to bother you, but everyone's waiting."

With great reluctance Zsuzsanna released Katalin, but didn't let go altogether until she dabbed her niece's eyes with a handkerchief pulled from the sleeve of her dress. "Would you take care of Katalin?" Zsuzsanna asked Sophie.

"Sure."

While Zsuzsanna went off to initiate the festivities, Sophie led Katalin through the bar into what looked like a studio apartment—one small room furnished with a bed, a dresser, and a nightstand, and an adjoining bath. From the minute Sophie opened the door, there was no doubt who lived there. Clothing was everywhere—coat racks, hooks, curtain rods hung between doorways and above windows, doorknobs, bedsteads, and every inch of floor space. Katalin felt as if she had been invited to crawl inside a little girl's chest of treasures. Though it appeared as if Sophie stood at the doorway, tossed an article of clothing and let it reside wherever it landed, Katalin began to detect a certain sense of order within the chaos. The mirror over the dresser held belts and scarves. One coat rack housed blouses; the other, dresses. The doorway leading to the bathroom was reserved for skirts, the rod hanging over the window designated for slacks. Sweaters were folded one on top of the other over the end of the bed. Shoes and boots lined the walls and the bottom of the minuscule closet, where Sophie kept coats and other things too bulky for open storage.

"Welcome to Paradise Lost." Sophie splayed her arm and curtsied, urging Katalin to leave the hall and enter the room. "It's not much, but it's mine."

Katalin looked confused. Sophie divined her question immediately and answered it before it was asked. "My parents are alive, as well as they're ever going to be, and living on Twenty-seventh Street with two of my brothers. Once a week I visit them. They never visit me."

Katalin wanted to probe deeper, to find out why a young woman would choose to live away from her family, but Sophie's matter-of-fact tone discouraged conversation.

"I'm supposed to be making you party-pretty," she said, drawing Katalin in, turning her toward the dresser so she could see her reflection in the mirror.

"I look awful!" Katalin said, appalled at the sight of her red, puffy eyes and blotchy skin.

"Well, to be honest, I don't think *Vogue's* going to knock down your door to get this look on the cover of their magazine. Go splash some cold water on your face. I'll take it from there."

Katalin did as she was told, but she suffered a few misgivings when

Sophie opened the top drawer of her dresser and revealed an awesome collection of makeup, cosmetic brushes, and hair accessories.

"I don't wear . . ."

"I noticed." Without asking permission, Sophie dipped a fat yellow-bristled brush into a plastic tub of powder. With two quick flicks of her wrist, she dusted Katalin's cheeks, leaned back to check the effect, dipped and dusted once more. Then she dived into the drawer again and extracted another brush, this one smaller, thinner, and with a hot pink bristle. Dunking it into a tiny capsule filled with a gelatinous glob of green, she swabbed Katalin's eyelids, blending the color with the tip of her finger. A third brush daubed her lips with pink. A wand drawn from a long tube flicked along her lashes, coating them with a single layer of thick black goop. "Much better," Sophie said, standing back to admire her handiwork. "Don't you think?"

Katalin was afraid to look. Judging by Sophie's own heavy-handed appearance, she anticipated a circus clown laughing at her from within the glass. Instead, a pretty young woman stared for a bit and then smiled delightedly. To her surprise, the maquillage hadn't curtained her beauty; it had enhanced it. The green on her eyelids was softer than she had imagined; the pink on her lips and cheeks, much lighter. Where she had expected to see a row of black, garishly fringed lashes, the mascara was delicate, acting like an invisible outline that emphasized the mysterious Oriental shape of her eyes.

Everything seemed so right that when Sophie undid Katalin's braid, freeing the burnished mane so it could float down her back, Katalin didn't raise even the slightest objection. Nor did she protest when Sophie insisted she roll the waist of her skirt, hiking the hem about two inches, and loosen the tie on her blouse so the soft cotton fabric lounged on her shoulders rather than sitting stiff and prim. She even surrendered her shoes and socks in favor of a pair of woven sandals when Sophie retrieved them from beneath her bed and placed them in front of Katalin.

"Thank you," she said, appraising the final product, appreciative but still unsure. "I . . . we . . . in Hungary we don't dress like this."

"Somehow I guessed that," Sophie said, picking up Katalin's shoes, holding them out in front of her as if they needed fumigating. "I'll leave these here. You can pick them up tomorrow. Grab a piece of bed while I go to the bathroom, okay?"

Katalin nodded, but instead of doing as she was told, she found herself in front of the mirror again. Katalin wasn't a person of vanity. If anything, her habit was to downplay her physical attributes, subordinating them as she did everything else to her music, her overwhelming strength. It felt odd to be so intrigued by her own image, but the fascination was undeniable. The girl before her was a stranger, yet familiar; new, but with the same features as the unadorned, unmade-up young woman who less than a day before had boarded a Malev airplane bound for Frankfurt. Preening a bit, she tilted her head this way and that, watching as her hair swayed like long, graceful blades of grass. She blinked her eyes as quickly as a camera lens, surprising herself, catching herself in one pose after the other, as if she and her reflection were indeed two separate people and each was assessing the other. For her part, she liked the way the girl in the mirror looked. More important, she liked the way that girl made her feel. She felt different. Usually, Katalin hated feeling different, because it had always meant a sense of alienation, of being outside the norm. This time, however, different was good. It meant independence. It meant change. It meant new beginnings, new opportunities.

The toilet flushed in the next room. Katalin snapped out of her trance. She was about to turn when her eye caught a couple of small picture frames hidden behind a collection of perfume bottles. Each was a family shot—a round-faced, large-bodied woman; a square-jawed, broad-shouldered man; two husky boys; and a gangly young girl with long blond braids.

"Is this your family?" Katalin asked as Sophie exited the bathroom and started for the door to the restaurant.

"That's them. The noble Wisnewski clan."

Katalin's English wasn't good enough for her to know whether Sophie was being sarcastic or her tone was simply tinged with an inflection indigenous to New Yorkers.

"They look very nice."

Sophie narrowed her eyes, tipped her head and chuckled. "Is that your not-so-subtle way of asking why I don't live with them?"

Katalin blushed. "I guess so."

"It's really quite simple," she said as she opened the door to the hall. "We all have a problem with our vision."

"I'm sorry," Katalin said, suddenly embarrassed that she might have pressed Sophie to reveal some tragic genetic affliction. "Is it serious?"

"The doctors diagnosed it as *familias indigestivitis,*" Sophie said with a straight face. When Katalin looked confused, Sophie translated. "We can't stand the sight of each other!" Before Katalin could hide her shock, Sophie laughed and grabbed Katalin's hand, steering her out of the disorderly room. "Now before Zsuzsanna calls the police and accuses me of niece-napping, let's join the party."

As Katalin followed, she couldn't help wondering about the girl bouncing along in front of her. In the half hour they had known each other, Katalin had deduced that Sophie was funny and dramatic, generous and friendly. As appealing as that was—especially to one feeling so unmoored and so in need of a friend—instinct warned there was more to Sophie Wisnewski than she allowed the world to see. Katalin had lived with Zoltán and his ghosts too long not to recognize someone driven by darkness. The clues were slight, barely noticeable, but there, bleeping like a coded message feeding into a receiver. Katalin's sensitivities had picked up the signal. Something in Sophie's past was creating her future. Katalin was curious, but she knew better than to expect immediate answers. Most people fueled by the pain of a continuous nightmare didn't share easily. Some never shared at all.

In the month preceding the start of school Zsuzsanna took Katalin sightseeing; Sophie took her shopping. Between the two of them, Katalin covered most of the city in record time, gorging her eyes and her taste buds on whatever was put before her. She ate moo shu pork at King Wu's, cannoli and tortoni at Ferrara's, a knish at Katz's, a hot dog with mustard and relish at Yankee Stadium, a salted pretzel from a street cart, a tuna sandwich that slid out of a hole in the wall at the Automat. She tried pizza at Luigi's, cheesecake at Lindy's, and steamed clams at Lundy's in Brooklyn. When she wasn't eating, she was climbing, hiking to the top of the Empire State Building, the Statue of Liberty, and the Chrysler Building. She traipsed down to Wall Street, through Rockefeller Center, up to the Bronx Zoo, then down again to Central Park, the Planetarium, the Metropolitan Museum of Art, and the Museums of Natural History and Modern Art. She rummaged through the racks on the Lower East Side, toured Orbach's, Macy's, B. Altman's, and a slew of Sophie's other 34th Street haunts. Uptown, she tiptoed through glamorous emporiums like Saks Fifth Avenue, Lord & Taylor, Bergdorf Goodman, and Bloomingdale's, intimidated by the luxe and elegance she saw on their shelves and in their displays. She rode the buses and stared at the buildings that tickled the sky. She walked the streets and marveled at the elegant apartments that lined Park Avenue and upper Fifth, at the bohemian atmosphere of Greenwich Village, the quaintness of Murray Hill, the tacky hustle-bustle of 42nd Street.

Katalin felt as if she had been confined to a closet for most of her life. Now the door had swung open and she had stepped out into a world bursting with plentitude and abundance. The key word to life in America seemed to be *more*—more options, more space, more money, more avenues of success, more chances of failure. In New York there was more of everything, including people. While it was true that the population of the city's five boroughs was almost as large as the population of the entire Hungarian nation, it was the variety of people walking the streets that amazed Katalin. In Hungary there were the Magyars, the Slavs, and the gypsies. It was easy to pinpoint a man's ancestry or a woman's parentage. In New York there were so many skin tones, so many eye shapes, hair colors, body types. She had never seen a black person before, nor an Asian.

Initially, she had been confused by the conflux of cultures. Though Zsuzsanna's neighborhood looked nothing like Budapest, the sights and smells and language were Hungarian. Inside, Zsuzsanna's apartment looked Hungarian, but the sights and smells outside her window were pure New York. When Katalin ventured beyond the invisible borders of Little Hungary, however, she discovered that Zsuzsanna's community was not unique.

"New York's made up of hundreds of little ethnic pockets," Zsuzsanna explained. "Yorkville. Little Italy. El Barrio. The Lower East Side. Harlem. Chinatown. Each one is a separate enclave with specialty butchers and grocers and restaurants and whatever else makes the people who live there feel at home."

"I thought people come here to get away. I thought they wanted a new home."

"That's true, Katya, but most immigrants don't cross an ocean on a whim. Usually they're running from some form of tyranny, and so they behave like frightened sheep. They bunch together, finding comfort in the sounds of a familiar language or the sight of a familiar face. They bring with them the traditions that make them feel good, like their food, their humor, and their music. Other customs—like politics and caste systems and habits of repression—they gladly leave behind. That's what the New World means. It's what this country's all about. Even the Mayflower was just another ship filled with immigrants."

Katalin smiled. It was comforting to know that no one paid attention to her accent or the fact that she didn't look like the person sitting next to her. In Budapest a foreigner stuck out like a cattail in a wheat field. In New York there was no way of distinguishing a visitor from a native.

When Katalin started Juilliard she felt at ease immediately. Though there were dozens of nationalities represented and dozens of languages spoken in the halls, the main language, the common language was music, and that she spoke fluently. So much so that, after hearing a tape of her performances in Salzburg, the dean of the Music Division decided that instead of pursuing a standard four-year Bachelor of Music curriculum, Katalin should enter the three-year, performance-intense Certificate program. At first Katalin objected.

"I wanted to come here because I thought Juilliard would give me a well-rounded music education. I wanted some liberal arts classes, music history, music literature, things like that."

The dean, a wiry man with long, tapered fingers and gray, wolverine eyes, studied the young girl seated across from him. Rarely did a student object to being singled out for her superior ability.

"Everyone who has reviewed your work has concluded that you have the makings of an outstanding concert pianist. Our feeling is that the faster we prepare you for your destiny, the better for you and the better for the public at large."

Katalin's face registered her disappointment. The dean was moved. More often than not, pianists had no desire to study anything but technique and musicianship. They had no impulse to round themselves or to expand their intellects beyond the keyboard. He and others involved in the training of gifted musicians accepted that sort of unilateral focus as the norm. Musicians existed in a world of feeling and, as a class, were required to sacrifice much on the altar of their artistic goals. That was why most music schools neglected the cultivation of scientific and abstract thinking, preferring to concentrate on more closely related topics instead. Yet here was a young woman with a unique duality—an extraordinary talent paired with a curious mind. It would be a sin, he decided, to feed one and starve the other.

"Perhaps we could alter your schedule to include one elective each semester. How does that sound?"

"That sounds great!" Katalin said, taking his change of heart as a reaffirmation of the rightness of her decision to come to his school. "In case you're concerned, sir, I won't allow this exception to create a problem. I won't cut my practice time. I won't let you or the school down."

"I'm sure you won't, but you're here on a tuition scholarship, Katalin. Don't you have to work to supplement your funds?"

"I live with my aunt. She owns a restaurant. I waitress there part-time so I can earn extra money."

"Taking extra classes, practicing, working." He leaned back in his chair and eyed her with a mix of sympathy for her plight and admiration for her ambition. "When will you have time for a social life?"

Katalin blushed, but answered without a hint of regret: "I won't, but since I've never had a social life, I won't miss it."

As the dean watched her rise and go, he recalled a line from *The Merchant of Venice*: "Sufferance is the badge of all our tribe." Shakespeare might as well have been writing about musicians, he thought.

•   •   •

Though still officially called the Institute of Musical Art and still housed in an elegant building on Claremont Avenue near Columbia University, in 1968, Juilliard was in the midst of a period of enormous change. Founded in 1905 by Dr. Frank Damrosch, the godson of Franz Liszt and the head of music education for New York City's public schools, the Institute had been created with the purpose of establishing a music academy that would rival the major conservatories of Europe and provide Americans with the specialized, intensive training required by the musically gifted. Though Dr. Damrosch had planned for perhaps one hundred students, within the first year enrollment reached more than five hundred, forcing them to expand beyond their original quarters on Fifth Avenue and Twelfth Street to the more spacious Claremont Avenue building.

In 1919 a wealthy textile merchant, Augustus Juilliard, died. In his will he dowered a foundation for the advancement of the musical arts, the largest of its kind until that date. In 1924 the trustees of his estate formed the Juilliard Graduate School. In 1926 the Graduate School and the Institute merged under one president and one board of trustees, maintaining separate deans and separate identities. Gradually, the two schools amalgamated. In 1951, under the direction of William Schuman, the Dance Division was added. When Schuman resigned his office in 1962 to become the first president of the newly constructed Lincoln Center, he handed over the reins to Dr. Peter Mennin. One of Mennin's more significant changes—aside from implementing plans to have Juilliard join the center—took place the same year Katalin entered the school: A Drama Division was created.

"Transfer," Katalin said one evening as she and Sophie set up for the dinner crowd at Csárda. "It would be such fun."

Sophie dropped the silverware she was holding and stared at Katalin. Appearing completely aghast at the suggestion, she gripped the table, raised an eyebrow, and sucked in her cheeks. "Fun? Did you say fun? You may be Queen of the Ivories, but alas, how little you know about those who walk the boards." Clucking her tongue in dismay and disbelief, Sophie lifted a hand to her forehead and slowly shook her head, a gesture designed to convey a ponderous frustration at age-old misconceptions about disciples of Thespis. "Drama is not supposed to be fun. Acting is not a cloak of mirth; it is a cross to bear. It is a way of life. It is a way to make a buck. It is all of those things. But, my naive paprikas, it is not fun."

Katalin tried to keep a straight face, but laughter spurted from her mouth. Without a doubt Sophie was the funniest person she knew. She was always making jokes or wisecracks. Sometimes Katalin recognized Sophie's humor as a carefully calculated vehicle of avoidance, a way of detouring around revealing anything about herself. Sometimes it was verbal armor, protecting her from the jibes and insults proffered by insensitive customers who thought that because they were paying for their dinner, they were entitled to take a bite out of the waitress's pride as well. Most often, though, it was simply an impulse, a response as natural to Sophie as breathing.

"They're holding auditions at the end of this mouth," Katalin persisted. "You need to prepare two monologues that together are about four minutes long. One has to be from the classical repertory and one from a play written in the last hundred years." She waited for that to sink in before adding her own punch line. "You also have to prepare a song, which you may be asked to sing *a capella*."

It was Sophie's turn to laugh. "That's perfect!" she said, pausing between raucous peals long enough to call over Zsuzsanna, Sándor the bartender, and György the chef. "Okay, guys, get this: Katalin wants me to apply to the new drama school at Juilliard. To get in, I have to do two minutes of Shakespeare, two minutes of Tennessee Williams, and two minutes of the Vienna Boys' Choir. Katalin has never heard me sing. Those of you who've had that distinct pleasure and who think that a group from Juilliard would get a tingle from my dulcet tones, raise your hand." She stopped, looked around as if her audience numbered in the hundreds, and said, "No hands showing? How odd."

Then, with her usual flourish, she began to sing the Beatles' latest hit, "Hey Jude." It was not a pretty sound. In fact, Katalin didn't think she had ever heard an innocent group of notes so horribly tortured. Sophie was completely tone deaf.

"They said you *might* be asked to sing," Katalin said in a way that conceded Sophie's singing amounted to a definite minus.

"C'mon, Katya! You're a sweet kid, but . . ."

"I think it's a wonderful idea." Zsuzsanna had plunked her body down in the nearest chair so she could have a front-row seat for Sophie's latest performance. When there had been enough chatter on the subject, she interrupted. "You're trying out for the Drama Division, not Maria Callas's spot at La Scala."

Sophie studied the group in front of her. She felt encouragement and confidence radiating from Zsuzsanna and Katalin. She read approval and cheer in the eyes of Sándor and György. Even Juan the busboy had poked his head in to listen and was flashing her the high sign.

"You'll be sorry," she said, dismissing them with a wave of her hand, grabbing a stack of forks and, with rapid-fire precision, depositing them next to Csárda's white plates with the red-and-green borders. "I'll do it just to get you all off my back, but you'll see. You'll be sorry."

"I don't think so," Katalin said softly.

"Neither do I," Zsuzsanna agreed.

Because her back was to them, no one saw the tremulous row of tears that trickled from Sophie's eyes down to a mouth struggling to hold a grateful smile. She wouldn't let them see how much their friendship and support meant to her. She couldn't. If she did, they'd do what everyone else she had ever cared about had done. They'd reject her.

Katalin had cut her practice session short to run home and wait for the results of Sophie's audition. Standing in the small foyer inside the door to Csárda, she stomped the snow off her feet and yelled to Zsuzsanna. "Any word yet?"

"*Nem*. No. Nothing."

Katalin was freezing. As she walked through the bar into the dining room, she blew warm breath onto her hands, rubbed them together, and then patted her cheeks. Zsuzsanna motioned to join her in the front booth.

"Here. Have a cup of tea," she said, totaling a column of figures before pushing her ledgers aside. "She'll be here soon."

"I hope they say yes."

"You like Sophie, don't you?"

"Very much." Zsuzsanna nodded and smiled, as if she had known the answer all along but simply needed to hear it. "I think of her as a friend," Katalin said.

"Good. I'm glad. What about at school? Have you made friends there?"

"I have many acquaintances, but it's hard, Aunt Zsuzsanna, to make friends when you spend most of your day locked in a small room with a piano."

Zsuzsanna nodded, remembering how Zoltán used to bury himself in his room, sometimes the barn, playing his violin for hours at a time. She recalled the discussions she and Zoltán had up in their special tree, how frequently he talked about his feelings of isolation and separateness, how thankful he was that he had a large family to surround him. Zsuzsanna knew that in Budapest, Katalin's only real friend was Judit Strasser. She also knew that as difficult as it was for a prodigy to have a normal complement of friends, it was practically impossible in a place crawling with spies. There, she supposed, though it was undesirable, it was natural for Katalin to be limited to one playmate, one confidante. But this wasn't Budapest. Katalin was young. She should have lots of people to party with, to talk with. And, Zsuzsanna thought, noticing again how beautiful Katalin was, feeling as she always did that this girl, her godchild, was one of God's most special creations, she should have lots and lots of boyfriends.

"How about the boys at school? Any lookers?"

Katalin giggled. In the six months since she had come to live with Zsuzsanna, she had seen a very different person from the aunt she remembered. Zsuzsanna loved being a woman. She reveled in her femininity, oozing femaleness from every pore. She doused herself in flowery perfumes and wore low-cut blouses and maribou-trimmed peignoirs and high, high heels. She flirted with every man who walked through the door of Csárda, whether he was married or not, whether she was interested in him or not. It wasn't the conquest she liked. It was the hunt, the teasing, the tempting, the sniffing out of another animal's scent. And if half the gossip Katalin heard from the neighbors and steady customers was correct, her aunt was a superb hunter.

"Well?" Zsuzsanna pressed, flicking her hand in a backward wave, urging Katalin to bare her nighttime fantasies.

"I don't even have the time to think about boys, Aunt Zsuzsanna, let alone moon over them. There's no one."

Katalin's reddened cheeks branded her a liar. There was someone. Zsuzsanna was about to probe further when Sophie burst into the room with all the suddenness of a flashbulb. She whipped off her hat and tossed it into the air, revealing a head of hair charged with electricity, frizzing about her head like a static halo. Her outfit was a blinding rainbow of psychedelia—a green Day-Glo sweater over an orange skirt over tights that covered her legs in a wild, neo-Nouveau pattern.

"Okay. You want to blow your minds," she announced, her expression too much a cross between fury and excitement for Katalin and Zsuzsanna to pinpoint. "I did two minutes of Shakespeare. I did two minutes of Maggie the Cat. And I did my own personal rendition of 'Sergeant Pepper's Lonely Hearts Club Band.' "

Zsuzsanna groaned. The ensemble was frightening enough. The thought of Sophie singing to what was probably a very conservative jury had to be an act of deliberate self-destruction.

"And?" Katalin had tried to maintain a hopeful smile, but she was thinking the same thing Zsuzsanna was thinking.

"And? You ask as if there is a question about the ferocious talent caged within this voluptuous body. God save me from those of little faith." Sophie crossed herself, threw herself onto the table, stretched out before them, and emoted for all she was worth. "You were the ones who insisted that I subject myself to this trial by fire. You were the ones who decided that City College was not school enough for me. Well, you were right. I, Sophia Clara Wisnewksi, am now a student of the Drama Division at Juilliard. And on this auspicious occasion, I have only one thing to say." She rose to her knees, lifted her chin skyward, placed her hand over her heart, and said, "Katharine Hepburn, watch your ass!"

13

*T*he Juilliard building at Lincoln Center was finally completed in 1969, allowing the school to move into its new quarters off Broadway on 66th Street, and not a day went by that Katalin didn't meander around the corner into the plaza at the heart of Lincoln Center. By positioning herself at the fountain, she could gaze at the three buildings surrounding the square without moving. Ahead of her, through the massive expanse of glass that fronted the Metropolitan Opera House, she could see the majestic winding staircases, the glittering chandeliers, the rich red carpet, and of course the extraordinary Chagall tapestries that distinguished the new Metropolitan. On her left, marked by a soaring colonnade, stood the New York State Theater, home of both the New York City Ballet and the New York City Opera, while to her right, Philharmonic Hall, combined the colonnade of the New York State Theater with the open edifice of the Opera House. Inquisitive souls like Katalin could peer through its banded glass to the elegant but austere interior, with its sleek balconies softened by oases of leather benches and tall, leafy trees.

Several times—during the day when there was no audience and no scheduled rehearsals—Katalin had ventured inside. She had tested seats all over the gold-toned auditorium, trying a box, the front row of the mezzanine, the middle of the orchestra, the side of the upper tier. Wherever she sat, her eyes focused front, picturing herself behind the incredible Steinway concert grand offered to soloists, seeing herself the way others would see her.

Some day, she told herself, *some day, I'll walk out on this stage and my music will fill this magnificent hall. My name will be inside the programs distributed at the door. My name will be on the posters lining the lobby and in the placards on the street. My name will be in bold type in the advertisements appearing in the arts section of* The New York Times. *Some day.*

Still wrapped in her dream, Katalin walked through the plaza toward Juilliard and her class in piano literature, acknowledging the changes she felt taking place within her. A year ago she might not have been so admiring of these starkly modern structures. Then, her aesthetic had been firmly rooted in the European style, but her months in New York had refined her tastes, and as her eye grew more accustomed to steel and glass, she found herself admitting that there was an energy and vitality in the American style.

Also, she was beginning to enjoy the hurried pace of the city. Though some called it frenzied, to her it felt deliciously free. Americans rushed from one place to the next, as if they couldn't wait to get wherever they were going. In Budapest no one was ever in a hurry. There was little reason to rush; there was no place to go.

Racing through the lobby, Katalin spied a small crowd of students gathered in front of the elevators. Some were engaged in conversation; others appeared lost in their own thoughts. One girl stood off to the side vocalizing, not caring who listened as her contralto laddered up the scale, gaining in vibrato the higher she went. In front of Katalin were three dance majors, twig-thin, their hair slicked into neat neck-hugging buns, their legs dressed in colorful layers, and their feet splayed outward in a stance that read *second position.* Two orchestral musicians, easily identified by the odd-shaped boxes they carried, were arguing loudly about the current World Series, where it appeared a miracle was taking place—a local team called the Mets was winning. As others joined enthusiastically in the discussion, Katalin reflected on that passionate penchant of Americans for taking sides. There was something incredibly infectious about American zealousness. They were perennial fans, perpetual idealists, and permanently committed to the ideal put forth in the "Superman" comic strip—the defense of truth, justice, and the American way. They were, as Sophie had taught her to say, gung-ho!

But, she thought as abruptly, they weren't always consistent. She would never understand why the United States government—despite mass demonstrations of public dissent—insisted upon championing the cause of the South Vietnamese. The government's answer was that American soldiers were needed to help prevent the spread of communism. They claimed the troops were there to make certain that those who wanted democracy had democracy. But where had the Americans been in 1956 when the Hungarians had needed them? Where had they been just last year, in August of 1968, when Russian tanks roared into Czechoslovakia? For those whose homes were behind the Iron Curtain, it was difficult to understand how the United States could have been so deaf to the loud rumbling of tanks crushing another nation's spirit.

For Katalin, the brutal end of the "Prague Spring" had had an effect. Letters from home had slowed. Having read reports that Hungarian soldiers had participated in the effort to subdue the Czechs—a notion that filled Katalin and everyone else in the Hungarian sector of New York with shame and disgust—she could only assume that the Hungarian government had tightened its restrictions as a way of showing good faith with the Soviets and avoiding any fallout from the Czechoslovakian "situation." She had heard from Mária twice in the past nine months, and both of those letters had been hand-delivered from a young man who worked at the address Zoltán had told her to use only in an emergency. That address had seemed a puzzlement at the time, but between packing and saying good-bye to everyone, she hadn't pursued it.

When she received the first of these surreptitious letters, she questioned Zsuzsanna, asking her if she knew these people, why they were delivering her mail, who they were dealing with in Hungary, and why it was such a big secret. Her aunt had sloughed it off as simply another example of Zoltán's excessive paternal caution and nothing for her to worry about. But then, last week, three Juilliard students—two Czechs and a Hungarian—had asked for asylum. Word was that in each case a family member had been arrested on trumped-up charges. The students had been advised not to return home but to stay in the United States indefinitely. Katalin panicked. She knew how vulnerable Zoltán was, how visible he and Mária were. What if the AVO decided to set an example? What if they went on one of their infamous hunts? Sophie, in her usual way, attempted to calm Katalin by bombarding her with clichés Katalin didn't fully understand, telling her not to borrow trouble, that no news was good news, that she had to keep a stiff upper lip. Zsuzsanna, using different words, had offered essentially the same advice.

Thank goodness for school, Katalin thought as she boarded the elevator, headed for Paul Greco's class. Between classwork, piano studies, practice, and her job at Csárda, she was left precious little time to be depressed or worried.

•   •   •

Paul Greco was a man who had been born in the wrong place and time. While his mode of dress was modern-day and his speech was of the moment, his soul resided in another century. He decried the results of the Industrial Revolution, blaming progress for the death of letter-writing and the therapeutic benefits of silence, among other things. He loathed the telephone, the car horn, Muzak, and of course, television. To him they were intrusions on a world he believed had been made poorer by their invention. As if to prove his case, he often demanded that his students or his critics present him with a list of modern composers that would match in number and genius the listing from the nineteenth century, when Beethoven and Brahms and Schubert and Schumann and Liszt were committing their brilliance to paper.

"Today, all I hear is 'I don't have time,' " he ranted during one class, his black eyebrows arched in his handsome, olive-skinned face. "Schubert died at thirty-one, and in those few short years he composed more than six hundred songs, nine symphonies, twenty-one sonatas, six operas, and hundreds of other pieces of music. Obviously, he found time to do what he had to do."

It was always like that. Greco was always expounding on something, his conviction so great that he seemed always to overwhelm whatever space he occupied. One day it was the dearth of concerts, another day the overabundance of drugs. One minute he was extolling Beethoven's ability to shape sounds; the next minute he was lamenting the inability of audiences to listen.

This morning, Greco's aspect loomed dark and foreboding. For a moment Katalin wondered what had caused the storm that raged behind his eyes. He waited for the last student to take his seat before he spoke.

"Last night, Madame Muzijevic was savagely raped and murdered."

Cries of grief and shock were heard throughout the room. Several students wept. Katalin felt as if her heart had ceased to beat. Stella Muzijevic had been her tutor. She was a woman in her late sixties. Slavic, Jewish, she had come to this country just before the outbreak of World War II.

"If the Nazis hadn't killed me," Katalin had heard her say, "surely the Russians would have. Better to be poor here than dead there."

Struggling to control his ferocious anger, Greco gave the class what few details he had. The assailant had accosted the elderly woman with a knife and forced her into an alley off 90th Street. After he had raped and sodomized her, he had mutilated and robbed her.

"We had dinner together," Greco said, his voice trailing off into the distance, as if he were speaking more to an unseen audience than to those seated before him. "I paid because she said she was short of cash. She had twenty dollars in her wallet. Some lowly drug-crazed dog killed her for a meager twenty dollars!"

There was an edge to his fury, something that led Katalin to believe that his suffering was not born of loss alone, but also from a sense of guilt. Though she didn't know him well, she knew enough to know that a man of his exceptional sensitivities would have felt that he could have saved his friend, that he should have done something to try to prevent such a heinous crime.

"Those of you who knew Madame Muzijevic know how stubborn she was," he said, as if reading Katalin's thoughts. "I begged her to let me take her home, but she refused."

"Have they caught him?" a boy to Katalin's left asked. "The pig who did it?"

"Not yet," Greco said in a voice that hinted at his wish to get to the killer before the police did and extract his own punishment. "But they know who it is. He left his fingerprints on her purse and the knife he used to cut her." His mouth tightened and he shuddered, horrified that something like this had happened to someone he knew, that something like this had happened to anyone.

Greco's obsidian eyes blazed with rage, and for a few moments everyone fell silent, fearing that the slightest sound would set him off. Abruptly, he dismissed the class. As Katalin rose to leave he stopped her. The storm appeared momentarily stilled.

"If it's all right with you, Miss Gáspár, I've been asked to take over as your instructor."

"It would be an honor," she said, torn between an ineffable sadness over Madame Muzijevic's death and an almost uncontrollable delight at having been assigned to Paul Greco.

"There will be a memorial service for Stella tomorrow morning at eleven. Your regular tutorial is at two. I'll expect to see you at both."

Without waiting for a reply, he grabbed his briefcase and his coat and strode out the door and down the hall, leaving Katalin alone in the empty classroom. For a few moments she stood there, absorbing what remained of his aura, for despite her horror at what had happened, the air felt positively electric, as if his personality had charged the atmosphere with energy. Perhaps it was the intense concentration of that energy that made him so unusual. Nothing about him was diluted; nothing was watered down by fear of what others might think or concern about whether he fit a particular convention or mold. He thought what he wanted. He said what he thought. He did what he said. And he did what he believed was right.

Paul Greco was one of the most eccentric men she had ever met. Yet Katalin understood him. He was a kindred spirit, a singularly directed soul who, like Katalin and her father, existed not on oxygen or any other form of human sustenance, but rather on the life-giving force of music. To him, it was his talent that made him strong; being able to produce music was a gift that, he felt, rendered him invincible. His abilities set him above and apart, as if he had been chosen by some omnipotent being to complete an earthly mission. But Katalin knew that, like Zoltán, if the day ever came that Greco thought he might fail in that mission, that he was no longer able to teach or to translate his godly endowments into credible performances, he would feel as drained of life as if he, too, had been stabbed and violated and left to die in a dark, trash-littered alley off 90th Street.

Sophie was in the student lounge, deep in conversation with Predrag Lauc. A piano major more commonly known by his nickname, Pedjá, he was a Yugoslavian in his second year of the Master's program. Tall, blond, exceedingly handsome, he exuded a searing Byronic presence, dressed in his habitual costume of head-to-toe black. His face was angled and planed, with a deliberate jaw and a forceful brow. His eyes were blue and always intensely focused. Every gesture, every facial expression was concentrated, calculated, as if designed especially to match his image of the romantic poet.

Katalin had first met Pedjá when Paul Greco had invited him to play for her piano literature class. What had struck her then, and continued to interest her, was the magnetism of his personality. From the moment he had entered the classroom, he owned the complete attention of everyone present. He played Bach's "Chromatic Fantasy and Fugue" with expression and enough virtuosity to impress, though without true greatness. Nonetheless, she—and every other person in that room—had appeared mesmerized.

Later, over coffee, he had explained that in fact people were always more taken with his image than his talent, although in his view, both were exceptional.

"Image is everything," he had said, taking time away from their conversation to shake hands with other members of her class and thank them for their words of praise. "I've been here three years, but it doesn't take long to see that in New York, it's not what you play or even how you play it that counts as much as how you look."

Katalin had scoffed at such an elementary and unflattering assessment of the New York musical community. They were hardly dilettantes, she reminded him.

"No, but they are Americans," he said pointedly. "In Europe, when you're seated behind a grand on a concert stage, audiences don't care about clothing. They know the music. There, you have to compete with tradition and history for recognition. Here, you're fighting *The Beverly Hillbillies* and *Star Trek.*"

"Did you hear about Madame Muzijevic?" Katalin asked now as she slid onto a chair next to Pedjá, across from Sophie. Their faces telegraphed ignorance. "She was raped."

Pedjá's mask cracked. His blue eyes darkened. Stella was from Yugoslavia. Often, she and Pedjá dined together and exchanged stories about their homeland. She told him how it had been before the Germans; he told her what life was like since. It was, as she called it, "a pleasured heartache" to hear about the changes in Belgrade, despite the terrible things that had happened in the capital since she had left.

"Is she going to be all right?" Pedjá asked, already flipping pages in his black leather appointment book, ready to pencil in a hospital visit.

Katalin shook her head. "She's dead."

For the first time since she had known him, Pedjá allowed himself to display an honest emotion. His head fell into his hands as he grieved for an old woman he had called friend. Allowing him whatever privacy could be had in a public place, Katalin turned to Sophie, who had said nothing. She had asked no questions, expressed no feelings, declared no grief or shock or dismay. Instead, she remained preoccupied with her tuna sandwich.

"Did you know Madame Muzijevic?" Katalin asked.

"By sight and reputation," Sophie replied between bites.

Her callous, almost cavalier, attitude about this poor woman's murder was beginning to annoy Katalin.

"Don't you have anything to say about what happened to her?"

Sophie stuck a straw into her Coke, sucked up several mouthfuls of the bubbly cola, and said, "She was asking for it. I've seen Stella Muzijevic and I'm telling you, it's no wonder someone ravaged her body. When she's strutting her stuff in those funky Red Cross shoes, just letting her ankles hang out the way she does, whoa! She's a real turn-on. And if she had on that far-out print dress I saw her in last week?" She shook her head. "It would take an iron man to resist such a blatant come-on."

Katalin's mouth hung open. Pedjá was staring as well.

"Sophie," Katalin said, "you're being disgusting. This is a tragedy. Don't you understand? Madame Muzijevic was raped and murdered."

Sophie wiped her mouth with a napkin, crumpled the used paper into a ball, tossed it into a wastebasket five feet away, and pushed herself back from the table. Without any change in attitude, she rose, picked up her books, tossed them both a wave, and trotted out of the lounge.

"I don't get it." Katalin appeared dumbstruck.

"Ignore her." Pedjá, perhaps because he championed eccentricity, inventing idiosyncratic behavior patterns to fill in what he considered to be the ordinary blanks in his personality, dismissed Sophie's peculiar performance as an anomaly. It had been insensitive and crude, but, he reasoned, everyone was entitled to a mood quirk. "Is there going to be a memorial?"

"Tomorrow morning at eleven."

Katalin felt his hand on her arm. When she looked up, his blue eyes were fixed on her. Within them, she saw sympathy and a streak of compassion she had never expected to find in his emotional repertoire. "We'll go together," he said.

"That would be nice."

Katalin allowed herself to fall into step beside Pedjá as they left the lounge and headed for their respective practice rooms. From the time they had met, Katalin had considered Pedjá an acquaintance. Today, he had declared himself a friend. It felt good, especially since someone she had believed carried that title with pride had just disappointed her.

For a month Katalin and Sophie avoided each other. Knowing each other's schedule at school made it easy to be somewhere else. Actually, for Katalin, staying away from the lounge where Sophie held court was less a conscious decision than it was a necessity. Paul Greco was working her to a frazzle. Without saying so, he made it clear that he felt Madame Muzijevic had been proceeding too slowly, that she had been babying Katalin's talent instead of demanding that it mature.

"You've been getting by," he told her the first day. "You're exceptionally facile and obviously were born with a musical gift, but you haven't pushed yourself much beyond the cradle."

Katalin was shocked. She started to protest, to count the millions of hours she had spent doing scales and arpeggios and octaves, to run through her vast repertoire and dazzle him with the power of her memory. But then, anticipating her defense, he went on.

"Facility is not technique. You must dig deeper, try harder. You must learn musicianship."

He was so definite, so unflattering that Katalin felt herself growing alternately angry and nervous—angry because she felt he was belittling a talent others had praised, nervous because perhaps he had noticed a tragic flaw, something Andras and her father had been too blinded by affection to see.

"In order to add reason and authority to your playing, you have to examine a score more thoroughly than you do. Because you sight-read so superbly, you've gotten into the habit of exerting yourself on the more difficult passages while neglecting those you've dismissed as easy. If you intend to make an indelible mark on an audience every single time you play, nothing is easy!"

He commanded that she select a composer. Instead of working on individual pieces, his plan was that she study and commit to memory a complete cycle, like Mozart's concerti or Schubert's sonatas or the solo works of Chopin.

"Concentration on the products of one great mind is a way of prodding another mind into greatness," he said. "It's the difference between squinting and seeing through the whole eye. When you know the entire *oeuvre* of a composer, your view of his works is clearer and brighter than if you played only a few favorites."

Because of her musical heritage and because she knew that certain composers were banned in Hungary and she would never be permitted to perform their music onstage, she selected Liszt. Convinced she had already mastered the "Paganini Études," she selected the "Mephisto Waltz No. 1" as her first project under Greco's tutelage. When she brought the piece to her lesson and began to play, he removed her hands from the keyboard and the score from the music stand.

"You are not ready to play."

"I've looked it over." She had thought being his student was going to be an excursion into a land of musical ecstasy. Instead, it was turning into an exercise in torture and humiliation. "I thought I'd run through it with you before I started breaking it down."

"I don't want to run through it and I don't want you breaking it down. What I want is for you to take this home and, every night when you get into bed, read it as you would read a novel. Study it. Find the different themes. Search for the composer's message. When you understand the character and mood of the material, when you know every change in tempo, every place where one phrase ends and the next one begins, then you will be ready to play the 'Mephisto.' For the time being, practice scales, arpeggios, trills, thirds, sixths, and octaves."

Katalin was incensed. Rising in a huff, her skin pink with indignation, she turned to Greco. "I am not a beginner, Mr. Greco. I am an accomplished pianist. I came to Juilliard because I want to move forward in my musical training, not backward. If you are not willing to help me, I'll find someone who is!"

When the air aroused by her departure had settled, Greco moved in front of the keyboard. Without any sign that he had been disturbed or upset by her exit, he raised his hands and prepared to execute the daring, dramatic opening of Liszt's most famous waltz. As his fingers touched the keys a smile outlined with arrogance overtook his face.

"Just as I've waited all my life for a student like her," he assured himself, "she's waited all her life for a teacher like me. She'll do what I want, because she wants to be great. And I am the means to that end!"

"What do you say? Can we declare a truce?" Sophie stood in front of Katalin waving a white napkin.

Katalin stopped laying out silverware and turned toward Sophie. She was still riled from her argument with Greco. "You were heartless and cruel and I don't like people who don't care about other people."

"Other than that, I'm a hell of a gal, eh?"

"Everything is not a joke, Sophie."

Sophie's face grew somber. "Maybe not, but life's not an ongoing Shakespearean tragedy either. Maybe you should lighten up a little."

"And maybe you should have understood that an innocent old woman was savaged and that some of us felt bad about it even if you didn't!" Katalin slammed the knives she was holding down onto the table. Her eyes flamed and her body shook.

Sophie didn't know about Katalin's contretemps with Greco. She didn't know that Katalin still hadn't come to terms with the death of her friend Vera and the accumulated losses of her uncle Mihai and two young boys known as Mátyás and István. She didn't know that although Katalin was happy in New York, she was besieged by long-lasting episodes of homesickness. All Sophie knew was that she cared about Katalin too much to allow a spate of foolishness to put a wedge between them.

"I was awful," she said at last, her tone and her manner properly contrite. "I said all the wrong things at exactly the wrong time. I'm sorry I offended you."

"I just don't understand how you . . ."

"I knew someone who was raped, and to this day that girl is—pardon the pun—totally fucked up. I guess I was reacting to her situation more than to what happened to your friend Stella."

It was rare that Sophie maintained a dour visage. Usually, a pose of sobriety was simply a setup for a punch line. Katalin waited, but the payoff didn't come. Sophie's apology was sincere.

"I'll wait two of your tables and give you the tips." Sophie sensed a softening in Katalin's attitude. She smelled forgiveness and pounced before Katalin could reconsider. "Okay, how about my Woodstock T-shirt, my love beads, and, because I really do love you, I'll dye your hair purple and spike it for your first big concert. Now really, Katie my girl. I don't care if you are a mad Hungarian. No one can turn down an offer like that!"

Katalin shook her head, completely helpless against Sophie's jests. "I'll take the T-shirt, the beads, and the tips. The hair is out of the question."

"Suit yourself," Sophie said, lifting her eyebrows in a show of incredulity. "But you're making a mistake. Purple hair makes headlines!"

Katalin laughed and held out her arms. Sophie fell into Katalin's embrace, hugged her quickly, and then, just as quickly, pulled away and headed for the kitchen. Why, Katalin wondered as she watched Sophie disappear behind the thick wooden door? Sophie had felt the need to express something intimate. She had responded to Katalin's offer of closeness with spontaneous warmth. But then, that resounding need she had to be distant had overwhelmed her once again. This was not the first time Katalin had sensed an insistence upon coldness lurking just below the surface. How often in the past year had Katalin witnessed incidents in which Sophie had barricaded her emotions behind a barrage of snappy comebacks? How many times had Sophie refused Zsuzsanna's invitations to spend holidays or Sundays with her and Katalin, opting to spend those occasions alone in her room rather than in the company of people who cared for her?

A lifetime of experience had taught Katalin to recognize the signs of calculated alienation. In Hungary, when she, her family, and friends had practiced the art of emotional and intellectual quarantine, she knew why. There were harsh consequences to speaking one's mind or baring one's soul. What truth was Sophie protecting? What was she hiding behind that impenetrable wall she had erected around her heart?

The dining room of Csárda was a spacious but cozy den. Dressed in dark cherry wood and humble hand-carved furnishings, it felt like a clubhouse for those who longed to steep themselves in the traditions of the Magyar. Red and green were the predominant colors; the Hungarian countryside, the dominant decorative theme. Wooden booths, their gracefully arched backs punctuated with tulip and bird cutouts, recalled the hearthside tables of the *puszta*. Small lamps with crisply pleated shades cast a rosy glow on diners; a metal tray provided salt, pepper, and the ubiquitous paprika; squat stoneware vases, emblazoned with the bucolic patterns of the plains, bulged with flowers. Garlands of paprikas painted the scene with splashes of red, while sprays of dried wild flowers enlivened the niches that guarded each doorway. Here and there, the black hat and whip of the *csikós* created a rustic still life; a violin, a mandolin, even an accordion held a place on Csárda's walls. Because this was Zsuzsanna's place and there was nothing Zsuzsanna liked better than attaching herself to a star—no matter how distant the connection— photographs of famous émigrés covered every other available inch of wall space. Georg Solti. George Szell. Vasarely. Peter Lorre. Adolph Zukor. Sir Alexander Korda. The Gabor sisters. Paul Lukas. And of course, Katalin Gáspár.

That night the restaurant was exceptionally busy. Every booth was filled. Four tables stood vacant, but RESERVED signs earmarked them for late diners. While Sophie raced by her on her way to pick up entrees from the kitchen, Katalin tried to coax a dessert order from the party in booth number 2. She hated when she had a group that insisted upon digesting each course before they ordered the next. Such acts of gustatory dawdling eliminated a turnover and reduced tips. But, Katalin thought as she waited for the two women to fuss over whether or not they should get individual pieces of the apple strudel or pick at their husbands' *palacsinta*, Zsuzsanna had created an atmosphere that begged customers to linger. The lights were dim, the ambience was enticing. The food was delicious. There was a promise of music. Why leave?

"One *palacsinta* and one apple strudel. How many coffees?"

Katalin had started for the kitchen when she noticed him talking to Zsuzsanna. She could hardly believe it. Paul Greco was standing with her aunt beneath the archway that led to the bar, laughing, chatting, flirting, behaving as if he were simply a patron stopping by for a brandy and a plate of goulash. But he wasn't just any customer—he was her tutor, and that afternoon she had challenged him.

What is he doing here? Katalin became so flustered, she pushed open the wrong door into the kitchen and collided with Sophie.

"I know English is a tough language," Sophie said, righting two bread baskets that had spilled over onto her tray, "but these are basic, Katalin. See," she said, pointing to the words on the doors with the vacant, yet omniscient half-smile of a kindergarten teacher who has said the same thing twenty times before. "In. Out. You don't go out the in door. And, my little *galuska*, you don't go in the out door. If this had been *pörkölt* you would now be counting the seconds before your last breath."

"Sorry," was the best Katalin could do.

Shaking her head, Sophie left to deliver her bread. Katalin remained distracted. She watched as Zsuzsanna led Greco to a table. He sat. She sat with him. He smiled. She signaled for a bottle of wine. He said something. She laughed. Katalin's stomach knotted. Making certain she had the correct door, she escaped to the kitchen and shouted out her orders. It was only a matter of seconds before her tray was filled, but to Katalin it felt as if the kitchen had slowed to three-quarter time. What was going on? she wondered as she maneuvered her way out the door and over to booth number 2.

In the far corner the band had begun their first set of the evening. Violin, piano, and bass, played by three men with cappuccino skin and licorice hair. Bedecked in gold earrings and layers of golden chains, they wore billowy zoave pants, wide-sleeved shirts, midcalf boots, and scarves inventively wrapped and tied around heads and waists and hips. Within seconds the air sizzled with the frisky rhythms of the gypsies. As always, when a *csárdás* was played, the audience perked up, as if each note were laced with vitamins. Soon, hands came together and toes began to tap.

Katalin peeked at Greco. It was difficult to read his face. She couldn't decide if she saw genuine amusement or benign disdain. Though she wasn't entirely clear about why, she found herself hoping that it was the former. It was suddenly very important to her that he like Zsuzanna's trio. Perhaps it was because somehow she felt as if they gave her a shading Greco might not have seen before, as if when he listened to them, his definition of her would become sharper and more on target. True, her training was classical, but these folk tunes belonged to her ancestral repertoire and therefore explained her in a way nothing else could.

"You'll never know why he's here if you insist on playing hide and seek." Sophie's voice edged past Katalin's thoughts. "Say hello. It's another one of those easy English words I know you know." A hand placed on the small of Katalin's back nudged her forward.

"Good evening, Mr. Greco." Zsuzsanna was no longer at the table. In a way, her absence was a blessing. Katalin felt awkward enough. The last thing she wanted was her aunt observing the strain between Katalin and her tutor. "I hope you're enjoying your evening at Csárda."

"I am indeed," he said, gifting her with a smile. "The food is superb."

"I see you had the *gulyás*." Katalin hated herself for sinking to such banalities, but she was struggling to knit sentences together to create conversation. Fortunately, Zsuzsanna returned.

"So, Paul. What do you think of my gypsies?"

Katalin couldn't help but note the familiarity in Zsuzsanna's tone and the fact that midway through the wine they were already on a first-name basis.

"I'd prefer a cimbalom to a piano," Greco said, as always preferring brute honesty to gentle politeness. "If you're going to present them as an authentic gypsy orchestra, they should be using authentic instruments."

The cimbalom, a cross between a harp and a xylophone, was used, as Greco had said, in gypsy bands all over Europe, most particularly in Hungary. It was the very piece that gave the music of the Rom its distinctive sound.

"I would love a cimbalom," Zsuzsanna said, "but finding one is almost as hard as finding an honorable man."

They both laughed. Katalin shifted about in embarrassment. She felt as if she had intruded on their privacy.

"By the way," Greco said, speaking now to Katalin, "you forgot this." He reached to the chair next to him, retrieved his briefcase, and extracted the score to the "Mephisto." "I was certain that when you crawled into bed tonight, you would be upset with yourself for leaving it at the studio. I know how serious you are about your work."

Katalin took the music and mumbled her thanks, not entirely pleased that he had tracked her down simply to prove his point.

"Paul said you've decided to study Liszt." Though Zsuzsanna was speaking to Katalin, she was smiling at Greco in that Pompadourish way she had, half elegant lady, half well-seasoned courtesan.

"Liszt and only Liszt," Katalin said, uncomfortable with the intimate rapport Zsuzsanna and Greco appeared to have established. "It's Mr. Greco's theory that students should limit themselves to one composer." That sounded argumentative, but that was how she felt.

"Imagine calling the study of Liszt limiting!"

His laugh was irritating, more so because they both knew he had bested her. He had stabbed her with her own words. How could any real musician categorize the output of a composer of Liszt's stature as being a study hampered by boundaries? His vision had been limitless. If hers was less, she did not deserve the privilege of his music.

"I have orders waiting." Katalin had erred, but something inside her refused to apologize. "Thank you for bringing me my music."

Zsuzsanna watched as her niece turned and walked toward the kitchen, marveling at the changes that had taken place in Katalin in one short year. She had forsaken her braid so that her burnished mane now fell down her back in a glorious cascade of silk. She had allowed Sophie to teach her the art of maquillage, but had translated her lessons into a flattering softness that emphasized the paleness of her eyes and the lushness of her lips.

"Beautiful, isn't she?"

"She is a striking young woman, that's true."

"Striking and talented," Zsuzsanna said, detecting a tinge of criticism in his tone. "She's my brother's child. I don't know if you ever heard of Zoltán Gáspár, but he—"

"I know all about Zoltán Gáspár. I also know all about Mária Gáspár."

"Then you know Katalin comes by her genius naturally." When he didn't respond, Zsuzsanna knotted her brow and pursed her lips in an expression that dared him to refute her. "Tell me you don't think she has talent."

"Of course she has talent, Zsuzsanna. If she didn't, she wouldn't be at Juilliard. But genius is ten steps above talent."

"In Hungary, most people think she *is* ten steps above."

"Not to insult you, but so what! The goal is not to be considered exceptional in one's native land, but to be hailed as the best in the world."

"And you don't think my Katalin has what it takes?"

"Being the best takes more than mere ability, Zsuzsanna. It also takes Herculean dedication and diligent, expert instruction."

"Since she was three years old she's been tutored by Andras Strasser, one of the finest piano instructors at the Franz Liszt Academy. They don't come too much better than that!" She hoped he caught her intended slap.

"That may be true, but Strasser's your brother's closest friend, yes?"

"He loves her like his own."

"And I'm sure your brother has also helped to guide Katalin's training."

"Of course he has. She's his progeny." Zsuzsanna thought she was making a point in Katalin's favor.

Instead, Greco's black eyes darkened as quickly as a summer sky overcome by an unexpected rain.

"Let me tell you the cold, hard facts about family members judging musical ability, my dear Mrs. Pal." His voice trembled a bit, as if he had hit himself in the wrong place and reopened an old wound. "No matter how detached you think you are, no matter how objective, it's impossible to listen with the ear of a stranger. You hear what you want to hear. You see what you want to see, because the person at the piano is an extension of yourself. For you to succeed, they must succeed." His mouth curved, but the result could hardly be called a smile. "Take it from me, Zsuzsanna. I know you love Katalin, but often, love is not only blind, it's deaf as well."

A week later a cimbalom was delivered to Csárda. Zsuzsanna reacted like a young maiden receiving a gift from a suitor, fluttering about the instrument as if it were a nosegay of violets instead of a large arrangement of metal strings on a stand. She fussed over it endlessly, shifting it an inch here, a foot there, until finally she was satisfied it had a place of prominence in the dining room.

"Now all I need is someone who knows how to play it."

Though Katalin had never actually played a cimbalom, she had seen one or two at the Academy and had watched several performances in which it was used. She also understood the principle of the strange instrument, because she knew its history.

In the Middle Ages, the lyre and the harp spawned many children. Among them was a triangular or, sometimes, rectangular instrument called a psaltery. More musical than a zither, when it first appeared in the eleventh century it was little more than a simple sounding board with strings stretched across its middle and supports beneath its edges, the strings plucked with quills to create sound.

The psaltery developed into the dulcimer, the difference being that the strings of the dulcimer were hit with beaters instead of plucked with quills, clearly establishing it as a precursor of the piano.

In eastern Europe the dulcimer found a home with those who played folk music. In Hungary, where its specialist performers were gypsies, it evolved into the cimbalom and, eventually, a national symbol.

Pulling a chair up to the cimbalom, Katalin picked up the pair of slender leather-covered hammers that lay across the top and cautiously began to tap the strings, relying on her sense of pitch to determine which notes were which.

"Give me some time with it," she said to a grateful Zsuzsanna.

Before afternoon had turned into evening, Katalin had managed to reproduce two or three songs. By the next day she was able to accompany the gypsies on their more elementary pieces. Within a month she was fluent.

During that same month, while learning to create music on a new instrument, Katalin had also learned the importance of silence and introspection to the creation of sound on the piano. Though she hated to admit it, Greco had been right: There was much to be gained from spending quiet time with a piece of music, absorbing its spirituality before molding it with one's fingers.

Night after night, she studied the "Mephisto" the way she might have studied Tennyson. Slowly she began to ferret out the emotional messages Liszt had hidden in the notes penned on his score. She began to divine how he wanted those messages translated and delivered—which passages demanded attack, which preferred a caress. She began to feel an intrinsic rhythm and movement to the piece, as if it were a creek twisting and bubbling from one end of a valley to another. If she listened carefully, with her inner ear and her heart, she could tell when the water was rushing over a clear-bottomed bed and when it was being slowed by a gathering of rocks or streamside brush. She could sense when the water had pooled into a restive blue, when a sharp descent demanded that it crash into a flurry of white-capped waves.

Still, it wasn't until Greco invited her to play the piece in front of his class that she realized just how effective this mode of study was.

"Horowitz is a thinker," Greco was saying. "He doesn't simply bang out the notes. He thinks the piece through, studying it until he has total control. Miss Gáspár has been thinking Liszt's 'Mephisto Waltz.' I think it would be interesting to see how far she's gotten." He pointed to Katalin, who furrowed her brow in protest. "Come. Come."

During her tutorials she and Greco had been working on fingering. They had discussed the use of the pedal, but as yet had reached no definite conclusions. In her mind, the "Mephisto" was a work in progress, not part of her stage portfolio.

"I don't think I'm ready to perform."

"A performer is always ready to perform." Denying her the opportunity to argue further, he turned his back, walked to his desk, and took his seat. Then he waited.

Having been given the choice of embarrassing herself by doing nothing or something, Katalin elected to play. As she took her place behind the Steinway and adjusted the stool, she considered asking for her sheet music, but quickly rejected the notion. She was a veteran concert pianist. She had a photographic memory and everyone in that class knew it. In truth, he had given her no choice.

Since there was no working one's way into this piece, Katalin launched her pianistic attack, retelling the famous tale of Faust, Mephistopheles, and Marguerite, first with daring, distinctive phrases and then with beguiling, provocative passages. Closing her eyes so she could hear the music better, Katalin listened as the story unfolded with a new voice, her voice. The words her fingers spoke felt familiar, but they had been edged with a sharper accent than she ever remembered using. She heard herself underlining some passages, shading others, giving still others a parenthetical twist. She had played this piece of music a dozen times before, but never like this.

When she had finished and heard the appreciative, respectful applause of her classmates, her face glowed with satisfaction. Turning to Greco, she steeled herself for his expected *I told you so*. Instead, he made his way toward the piano. Lifting her hand to his mouth, he kissed it.

"*Brava!*" he said.

It was only one word coming from one man, but to Katalin it sounded like an ovation.

As she returned to her seat, still glowing from his tribute, compliments fell at her feet like rose petals. The consensus was that her interpretation had been unique and therefore startling. As Katalin listened to her fellow students—and therefore competitors—rave about the newness of her "Mephisto," she projected their enthusiasm on to a concert audience and further, to a critic's pen. Would the impact be as favorable? she wondered. Would another audience find it exciting or unnerving? Then she recalled Greco's words: "If you intend to make an indelible mark on an audience every single time you play, nothing is easy!" An indelible mark. Every time. That was exactly what she wanted. That was greatness.

When she looked up, he was standing over her with another piece of sheet music. Though he spoke in a tone that brooked no arguments, his eyes smiled when he said, "Tonight, you begin the 'Spanish Rhapsody.' "

The relationship between musician and tutor was a special one. In a way it was like a marriage, in that trust and commitment were essential to its success. Though Katalin and Greco had not come to this union easily, that impromptu classroom performance had acted like a bonding ceremony. He had proved himself to her, and, she hoped, she had proved herself to him. Without taking vows or exchanging tokens, they had pledged themselves to each other, for better or worse.

Though he worked her very hard, Katalin grew to love every moment she spent with him. He was so scholarly, so learned about the world of music that information streamed from him like the overflow from a glass poured too full. Better than that, his knowledge was not attached to his surface, but rather had been absorbed by his soul. He didn't simply have facts on hand; they had become an intimate part of his being. He spoke of composers as if they had been personal friends. He gossiped about pianists as if they, too, had visited him just the other night.

When Katalin bemoaned the hours it took to memorize a piece, he blamed Liszt and Clara Schumann. "They thought it was more romantic to play without music, and so now we pianists are doomed to follow in that tradition." Once, during a practice session, when a fly landed on her hand and refused to leave, he told her a story from Paderewski's memoirs about a spider that for months left its web whenever Paderewski played the Chopin étude in thirds. The spider would linger, listen, and then, as soon as Paderewski was finished, climb back up. When he suggested that she add more muscle to a particular measure and she fretted about its being too loud, he reminded her that Liszt was called a "piano pounder" and that in his day, before the iron frame, he often performed with seven pianos on stage at a time so that when he broke one, they could wheel in another.

Though he didn't totally approve, Greco located someone to help Katalin learn the cimbalom. He even condescended to coming around now and then to hear her play. By summer, he was a regular fixture at Csárda and an intrinsic part of the tiny circle that had become Katalin's life.

Zsuzsanna couldn't have been happier. First of all, Greco was a celebrity. He was, as the press had dubbed him, "New York's Music Man." Whenever a soloist arrived in town for a concert, Greco was called in to do interviews for both radio and television. Several times the tables turned and he became the subject. Johnny Carson interviewed him on the *Tonight* show, Hugh Downs on *Today*. Because he was a known commodity, where he went and what he did was news. When the gossip columnists heard he was frequenting a small Hungarian restaurant on the East Side, Csárda received a mention in their columns and Zsuzsanna had a waiting list for reservations.

But there was another, more personal reason Zsuzsanna was so delighted with Greco's increased presence. She wanted him. His olive skin and obsidian eyes had bewitched her. Paul Greco's smoldering sexuality hit her like a January hot spell—totally unexpected, but very welcome. As experienced as Zsuzsanna was, the depth of his sensibilities affected her so, she found herself behaving like a virgin. Here was a man who used his intelligence to stroke her in a way that other men's hands never had. When he smiled, she swooned; when he spoke, she shuddered. She wanted him. And she intended to have him.

If Katalin was aware of her aunt's intentions, she showed no sign of it. Not because Zsuzsanna had made any effort to conceal her feelings. Quite the contrary. Her admiration for Paul Greco was blatant. But Katalin, despite the fact that she was approaching twenty-one years of age, was still incredibly innocent. Sheltered by her music and dedicated to the perfection of her art as she was, her womanhood remained underdeveloped. She didn't date. She didn't even flirt. And because she spent so much time at Juilliard, she never met anyone but musicians. Without meaning to, she had whittled away all extraneous pleasures from her life, save those nights when she played cimbalom for the diners at Csárda.

Those nights were special. There was something so liberating and so exhilarating about not using any music, about improvising notes and creating melodies. She loved the feel of those leather beaters on the taut metal strings. She loved the sensation of wearing a costume and playing a part. Most of all she loved the freedom of indulging her moods by simply expressing them musically. It was fun, which for Katalin was something rare indeed.

Adding to her enjoyment was the fact that Pedjá had joined the Csárda coterie. He filled in as a waiter, sometimes as a pianist, and occasionally, when Zsuzsanna booked a private party, as a bartender. He and Sophie and Greco and Katalin and Zsuzsanna had become a unit. If one needed help, the others offered assistance. If another felt blue, the others did whatever they could to add spice and color. They were together so often that Katalin had come to believe that each of them had ceased to be an individual entity, but rather had become elements merged into a single component. That was why she was so rocked by what happened the night Sophie opened in an off-Broadway show.

Billed as Sophia Wise, Sophie had the lead in a play called Monkey See, Monkey Do. It was a tragedy about a young woman doomed to follow her mother's path toward suicide. Katalin sat riveted in her seat as she watched Sophie create the character of beautiful but self-destructive Leda Swann. By the second act she was so mesmerized by her friend's performance, she hadn't noticed that Greco and Zsuzsanna had gone. By the end of the third act, overwhelmed with the emotions stirred by the play, she neglected to notice that Pedjá had fallen in love with its star.

As soon as they could, she and Pedjá headed backstage to Sophie's dressing room.

"You were brilliant!" Katalin exclaimed as she took Sophie in her arms and hugged her.

"And then some," Pedjá said as he moved toward Sophie. He, too, took her in his arms, but his embrace was different from Katalin's. He held Sophie close and when his lips touched hers, Katalin couldn't help but see the yearning that had chalked itself onto his face. When they separated, their eyes continued to transmit seductive messages.

Katalin felt disoriented and displaced, as if a second play were being performed. Again, she was the audience, but this time Pedjá had joined Sophie onstage. They had become a duet. Though they pleaded with her to come with them to the cast party, Katalin begged off, claiming a headache. She didn't care how lame her excuse sounded. She wanted to make her exit now, rather than bidding them good night at Sophie's door. Outside the theater as she hailed a cab, and then on the long ride uptown, she tried to identify her feelings. Did she feel betrayed? Abandoned? Jilted? None of those seemed to fit. She had no romantic feelings toward Pedjá. And if the truth be known, he and Sophie would probably make a good couple. No. If she was feeling jealous, it was only because they had found each other, while she was still alone.

As she trudged up the steps to Zsuzsanna's apartment, it struck her that apart from her long-ago crush on a nine-year-old boy, she had never allowed herself to care for anyone. Whether it was due to lack of opportunity or the forced myopia of her career, she didn't know. What she did know was that she felt very, very lonely.

The minute she opened the door, she sensed that she had walked into the middle of another act in a continuing drama. The lights were dim. Rachmaninoff was playing on the stereo. An empty wine bottle confronted her from the center of the cocktail table. Strange sounds filtered through the door to the bedroom. Since she was certain she already knew the characters, Katalin didn't know why she bothered to check the man's jacket strewn over the arm of the couch, but she did. In the pocket was Greco's signature—a red silk handkerchief. Not wanting to disturb them or embarrass herself, Katalin slipped out the door and down the stairs.

Standing in the dingy lobby, unsure about what to do and where to go, Katalin admitted that she had never felt as lonely as she did at that moment, with a strange loneliness she had never experienced before. When she soloed onstage, it was a solitary but familiar sensation; when she imprisoned herself for hours on end in a practice studio it was a companionless but comfortable time. She had felt a frightening loneliness when she had arrived in New York and had searched the gallery for Zsuzsanna and Mihai. Then, she had felt unprotected, but still she was able to hold out hope that soon she would be claimed by someone who loved her, who would make her feel safe and connected. Tonight, she felt adrift and alone. Everyone had someone to love—everyone but her.

Wiping tears from her eyes, she stumbled out of the building onto the street. Without even thinking she headed for Csárda and the one certainty in her life—the piano.

14

Saigon, July 1970

The first face Steven saw when he awakened was black. Blurred. Out of focus. Yet familiar. Steven struggled against the darkness. He fought to see more clearly, to sort out the pieces floating by him like so much flotsam and jetsam, to pull them together and create a whole image. He fought, but failed. He was lost in a fog of drugs. Lost in a jungle that wanted to consume him. Lost in a war that wanted to kill him.

Time passed. He knew, because the space beyond his eyelids was suddenly brighter. Somewhere in the back of his mind, where he had stored his sanity, he knew the sun was shining. That meant it was day. The last time he had regained consciousness it had been night. But how many nights ago? What day was this? What month? He blinked. The black face was there again. It leaned closer. Warm puffs of air powdered his cheeks. He blinked again. A hand touched his. He heard his name being repeated. The voice pleaded with him to wake up. He wanted to, but couldn't. The dreams wouldn't let go. They were holding him back, keeping him in that place. That horrible place.

He didn't know what *now* was, but *then* was June. *Then* was Cambodia. Siem Reap. A small town eighty miles northwest of the capital, Phnom Penh. Communist forces had attacked there and at Kompong Thom, to the north. His First Mobile Guerrilla Force was sent to Siem Reap, just outside of Angkor, once the seat of a mighty empire that stretched from the China Sea to the Indian Ocean and reigned for six hundred years. Now, ruins. Angkor Wat. Bayon. Bantéay Sreï. Ta Prohm. Angkor Thom. Temples built by the ancient Khmer. More than a hundred of them tangled in the thick web of an ambitious landscape. He remembered thinking how beautiful they were, how serene, with their conical, multi-tiered towers protruding into the cloudless sky. Terraces. Galleries. Vast stone labyrinths that threaded through areas of sunlight and shadow. The carvings were exquisite. Lion-dogs. Seven-headed serpents. Heavenly dancing girls.

So much fighting. So much death. Four days. Nonstop. On the fifth day the allies recaptured the area. He had been hit, left for dead. Buried beneath a pile of bodies. So dark. So close. Hard to breathe. He kept choking. Fighting for air. The air was foul. Rank with the stink of rotting flesh. Had to be quiet, though. Couldn't cough. Couldn't turn away. Couldn't run. Had to lie still and wait. Hours went by. His shoulder throbbed. Other men's blood dripped on his face. Other men's waste clung to his clothes. Finally, there was silence.

With great respect he removed the dead from his back. It was dusk. Within the hour it would be black as the bowels of a coal mine. Quickly, he patched his wound and dropped to his knees. The land surrounding the temple was open, cleared of everything except clusters of tall, graceful palms. With narrowed eyes he studied the horizon. Everything was flat. Except those palms.

Stay low, he told himself. Belly along the ground. Keep moving, no matter what. Couldn't help the dead. Had to help the living. Had to hook up with his men. Had to complete his mission.

He was part of the Special Forces Group. He wore the Green Beret. The SFG had come to Vietnam in May 1961 as advisers. Now they trained and commanded the Civilian Irregular Defense Group—CIDG— a conglomerate of local strike forces and hamlet defenders. In a perverse way, he preferred being part of CIDG, being a Beret. Standing side by side with the South Vietnamese, helping them defend their land, seeing the enemy from their end of the gun—the war made more sense. These people had names and voices. They carried pictures of their families. They talked of their homes, their ancestors, their holidays. They gave the war a face.

Six months ago he had volunteered for the super-specialized SOG—

Studies and Observation Group—headed by Colonel "Bull" Simons, World War II Ranger, jungle specialist, Green Beret. SOG monitored locations of allied POWs and downed airmen for escape and evasion (E & E) raids. They also performed a variety of "black" missions—kidnappings, assassinations, document retrievals. He was here as part of Daniel Boone, the cross-border operation in Cambodia. In Laos it was called Prairie Fire. In North Vietnam, Kit Cat. SFG had come looking for the black box from a downed U-2. The last thing the United States needed was for secret codes to fall into Soviet hands. His team had been combing the jungle in search of the missing container when they had walked into this ambush. Now, he had to find both the black box and the survivors.

For two days he tracked them, using much that he had learned from the Montagnards, the tribesmen who worked with the Special Forces. He followed a trail of broken twigs, constantly on alert for camouflaged mines. He watched for footprints, bent leaves, disturbed soil, signs of bodies being dragged, of equipment being lugged. Anything. Everything. He listened with the ears of a deer. He looked with the eyes of an eagle. He went deeper. Into the thick, where there were no clues to point the way. Only ghosts of those who had gone before.

God, he hated it there! The air was so hot it burned his lungs; so wet, his clothes felt like plaster next to his body. He had been in Southeast Asia for almost two years. Two years of inflicting and avoiding death. He remembered landing in Saigon, dressed in a uniform of optimism, carrying a duffel filled with hope. That was gone now. Buried alongside military companions and civilian strangers, human sacrifices in a battle of ideology. It wasn't a war, they said. It was a conflict, an involvement, an insurgency. We weren't looking to engage China or the Soviet Union. We were assisting the South Vietnamese. We weren't poisoning the landscape. We were clearing brush to ferret out enemies. We weren't ravaging villages. We were destroying Viet Cong headquarters. Lies. Dangerous lies.

He was there. He saw. Guns. Bombs. Poison. Death. That was truth. That was reality. The rest was words.

Reading the sun, he burrowed his way through the green cesspool of vines and undergrowth. Finally, he found his SFG team and the downed plane. Together, they picked at the wreckage like vultures at carrion. No pilots. No black box. With only four Americans and one hundred Cambodian mercenaries remaining, he deployed four teams. Following sandal tracks, they spread out. He led a group headed east. Two miles. Four. Seven. Suddenly his point man spotted an NVA base camp. He sent one of his Cambodian "hunters" to reconnoiter. Three huts. Six prisoners in one off to the side. He remembered giving the order to cover him as he got into position. At his signal, they were to attack. Risky, they said. He would be killed, they said. Maybe. But there were six people in that hut. Someone had to take the risk to save them.

Gunshots popped like firecrackers. Grenades exploded. Straw roofs burst into flame. Screams lanced the atmosphere as one group attacked, another fought back. Inside the prisoners' hut six soldiers—four Cambodians, two Americans—hung from crosstrees, trussed like pigs. Naked. Face down. Fair game for the red ants and venomous snakes that patrolled the jungle floor. He saw one North Vietnamese guard. His pistol was drawn. Aimed at a black soldier whose knee had been shattered.

He heard the enemy say, "White man don't care about you. Charlie don't care about you. No one care about Negro." He remembered watching that small yellow hand line up the shot, that skinny finger cock the trigger. He remembered shouting, "I care," and blowing the NVA soldier's head off. After that, he couldn't remember a thing.

Steven's eyes fluttered open. They stared at the man hovering over his bed. That face. That voice. Finally, they came together. His lips wobbled as he recognized the man he had saved.

"You smilin' at me, Cap'n?"

Steven forced his eyes to blink.

"Well, look at that! That man even blinks with an accent."

Steven's mouth tried to smile. Then he tried to speak.

"Where . . . who . . ."

"We're in Saigon. You're the Hunky Honky who saved my ass. This here is Melody. She's the luscious nurse who saved your ass. And I'm Shadow, only one of hundreds who wants a piece of her ass."

It hurt when he laughed, but to Steven the pain was welcome. It meant he was alive. He must have groaned, because the woman called Melody bent over him. Her face had lost its merry blush. She pressed her wrist to his forehead and thrust a thermometer in his mouth. She strapped a cloth band around his arm, tied it in place, and began pumping a small rubber ball. Holding the metal disc from her stethoscope against the inner flesh of his elbow, she watched the meter that registered blood pressure. He watched, too, having no idea what he was looking for, but looking just the same.

Melody untied her contraption, removed the thermometer from his mouth, shouted something unintelligible to another nurse, and began to probe his upper torso. Suddenly, his pain localized.

"You have a bullet wound in your left shoulder and four broken ribs," she said, explaining the layers of tape banding his shoulder and chest and the excruciating spasms radiating from his rib cage outward. "And," she went on, "a full-blown major-league case of malaria."

The second nurse handed Melody a needle, which she promptly stabbed into his right arm. "Quinine," she said, swabbing the spot with alcohol. "We tried giving you chloroquine but you didn't respond, so we moved on to the hard stuff."

Steven nodded. Again, he wasn't clear on everything she was saying. All he knew was that he felt hot.

"You've been one sick bastard," Shadow said, shaking his head. "By the time we found the choppers, you were pretty near out of your mind."

Words formed images. Images became pictures.

"Your knee?" Steven asked, seeing again that butchered joint, recalling how even after they had packed it and bandaged it, it had insisted upon bleeding. He remembered how brave this man had been, marching despite the pain, refusing to be carried, accepting only occasional assistance.

"The docs patched it. I won't be doing deep knee bends for a while, but hey! I'm walkin' and talkin' so what the hell!"

Steven started to smile. Another picture insinuated itself onto his consciousness. He tried to sit but fell back onto his pillows, breaking into a sweat. "The box," he said, panting. "Did we get the box?"

Shadow patted Steven's hand gently. At the same time, he laughed uproariously. Groggy as he was, Steven knew one gesture was private, just between the two of them. The other was for public consumption.

"Did we get the black box? Fuckin' A! We're heroes, Captain Kardos. Grade A, number-one all-American heroes!"

"What happened?"

"After you splinted my leg, we untied the rest of our boys. Then we strip-searched the gook who seemed determined to have my rump roastin' on his barbecue. After that, we dug around in the mud. It took a while, but we found it buried just below where my pecker was hangin'. Can you beat that? If you hadn't showed up, for sure I would've wound up pissin' all over our nation's secrets." He paused, waiting for a slow smile to settle on Steven's lips. When it did, he winked. "They would've court-martialed me, but it would've been worth it." He laughed again. He had attracted an audience by now and they laughed with him. "Would've served Uncle Sam right, though, for being such a bigot. If he'd left his precious codes with me in the first place, they never would've been lost. Once I get my hands on a black box, brother, I don't never let go!"

The entire tent whooped and hollered. Shadow took a bow. Melody swatted the side of his head.

"You're disgusting."

"You're jealous," he said, pinching her butt. "How long's it been since you've had a good hump?"

"My private life is none of your business."

"It's not your life we're interested in," someone shouted from across the room. "It's your privates!"

"I don't do anything with privates," Melody countered, feigning an attitude. She knew she was helpless to stop the ribald banter, but she was used to it. It was harmless and, in a strange way, therapeutic.

"You better get better quick, Cap'n," Shadow said, looking over at Steven, whose face was drenched in sweat. "This woman is ripe."

"I'll remember that, Sergeant."

Shadow beamed. It was the first sentence Steven had spoken in a week. When Shadow looked over again, Steven had drifted back to sleep, but this time his face wasn't contorted and his body wasn't twitching around the bed.

The next time Steven awoke, four hours later, he was more alert and more curious.

"Don't you ever leave?" he asked his companion, truly concerned.

"That's why they call me Shadow," the black man whispered, patting Steven's shoulder. "Don't you pay me no mind. I'm here 'cause I want to be. You saved my life, Captain. The least I can do is baby-sit you till you're strong enough to get up and out of this here bed. Besides, thanks to you, we've got some R and R coming to us. Uncle Sam has decided we did such a great job saving his butt, we're worth two deluxe tickets to the Big Apple." Steven's eyes widened in amazement. "That's right! We're going to New York City. Man! If that's not hot shit, I don't know what is!"

"New York City." Steven said it the same way he might have said Tanzania. He had never been to either place. Both were exotic. Both were very far away.

"All you have to do is kick this damn fever and we're outa here!"

"I'm working on it, Shadow."

"I know that, sir. I surely do know that."

A week later, Captain Steven Kardos and Sergeant James Jackson boarded a medical plane bound for Johns Hopkins Hospital in Baltimore, Maryland. After a month's stay Steven's malaria was said to be cured; his shoulder wound and his ribs were healed. Shadow had undergone reconstructive surgery on his knee and was able to get around with the help of a cane.

The third week in August, Steven and his self-appointed bodyguard-for-life were sent to New York for two weeks' R & R, courtesy of the United States government.

•   •   •

"If I ate chitlins and collard greens and survived, you can suffer through a bowl of *gulyásleves* and a plate of *káposzta*."

As Shadow grumbled about the fate of his stomach, Steven inspected the menu of a small restaurant in the Hungarian section of New York, decided it was to his liking, and pushed open the door.

He and Shadow had been exploring the area all afternoon, with Steven translating names and relating a few tales of his days in Hungary and his escape to America. The day before, they had visited Harlem at Shadow's insistence. Each had proved an eye-opening experience for the other.

Uptown, according to Shadow, was everything above 96th Street and below the Bronx. Uptown was black, except for the area around 110th Street known as El Barrio, which was Latin. Uptown was—especially to those from midtown—foreign territory, another city from the one where women spilled out of taxicabs and limousines to shop on Fifth Avenue, and businessmen with leather attaché cases bustled about in linen suits and silk ties on their way to air-conditioned offices and executive bathrooms. It was another land entirely from the one where doormen guarded the entrances to elegant cooperatives and children skipped in the park while their mommies or governesses sunned themselves on nearby benches.

Where Shadow came from, on the South Side of Chicago, there were no doormen and no parks.

"My mother was a prideful woman who refused to take welfare," he told Steven. "Instead she worked as a maid for a family in Evanston. My sisters and I wore their hand-me-down clothes and ate their leftover food. Lucky for me their boy was about two years older, so I got his shoes."

"Sounds familiar," Steven said. "My brother and I lived off my aunt and uncle, eating from their table, dressing in whatever the neighbors had no use for. The difference was," Steven said, thinking back, trying to remember what his shirts and pants had looked like before they turned colliery gray, "I'll bet your clothes were better, used, than our clothes were when they were new!"

Steven went on to describe how he and Matthew had saved to buy one extra sweater to share between the two of them, or a second pair of shoes. He recalled the drafty garage apartment, the long walk to school, the tedious hours in the mine after school. He even told Shadow how he and his brother had been bullied because they had been immigrants and spoke with accents and therefore were different from the majority.

To Shadow, all of this was a revelation. Though he supposed that in a barely used pocket of his consciousness he knew better, he had never met a white man as poor and disadvantaged as a black man.

"This was in Kentucky?"

"A little town called Woodridge that was no more than a fat bend in the road."

"Any dudes like me in Woodridge?"

"Every day at five o'clock there were hundreds of men who looked just like you."

It took Shadow a minute, but he laughed. Then, his face grew serious. "Why'd you save me? I mean, that gook in Cambodia wasn't far from wrong. We blacks aren't the favorite sons, you know, 'specially in the South. Some white folk there would rather shoot us than look at us."

Without breaking his stride, Steven draped his arm around Shadow's shoulder. "Not this white folk."

That night, Shadow had treated Steven to dinner and jazz at a popular uptown club called Small's, a dark, smoky place filled with all the seething vitality that was Harlem after the assassination of Martin Luther King, Jr. Steven had a wonderful time. He wasn't the only white man in the place, but as a white man in uniform sitting with a black man in uniform, he was getting more than his share of attention. The women flirted with him. The men seemed suspicious of him. Shadow advised him to ignore all of them and "just dig the music."

"Tonight I want you to dig *my* music," Steven said now as he and Shadow walked into the dimly lit bar of Csárda. "*Cigányzene*—gypsy jazz."

A small woman, with peroxide-blond hair fluffed around a pretty face struggling to hold on to its youth, approached them.

"You two boys here for dinner or just drinks?"

"How about drinks and then dinner?" Steven asked. He wouldn't voice it, but all afternoon he had been suffering an attack of nostalgia. Though he was hungry, he wanted to stretch the evening out for as long as he could. This woman, this restaurant, this neighborhood—they were infecting him with a gnawing homesickness for a place he barely remembered.

"Grab a barstool and tell me your pleasure."

Steven and Shadow mounted the wooden stools and ordered: bourbon and water for Steven, scotch neat for Shadow.

"*Egészsünkre!*" Steven said, raising his glass, including Shadow and the friendly woman behind the bar in the sweep of his arm.

"Is that what you Hunkies call a toast?"

"That's it," Steven said, chuckling as Shadow tried to imitate what he had said, mangling the word beyond recognition.

"Before I take one sip, tell me what that egesh-clunker stuff means, 'cause if this tastes like that sounds, it's gotta be poison!"

"It means 'cheers to all of us,' " Steven explained. "And if you want to taste Hungarian poison, have a glass of plum brandy."

The woman behind the bar laughed. It was a lusty sound, one that struck a familiar chord in Steven's ear. "Guaranteed to make your socks roll up and down," she said, refilling both their glasses. When they protested, she said, "This is on the house."

"That's nice of you, but you don't have . . ."

"I know he's not Hungarian," she said, tilting her head in Shadow's direction, "but you are. This is my way of saying *szia* and glad to have you here."

Steven smiled his thanks and drank his bourbon. As Shadow and the barkeep chatted, Steven indulged himself in the thick Magyar atmosphere of Csárda, letting the sights and sounds and smells transport him back to his childhood. A mural on the opposite wall depicted Lake Balaton and *Rózsakö* on the southern shore. Steven remembered visiting the Rose Rock with his family the summer before Béla and Margit were killed. He remembered Margit telling him that it was believed that if a man and woman sat upon the rock with their backs to the lake and thought about each other, they would be married by the end of the year. He smiled at the memory. That day, Béla had taken Steven aside and told him that when they had been young, he and Margit had sat upon that rock and, true to the legend, had wed before the year was out. Steven recalled how grown up and important he had felt receiving his father's confidence.

Behind the bar, hidden beneath the wooden rack where Csárda's glasses were stored, a row of photographs caught his eye. They were mostly black-and-white snapshots and not very large, but they, too, felt familiar. There was one of a group of babushkas—older women with colorful scarves tied around their heads, pie-round faces and bulbous cheeks that in real life had probably been bright pink. There was one of a boy playing a violin, another of a young girl playing the piano. Next was a woman and a large man with a worker's cap tilted at a rakish angle. Steven stopped. Something about that picture held his attention. While he stared at it, wishing he could get closer, the woman's voice changed. She was speaking Hungarian to the other bartender. Suddenly his heart started pounding. When she switched languages, the pitch of her voice altered. He turned and gaped at her.

"May I see that picture?" he said, pointing to the one of the couple. His hand was shaking.

"Sure," she said, thinking he was having an attack of battle fatigue, wondering if he was going to turn violent. Slowly, so as not to upset him, she took the photograph off the wall and handed it to him. He stared for several minutes.

"Your name," he demanded, gazing at the picture, then at her, mentally trying to scratch away the years. "It's Zsuzsanna, isn't it? Zsuzsanna Pal!" She nodded, afraid to do more. "It's me, Zsuzsanna! István! Kardos István."

Zsuzsanna dropped the glass she was holding. She might have fainted if Sándor hadn't caught her.

"István?" Her voice was a whisper, almost a prayer. He leaned closer so she could see him better. Within seconds her hands had clasped his face and drawn it to her. "István," she murmured as she studied his features. The handsome man in the khaki uniform with the thin black line curving around his left eye faded and a small boy from another time emerged. As the memory grew stronger and the resemblance sharper, she nodded her head, allowing a flood of happy tears to dance down her cheeks. "I can't believe it's you. I thought maybe you were dead. I . . . I didn't know what to think. . . . I didn't know where you . . . Mátyás! How is Mátyás?"

Steven walked around to the other side of the bar, wrapped his arms around Zsuzsanna, and hugged her. She was trembling, so even after they parted he kept his arm around her waist to steady her. "Mátyás is fine," he said, taking a cocktail napkin from the bar and gently wiping the tears from Zsuzsanna's face. "In fact, I called him last night. He's coming to New York this weekend."

Again, Zsuzsanna's eyes pooled.

"If you two want to have a private reunion, maybe this Sándor guy can show me to the nearest table." Shadow's emotions had roller-coastered from fear for his captain's sanity to embarrassment at watching something so personal and so moving as the scene being played out in front of him. "Come on, Sandy. Get me some grub!"

"Would you mind, Shadow?" Steven hated the idea that he was making his friend uncomfortable, but he couldn't help it.

"Any pretty women in there, Sandy, my pal?" When Sándor winked, Shadow slid off the stool, leaned on his cane, commandeered the bartender, and saluted Steven. "No need to hurry, sir. Those gypsy girls are gonna take one look at this chocolate soldier and rip this joint apart trying to get a piece!"

Zsuzsanna and Steven filled each other in on those blank years. They talked about Mihai and Vera and Mátyás and what life had been like in the hills of Kentucky and on the side streets of New York. Now and then Zsuzsanna wept, unable to control the waves of emotion tiding inside her. For years she'd believed that she had dealt with the pain of leaving her family behind, of leaving Hungary, of having Mihai leave her. She believed that she had stored those emotions away, that she had secured them beneath a pane of glass, framing them like the pictures she hung on her walls. It was easier keeping them contained that way. Then she could look at her memories without touching them, deal with them for a brief, painless moment and move on. Never did she allow them to edge beyond those frames, to overflow their boundaries and seep into her heart. If they did, she feared her heart would break from the weight of regret and loneliness for what was and what might have been.

"Do you hear from your brother?" Steven asked.

"The censors work overtime on correspondence between dissidents and traitors." Her response was honest, but deliberately vague. She knew what he was going to ask next, but she had to hear how he was going to ask before she answered.

"How's Katalin? Is she still playing the piano? Is she all grown up and beautiful?"

Zsuzsanna heard the shy hopefulness in his voice. To know that the unspoken name in all of Katalin's dreams was standing here in the flesh, and that he had thought of Katalin more than once during the intervening years, was a great relief.

"She is still playing the piano, and yes, she's all grown up and beautiful." Zsuzsanna linked her arm through his before he could interrogate her further and steered him toward the dining room. "But we have lots of time to reminisce. Right now, your friend is waiting."

She had seen the disappointment on Steven's face then, and the three other times he attempted to raise Katalin's name. Each time, she deflected his questions. He'd get his answer soon enough.

Shadow had polished off an appetizer of cabbage stuffed with meat and rice, a bowl of lentil soup, a helping of cucumber salad, and steak "Hortobágy style"—beef braised in stock with a large dumpling. By the time Steven joined him he had drunk most of the Bull's Blood by himself and was now offering his glass up to Sophie, who had uncorked bottle number two.

"They starve you in the army?" Sophie said as she poured the dark wine into his glass.

"In more ways than one, sugar. You want to help fill my other needs, you just say the word!" Shadow laughed. It was a deep, mirthful baritone that said: here was a man who had experienced more than his share of serious moments and therefore knew how special honest laughter was.

"Don't hold your breath, soldier boy." Sophie pretended to be annoyed, but she couldn't hide the smile that lurked just beneath her scowl. "Where'd you find him?" she asked, turning to Steven for sympathy.

"He was hanging around a hut in Cambodia. I just happened by. I saved his life. He saved mine. You know how it is."

Sophie looked from one to the other. The affection between them was genuine and palpable. "Yeah," she said, deciding she liked them both. "I know how it is."

Sophie disappeared into the kitchen to collect another order. Zsuzsanna returned. Though she didn't say anything, Steven thought he noticed a change in her demeanor, a skittishness that could have been nerves or impatience. She was gulping her wine, looking toward the curtain at the other end of the room. Occasionally she checked her watch. When the gypsy band entered from behind the curtain, she jittered in her chair so badly, she almost spilled her wine.

Steven shifted to gain a better view of the quartet. Waving his hand, he encouraged Shadow to do the same. As the *prímás*, or band leader, held his violin beneath his chin and began to play the slow introductory part of the *csárdás* known as the *lassú*, Steven felt a strange excitement overtake him. The lights in the room had dimmed, diluting his sense of place. For a moment the specific vision blurred, dissolving into a generic tableau of diners and entertainers. The scene was so familiar it had a taste to it, a pungency that made him feel as if he were being held in limbo, caught between the present and the past.

A powerful sense of *déjà vu* enveloped him. Instead of fighting it, he closed his eyes and allowed himself to be swallowed by it. The lush romanticism of the violin transported him back to his uncle János's house, where on Sundays, Rosza played records from the old country. As the other violin and the bass joined in, Steven drifted further back into his history, to Budapest and a time when he felt sheltered and loved and attached, that special time before Margit and Béla had died and his life had been forcibly shunted onto a different path.

The *prímás* stroked the strings of his violin, drawing from the wooden box a sweet sadness that cried and exulted at the same time. It was a special sound that only a violin could produce. Like the keen of a mourner at the grave of a loved one, it sang a plaintive, pathetic duet of bitterness for what death had removed, thankfulness for what life had left behind.

The rhythm quickened. The cimbalom set the pace, filling the air with a jaunty wildness that soon became a frenzy. The two violins flamed with the heat of the tune, bows flying across strings. The bass reveled in a lower, darker register, but even there in the depths of the scale, the notes were picked and strummed with lightning speed.

Steven clapped his hands along with the rest of the audience, but he was experiencing more than simply a musical high. He felt reborn, energized by a drug that had miraculously expunged every unhappy, unpleasant second of his life. For these few moments, there was no pain, no uncertainty, no heartache, no loneliness. Only joyousness and sunshine remained. As he glanced over at Zsuzsanna, his mind transposed her to another place, a large apartment with a spinet piano and a sparkling chandelier. Seeing her there, seeing himself, he found himself thinking of Zsuzsanna's family, of Zoltán with his mangled hands and Mária with her small form and huge talent and, of course, Katalin.

Her name flashed across his brain. His head turned. The young woman playing the cimbalom! She was dressed in the garb of the gypsies, with layers of colorful skirts, an oversized white blouse, and a bib of golden chains. But the scarf tied about her head covered only part of her hair. The rest hung down her back like a golden curtain, soft and shimmery against her skin. Gypsies didn't have tawny hair. They didn't have velvety white skin that rivaled the petals of a calla lily. And they didn't have eyes the pale green color of Siamese celadon.

Steven closed his eyes again. He had dreamed of her a thousand times, but his dreams had remained shackled to the only reality he dared allow himself to save. He was nine years old. He was in an auditorium listening to a seven-year-old play an obscure piece by a French composer. He had always been afraid to dream beyond that moment, afraid that his dream would leap forward into a nightmare of death and burials and good-byes and never-again. His eyes shot open. He turned to Zsuzsanna, his question forming on his lips. Before he could speak, she smiled and nodded. Katalin! His hand went to his chest. His fingers sneaked between the buttons of his shirt and grasped his good-luck charm—the key he had carried with him every day since she had given it to him so many years before.

For the rest of the set he sat transfixed, trying to drink her in without drowning. As he watched her play he couldn't believe that the beauty before him was the little girl he had left behind in the city by the Danube. He couldn't believe any of it—that she was here, that he was here. He had wandered into Csárda by chance, had found Zsuzsanna by chance. Was it chance? he wondered as again his fingers sought the familiar comfort of the key. Or that word people often used to explain the inexplicable: *destiny.*

• • •

As Katalin walked toward him, part of him begged her to recognize him immediately so there would be no awkward moments, no uncomfortable pauses. Another part of him needed time to consider what he wanted to say. When she was merely steps away, he stood.

"Katya?" She stopped. The smile that had graced her face disappeared. It was rude to call a Hungarian by her nickname. *Katya* was something only family and those very close to her would have used, and even then only in private. "Katalin," he said, realizing his gaffe, addressing her properly. "I'm sorry. I didn't mean to offend you. I'm an old friend. We knew each other a long time ago. In Budapest. I used to live on Dozsa György ut. In 1956 my parents were killed. My brother and sister and I left Hungary."

As he spoke, her eyes contracted with suspicion, but then, as she began to intuit who he was, they widened with growing disbelief.

"The night we left, you gave me this." He reached inside his shirt and pulled out the key, which hung on a chain alongside his dogtags. Sophie, having been told by Zsuzsanna who Steven was, had positioned herself next to Katalin. When Katalin began to tremble, Sophie slipped her arm around her friend's waist to steady her. "You told me I would always have a place to come home to. I haven't made it back to Budapest as yet," he said, shrugging his shoulders, as if he had just surrendered to fate. "But if you're here, I have no need to be there."

A slow smile inched its way onto his mouth as he followed her eyes on a hesitant path to his pocket and the name tag above it: KARDOS.

"István?"

Recognition flooded her face; his smile grew. Her lips mimicked his, curling upward in a delighted arc. His eyes locked on hers and remained there, unblinking, holding her tight in his line of vision as if she were a mirage from the Hortobágy steppes and any second might fade from view. Though they couldn't see it or feel it, others noticed that their bodies had tensed. They appeared poised on the precipice of a moment, like runners awaiting the pop of a starter's gun. Instead of moving toward each other, however, they stayed frozen to their marks, paralyzed by the adult emotions that had erupted at the realization of their childhood dreams.

Then Steven bridged the years and folded Katalin into his arms. It amazed him how perfectly they fit. She was tall and graceful, with long arms and legs. Though spare of flesh, even through her clothes he could feel a lean lushness of form. The embrace lasted only seconds, but for Steven it was time enough to fall in love. To see her, to hold her, to breathe the air around her, was to have each of his senses fully charged. Everything she did, including the subtlest of movements, elicited a near-electric response. The gossamer feel of her hair caressing his face. The delicate blend of hyacinth and jasmine tickling his nose. The sensation of down feathering his skin as her cheek brushed against his. The taste of her lips. He felt as if he had been transported from the reality of Csárda to the enchanted world of Prospero's island. There, empowered by the magic of the place, a figment of his imagination had been transformed into this beautiful creature of warm blood and soft flesh.

As they parted he closed his eyes and reopened them quickly, testing, affirming that the woman in his arms was truly the girl from his past. She looked different, of course—older, more developed, more sophisticated—yet, looking at her eyes with their exotic Magyar shape, her lips with their sensuous fullness, he believed that close up, he would have known her anywhere. As they joined the others at the table and excited conversation eddied around them, he observed hand movements that struck a chord, expressions that jogged a memory. Her voice had changed, dropping half an octave, conjuring a haunting echo of her mother, Mária. Her laugh, also achingly familiar, made him want to cry for the pictures it retrieved and the feelings it evoked.

He never knew when the music ended and the crowd dispersed. He never heard Shadow or Sophie say good night. He never felt Zsuzsanna buss his cheek as she left, to close the register and then go to her apartment and to sleep. He wasn't even certain that he heard a single word of the conversation between himself and Katalin. He was too absorbed in the miracle of being in her presence, immersed in the simple wonder of having found her again after all those years and all those miles.

When, finally, she called a reluctant end to the evening, shyly reminding him that she had school the next day, he damned the frailty of the human condition, cursing the need to sleep in order to function. If only the body could respond to the will of the heart, he thought. He knew it was foolish and probably unnecessary, but he had been gripped by an urgency that warned him to stay with Katalin. Pulsing just below the level of normal behavior was the irrational fear that he would leave her at her door only to find that the door was a facade, that she was an illusion, that the entire night had been a chimeric vision, a malarial hallucination. If he let her go, he was certain she would fall through the looking glass and disappear forever.

Outside, a fire engine shrieked up the avenue. Somewhere near her there had been a call for help. Someone was in danger. Blanketed by the heat of the summer night, Katalin listened to the sounds of the city as they drifted in through the window and mingled with her aunt Zsuzsanna's light snoring. She supposed that if asked, Sophie and Judit would probably advise caution. They would remind her that she and István had known each other as children, and then only for a few years. They would point out that now they were adults and that puppy love was not something upon which to base a relationship. They might also present the argument that his attentions had been kindled not only by the coincidence of finding her again, but also by the natural urgings of a soldier on leave.

Katalin listened to the silence that spoke to her. Then she listened to her heart and dismissed the gloomy prophecies of her two Cassandras. She was innocent and frightened of the stirrings she felt—that much she was willing to admit. But she had loved István since she was seven years old. He had left her then, yet she had continued to think about him even when the odds of their ever seeing each other again were slimmer than a spider's thread. Tonight, just as suddenly as he had exited her life, he had walked back into it. If tomorrow or next week he left again, so be it.

Up to now her life had been characterized by isolation and hard work. Though she loved her music and would never have described herself as a martyr to its cause, the piano had demanded, from the time she was three years old, that she be locked away with a keyboard, practicing for a tomorrow that had yet to come.

That night, peering into the dark and seeing István's strong face before her, feeling his arms around her, she decided that, for once, she was going to live for today. She was going to put pleasure ahead of diligence, love ahead of duty. István had one week remaining to his leave. Seven days. One hundred and sixty-eight hours. An incalculable number of wonderful moments.

While the tiny voice that lived inside her tried to justify this radical shift in behavior, another voice, that of her mother, spoke, overwhelming her nagging conscience. Just before Katalin drifted off to sleep, she remembered something Mária used to say: "Time enjoyed is time well spent."

15

Since, as Shadow put it, Steven had been rendered senseless by an overdose of paprika and was doomed to spend the rest of his leave in Little Budapest, Shadow had decided to fly to Chicago to visit his family.

Steven watched the taxi pull away from the curb and into the traffic headed for the East River Drive. He trained his eyes on the cab until it turned and disappeared behind a row of buildings. When it did, an incongruous chill gripped Steven's body. He shivered as if an arctic wind had lost its way and surfaced on an August afternoon in the middle of New York City. Recognizing it for the spate of loneliness that it was, he attempted to shake it off, but try as he might, he missed Shadow already.

Steven had never had any real friends. There was Mátyás—but he didn't count, because he was a brother. There had been Vera, of course, and Katalin, who he supposed didn't count either, because back then she was just a girl and therefore an unseemly confidante for a rough-tough boy like himself. Now she was a woman he wanted as something more than a pal. He had cared deeply for Mihai and Zsuzsanna, as guardians and saviors. There had been Nell Mahoney, but she had been a teacher-friend, which was very different from a buddy. Shadow was a buddy.

Funny, he thought, one never realized how large the holes in one's life were until someone dived into them. Until Shadow, Steven hadn't identified certain of his emotional rumblings as a longing for companionship. Perhaps to do so would have seemed disloyal to Matthew. Perhaps it would have exaggerated the insulting behavior of his cousins. Perhaps it simply hurt too much to think about it.

Over the past couple of months, like a foal taking his first steps, Steven had allowed Shadow to lead him and to teach him the art of friendship. Because he was so needy and Shadow was so generous, they leapfrogged over the early stages of fellowship, jumping feet first into the heart of it: the spontaneous, nonobligatory caring of one for another, the give-and-take that has to exist between two who have no family bonds. Within a very short time he and Shadow amassed a file of experience that cemented their relationship. For Steven, the hardest part was learning to trust. Growing up in a communist state, where often even family members were government spies, and then with the Vas family, who never succeeded in making him feel completely welcome, he trusted few, and never counted on anyone one hundred percent except Matthew. Until Shadow. He trusted him implicitly. After all, he thought, chuckling at the irony of the situation, how many friends had been compelled to depend on each other for their very lives before one even knew the other's name?

Out of the corner of his eye Steven caught a glimpse of himself in a storefront window. There was no one in the picture with him—no one behind him, no passersby, no stopped cars, no one to help fill the lens. He stood alone, and just then he felt alone. In that moment he experienced an epiphany of sorts. Apart from Matthew, Shadow was the only man Steven felt he could confide in and rely on. In a moment of flashing prescience, he knew that for the rest of his life, no matter how many men he met, he would continue to feel exactly that way.

It was twelve-thirty. Steven was supposed to meet Katalin at Juilliard at three o'clock outside her practice room on the fifth floor. He would be ridiculously early, but so what, he decided as he hailed a cab and raced crosstown. When he located the room, he peered through the narrow rectangular window in the door. Her back was to him. For several minutes he watched as her hands gamboled over the keyboard. Lightly, yet with authority, her fingers sounded the notes of what he thought he recognized as a Liszt concerto. Now and then, in a forte passage, her body responded to the exertion of power. Her hands rose and fell in balletic leaps. Her head snapped, swishing her braid across her back like a horse's tail swatting flies. He couldn't see her face, but he knew her eyes were closed, just as they had been when she had played the Poulenc so very long ago.

Pirating a chair from a hallway lounge, Steven planted himself just outside the door, where he could listen to her play without creating a disturbance. For an hour and a half he delighted in his private concert. Several times he heard her repeat sections, altering the emphases, changing the pedaling or, he assumed, the fingering. It all sounded marvelous to him, but he knew his was an ignorant ear, while hers was attuned to perfection.

Could he meet her exacting standards? Certainly he wasn't perfect. Actually, he thought, letting a self-deprecating grin insinuate itself on his lips, he was far from it. He was twenty-three years old and dead broke. He had no formal education beyond high school, another year to his hitch in the service, and only a vague notion of what he wanted to do afterward. He intended to go to college. That much was definite. Nothing else was. The only absolutes: He would never make his home in Woodridge and would never return to the mines.

"May I help you?" A man garbed all in black stood over him like a raven seeking a perch.

Steven bounded to his feet, instantly at attention. "I'm a friend of Miss Gáspár's. I was supposed to meet her here at three."

"It's two-thirty."

"I'm early."

"I see that." The man considered Steven before granting him the honor of an introduction. "I'm Paul Greco, Katalin's tutor." He offered his hand for a brief handshake. "You must be Steven Kardos."

"I am," Steven said, wondering whether it was Katalin or Zsuzsanna who had told Greco about him. "Pleased to meet you."

"I understand you're here on R and R. How long will you be in New York?"

"Five more days."

Again, Greco's face exhibited signs of internal debate. "Zsuzsanna tells me you're an old friend from Hungary. Because of that, I'm going to permit Katalin to forgo several of her lessons so she can show you our city, but please remember, she does need time to practice."

Though Steven said he understood and returned to his seat like an obedient schoolboy when Greco went into the room to speak to Katalin, Steven's reaction to Greco was to be instantly jealous. He hated the thought that this man—or any man, to be honest—was in a position to exercise such control over Katalin's life. Who was this Greco to decide whether or not Katalin was able to spend time with Steven? Had she empowered him to take such liberties? Was Greco taking advantage of Katalin's dependency on her tutor? Or his relationship with Zsuzsanna? When Katalin had told him about it, he had been shocked. He still was. How could she! Steven thought with self-righteous indignation.

Greco was almost ten years younger than Zsuzsanna. What was she thinking?

Stop it! he reprimanded himself. Their affair was none of his business. Knowing that didn't keep him from pacing the hallway like a cadet on report. As he did, he thought about his anger. It didn't take long to give it a name: Mihai. He had no right, yet he was annoyed that when, after all these years, he had finally found Zsuzsanna, she was not with Mihai. Steven cared deeply about Mihai. The man had saved his life. Steven would have liked to have seen Mihai, to talk to him, to exchange stories with him, to show him the kind of man he had become. In his mind, Paul Greco was not a viable subsitute for Mihai Pal.

You're being ridiculous, he mumbled to the air around him. *You're being selfish and immature. They divorced because they weren't happy. It's been years. Whatever Zsuzsanna wants to do and with whomever she wants to do it, is none of your goddam concern.*

He hadn't realized the music had stopped until the door swung open and Katalin was standing before him, smiling. Then she was taking his hand. To his immense satisfaction, she tossed Greco a casual good-bye.

For the rest of that afternoon and two days after that, Steven and Katalin were inseparable. Though she made an admirable guide and he a creditable tourist, sightseeing was only the surface. Their real exploration was of each other. Buildings, monuments, parks, statues—they were simply landmarks on a personal odyssey.

Steven and Katalin had known each other once, but because they had been so young, their past had become backdrop for a new drama played on a new stage. They played their parts believing they were acting on instinct, reveling in the process of discovery, completely unaware that they were following a script written long ago by the ancient gods of love.

They talked about everything, each new topic performing the task of a probe, exploring beyond the facade of conversation, delving into the deeper realms of honest thought. He spoke about Vietnam and how he felt about being a Green Beret.

"Signing up for extra tours was my way of paying back," he said, refusing to explain further, unwilling to share with her the slow descent into hell that was every soldier's nightmare.

When she confessed that several months before, she and Sophie had marched in a demonstration against the war, his reply was gentle but pointed.

"Didn't it feel great knowing you were free to protest?" She nodded.

In fact, the day had been exhilarating. "In Hungary, you wouldn't be free to say anything the government didn't want you to say. Here, we are."

She spoke about Juilliard and Paul Greco and what it was like living with Zsuzsanna and being friends with someone like Sophie. He asked and she told him about Zoltán and Mária, Andras and Ilona, and Judit.

"Judit hasn't changed a whit. She's still very much the rebel," Katalin said with obvious admiration. "I think right after she spoke her first word, she took a solemn vow never to accept the status quo, no matter what it is. If she can challenge something, she does."

"Well, I say okay to that!" Steven grinned and flipped Katalin a thumbs-up. "If Judit can rattle cages without getting thrown into one, I say, go for it!"

"You're so American," Katalin said, giggling, amused at how easily colloquialisms dripped from his tongue.

"I am an American."

When Katalin winced, it struck him that never before had he felt self-conscious about his dual nationality. He was Hungarian by birth, American by declaration. Many Americans had waved another flag before the Stars and Stripes. No one paid attention to things like that. Katalin did, because she had known him, and still thought of him, as Magyar. And why not? Ethnically, he was. He looked Hungarian, ate Hungarian whenever he could, and occasionally, as he was doing with her, spoke Hungarian, not because he felt more comfortable, but because with certain people, like Matthew and Zsuzsanna, it felt natural.

"Don't you ever want to go back?"

It was such a short sentence, but with so many subtle shadings, he had difficulty sorting them out. He heard the programmed defense of the motherland. He heard an anticipated sense of loneliness for the time when she returned and he stayed. He suspected that lurking in a corner of consciousness, there was an admission that perhaps there was more to hold him here than to lure him there. And though he couldn't be certain, he thought he heard a whisper of indecision, a hint that it had occurred to her that making her home in the United States was not completely unthinkable.

"No. I don't want to go back," he said, in a way that was definite but gentle. "Even if I did, I'm an American citizen now. If I returned for a visit, the minute I crossed the border they'd take my passport and I'd never get out."

It saddened Katalin to agree, but he was right.

The first night, they partied with Zsuzsanna at Csárda. Pedjá was playing the piano and so, naturally, he and Sophie joined them for a late supper. It was immediately apparent that the three women at the table thought Pedjá charming and adorable. Steven found the blond Slav unctuous and excessively self-involved.

"You think that because he's a Slav," Katalin said later, when Steven indicated that he had been less than impressed. "I have to admit, at first I was guilty of the same prejudice," she said, referring to the universal Hungarian belief that Magyars were patrician; Slavs, peasants. "Then I got to know him. He's very talented and, despite his quirks, a lot of fun."

Indeed, Steven thought.

The next night, they attended a concert at Philharmonic Hall.

"Paul gave me the tickets," Katalin said, curious about the suspicious look on Steven's face. "He thought you'd enjoy seeing the stage where one day I hope to perform."

"That was nice of him."

Katalin stifled a smile. There was no mistaking the greenish tinge washing his words.

"You don't like him, do you?" she said, during the intermission.

Since Steven had no acceptable explanation for his feelings, he opted for the truth. "I'm out of line and I know it, but I can't help myself. I'm jealous. There you have it. I don't like the fact that he gets to spend hour after hour, week after week alone with you and I get a lousy five days, two of which are gone."

He plunked his elbow on the arm of the chair, rested his chin on his hand, and pouted like a petulant child. Katalin found him irresistible.

"Would it help if I told you I care more about you than I do about him?"

"Depends on how much," he said, keenly aware of her closeness. Unable to restrain himself, he leaned forward until their lips met. "How much more?"

"A lot," she said, marveling that such a simple brush of flesh could provoke such volcanic sensations.

"Good" was all he said. It was all he could trust himself to say.

Friday night, after dropping Katalin at Zsuzsanna's, Steven traveled to LaGuardia Airport and waited for his brother's plane to arrive. As the 707 taxied to the gate, Steven bobbed up and down like a cork in a bucket of water, so anxious to see Matthew he could barely contain his excitement. Until he spotted that ruggedly familiar face and that solid, square body strolling into the lounge, his heart started and stopped at least a dozen times.

Steven broke through the crowd and attached himself to Matthew, clinging to him as if he were a life source. "God, it's good to see you!"

"You too, baby brother," Matthew said, too shaken to bother about the tears sneaking onto his cheeks. "How about you? How's your shoulder? What about your ribs? Is the malaria gone?"

Matthew poked and prodded like a rancher examining a prize bull. Steven grabbed his brother's hands, held them tightly in his own, and laughed. "I'm in one piece. I swear it! Got any baggage?"

Matthew nodded impatiently and then returned to a subject he considered more important than luggage. "Why didn't you call me from Baltimore? I would've visited you in the hospital."

"That's why I didn't call." Steven piloted Matthew through the terminal, down the escalator, toward the baggage claim. "Hospitals are dreary places. It's more fun visiting here. Especially since I found Zsuzsanna and Katalin. Wait till you see them. They look terrific!"

Steven had called Woodridge twice: once when he arrived in New York to tell Matthew where he was, why he was in the States, and why Matthew shouldn't worry; a second time to relate the fabulous story about his serendipitous reunion with Zsuzsanna and Katalin. Over the phone, Matthew thought he detected in Steven's tone a special glee about finding Katalin. Now, the sparkle in his brother's eyes as he spoke her name verified the speculation.

As they waited for Matthew's suitcase and then during the cab ride into Manhattan, Matthew continued to interrogate Steven. He seemed desperate for every detail concerning Steven's health—both mental and physical—how he had fared in Vietnam, whether or not he was going back to active duty, what he wanted to do when he was discharged. He demanded that Steven open his shirt so he could see where they had removed the bullet. He pressed on Steven's ribs to assure himself that they, too, had mended. Then he proceeded to quiz Steven about his case of malaria, having borrowed a dozen medical books in order to research the disease thoroughly.

By the time they reached 74th Street, Steven was exhausted. He felt as if he had just lived through the Spanish Inquisition. It wasn't until Zsuzsanna opened the door and she and Katalin flung themselves at Matthew that he realized his brother had managed to neatly sidestep every question Steven had asked about him.

Matthew loved Csárda—the atmosphere, the music, the food, the people, everything. It felt like home, he said the first time he walked in, as though he could reach back in time and touch a part of his life he thought he'd never experience again. While Matthew, like Steven, had become a naturalized citizen, unlike Steven his soul was and would always be more Hungarian than American. Part of the reason was he had been older when he and Steven had left Budapest; his memories had been sharper, his tastes more ingrained, his habits more entrenched.

Yet he harbored no secret wishes to return to the land of his ancestors. He cherished his freedom. He admired the American work ethic and the seemingly endless American capacity for compassion and generosity toward those outside their borders. But Matthew had never glossed over American failings the way Steven liked to do. He had listed them on the same side of the ledger where he had listed Hungary's shortcomings. Deficits were deficits, no matter what the currency.

He had come from this, he thought as he delighted in the evening. Just as she had when Katalin had arrived, Zsuzsanna had invited many of her neighbors to meet her "nephews" and celebrate their homecoming. Over and over again she recounted the story of their escape. Matthew laughed as he heard the perils of their journey escalate and the bravery of Zsuzsanna expand with each telling of the tale. By the time she had completed her rounds and had deposited Matthew at his table, he was as convinced as anyone that if Zsuzsanna had stayed in Budapest, she would have defeated the Russians single-handedly.

Quiet by nature, Matthew was an inveterate observer. As he surveyed the crowd at Csárda, many of Zsuzsanna's friends insisted upon sharing their individual stories with him. Each biography contained chapters about suffering, about surmounting terrible odds, about the raw determination to keep a family together despite the costs of such commitment. The fact that each author considered the ending of his or her story a personal triumph and therefore happy—whether it would be judged the same by anyone else—did not surprise Matthew. When one is born of an ancestry forced to confess a thousand years of foreign domination—an ancestry that nonetheless survived, with its ethos and customs and sense of itself intact—one is born with an innate inability to be cowed.

In every stranger he found a familiar trait: vanity, hilarity, an intense capacity for enjoyment of the littlest pleasure, a love of music, a respect for intellectuals, a wariness of politicians. In every plate of food and glass of wine, he tasted his heritage.

When the gypsy band began to play, Matthew grew drunk with nostalgia, gripping Steven's hand as, inside, he grieved again for Béla, Margit, and Vera. Watching Katalin at the cimbalom, he found it hard to connect the magnificent young woman in front of him with the skinny little girl he remembered. Harder still were his attempts to picture Zoltán and Mária and what they might look like today. He tried, but his mind denied the request. To fill it might have prompted another demand: that he project the images of his parents and his sister onto his screen. Mercifully, his brain protected his heart.

The single jarring note in this otherwise harmonious evening was Sophie Wisnewski. Matthew didn't understand her. What's more, he wasn't certain he liked her. Probably because, from the outset, it seemed clear she didn't like him. When Zsuzsanna introduced them, Sophie peered at him as if he were an amoeba on a microscope slide. Her cornflower eyes moved from one part of his anatomy to the next, lingering as if assessing and then moving on as if she had found him lacking. When she had completed her appraisal, she looked down her cumbersome nose at him in a way designed to make him feel he was the subject to her monarchy.

Yet he saw the affection Zsuzsanna lavished on Sophie, sensed the affinity Katalin felt for the Polish girl. He couldn't help but notice the attraction she held for that other friend of Katalin's, Pedjá Lauc. The customers seemed to adore her. György and Sándor were protective of her. Even his brother displayed a positive response. Was it his reaction to her that was the problem? he wondered. Or her reaction to him?

Sophie's abrasive behavior toward Matthew had not gone unnoticed by Katalin. The first chance she got, she pulled Sophie off to the side.

"What's stewing?" she said, trying to sound casual.

"Cooking," Sophie corrected. "What's cooking?"

"Okay. So what's cooking?"

"Ask György. He's the chef."

"He's not the one giving Mátyás a hard time. You are."

Sophie drew herself up in a huff. "I'm doing no such thing."

"You're being nasty, Sophie, and you know it."

"Did he say that?" Her face scrunched into an expression Katalin couldn't read.

"He wouldn't say anything. You're my friend and he wouldn't want to insult me by insulting you."

Sophie raised her hands. Her laugh was loud and self-conscious. "Boy, for someone who doesn't speak a well English, you sure do know how to sock it to ya. I got your drift, Katalin. Okay. I got it. From now on, I'll be so nice to the coal minin' man, he'll think that cheap cologne he splashed on his kisser really does drive women wild."

"Thanks." Katalin fought the smile that wanted to rest on her lips. Sophie didn't deserve one. Not this time.

As Katalin turned and walked away, Sophie gritted her teeth. She wanted to call Katalin back and explain, but what would she say? That she knew her reaction seemed bizarre, but she was afraid of Matthew Kardos? That he was simply too handsome for her. Too nice. Too mature. Too perfect. Even if she told Katalin exactly how she felt, Katalin could never understand. Not unless Sophie told her the rest of it. And that she couldn't do.

It was late by the time Katalin and Zsuzsanna bid everyone good night. Though her body was exhausted, Katalin was too keyed up to sleep. Grabbing her music and a light throw, she ensconced herself on the sofa, curling her feet beneath her, trying to lose herself in one of Liszt's Rhapsodies. Sharps and flats, quarter notes and half notes traipsed before her eyes like a beginner's ballet class. Inherently graceful, they seemed clumsy and awkward, as if they had locked into a rhythm that kept them jammed a half-step behind. She wanted them to dance without inhibition, to pirouette and jeté across the page. Instead, they plodded about as if there were weights in their shoes dragging them down until they could do nothing but lie there in an overtaxed heap.

Sensing that her niece needed to talk, Zsuzsanna fixed a pot of tea for the two of them. Without tiptoeing about or pretending that she didn't wish to intrude on Katalin's silence, Zsuzsanna placed the teapot and its accouterments on the coffee table, served them both and, without apology, began to speak.

"Mátyás looks wonderful, don't you think?" Neither Zsuzsanna nor Katalin could bring herself to call Steven or Matthew by their English names.

Katalin nodded absently, still trying to conjure an interest in her music.

"István looks wonderful too. Or hadn't you noticed?" The involuntary blush that rouged Katalin's cheeks belied her outer calm. "It's too bad about that scar," her aunt continued, "but in a way, I suppose it only adds to his appeal. What do you think?"

Katalin gave up. Dropping the manuscript into her lap, she looked squarely at Zsuzsanna. "I think he's devastatingly handsome, scar or no scar. Are you happy now?"

"Are you?"

Katalin was thrown by Zsuzsanna's directness. "Yes. No. I don't know." Fussing with the fringe on one of the sofa's mob of pillows, she tried to straighten her thoughts at the same time she straightened the tangled silken threads. "I feel so strange when I'm with him. Wonderful, but scared. Excited and nervous at the same time. Giggly and silly. Oh, I don't know. Does any of it make sense?"

Zsuzsanna laughed. "Only if you recognize the symptoms of love."

Honest confusion clouded Katalin's eyes. "How can you love someone you haven't seen since you were seven years old?"

"How can you love someone you've known for only seven seconds?" Zsuzsanna replied knowingly. "It happens, *dragam*. It happens all the time."

"Are you in love with Paul Greco?"

Zsuzsanna's laugh was light and flirtatious, as if she believed Greco were hiding behind the drapery and would hear her answer. "No. And he's not in love with me. But we are lovers. We care about each other. We enjoy each other. But we've made no commitments, taken no vows."

"You're so different," Katalin said, trying to be tactful.

"Not as different as you think," Zsuzsanna said wistfully. For a second, while her physical presence remained, her spirit visited elsewhere. She arched an eyebrow and puckered her lips. She squiggled in her chair and pulled her robe across her chest. A slow, sultry smile insinuated itself on her mouth. It lingered and then, when the dream was done, disappeared. "The beautiful thing about Greco," Zsuzsanna said, continuing as if there had been no lapse, "is that he sees with his soul and not with his eyes. When he looks at me, he doesn't see a woman burdened by age. He sees that part of me that will never grow old, the part that still giggles at silly things and skips down the street and embraces life with a gusto that's eternal. But you should know that. After all, it's his ability to hear beyond the keyboard into the heart that makes him such an exceptional tutor."

Katalin nodded, but midway through Zsuzsanna's monologue, she had drifted. "István has to go back to Vietnam," she said.

"I know."

"What if something happens to him?"

"After everything you've seen and everything you've lived through, how can you not have learned that the only way to get the most out of life is to take it day by day?"

Katalin nodded. She did know that, but suddenly, for her, the days seemed to have fewer hours. "And then when he's discharged," she continued, her speech becoming more rapid, as if she were racing with her imaginary clock, "it'll be time for me to return to Hungary and then what'll I do? He can't go with me."

"Why can't you stay here?" Zsuzsanna heard the longing in her voice, as well as the betrayal of her brother. As if Zoltán were in the room with her, she immediately reassured herself she never would have suggested such heresy if Katalin hadn't prompted her.

"What about Mama and Papa?"

Zsuzsanna noticed that Katalin hadn't said she was opposed to the notion of staying. "Your father will never leave Hungary." Though it still pained her, she had come to terms with that reality years before. "Your mother will never leave your father."

"Then how can you expect me to leave them?"

"It's not what *I* expect or what *I* want, Katya. It's what you want. I know how difficult a decision like this is. Remember, I, too, once had a painful decision to make. But you wouldn't be alone. You'd have me and István and Mátyás and Sophie and Greco and all the other friends you've made. You'd also have the entire free world as your stage."

An odd look seized Katalin's face. Her mouth twitched, tilting from a half-smile to a half-frown, as if only part of her thoughts were pleasing. Her eyes narrowed in concentration; even her cheeks drew in as a revelation occurred to her.

"All my life I've done things because of my music. I've changed schools, given up playtime, sacrificed friendships, missed good movies, good books, school functions, and holiday celebrations." Zsuzsanna's nerves grew taut as Katalin's eyes glossed and her lower lip quivered like a rose petal in a rainstorm. As she waited for Katalin to continue, Zsuzsanna could only pray that her niece was not building up to an announcement of her retirement. "Just once, I'd like to do something for reasons other than music."

"Love is a good reason."

Katalin smiled at Zsuzsanna's lack of subtlety.

"I'm not certain I'm in love," she said, too fearful to admit the intensity of what she felt to herself, let alone someone else. "If and when I am, then we'll talk."

Zsuzsanna didn't comment when Katalin rose from the couch and escaped to the bedroom, but as she put the teapot and cups in the sink she smiled and quoted her favorite TV show: "You bet your bippy we will!"

The next night, at Sophie's suggestion, the Kardos brothers, Katalin, and Sophie hit the Joke Joint, a comedy club on the West Side. Like its main competition, the Improv, it was a cabaret that gave budding comics a chance to try their routines before an audience. Roy Diamond, the owner of the Joke Joint, acted as the emcee, and tonight the club featured Ricky Pearl, a young comic who had begun at the Joint and had returned a star. He was a veteran of the The *Tonight* Show, *The Carol Burnett Show*, and *The Ed Sullivan Show*. He had done guest shots on everything from *Get Smart* to *Green Acres* and he was a headliner at the Sands

Hotel in Las Vegas. Sophie thought he was fabulous. Matthew wasn't impressed. Pearl was an insult comic. Matthew didn't think making fun of people was funny.

"What is it?" Sophie said, after Pearl had finished his act. "Is there some state law in Kentucky that says if you laugh they raise your taxes? Christ, Matthew, loosen up."

"This is as loose as it gets," he said, unperturbed.

"You call this loose?" Sophie threw her head back, rolled her eyes, and grabbed her heart, as if her body had been jolted by an electric shock. "I'd hate to see you when you're uptight."

"He's not that bad," Steven said, defending his brother. "When he didn't think we were watching, I caught him chuckling at that chunky lady who came on before Pearl."

"Yeah, right. Me too. Next to him, Richard Nixon is a regular laugh riot."

Steven smiled and patted his brother on the back. "Matthew's just a bit on the serious side."

"A bit on the serious side," Sophie mimicked. "I would call that a gross understatement. This person sitting to my left is beyond serious. He's into stiff. Look at that face," she said, leaning forward and staring into Matthew's eyes. "Next stop, Mount Rushmore."

"Are you having fun?" Matthew asked, keeping his eyes fixed on hers.

"I always have fun," Sophie retorted, wanting to escape his gaze, unable to turn away. "Unlike you, I don't take anything seriously."

"I don't think that's true."

"I don't think I care what you think."

Sophie bounded to her feet and stormed out of the room. Steven ordered another round of drinks and quickly involved Matthew in a discussion about people back in Woodridge. Katalin retreated into an uncomfortable silence. The bad chemistry between Sophie and Mátyás upset her. She knew it had been naive to expect that simply because she wanted them to like each other, they would. Still, this instant intense antagonism struck her as peculiar. Something was off.

Knowing Sophie as she did, she had to agree with Mátyás's assessment: There were lots of things she took seriously. The problem was, she wouldn't tell anyone what they were and why they affected her the way they did. As for Mátyás, he, too, had his share of secrets.

The night before, Katalin had lured him away to the back of the bar at Csárda for a private talk. While asking him about what he was doing, coyly trying to understand why he hadn't left Woodridge in search of a better situation, she had noticed that his suit was new and of finer quality than she would have expected for someone in his line of work.

"I've managed to build a small nest egg just for special occasions like this," he had said.

When she probed further, he confessed that he had a modest stock portfolio that was doing quite well. If he stayed lucky and his investments continued to pay off, he confided, it might not be too long before he'd be able to quit the mines. His assessment of his finances had not been completely accurate. What he hadn't told her was that, thanks to Walter Perry and his own newly discovered gift for working the market, the two accounts he had established the day Steven had left for the service had more than tripled.

When she asked him if he was seeing anyone special or if he just played the field, he revealed that he never went out.

"It might sound ridiculous to you, but until István comes home safe and sound from Vietnam, the most I can see fit to do is have an occasional meal with the boys at O'Brian's. I don't think it would be right for me to be out kicking up my heels while my brother's getting shot at in some jungle."

Katalin didn't think it sounded at all ridiculous. In fact, it was precisely what she would have expected from Mátyás. While it was true that he was a reflective, somber being, she also knew him to be tuned like a highly sensitive alarm; the slightest provocation aroused his primary instinct, which was to protect. Mátyás was a caretaker. He always had been and, Katalin thought with assurance, always would be, which meant he might never laugh as much as Sophie would have liked him to. Caretakers always bore the burdens of others. It was their nature. It was their curse.

Maybe it was that difference that was at the root of the friction between him and Sophie. Sophie's signature was fierce independence. She couldn't tolerate assistance. She wouldn't accept help. Her antennae must have homed in on Mátyás's protective instincts. Before he could say "What can I do for you?" she had said, "No way."

Sophie returned just as the next comic mounted the stage. Fat, costumed in army green, his face painted in a traditional camouflage pattern, using a machine gun as a prop, he shouted at the audience, yelling about the war, the government, drugs, his sex life. Sprinkled among his invective were obscenities of the foulest order. Every now and then he paused, listening for the laughter and the applause he expected. When the crowd didn't reward his ability to string four-letter words together, he resorted to pointing the gun at them, screaming even louder.

Sophie leaned close to Matthew. "I don't think he's going to make it in prime time."

Without taking his eyes off the raging lunatic on the stage, Matthew said, "If he does, we're in a lot of trouble, because I'm funnier than he is."

It was hard to tell who was more surprised by Sophie's uproarious response to Matthew's quip: Steven, Katalin, or the so-called comic.

"I knew there had to be at least one intelligent life form in this pile of shit known as an audience," he railed, ignoring Roy Diamond's signal to exit the stage. "See that broad with the big schnoz and the Technicolor hair? She knows what's good."

"That depends on how you look at it," Sophie shouted back. "I'm Polish!"

The place rocked with laughter. Sophie loved it, especially when everyone turned and applauded her. Everyone, including Matthew Kardos.

"It went too fast," Steven said to Katalin in the cab on the way back to the city from the airport. "I feel as if I barely spent any time with him."

"That's because there were always so many other people around. Zsuzsanna and I should have left the two of you alone."

Steven took her hand. "Stop looking so guilty. He loved seeing you and Zsuzsanna, and in spite of how it appeared, I think he enjoyed meeting Sophie."

At Zsuzsanna's insistence, Sophie had deigned to join them at Sunday breakfast—for her, a rarity. Though Sophie made a show of trying to restrain her impulse to gibe, she couldn't resist slipping a few wisecracks in between the salami and eggs and cheese and rolls and coffee and streusel cake. Still, Matthew had kissed her good-bye. And Katalin was certain she had noticed a faint blush pinking Sophie's cheeks in the aftermath of that kiss.

Katalin felt her own cheeks warm as Steven shifted position and his leg brushed hers. While he talked about Matthew, she fought to concentrate on what he was saying instead of what she was feeling, but it proved an impossible task. Never had she felt so conscious of another person's being. Sitting next to him, breathing his scent, touching his hand, she began to feel as if the sensual side of his spirit had separated from his body, was reaching toward her and demanding that she take notice.

She almost laughed at herself. *Take notice.* That was funnier than anything Sophie had ever said. From the moment Katalin had affixed István's name to that glorious face, she had not simply taken notice of him, she had become acutely, intensely aware of him. That awareness had grown like a swamp weed in the days that followed, spreading until it had completely taken over Katalin's consciousness. When she wasn't with him, she thought about him. When she was with him, she couldn't think of anything but him. When they talked or occasionally touched, an odd tingling sensation rose like goose flesh on her skin, a pleasant, enticing feeling, one she had never experienced before.

Steven had introduced her to an entirely new menu of responses. All he had to do was look at her the way he was looking at her now and her heart fluttered with alarming irregularity. If he kissed her, and he had once or twice, or held her in his arms, she felt a radiating heat within and a hibernal chill without. Admitting her innocence in matters sexual, she suspected she had not even skimmed the depths of her ability to feel. She was merely sampling her physical sentience.

When they returned to Zsuzsanna's apartment, Katalin was so absorbed in defining what she wanted and deciding what to do if it was offered to her, she never saw the bottle of champagne icing in the silver bucket and the note that had been placed between two crystal flutes until Steven showed it to her: "See you tomorrow. Enjoy tonight. Z."

Katalin blushed. Chopin was playing on the Victrola. There was food warming in the kitchen. The drapes were drawn. And on the fireplace mantel, a row of short, fat candles waited to be lit.

"Hungry?" Steven asked, deliberately strolling into the kitchen, away from Zsuzsanna's tableau of seduction.

Grabbing a towel, he lifted the lid to the large black pot simmering on the stove, stuck his nose close to the steaming contents, and declared excitedly, "Seven Chieftains stew!" He hadn't had this concoction of three kinds of meat, bacon, green peppers, tomatoes, and sour cream in years. According to legend, each of the seven tribes of Hungary had contributed one of the ingredients of this stew. True or not, *hét vezér tokány* was a dish fit for kings—or at the very least, a captain and his lady. Without waiting for an answer from Katalin, he scouted the cabinets, found two large bowls, and filled them with the hearty stew. Opting to save the champagne for later, he uncorked the bottle of Leányka conveniently cooling in the refrigerator, piled everything onto a tray, and carried his feast into the living room.

Continuing to heed Zsuzsanna's unwritten instructions, he lit the candles, shut off the overhead light, and made himself comfortable on the sofa. When still Katalin hesitated, he patted the cushion next to him. "You don't want the chieftains to get cold, do you?"

"Certainly not." She smiled, finding his easiness infectious, and then took the seat and the glass proffered her.

"Leányka," he said, swirling the delicate white wine from Eger, watching it ebb and rise in the goblet. "How appropriate. A wine called Little Girl." He clinked his glass against hers and stared deep into her eyes. "Here's to the little girl I left in Budapest and to the beautiful woman I found in New York."

Though Katalin knew life didn't require an explanation for why someone fell in love with someone else, or a statement of time when the actual fall occurred, if ever she was asked, she would have cited this night and repeated that toast. In a few words he had managed to encapsulate years of dreaming and wondering whether her dreams would find flesh or simply fade with the dawn of an empty reality. In a single sentence he had given shape to years of amorphous infatuation, put into focus endless hours of trying to make sense of nagging sensations of longing, inexplicable feelings of loss. She had not been certain before, but she knew clearly now that she had been waiting for him, for this night, for this precise moment to relinquish her heart.

They ate, drank, laughed, talked. By midnight the candles had burned to a flicker. The music had changed from Chopin to Brahms to Rachmaninoff. The mood had changed as well. The air had thickened. Desire filled the space between them, so dense it was almost palpable. Steven searched Katalin's face, probing beyond the cool green of her eyes to her core, where the flaming red of passion lay. She returned his gaze with a trusting, steady stare. Keeping his eyes locked on hers, he reached behind her and unpinned the braids she had coiled about her head. Loosening one and then the other, he ran his fingers through the tangled silk, unplaiting it, luxuriating in it, smoothing it out over her shoulders onto her back.

As Rachmaninoff serenaded them, Steven took Katalin in his arms and kissed her. His mouth fell against hers softly, gently inviting her to join him on an intimate adventure. He didn't press. He wouldn't push. From the start he had divined her state of innocence. It hadn't been difficult. Katalin carried it as openly and naturally as a rose carried its scent.

Her lips quivered beneath his, but he tasted no fear. Lightly, his tongue traced the sensuous line of her mouth, drawing it open. As their kiss deepened, he felt her body shift. His arms closed around her, drawing her in until they sat a breath apart. He held her, stroked her hair, and marveled at the miracle of it all—of finding her, of being with her and being able to love her.

For Katalin, his embrace became her world. There was no sound, no feeling, no movement other than what occurred between the two of them. As his hands eased their way onto her breasts, her head filled with music composed by her heart. He led. She followed, feeling neither inhibited nor shy. With anyone else she might have worried about her lack of experience or her lack of knowledge; she might have wrestled with questions of morality or propriety. With István, she exulted in the extraordinary new sensations being seduced from her body, relishing the euphoric appasionata rising within her.

Steven was beginning to feel the heat of his own passion. Even through her clothing, his fingers had discovered a surprising lushness. Rounded and full, her breasts rose from her slimness like sand-swept dunes on a quiet beach. One by one he undid the buttons of her blouse, deliberately lingering over each tiny white pearl. He had waited a lifetime for this. He refused to rush. Pushing the light cotton fabric aside, he slid his hand beneath her brassiere, touching her with near reverence.

Soon, her fingers imitated his, undoing buttons, sliding hands onto flesh, wanting to feel, wanting to be felt. His breath had grown short. Hers, too, had become staccato. Taking her hand, he rose from the couch and led her into the bedroom. There, on Zsuzsanna's bed, they found themselves again, only to become lost in a garden of lacy pillows and flamboyant chintz and the heady scent of consummation.

Steven's mouth sought hers with an avidity that bordered on obsession. Like a man denied water, he thirsted for the moistness of those generous lips. He'd kiss her and then look at her and then kiss her again, astounded by the reality that when he opened his eyes she was still there, still wanting him as much as he wanted her. When he began to remove her clothes, she complied, eagerly shedding her blouse and her brassiere, kicking off her skirt and her slip, feeling free and wonderful in her nakedness.

Again, Steven's hands traveled her flesh, but this time the voyage extended. Her body trembled beneath his as his fingers sailed down from her neck, mooring on lusher shores. His mouth journeyed as well, closing around the soft pinkness that tipped her breast, feasting on her, savoring her, devouring her. He, too, had undressed, and now, spurred by primal urges that needed no instruction, she had begun an exploration of her own.

Stroking his skin with dampened palms, her body had developed a rhythm as slow and sensuous as the most haunting *lassú*. Sensing that their bodies and their souls were moving in concert, he started toward the softness that could be found only in that special female crevasse. As he neared the source of her heat, she froze. Her flesh tightened. Her breathing, which had already grown shallow with excitement, grew shallower still, coming now in nervous puffs.

"What is it? What did I do? Did I hurt you?" He propped himself up on his arms and quickly snapped on the light. He had turned it off only moments before.

"I'm afraid of the dark," she said.

His hands caressed her face. His mouth kissed away her embarrassment. "Close your eyes," he said. "The way you do when you're playing the piano."

When she did what he asked, he took her face in his hands and kissed her eyelids, chasing her fears, reassuring her of his presence and his love. Again, his hands traversed her body, touring the satiny landscape of her skin, but this time, as he touched her he whispered to her.

"See the colors. There, on the inside of your eyelids. Concentrate on them, on this moment, on what you feel, on how you make me feel."

Soon, with his voice in her ear, she felt encouraged to find him again, to hold his strength in her hands, to guide him toward the place where she burned. She had never experienced such need, such pressure, such intense, desperate longing. He had to fill the void within her, the blank she was without him. She arched and he completed her, taking her with him on a ride that made her feel as if a thousand cymbals were crashing inside her head. Rising, falling, sensing the exquisite building of a crescendo, she felt as if her body had fused with his, as if her flesh had been grafted onto his, as if she had become one with him.

Afterward, when his lips had reluctantly separated from hers, then and only then did he allow her to open her eyes. She didn't know when, but at some point, he had again turned off the light. The room was black.

"I just wanted to show you that beautiful things can happen in the dark," he said.

"I love you," she said, a sob escaping her throat.

"I love you too. But that's not something to cry about."

"I can't bear the thought of being without you."

Steven switched on the light. Tears glistened on her cheeks. He kissed her and smoothed a strand of dampened hair off her face. "You'll never be without me. I'll be right here." He leaned down and pressed his lips against the flesh above her heart.

"What if something happens to you?"

"Nothing's going to happen. I've got my lucky charm with me." He held up the key to her flat in Budapest. Next to it hung his dogtags. To Katalin, both were symbols of potential loss. Steven saw the green of her eyes darken. He read her thoughts. "Katya, my precious Katya. Please. Tonight is a magical night. For us, there is no tomorrow. There is no other place than right here, no other time than right now. I love you. You love me. That's all that's important."

As his lips met hers she clung to him, wanting to believe in the power of love and the magic of the night. Yet behind her eyelids she saw no rainbow. Instead, she saw the tomorrow Steven wanted her to ignore. There was no rosy glow suffused around a couple brimming with happiness. There was no sunshiny yellow beaming down on children scampering about a verdant yard. There was no blue she could ascribe to the river that rolled through Budapest or the sky that hovered over New York. There were no colors except the menacing, empty blackness that had terrified her as a child. It terrified her now.

16

"W hy would you do something like that? Especially without discussing it with me first?" Andras's face flushed crimson.

"What's there to discuss? It's what I want to do." Judit met her father's anger head on, refusing to be cowed by his disapproval. "Besides, if I had come to you, you would have tried to talk me out of it, just as you're doing now."

"Of course I would have dissuaded you. With talent like yours, how could you even think of changing your course of study from soloist to accompanist?"

"It was easy."

Andras looked at her as if she were a complete stranger. Not that he was unfamiliar with his daughter's rebelliousness and her penchant for surprise, but in his wildest flights of imagination he had never dreamed she would do something as foolish as this. He stared at her, trying to understand when she had changed, when he had lost control, when they had grown apart.

"You're too good to waste your time playing backup for someone else."

"First of all, I don't consider it a waste of time," Judit said. "To me, the hundreds of hours I used to spend memorizing endless sonatas and concertos were a waste! Where did it get me? Nowhere!"

"That's not so. Your playing is exquisite, much too good to squander on an accompanist's chair."

Judit leaned forward across his desk, eyeing him. "Since when?"

"What?"

"Since when do you think I'm this incredible talent?" Judit's tone was bitter. "Since Katalin went to New York?"

Andras felt as if she had sliced his wrists and emptied his veins. The color drained from his face, leaving him ashen and shaking. Judit didn't seem to notice. She was standing now, quietly raging, addressing him in a voice quaking with cold fury.

"When Katalin was around, I was always second. And do you know why? Because you put me there, Papa. You! Since we were three years old you've always put her first. She was the genius. She was the prodigy. She had the hands that were going to affix a star to your name. And me? I was the also-ran. The runner-up. The one who always came in second. Now you want me to believe that all the time you appeared so obsessed with Katalin, you considered me center-stage material as well?"

"Yes! Of course I did. I do. Because you are. You could be brilliant, Judit. Please, I beg you. Don't throw your gift away."

Andras stood and started around his desk. Judit shook her head and walked toward the door. When she turned and looked at him, the anger was gone. In its place Andras read something that to him was far more devastating—disaffection and disbelief.

"You should have told me that years ago, Papa, when it would have made a difference. Now, it doesn't matter. I'm used to being second best. I've been doing it for so long, it's what makes me comfortable. If you want me to be first, I'm sorry. You're too late."

As she closed the door behind her, Andras felt a grinding pain in his heart. He sat and clutched his chest, but he knew the source of his agony was spiritual, not physical. Through teary eyes he looked at the spot where his only child had stood, pointing an accusing finger at his fatherhood. He tried to defend himself, but his lips remained silent, sealed by the knowledge of his guilt. The pain sharpened. His vision blurred. His head screamed with sounds he should have heard, words he should have spoken, endearments he should have delivered.

For most of his adult life, Andras Strasser had considered himself a man of standards, a man of priorities. He believed in family, God, scholarship, and music. He adhered to a vigorous work ethic and considered charity an obligation. Despite his one skirmish with Zoltán, he had always viewed himself as exceptionally loyal and devoted to those he deemed part of his inner cadre. Yet his daughter had just charged him with violating every one of his precious codes. According to her, he had committed emotional treason. He had lavished his devotion and affection and attention on another child at the expense of his own. He had invested his ambitions and his dreams in a bank with a different name.

Judit had a right to be furious. Asking a child to assume her father's approval was callous. Feeling but remaining silent about one's love didn't count. Instead of grabbing every available opportunity to tell her how beautiful he thought she was, how talented, how clever, how perfect, he had done exactly the opposite. She had been reared by the well-meaning, yet impersonal hand of benign neglect. He had patted her head now and then, but rarely had he taken the time to nourish her self-esteem. He had given all of that to someone else, creating the impression that she was not and would never be the main source of his pleasure and his pride, that she would never be anything more than just good enough. He had done to her what his father had done to him.

The difference was, Andras told himself, seeking consolation, for him and Judit there was still time to make amends. For him and his father, it was too late.

Though Judit had anticipated her argument with Andras and, in truth, provoked it, the exchange upset her. She loved her father, she knew he loved her, but this discussion had been brewing for a lifetime. He wanted her to be a concert pianist. It used to be that she wanted to be whatever he wanted her to be, but lately, all that had changed. She was beginning to assemble her own priorities, to sculpt her own future, and being a soloist simply didn't fit in with her plans.

Besides, she mumbled to herself as she turned the corner and headed down the corridor toward Ilona's office, at twenty-one she was old enough to be making decisions by herself, for herself.

Normally, Judit would have burst into Ilona's office unannounced. Distraction had slowed her pace, so that when she went to open the door and heard Ilona's voice, she hesitated. Her mother was speaking Yiddish. Judit didn't speak Yiddish, but she understood it. What she heard confused and upset her.

"Don't worry. Somehow, I'll find a way to get the drugs to Prague. When I know who and when, we'll arrange a drop and a pickup. . . .

Of course I'll be discreet. Aren't I always? . . . Yes . . . Yes. I'm always careful. Speak to you soon. Shalom."

Judit waited just long enough to hear the telephone receiver being replaced in its cradle. "What was that all about?" she asked, closing the door securely behind her and speaking in a nervous whisper. "What drugs? What sort of drop? What are you picking up? And from where?"

Ilona's face blanched. Shocked as she was to discover that her daughter had been eavesdropping on her call, she was more disturbed to realize it could have been anyone. It wasn't wise to be so lax about her own security.

"It's nothing, dear. Just hospital business." Ilona made a show of riffling through a sheaf of papers on her desk. Judit was buying none of it.

"Just hospital business," Judit repeated, taking a chair and pulling it next to Ilona. "Drop-offs and pickups and being discreet and careful. Those are words commonly used between hospital personnel, are they? And since when has Yiddish become the national tongue?"

Ilona dropped her pose. "Forget what you heard."

"No."

"I'm telling you, Judit. It would be better for everyone concerned if you blotted that conversation out of your memory."

"What if I'm concerned about you?"

Ilona reached across her desk and took her daughter's hand. It was cold with fear. "The less you know, the better."

Suddenly, Judit remembered the recordings Ilona had given her and Katalin. She remembered wondering who had gotten Zsuzsanna's address for Zoltán and how. She recalled overhearing snatches of other conversations concerning patients who had been critical and had experienced miraculous turn-arounds.

"I think I just put two and two together and figured out enough to know that you are operating some sort of medical black market." Ilona didn't respond. Her expression remained neutral. "Maybe I can help." Still, Ilona continued to be close-mouthed. "I'm going to Prague this weekend."

Ilona's voice was level, but Judit had noticed an immediate change in her mother's eyes. They were alert, curious, yet cautious. "Why are you going to Prague? And why didn't I know anything about it?"

"Well, actually," Judit said, knowing that Ilona's reaction to her news would be muted by whatever had precipitated her secret phone call, "that's what I came to talk to you about. I know it seems very last-minute, since I'm supposed to graduate at the end of the year, but I've decided to be an accompanist instead of a soloist. My new adviser felt that the best way for me to be certain this is the right move is for me to perform in my new capacity immediately, and so I'm going to Prague to accompany Emke Sándor in a recital."

An opera fan, Ilona knew of Sándor Emke. He was one of Hungary's best tenors.

"Does your father know of this shift in focus?"

"He didn't, but he does now." Judit's voice had already told Ilona what she wanted to know, but she asked anyway.

"How does he feel about it?"

"He hates it, but you know what, Mama? I did this for me. Not for him. I don't want to be a soloist. I like having time to do other things and indulge other interests besides music." She lowered her head and shifted in her seat. When she looked at Ilona again, it was with a more childlike visage than the one she had worn moments before. "I'm not as single-minded as either you or Papa. I'm fractured. Though I love music, I feel the pull of a hundred other things. I used to feel guilty about taking time away from the piano to read a book or attend a lecture or go to a reading. I don't want to feel guilty anymore. I want to feel useful and productive and fulfilled. Can you understand that, Mama?"

Ilona rose from her chair, walked around her desk, and hugged her daughter. "Of course I understand. What's more, I applaud you for taking a stand and finding your own voice. As for your father, give him time. It may take him longer, but he loves you. Eventually, he'll understand as well."

"Would he understand what you're doing?" Judit asked.

Ilona had begun to return to her desk, so her back was turned, preventing Judit from witnessing the debate going on inside her mother's soul. When Ilona took her seat and faced Judit, the debate was over.

"No, he wouldn't, and I don't want you saying anything to him."

"I won't." A slow, conspiratorial smile sneaked onto Judit's face. "Now, let's get back to Prague. What am I dropping off and what am I picking up?"

Another woman might have continued to refuse her daughter participation in something as dangerous as smuggling, but not Ilona. Though it appeared incompatible with someone whose life was dictated by scientific fact, she viewed certain circumstances with a more spiritual eye. Things didn't just happen. They happened for a reason. In Yiddish the word was *beshart*—meant to be. Others called it kismet or fate or providence. However one said it, Ilona believed that while one coincidence could be discounted as serendipitous, two and three fortuitous events piled on top of one another demanded attention.

For Judit to have made this decision at this time. For her to be sent to Prague just as Ilona was being asked to ferry goods back and forth from that particular city. It was simply too much to ignore.

"Ever since that horrible debacle in Czechoslovakia three years ago, there's been a decrease in the number and variety of medical supplies coming into Prague. Unfortunately, lately there's been an increase in industrial accidents. Tyrothricin is an antibiotic used in preparing surgical dressings. It's not very plentiful to begin with, but thanks to the Czech uprising in '68, in Prague it's become practically nonexistent. A doctor friend of mine in one of the hospitals there needs tyrothricin for his more serious surgeries. That's what you'll be dropping off."

"Where do you get it?"

"From the United States mostly. Sometimes from West Germany, France, and England. It depends on how much I need and who can get it to me fastest."

Judit was impressed. "What am I picking up?"

"A Torah."

Judit's eyes widened. A Torah was a parchment scroll containing the body of Jewish teachings and traditions. It was considered sacred. "Whose is it?"

"It was found buried in a wall in a secret tunnel beneath a church in a town on Prague's outskirts," Ilona said. "The scholar who examined it thinks it dates back over a hundred years. It's small, so they believe it was used either in a home or a provincial synagogue. The writing is Hebrew, but the dressing is an old design with Hungarian and Slovak imagery, which makes them think it might have come from that part of Slovakia that used to belong to Hungary before the war."

"How did it get to Prague? And how did it get buried in a cave?"

"I don't know, Judit. Maybe some of the Hungarian Jews who fled the Nazis carried it over the border into Czechoslovakia. Maybe they made it to Prague, where they were hidden by a good Christian family. Maybe the family, recognizing the religious significance of the Torah, decided to put it somewhere where it would be safe." Ilona's voice had drifted. Her brown eyes had blackened, as if today had disappeared behind the dark clouds of yesterday. "It doesn't matter how it got there or how it was discovered," she said, snapping back to the present. "Since there's no yeshiva in Prague, the Torah must be brought here."

Judit already knew how few Jews remained in Czechoslovakia and Poland. She knew, too, that the only training ground for rabbis and Jewish scholars was in Budapest. What she didn't know just then was how she was going to smuggle a Torah past immigration.

"Don't worry, Mama," she said, frightened but at the same time oddly excited. "We'll work it out. Somehow we'll work it out."

·   ·   ·

For the first time since she had come to Attila Kovács's bed, Judit felt as if she was worthy of the honor of receiving him. As he hunkered over her, she opened herself to him proudly, knowing that just a few hours before, she had committed herself to a courageous act of rebellion. She rejoiced as his mouth sucked at her breasts and his hands sneaked down between her thighs. His fingers invaded her privacy, but she felt no sense of violation or trespass. She felt blessed, as if her body were being sanctified by the hand of one who had been declared divine.

To Judit, Attila Kovács was the personification of supernal power. Like a Crusader, everything he did, everything he said bore the mark of omnipotence. With his pen as his only weapon, he bombarded the blasphemy of communism. He swiped at the hypocrisy of the system. He hacked away at the dense forest of false promises. And when he became too much of a nuisance and they were bound to silence him, he suffered their punishments with a stoic's indifference to pain, refusing to be tamed.

For two years, these hands that had wielded both a prisoner's hammer and a playwright's pen had coaxed passion from Judit's body. She had come to him willingly the first time he had asked and every other time he had asked. She had closed her eyes to the fact of his wife and the scandal that would befall her and her parents if this illicit liaison were discovered, just as she had avoided the knowledge that she would never be anything other than a vessel to him, a receptacle for the overflow of his sexual needs.

Afterward, when he was sated, she wrapped a blanket around herself and went to fix his coffee. Since they rarely met in the same place, she had to search the kitchen for a pot and cups. As she looked around the small room of yet another "apartment of a friend" and waited for the strong kávé to brew, she wished again that they could have their own place. It didn't matter to her whether it was a shack, a rundown apartment in town—anything, as long as it was theirs. On the rare occasion when she broached the subject, Attila told her they couldn't do that because he was always being watched and hunted, that going to the same place all the time would attract unhealthy attention to her as well as to him.

"If you consort with a criminal, you are a criminal," he had said to her more than a dozen times.

It was bitter cold in the Óbuda flat, yet when she carried his heavily sweetened glass of coffee into the bedroom along with a plate of cheese-filled pastry cones, she wasn't surprised to find him sitting above the covers, completely naked. As she always did, she hesitated in the doorway just to marvel at the fact of him and the knowledge that she was the mistress of the man they called Freedom's Playwright.

She served him and then took her place beside him, pulling her own blankets closer. It was like a ritual. They made love and then they snacked and then they talked.

"How can the people believe that Kádár's reforms are steps toward freedom?" he asked, his lapis eyes sparked with outrage. "If they are, he is moving sideways, like a crab. Yes, he has eased his grip on a few businesses. So what! While his hand is in their pockets, skimming the capitalistic profits he's supposed to abhor, his fist still strangles the necks of men like me."

Judit was used to his sermons. It was one of the qualities she most adored. He was consumed by his passions. There was never a second that he was not on fire. Whether he was pounding away at her flesh or at her mind, the intensity was the same. She listened as he ranted about János Kádár and the house of cards he was building for the Hungarian people. As he spoke, Kovács combed his fingers through his mane of long blond hair, which had grown snarled and knotted from their love-making. His moustache bowed about his lips, drooping downward toward his chin and lending him the aspect of a golden walrus. He had no body hair, except the blond tuft that haloed his genitals and a light fuzz on his legs, yet he exuded an aura of brutish strength.

"If he were a true reformist, he would ease the censorship of his nation's writers. But he refuses to allow the truth to be told. He is afraid. All oppressors are afraid of the truth."

Judit's attention strayed. A thought rapped at her consciousness, begging for her consideration. How many times had Attila railed about the constant persecution of himself and other Hungarian writers bent on championing freedom's cause, of Solzhenitsyn in Russia, of Havel in Czechoslovakia. How many times had she listened to him bemoan his lack of access to the stages of the West.

"Our voices need to be heard. Somewhere, someone has to be made to listen. Until the muzzles are taken off here, the West is our only outlet."

Judit thought about her upcoming trip to Prague. She recalled what her mother had said about the American organization she dealt with, the pouches she sent to New York, the contacts she had made through a man named Phil King.

Kovács had worked himself into a state. He reached for Judit, flinging aside her blanket and pawing at her flesh. There was no foreplay, no loving, no stroking. Attila mounted her and entered her, reaching down to hoist her hips so he could drive himself deeper and deeper into her core. For once, Judit felt neither pleasure nor pain. Her mind was elsewhere.

She was in Prague, leaving a package at a prearranged drop, picking up another package and ferrying it across a border. Scenes of potential disaster synthesized with images of possible success. She envisioned getting caught, being interrogated, being imprisoned. She visualized the Torah in the old synagogue on Dohány utca. She saw her mother's pride, the rabbi's gratitude, and in another vision she saw something on Attila's face she had never seen before—respect.

Courage wasn't something donned like a coat, but suddenly Judit felt stronger, braver, more daring than she ever had before. There was no fear, no hesitation, no compunction about what she was about to attempt. As critical as this weekend was, it had just gained significance. It had become a trial run for an even more important mission—getting Kovács's plays out of Hungary.

Judit learned many things on her journey to Prague: that she enjoyed being an accompanist, that flowers did grow in the dark, that Sándor Emke was an egotistical jerk and thank goodness for that, and that she could make a difference.

The afternoon she arrived, the taxi dropped Emke at the Alcron off Wenceslas Square in the New Town and then drove to the Old Town, depositing her at the Karlovo, a modest *pension*. She unpacked and then took to the streets, keeping an eye on the time while trying to behave like any other tourist. She strolled by the monument to John Huss in the center of the Old Town Square. In 1402, Huss preached his "fighting words," advocating church reform and the supremacy of Czech national aspirations above German influences. When, in 1415, he was burned at the stake, his martyrdom triggered the religious Hussite wars.

Judit wandered past the Old Town Hall, where every hour on the hour crowds gathered to see Prague's great landmark—the astronomical clock built in 1490—and to witness the solemn march of Christ, the twelve apostles, Death, and a host of other allegorical figures. She wended her way through the narrow, winding cobblestone streets of the Staré Město, from the Powder Tower once used to store gunpowder, past a host of facades, some graced with the curving forms of the Baroque, others with the pointed arches and flying buttresses of the Gothic, until finally she reached her true destination.

The Prague ghetto had been founded by Jewish traders as early as the ninth century. By the seventeenth century it had become a hub of Jewish culture. Now, its central focus was a cemetery where fifteenth-century tombstones leaned and jostled against one another, cramped and crowded with too many markers in too little space. Beneath them, entombed in this small patch of land, rested the remains of twelve thousand people, stacked layer upon layer. Judit tiptoed around the tumbled memorials, careful not to jog any of the precariously tipped shrines. Though she didn't recognize any of the names, and the dates of death had all preceded her birth, she felt a connection with the people lying there. None of them had died at the hands of the Nazis—there were no individual graves for the victims of that madness, only mass remembrances—yet it was difficult to be in Prague and not feel a tie.

It was here in this section of the city that the Nazis had stockpiled all the remnants of Jewish life—religious and secular—that they had stolen from Jewish homes and synagogues throughout Europe. After the war they intended to open a museum to display the artifacts of the culture they had destroyed.

Before coming to the cemetery, Judit had visited the nearby Pinkas Synagogue, where the names of 77,700 Jewish men, women, and children murdered by the Nazis had been painted on the interior walls. She visited the Old-New Synagogue, built in 1270 and believed to be the oldest surviving synagogue in Europe. That proud, magnificent temple, a masterpiece of early Gothic architecture, had once served a vital, thriving community. It stood empty now, tending an almost extinct congregation. Its disuse upset Judit more than its disrepair. One could fix a sagging arch, but how did one restore a population?

Slowly, she found her way to the tomb of the scholar Rabbi Low, who died in 1609. She folded her hands and stared at the stone memorial, counting the innumerable scraps of paper stuck in the cracks of that tomb. It was said that many of the Jews of Prague had scribbled prayers onto those papers, hiding them at the same time they came to hide their valuables in the cemetery, before being transported to the camps. It was hard to look at those unfulfilled prayers and these tombs and not to feel attached. She shared the same blood. Had she lived in this place at that time, she would have shared the same fate.

Unless, of course, she had been lucky enough to know people like Luba and Vasil Benes. They were her contacts in Prague. Vasil was a doctor. Luba had been a nurse. During the German occupation they had been revolted by the wholesale killing of the innocent. Knowing that to speak out or to challenge the regime was to invite certain death for themselves and their children, they took a more private, no less dangerous, stand. They managed to hide the children of a Jewish colleague in their attic for the duration of the war. Both parents were destroyed in a concentration camp. One of the boys died of typhus in the Benes house, but the two girls had survived. After the war, Luba and Vasil had relied upon an underground organization similar to the one Ilona worked with to resettle the girls in England. From what Ilona had told her, the girls were women now, married, with children of their own and safe.

As Judit studied the scraps of paper crammed into Rabbi Low's tomb, looking for the one she had come to find, she felt tears of admiration glide down her cheeks. She didn't even know these people, yet she knew that she owed them. She dug into her coat, found a handkerchief, and dabbed at her eyes. It was then that she noticed the slip of paper with jagged edges cut by a pinking shear. Using her handkerchief as a blind, she held it to her eyes and looked about, checking to be certain she was alone. When she felt relatively secure, she allowed the handkerchief to drop to the ground in front of the tomb. As she bent to retrieve it, her fingers snatched the specially marked piece of paper, tucked it into the center of the linen square, and stuffed the wad back into her pocket. Maintaining her guise, she lingered another few moments, then turned and headed back to her room at the *pension*.

IF YOU NEED ANYTHING, CALL THE MAID was all the note said. Taking a deep breath, Judit buzzed the front desk and asked if someone from housekeeping could bring her some extra towels. The waiting was torturous. How would she know if the woman who came was the woman she was supposed to speak to? What if she was about to open the door of a trap? She had no training in this sort of thing. Why had she agreed to this?

Because you've always been an impulsive ass, she muttered. *Why don't you ever think things through? Why don't you look before you leap?*

The knock on the door startled her. Her breath caught in her throat. Her hand was damp as she clasped her fingers around the knob. Breathing deeply, she donned a mask of sang-froid and opened the door. Before her stood a tall, spindly woman with an angular, ascetic face, holding a stack of white towels. There was no hint of friendly conspiracy, no clue as to what lay behind those cool blue eyes.

"You asked for towels."

"I did."

The woman strode past Judit with the no-nonsense gait of an infantryman. She placed the pile of towels in the center of the bed and turned up the sound on the radio. A flick of her hand ordered Judit to close the door. A finger raised to her lips warned about keeping voices low. Without speaking, she lifted off the top three towels. There, in the center, was the Torah. The size of a large reference book, the ancient scrolls

316 / DORIS MORTMAN

were wound around dark wooden spindles and encased in aged white silk, lavishly embroidered with a fanciful design of flowers and birds. Gingerly, lovingly, Judit ran her fingers across the carefully stitched threads.

"It's beautiful," she whispered, speaking in English as Ilona had instructed her to do.

"So are you," the woman said, easing for a moment. "You look like your mother."

Judit smiled. "Luba?"

The woman nodded. "How are you going to get this out?" she asked, scrutinizing Judit, searching for signs of weakness or incompetence.

Judit had thought about nothing else, yet until this very moment she hadn't been certain of her plan.

"Can we remove the scrolls from the spindles?"

Luba eyed Judit suspiciously. "Yes, but why?"

Judit didn't answer. She went to the closet and took out her jacket. It was a big, bulky down anorak. She laid it out on the bed and then rummaged about her purse, where she found a sewing kit. Using one side of a scissors, she slashed open the inner seam of the jacket lining and scooped out the filling. Gently removing the casing, she and Luba removed the Hebrew scrolls from the wooden spindles. Placing a few towels against the outer shell, the two women laid out the parchment as smoothly as they could. Then they added another layer of towels and filled in around the Torah with the stuffing Judit had removed from her jacket. Then she restitched the seam and admired her handiwork.

"You'd never know, would you?"

Luba took the jacket and examined every inch of it, probing, checking, inspecting, as if it were a child and she was looking for deadly ticks. Though Judit had not been at all cavalier about her mission, watching Luba had a sobering effect. The older woman made it clear with every move that this was indeed serious business.

"Is good." She smiled, but so briefly that Judit almost missed it. "Be careful not to rip it."

"I will."

Luba nodded and looked at her watch. Without saying a word, Judit went to the bathroom and brought out a bag filled with dozens of hair rollers. "The tyrothricin is in tubes." She took one of the rollers and showed Luba how she had stuffed a tube into the center. The pink foam rubber that was supposed to keep the curler from digging into the scalp had closed around the medicine, providing a natural cover.

"I can't take all of them at once," Luba said. "It looks too suspicious."

"Take some now, some when you come in to make up the room, and the rest Sunday morning before I leave."

"Good." Luba patted Judit's cheek. "You be safe," she said as she took the bag and opened the door. "Just be safe."

Judit never saw Luba again.

The next night, when Judit walked onto the stage of Smetana Hall, she experienced a moment of awkwardness. She was introduced, there was a smattering of applause, and then she was expected to take her seat at the piano and await the arrival of the main attraction, Sándor Emke. Judit had never brought music onto a stage. She had never had to wait for anyone other than a conductor. Nor had she ever felt the need to remind her ego that someone other than she was the prime reason for the fullness of the house. The moment came and then it passed. After that, the evening went exceedingly well.

She enjoyed her role more than she had hoped. She did not feel at all insignificant or as if she were selling her talent short. Quite the contrary. Aside from providing essential instrumental enrichment, it was she who kept the pace of the performance, she who controlled the nerves of the soloist, she who decided the order and number of the encores. True, she was not the focus of the applause, nor was she the one feted and spotlighted at the after-concert soiree, but she was appreciated—and at this particular juncture in her career, that seemed enough.

The next morning Judit packed and then practiced wearing her coat. She studied herself in the mirror, adopting different poses, checking each one to see if there was a giveaway bulge or a telltale gap in the stuffing. When she was satisfied, she waited downstairs for the taxi that would take her to the airport. She had left the rest of the hair rollers in a bag. Now she had to hope that Luba, and not some other maid, retrieved them, and that when Judit arrived in Hungary she was not the victim of an overzealous customs officer.

Throughout the plane trip Judith had to restrain her growing sense of panic. She had folded her jacket and stored it in the overhead bin, but still she fretted that something might happen to it. Things had gone so well. Almost too well. When the plane landed she decided not to wear the jacket but to carry it over her arm. When she and Emke had their baggage, they both proceeded toward Immigration. Emke slid Judit's bag onto the table first. The officer, a young, eager communist with every crease in his brown uniform perfectly pressed and every word of his rule book memorized, asked Judit the usual questions about where she had been, how long she had stayed, and what she was bringing into the country. She answered without a problem. When he opened her suitcase and rifled through it, she had no problem there either. It was when he took her coat and began shoving his hands into the pockets that beads of sweat dotted her brow.

"Does this have inner pockets?" he demanded.

She nodded and took the coat from him, praying that when he had grabbed it from her, he hadn't ripped the scrolls. Carefully, she held open the coat and unzipped the inside pocket. Suddenly she noticed that one side of the lining was neatly stitched with a navy-blue thread that matched the jacket, while the other side was ablaze with crooked red stitching, the results of a her own clumsy stitchery. When he didn't seem to notice, Judit decided that in a nation where few bought new clothes for every season, patching must not be a big deal. Just as she was beginning to feel safe, he ran his finger over the zigzag red threads.

"This repair is new."

Her brain was scrambling for an excuse when Sándor Emke rescued her.

"Maybe," he said with an arrogant sniff. "But I'm growing old waiting for you to get on with it."

The young officer stared at Emke.

"Do you know who I am?" Sándor asked in his most imperious manner. "I am Emke Sándor, lead tenor of the Hungarian State Opera." When he saw no sign of recognition on the officer's face, Emke simply attributed the young man's unawareness to the native ignorance of the communist bureaucrat and continued with his harangue. "The young woman is my accompanist and we've just returned from a highly successful concert in Prague. I can assure you that she had neither the time nor the inclination to shop for contraband. She was much too busy preparing for her evening as my assistant. Now, please, can we hurry it up!"

As the officer stamped their passports and waved them through, it was all Judit could do to keep from laughing. If she had said what Emke said in the way he said it, she would have been hauled off to Fő Street prison.

Only in Budapest, she thought as she ran for a taxi, folded her jacket on the seat beside her, and gave the driver her address, *could a tenor intimidate an officer of the State Police. Only in Budapest.*

One month later Judit was asked to go to Vienna to accompany a quartet from the Opera Company. Judit was only too happy to accept. This was the opportunity she had been waiting for. First, she went to Ilona and asked if she needed a courier. She did. This time, aside from medical matters, Ilona wanted to send Katalin and Zsuzsanna news clippings about Mária's latest film. To accomplish this, Ilona gave Judit a pouch and an address. She was to take the pouch to a booth at the Flohmarkt, a flea market held every Saturday south of the Opera Quarter, near the fruit and vegetable market. There, she was to ask if the dealer had an old zither. If he said he had only a dulcimer, she was to leave him the pouch.

Judit's next stop was to get Attila to give her a few of his manuscripts and the names of several producers. He was dubious.

"I'm telling you I can get these to New York," she said, piqued that he showed so little faith in her ability to accomplish the very thing he longed for.

"I don't know if I can afford to take the chance."

"It's not you who's taking the chance, Attila. It's me. Now if you're not interested, just say so. I'm going to Vienna anyway. I'm making contact anyway. It's up to you whether or not your plays go into the pouch headed for New York."

He fussed a bit, more uncomfortable with the inevitable changes this act would bring to their relationship than with the inherent danger to Judit, but in the end he capitulated. Just as Judit had suspected he would.

Two weeks later, Judit met the man in the Flohmarkt and told him where she had left the pouch. Everything seemed to go smoothly. Just as she had hoped it would.

Later that day, when the man called to tell her he had found the zither she had asked about, she felt so joyous, so significant, so proud of herself, she practically flew to the Kärntnerstrasse, determined to buy herself a present. As she went from one clothing store to another, one perfumery to the next, searching for just the right reward for her job well done, a man followed her. He was the same man who had followed her from Ilona's office to Attila's flat, the same man who had trailed her to Vienna and the flea market and then back to her hotel. She was too absorbed in the success of the day to notice him.

Just as he had known she would be.

17

New York, 1972

It seemed impossible that three years had passed since Katalin's first days in New York. Even more impossible was trying to adjust to the notion that soon she would receive her certificate and her term at Juilliard would come to an end. They had been wonderful, productive years and she was loath to let go. There were the peripheral pleasures—living with Zsuzsanna, her friendships with Sophie and Pedjá, her growing love of the city, her proximity to Mátyás, and, of course, the prospect of being close to István when he was discharged in August.

Weighted with no less importance was the sense of enormous professional accomplishment. Katalin could feel her own improvement. While she had come to Juilliard technically advanced, her musicianship had been lacking; her ability to channel the composer's intent through her emotional network and to deliver a joint musical message had needed sharpening. Greco's method of preparation—unbearably annoying at first, now an integral part of her absorption process—had sensitized her to the nuances and subtleties hidden within a composition, the shadings that made the difference between an adequate outing and a brilliant performance. Now when she played, she was keenly attentive; her ears remained open, her mind receptive. In effect, she joined her audience, listening to the musical interpretations being offered at the keyboard, appreciating and responding to the emotional generosity of the instrument creating the sounds.

Though they fought with irritating regularity, she accorded full credit for her advancement to Paul Greco. While pride prohibited confession, in private she acknowledged that part of his genius rested in his unique ability to impress a concept on her by battling with her. She had once described this particular form of combative edification to Zsuzsanna as "practicing the Socratic method with boxing gloves on." He provoked her and delighted in it.

Once, for instance, she commented that—despite her having the B-flat major in her repertoire—she believed most pianists neglected the Schubert sonatas because they were too long. Greco took issue.

"A great painter never makes a mistake about the size of a canvas," he bellowed.

Katalin snickered, but Greco continued, more determined than ever to prove her wrong—or, to be more precise, to prove himself right.

"Michelangelo was never at a loss as to how to fill his space. Renoir never had too much structure, too little subject. Picasso never had a canvas that was too big or too small. Was 'Guernica' too big? Were Renoir's portraits too small?"

Katalin had refused to nod or to speak or in any way to validate what he was saying. She had made a simple statement. He was elevating his response into the Sermon on the Mount.

Another time, they disagreed about the way she was playing a Chopin mazurka.

"This is not a percussion piece," he said.

"I understand that," she said.

"Then where is the voice?" he said.

"In my hands," she said.

"Then why don't my ears hear it?" he said.

Back and forth they went, he insisting that she was not thinking vocally, she continuing to pound the keys. When they reached an impasse, he left the classroom. Several minutes later he returned with one of the opera majors, a young Lithuanian soprano. He handed her the music and asked her to vocalize the melody. Katalin was outraged. The rest of the class was curious. The soprano sang Chopin, lifting the flirtatious melody off the page, infusing the atmosphere with the moodiness of evening so befitting a mazurka, which was in fact a night dance.

Her breathing, her vocal treatment, the sense of emotion her voice conveyed, combined to create a vastly different effect from the one Katalin had produced. In this version there was more to hear: the choreography of the dance, the romance of courtship, the exoticism of Chopin's fascination with Oriental themes, the haunting sound of the *dudy*, Poland's beloved bagpipe. At the end of the impromptu performance, Katalin waved a white handkerchief in surrender.

Again, Greco was right. "The great pianists, like Paderewski and Horowitz and Rachmaninoff, don't simply play. They sing."

It was through incidents like these that Katalin learned to trust Greco, to understand that he was rarely capricious in his pronouncements, rarely careless about his criticism. That trust came in handy when suddenly she realized that in June her scholarship was finished and that unless she continued in the Graduate Program, her student visa would be revoked and she would have to return to Budapest.

"You really should consider staying," Greco said one night over dinner at Csárda.

Katalin nodded, but she couldn't speak. Her head was swimming and her heart was full. She loved New York, but lately the tug of her homeland had grown stronger. Maybe it was because recently, after receiving perhaps one letter every few months, she had been bombarded with mail. Letters from Mária, funneled through Ilona's network, came filled with news of the family, clippings advertising Mária's films and plays, photographs of her and Zoltán, Andras and Ilona. There were letters from Judit as well, but these were political updates, reports on the so-called Kádár reforms, along with Judit's commentaries on the real impact and import of those reforms. She saw no visible improvement in the quality of Everyman's life since the inception of the New Economic Mechanism, no easing of censorship or border restrictions or the granting of travel permits. What she did see were government bureaucrats growing fat and rich on the profits they made off what Judit labeled "Kádár's Kompromise Konsumerism."

Six months ago, one of Judit's letters had asked Katalin to keep her eye out for word on the first Western production of one of Attila Kovács's plays. Checking the newspapers every day, Katalin finally found a short squib announcing that Joseph Papp had agreed to stage *The Zoo*. Katalin conveyed the information to Judit, who responded with an excitement that transcended the cold black-and-white of the typewritten letter. Reading between the lines, Katalin gleaned that Judit's involvement with Kovács had moved beyond the coffeehouse. Also, that Judit had been in some way responsible for Kovács's plays getting to Papp.

How had Judit arranged something so complex? Katalin wondered. She had to have had help on both sides. Putting two and two together,

Katalin realized that on this side of the Atlantic, that help had to have come from the people who delivered Judit's letters and picked up whatever Katalin wished sent to her family in Budapest. Though she had tried pumping Zsuzsanna, who proclaimed total ignorance, as well as the various messengers on the few occasions when she had been around to greet them, Katalin still had no clue as to who they were and why they did what they did. More perplexing was who was helping Judit on the other side? Who was her contact in Budapest?

"I can't stay without a scholarship," she said now, pushing her food around on her plate, "and from what I hear, scholarship money is very, very tight."

"That's true," Zsuzsanna said. "Look what happened to Sophie."

The foundation that for three years had helped fund Sophie's education had gone under. Instead of applying for another scholarship, Sophie had stunned Katalin and Zsuzsanna by opting to leave Juilliard, work the day shift at Csárda, and try her wings on the off-off-Broadway circuit. She had garnered a few minor roles in some very minor productions.

"I know a way." Greco said it quietly, as if the thought were embryonic and needed silence during its gestation. "The Chickering."

"What's the Chickering?" Zsuzsanna asked.

"It's a piano competition named for Jonas Chickering, who, along with his partner John Mackay, patented a one-piece iron frame for grands in 1843. First prize is ten thousand dollars, a solo recital at Carnegie Hall, and a year's concert bookings. If you win, Katya, you could afford tuition and kick off your concert career, all in one wild arpeggio."

"When would I have to audition for the advanced program?"

"March." He had anticipated the groan that followed. March was only two months away. In order to fulfill the audition requirements, she had to memorize a Bach fugue, a Beethoven sonata, substantial compositions by both nineteenth- and twentieth-century composers, as well as an additional work from the Romantic period. "Don't look so tragic. You already have the Bach and the Beethoven in your repertoire. Any one of the Liszts fulfills the nineteenth-century requirement, and the Rachmaninoff 'Preludes' fulfill the twentieth. As for the Romantic work, you have the Schubert. So you see? You have nothing to do except practice."

A slow, hesitant smile lingered at the edges of his mouth as he waited for a positive response. He should have known better. Katalin was not a woman propelled by impulse. She considered every plus, every minus, every contingency, every possibility before making a commitment. It was one of the qualities he most respected about her. Right now, however, it was bothering the hell out of him.

"When is the Chickering?"

"Last week in August, first week in September."

"That's too late," Katalin said, shaking her head with frustration. "Without the money for tuition, I can't continue at Juilliard and I can't extend my visa without having a notice from the school that I'm a student."

"Number one, you don't have to pay until you register—which would be mid-September. Number two, I'm quite certain the president of Juilliard would be more than happy to list you as a student for the purpose of stretching your visa. You're a credit to the school, Katalin."

Greco reached over and patted her hand. It was cold and limp. He looked into her eyes. They were vacant and fixed, as if she had put all her senses on hold while she retreated into the realm of intense thought. While he knew without doubt that the best thing for Katalin was to enter this competition so she could begin to forge a career with New York as her home base, he knew that for her, it was not that simple. She had family in Budapest, friends, ties, loyalties. And because of who they were and where they lived, regular visits were not a realistic option. This was not about a contest. This was about her future.

"What are my chances?" she asked, still distracted.

"Big prizes draw big talent. You'll be competing against the finest young pianists in the free world."

He could almost see Katalin's thoughts tumbling over one another inside her brain. She was assessing both her ability and her desire. She was experienced enough to know it took more than virtuosity to triumph at a competition of this caliber. It took extraordinary effort combined with gladiator strength of mind and purpose. To win you had to be not only capable of winning, you had to view winning as the only acceptable end. Zoltán Gáspár's daughter didn't enter competitions to place or to show.

"Let's do it," she said.

Greco's smile left the shadows and burst onto his lips. "Let's do it indeed!"

While Katalin trained for her Juilliard exams, Greco mailed her application to the Chickering committee. A month later they were notified that out of 285 hopefuls, she was accepted—one of 125. The next step was to submit a twenty-minute audio tape, recorded during a fifty-minute recital performed before a team of Chickering representatives. As soon as the recital ended, Katalin was asked to select which twenty minutes she wanted the judges to hear. Six weeks after that, she received notice that she had advanced to the next round of 35. But she was not the only quarter-finalist from Juilliard. Pedjá Lauc had also made the Chickering cut.

Katalin's March audition went smoothly. Since it also served as her graduation exam, once it was over and she knew her admission to the Advanced Certificate Program was secured, she was free to concentrate on her preparation for the Chickering. And concentrate she did, almost to the point of fanaticism. Once Katalin had made the decision to try to stay in New York, she became obsessed with winning. It was as if her soul had been taken over by a spirit that preyed upon her, taunting her about not returning home, not caring about how Zoltán and Mária might feel. The voice tormented her with accusations of disloyalty and selfishness, goading her into the belief that she owed her parents the victory; that anything less was a betrayal of their understanding, their patience, and their love.

Knowing that Pedjá was one of her competitors colored her perspective. Normally, she viewed all contestants as one contestant, one nameless, faceless, anonymous person. To lump everyone together made it easier than to vie with thirty-four individual pianists. But she knew this pianist and she knew him well. Pedjá was good. Very good. He also had tremendous style. Since even the judges acknowledged that a major part of the allure of the Chickering was its history of attracting top record producers, concert-series managers, and booking agents, and since even the press boggled at its consequent success rate at spawning concert stars, the winner was always someone with enormous stage presence. Katalin believed that gave Pedjá a definite edge over a hayseed from Minnesota or an émigré from Budapest.

Her first task was selecting the program. It also proved to be her first obstacle. She and Greco were in full agreement about Liszt's E-flat major as her concerto selection for the finals. They also concurred on Bartók's Sonata for Piano and Chopin's "F-minor Ballade" for the semis. It was the beginning round where they differed, sharply. In addition to Mendelssohn's Six Preludes and Fugues, and Brahms's Two Rhapsodies, she wanted to reprise Liszt's "Paganini Études."

"Absolutely not!"

"Why not? It's a perfectly balanced offering."

"I hate the way you play the Études."

"Why? Because it's not traditional?"

"I suppose."

"Since when are you such a purist?"

"Since your career depends on this competition."

Katalin couldn't tell him that playing the "Paganini Études" was her way of assuaging her guilt about not going home, that again she felt the need to remind the world about the existence of Zoltán Gáspár and to remind Zoltán of his monumental talent. She didn't care what Greco thought. This was for her father.

"I take full responsibility, okay? If I'm eliminated after the first round, I promise I'll announce to the press that I selected my program and that my tutor complied under duress. There, are you happy?"

"No."

She leaned over and kissed his cheek. "You will be," she said as she scooped up her music and prepared to bury herself in a practice room, "when we take first prize at the Chickering!"

As the date of the contest neared, Katalin turned reclusive. If she wasn't playing—which she did ten hours a day—she was studying her music, sitting up in bed at night, reading scores or fingering the coverlet as if it were a keyboard. Zsuzsanna rarely saw her niece anymore. When she did, she fretted about the strain lining Katalin's face and thinning her frame. Worry prompted Zsuzsanna to declare July 24th a holiday.

"What's July twenty-fourth?" Katalin asked that morning when Zsuzsanna asked her to get home before five.

"It's Make-Your-Old-Aunt-Happy-by-Taking-a-Night-Off Day."

Katalin laughed. "And what does my old aunt want to do on this very special holiday?"

"I want to have a celebration. Sophie's still in that avant-garde piece of garbage they call a play, so she can't come, but I've asked Paul and Pedjá to join us." At the mention of Pedjá's name, Zsuzsanna caught the almost imperceptible twitch of Katalin's eyebrows. "I know you and Pedjá think you've become rivals, but as far as I'm concerned, until you mount that stage a month from now, you're still friends." Katalin acquiesced. Zsuzsanna was delighted. "Tonight, we celebrate friendship! You come home and get dressed in something cool. I'll take care of everything else."

They had champagne at Csárda and then moved on to dinner at a nearby Italian restaurant where Zsuzsanna knew the owner. Judging from the number of times the man came over to the table, it was easy to surmise that he and Zsuzsanna had known each other very well.

"What now?" Zsuzsanna said as they lingered over their coffee. "It's too early to call it a night."

"One of my columnist friends told me about a place called the Joke

Joint," Paul said, rimming the top of his cup with a lemon rind before sipping his espresso. "She said it's fun."

"I've been there," Katalin said, excitedly. "It was fun."

"Then the Joke Joint it is," Zsuzsanna declared, rousing her troops for the march crosstown.

The Joint was packed. Not only were all the tables filled, but people stood three deep at the bar. Uptown swells bumped up against middle-class folk. Future comics hid in the corners trying to build the courage to get up and do their thing during Diamond's legendary Tryouts. There was so much noise one could hardly think and so much smoke one could hardly see. Glasses clinked on trays precariously balanced on the shoulders of inept waiters. Chairs scraped against wooden floors. The lights were hot, the air conditioning sporadic. None of that mattered. The Joint had become part of the New York scene. It was theater, and everything and everyone was part of it.

Thankfully, Roy Diamond recognized Paul Greco. Snapping his fingers and shouting in shorthand, he caused a small table and four chairs to appear. A caravan of busboys lifted the furniture above the crowd, squeezing the setting into an already jammed front row. Zsuzsanna, delighted to have been granted such a prominent spot, cooed with pleasure. Greco seemed unnerved. He was slightly claustrophobic, and the airlessness and narrowness of the room was making him edgy.

"Calm yourself," Zsuzsanna said, snuggling against him. "We're going to have a great time. Aren't we, kids?"

During dinner, Pedjá and Katalin had fenced with each other, each trying to discern how the other was coming in his preparation, what each intended to play, whether or not either had been approached by anyone in the music industry in advance of the competition. Several times Zsuzsanna tried to interrupt, but Greco warned her off.

"Leave them alone. Their curiosity is natural. Their competitiveness is healthy."

By the time they'd reached the Joke Joint, however, they couldn't probe another inch. Exhausted, they sat back and relaxed, reverting to old habits of friendship instead of their more recent venture into verbal tug-of-war.

As the show began, all four agreed that the dentist-by-day, stand-up-by-night would never make the big time with jokes about flossing and laughing gas and sex while drilling. Pedjá thought some of the material used by the next comic, a fat black woman, was hilarious. Zsuzsanna thought she was too dirty. Katalin thought she was too hostile. Greco thought if she intended to make it at all in the barbaric, antediluvian world of prime-time TV, she wasn't hostile enough or dirty enough.

When Roy Diamond took the stage to introduce his current star, excitement buzzed the room. From what snippets they could hear, Zsuzsanna and the others gleaned that it was this performer everyone had come to see.

"Every now and then," Diamond was saying, "we get lucky. Not that way, you horny old man," he said, pointing to a dapper gentleman in the third row. "Every now and then there comes along a comic with a unique eye on the world. We found this lady right here in our audience. She was a wise-ass out there. She's a wise-ass up here. Ladies and gentlemen, the Joke Joint is proud to present Poland's answer to Phyllis Diller—Sophie Warsaw!"

They heard the name, but the connection wasn't made until they saw her standing onstage—wearing tights (one leg purple, the other leg yellow) under a red crinkle-patent mini-dress, her hair spiked, sprayed, and dyed shocking pink with an occasional swatch of orange. Her eyelashes made Twiggy's look natural; her lips were glazed fuchsia.

"Is that who I think it is?" Katalin said, her expression a montage of shock, pride, and amusement.

"If I didn't know better, I'd swear that was our own Sophia Clara Wisnewski," Zsuzsanna said, she, too, feeling a bit dazed.

"Or," Pedjá added, "could it be Sophie Wise, lead actress in the supposed off-off-off Broadway production of Goose Bumps?"

"Good evening, ladies and gentleman. I'm Sophie Warsaw."

"Yeah, right!" some guy yelled from the back of the room.

"And who might you be?" Sophie asked the heckler. "John Denver's brother, Grover Cleveland?" The audience applauded. "Okay, let's get it over with. Just because I'm Polish, you think I'm stupid, true? Well, think what you will. It doesn't matter. I won't understand it anyway."

She waited for the laugh before continuing.

"Do you like Polish jokes?" The crowd hooted and cheered. "Sure," Sophie said, slapping her thigh in a gesture of exasperation. "You don't have to live with them. You think it's a joke having a grandmother who went on the pill because she didn't want any more grandchildren? Or a brother who didn't know how to write the number eleven because he didn't know which one came first? Have pity!"

As she stalked the stage, staring out at faces rounded in laughter, Sophie felt her nervousness calm. She was always a wreck before she stepped onto the stage and told her first few jokes. Standing on the dark side of the spotlight was terrifying, like being in a courtroom waiting for the jury to file in with their verdict. Guilty, not guilty, funny, not funny, it all came down to strangers passing judgment on strangers.

Before becoming a comedienne, Sophie had abhorred being in a position where others who had no right assessed and appraised her. In her mind, no matter what they thought, she believed she always came up wanting. She wasn't pretty. She didn't come from a family that could be even remotely defined as classy or notable. She had no immediately visible talent or overwhelming scholarship in a particular area. All she had ever been was funny. She had been the funniest one in school, the funniest kid on her block, the one who always made others laugh.

She remembered the first time she ever told a joke. She was in grammar school. She had just moved into the neighborhood, and for months she had hung on the sidelines, watching, observing, trying to pick out the least intimidating girls, the ones who might accept her into their clique. One girl, Rosy McDowell, seemed to be the center of attention, the one person everyone gathered around. In time, Sophie realized it was because she made them laugh. They liked her and wanted to be her friend. *If I made them laugh*, she recalled thinking, *they would want to be my friend*. And so she did.

Sophie walked to the front of the stage, leaned over, and stared at a man in the front row. As she bent over, her eyes caught a glimpse of the people seated four tables away. Her stomach jolted. She had never performed in front of friends. She wasn't certain she could do it. Panic washed over her like a sudden fever. She started to stand. She wanted to run. She did neither. Instead, she decided to show them what she was all about. Quickly, she summoned her forces and concentrated on the man who was looking up at her expectantly.

"How many Polacks does it take to pull off a kidnapping?"

The man blushed and shrugged his shoulders.

"Ten. One to steal the kid and nine to write the ransom note."

She paced the small stage, carefully avoiding Zsuzsanna's table, gauging her timing, assessing her audience.

"Did you hear about the Polack who cut off his hands so he could play the piano by ear? Or the Polack who cut off his left leg and left arm so he could be all right?"

Back and forth she walked, staring into the crowd, making eye contact with first one patron, then another.

"I had a cousin who went to register at the desk of the Waldorf Hotel. Poor thing. She signed the registration card with an O. 'Why'd you put a circle there,' asked the clerk. She explained that she didn't know how to write. 'Then why not sign with an X?' 'I used to, but when I got my divorce, I took back my maiden name.' "

Sophie climbed onto a wooden stool, took a sip of water from a glass left on a nearby table, and faced her fans.

"I know this is going to upset you, but it's time you grew up and faced facts. Santa Claus is not a nice Waspy guy. He's Polish." She scanned the room. It was as if the audience were holding its collective breath, afraid that if they breathed they would miss the next line. "Yes, ladies and gentlemen, jolly Saint Nick is a Polack. How do I know?"

As if they had been primed for the moment, everyone echoed, "How do you know?"

"There are two doors and at least eight windows in the average house, right? This putz comes down the chimney. You want to tell me he's not Polish?"

The crowd roared. Sophie turned and, for the first time, looked directly at Katalin's table. She smiled.

"I have some friends here tonight." She pointed at them. "Two Hungarians, a Slav, and a man of undetermined origin. Add a little lettuce, a touch of mayo, and it sounds like a sandwich at the Uptown Deli." Nervously she waited until Greco, Zsuzsanna, Pedjá, and Katalin all wore smiles. "And you guys thought I was a serious actress. Now who's Polish?"

She was onstage for close to an hour. She gibed people in the audience. She snap-crackled jokes until the crowd was breathless. Though the meat of her routine was her astounding array of Polish jokes, she didn't neglect the ethnic foibles of the Irish, the Italians, the Jews, the WASPs, the blacks, or the Latinos.

"If you want to pick," she said, "let's pick."

By the time she finished her act, people were on their feet, screaming for more. She took her bows, did a two-minute encore, and then, sweaty but elated, she snaked her way to her friends.

"So? What'd you think?" she said, thanking the waiter who brought her a chair, a soda, and a napkin.

Katalin hugged her. "You were fabulous! I saw it, but I still can't believe it. You're so funny."

"My little Sophie," Zsuzsanna said, so thrilled she was laughing and crying at the same time. "I'm so proud of you. But where did you get the idea for that name and this act?"

"Easy. Everyone was always hitting me with Polish jokes. I decided to hit back."

"Well, now you are a hit. A huge hit!" Pedjá was beyond impressed. He was utterly beguiled. To Pedjá, there was nothing quite as attractive as stardom. Suddenly, this waitress, this pseudo-actress, this large-nosed, clownish girl he had dated and dismissed was glowing with the dust of certain celebrity. "Are you finished now?"

"No. I have another show at midnight." Inside, it was Sophie's turn to laugh. Pedjá was so obvious he was pathetic. But it felt good. The recognition, the look of respect, the touch of regret in his voice. It felt great.

"I'd be happy to stay and see you home," he said.

"Thanks, but no need. After the place closes, we all hang out and review the night."

"It is late," Zsuzsanna said, ever the protector. "Maybe we should all stay and wait to take you home."

Sophie leaned over and kissed Zsuzsanna's cheek. "I love you for being so concerned, but I've been doing this for months. Trust me, I'll be fine."

"Is this why you left Juilliard?" Katalin asked. "I thought you wanted to be an actress."

"I thought so, for awhile." Sophie understood that Katalin's question went deeper than it appeared. Katalin was steeped in the classics. Because of that, Sophie knew that sometimes her friend's vision was myopic. "Katya, I don't like being serious. You know that. I like having fun and making fun happen."

"I know, but . . ."

"Do you remember the night we came here with Steven and Matthew?" Katalin nodded. "I made that one comment and everyone laughed."

"They certainly did," Katalin said, remembering.

"I loved it. I loved hearing that sound in my ears. A few nights later I came back here on a whim. It was Tryout night, when you volunteer to stand up and take your shot. I don't know what possessed me, but when Roy asked who wanted the mike, my hand was up and waving." Sophie's voice had dropped. She sounded almost mystical, as if she believed that what had happened next had occurred thanks to divine guidance. "I walked onto that stage having no idea what I was going to say or do. But then I turned and looked into the eyes of the people at the tables. They were giving me the same indulgent, patronizing stares I always get. My nose, my clothes, my heritage. They've always been the butt of jokes—so, I figured, let 'em have it. I began to tell every Polish joke I knew. They loved it because I was Polish and somehow that made the humor less cruel. It also made it okay when I poked fun at them. It was like we were all in it together, like 'I'll show you mine if you show me yours.' Do you know what I mean?"

Paul, who had been silent throughout, surprised everyone by taking Sophie's hand and kissing it. "They say that great comedy is born of great pain. I don't know whether that's true in your case," he said, "but I do know that in addition to a quick wit, it also takes intelligence and sensitivity to be a comedienne. You have both in large quantities and because of that, you're going to make it, Sophie Warsaw. You're going to make it big."

It was almost four o'clock in the morning when Katalin got the call that Sophie had been mugged and was in the hospital. She roused Zsuzsanna. They both threw clothes on and raced downtown. When they got to the emergency room, they were ushered into a tiny cubicle. There, hooked up to a horde of frightening machines, was Sophie, her face bandaged, her arm set in a cast, her skin blue and bruised. She was unconscious.

"She has some internal bleeding," the nurse told them. "We've been waiting for her vital signs to stabilize. Once they do, she's going in for surgery."

"Is she going to be all right?" Katalin couldn't take her eyes off Sophie.

"We think her spleen's been ruptured, but we won't know the full extent of her injuries until she's opened up."

"How did this happen?" Zsuzsanna said, her own color pasty and wan.

"According to the police report, she was leaving a comedy club on the West Side when two men mugged her. The police think she was beaten with baseball bats. The crooks took her money, but left her wallet. That's how we found your number."

"Has her family been notified?" Katalin asked.

"We assumed you were her family."

Suddenly, an alarm went off on one of the machines. The nurse ran to Sophie's side, checked her, and shouted for an orderly. Within seconds Sophie's gurney was being wheeled down the hall toward an elevator. Something terrible had happened.

"*Jézus Mária!* Please, God, keep my Sophie safe," Zsuzsanna sobbed.

Katalin, whose innards were in such turmoil it felt as if it would be weeks before they righted themselves, couldn't bear to stand by and do nothing. She needed to keep busy, to stay active, to feel as if she were contributing to Sophie's recovery.

"Where does her family live?" she asked Zsuzsanna.

"Sophie and her family don't speak," Zsuzsanna said quietly.

"If Sophie dies, they'll never speak again. They deserve to know. They deserve the chance to make amends."

"I don't disagree, but let's wait until Sophie comes out of surgery. It's five-thirty in the morning. We don't know anything for sure. Wait. When we have something concrete, you'll notify her people."

Katalin found the waiting intolerable. Though she tried to remain optimistic in front of Zsuzsanna, inside she was angry and frightened. She kept picturing Sophie onstage, alive and vibrant. She saw her at the table afterward, glowing with pride, basking in the glorious light of her success. Now she lay in an operating room, her body damaged, her life threatened. Katalin couldn't shake the image of Sophie's face, a collage of white gauze and purple welts and dried blood. When finally the doctor appeared, Katalin was prepared for the worst.

"She's critical," he said in that matter-of-fact monotone doctors use with the potentially hysterical. "We had to remove her spleen and repair the left lung, which had been punctured by one of her broken ribs. She suffered a lot of internal bleeding, but the prognosis is positive. We'll know more when she comes out of the recovery room."

"How long will she be in there?" Katalin asked.

"Several hours." He looked at the two women standing before him. Neither one looked too healthy. "Why don't you go home and get some sleep. When you come back in the afternoon, she'll be settled in a room and you can visit with her."

Zsuzsanna nodded politely and thanked him, but she had no intention of going anywhere. Katalin did.

The Wisnewskis lived in a run-down building on 27th Street, between Second and Third avenues. It wasn't a tenement exactly, but it was close. An eight-story apartment house of unimaginative brown brick that, even in its heyday, had never been anything special, it exuded an aura of fatigue and defeat, as if the demands of the city and the needs of the tenants had sapped whatever energy had once been contained within its walls.

Apartment 1A was not easy to find. Tucked behind the elevators in the back of the building, it appeared to be the only apartment on the floor. Katalin pressed the buzzer and waited. No one came. She pressed the buzzer again. And a third time. She was about to leave.

"Who are you and what do you want?"

"My name is Katalin Gáspár. I need to talk to you about your daughter, Sophie."

"I don't have a daughter."

"Yes, you do, Mr. Wisnewski. Her name is Sophia Clara. I know you aren't on the best of terms, but I'm her friend and I need to see you."

"I don't care what you need and I don't care what she needs."

"Mr. Wisnewski. I'm not leaving here until you open the door."

"Go away." His voice sounded different, distant, as if he had moved farther into the room, away from the door.

Katalin pressed the buzzer again and again and again.

Something bumped against the door. She heard a chain being unlatched. The door opened. Staring up at her with pale, rheumy eyes was a rawboned man in striped pajamas, seated in a wheelchair. His body was bent, hunched over, and very weak-looking, but his visage was like a steel mask welded together with anger and rage.

"Now what the hell do you want?"

"Sophie was mugged," Katalin said, ignoring his hostility. "She's badly hurt. They beat her with baseball bats and left her to die. She's in the hospital, on the critical list. I thought you should know."

"So now I know. I still don't care."

Katalin was shaken. She looked past him into the apartment, noting the shabby furniture and the littered floor. It smelled of sauerkraut and stale sausage. So did he. But there was another odor coming from this man—a bitter, acrid scent, rank with resentment and unavenged hatred.

"You can't mean that, Mr. Wisnewski," Katalin continued, knowing it was hopeless, yet unwilling to accept a father's total dismissal of his child. "Whatever went wrong between you and Sophie, does it really matter now? She's hurting. Won't you go to her?"

He laughed. It was a mean cackle, the kind one would have expected from a crow. "Even if I could, I wouldn't take one step to help her. I helped her once. And look where it got me."

Before she could follow up, he slammed the door in her face, bolted the locks, and hitched the chains. Katalin considered leaning on the buzzer again, but didn't. He had heard all he intended to hear and said all he had to say.

Fortunately, Zsuzsanna had given her the address where Mrs. Wisnewski worked. Flagging a cab, Katalin raced across town to a factory on 18th Street and Ninth Avenue. It took some talking to convince the foreman that Katalin's mission was an emergency, but after several minutes a short, lumpish woman with a flowery scarf tied around her head and blue eyes that could only belong to Sophie's mother appeared at the door.

"Mrs. Wisnewski?"

"Ya." She continued to hold onto the door as if she needed the support, or perhaps a quick escape.

"I'm Katalin Gáspár. I'm a friend of Sophie's." She watched. The woman's eyes flickered. Not with the hatred Katalin had seen firing her husband's eyes. This was a mix of emotions: fear and love and uncertainty. "Sophie's in the hospital. She was mugged and badly beaten. She came out of surgery less than two hours ago." The eyes darkened and tears formed in the corners, trembling there as if afraid to fall. "I went to see your husband. I told him there was a chance Sophie might not make it, but he says he doesn't care, that he won't go visit her. You care. You'll visit her, won't you?"

Frieda Wisnewski's eyes darted about the room and her body trembled, making her look like an animal caught in a trap. Her hand let go of the door. She held it out toward Katalin, grabbed the younger woman's hand and shook it.

"No. No, I can't. If Leo won't go, I can't." The tears began to fall, flooding her face with a sea of remorse. "I do love her and I do care, but I can't go. If Leo says no, I can't."

Katalin helped the aggrieved woman to a chair and sat next to her, comforting her.

"Mrs. Wisnewski, tell me what happened. Tell me what could possibly be so awful that it would keep you from visiting your daughter."

Frieda looked at Katalin with searing intensity. She appraised her, assessing whether Katalin was worthy of hearing confession, whether the circumstances were worthy of betraying her husband.

"I love Sophie too," Katalin said, still trying to coax the truth from the agitated woman. "I only want to help her. You're the only one who can help me."

"You can't tell Leo I told you," she said, grabbing Katalin's hand as if she needed to seal their bargain with a meeting of flesh.

"I won't. I swear on my parents, I won't say a word."

Frieda nodded. "Then I'll tell you."

Sophie was thirteen years old. Infatuated with the bizarre even then, she was known in the neighborhood for her wacky wardrobe and her sassy ways. She was also known as the little mother of the Wisnewski family. At night Frieda worked as part of the cleaning crew for a big office building in midtown. During the day she ran a sewing machine at a dress factory. Leo was the resident superintendent of their building on 93rd Street. Her two older brothers, according to some of their neighbors, were no-accounts. One was supposed to be apprenticing with an electrical contracting company. The other was supposed to be in school. Rarely did either of them do what he was supposed to do.

Sophie's day started early. She was up at six so she could get to the bathroom before her brothers. Then, while Frieda fixed breakfast Sophie packed lunches. After school Sophie raced home to do the food shopping and the laundry and the cleaning. She was also in charge of starting dinner. The only time she could study was between chores or late at night when the rest of the family had gone to sleep. In her stolen moments Sophie dreamt of being rich and famous and having someone else do the chores for her.

Sometimes, when her father decided he had done enough to earn his keep and took off to a local bar to reward himself, Sophie found herself answering the calls of the tenants. The excuses she invented to explain why her father was unavailable were legendary. Though she defended his absences in public, in private she hated him for spending her mother's hard-earned money. It killed her that he thought nothing of disappearing for a few hours, wandering in around dinnertime tipsy and insulting. It infuriated her even more to know that he encouraged her brothers to follow suit.

One day, after Sophie had left the local supermarket and started home, she heard some Spanish boys taunting her. She didn't know what they were saying, but she knew it wasn't anything she wanted translated. Keeping her eyes straight ahead of her, she quickened her pace. Though they didn't get any closer to her, their pace quickened as well. For five blocks they whistled and clucked their tongues and made rude noises at her. She thought about running, but she looked around and saw no one to help her if they attacked. Step by step, she proceeded toward her building, praying that today Leo would be home. That Jan was home. Or Eddie. That they were sober.

She pushed the door open and hastened down the steps into the basement apartment where they lived. Before she could fix the locks, the three youths, all high on drugs, slammed into the apartment, throwing her to the floor.

"Papa!" she screamed, hoping he was in the bedroom taking a nap. "Papa! Jan! Somebody! Help me!"

But no one came. One of the youths ripped off her skirt and tore her panties from her body. While the other two held her, he unzipped his fly and relieved himself on her belly. When he was through, he mounted her, pushing his half-hard penis into her, seesawing back and forth, trying to make himself virile. All the while, Sophie screamed and kicked. When she cried, they smacked her, yelling at her in Spanish.

While the one pumped her, the other two laughed at her misery and played with her budding breasts, pinching her nipples, tweaking them, twisting them, biting them until the pain was so great she thought she'd pass out.

When the first one was finished with her, the other two used her, one in front, one sodomizing her in back. They changed positions. Two would go at her while the third one forced himself into her mouth, pushing himself down her throat until she gagged. One of them found a broomstick and shoved it up her until blood gushed onto the floor. Each time she cried they found another way to punish her. Eventually she sought refuge in unconsciousness, fainting, fading in and out as they fucked her and beat her and humiliated and abused her. She had no concept of time, but once, when she was awake, she noticed that the light outside the window had grown gray. Knowing what time she had left the market, knowing what time it got dark that time of year, she guessed that they had been tormenting her for at least two hours.

Sophie never heard the door open. She never saw the horror on her father's face as Leo saw the blood and the mess and the three crazed animals rutting about with his daughter. Her attackers were so lost in her and in their drugs, they didn't hear him either. Trying not to make any noise, Leo reached behind a chair where he kept a lead pipe in case of intruders. Charging them, he slammed the pipe down on the rump of the first boy he came to. Unfortunately, Leo was drunk. He was as rocked by the blow as was his victim. He stumbled. The other two bounded up like springboks, leaping on Leo and beating him with his own implement. They beat him again and again with the lead pipe, crushing his spine, leaving him a pathetic heap in the middle of the floor.

When they left, Sophie crawled to the telephone and dialed 911. Then she crawled to Leo, who lay frighteningly still.

"I'm so sorry, Papa," she cried, wanting to put her head on his chest, afraid that if she did she would make his injuries worse. "Thank you for protecting me. Thank you for saving me. Thank you for showing that you love me."

It was later, when they were in the hospital and he refused to see her, that the bitterness set in. How could she have been stupid enough to think he loved her? She would go to his room and he would shriek at her, demanding that she be taken away. She appealed to her brothers, but they sided with their father. Her mother was too tortured to venture an opinion. Not Leo. He had very definite opinions about what had happened. Leo blamed her for the fact that he was crippled for life. He blamed her for wearing provocative clothes that incited her attackers. He blamed her for everything.

She blamed Leo, because she believed that if he had been home, she wouldn't have been raped, she wouldn't have had her uterus punctured by a broomstick, she wouldn't have been beaten, she wouldn't be plagued by nightmares, and she wouldn't have to feel as dirty and worthless as she did. The difference was that Leo voiced his accusations to anyone and everyone who would listen, calling Sophie names most men didn't ascribe to strangers, let alone their own children. Sophie kept her denunciations to herself.

The day Sophie was discharged from the hospital, no one came to pick her up. She went home, packed her belongings, and left. For six months she lived in a shelter. While she was there, one of the volunteers took her under her wing. Eventually, Zsuzsanna took her from the shelter and gave her a home. Though she tried to reunite Sophie with her family, her efforts were fruitless. Deciding that the best thing for Sophie was to stay with her and not be returned to her kin, Zsuzsanna established a few rules. She insisted that Sophie go to school. Sophie agreed. Sophie insisted that she work and pay her own way. Zsuzsanna agreed. She set Sophie up in the little apartment in the back of Csárda, checked Sophie's homework, trained her as a restaurant jack-of-all-trades, and offered her as much affection as Sophie could handle. Most of all, she made her feel safe. Over the years, Zsuzsanna returned to Sophie a sense of purpose and a sense of self-worth. The one thing she could never do, however, was help Sophie to feel clean.

Frieda was weeping, as was Katalin.

"Leo was always an angry man. He was angry that the war made him leave Poland. He was angry that he couldn't find a good job here. He was angry that he had to struggle and pinch pennies." Her voice trembled, telling Katalin more about the hardship of her life with Leo than words ever could. "After that day, it got worse. We had to move from that building because he couldn't do the chores, so he couldn't keep his job as superintendent. In this place, the boys do his chores for him. Leo hates that too."

"But it wasn't Sophie's fault."

Frieda covered her eyes with her hands and sobbed, her pudgy body shaking with the horror of it all. "I know that, but what can I do?"

Katalin put her arm around Frieda's shoulders and held her close. "You can go see Sophie now and tell her that."

• • •

Katalin tiptoed past three other women to the end of the room, where Sophie lay in a bed hidden by curtains. She was still asleep, still hooked up to monitoring devices, but the nurse had assured Katalin she could be awakened. Katalin stood over Sophie, looking at her as if she had never seen this pale, blond woman before. In a way, she hadn't. She had never realized it until now, but the person Katalin knew was not complete. She was an act, not a reality. The Sophie that Katalin knew was the Sophie that Sophie wanted Katalin to know. It was different now. The truth had added substance to the act.

Things were so much clearer. No wonder Sophie never cried, made everything into a joke, and was intensely loyal to Zsuzsanna and very untrusting of men. No wonder Sophie was such a good actress and such an adroit comic. Katalin's mouth twisted into a wry smile. Greco was right again. Great comedy was born of great pain.

Sophie stirred. Her eyes didn't open, but she moaned. Katalin touched her arm. "Sophie," she whispered. "Sophie, it's Katya."

Sophie's eyelids fluttered and she blinked, trying to focus. When she did, she offered Katalin a wobbly replica of a smile.

"Hell of an encore, don't you think?"

"It got everyone's attention," Katalin said, stroking Sophie's arm, hoping that what she was about to say next didn't upset her friend. "Including your mother's."

A long awkward silence ensued. The anesthesia had slowed Sophie's thought processes. Katalin could almost see her thinking about what her response should be.

"She's sitting with Zsuzsanna in the hall. I'm going to get her."

"No," Sophie said. She was agitated. The machine monitoring her heart blipped faster and louder. "I don't want to see her."

Katalin held Sophie's hand in hers, trying to calm her. "Yes you do. And she wants to see you. Very badly."

"No." Her heartbeat had leveled. The protest had weakened. "I . . ."

"Give her a chance to say she's sorry." Sophie tilted her head. Katalin took that as consent. She leaned down and kissed Sophie's forehead. "We'll be right back."

Frieda, almost as hesitant as Sophie had been, hung back, stalling the moment of reconciliation. But as she neared her daughter's bed and saw that pale face and those deep-blue eyes that so resembled her own, she forgot her fears and all the misunderstandings and slights and wedges that had come between them. She ran to Sophie's side and hugged her. Katalin held her breath until she saw Sophie hug Frieda back.

It began slowly, but within minutes mother and daughter were chatting away in Polish, their hands tightly clasped, Frieda's other hand caressing Sophie's brow. As Katalin pulled the curtain around them, she was surprised to feel tears dampening her cheeks. Though she wanted to believe that it was their reunion that had provoked her tears, in her heart she knew—those tears were for Mária. Katalin missed her mother.

18

*T*he next several weeks were filled with surprises, not all of them wonderful. Displaying unusual compassion—considering that the Chickering was less than a month away—Greco actually encouraged Katalin to spend time with Sophie. Instead of hounding her about practicing, he urged her to do everything she could to help heal her friend's emotional wounds while the doctors tended to the physical ones. Not only did he send flowers, but he actually went to visit Sophie. It was a side of Greco that Katalin had suspected existed but had never seen.

Pedjá, however, came once to the hospital, stayed for an hour, and never came again.

"I thought you were lovers," Katalin said, truly confused.

"You think everyone who takes off their clothes in front of each other are lovers," Sophie said, exhibiting no sign of anger or hurt pride. "I've been naked in front of half this hospital and I assure you, I haven't made it with any of them. Pedjá and I rolled around a few times. It was sex, Katya, nothing more. He wanted it. I gave it to him. I don't owe him and he doesn't owe me."

The biggest surprise was Matthew Kardos. The morning Sophie was scheduled to leave the hospital, he appeared at her bedside.

"Zsuzsanna told me what happened," he said, smiling at the frail girl sitting on the edge of the bed, her feet dangling several inches above the floor. Her nose was still bandaged. Her arm was in a cast. Beneath her blouse he could see the bandages on her abdomen. "I figured that with you out of commission, Csárda might need an extra waiter. Besides," he said, winking at Katalin, "With everyone else treating you like some sort of empress, I thought you might need a representative of the common folk around to suffer your abuse. Here I am."

"Well, they don't come much more common than you, coal mining man," Sophie said. But she could not repress a smile.

"Does that mean you're going to be nice to me?" He had brought her flowers. Without comment, he handed them to her.

"Probably not," she said, accepting the bouquet with a shaky hand. "You're the kind of sap who simply begs to be abused." Her voice cracked, and when she held the blossoms to her nose, Katalin was certain she had used the petals to catch a few disobedient tears.

"Right now, I'm begging you to slide off that bed so I can help you into that wheelchair. It's time we got you out of here."

"No wheelchair." Sophie's eyes turned flinty, her pose unyielding.

"I think it's a hospital requirement that they take you to the door in a wheelchair," Katalin said gently, seeing Leo, knowing Sophie was seeing Leo.

"I don't care."

Zsuzsanna had told Matthew very little, only that Sophie had been mugged and severely beaten. She had been too upset to go into detail about the extent of Sophie's injuries, let alone any of Sophie's background. Matthew knew nothing about Leo, but it was clear that something had spooked Sophie and that no amount of coaxing was going to get her into that wheelchair.

"I've got an idea," he said, lifting her into his arms, careful not to jostle her. Instinctively, her arms wrapped around his neck. "I'll sit in the wheelchair. You'll sit on my lap. Katalin, you push. How's that?" Without waiting for an answer, he settled himself in the chair, maintaining his grip on Sophie. Katalin, taking his cue, got behind them and quickly started moving them down the corridor toward the elevator.

"Stop!" Since Sophie's voice was only a single decibel level below a screech, Katalin obeyed. The trio parked in the middle of the hall. Katalin and Matthew eyed Sophie carefully. She seemed to be struggling to find the right words. "I just want to say . . . thanks . . . for being so nice . . . and all that."

"You're welcome," Matthew said, wishing she would show this face more often, wondering why the endearing, delicate young woman he was holding in his arms kept herself hidden behind such a thick, dark wall.

"Okay," Sophie said, refitting her mask. "Enough of this maudlin bullshit. Start pushing, Katalin. I'm beginning to get lap sickness."

With Sophie comfortably ensconced in her apartment, attended by Zsuzsanna, Matthew, and the Csárda crew, Katalin felt free to return to her normal routine. It took nearly a week until she felt on top of her form again, but that afternoon, when she was leaving Juilliard and ran into Pedjá, she was brimming with confidence. Though she shouldn't have been surprised at what he said, and how insecure it made her feel, she was.

He was lugging a huge box and several shopping bags into the building. She could have sworn that he tried to avoid her and that when she stopped him, he was in a rush to get away from her.

"How're you coming?" she asked, glancing at his packages, noting that they were from Paul Stuart, a very tony men's shop on Madison Avenue. "Are you ready?"

Several times she had gone looking for him to tell him Sophie was home and that he could, should, visit her. Each time, his practice room had been empty.

"Now I am," he said, lifting his parcels and holding them out to her like a fisherman with a prize catch. "Now that I have my outfits, I'm ready to take the stage."

Katalin couldn't keep from chuckling. "Now that you have your outfits?"

"Katalin, my naive pet. I've told you over and over again. In America it's image that counts. I've practiced my pieces until my fingers are limp. So have you. So has every other contestant. We're all good. We all know we're good. But good is not going to take first at the Chickering."

"I guess I am naive," Katalin said, thoroughly disliking his patronizing tone. "I thought they awarded first prize to the best, not the good."

"Touché, but what is the definition of best? Is it the most technically astounding pianist, the most soul-wrenching musician, or is it the most appealing stage artist? I'm going for the last. When I take the stage, Ms. Gáspár, watch out! I'm gonna grab that spotlight and shake the shit out of it!"

"Wearing what?"

"You'll see, Katalin. Soon enough."

With an irksome wink, he turned and headed for the elevators, leaving Katalin with a bad taste in her mouth and a knot in her stomach. The Chickering was in two weeks. Not only hadn't she thought about what she would wear, but she hadn't thought it was important. Suddenly, it became vital. Pedjá was talented. In her heart Katalin felt she was more talented than he, but there was a ring of truth in his words. All the contestants—certainly the finalists—were exceptional pianists. What if Pedjá was right? What if at that level, mere technique was not enough? She would simply have to create her own image. After all, she told herself, if she was going to compete, she had to compete in all areas. And if she intended to win—which she did—she had to be prepared for all contingencies.

It took days of looking and thinking and deciding. Finally, with less than a week before the start of the Chickering, Katalin unpacked her purchases and assembled her outfits on Zsuzsanna's bed. A little hair and makeup advice from Sophie, a little encouragement from Zsuzsanna, an oath of silence extracted from each of them, and she was set.

Pedjá Lauc wanted to compete with image? Fine! Now she, too, had image.

Three days to the Chickering and still more surprises. Steven had been discharged and was home for good. When she saw him standing outside her practice room, the dam on her emotions burst. As he hugged her, she laughed and cried at the same time, touching him, holding him, kissing him, unable to believe that the flesh she felt beneath her fingers was his and not an illusion. She bombarded him with questions, not able to stand still for the answers. When had he gotten out? When had he arrived in New York? Why hadn't he called? Where was Shadow? What was he going to do for the rest of his life? For the next few weeks? For the rest of the day?

Steven had stopped at Csárda first. Matthew and Zsuzsanna had filled him in on what Katalin was doing, how important it was, and how soon it was all scheduled to begin. Before going to see her, he detoured to Paul Greco's office.

"I know about the competition," Steven said to him. "I came to see you first because I don't want to do anything that would hurt Katalin's chances."

"That's good. Especially since you're one of the reasons she wants to win so badly."

"Should I not see her? Should I slip out of town and come back when it's all over?"

Greco considered the question. His first instinct was to say yes, to remove this potential distraction until his presence could not possibly be damaging. But he couldn't do that to Katalin. She loved this man, and clearly he loved her. What would be served except to hurt them both and cast himself in the role of heartless villain?

"No, that's not fair. But if I might, could I ask you to use some restraint?"

Steven chuckled. "You can ask. I don't know if I can," he said honestly. Then he cleared his face of humor and grew serious. "I do have to go to Washington. What if I schedule it immediately?"

"I would appreciate that. She needs to get the proper mind-set early on. Once she's past the early rounds, she'll be on course."

"I can watch her compete in the semis, can't I?"

Greco smiled and nodded. "I wouldn't dream of denying you the pleasure and the privilege of seeing Katya perform. She's going to win, you know."

Steven rose and shook Greco's hand. "Yes," he said. "I know."

Now, holding her in his arms, he did experience a few pangs of regret. The thought of leaving her for a moment, let alone several days, was so painful, he knew that if he didn't tell her right away, he would capitulate to his desires and not tell her at all.

"I have to go to Washington tomorrow," he said as they walked toward the fountain in Lincoln Center.

"Why?" One word, yet plumped with such an obvious mix of anger and disappointment and rejection, it sounded like a chorus.

They sat on the rim of the stone fountain, catching the sunshine on their faces, the water mist on their backs. He took her hand and kissed her fingers.

"Let me go back and tell you what I did this last year. You need to know that to understand. Okay?"

She nodded, but still, he could see that nothing he said was going to make his leaving any easier.

"When Shadow and I went back to Vietnam, we were assigned to desk duty at U.S. Command Headquarters in Saigon. As an adjutant, I played nursemaid and secretary to Lieutenant General Hutchinson, one of the men who took over after Westmoreland was sent stateside. Hutch was not a very imaginative sort, and so he continued the same smoke-screen policies Westmoreland had initiated. Press releases lied about body counts and injuries so that we could continue to look like winners, when in fact everyone knew we were getting our asses kicked. Suddenly everyone was talking about de-escalating. They tried to make it sound as if it had been a brilliant military decision, but that wasn't the reason. There was no heart left. There were no men left.

"One of my jobs was to escort government officials around when they came to Saigon. About six months ago, one of those Congressional fact-finding committees came over. The head of it was Owen Rhinehart, the senator from Kentucky. I guess because we were from the same part of the world, he sought me out and pumped me for information. There was something about him that said he wanted what didn't go into the press releases. While Shadow took the other senators and congressmen to see the so-called safe zones—places we could take the officials where they could think they saw the war, but could never really be in any danger of coming close to the war—Senator Rhinehart and I talked. We hit it off right away. I told him how much I hated the fact that we were lying to the American public, that they were sending us their sons and we were repaying them with bullshit. He was as upset as I was. He's pompous, Rhinehart. In fact he's lampooned in the press as one of those Washingtonians who's a dedicated party man—as long as the party is black tie. But he's bright and able and has a good record on liberal, socially conscious issues."

"In other words," Katalin said, "you like him."

Steven smiled. "Yes, I do. Anyway, during the course of our conversations Senator Rhinehart encouraged me to apply to college—specifically, Georgetown University. I told him I'd have to go wherever I could get a scholarship and a job. He told me he'd arrange both. He did. I have an interview with the admissions office at Georgetown and a job in his office. If I'm accepted, I can start in September."

Katalin tried to look enthusiastic, but she wasn't certain how far away Washington was. Here she was looking to stay in New York and he was planning on living somewhere else.

Tuned in to her thoughts, Steven said, "It's only four and a half hours by car, an hour by plane, and three and a half hours by train. We can see each other on weekends, which we couldn't do when I was in Vietnam and you were here. And we wouldn't be able to do if I was here and you were in Budapest. Right?" He leaned over and kissed her.

"I guess," she said, still not totally convinced.

"And now," he said, standing, taking her hand and leading her from the fountain, "I think we should stop talking about being apart and start discussing getting together. If you have no objections, I've rented a gorgeous room at the Plaza Hotel overlooking the park. It's just for us and just for the night. Care to join me?"

He slipped his arms around her waist and held her next to him. His eyes were like blue crystals, hypnotizing her until she had no independent thought, no feelings other than those that started and ended with him.

"When are you coming back?"

"I'll be there when you take the stage for the semifinals." The hint of a smile tickled her lips. "I'll be the guy in the front row with the I LOVE YOU button pinned to my lapel." Her smiled broadened. His lips touched hers. "Am I going to have to make love to you right here?" "An intriguing thought, but no. The Plaza it is!"

Katalin's sensuality had always been tied to her music. The sensations she felt when she thought about love had never been linked to a person or to an actual physical experience. They had never been feelings she recalled from the past, conjuring them as companions for a lonely night, bathing in them the way women with more savvy were able to do. Rather, they had been visceral promptings, earthy preludes to the ethereal sounds she would create at the keyboard. For the first time in her life, those feelings had a name and the music had no sound.

Making love with Steven was an experience that defied comparison. Nothing she had ever done had managed to arouse such explosive responses. Lying in his arms, her body lavished by his hands, she felt as if her flesh had been hulled, exposing every nerve ending. Whatever he did, whatever he said, rocked her to the core. Her body shook as his lips descended from her mouth to the soft folds of her neck, to the eager tips of her breasts. She moaned as his fingers played on her sex. His body trembled as her hands encouraged his manhood to flourish. Never had she known such pleasure. Never had she realized she was capable of dispensing such pleasure. As his body covered hers and she opened herself to him, she felt as if in some cosmic way, she understood the Creation, as if the light of Paradise was beaming down upon them, diminishing everyone and everything except them, concentrating all the energy of the universe into this one magnificent union. They touched. They caressed. They inhaled each other's flesh. And when they came together, their bodies joined in such a volcanic tangle, their emotions spiraled, swirling, whirling, eddying higher and higher until they were caught in the cyclone of their passion. Still, she felt insatiable, unquenchable, as if there could only be a crescendo to this composition, never a diminuendo and never an ending.

"*Szeretlek*, Katya," he said over and over.

"I love you, István." She, too, felt the need to say the words, to feel them on her lips, to hear them, to see his reaction to them, to emphasize the meaning behind them by surrendering herself to him again and again.

By morning there was not a freckle on either one's body that hadn't been explored. There was not a topic that had not been discussed. And not a decision that had not been made. Steven would go to Washington. Katalin would ready herself for the competition. If Steven got his scholarship, he would go to Georgetown and work for Senator Rhinehart. If Katalin won, she would continue at Juilliard, fulfill her concert dates, and begin to carve out a career. Yes, they would marry. Of course they would marry. But there was no need to rush. They were young. They were in love. They would be in love forever. They had plenty of time.

Steven was true to his word. The first night of the semifinals he sat in a box on the right, a red button with I LOVE YOU in fat white letters pinned to his lapel. In the box with him were Zsuzsanna, Matthew, and Sophie, all waiting for the master of the competition to begin the evening.

The day before, each of the ten seimfinalists had been asked to reach inside a large glass beaker and pick a number. That number would determine the order in which they would play. Katalin suffered the misfortune of drawing the number one slot. Most entrants feared the judges were hardest on the first and last positions. Given a choice, most would choose three, four, or five.

Backstage, Katalin was too nervous to think about numbers. She was focused on her program: Chopin, Bartók, Liszt. Despite Greco's worries, Zoltán's interpretation of Liszt's "Paganini Études" had brought the crowd to its feet in the opening round. Her father had brought her luck—just as she had known he would. Tonight, Katalin was relying on her mother for an extra blessing.

For this evening's performance Katalin had elected to wear the same white dress and embroidered shawl she had worn for the Salzburg. She had plaited her hair into two braids that she wound around her head like a crown and decorated with small sprigs of baby's breath. On her legs she wore white tights; on her feet, red ballet slippers with ribbons that laced around her ankles.

"Smart move, doing the ethnic thing." Pedjá, who was playing in third position, had come up behind her. Looking positively leonine, his blond hair and pale skin providing the perfect ground for his sharply edged cheekbones and sky blue eyes, he was a portrait in ebony, garbed, as he usually was, in head-to-toe black. The suit, loosely cut yet finely tailored, was of a silk that even in the dimness of backstage possessed an elegant shimmer. His shirt, also made of black silk, was buttoned to the neck, the collar rising behind his gleaming mane. He wore patent-leather shoes and thin silk socks. His only concession to the expectation of formality was a thin black grosgrain ribbon looped into a casual bow tie.

"With all of you Americans in the semis," Katalin said, "I thought I'd remind the audience that the Chickering is an international competition."

"Since when did I relinquish my Yugoslavian citizenship?" he asked, miffed at what he perceived as a slight.

"Pedjá. Other than that perfectly gorgeous Slavic face, there is nothing about you that says Dubrovnik. Everything about you simply screams Hollywood."

"Everybody's got to be some place," Pedjá said, laughing at the truth she held up in front of him. "Play well, Katalin."

"Thank you, Pedjá. You too." She heard the master begin his introductions and took a few steps closer to the stage. Pedjá touched her arm.

"Just do me a favor," he said.

". . . *our first semifinalist, from Budapest, Hungary . . .*"

"What?" Katalin wondered if he was deliberately breaking her concentration or if it only seemed that way.

"Don't play great."

"*Miss Katalin Gáspár!*"

She started for the stage and stopped. "I gave them great in the opening rounds," she said, flashing an irresistible smile. "Tonight, I'm going to give them brilliant."

When she walked onstage, Steven gasped. It wasn't that she looked so beautiful—which she did—or that she appeared so self-possessed and mature and professional—which she did—it was her costume and the aura she exuded. Katalin was the embodiment of his place of birth, the incarnation of so many memories he kept filed away in a drawer marked DO NOT OPEN. Her tawny hair, the braids laced with flowers, her vaguely Oriental eyes, the shawl, the shoes—all of it was so poignantly familiar, Steven had to remind himself that he had not seen its like for more than sixteen years. When he turned and looked at Matthew, he saw that his brother had been affected also, that he, too, had been taken back in time on the wings of nostalgia.

Katalin took her place at the piano. She lifted her eyes toward the box where her supporters sat, took a minute to bask in the warmth generated by their gestures of love and encouragement, nodded, closed her eyes, bowed her head, and readied herself for her performance. Steven held his breath. As she raised her hands he clasped his together, praying that all would go well. It had to. It was the only way she could stay in the United States. Unless, of course, he realized suddenly, he married her. Inside, he smiled. It wasn't what they planned, but it could hardly be considered a nasty alternative.

The enormous hall was only a quarter full. The audience consisted of the twelve judges, assorted members of the press, friends and families of the contestants, dozens of Juilliard students and other young people Steven judged to be either aspiring musicians or classical-music groupies who simply loved being treated to something as delicious as well-played Chopin.

And this Chopin was being played extremely well. Katalin's fingers frolicked over the keys, charming from them the delicate sentimentality that marked Chopin's work. She was at one with the poetic Pole, clearly in agreement with his nineteenth-century sense of elegance and refinement. Just the other night she had told Steven she believed Chopin would have been astounded at the way people lived today, horrified at the cacophony, the filth, the disarray, the constant state of upset that characterized the everyday existence of the modern world. Frédéric Chopin was a man who insisted upon harmonic beauty, accepting nothing less. From wallpaper to buttons to the way a table was laid to the way his compositions were performed—everything had to be exquisitely done.

As Steven listened to the unparalleled beauty of the "Ballade," he tried to imagine someone with the extraordinary greatness of Chopin being jealous of another man's physical strength, as Chopin was of Liszt, or to imagine such a fragile, ethereal dandy—as the composer had been—involved with the cigar-smoking, ultra-feminist novelist George Sand. As he watched Katalin swoon over the keyboard, she, too, lost in the magnificence of the piece, he recalled something else she had told him. Trying to explain rubato to him, she had read him what Chopin said about it: "The left hand is the conductor, it must not waver or lose ground; do with the right hand what you will and can." Then she read him Liszt's definition: "Do you see those trees? The wind plays in the leaves, life unfolds and develops between them, but the tree remains the same—that is the Chopin rubato!"

When Katalin's hands fell into her lap, the audience roared its appreciation. Sophie was weeping. A look around the hall showed that others had experienced the same intense wave of emotion that had moved her. Steven could barely contain himself. As Katalin rose to accept her applause, he stood, shouting *"Brava!"* at the top of his lungs. She stifled a smile, bowing gracefully, keeping her attention focused on the judges. When she took her place once again, he settled back in his seat, unable to believe how fortunate he was to have this precious jewel as his beloved.

When her hands struck the first discordant notes of the Bartók, he jerked. Still feeling safely cocooned within the gossamer softness of the Chopin, the jagged dissonance of this sonata sliced through him like a serrated knife. This piece was the polar opposite of the Chopin. There was little that could be defined as lyrical or poetic or gentle. This was a composition of clashes, of asymmetrical phrase groups, irregular meters, a dark, droning bass. At first Steven found himself disturbed by the music, agitated almost. He had to strain to understand it, but the more he listened, the more he heard. Certain passages spoke of Bartók's heritage, recalling Magyar folk tunes and rhythms. Other passages displayed his lush singing tone, his elegant virtuosity, his twentieth-century definition of harmony.

Katalin attacked the piano, treating it the way Bartók treated it—as a percussive instrument, as a true hammer clavier. Yet, Steven noticed, she wasn't banging the keys. She wasn't pounding out the music; she was demanding that it be heard, issuing commands from a position of strength and power. He was amazed that such a feminine creature could produce such mighty sound, but she was doing precisely that. Again he was awed, but not simply with the way she executed the piece. He was impressed with the way she had planned this segment of the competition. It was contrapuntal, but it was effective. When she finished the sonata and rose, the applause was as thunderous as the music had been. Steven didn't care how many followed; assessing the honest enthusiasm of the crowd and the undisguised admiration in the eyes of the judges, he knew that Katalin had just secured her place in the finals.

For the finals, Pedjá drew the first position, Katalin the last. Again, the twelve judges and the press occupied the premier rows. Again, Steven and Zsuzsanna sat in the first box on the right. Because, like the semis, the finals were spread over two nights, this evening they were joined by Katalin and Greco. Sophie and Matthew sat in the adjacent box. The audience had grown, filling most of the 2,200-seat auditorium, for the finals of the Chickering were an annual social event.

Onstage, the New York Philharmonic Orchestra waited to play backup to the five young pianists who had come to this city to offer their talent to the world. At precisely six o'clock Pierre Boulez, musical director of the New York Philharmonic, entered to respectful but restrained applause. A few years before, when Boulez had replaced the popular Leonard Bernstein, he also began to replace the more traditional Philharmonic repertoire with compositions more in keeping with his modern tastes. The subscribers, the bulwark of any orchestra, objected. They wanted the masters, the classics, the tonal presentations that made them hum and lulled them to sleep and gave them the pleasures they wanted from their music. Boulez insisted that they learn something new, that they train themselves to appreciate music that dared to be different from that which had always been popular, music that reflected the dissonance of the twentieth century. It was a battle—one fought with white gloves and politesse, but a battle nonetheless.

When Boulez introduced Pedjá Lauc and announced that he would be playing Prokofiev's Third Piano Concerto, his pleasure was obvious.

"I don't like the fact that Boulez is so happy with Pedjá's selection," Greco muttered, glaring at the French conductor.

"What difference does it make?" Katalin asked.

"I don't want him giving Pedjá his all and you his leftovers."

Katalin kissed his cheek. "If Boulez doesn't want me to outshine him, he's going to give me what I want or I'm going to play right over him. Okay?"

Greco looked at his protégée. When she had come to him she had been a shy, fragile bud, so hesitant and so tentative that he had worried that she might never achieve the stardom she deserved. He worried that she wasn't tough enough or aggressive enough or resilient enough. Though concert performers were called artists and were handled with care, the business of concerts was as cutthroat as any other. With so few major concert halls in which to play, with funding shrinking and the size of audiences diminishing rapidly, managers had to be almost ruthless in booking their clients. Too, the performers had to participate in their own careers. They had to be willing to go that one extra step to differentiate themselves from the rest of the pack. Greco had worked very hard to augment Katalin's self-image, to help her see all that she had to offer and to teach her the best way to present herself. Though he pretended to disapprove of her choice of costume, secretly he had admired her initiative in breaking with tradition and wearing native dress. Whether he liked it or not, there was more to the world of the piano than the piano.

Pedjá entered with all the pomp and majesty of a conqueror. His hair gleamed. His chin was lifted in an imperious tilt. His coattails furled behind him like a heraldic pennant. When he came center stage and faced the audience, Katalin chuckled. He was wearing the required tails, but his shirt, vest, and tie were black. He was the Prince of Darkness.

When he played, however, he managed to turn the darkness into a light so powerful it illuminated the entire hall with its brilliance. He had chosen the perfect concerto to exhibit his percussive skills. Prokofiev's Third was diabolical, fearsome in its austerity and power. There was no romantic color, no wide-spaced arpeggios, no pretty melodies. This was the music of revolution and Pedjá played it the way Katalin imagined Prokofiev had played it: railing at the keys with a controlled savagery.

Unable to resist the pull of the music, Katalin leaned forward, marveling at the rightness of his selection. This piece was so Pedjá. Prokofiev was so Pedjá. Called "the pianist of steel," Prokofiev was vigorous and exuberant and completely anti-Romantic. He believed that if the piano was a percussive instrument—which it was—then it should be played that way. He hated Chopin, said terrible things about Mozart, and even went so far as to breach the rules by refusing to play a classical concerto as his graduation piece from the St. Petersburg Conservatory. Instead, he premiered his own D-flat Concerto. He won the Rubinstein Prize anyway. The way Pedjá was playing, Katalin worried that Prokofiev's Third might win him the Chickering.

Rather than join the others for dinner and the post-concert critique, Katalin retired to her room. She had a great deal to think about. The other two contestants had been wonderful, but Pedjá was the standout. He was the one to beat. Katalin made herself a cup of tea, decompressing, forcing herself to shed any personal doubts Pedjá's performance had raised. He was unimportant now, she told herself. He was finished. He had done whatever he was going to do. The judges had scored him. The evening was over. He had had his night. Tomorrow was hers.

When her body had calmed and her mind had cleared, she lay down on her bed and visualized the Liszt, going through the piece measure by measure, bar by bar. Her fingers fluttered; her head moved from side to side as the music raged in her head. She could feel the sound pulsing through her veins, the energy of the orchestra feeding her, pushing her, prodding her to be better than she had ever been before.

It was late when she fell off to sleep, but even then, even in the arms of Morpheus, she heard the music. It continued to play throughout the night, serenading her, caressing her, hypnotizing her into believing that as long as the music flowed, she was safe. Suddenly, near dawn, a voice interrupted. It was crying or maybe shouting. Katalin couldn't tell. Neither could she make out what the voice was saying. The only thing she knew for certain was that the voice belonged to her mother.

Greco escorted Katalin to the door leading onstage. The fourth finalist had just completed Beethoven's "Emperor" concerto and was taking his bows. Katalin, wrapped in a long black cape, bowed her head and began to rub her hands together and stretch her fingers. To control her nerves, she took long, deep breaths—inhaling, exhaling, inhaling, exhaling.

"He was fair," Greco said, rubbing her shoulders, loosening her arms, doing what a second does for a fighter.

Katalin heard Greco's assessment. Others might have thought he was only saying that to lift her spirits. She knew Greco was an honest judge of music. The Korean from San Francisco had been just fair. The orchestra had overwhelmed him, which was something a pianist could not allow.

Abruptly, Katalin grabbed Greco by the arms. "Tell me the truth," she said, her eyes wider and wilder than he had ever seen them. "Am I good? Am I really good?"

He took her face in his hands and looked her squarely in the eye. A gentle smile claimed his mouth. "No," he said softly. "You're not good, Katya. You're the most extraordinary musician it's ever been my privilege to teach."

Tears welled in Katalin's eyes as she felt the warmth of his hands on her face and the sincerity of his words in her heart. They both heard Boulez begin her introduction.

Greco kissed both her cheeks and let her go. As he did, he noticed a change in her expression. She looked almost mischievous. Taking the corner of her cape, she dabbed at her eyes. Pure, clear, luminously green against her white skin, they glistened like peridots against pearls. Her hair, gleaming like so many strands of spun gold, hung down her back, held by a black satin ribbon. It dawned on Greco that he hadn't seen her gown. When he picked her up she had been wearing that cape. She hadn't removed it or opened it. His stomach twisted. He knew without asking that whatever was beneath that cape was, as he had feared it would be, newsworthy.

She stood with her back to him, facing the door to the stage. Boulez called her name. In one dramatic turn, she flung open the cape, slid it off her shoulders, and tossed it to Greco, who stood staring at her, mouth agape. Her dress was long and black. It was also strapless. A tube of black silk that banded her breasts and then flowed in a gentle drape to the tips of her toes, it exposed an expanse of smooth, pearlescent flesh. With her hair shimmering behind her, she looked like a goddess, a muse, an elegant figurehead perched on the bow of a ship.

"Wish me luck," she said, blowing him a kiss as she walked out.

"Luck," he whispered to the space where she had stood. "You have as much beauty as you have talent," he said as he huddled by the door so he could watch the reaction to her entrance. He heard the gasps. He saw the looks of shocked admiration on the faces of the orchestra. He even heard a smattering of applause. "You don't need luck," he thought as he closed the door and headed for the stairs that led to the auditorium. "You've got it all."

Aware of the stares her dress had attracted, keenly aware of Boulez's disapproval, Katalin swept past him to the front of the stage, where she gave a deep, debutante curtsy. Rising, straightening her shoulders and adopting a regal posture, she took her place at the piano. With deliberate slowness she shook her head, sweeping her hair onto her back, smoothed the skirt of her gown and touched her feet to the pedals, giving the audience time to adjust to the way she looked so that when she began, they could enjoy the music without distraction. Her face was all business as she nodded to Boulez. His eyes wandered to the lush mounds rising above the pleated black bodice. Her eyes fixed on his with an impatient glare. Embarrassed, he turned, tapped his baton on the podium, and raised his hands, taking control of the orchestra.

From the instant Katalin's fingers touched the keyboard, however, it was clear that she was the one in control. Katalin had been studying Liszt for most of her life. For the past few years, at Greco's insistence, she had become his intimate, living with him, sleeping with him, learning every single thing about him, from little-known facts like the unusually large size of his thumbs or the even more curious fact that though he was Hungarian-born, he couldn't speak his native tongue, to the more documented details of his remarkable career, like the fact that he had invented the solo recital, giving performances he called "soliloquies," and—always—playing with unprecedented bravura.

There, on the stage of Philharmonic Hall, Katalin was the very essence of bravura: her elegant, yet slightly exhibitionist attire, the flash of her arpeggios, the thunder of her chords, the sinuous sway of her body, the emphatic jut of her chin.

As Greco watched Katalin take the daring leaps and breathtaking risks that were the hallmarks of the Lisztian style, he found his mind drifting. He fought it, but suddenly his mother's face materialized before his eyes. Through her ghost he continued to watch Katalin, seeing his pupil's hands superimposed over his mother's lips urging him to practice harder, to play better, to become the star she so desperately wanted him to become. How many times had he sat where Katalin sat, in the finals of a competition? How many times had he looked into the audience and spotted his mother with her eyes closed and her hands gripping the arms of her chair as he took his seat and prepared to disappoint her once again?

Malva Greco never understood the difference between talented and gifted. Paul was talented, but the space between what he could do and what Katalin was doing on this stage, this night, was virtually immeasurable. If only Malva had borne a child with the extensive skills and the heightened sensory capacity of a Katalin Gáspár, instead of a son with good skills but a greater ability as a teacher, her dreams would have been fulfilled.

Malva was a piano teacher, a humble instructor of small children and cranky adolescents. When Paul displayed an interest in the piano, coupled with an ability to play, Malva was certain that God had decided to rectify His mistake. He had short-shrifted Malva, she decided, so He could give Paul an extra dollop of talent. The truth was that what Paul had inherited from Malva was her ability to teach. Unfortunately for both of them, that's not what she wanted. She wanted her son to be a concert pianist, a star, a name that would find its way into the permanent listings of musical greats. It was not to be.

He was admitted to the Curtis Institute and graduated with honors, but when he tried to explain to Malva that there, too, he had been told his real calling was teaching, she dismissed them as fools. For five years, in an attempt to please his mother, he endured the tours she organized, playing in second-rate halls with third-rate orchestras. He played in the competitions she selected for him, coming away with the bronze medal or no medal at all. The day of his thirtieth birthday he declared his independence. There would be no more competitions, no more tours. He accepted a teaching job at Juilliard. Malva refused to accept his decision. She took it as an act of filial disobedience and refused to speak to him. To this day, she insisted upon maintaining an icy distance from the son she believed had betrayed her.

Too bad, Greco thought as Katalin dropped her hands into her lap and the crowd rose to its feet. *You would have loved this, Mama. You would have loved standing with this tumultuous audience watching that magnificent creature take her well-deserved bows.* "What's more," he said, as tears of joy for Katalin's success mingled with tears of sadness over his own failures, "you might have been proud of me. I helped put her on that stage and that, Malva Greco, is a talent in itself."

By the time the ovation subsided, Greco's hands were sore. He looked up into the box. Zsuzsanna winked at him and held up two hands with crossed fingers. Steven, Matthew, and Sophie had their eyes glued to the microphone where Boulez was calling a brief intermission for the judges to make their final tabulations. No one left his seat. Greco held his breath. Ten minutes later, Boulez invited the five finalists to join him onstage.

Pedjá led the procession; Katalin brought up the rear. Each face was a study in nervous anticipation. From the Prince of Darkness at one end, to the Princess of the Piano, as the press was already calling her, at the other, there was a palpable tension, as if they were all being held together by a wire that was being pulled tighter and tighter.

"The bronze medalist, winner of a check for twenty-five hundred dollars, is Martin Rubinsky of Houston, Texas."

Martin claimed his prize and stepped back into line.

"The silver medalist and the recipient of a check for five thousand dollars, Pedjá Lauc."

The audience approved the selection, clapping wildly as their man in black came forward to accept his prize.

"And the winner of this year's Chickering Piano Competition, the gold medalist who will receive a check for ten thousand dollars, a recital at Carnegie Hall, and a year's concert bookings, Miss Katalin Gáspár!"

Not a single person didn't rise to hail the queen of the evening. As Katalin approached Boulez, he held his hand out to greet her. As her way of showing her appreciation for his part in her win, instead of allowing him to kiss her hand, she did what women had done to Liszt: She reversed tradition and kissed his hand. Boulez, who had understood and accepted the gesture with genuine grace, placed the medal around her neck, bowed, and backed away, giving her the spotlight and the acclaim she deserved.

Katalin stepped forward to meet her public. With the finesse and polish of an experienced diva, she accepted it all—the prize, the money, the adulation, the respect, and of course the glory. For herself, but most especially for her father.

There was barely room to breathe in Csárda, let alone to dance. Despite the crush of humanity, Zsuzsanna instructed her gypsies to play. When no one took the floor, she grabbed it for herself, lifting her skirts, whirling and twirling, doing the *csárdás* the way she had seen her mother and her relatives do it on the farm in Debrecen.

It was right to remember Eva on this night, Zsuzsanna told herself as she spun about, leaning her head back and wantonly shimmying her shoulders until her breasts bobbled like apples in a barrel. This was a night to celebrate the Gáspár genes, the music that had flowed from father to son, to daughter. Without thinking, she reached for Greco, enticing him onto the floor, pulling him next to her and demanding that he dance.

Katalin and the others shouted encouragement as Greco shed his jacket. Quickly, he caught the spirit of the dance, bumping his hips against Zsuzsanna's, grinding against her as she shimmied up against him. Shadow, who had flown in from Chicago for the finals, was hooting as if this were a basketball game, clapping his hands, making wild animal sounds. Steven and Matthew raised their hands above their heads, clapping, stomping their feet, letting the rhythms of the gypsies fire their souls. Even Pedjá, who had been lavish in his congratulations on Katalin's victory, had dropped his mask. Grabbing the nearest available female, he joined Zsuzsanna and Greco on the dance floor, letting go of his concerns for image, just snapping his fingers and swinging his hair and wiggling his body.

The mood was euphoric. Katalin felt as if she had been catapulted to heaven and was adrift on a raft of white, puffy clouds. She wore her medal with the same pride as she wore Steven's love. She didn't think she had ever been happier. Earlier, after she had finished with the press, she and Paul had shared a private moment during which she had thanked him for all he had done. They had cried together and hugged each other and giggled over her new sobriquet, the Princess of the Piano. They were a team, she had told him, assuring him that she did need him and would continue to rely on him.

"If I'm the best," she had said, "it's only because you're the best."

Watching him now, romping with Zsuzsanna, looking relaxed and self-satisfied and joyous, her heart swelled with affection. She looked at Sophie, safely tucked into a corner where she couldn't get hurt. She, too, was slapping the table with her good hand and shouting. Every now and then, Katalin noticed Matthew checking on her, caring for her, caring about her. She smiled at that, as well as the way Shadow had attached himself to Steven. At Steven's insistence and with Rhinehart's help, Shadow had applied to and been accepted at George Washington University. He and Steven were going to share an apartment, but, as Shadow told her, "If you're a good girl, I'll find me a bad girl to keep me occupied on the weekends."

Everything was so perfect, Katalin thought, hugging herself. So deliciously, wonderfully perfect. It was like a bubble, blown from a pipe, all round and translucent and iridescent, floating effortlessly into the air. When, a few moments later, Steven wrapped his arms around her and pressed his lips against hers, she thought for sure, the bubble had to burst. And it did.

A young man approached her. There had to be more than two hundred people jammed into the restaurant. Still, he looked unfamiliar.

"They said you were Katalin Gáspár. That right?"

"Yes."

"I've got a telegram for you. Sign here."

As she signed her name her heart began to thump inside her chest. Telegrams were bad news.

"I don't want to read it," she said to Steven. "It's something terrible."

"You just won a major competition. It's probably congratulations from the president of Juilliard or maybe even the President of the United States."

Mollifed, she ripped open the envelope. It was from Budapest. Had Greco telegraphed her parents the good news? Was this their response?

She lowered her eyes, expecting to read words of congratulations and love and pride. She scanned the pale-yellow slip of paper.

"I have to go home," she said, sounding like an automaton, looking at Steven through vacant eyes.

"Okay," he said cautiously, hating what he saw, what he feared might be in that telegram. "I'll go with you."

"You can't go." Her skin had chalked. Her voice was flat. "And I can't stay."

Her eyes filled with tears and her body began to shake. Steven took the telegram from her hand and read it.

KATALIN. YOU MUST COME HOME IMMEDIATELY. MAMA IS DYING. I NEED YOU. PAPA.

III

Scherzo

1972–1977

19

Budapest, Hungary

Within hours of her landing, Katalin sensed that she had not simply crossed an ocean; she had journeyed back in time. It was as if, over the long flight to Frankfurt and the subsequent journey to Budapest, a giant eraser had slowly but surely rubbed out everything she had gained from her experiences in New York. She had matured there, gained in confidence as both a performer and a woman. She had tasted the bittersweet wine of independence, the delicious, honeyed flavor of love. She had entered the fray of the professional pianist and emerged the victor. Then, she had boarded that plane at Kennedy Airport.

Now the last three years of her life had been swept away, as if they were nothing but so many particles of dust. She wasn't the gold medalist of the Chickering Piano Competition, an honor graduate of Juilliard, a highly regarded pianist with a bright future on the international concert stage. She was only a Hungarian citizen coming through customs after a long stay in the dubious West.

The immigration officer took her passport, checked her other papers, and whisked her out of the line, into his office. Immediately, Katalin discovered that while freedom was an easy habit to acquire, it was a difficult one to break. Things she had come to accept as ordinary were suddenly exceptional—moving about without looking over one's shoulder, speaking without a mental censor, looking to the police for help. She had almost forgotten what it meant to live in an occupied country. The hassle at customs, the suspicious leers, the intrusive questions, and the rudeness of the officials brought it all roaring back. Determined to maintain her dignity despite an hour and a half of meaningless interrogation designed to do nothing except intimidate her, she endured the reindoctrination process. When it was done she turned and walked away—no comment, no change in expression, no chance for them to look inside and know whether or not they had succeeded in browbeating her.

Outside, she hailed a taxicab to take her from Ferihegy to the hospital where Mária lay. On the ride into town, Katalin tried to shake off the shock of reentry and prepare herself for what she was about to see, but she couldn't. How could she ever be prepared to witness her mother's dying? Mária had never been sick. Katalin had never even seen Mária sleep late. Her mother was a veritable dynamo, the personification of kinetic energy. Trying to imagine her weak and incapacitated was as impossible as imagining life without Steven and Matthew and Sophie and Zsuzsanna and Greco. At that moment, Katalin was incapable of facing either truth.

Instead, she found herself staring out the window of the rickety Russian-made Lada at the landscape. It was like a photograph in a scrapbook, a sight she remembered from the past that remained unaltered in the present, frozen into a permanent tableau of sameness. There was a time when, like most Europeans, she had considered that sameness an admirable quality, a sign of continuity, a symbol of longevity. Now, she saw through eyes exposed to New York, with its constant flurry of construction, where the skyline was forever changing, adding a new spire here, a taller tower there. She had been gone from Budapest for three years. Nothing had changed. Despite Kádár's reforms, despite his "New Economic Mechanism," the iron fist was still holding progress at bay.

Dropping her luggage at the hospital's front desk, Katalin headed for her mother's room. Dread and fear accompanied her as she walked the long, dimly lit corridors of the hospital with their acrid antiseptic smell. Moans of loneliness, cries of pain filtered out of the patients' rooms into the hall. By the time she found Mária, she was shaking.

"Mama," she whispered, not knowing whether Mária was asleep or awake.

An old man sat in a chair next to the bed. His back was bent. His head was lowered, buried in his hands. At the sound of her voice he rose and turned his face toward her.

"Katya!" Tears streamed from Zoltán's eyes like an April cloudburst, quick and torrential.

How he had aged. It hurt Katalin to see him so thin, so frail he appeared almost brittle. He tried to rise to greet her, but he was too weak, too overcome with emotion. Katalin went to him, folded him in her arms, and let his tears wet her shoulder. She had yet to look at Mária.

"Let me see you." Zoltán separated from her but refused to let go. His hands held her at arm's length as his eyes reconnoitered. His graying brows arched in confusion. The person before him, while clearly familiar, was very much a stranger. Beyond the surface differences of clothing and makeup, he intuited an inner transformation, a spiritual conversion. Katalin was possessed of an aura that spoke of assuredness and personal definition.

Over the past several years they had corresponded, but only sporadically. Because Zoltán was a listed dissident, mail to and from the house on Tárnok Street was usually confiscated and destroyed. While Phil King's underground had provided an alternative postal system, its efficiency was limited by fear of discovery. Only when vital packages were sent in or out of the country were letters delivered, and then usually in bunches that spanned several months. From those bunches however, Zoltán knew about her success at Juilliard, about her rewarding tutorials with Paul Greco. From Zsuzsanna he had heard about István and Mátyás Kardos, how they had reappeared in Zsuzsanna's life, how important they—particularly István—had become in Katalin's life. When he had sent the telegram about Mária—having secured official permission to do so—he had been loath to interrupt Katalin's rising star. Looking at her now, knowing he would have her by his side when the worst of this ordeal occurred, he had no regrets.

"You look very beautiful, _kicsi szilva_." His hand caressed her cheek. It was trembling. "You're so grown-up I hardly recognize you."

"It's me, Papa." She hugged him again, letting him feel the reality of her presence. She adored this man, yet as she said the words "I'm home" she was certain she heard the horrifying clang of the Iron Curtain slamming behind her.

"Let Mama know you're here."

Katalin allowed her eyes to travel to the pillow. Mária's eyes were closed. At first she appeared peaceful. A second glance drew attention to both the slackness of her skin and the grayness of it, the darker, charcoal color of the hollows beneath her eyes. Mária's skin had always been so pink, so fresh-looking. A chill took hold of Katalin's spine until she grew faint with apprehension. Mária's skin looked dead. Gingerly she reached out and let her finger graze her mother's forehead. The flesh was warm. Katalin felt relieved. She moved closer.

"Mama," she said, petting Mária's cheek, half-hoping that her touch held the miracle that would revive the color in her mother's face, unaware of the tears trickling down her own. "It's Katya. I've come home to be with you. Mama, please. Open your eyes and look at me."

Zoltán backed away, making room for his daughter, who filled the void by Mária's side. Leaning over her mother, she crooned to her, cajoling, begging her to waken. When Mária's lids fluttered, Katalin's heart drummed inside her chest. With great effort, Mária opened her eyes. She blinked and tried to focus, slowly moving those dark orbs of sight in the direction of the soft voice that had lured her out of her torpor. When eye and mind connected, Mária's lips quivered in an unsteady smile.

A hand emerged from beneath the covers. As the bony limb reached for her, Katalin had to fight not to retreat from it. She took the unfamiliar paw and held it, feeling bone where once there had been flesh and strength and softness.

Katalin bent down, allowing those fingers to caress her face, touching her features as a blind man might. As she lowered herself to receive her mother's kiss, she was confronted with another manifestation of Mária's decaying state. For as long as Katalin could remember, her mother had always smelled like a garden at the height of its bloom. Mária was a woman who adored scent, dousing herself with light floral colognes. Katalin wanted to weep as the odor of spoilage, of rotting, of something that had once been fresh and vital, now deteriorating, assailed her.

"I'm sorry, Katya." The voice was strained but recognizable. "You were so happy with Zsuzsanna in New York. I'm sorry to bring you here."

Katalin couldn't speak. She bit her lip to stem the sobs. All she could do was shake her head.

"Szép, Katya. My beautiful baby. I know it's selfish, but I'm so happy to see you." The shadow of a smile flickered across her lips. "Come. Talk to Mama."

Zoltán moved a chair by Mária's bedside so Katalin could sit. He stood behind her, watching, praying that perhaps his daughter could do what medicine could not.

Katalin took Mária's hand. The smile broadened and for an instant Katalin thought she saw a flash of light in Mária's eyes. When she said, "Tell me about István," and the flash turned mischievous, Katalin was certain. The light was dim, but thank God it was still burning.

"You wouldn't believe how handsome he is, Mama," Katalin said, her voice filled with surprise, as if she had not yet accepted the miracle of their finding each other after so many years. "He's tall and strong and his eyes are still as blue as the Danube is supposed to be."

Mária's mouth quivered. Katalin fretted she had said something wrong. It took a minute to recognize the movement as a halting effort to smile. Relieved, she went on.

"He looks like Margit, I think."

Mária nodded. Her mouth quivered again. "He always did. Mátyás looked like Béla."

Katalin thought about that for a second, retrieving a picture of Béla Kardos so she could stand it next to a mental image of his eldest son. "He still does," she said, moving closer and taking Mária's hand, grateful that she was able to evoke the look of contentment currently residing on her mother's face.

Buoyed by what she saw, Katalin continued to describe the boys as men, detailing their childhood in Kentucky, the mines, their life with the Vas family, Steven's tour of duty in Vietnam. As long as she kept talking, reality remained sheltered in the background. By focusing only on Mária's face, Katalin was able to ignore the fact that they were in a hospital, that Mária was seriously ill, that her father appeared as ravaged by grief as her mother was by her leukemia, that she had been summoned home to Budapest because there appeared to be little hope of remission.

"I see something in your eyes that hasn't passed your lips," Mária said, squeezing Katalin's hand. "You love him, yes?"

Katalin flushed, suddenly embarrassed. Instinct prompted her to look over her shoulder. She knew it was silly, but she felt odd talking about her feelings for Steven in front of her father. She needn't have worried. Zoltán had gone.

"Well?" Mária pressed.

When Katalin turned back toward her mother, a wave of sadness washed over her, momentarily paralyzing her. This woman was her confidante, the parent to whom she had always gone for comfort, for advice, for guidance. What would she do when Mária was gone? How would she handle the rest of her life? Who would dress her on her wedding day and teach her how to bathe an infant and teach her to cook and give her hints on how to make a husband happy and do all the other thousand and one things mothers did for their daughters? Never, in Katalin's wildest imaginings, had she envisioned a future without her mother. It wasn't that she didn't love Zoltán—only God knew how deeply she felt—but Mária was the source, the fountain, the headwaters from which Katalin's life flowed. Katalin had come from her and was still, despite her age, emotionally nursed by her.

Again, Mária squeezed her hand. Concern masked her face. Katalin snapped to.

"Yes, I love him," she said, smothering her fears, setting them aside for a time when she was alone and could deal with them. "And he loves me."

"You should be with him," Mária said.

Katalin saw the guilt. She heard the agitation. Gently, she leaned over and kissed Mária's cheek. "I'm where I want to be."

Mária's eyes pooled and she shook her head, debating her daughter. "Go back."

"You think I'm here because you need me and Papa needs me."

Mária nodded. She wanted to speak, but her heart had filled her throat.

"I'm here because *I* need you," Katalin said. Mária started to speak, but Katalin put a finger to her mother's lips, stopping the protest before it began. "I love István, but always remember, Mama, I loved you first."

Katalin had lost track of time. She had spent hours talking to Mária and Zoltán, distracting them from the all-consuming process of death by telling them stories about New York. Mária wanted to hear about people—who, what, where, when. Zoltán wanted to hear about music. He needed to know about Greco, about Juilliard, about the Chickering. Katalin danced around the competition, knowing that to tell them of her win would only add more guilt to their burdens. Though he pressed her at first, three turns and Zoltán sensed the reason behind her avoidance of the subject and dropped it.

Toward morning, Katalin left Zoltán with Mária and, claiming a need for coffee, went searching for Ilona. She didn't have to go very far. Ilona was on her way to Mária's room. When she saw Katalin, she ran down the hall and embraced her.

"I'm so glad to see you," she said, beaming at Katalin, squeezing Katalin's arms, as if testing to be sure the young woman was not a mirage. "We wanted to pick you up at the airport, but your father said you didn't tell anyone when you were coming in."

"I didn't want to take anyone away from Mama."

Ilona nodded. Her eyes narrowed, as if weighing the impact of what she had to say. "She's very sick, Katya. Very, very sick."

The words hit Katalin with double-barreled force. It wasn't one voice she heard, but two: Mária's doctor and Mária's best friend. Both were telling her the same thing. It had to be the truth.

"Aunt Ilona." Katalin's voice had dropped to a whisper. "Please. I'm begging you. Contact your friends. Those people who delivered mail to me in New York. Those people who work underground. Ask them to get medicine for Mama. Tell them to go to the best doctors in America and bring back something that will help her." She grabbed Ilona. Fatigue and grief and fear had gathered in her eyes, blending into fat, hot tears of frustration. "I don't know who they are or what you do with them and I don't care. I need you to help Mama."

Ilona pulled Katalin to her and cradled her, smoothing her back, whispering into her ear. "I love your mother, Katya. She's my sister, my closest friend. You know I would give anything, including my blood, to save her, but the leukemia is too virulent, too advanced." She took Katalin's face in her hands and held her so that their eyes were fixed on each other. "I've already spoken to those people. They've already sent me whatever they had. There's nothing more to send. There's nothing left to do."

Over the next several weeks, the pieces of Katalin's life fell into the grinding pattern of vigil. She and Zoltán split their time at the hospital. Katalin went early in the morning. Zoltán joined her after work, bringing food so the three of them could have dinner, such as it was, as a family. Often, after dinner, Zoltán insisted that Katalin go home, go out, do something, anything to break the tedium of devoted care. Frequently, Katalin refused, surrendering to the irrational fear that her leaving would provoke Mária's last breath.

One night, however, she aquiesced. She was tired, both physically and spiritually. Ilona, who was in and out of Mária's room, said she would spell Katalin. Andras was coming later. He would watch over Zoltán. Katalin needn't worry. The question remained, however, where to go? Judit was on tour with Sándor Emke. Katalin had no other friends, and even if she had, she had nothing to say.

She left the hospital and wandered, gulping at the breeze, forcing the crisp autumn air into her lungs, hoping to displace the stale hospital air that filled them. Her eyes looked without seeing; her feet walked without any destination other than a path that led away from that dark gray house of illness and death.

Ilona had admitted Mária to Shalom Hospital. The Pest Medical Center was newer and bigger, but Ilona felt more secure at Shalom, better able to treat Mária with whatever she needed, legal or otherwise. Though the Strassers didn't live in the Jewish quarter, Katalin knew the area well. She roamed the streets with an easy familiarity, past shops where she and Judit used to pick up inexpensive shoes and clothing, past

370 / DORIS MORTMAN

restaurants where she and Andras often shared a sandwich and a coffee. Without caring where she was headed, she turned onto Rákóczi Street, toward Keleti station. After several blocks Katalin left the main thoroughfare. The neighborhood changed. Buildings with grimy facades and bullet-scarred walls lined the streets. A woman and a child ran past her. They were dark-complected, large-nosed, and barefooted. A large man followed, shouting at them. Katalin saw none of it. She was lost in thoughts of another city, another time.

A sound filtered through the fog of her trance. Small, muted, indistinct, it amplified as she walked, growing inside her head until she could no longer ignore it. She stopped, listening. Mesmerized, she followed the sound inside a courtyard to the open window of a first-floor apartment. Inside, she saw a tiny band: a violin, a viola, a clarinet, and a cimbalom. The musicians were gypsies, as was the raven-haired woman dancing the *csárdás* in the center of the room. Her black eyes were ablaze with the untamed savagery of the music. Her waist-length hair flew about her face like the devil's veil as she whirled in a Dionysian frenzy. Her hands stretched above her head. Her back arched. She clapped. She flung her hair. She stomped her feet. Encouraged by the calls of the other gypsies in the room, she twisted her body into an erotic curl, pumping her pelvis, thrusting her bosom, offering herself to the *primás*, the roguishly handsome violinist responsible for the musical aphrodisiac.

Katalin watched the lusty dance in complete thrall, helpless against the seething hot rhythms of the *csárdás*. The music had fired her blood, reviving sensations and feelings she had only experienced in bed with Steven. She couldn't see his face—her eyes were too filled with the scene before her—but she could feel his hands on her body. He was thousands of miles away, but standing there, Katalin responded as she had when he was no more than a breath away, and she shuddered when the gypsy woman pressed her pelvis against the violinist's groin. Katalin knew she should leave before she was discovered, but her passions held her there. Her desperate need to be near Steven held her there.

When the music finally stopped, Katalin leaned exhausted against the cold stone of the building, trying to understand what had just happened to her. On some level, she knew she had been bewitched by the tantalizing demon of rhythm. She had been possessed by the mythical ghost she had heard about, the one gypsies summoned with their music. The musicians played while the dancers waited for the *duende* to make his presence felt, to invade their bodies, finding entry at the soles of their feet, using the bloodstream to rush upward into the heart, bursting with a tidal wave of inspiration. Katalin had fallen victim to the power of the *duende*. She had surrendered to the magic moment, allowing it to do with her what it would. Now, she was spent, and wrapped in the solitude of that small courtyard, strangely calm.

Relieved of the tension that had been her only companion of late, Katalin's mind opened to thoughts she had been struggling to avoid. She had received no letters from Steven, no word from anyone in New York. She had written him dozens of times. True, she had no way of knowing whether or not he received them, but still she hungered for a message, a line, a sentence that reaffirmed his love for her, his commitment to her, his promise to wait as long as was necessary to marry her.

Like a machine revved up after a long period of inactivity, her brain sped from one thought to another. Listening to those musicians play reminded her about her own music. She hadn't touched a piano in weeks. She hadn't even thought about a piano until tonight. Thinking about it now, a sharp pang cut deep inside her chest. She missed her music. She missed the feel of the ivory on her fingertips, the feel of the music pouring from her soul onto the keyboard and into the air. She missed Greco and their tutorials. She missed the band at Csárda, her evenings at the cimbalom. She missed Zsuzsanna. She missed Sophie.

Tears she had kept dammed poured down her cheeks like a raging brook. Sliding to the ground with her legs hugged close to her chest, hiding her head in her hands, she sobbed her sorrows onto her knees. She had fought it, she had avoided it, she had denied it, but now, whether she liked it or not, Katalin confronted the truth. She would not be returning to New York, or to Zsuzsanna or Sophie or Steven any time soon . . . if ever. She was a prisoner here, held by a love of family as well as by a government that would never let her leave again. As reality struck, her heart broke.

She never noticed the gypsy violinist with the obsidian eyes standing at the window, watching her weep.

Katalin returned to that courtyard every night that week, drawn there by a metaphysical cord that pulled her toward the music. Though she never told anyone where she was going, using a head-clearing walk as her excuse for leaving, her behavior didn't strike her as the least bit unusual. After all, music had always been her balm, the one element in her life on which she could depend. Though this was not music of her making, it was sound nonetheless.

Each night she stood outside that window, dressed in darkness, hidden behind a shadow of lamentation. As the gypsies played, Katalin clung to the walls and listened, imploring the seductive sonority to disturb the silence that had taken hold of her soul, to infuse her blood with a vitality she didn't feel anywhere but here. What a relief it was to surrender to the slow, sad melody of the *lassú*, and then to purge her anguish about Mária's steady deterioration in the exhilarating rush of the *csárdás*.

It was only after she had returned to the courtyard several times that it struck Katalin that aside from the emotional catharsis she experienced at this window, she was returning because she was entranced by the musicianship of the violinist. Katalin had heard dozens of gypsy bands in her lifetime. She had also heard dozens of violin virtuosos, including her father. Katalin had a trained ear. This man was an exceptional talent. With the proper tutoring, this young, handsome gypsy could be a master of the string and the bow.

One night, as she hovered beneath the window in a quiet moment after the dancers had depleted their energies, she heard him begin a piece she recognized. He was improvising, changing the melody slightly, but it was still the romantic, lush sound of Johannes Brahms. She closed her eyes and offered her battered spirit to the gentle care of the musician, allowing the sweetness of his violin to wash over her and anesthetize her to the coldness of the night and the chill that had attached itself to her heart. She was deep in a rhapsodic daze when a harsh voice crashed through her reverie.

"What are you doing here?" the voice demanded.

Katalin snapped to attention and stared at the face behind the voice. It was the dancer, the gypsy woman with the nubile body and the curtain of ebony hair. Up close, Katalin could see that she was quite beautiful, in an exotic way. Her skin had that brownish tinge that distinguished the gypsies, looking as if someone had dropped a teaspoon of black coffee into a cup of cream. Her nose was long and prominent, pierced on one side at the tip and marked with a jewel. Her eyes were black, almond-shaped and heavily lidded, her brows thick and dark and furrowed now in an angry line.

"I was just listening to the music," Katalin said quietly.

"In case you didn't notice, we're gypsies. The last thing we need is a *gorgio* hanging around making trouble. You're just the kind of excuse the police need to harass us."

"I'm sorry," Katalin said, scrambling to her feet, thoroughly embarrassed. "I didn't mean to cause a problem, I just—"

"Get out of here. Go away." The gypsy folded her arms across her chest in a gesture of insistence. "You don't belong here." Her mouth, a broad arrangement of full lips and slightly yellowed teeth, formed an impatient snarl as she waited for Katalin to do as she was told.

Katalin obeyed, quickly gathering her belongings and turning toward the archway that led out of the courtyard.

"And don't come back," the angry voice called after her.

Though she knew she was overreacting, Katalin felt she was being banished from a place of pleasure. She exited the dingy courtyard consumed by melancholy, the gypsy's words echoing in her ear: *You don't belong here.* She didn't, that was true. But where did she belong? In a hospital watching her mother die a horrible premature death? In New York, making her recital debut at Carnegie Hall? In Steven's arms? By her father's side?

As she crossed the street and headed back to the hospital, she knew there were no answers for her questions. Neither were there answers for the questions being asked by the dark-eyed man at the window who stood and watched long after she had disappeared into the night.

Three days later, Mária came home. Her cycle of treatment had been completed and Ilona felt she would fare better in more comfortable surroundings. For Zoltán and Katalin, it was a blessing. Being able to bring Mária tea in her favorite Herend cup or to serve her soup in a bowl with a delicately painted floral made everything seem brighter and more positive. They fluffed the pillows behind her and tucked the blankets around her, enveloping her with happy pictures and pretty flowers and pleasant mementos, as if each item contained magical powers that would nullify the evil disorder that was devouring her body.

When Mária felt able, they moved her into the living room, where, at Mária's request, Katalin played the piano for hours on end. It seemed to soothe her mother, and so Katalin imbued her playing with as much heart as she could, praying that Plato and Aristotle were right, that harmony would dispel disharmony, that music had the power to heal, that maybe, just maybe, a continuous inundation of melody would do what medicine could not.

Sometimes during the afternoon while Zoltán was at work and Mária was asleep, Katalin would take out her mother's scrapbooks and relive the glorious history of Mária Gáspár's life behind the footlights and before the camera. Her mother's clippings never ceased to impress Katalin. In all her years in front of the public, she had never had a poor review. Her talent was that mighty, the power of her personality that extraordinary. Even during the worst times, during the war and during those years afterward when Stalin's toadies stomped on everything—especially those who called themselves entertainers—the critics refused to denigrate her. She had been their light in the blackness of those horrible years and they never forgot it. When she made the transition to film, they welcomed her with unabashed joy.

At the end of each of these bittersweet visits with her mother's past, Katalin found herself facing the empty page that was the future. Unless a miracle were visited upon Mária, that page would contain her final notice—an obituary.

"I know it's not how you wanted it," Judit said, "but I'm glad you're home."

Having finally returned from what she dubbed "the endless aria," Judit ran to see her friend. The two young women spent time with Mária, but then when she fell off to sleep, they removed themselves to another room to catch up with each other's lives.

"I can't believe this is happening to her," Katalin said, relieved to be able to talk about her mother's illness. "She looks so terrible and she's in such tremendous pain. Some days I think she's getting better. Really, I do. But then, when she's alone and she thinks I can't hear, she cries, Judit. She cries from the pain."

Judit hugged Katalin, wrapping her arms around the person who had been her friend from birth, trying to surround her with the security of that friendship.

"Mama says she and the other doctors have done everything they can do."

Katalin nodded. "I know. We speak about it all the time. In fact, I've done you a great service."

"You have?"

"You know how your mother always says you're the world's biggest pest? You've been replaced."

"Again, you take first place! I can't stand it." Judit let loose with a hearty laugh. Katalin laughed too, and for one brief moment the eclipse that had cast a perpetual shade over their lives passed and the sun shone.

"I've missed you," Katalin confessed.

"I'm sure you made a thousand new friends in New York."

"I did, but you can only have one best friend," Katalin said, recognizing Judit's need.

Judit smiled. "Because you said the right thing, I have a present for you."

She rummaged about in her bag and pulled out a thick manila envelope that looked vaguely familiar. Katalin's heart raced. As she reached for the envelope, her excitement was stemmed by a question that poked at her consciousness.

"Where did you get this?" Instinct had lowered her voice. "Are you the mysterious courier who funneled my mail back and forth?"

"Just open the envelope and close your mouth." Judit's tone was light, her eyes were not.

"Tell me what you've been up to."

"It's better for you if I don't." Judit squirmed in her seat, turning away from Katalin to avoid her friend's unremitting gaze. When Katalin still didn't pick up the envelope, Judit looked at her squarely and said, "It's safer for me if I don't tell you. Okay? Just trust me. I know what I'm doing."

They stared at each other for several minutes, neither of them speaking, neither of them looking away.

"Does this have anything to do with Kovács Attila?"

"In the beginning, it did," Judit said honestly. "Now it has to do with me. And this," she said, waving the envelope in Katalin's face, "has to do with you. Are you going to open it or shall I?"

"Okay, okay."

Sensing that she wasn't going to get anything more out of Judit, Katalin emptied the packet onto the couch. It was filled with news clippings about the Chickering. As Judit rifled through them, reading, whistling at the pictures of Katalin in her strapless gown, Katalin noticed a small piece of note paper clipped to a photograph at the bottom of the pile.

Thought you might want to see the impression you made on New York. They loved you! I love you. Zsuzsanna, Sophie, Matthew, Shadow, and Greco love you. We all miss you and we're all praying for Mária. Tell her that. Tell her we're pulling for her. Maybe it will help. Please God.

Trying not to cry, Katalin looked at the picture. It had been taken at the party at Csárda after her victory. She and Steven stood arm in arm, grinning into the camera as if they had just been told that they had been granted a universal reprieve from all things sad and unpleasant, that from that moment on life would be nothing but champagne and chocolates.

"Who's the fabulous-looking guy in the picture?" Judit asked after awhile, feeling the need to break the terrible silence that had descended.

Katalin looked at Judit, looked at the photograph, and then, brightening, looked at Judit again. "Guess."

"Two seconds ago you looked as if someone stuck a knife in your heart and now you want to play games? Katalin, what's going on?"

"Guess who this is." She thrust the picture under Judit's nose.

"I have absolutely no idea."

"Look at it carefully."

Judit took the photograph, studied it and returned it to Katalin. "Richard Nixon?"

"Hardly. It's István. Kardos István."

Now it was Judit's turn to gape. "István?" She snatched the photograph away from Katalin and stared at it in disbelief. "This unbelievably handsome man is little István?"

Katalin laughed and nodded. "They call him Steven."

"Do you love him?"

"Yes. Very much."

"Are you going to marry him?"

"I thought so. Now, I'm not so sure." Without meaning to, Katalin's gaze drifted toward the bedroom where her mother slept.

"Things will work out, you'll see."

"Have things worked out between you and Attila? Has he divorced his wife?"

"Yes and no." Not talking about her relationship with Kovács was such an ingrained habit for Judit, that even with Katalin, she found it difficult to answer openly. "I worship him, Katya. That's the only way to describe it. He's the most exciting, powerful man I've ever met. I view every second I'm able to spend with him as a privilege. As for his wife? She's still his wife."

"Don't you care about having a future with him?"

Judit shrugged her shoulders and laughed. "You've been away too long. You forget that, here, nobody's future is sure. Especially if you speak out against the system and Attila does."

"Do you?"

"In quieter, more subtle ways."

The two friends stared at each other. When they were children, they had known everything there was to know about each other. As Katalin focused on what Judit had just said—more importantly, all that she refused to say—she realized that the difference between the friendship of children and the friendship of adults could be encapsulated in one word: secrets. Children had no secrets.

"Do I have to worry about you?" she said softly, telling Judit in her own way she wouldn't pry or trespass where she didn't belong.

"I love you for caring, but no." Judit hugged Katalin, grateful for her understanding. "Besides," she said, her voice brimming with sympathy, "you have enough to worry about."

Mária clung to life, hanging on to the brink of existence with hands too weak to hold a comb. Each day, Katalin tended her mother as a mother would tend a child—feeding her, bathing her, reading to her, talking to her, making her as comfortable as she could. Ilona came by three times a day to administer morphine. Though Mária's flesh was withering, her pain was growing more and more intense.

With Katalin and Ilona seeing to Mária's physical needs, Zoltán could only try to soothe her soul. Often, he simply sat holding her hand, not speaking, just making certain she could feel his flesh near hers and know that he was, as he had always been, by her side. His eyes had grown hollow from the strain of his vigilance and his frame had dwindled so that he looked almost as frail as he had when he had been released from Recsk, but his will remained strong, as did his love for his wife.

Sometimes Katalin overheard her father crying in the bathroom. Though she tried to get him to confide in her, to share his grief and to divulge his fears, she knew that he felt he had to maintain an appearance of control, that it was important for him not to break down in front of Mária or her. She understood, but it pained her nonetheless to think that he had no other release but to sob into a towel, alone and frightened in his own home.

"How much longer does she have?"

Even under normal circumstances, for a doctor this was the most difficult of tasks. Facing Zoltán required additional strength. Ilona said, "It's a matter of weeks," and immediately felt a searing pain grip her heart, one born of her own grief, her own sense of helplessness, her own inability to accept that which was inevitable.

Zoltán said nothing. He kissed Ilona and returned to his wife's bedside. Mária was awake, as if she had overheard their conversation and had been expecting him.

"Lie with me."

She moved her hand to the side of the bed that had always been his. Taking care not to jostle her, Zoltán did as she asked, settling himself on the bed, resting his body next to hers. Her hand found his and for a few moments they lay in silence, communing in the telepathic way of two who had loved for a lifetime and didn't need words to communicate.

"I don't want you to die." He said it simply, but it was far from a simple statement. It was a declaration, a challenge, a plea, a prayer.

"I don't want to die, but since it appears as if that's exactly what I'm going to do, I want to talk."

Though her voice sounded stronger than it had in weeks, Zoltán worried that any undue exertion would hasten the end.

"I want you to save your strength," he said, shushing her as he fluffed the pillows that supported her back.

Mária smiled and stroked his cheek. "For what?" In spite of himself, Zoltán smiled. It was macabre, but she had a point. "I want to talk about Katya," she went on. "She's in love, Zoltán."

"I know."

"I think she and István had made plans to marry. I interrupted those plans." He started to protest, but she quieted him. "Help them find their way back to each other. I don't know how you're going to do it, but promise me that you'll try."

He pressed two fingers to his heart, brought them to his lips, kissed them, and touched them to Mária's lips, sealing his vow to fulfill her request.

"I want her to have it all, Zoltán. Love. Marriage. A family. Her music. I want her to have what we had."

It was then that he wept, when the full force of his loss slammed against his heart.

"I've lost much in my life, Mária, but so long as I had you, I knew I'd survive. You were always my strength, the light in my darkness, the song that sang in my soul. What will I do when you're gone?"

"You'll mourn for me," Mária said, wishing there was a drug that would soothe the ache in her heart, "but then you'll dip into that deep well of courage that has served you in the past. I know you think that well is dry, Zoltán, but it's not. Drink of it, my darling, and be strong. For Katalin. For yourself. And for me."

Zoltán lowered his head onto Mária's chest and cried. No matter what he had suffered in the past, he was certain that he had never experienced agony this fierce, this immobilizing, this depleting.

"There's something else I want you to promise me."

Her voice had grown weaker. Zoltán raised himself up and looked at her, his chest pounding with fear.

"I want you to open the door to the prison where you keep your music. I want you to let it out."

His first response was that she was being unfair to try to extract a deathbed promise she knew he couldn't fulfill. His second response was anger.

"I can't make music anymore. Just as I can't open the door to your body and chase away death."

Mária's eyes watered as she looked at this man she had adored every single second of their life together.

"You're using Katya to make your music for you," she said, knowing she was hurting him, hating herself for doing it, but needing to say what she felt had to be said. "Let her decide her fate. Allow her to control her life. You take control of yours."

Angry, frustrated, confused, Zoltán lifted his hands and held them in front of his wife.

"They crushed my ability to control my life."

"No! They took away your ability to play the violin, but they couldn't crush who you are." Mária clasped his hands in hers and held them up between them. "I didn't fall in love with these," she said. "You haven't played a note in years and I still love you as much as I did when you were in the famous Gáspár Zoltán." Her voice trembled as she grappled with remembrances of what their life had been, regret over what it would never be. "I fell in love with a man whose being was lyrical, a man with music in his soul. In spite of what they did, in spite of what you did to yourself, you still have that music, Zoltán. You just have to set it free."

Zoltán looked beyond the sharp lines that pain had scratched onto her face, into eyes still soft with love. Gently, carefully, he lifted her into his arms, pressing her frail form against him.

"I love you," he said in a voice that had diminished into a whisper.

Her body went limp. He pressed her closer, crying with relief when he felt the warmth of her breath on her his neck. Though he knew she had slipped back into a soporific fog, he continued to hold her and to say, "I love you." As long as there was a slim chance that she might be able to hear him, he repeated it over and over and over again. Soon there would be no chance.

The intervals during which Mária was lucid became shorter and fewer, but when she was alert she bombarded Katalin with questions about America, as if she couldn't die until she had heard it all. One day, she seemed particularly obsessed with the subject.

"What are their movies like?" she asked.

"There are so many of them, Mama, you wouldn't believe it. Most of them cost a fortune to make, but if they become hits, everyone involved becomes very, very rich."

"Not like here," Mária said with sudden lightness.

"No, Mama. Not like here." It had been so long since Katalin had seen Mária smile. Something told her to cherish the moment. "You know what else is different? Watching the credits roll. You know how here every name is Hungarian. There, every name is different. Spanish. Hungarian. English. Scottish. Jewish. Polish. Japanese. Chinese. You

about life in the New World, prattling on about everything from the cost of beef to the number of women with bleached-blond hair, anything she could think of to stave off the inevitable. When Mária's hands fell limp and her chin drooped, Katalin knew. She stopped talking and let go of her mother's hands. If only letting go of her mother was as easy.

She shed no tears at that moment of death. Instead, her grief took the form of a ghostly, efficient calm. Rising, she went to the bureau, took Mária's comb, and fixed Mária's hair. She straightened the blankets, opened the window to let in some air, tidied the room and then, when all was neat and orderly, prepared to telephone her father.

Before she did, however, she indulged herself in one final moment alone with Mária.

"You're free, Mama," she said, kissing Mária's cheek. "For the first time in your life, you're really free. Now you know how wonderful it feels."

20

*T*hough the wind blew bitter cold, the air was unusually clear. The
March 1973
sun was full, the sky blue. The Danube flowed through the city at a
slow, majestic, respectful pace, its waters a little less silty, a little less
gray. So that no one would be denied the serene beauty of the funeral
Mass, speakers had been set up in Trinity Square, outside the heavily
spired Matthias Church high in the Buda Hills. Nearly fifty thousand
people, including many members of the reigning Politburo, had come to
bid Mária Toth Gáspár farewell.

Inside, above the rapidly filling pews, beacons of sunlight filtered
through a massive rose window onto the richly decorated church, casting
a prismatic rainbow. Its walls, luxuriously painted with leaves and animals, as well as its towering columns and high vaults, were emblazoned
with geometric motifs, recalling the church's use as a mosque during the
Turkish occupation. The refracted brightness also fell on lushly gilded
altars, sparking them with such uncommon brilliance that many of the
mourners were moved to remark that the light must have come from
Mária's star.

Zoltán and Katalin sat in the first pew, heads high, shoulders straight, eyes dry. They would not grieve in front of this throng. Instead, they would do what her admirers had come to do—honor Mária by celebrating her life. As the priests intoned the pious words of the Mass, Zoltán, who had no use for God, endeavored to find some element of solace within the ritual. As a disbeliever, however, his only comfort derived from the knowledge that Mária, who had been born and baptized a Catholic, would have wanted to be buried a Catholic.

Being presented a prescribed liturgy made it easier for Zoltán to endure this part of his wife's funeral. He was not required to participate and so he didn't. Instead, he used the time for his own musings, letting the priest's words waft over him like so much clatter. To Zoltán, they were meaningless incantations to a powerless God who had been unable to spare his torment in Recsk, unable to spare Hungary its national torture, unable to save the innocent and undeserving Mária. He refused to accept the standard postmortem bromide: "God works in mysterious ways," or the well-meaning counsel of those who encouraged him to seek consolation through a greater understanding of His universal plan. As far as Zoltán was concerned, there was nothing mysterious about the fact that his precious wife had suffered a gruesome illness and had died a horrible death. And if His plan demanded acceptance of that sort of ghastly involvement, Zoltán wanted no part of it.

He must have shuddered, because suddenly he felt Andras's arm on his shoulder. He squeezed his friend's hand to let him know he felt and appreciated his presence. A quick glance sideways took Zoltán by surprise. He supposed he hadn't really looked at Andras in months. His face was gaunt and ashen, ravaged by deep, soul-searing grief. Andras had always displayed great affection for Mária. An artist himself, he was a corseted man who had stood in awe of her talent, of her ability to move the emotions and stir the passions civilized people tended to closet in the name of propriety. Watching him now as he stared at Mária's flower-draped casket, seeing the raw anguish etched on his face, it was apparent that even in death Mária had moved him.

Zoltán turned and looked beyond Katalin and Judit at Ilona. Her shoulders were stooped, bowed by the unreasonable burden he knew she carried. Ilona believed she had failed Mária, that it was personal inadequacy that had caused her friend such a painful, premature death. Zoltán knew better. He knew how much Ilona had risked to save Mária. She had used drugs unheard of in Hungary, administering them despite the prying eyes of nurses and residents. Toward the end, when she had felt desperate, compelled to resort to highly experimental drugs—obtained, as the others had been, from her underground network—she played both doctor and nurse, refusing any assistance so as to avoid any troublesome questions. Afterward, though Zoltán and Andras had tried to convince her otherwise, Ilona maintained that Mária had died because she, Ilona, had been deficient in some vital way. Zoltán countered by reminding her that the cancer had simply been more efficient in every way.

Zoltán was so lost in his own thoughts, he hadn't noticed that Andras and Katalin had left their seats. It was only when the strains of Mozart's *Missa Solemnis* filled the church with its sacred tones that he realized his daughter and his friend had begun their personal tribute to his beloved.

Katalin played the piano, Andras the mighty organ. They had selected this particular piece because it was unfinished, as was Mária's life. Dark, brooding, yet with an exultant feeling of transcendence, the music exuded the spirit of resurrection. Sitting there, letting himself float atop the notes, Zoltán almost believed he could see Mária's soul drifting toward heaven. It was the only moment during that long day when his eyes teared. Because it was at that precise moment, certain that he was witnessing the ascent of her spirit, that he said good-bye.

When the Mass concluded, Mária's casket was placed in a simple farmer's wagon drawn by two workhorses dressed with flowered wreaths, red and green ribbons, and embroidered blankets. Mária had always said that her favorite place on earth was the Gáspár farm in the heart of the *puszta*. She adored the simplicity of life as lived on the Great Plain. She loved the romance of the place, the mystery of the fabled Fata Morgana, the way the farmers and *csikós* found release through bold, uninhibited revelry. Though the smallholders who had traveled from the little village outside Debrecen where the Gáspárs once lived had lined the cart with straw, Mária Gáspár's love of flowers—an affinity shared by most Hungarians—was well-known. The florists of Budapest, as their tribute to Mária, had requested that they be granted the privilege of surrounding her coffin with the flower of the Magyar, the Whitsun rose, or peony. Though out of season, the florists heaped mounds of the fragrant flower onto the humble cart, creating a fluffy bower of velvety aromatic blossoms.

With Zoltán holding the reins, Katalin walking alongside, and the Strassers directly behind the cart, the procession started down Tárnok Street, winding around the curving hills of Buda, across the Chain Bridge into Pest. Slowly, the quiet, respectful horde walked through the Balváros, the Inner City, making their way to the Convent of the Blessed Virgin where a young orphan named Mária Toth had been raised. Two elderly nuns stood by the entrance awaiting Mária's return home. When she arrived, they tugged at the ancient metal rings in the center of the thick wooden doors, pulling and heaving until at last they were open. Zoltán led the cart inside the high walls, through the courtyard, around the abbey, to the cemetery. There, Mária's casket was removed and carried to its final resting place.

As the crowd assembled, Katalin and Zoltán stood by the open grave, their hands tightly clasped, their eyes locked on the chasm that was going to house Mária for eternity. In his pocket, Zoltán closed his fingers around a packet of photographs—Eva, György, Zsuzsanna, Miklós, Sándor, Tomás, Imre, Béla, Margit, Mihai. That morning, he had added his favorite snapshot of Mária to his gallery of those he had loved who had passed out of his life. He carried this pictorial portfolio with him wherever he went. Though he claimed no religion he was a spiritual man nonetheless. He believed that by carrying their likenesses, he carried a piece of their souls.

When silence prevailed, the Abbess, followed by the nuns and novitiates who inhabited the convent, filed out of the abbey where they had offered their own Mass for their sister, Mária, and proceeded through the hushed gathering to the burial site.

The Abbess had just taken her vows when Mária had been brought to this place. Wanting to prove herself worthy of her habit—and recognizing in the rebellious child much of the anger and confusion she had felt when she, too, had been orphaned—Sister Thérèse had taken the Toth girl as her personal charge. Though she had never spoken it aloud until today, when Mária had run away to join a theater company, Sister Thérèse had rejoiced, considering it God's will and her own personal triumph.

After the Abbess gave the benediction, three actors from Mária's theater company read from several of her best-known plays. As their words filled the stillness with both past remembrance and future inspiration, Katalin allowed her eyes to wander. She panned the hundreds of faces within her view, noting a common veil of grief masking most of those who stood there. She was about to return to the speaker when something off to the side, near the wall, caught her attention. It was a face, oddly familiar yet definitely unknown. He turned. She fixed on him, demanding that he look at her and jog her memory. Umbered skin, obsidian eyes, hair the color of pitch. The gypsy violinist. The gypsy from the courtyard apartment. Katalin stared at him, telegraphing questions: *Who are you? What are you doing here? Why have you come?* With a polite bow of his head, he turned away, refusing to answer, preferring to remain void of all expression other than condolence.

Perplexed, her gaze traveled. Again it stalled on the face of a stranger. This one did not look away. Instead, he stared directly at her, as, she realized somewhere in the periphery of her consciousness, he had been since they had arrived at the convent. Tall, handsome, clothed in the uniform of an officer of the Hungarian Army, he beckoned her attention with seal brown eyes that appeared soft and sympathetic. While his mouth was set in a grim line of consolation, his body language transmitted other, somewhat mixed signals. In his hands, folded before him in the manner of a choirboy, and his chin, ever-so-slightly bowed, she read sadness at her mother's passing. From his stance, she read ceremonial obligation and distance from the emotional reality of the moment. While she scrutinized him, trying to discern which signal was the stronger, he continued to stare at her. It was when she tried to free herself from his visual grasp that she discovered the full power of his attraction. His hold was so tight, she had to summon her reserves to change perspectives. As she did, she wondered whether she should be flattered or frightened by a man with such intense magnetism.

When the service concluded and Katalin escorted her father outside to a waiting car, she saw something else that disturbed her. Away from the gates, yet not far enough so that Katalin couldn't see their faces clearly, Judit was being questioned by two policemen. Though neither man touched her, Judit recoiled, backed up against the stone wall, and adopted a pose of utter defiance. Katalin watched as Judit's spine grew rigid and her face blanked. The police wanted to know something. Judit was determined not to tell them.

Someone helped Zoltán into the car and then offered to do the same for Katalin, but she shook him off, needing to delay her departure until she was certain Judit was all right. Just then, one of the officers grabbed Judit's wrist. Whatever he said to her had the desired effect. Though the policeman might not have been able to read the miniscule change of expression, Katalin knew Judit was gnawing at the inside of her cheek, a sign of fear. What did they want from her? What was she involved in that was serious enough for them to confront her on such a public occasion? Katalin watched Judit respond with a disgruntled nod, as if she understood the implications of their threat—Katalin was certain they had issued a threat—and would comply. Only when the policemen had left did Katalin slide into the car next to her father. As the driver pulled away from the convent, Katalin pressed her face against the window, determined to catch Judit's eye. She did. For a second they made contact. Then Judit looked away.

It's safer for me if I don't tell you, she had said when she gave Katalin the packet of clippings. Though Katalin was eager to know why those policemen had accosted her friend and why Judit's safety depended on keeping secrets from one she had trusted all her life, Katalin had lived in this country too long and seen too much to tempt the system. Much as she hated it, she would respect the rule of silence. Judit's life depended on it.

• • •

Zoltán had lapsed into an inconsolable depression in the month since they had laid Mária to rest. He ate only when necessary, spoke only when necessary, and slept only when his body begged for relief from perpetual emotional agony. He dragged himself to work and went through the motions of his job, but at home he remained spiritually paralyzed. Katalin tried everything to shake him loose from his grief, but to no avail. One night, Ilona insisted that Zoltán come to the Strasser apartment for dinner. Zoltán tried to beg off, but Ilona would have none of it. She sent Andras to get him and with a great deal of coaxing from both him and Katalin, finally got Zoltán to agree to an evening out.

It felt so strange to be there alone. Katalin hadn't been alone in that apartment since before she went to New York. It hurt that she didn't feel more at home there, but it had ceased to be the place where she lived. It had become the place where her parents lived, her mother had died, and her father was passing time. There was little there that felt as though it was hers. Her room was unchanged, but she was significantly different. She wasn't the girl who had inhabited that space, the youngster who had been sheltered and coddled and taught that, despite what was going on in the world around her, she had nothing to concern herself with but her music. Now she was a young woman who felt enormously burdened, beset by feelings of untimely loss and unremitting obligation. Instead of finding comfort in familiar surroundings, she felt chained to a past that no longer gave her succor. Without thought as to where she was going or what she intended to do when she got there, Katalin grabbed her coat and took to the streets.

It was raining as she walked to the bus stop. Without looking at the number on the front of the bus, she climbed on, letting the driver take her away from where she was to someplace else. The roads were slippery. Despite the weight of the cumbersome vehicle, the bus slid partway down the hill. Once over the bridge, on the flatter surface of Pest, it regained its equilibrium and proceeded at a slow but steady pace. Katalin noticed a familiar street. Pulling the cord overhead, she signaled the driver to stop.

Outside, memory directed her. When she reached the courtyard of the gypsies, she didn't hide outside the window. She walked into the building and down the hall until she came to the door that stood between her and the music. She knocked but no one answered. Taking a chance, she turned the knob. The door opened. The music ceased. Without waiting for an invitation she entered, walking past the fiery dancer straight for the violinist, who looked as if he had been expecting her.

"Why were you at my mother's funeral?" she asked, keeping her voice low.

"I went out of respect. I'm a great admirer of both your mother and your father."

Katalin's eyebrows lifted in surprise. "How do you know about my father?"

"Every violinist knows about your father. He's this country's finest." He said it simply, definitely, as if there was no debate. Katalin liked that. "I had to be there."

On a primitive level, Katalin understood. As a musician she accepted the notion of a mystical connection between those who produced sound. She nodded her acceptance of his explanation.

"I know about you too," the gypsy man said. "Your talent is well-known and well-respected."

Katalin looked at him through curious eyes. Having grown up in Hungary, she had been exposed to all the prejudices against gypsies: They were a dirty, thieving, unscrupulous lot of beggars. They were to be shunned and avoided. They stole babies, would do anything for money, including allowing themselves to be hired as executioners. And, though no one ever verified this, they had once borne the reputation of being cannibals. She knew by the lighter tone of his skin that the man before her was one of the elite Musician-gypsies of Budapest and not one of the squalid, foul-smelling Walachians who soiled the gutters of Esztergom or the questionable horse traders of the south known as the Lovári. She could tell by the way he spoke that he was probably more educated than the rest of the lot who stood in a circle staring at her, but his learning would have come from books and not from schools. Gypsies saw no need for schools.

"My name is Tar Tibor." He held out his hand. Katalin knew this was more than a simple gesture of politesse. If she refused, she would be insulting him, insinuating that he was too filthy to touch. If she accepted, she would be defying one of the basic rules of social conduct between gypsies and *gorgio*—no physical contact. She accepted, grasping his hand and shaking it firmly. Without taking her eyes off his, she could hear by the gasps that she had shocked everyone, including, she supposed, herself.

"What are you doing here?" he asked gently, recognizing that for her to come to this part of town was a journey, not only over distance but over unwritten boundaries that extended over several centuries. "I know you've been here before. I know you were asked not to return." He glanced quickly at the exotic woman who had sidled next to him and was glaring at Katalin. "Why did you?"

Katalin ignored the dancer and the hostile stares of several of the other gypsies. She concentrated only on Tibor. "Just as you needed to come to the funeral and pay your respects, I needed to come here and play with your band."

He looked at her quizzically. "We don't have a piano."

"I know." His tone had signaled acceptance of her request. Without waiting for confirmation, she slipped out of her coat, tied her hair back into a ponytail, and took her place behind the cimbalom. When she was settled, hammers in hand, she looked to him as any player would look to the *prímás* for direction, and waited. Tibor's full, lush lips spread into a broad, delighted smile. A quick nod to his associates put them at the ready as well. Still keeping his eyes fixed on Katalin, Tibor raised his violin, rested it beneath his chin, and drew his bow across the strings.

As always with the *csárdás*, it began slowly, sadly. Tibor stared at Katalin, watching to be certain that the sorrowful melody didn't elicit the tears he sensed lay just beneath the surface of her calm. As the tempo of the rhapsody accelerated, he held back, giving Katalin the stage, allowing her the catharsis he knew she was seeking. Her hands flew over the metal strings, demanding they release the sound they held within their tautly wound wires. Tibor saw her submitting to the demon, surrendering herself to the power of the music. He saw her eyes close as her hands continued to seduce melody from metal.

Suddenly, the gypsy girl, Farah, took to the floor. In a wild rage of jealousy she spun before Tibor, looking to distract him with the erotic twists and turns of her body. As the music snapped, she jolted about, shaking her breasts and pumping her pelvis in a way that went beyond mere suggestion. This had become a physical demand, a dare, a confrontation between the creator of the music and the interpreter of its rhythm.

Though Katalin was keenly aware of Farah's crude challenge, she ignored the seductive dervish, involving herself in something far less corporeal, far more ethereal. She and Tibor were communicating on a higher plane than the simple playing of a tune. They were coming into concert with each other via the bond of harmonics. He was a wonderful violinist. Her evenings at Csárda had taught her how to play the cimbalom well. Together, they were forging something so powerful, so moving, that in spite of whatever inbred bias had greeted her upon her entrance, Tibor's clansmen were now on their feet, stomping and clapping and clicking their tongues as they would for one of their kind. When the music ended, they hooted their approval, clamoring around her to slap her back and pump her hand.

Yet Katalin was shaken. She felt as if she had just awakened from a hypnotic trance, as if her appearance had been manipulated by a force greater than her own, as if her playing cimbalom with a bunch of gypsies had been an act against her will, at the behest of the devil himself. She looked around, confused and befuddled. For the moment, she didn't remember her name, let alone the name of Tibor Tar.

"Let me see you home," he said, not waiting for an answer but grabbing her coat and gently steering her toward the door. "I think you need to rest."

Numb, she obeyed, following him into the hall where he helped her on with her coat. Hiking her collar up over her ears and covering her head with a scarf he pulled from a pocket, he led her into the night. For a long while they walked in silence. Perhaps it was the cold dampness on her cheeks. Perhaps it was the effect of the music wearing off. Whatever it was, several blocks past the gypsy apartment, something made Katalin stop beneath a streetlamp and stare into the black eyes of her escort.

He expected her to turn against him then, to tell him to get lost, never to come near her again, to forget what had just happened. Instead, she proffered a shy smile. "Thank you," she said, her peridot green eyes misting with gratitude. "I needed the release of the music."

"I know."

She paused, unsure about what to say, what to do. "You're very good." He tilted his head in a gallant gesture of appreciation. "Have you ever been tutored?"

He laughed. It was a deep, throaty sound. "Gypsies don't go to the Academy."

Katalin nodded and smiled. "Right. I forgot."

"It's getting late." Tibor pushed up his sleeve and looked at the time on his watch. Katalin hated herself for wondering if he had stolen it. "I think we have to get you home."

They walked most of the way, taking a bus when they found one. About a block from Katalin's apartment, Tibor stopped.

"I'll leave you here."

"Don't be ridiculous. It's freezing out. Let me give you a cup of coffee before you start back."

Tibor shook his head. "Your father will be home. Your neighbors will be home. It wouldn't look good for you to be bringing a gypsy into the building."

Though she knew what he was saying, something in her needed to reject it. "I like you, Tibor. I'd like to be your friend and maybe, if it's all right, to play with your band every now and then."

"I like you, too, and I'd be honored to be your friend. It's just that I think, for your sake, it's better if we keep our friendship secret. As for playing cimbalom, anytime you want. You know where we are."

She bid him good night, waiting until he turned the corner before entering her building. When she walked into the apartment, Zoltán was waiting for her. His face was chalked with worry.

"Where were you?"

She wanted to tell him where she had gone, believing that he, of all people, would have understood her need to purge her grief through music. She wanted to tell him about Tibor, what he said about how talented he thought Zoltán was, how much fun it had been losing herself in the spell of his energy.

"I needed some air so I went out for a walk," she said instead, knowing instinctively that Tibor was right and that in her father's eyes he would forever be an untouchable. "I feel better now."

"Good." Slowly, a tinge of color returned to Zoltán's cheeks.

"Did you have a nice evening, Papa?"

"It was all right," he said dully. "And yours?"

"Quiet."

He nodded, his eyes distracted, his manner that of an automaton. Then, kissing her cheek lightly, Zoltán rose and walked slowly off to the bedroom, a ghost of a man in search of the ghost of his wife. Katalin remained in the living room, sitting in the dim light of what had become a living tomb.

So much had changed. Things that used to provide joy had become burdens. Things that used to produce pleasure now caused depression. Having dinner with her father, spending an evening at home, reading or listening to music used to be some of life's simpler delights. Lately at dinner they ate in silence. Afterward, Katalin would clear the table and wash the dishes while Zoltán mourned. Katalin would read. Zoltán would continue to mourn. He refused to listen to music or to allow himself even the slightest diversion from the all-encompassing task of grieving. Certainly, Katalin understood. There would always be a hole in her heart where once her mother had dwelled. But she had moved beyond that sadness and accepted the notion of remaining, the reality that she was still part of the world Mária had left. She had recognized that she didn't have to fill the space where Mária had existed, she merely had to learn to adjust to the emptiness. Zoltán had accepted nothing.

He had grown so distant and so removed, Katalin began to feel as if she had lost both parents. Day after day, the silence between them grew louder. What frightened her was that the further he withdrew into himself, the more time she had to think about how to go about filling the void. Though it felt like an act of infidelity, she found herself dreaming of leaving Hungary, of returning to Steven and her friends at Csárda, of taking her Masters at Juilliard and fulfilling the concert dates she had won as part of the Chickering. In those dreams, while she imagined herself on the spotlit stage of Carnegie Hall or in a candlelit room with Steven, she never allowed herself to see Zoltán sitting in this room alone. She never permitted herself to watch her departure, to witness herself leaving her father behind.

Yet despite the enormity of her love for him and her overwhelming compassion for the loss he felt, she, too, was suffering. That morning, after Zoltán had left for work, Katalin had gone to visit Judit to ask about getting a letter to Steven. She was desperate to hear from him, to know how he was doing without her. She knew she was miserable without him. Mindful of the scene she had witnessed outside the convent, however, she wasn't at all surprised when Judit told her it was impossible; that for now, all lines of communication were closed.

That afternoon, she applied for a visitor's visa, thinking that if she asked for a limited leave with a guaranteed return, perhaps her request would be granted. It was denied.

When she returned to the empty apartment, she was struck by the realization that in effect she was a prisoner, locked into an inescapable situation by personal loyalties and political happenstance. She had been stripped of her freedoms, the most important of which was the freedom of choice. Like it or not, she was here to stay.

Retrieving the picture of herself and Steven, she sat on her bed and stared at it, branding the sight of them together and happy and in love onto her memory, knowing that the future that had glowed so brightly in their eyes that night had flickered to a fading ember.

Tonight Katalin had responded to her frustrations by choosing to cross an internal border. She had mingled with gypsies. She had made friends with a gypsy. And she had lied to her father for the first time in her life. What pained her most was that she knew with absolute certainty that it wouldn't be the last time. If her return to Budapest had taught her anything, it was the weight of loneliness, the importance of secrets, and the necessity of lies.

Three weeks later, Katalin went to see Andras.

"Uncle Andras, I don't know what to do," she said, unable to stem her tears or the panic rising in her throat. "I feel as if I'm standing by watching him commit suicide."

"How? What's he doing?"

"Nothing. That's the point. He's simply allowing himself to waste away. It's like he's hurrying his own death so he can join my mother." A sob caught in her throat. "I don't know how to stop him."

Andras led her to the couch in his office and sat her down, trying to comfort her.

"He's just grieving, Katya. Give him time."

"It's more than that."

"What do you mean?"

Katalin wiped her eyes slowly, rehearsing what she was about to say. Even to her ear it sounded strange, but she was certain it was true. "Papa's mourning more than Mama's death, Uncle Andras. He's mourning his life."

Andras looked at her quizzically.

"Now he refuses to listen to music. Not only won't he let me put the radio on or soothe him with some of his favorite recordings, he doesn't even want me to play for him." Katalin couldn't bear to tell him how on several occasions when she had sat down at the piano—wanting to please him, needing to play for herself—Zoltán had walked out of the apartment. "I think Mama's death set off an emotional avalanche. Everything's crashing in on him. The past and the present have somehow collided with each other and he's too confused to be able to separate them. The fact that he can no longer play the violin and the fact that Mama is no longer around to assure him that it's all right is pushing him over the edge. I'm afraid, Uncle Andras. Truly afraid."

"What can I do?"

"I don't know," Katalin said, hating how helpless Andras looked, hating how helpless she felt. "But you have to try to help him."

Andras rose from the couch, circled his desk and then turned to Katalin. "We're not as close as we once were. Since Salzburg, there's been a distance between us. I regret it, but I'm not certain I can bridge it."

Katalin stood. "You have to," she said, meeting his gaze head on. "I don't care what it takes. You have to pull him out of this. After all, Uncle Andras, you owe him."

For a long while after Katalin left, Andras ruminated on what Katalin had said. Though they hadn't realized how serious it was, he and Ilona had both noticed Zoltán's decline. They had discussed the problem, but neither had arrived at a solution. Now Katalin was demanding one. She was charging him with the task of leading Zoltán out of his depression. It was a difficult assignment, but there too, Katalin was right. Whatever it took, he had to try. Because he did owe Zoltán. He owed him his life.

21

Budapest, 1943

Ilona Strasser was not a native of Budapest. Born and raised in Kaposvár, a small city in southwestern Hungary, her lifelong dream was to practice medicine alongside her father. The incomprehensible insanity that was the Third Reich interfered with her plans.

For Ilona the horror started on March 13, 1938, the day Germany occupied Austria. That night Ilona raced home from Pécs, where she was attending the university, to be with her parents. Together they gathered around the radio, tuning in the forbidden BBC from London, broadcasting in German reports of the invasion, as Hitler's armies swallowed Vienna. Listening, the Roths tried to assess how imminent the danger was, tried to judge how close the peril really was to their borders. Like most people, their first response was denial—it wouldn't happen in Hungary, it couldn't happen to them. But by the next morning, Radio Budapest, the voice of the Hungarian government, had become strident, the words parroting Berlin. And by May, discrimination was officially sanctioned by the First Jewish Law.

The condition of Hungarian Jews deteriorated rapidly. Students lost their scholarships. Economic hardships were imposed. History books were rewritten overnight, portraying Jews as the villains in every circumstance from Roman times onward. And anti-Semitism, which throughout Hungary's history had yo-yoed like a jungle fever, suddenly erupted in a heat of blinding hatred.

Though Ilona managed to finish her education, by 1941 the situation had worsened.

"You can't stay, *cica*," Laci Roth said, calling her "kitten," his favorite term of endearment for his precious Ilona.

"Do you think it's any better in Budapest?" Ilona asked, terrified at the notion of leaving her parents and traveling to the capital alone.

"It can't be worse." His words were punctuated with forced laughter. "Besides, it's more cosmopolitan there, more sophisticated." From Laci's tone it was clear he was hoping to convince himself as well as his wife and daughter. "In Budapest there's always been a reliance on Jewish professionals, a real respect for the standards of learning and practice of Jewish doctors and lawyers. Here, the people are more provincial, more prejudiced. Here, *cica*, there's serious trouble brewing."

Frightened, burdened with a sense of dread that felt too real to ignore, Ilona did as her parents wished, finding lodging behind the synagogue on Dob utca, in a small dormitory that in peacetime had housed yeshiva students. It didn't matter that the room was no larger than a broom closet or that there was little food and practically no heat; Ilona's days at the hospital were too long for her to do much else in her off-hours other than fall into a semi-unconscious sleep. Six months after she arrived, however, her sleep was sweetened with dreams of a young man.

He had brought his mother to the emergency room. For weeks the older woman had been spotting blood, but had chosen to ignore it. That morning the bleeding increased. Andras demanded to see a gynecologist. Ilona was sent to examine the elegant Judit Strasser. She was small, but imperious. Judit Strasser comported herself like the nobility she believed she was. After all, her father-in-law, Géza Strasser, had been ennobled by the king. He had been made a baron. His son Simon, her husband, was a baron. That, she reasoned, made her a baroness. Adolph Hitler was a paper hanger.

When Ilona told Baroness Strasser she had several large interuterine polyps and recommended a hysterectomy, Andras insisted upon a second opinion.

"If you need one, go talk to another doctor," the Baroness said. "Dr. Roth's examination was extremely thorough. I'm satisfied with her diagnosis."

"But she's very young," Andras whispered, intimating that in this instance, youth equaled stupidity.

"So are you," his mother whispered in retort.

Two weeks after his mother's surgery, a humbled Andras Strasser returned to Shalom Hospital. Told Ilona was in the operating room, he perched himself on a bench and waited. Three hours later he presented her with a slightly wilted bouquet of flowers.

"I insulted you and I'm sorry," he said, noticing that despite her obvious fatigue she was exceptionally pretty. Her hair, just released from the confines of a surgical cap, was in a state of disarray. Bouncy chestnut brown curls bobbed about her face, directing his attention to her rich dark eyes and her creamy skin. "You probably saved my mother's life."

Laboratory tests had proved the polyps malignant.

"I hope so," Ilona said, knowing that with the German army continuing its deadly advance, no one's life was truly safe. "How is she doing?"

"Very well. She asked me to invite you to Shabbat dinner."

Ilona laughed. "Forgive me. It's just that . . ."

"That's precisely why you should take a few hours off. In the midst of this chaos, it's important to recall how nice civilization used to be."

Andras was right. Civilization, especially as the Strassers practiced it, was delightful. They lived in a villa on the highest crest of the Buda mountains, a hill called Svabhegy. As Andras showed her about the front rooms, Ilona tried not to gape at the high ceilings and silk-covered walls, the thick damask drapes and lavishly upholstered furnishings, the polished parquet floors, the intricately patterned Turkish rugs, the gilded frames, the priceless art. Ilona was a country girl. This was a world so completely foreign to her, she was momentarily unnerved.

"This was my grandfather's country house," Andras explained.

"Country house?" Ilona said, astonished. "Where was his city house?"

"On Andrássy Avenue, in Pest."

Ilona shrugged as if to say, "Of course." Andrássy was one of the most exclusive neighborhoods in Budapest, an arcadian boulevard bordered at one end by the City Park, Heroes' Square at the other.

"Originally, just like the Kornfelds and the Fellners and the Herzogs and most of the other wealthy Jewish families in Budapest, Grandfather's money came from grain trading," Andras continued, enjoying the look of wonderment on Ilona's face. "Later on, he moved into light industry, manufacturing, metal cans."

"It's magnificent." Ilona couldn't keep the awe out of her voice. "I've never seen such a beautiful house."

Andras smiled. It was difficult for him to relate this shy provincial girl with the brisk, no-nonsense doctor who had expunged the cancer from his mother's body. "Come inside. I want you to meet my father."

Simon Strasser was an imposing man. Standing to greet her in the elegantly appointed drawing room, dressed in a finely tailored navy three-piece suit, sporting a hussar moustache and wire-rimmed glasses, he appeared every inch the baron. As Ilona looked at his dark hair and brooding eyes, she detected much of Andras residing in his father's face. But Simon's visage was harder, his back straighter. This was a man who wore his past like a uniform sashed with medals, each one a symbol of his loyalty to his country. He was proud of the fact that his grandparents had funded and manned soup kitchens for the indigent during World War I. He was proud of their contributions to the synagogue and the Jewish community. He was proud that he and his Judit had been able to carry on the Strasser tradition of charity and caring. He was proud of being a Hungarian Jew.

Yet in the set of his jaw and the tight lines around his mouth, Ilona read anger and outrage. This was a man who saw the future, abhorred its creators, and had determined that no matter what the circumstances he would not bend before them.

When Andras introduced Ilona, however, Simon softened. He kissed her hand, offered her a gallant bow, and thanked her profusely for saving his wife's life. As Ilona demurred, Judit sat in a velvet wing chair beaming.

As they talked and Ilona answered questions about her family, about life in Kaposvár, about her life as a doctor, she felt oddly detached, as if she were outside of herself watching with a certain amazement at how relaxed she was, how at ease she was with the Strassers, despite the intimidating surroundings. As the evening went on, she realized it was because on that primal level, that basic human level, they were very similar.

The Sabbath table at the Strassers' was no different from the Sabbath table at the Roths'. The setting was grander, the crystal was finer, and the flatware was sterling silver, but Judit covered her head with a lace chaplet and prayed over the candles just as Sarí Roth would have done; Simon blessed and sliced the *challah* almost exactly the way Ilona's father, Laci, would have. During the meal, there was the same general affection between family members that characterized a Roth gathering: Simon called his wife by the diminutive, Jutka, Judit fussed over Ilona and Andras, Andras teased his mother about her overly attentive behavior.

After dinner, Ilona fell in love.

Judit led the way to the music room, where red velvet walls, red brocade drapes, and thick Turkish carpets created an elegant cave. Despite the gilded crown moldings and glittering chandeliers, the focal point of the room was a remarkable nineteenth-century Bösendorfer piano of light mahogany, inlaid with kingwood in a Greek key design. The legs were plump angels of hollow-cast brass, exquisitely detailed and finished with gleaming ormolu.

Simon offered Ilona a chair facing the piano. Judit settled herself nearby on a small settee, resting her feet on a tufted ottoman. Simon eased into a wide, cushy chair that must have been his favorite since it seemed to mold immediately to his form. Andras seated himself at the piano. Without any introduction—clearly, this was part of their Sabbath ritual—Andras began to play.

Later Ilona learned that Andras had been one of those privileged to study with the great Ernö Dohnányi, considered one of Hungary's finest composers and most brilliant performers, then the conductor of the Budapest Philharmonic Orchestra. She also discovered that Andras had debuted at the Esterházy Palace in Fertöd at the age of fourteen, but had decided early on he disliked performing in public. Though he continued his study of the piano, it became an avocation. Carrying on his father's business was to be his life's occupation. Or so he thought.

Ilona knew none of that then. All she knew was that something about the quiet, introverted man seated before her touched a part of her no one had ever touched before. He was playing Rachmaninoff with all the pathos and melancholy required to interpret the moody Russian composer. Yet there was a surprising energy emanating from his music, a power she sensed he was unwilling to display in any other forum, a power she intuited he hid from most everyone, save those capable of seeing beyond his mild facade.

When he escorted her back to her dormitory, he took her in his arms and kissed her. As his lips pressed against hers, she felt that same powerful energy envelop her, wrapping itself around her, absorbing her into its aura. She had no qualms about surrendering to it. It made her feel loved. It made her feel safe.

From then on, whenever her schedule permitted, Ilona spent the Sabbath with the Strassers and whatever hours she could steal with their son. If their story had been written on another page in the annals of history, Andras would have conducted his courtship of Ilona in a more chivalric manner. He would have wooed and romanced her, reining his passions until after their love had been sanctioned by God and by law. But this was not a time that encouraged the slow unfolding of love. This was a time when every circumstance tested the fragility of life and every waking thought centered on its preservation.

Still, for almost five years, Budapest had been spared the worst moments of the war. While Hitler's Europe was suffering at his maniacal hand, Hungary remained set apart. Food rationing existed, but there were few shortages. There was censorship, but as late as the beginning of 1943, the voice of opposition still could be heard in books and plays and occasional editorials. There were restrictions on the freedoms of Jews and a rising incidence of anti-Semitism, but for the majority of Hungarian Jews there was still reason to believe they might escape the bloody hand of the dictator of death.

In April, 1943, Mária Gáspár desperately wanted a baby, but was having difficulty conceiving. Because she was a magnet for the press, who felt starved for any news unrelated to the war, she decided to seek advice from someone other than her regular physician, someone affiliated with an out-of-the-way hospital. In April, 1943, Shalom Hospital in the Jewish quarter was as out of the way as one could get. Through a friend in her theater company, Mária made an appointment with a young woman on staff at Shalom, Ilona Roth.

At first Mária felt embarrassed to be examined by someone her own age. Ilona neutralized that with a clinical, purely professional manner. It was afterward, in her office, that Ilona's warmth emerged.

"Judging from my examination, there's no physical reason you can't conceive a child," she said. "May I ask how long you've been trying?"

"Almost a year." Frustration and embarrassment flushed Mária's cheeks.

As a doctor, Ilona could have detailed dozens of impediments to conception, but because she suspected that the difficulty was emotional rather than physical or chemical, she spoke to Mária woman to woman. After she explained about the inhibiting effects of stress on the reproductive process and arranged a series of tests that would confirm her diagnosis, she counseled patience and a romantic weekend.

"Go away," she said to Mária. "Find someplace secluded and atmospheric. Enjoy each other. It's the best medicine I can prescribe."

That was the beginning of a friendship. On each successive visit Mária and Ilona discovered something else they had in common: an interest in folk art, a distaste for liquor, an affinity for wine, an admitted passion for the poetry of Sándor Petöfi, a secret love of the swashbuckling romances of Géza Gárdonyi, a lack of athletic ability, a lover gifted with musical ability. When finally Ilona was able to confirm that Mária was indeed pregnant, the two women arranged a celebratory dinner so that Zoltán and Andras could meet.

The men liked each other immediately. While Mária and Ilona talked about the baby, Zoltán and Andras gorged themselves on talk of music, exchanging opinions on teachers and conductors and theories and practices.

Over the next few months, the links of friendship began to form. The night Mária miscarried, the links were forged into an unbreakable chain.

It happened in the Strasser villa. Judit and Simon had invited Zoltán and Mária to join their Sabbath table. As a postprandial surprise, Zoltán and Andras invited everyone into the music room, where they played a duet. For that brief interlude, there was no war. There was no Hitler. There was no clock ticking, no ax threatening to fall. There was simply Mozart being played by two immensely talented men. There was simply the magic of the music filling the richly appointed red velvet room.

When Mária gripped her abdomen the first time, Ilona flew to her side. Three more spasms and Ilona insisted someone call for an ambulance. Next, she instructed Mária to lie down. Propping her legs with pillows, she waited for the sound of the ambulance. It never came.

"Shalom's one ambulance is out of commission," Simon said, his ever-present anger surfacing. "I called two other hospitals, but they won't dispatch an ambulance to a Jewish house. I explained that the patient wasn't Jewish. They didn't care."

Without debating the insanity of such a comment, Ilona told Zoltán and Andras to carry Mária to the nearest lavatory. Once inside the bathroom, she closed and locked the door so that Mária could have her miscarriage in private. Afterward, the two women huddled on the floor of the bathroom. Ilona held Mária in her arms, letting her spend her grief, cradling her as she might have cradled the child that now would never be.

In truth, Ilona knew that even if an ambulance had come, she probably couldn't have prevented the loss of Mária's baby—that once a miscarriage was in progress, it was almost impossible to impede. But that was not the point.

The next night, still reeling from the events of the evening before, Andras allowed himself to be persuaded to attend a meeting of Budapest's young Zionists. Andras was neither devout nor had he ever harbored any burning desire to emigrate to Palestine. Still, he went. There, in the basement of a building on Laudon Street, the street of leather tanners in the heart of the Jewish sector, he heard no prayers, saw no rituals, experienced no spiritual conversion. This was not a congregational gathering. This was a meeting of partisans.

Called the Hazalah—rescue—the group had formed originally to aid

Jewish refugees from Slovakia and Poland. The younger, more forward thinking among them, however, believed it was imperative that they shore up their defenses for the day the Nazis made Hungary another pearl on their bloody necklace of conquests. While they begged for support, the elders dismissed their pleas as needless hysteria. The war was winding down, they said; continued Allied victories would stop Hitler before he could wreak his particularly evil havoc on Hungary. The Jews of Hungary would survive his efforts to create a "Jew-free" Europe. The partisans spoke of what had happened in the Warsaw ghetto. They reiterated the rumors that abounded about death camps and labor camps and the whole-sale murder of women and children. The elders advanced the argument that it was different in Hungary, that here, the Jews were more assimilated than they were in the other Eastern European countries, integrated into Hungarian life: Their leading actors were Jewish, as were musicians, writers, and industrialists; the grand rabbi of Budapest was a member of the high legislative chamber. And if that wasn't enough, they pointed out that even Christian Hungarians were not mounting a Resistance. In their blindness the elders were making a tragic mistake. When the Nazis came, most Christian Hungarians would look away from the attempts to exterminate their "assimilated" Jewish neighbors. The Hazalah would be the one and only Resistance in Hungary.

Though Andras wanted to believe the elders, he, too, could hear the rumbling of the tanks; he, too, could smell the approach of death. When a secret meeting was called by the younger, more aggressive group for the following evening to form a defense unit, Andras went.

Listening to the reports of the Polish and Slovakian refugees, he understood that the Nazi system of elimination was an orderly and power-ful machine. Attacking its surface would do no discernible damage. If there was a chance to disrupt it at all, it had to come from some flaw within the structure itself.

"Why don't we upset their precious numbers?" Andras said, an idea forming.

"How?"

Andras could see that several men had already picked up on where he was headed. Confident in their support, he continued. "The Nazis count the number of people they kill, right?" Somber faces nodded agreement. "Each day they fill a quota. What if we flood their death machine with false identification papers? What if their dreaded lists show fewer Jews?"

"Then fewer Jews would be deported and killed," came the response.

Within a month, Andras was put in charge of one of the printing plants established in an apartment house basement, turning out false documents for that day when he and his family and his friends would have to abandon their identities and betray their heritage in order to escape a grim destiny.

On January 10, 1944, Ilona Roth and Andras Strasser stood beneath the *chupah* in the ballroom of the Strasser villa and were joined in marriage. Zoltán Gáspár served as best man for the groom; Mária Gáspár was the bride's matron of honor. Because in other times there would have been hundreds of guests invited to celebrate the occasion, Judit had insisted upon filling the mirrored room with chairs. Though they stood empty, she didn't care. As she watched Ilona walk down the aisle, wearing the dress Judit had worn at her marriage to Simon, the long ivory satin train trailing between the rows of vacant seats, Judit saw the smiling faces of those who would have been there, if they could have been there.

Ilona cared only that Sarí and Laci Roth were able to see her take her vows. It was the last time she would see them alive.

On Sunday, March 19, 1944, Hungary, an Axis ally, became an occupied country.

On Monday, as Eichmann's commandos settled themselves in the Majestic Hotel on Svabhegy, Operation Hazalah went onto full alert.

Telling only Ilona of his plans, mild-mannered, conservative Andras volunteered to become a messenger, one of those who, carrying Aryan identification, traveled outside Budapest to the provinces to try to awaken the Jewish populace to what was happening. In order to pass through the police checkpoints without detection, Andras costumed himself like a young Hungarian seminarian. For personal papers, he carried his streetcar commutation card, the only national document on which religion didn't appear.

His mission took him south, to several of the small towns surrounding Pécs. In each town, he had the rabbi gather the leading citizens together. He recounted what he had seen along the way: the arrests, the beatings, the loading of Jews onto trucks where many were executed. He told of the looting of Jewish homes, of watching old men forced to crawl in the mud, of rabbis forced to dance naked in the streets. He begged them to leave, to take the papers he carried sewn into the lining of his coat and escape before it was too late. As a way of underlining his message, he told them that as he had traveled through the countryside, he had noticed that even the storks, which for some unknown reason nested atop telephone poles, had left their traditional perches for safer ground.

Though he knew they believed him, though he could see the fear of death in their eyes, the pious refused to adopt Christian identities. Many of the younger generation hesitated, torn between saving themselves and abandoning their elders. Andras directed his most zealous efforts at persuading them.

"We are the future," he told them. "We are the vehicles of our own revenge. If we all die, the Nazis have won. If we fight and even a few survive, we win."

By the time he left, he had distributed enough false ID's to assure himself that at least some of the population would be saved. The others, he knew, were lost.

"Did you find out anything about my parents?" Ilona asked when Andras returned.

"They're alive and still living in their own home."

Ilona had desperately wanted to accompany Andras. She had wanted to be part of Operation Hazalah because she believed in its mission, but more than that because she had wanted to see Sarí and Laci; she had wanted to touch them, to assure herself that this blight that was descending on Hungary had not claimed them. Andras had convinced her that she would be doing the most good by remaining in Budapest to care for the ill and the injured.

Each day it was harder to concentrate on the matters at hand, because each day brought another ordinance, another prohibition: All Jews over the age of six were to wear a yellow star sewn to their clothing, even in their own homes; Jews could only sit in the rear of the streetcars; Jewish doctors could treat only Jewish patients; telephone service was suspended; practicing the Jewish religion was forbidden, as was having a bank account, using a radio, taking a taxicab, a train, or a boat. Regrouping began. Houses throughout the Jewish quarter were taken over. They became "Jewish houses," designated by Stars of David painted over their doors. Hundreds of families were taken from their homes and crammed into these prisons. Food rations were severely limited. Jews were no longer allowed regular allotments of paprika, fat, or poppy seeds. Cafés, pastry shops, public baths, even cigar stores were declared off limits.

On May 25, Andras and Ilona received word that all the Jews of Kaposvár had been herded into a ghetto.

The number of Andras's missions increased. Each time he left Ilona was certain he wouldn't return. When he did, she considered it a blessing and worked herself that much harder the next day to repay God for His beneficence. Then, two things happened that rattled the foundations of her belief in the Almighty.

On July 5, Hazalah messengers reported that the Jews of Kaposvár, including Sarí and Laci Roth, had been loaded onto a train headed for Auschwitz. All efforts to uncover their fate failed. Andras assumed they were dead. Ilona insisted upon believing they were still alive.

Then, at 1:17 P.M. on Sunday, October 15, Miklós Horthy capitulated, announcing over Radio Budapest that Hungary was ready to surrender "in order not to serve as a rearguard battlefield of the Reich." By nightfall, Horthy had been replaced by the Hungarian Nazis, known as the Arrowcross, who immediately wrested control of Budapest. As their first act of power, they raided the Svabhegy sector.

By the time Andras was notified, Simon and Judit had been dragged down to the banks of the Danube, along with all the other Jewish residents of Svabhegy. Using one of his disguises in hopes of being able to free them from their captors, Andras rushed to the scene and joined the crowd that had gathered along the quay. What he saw made him sick.

The Arrowcross—the Nyilas—uniformed in their green shirts and black pants, their red brassards marked with the arrowcross in a white circle and armed with their billy clubs, had corralled a group of frightened people dressed in nothing but nightclothes, demanding that they form a line along the quay. There were ten Nyilas and fifty Jews, many of whom had their hands tied behind their backs. Except for two small boys. They were ordered to push their parents into the river. Andras could hear the boys crying. He could hear their parents telling them to do as they were told, naively believing that if the boys obeyed, their lives would be spared. The boys continued to protest. One of the Nyilas shot the first boy in the neck, killing him instantly. Then, as he threw the dead child into the river, tossing him by the foot as one might skitter a stone across a lake, one of his comrades pumped bullets into the bodies of his parents.

Andras wanted to close his eyes, but all around him the crowd was watching in stunned silence. He couldn't give himself away. Instead, he forced himself to watch the other little boy push his mother into the river. He forced himself to watch the unholy agony on the father's face as his wife reached back and pulled her child with her into the freezing waters of the Danube. One by one, Andras witnessed the executions. Frantically, he moved closer, seeking an opportunity to do something, anything, to prevent what he knew was about to happen.

Suddenly, as if God had willed that they see each other one last time, Simon's head turned. For an instant that Andras would remember for a lifetime, his father caught his eye, blinked in recognition, and then looked away into the eyes of his executioner. The largest of the Arrowcross soldiers stood inches away from Simon. Andras watched with pride as his father straightened his back and stared at the illiterate thug with obvious, audacious disgust. Enraged, the Nyilas shouted at Simon, demanding that he reveal where he had hidden his fortune. When Simon remained mute, the animal slammed his club into the side of Simon's head. Simon staggered, but refused to fall. The Nyilas continued his ranting, but now he turned his club on Judit, crushing her ribs, breaking her jaw, threatening to rape her in front of Simon if he didn't tell him where he had buried his treasure.

Andras felt his heart rising in his throat, filling his mouth with a sour taste. It was all he could do to stand and watch his parents being brutalized. Before he knew what was happening, Simon grabbed Judit. With whatever strength they had left, both of them plunged into the freezing waters of the Danube. It was such a courageous act of defiance, Andras wanted to cheer. When he heard the gunshots fired into the water after them, he wanted to weep. Yet in an odd way, he felt grateful that his parents would die quickly from a bullet, rather than having to suffer the ravages of a callous river.

Inside his head, as he watched their bodies disappear, Andras recited the Kaddish, the Jewish prayer for the dead.

The next day, while Andras, armed with his Aryan papers, scouted for a place to live, Zoltán went to the Strasser villa to pick up some clothing for the homeless couple. They all knew it was hopeless to try to retrieve any valuables. Whatever Andras's father hadn't been able to hide, the Nyilas would have stolen. When Zoltán arrived, he realized it was worse than any of them had imagined. The house had been more than ransacked. It had been mutilated. Whatever hadn't been ripped off the walls or taken off the floors had been smashed beyond recognition. The mirrors in the ballroom had been shattered. The carpets had been burned. Drapes had been shredded. Furniture had been axed. But the sight that wrenched Zoltán's heart was the piano. Some feral brute had ravaged that magnificent instrument, hammering its innards until it had been rendered mute, pounding at its frame until the handiwork of dozens of craftsmen had been reduced to a pile of splinters.

As Zoltán made his way through the ruins, cataloguing the barbaric destruction of what had once been a magnificent home, he felt a sense of shame. He was a Christian. In *their* minds, he was one of them. He was supposed to be gloating at the Jews' fall from grace. He was supposed to approve their deportation, grateful to the Arrowcross for removing them from his space. He was supposed to be glad about their torture and their suffering. Zoltán didn't feel any of those things. Why? he wondered. He had been raised in the provinces where anti-Semitism had been part of the fabric of life. Yet something in his upbringing had wrought in him a sense of humanity, of responsibility to his fellow man; something that made him remember what his countrymen had forgotten—that he *was* a Christian.

When he came to the room where Andras and Ilona had lived, he saw that most of their belongings had been vandalized or stolen. The few articles of clothing he could salvage, he picked off the floor and stuffed into a bag. Just then, another man with a sack came into the room. His sack was huge and it was full.

"Good pickings," he said, scanning the debris like a vulture eyeing carrion. "Take what you want. Those filthy Jews won't be back." As he left, his laughter echoed down the hall. It was a sound Zoltán would not soon forget.

Hundreds were massacred in the streets. The Arrowcross had unleashed a reign of terror on the Budapest ghetto. Though some people were saved by the *Schutzpasses* issued by Swedish diplomat Raoul Wallenberg and the false papers from the House of Glass—a mirror company on Vadasz Street bought by Charles Lutz, the Swiss consul, and annexed to the Swiss legation—the collective murder of the Nazi regime continued.

Though Zoltán and Mária had offered sanctuary to their friends, Andras refused to endanger them with his and Ilona's presence. Besides, with her work in the hospital and his missions for Operation Hazalah, they were rarely in one place long enough to call it home. If ever they needed to contact the Gáspárs, as they had the night the elder Strassers had been killed, it was done through a Swiss courier. It was through that courier that Ilona learned Mária was pregnant again.

Though she would have liked to have examined her friend and to have shared the joyous news with her, Ilona was kept busy by hordes of patients both in the hospital and in basement clinics that had sprung up throughout the ghetto. Every day Ilona would sneak in and out, fearful that she would make that one false move, that single misstep that would either imprison her in the ghetto, away from Andras, or encourage a bullet that would kill her on the spot.

On November 16, Eichmann decreed that since the Russians had destroyed the train tracks that had been transporting his human cargo to Auschwitz, the Jews would walk to their deaths. The Russians were closing in on Budapest. Rumor had it that Hitler had denied Eichmann's request for deportation by foot. Despite that, Eichmann mounted his march. He claimed he was going to "concentrate" seventy thousand Jews on the Austro-Hungarian border as a last line of defense. The Hazalah knew otherwise.

Fifteen to twenty miles a day, they walked, sometimes without food, without proper clothing. Stragglers were gunned down. The old begged— in vain—for release. The Arrowcross raped women and tortured babies. If anyone was found with money on him, he was forced to strip and, at nightfall, to climb into a barrel. Then, the giddy Nazis would fill the barrel with water, letting their victim freeze into a block of ice.

In Budapest, the efforts of the Hazalah intensified. With the Red Army so close to the Hungarian border, the Nazis were accelerating their efforts to remove all witnesses to their bestiality. They began to kill for pleasure, shooting at random, growing suspicious of everyone, including their own. What had been insanity had become frenzy.

Andras joined his fellow partisans on the road to Hegyeshalom, the border town where the deportees were supposed to be turned over to the Germans. Hiding so that he would not be added to the deadly line, Andras photographed many of the atrocities committed on the march. He brought the film back to Budapest and showed it to the apostolic nuncio. Dumbfounded and horrified by what he saw, the cleric authorized Vatican safe-conducts, giving Andras blanks and approving, albeit implicitly, the counterfeiting of them. Added to the *Schutzpasses* provided by the staffs of Wallenberg and Lutz, the Vatican papers helped salvage a few more lives. Though Andras found the numbers spared pitiful, he recalled a passage from the Talmud: "Whoever contributes to the salvation of a single man is as worthy as if he had saved all mankind."

By early December, the Arrowcross had erected a wall around the ghetto, isolating the Budapest Jews from the rest of the world. Masses of people were jammed into safe houses, living in overcrowded rooms and stairwells. Burials were forbidden. Disease raged. Rations decreased to below subsistence level. And the Red Army drew closer. Though the Hungarian Nazis insisted upon claiming victory, most average citizens anticipated defeat. Many had begun to defy the government in anticipation of that defeat. Many, but not enough.

On December 17, Eichmann retreated, taking his staff with him.

On Christmas Eve, the siege of Budapest began. In the confusion of the Russian assault, Andras spirited Ilona to the Gáspárs, asking them to take her in and hide her. The nightmare was to last three weeks. Air strikes brought violent shelling. Opposing armies fought in the streets. Hungarians vacated their apartments, huddling in basements, trying to escape the onslaught. Still, the ghetto remained fenced. The Jews remained the targets of violence.

A decree was issued that any Jew living in the Christian part of the city and carrying false papers declaring himself a Christian was to be shot on sight. Andras and the others ignored the decree.

The Nazis were on a manhunt. Determined to eliminate those who could testify to their cruelty, they unleashed a hemorrhage of malignity unknown in history. Children's houses were attacked, the small inhabitants taken to the Raditzsky barracks, which had been converted into a veritable abattoir, or to the quays of the Danube, where they were shot. Death stalked the streets. It fell from the skies. It knocked down doors. Even at the House of Glass there was no security. The Nyilas, fresh from slaughtering residents of other protected houses, pushed their way inside the Swiss annex, opening fire, shooting into the darkness, not caring who or how many they felled. Only the arrival of the Hungarian police, called by one of Andras's cohorts, and the reminder that in the eyes of the world this particular attack was an affront to the Swiss, stopped the carnage.

Ten days after the siege began, Andras took the greatest risk of his life. He and other Hazalah partisans became "strollers." Equipped with fake police warrants, they donned Nyilas uniforms and visited the homes of party dignitaries selected for their cruelty. Naturally, the surprised officials protested, flaunting their service records by reciting their many heinous acts against the hated Jews. Without allowing their expressions to change, the strollers took their prisoners into the street where they continued their discussion. At the first intersection, the Nazi was executed. But not before the real identity of his kidnapper had been revealed.

On January 18, 1945, the Inner City of Pest was taken by the Russians. On that day, Andras appeared at the door of the Gáspár apartment.

"I feel like a quitter," he said after Zoltán had pulled him inside, "but I feared that if I didn't get away now, I'd never make it. I'd never see Ilona again."

Ilona flew into his arms. It had been weeks since she had seen him. Now, as she looked into his eyes, she tried to avoid the ghost she saw there, reflections of those he had watched die, those he had been unable to save.

"What's happening in the ghetto?" she asked, clinging to her husband's side.

"It's been mined, but for some miraculous reason, the bombs haven't been detonated."

Everyone in the room knew that didn't mean the dying had stopped. It simply meant that instead of collective murder, the deaths continued one by one.

"We have to hide you," Mária said. "The Arrowcross has begun to check every apartment."

She showed Andras the place where Ilona had been hiding, the place where both of them would stay for months, a small chamber secreted behind the wall of the closet, once part of the second bedroom. Inside, Mária had stockpiled food and blankets, candles and books. There were pillows and basins—one with water for washing, one for waste. During the day, Ilona and Andras kept the secret wall open just enough to let air in. They couldn't move around. They couldn't make noise. They couldn't alert anyone to their presence. All they could do was read.

Meanwhile, Zoltán and Mária joined their neighbors who had bivouacked in the basement to avoid being caught in the crossfire between the Germans and the Russians. There, everyone prayed that the air attacks would miss their mark and spare their lives. Zoltán and Mária added their own private prayers. The Nyilas, furious in their retreat, were executing people in the streets, raiding hospitals where they murdered doctors and nurses, along with babies and the infirm, carrying out blind massacres in revenge for their own defeat. They had made Buda a cemetery without gravestones. All Zoltán and Mária could do was pray they wouldn't bring their murderous vendetta to the Gáspárs' building and find their friends.

One day, Zoltán went alone to the basement. His ashen pallor attracted no attention. Neither did the fear that flickered in his eyes. Everyone in Budapest was pale and afraid. That morning, however, he had an added burden: Mária was crammed into the tiny chamber with the Strassers, suffering her second miscarriage. Though he had wanted Ilona to treat Mária in the bedroom where there was air and light and space to move about, the word was out that the Nyilas were combing the neighborhood looking for Jews with false papers. After helping his ailing wife into the darkened space, he had gone downstairs, hoping Mária's absence wouldn't arouse suspicion.

Upstairs, inside the darkened refuge, Ilona tended her patient. While Andras muffled Mária's cries with a towel, Ilona waited for the fetus to abort. Suddenly, the three of them heard a loud thud. No one breathed. They could hear the sound of heavy boots stomping throughout the apartment. Doors were opened and closed. Furniture was overturned. When the door to the closet was opened, Mária's eyes grew so wide, Ilona thought they would bulge out of their sockets. Andras pressed against her mouth, stifling the sound of her pain. Ilona, guessing that Mária's expression had been provoked by pain rather than pure fear, pushed the basin underneath her pelvis. Just as she had suspected, Mária aborted at the same time as her home was violated. Quickly, Ilona dressed Mária with bandages, swabbing her with disinfectant, her nose stinging from the smell of it in the closed, airless space. Andras, too, had to smother a cough. For hours, they remained confined. Ilona had given Mária something to help the pain, but nothing could ease the terror they all felt.

That night, when Zoltán came upstairs—having assured himself that, for the moment, the danger had passed—and opened the secret door, he wept at the sight of his wife lying in Ilona's lap, her hand limp and lifeless next to the basin where their second attempt at parenthood lay beneath a towel.

Later, after he had put Mária to bed, he unearthed a hidden bottle of brandy. Using only one glass—in case someone came—he shared the liquor with his friends.

"One of these days, when this is over," Zoltán said, "I'll repay your kindness."

A week later, he did.

It was early evening. The shelling had quieted. Zoltán and Mária had come upstairs. They had just checked on Andras and Ilona when two drunken Arrowcross burst through the door.

"We've been told you have Jews hiding in your apartment," one of them said, his whiskey breath souring the air.

"We do not." Zoltán stated it as a fact, believing that rabble only understood authority.

"Someone told us you did."

"Your informer is wrong," Mária said.

"Well, we'll just see, won't we." The two men staggered about the room, toppling lamps and vases, knocking into couches, elbowing walls. They opened cabinet doors, as if the Gáspárs had hidden grown people inside cupboards meant for dishes. They looked in the stove and other ridiculous places. Zoltán and Mária were able to endure that part of the search with relative ease. It was when they stormed the second bedroom that Mária's heart began to pound.

"Who lives here?" The shorter of the two demanded.

"No one."

"You have an empty bedroom?" He was shocked. "When the rest of the city is doubled and tripled up?"

"We're privileged," Zoltán said, stating another fact as though it should have been obvious.

The two soldiers huddled. Clearly, one was revealing the identities of the Gáspárs to the other.

"Why would someone tell us you were harboring Jews?" he asked, in need of an answer for his superior.

"I have no idea."

"Maybe because everyone knows that when Eichmann asked you to play for one of his parties and asked Mrs. Gáspár to do a reading, you refused."

That was true, but Zoltán was unaware that the grunts of the Arrowcross had been privy to such information.

"Just because I refused to consort with the Germans doesn't mean I'd lower myself to consort with Jews."

"Besides," Mária said, noting with disgust how pleased the two green-shirted men had been with Zoltán's slur, "I thought you had gotten rid of all the Jews."

"Most of them," the taller one said with great pride. "Unfortunately, the Russians came too soon for us to blow up the ghetto. We had it all mined and ready to go. A few more days and we would have annihilated every last one of them."

When they left, Mária went to the bathroom and vomited.

On February 13, after a vicious battle for Castle Hill, the Russians occupied Buda, completing their conquest of Budapest. Seven of every ten buildings had been badly damaged, with nearly all the windows of Budapest broken. That winter of '45 was unusually cold. There was no electricity, no gas, no telephones. Streets were strewn with rubble and the bodies of the civilian dead. Burnt-out vehicles blocked roadways and sidewalks. Only the waterworks functioned. As people came out of the basements and hiding places, they saw a city destroyed.

In the ghetto, while nearly 69,000 of Budapest's 125,000 Jews had been spared, the losses were staggering. Tremendous risks remained. Though the voices of the cannons had been stilled, the madness had not. Drunken Russian soldiers, mostly Mongols, raped tens of thousands of women in the dark cellars where they had been hiding. Houses and apartments were set on fire. Looters stalked the city. The war was over. The Soviets had liberated Budapest. But Budapest was not free.

It was a year before anyone ventured out on the streets at night, a year before some sense of normalcy descended on the battered city on the Danube.

During that time, Andras and Ilona found an apartment in Buda. María went back to work almost immediately, as did Zoltán and Ilona. Only Andras remained at odds. Many of his Hazalah cronies had emigrated to Israel. Those who remained returned to the religious life, studying to be rabbis or cantors. Since Strasser Manufacturing had been destroyed and there was no money to start it up again, Andras had no business to run. He volunteered to help in the resettlement of the Jewish quarter, but in truth, he had nothing to do. There again, Zoltán saved him.

"I've spoken to the head of the Liszt Academy," Zoltán said one evening after the four of them had had dinner. "He would like you to take a position on staff as a piano instructor."

Andras lowered his eyes, fixing his gaze on the dish before him. He was embarrassed that someone would feel the need to help him get on his feet. He was angry that he hadn't found something for himself. He was undecided about whether or not he would enjoy being a teacher. And he was frightened that if he didn't take this, there would be no other offers.

"I'm not a qualified teacher," he said, watching Ilona's face out of the corner of his eye.

"Tezsia remembers your playing. He also knows you were taught by Dohnányi. He considers you qualified and he's the only one who matters."

Andras laced his fingers together and squeezed them as if the answers to his future were hidden in his hands.

"You always loved playing," Ilona said, telling him in her gentle way that perhaps this had always been his future.

Andras laughed. The others looked at him in confusion. How could he tell them that he found himself ludicrous. For the past several years he had risked his life every minute of every day without thought of consequence. Now, someone had asked him to teach others to play the piano and he was stymied by questions. Was he good enough to teach? Would he like it? Would his students like him? Was this what he was meant to do? This was not a life-threatening situation, he told himself. There was no danger involved. The only risk was that he might make a fool of himself. So why was he hesitating?

Ilona rose from her chair and walked behind her husband. She slid her arms around his neck and leaned down so that her mouth was close to his ear.

"Simon and Judit would be proud," she said.

It was all she needed to say. The next day Andras met with Albert Tezsia. The following week the Academy arranged a small recital to announce Andras's joining the faculty. Before a full house, Andras and Zoltán took the stage. As they had that night so many years ago, they played Mozart. And, as they had that night so many years ago, they filled the hall with the magic of music.

Now, so many decades later, Andras looked out the window of the office he had first occupied in 1945. If it took every ounce of energy he had, every bit of imagination he could conjure, every contact, every source, every waking moment, he would pull Zoltán out of his depression. He would find the spirit of the man he once knew and restore it. He would repay his friend for his friendship—an eye for an eye, a life for a life.

22

Budapest, 1975

Katalin's loneliness had been a dull, hollow ache. When Mária died, the cut was rent larger; the ache became a stinging, searing pain that often awakened her in the middle of the night. Still, by treating the anguish of loss as one would any chronic illness—with stoic tolerance— she managed.

But loneliness had a cumulative effect, like snowfall on a cold mountainside, one layer blanketing another. Zoltán continued to sink deeper into the black crater of depression, closing himself in, shutting Katalin out, increasing her sense of isolation and despair. Andras and Ilona did everything they could—Ilona demanded that he dine with them at least once a week; Andras stopped by frequently with ideas about job changes and opportunities—but Zoltán remained committed to perpetual mourning.

In the past, Judit's friendship had provided diversion and relief from whatever was troubling Katalin. Now, Judit had her own career, her own romance, and her own problems. If she wasn't touring with Sándor Emke or another operatic soloist, she was working for or sleeping with Attila Kovács.

Though Andras rejuvenated Katalin's career by arranging several important concerts, their old nemèsis, Kocsis, was placing limits on where, when, and with whom she could travel. She either played inside the Iron Curtain or not at all.

Worse, while Katalin wrote dozens of letters to Steven, she had no way of knowing whether they reached him. Not only did she suspect that the government censors were disallowing her correspondence, but, after Judit had been threatened, the underground route temporarily closed down. She did receive two odd pieces of mail. One was postmarked Virginia, the other Illinois. Every single line had been blackened and the return addresses had been cut out of the envelopes. She desperately wanted to believe they had come from Steven, but she couldn't be certain. What if they weren't from him? What if he no longer loved her? What if he had never loved her?

Each time that ugly, unsettling thought arose, another of the bright, hopeful dreams she had entertained faded. As the days turned into weeks, weeks to months, and months to years, as promises dissolved and prospects dwindled, Katalin's life was enshrouded in a pessimistic fog.

In the midst of this gloom, her only source of pleasure was Tibor Tar. He was someone new, someone unassociated with her past in any way. He didn't provoke memories of her life with Steven or her life with Mária. He represented the world as she was being forced to know it, and because of that, his friendship meant a great deal. In truth, if it were not for him, Katalin believed she never would have survived those first two years after Mária's death.

A month after Tibor's invitation to play with the gypsy band, on a night when Zoltán had gone to the Strassers' and the apartment was filled with ghosts, Katalin returned to the rooms where the troupe gathered. She felt ashamed of her obvious neediness. Yet she was unable to turn back. She didn't care how it looked, she needed to be in that place with those people.

Tibor insisted she sit in with them. She did, and as she had the time before when she had jammed with the gypsies, she rejoiced in the wild, joyously free sensations that flooded her. That release was the reason she began to return regularly—despite Farah's open hostility—and why she didn't hesitate when, six months later, Tibor asked if she would play cimbalom with them in Martonvásár.

Though she hated lying to her father, what she hated even more was recognizing that when she told him she was spending the evening with Judit, he was only half-listening, only half-caring about what she did or where she went. It irked her that Zoltán never questioned where she had been or whom she was seeing. She supposed that if he thought about it at all—which she doubted—he assumed she had a lover. That irked her even more. If he had ever taken time out of his grieving to ask about hers, he would know that she, too, was without the person she loved, that she, too, felt horribly, irretrievably alone.

Taking what she needed, she made her way to Keleti Station, where she slipped into the ladies room, making certain no one followed her. Quickly, she tied her hair into a tight bun and covered her head with a flowered scarf, pulling it down on her forehead, wrapping it and knotting it behind her neck. She darkened her skin with makeup and kohled her eyes. She changed into a rainbow-tiered skirt, peasant blouse, and golden chains. She rouged her lips and dangled long golden hoops from her ears. When she was as gypsy as a green-eyed *gorgio* could be, she packed her real clothes into her bag and walked through the station, keeping her head down, shuffling like a beggar, trying not to look suspicious.

Waiting on the curb for Tibor's truck, she wondered about the sagacity of what she was doing. For a Hungarian woman with a burgeoning concert career to cast her lot with gypsies was not a smart move. Gypsies, even the lighter-skinned Musicians, might be welcomed inside Budapest's better restaurants, but close association, public fraternization, friendship—that was something else again.

Katalin debated the issue only as long as it took for Tibor to hoist her up onto the back of the truck. From that moment on, she had such a good time it didn't matter what anyone thought.

Old and rickety, off-balance, with bad gears and no shock absorbers, the truck jerked its way out of Budapest, onto route 70. On this hot, sticky night in August it was a relief to be headed away from the city into the pastoral countryside near Hungary's lake district. Though they would not be coming close to Lake Balaton, the "Hungarian Sea," or even the diminutive version of the Balaton, Lake Velence, the air still turned fresh and light the farther into the hills they went.

By the time they arrived in Martonvásár at the neo-Gothic castle where they were scheduled to perform, Katalin's spirits had lifted—somewhat. Looking at the manicured grounds and the elegant Brunswick mansion, imagining who might be in the audience, her stomach fluttered with second thoughts.

"What kind of crowd is it?" she asked, as she stood alongside the truck and watched Tibor's friends unload the instruments.

"Peasants. Farmers. Local townsfolk. No one who would recognize the famous Gáspár Katalin."

"Are you teasing me or criticizing me?"

"I'm stating a fact that I hope will put you at ease."

She looked into his eyes, those intense, opaque pools that always seemed to see beyond the surface. "I guess I am a little nervous," she said.

"A little?" Tibor laughed. "Believe me, it wasn't the truck that was shaking."

"Very funny."

"Well, ready or not, you're about to make your debut as . . ." Suddenly, his eyes narrowed. He stared at her, rubbing his chin and adopting a pensive mode. "You need a gypsy name. What are we going to call you, Katalin?"

"Why call me anything?" The last thing Katalin wanted was to attract attention to herself.

"Katalin is a Magyar name. Magyars don't play with gypsies, remember?"

She nodded dumbly. Obviously, there was no way out of it.

The others began to make suggestions. "Carnation. Liberty. Jubilee."

Tibor shook his head at each one. None of them felt right. Off to the side, something distracted him. While the others continued to invent suitable sobriquets, he walked over to the gate leading toward the main house.

"Vadrósza," he said as he plucked a flower from the ground, his mouth broadening into a slow grin. "The wild rose!"

The others must have agreed because they slapped Tibor on the back, congratulated him and Katalin, and then left to set up. Clearly, the matter of her name was settled.

"Why Vadrósza?" Katalin asked.

Tibor took her hands in his, the pink bloom still in his grasp. His ebony eyes fixed on hers.

"Because you're as beautiful as this flower, yet your music is wild. Your soul is soft like the petals of this rose, yet your spirit is sturdy, as if you, too, were protected by a cover of thorns. You're blossoming as a woman and as a musician, yet you don't want to be confined to the small space of a courtyard garden. You want to grow free, to wander wherever conditions allow." He lifted one of her hands and touched each of her fingers. "A wild rose has five petals, just like the fingers on your hand. Nature produces great beauty in those five petals. Your hand produces equal beauty with these five fingers." He handed her the wild rose, giving her time to examine it.

"Yes," he said, noting the soft smile that had curled her lips. "Vadrósza is perfect."

"I like it," Katalin said in a shy but delighted voice. "I like it a lot."

Tibor grinned as suddenly, quite unexpectedly, she snapped off the thorns and stuck the clean, green stem between her breasts, letting the flower peek out over the edge of her blouse.

"I guess that makes it official," she said, pleased with the effect.

Tibor responded by swooping down into a low bow. "Come, Vadrósza," he said with excessive gallantry. "Your public awaits."

The Brunswick castle had boasted no less than Ludwig von Beethoven as a frequent guest. Rumor had it that he came to see the mistress of the manor, Josephine Brunswick. According to Beethoven scholars, she was the "immortal beloved" to whom he addressed his love letters, the woman who was believed to have inspired both the "Moonlight" and the "Appassionata" sonatas.

For Katalin, the thrill of that particular evening was enjoying the secret irony of playing cimbalom with a gypsy band beneath the same bower of beech and sycamore trees where each summer the State Symphony Orchestra performed Beethoven symphonies and where—the summer before she had left for New York—she herself had performed the "Emperor" concerto.

As Tibor had predicted, the audience was made up of commonfolk, the kind who used a night like this to erase the hardships of a long, arduous week. As the band played, they clapped their hands and stomped their feet in time to the rhythm. During a slow *lassú* they became a human chain, linking arms with their neighbors, swaying from side to side along with the soulful melody. When Vadrósza and Tibor dueted on a lightning-fast *csárdás*, they leapt to their feet and demanded an encore.

For Katalin, the experience was like an electrical charge. When she performed with an orchestra, she felt different from when she soloed in a recital. There was a sharing in a concerto, a give and take between orchestra and instrumentalist, an inspiring of one to the other that didn't exist in a solo performance. Alone on a stage, it was a singular sense of power, a mastery of the moment when her hands could create the music that would control the audience. Each of these created a special feeling for her, but this . . . this was different.

As she struck the metal wires with her leather-covered hammers, watching several people take to their feet to dance on the lawn, she realized what set this performance apart. This was like those nights at Zsuzsanna's Csárda when she had played to an appreciative crowd. Then as now, the audience felt friendly, approachable, as if this were a party and they were all guests. Unlike a concert hall, where the audience's response was proffered from a distance, this was pure emotion. Katalin loved it.

And everyone loved her—just as they did each subsequent time she performed with Tibor's band. Whether she had planned it or not, whether she liked it or not, it wasn't long before Vadrósza, the wild gypsy woman of the cimbalom, had gained a reputation throughout the humble Hungarian countryside.

A year after Vadrósza's debut, on another night in August, Andras approached Zoltán with his latest idea. Though he had been rebuffed dozens of times already, Andras was convinced that this time, Zoltán would not—could not—reject him.

"The guest conductor for the Academy's annual concert has cancelled," he said casually, sipping his coffee.

"That's too bad," Zoltán said, biting into a piece of cherry strudel.

"It's worse than too bad. It's a disaster."

Zoltán flashed Andras a disbelieving look. "You're exaggerating."

"I don't think so. As chairman of the concert committee, I know that the biggest event of the Academy's season is only four months away and I have no conductor . . . what else could you call it other than a disaster?"

"You'll find someone," Zoltán said in his usual disinterested tone.

"How about you?" Andras dropped the question as casually as one might drop a spoon. The difference was, Zoltán might have picked up the spoon. He ignored the comment.

"Papa, did you hear Uncle Andras?" Katalin said, truly excited. "He asked if you would conduct."

"I heard him and I'm ignoring him," Zoltán said to his daughter, turning his back on his friend. "The heat has fried his brains."

"It's a wonderful idea, Zoltán, and you know it." Ilona rarely spoke sharply to anyone close to her, but she was growing impatient with Zoltán. He was making mourning a habit and she didn't like it. More important, she knew Mária wouldn't have liked it.

"Music is no longer a part of my life," he said, reciting the mantra he had chanted for years.

"Only because you won't let it be," Katalin said.

Zoltán's head snapped in her direction. He couldn't believe his own child would utter something so disloyal, so disrespectful.

"You don't need manual dexterity to be a conductor," Andras said, blunting an anticipated comment about his hands. "But you do need a musical soul, a genius for understanding how to interpret what the composer intended. You have that soul, Zoltán. You have that genius. Why not use it?"

Zoltán refused to answer. He couldn't. His head was throbbing with the memory of what Mária had said to him on her deathbed: *You still have that music, Zoltán. You just have to set it free.*

"This is a perfect opportunity for you, Papa. I think you should consider it."

"I'm a violinist, not a conductor." Zoltán's response was guarded and self-protective, like someone who knew he had been ambushed.

"You're a factory worker and a part-time taxi driver," Ilona said, correcting him, forcing him to see something he had blinded himself to for much of his life.

Her words were like a needle puncturing Zoltán's heart. His face creased from the pain of the truth in what she had said.

"Sometimes life compels us to make compromises." Andras had determined not to let up, even if later he were accused of badgering. "When you and I met, I wanted to be a businessman. Music was a part of my life, but I had never intended it to be my entire world. Yet here I am, a piano tutor. I was supposed to be running a manufacturing plant. It was taken from me. Fortunately, the talent God gave me wasn't. So I've used it. And do you know what? I've enjoyed it. Your hands were taken away from you, but the talent God gave you is still there. You've buried it and mourned it and tried your damndest to forget about it. But you can't. I'm offering you a chance to use that talent, Zoltán. So it's with a baton and not a bow. It's music and that should be all that matters!"

Open the door to the prison where you keep your music . . . let it out.

He heard Mária's voice. He tried to listen to what Andras was saying. In frustration, Zoltán shook his head. The barricades had gone up.

"I think you're being selfish," Judit said, astounding everyone at the table with her forthrightness. "For as long as I've known you, Uncle Zoltán, you've been wallowing in what happened to you in Recsk. It was a tragedy—no one disputes that—but you didn't die. You weren't crippled or maimed beyond recognition. Your fingers were crushed. It's been years. Isn't it about time you got on with your life?"

"That is what I'm trying to do," Zoltán snapped, annoyed at Judit's tone, equally annoyed that no one chastized her in his defense.

"That's not what I see. Papa's offering you an opportunity. Instead of jumping at it, you're turning your back on it."

"I'm happy the way I am."

"No, you're not." Katalin refused to be cowed by her father's growing anger. She saw it. She felt it. At one time she would have retreated from it, but not now. "You're miserable and you're making everyone around you miserable."

"Including you?" he said in the same incredulous tone as Caesar must have used when Brutus stabbed him on the steps of the Roman Senate.

"Yes, Papa, including me." Katalin fixed her father in her sights and took aim, knowing that by striking him she risked losing him. *Then again*, she told herself, arming herself, *weren't they doing all this because they feared he was lost already?* "I came back to Budapest because I love you and Mama. She was dying. I wanted to be with her and with you. But you were never with me. Not for one minute during Mama's illness or after her death. You were with her. And then you retreated into yourself, which is where you've remained. Not once have you asked me if I'm all right, if I miss Mama, if my life has been turned upside down. Well, I'm going to tell you what you haven't bothered to ask. I miss Mama terribly. I loved her and I'll miss her every single day for the rest of my life."

Her words tangled in a lump in her throat. She swallowed quickly, wiped her eyes and continued, firmly resolved that he should hear it all.

"There are others whom I miss. In New York, there's a man I had planned to marry. I love him very much, Papa, but our dreams have been squashed. I can't get to him. He can't come to me. I had friends, another year at Juilliard. I had a concert career poised and ready to fly. That, too, is finished."

Katalin and István had made plans to marry . . . help them find their way back to each other.

"Are you blaming me for all this?" Zoltán's face had flushed bright red. Though no one could see, his hands were shaking. Katalin had never spoken to him this way, even privately, much less in front of others. He was shocked—by how she spoke as well as by what she said.

"No. What I do blame you for is my interminable loneliness. We eat in silence. We sit in the same room in silence. You come and go without a word. I come and go without you caring where I've been. Sometimes I wonder if you care whether I come back. We aren't a family. We aren't anything. And the reason is that you refuse to be anything except a shadow of your former self."

Zoltán's face drained of color as the depth of his daughter's unhappiness, and the realization of his daily contribution to it, struck him. Judit was right. He was selfish. He had been wallowing in self-pity, and not just since Mária's death. For years he had indulged himself in pity, insisting that others go out of their way to compensate for his misfortune. Andras was right. Katalin was right. He was nothing more than a shadow of his former self.

"I don't know how to conduct," he said in a tone that asked forgiveness, more for his lack of understanding than his lack of training.

Andras and Katalin glanced at each other quickly, knowingly. They had gotten to him. Zoltán had cracked. He was willing, but afraid of saying so, afraid of failing—both them and himself.

"Ah, but you do." Andras rose from his chair and, like the teacher he was, stood apart so he could make his point more dramatically. "A fine conductor is first and foremost a fine musician. You are that. The best conductors are those who have reached a professional performance level on an instrument. You've certainly done that. You're capable of hearing orchestral colors and timbres. You're knowledgeable about the historical context of the great composers. You're a musician who always identified with the music both technically and emotionally. And, last but not least, you're someone other musicians would respect."

"Guilty as charged," Judit said, laughing at her father's summation to the jury, pleased to see how happy Andras was at the prospect of finally repaying his debt to his old friend.

"I don't know," Zoltán mumbled, still unsure, still struggling with his fears.

"You know, Uncle Zoltán, when I decided to become an accompanist, everyone thought I was selling myself and my talent short, that I should be a soloist or nothing at all." Judit spoke directly to Zoltán, though Andras and Ilona knew her words were meant for them as well. "The past few years have proved me right. I'm happy with what I do and how I do it. I'm using my talent. I'm making a contribution. And I'm recognized and applauded for my efforts."

Though Zoltán didn't want to acknowledge her words, he had never heard Judit express herself this way. She was baring a private part of herself because of him, because she cared enough to want to reach him. He owed it to her to listen.

"I wasn't meant to be in a spotlight by myself," Judit continued, her voice soft and introspective. "In truth, I don't think I was ever comfortable standing alone in the glare. At one time in your life you were, but that wasn't meant to be, either. You decided that was the end of it. I'm telling you it's not. Music is like a highway, Uncle Zoltán, with lots of lanes. One is faster than the other, that's for sure, but they're all going in the same direction. Either way, you're going to get where you want to go."

Without commenting, Zoltán rose from his chair. He walked over to Judit, took her face in his hands, and kissed both her cheeks. "Thank you," he whispered.

Andras waited for Zoltán to return to his seat before speaking.

"I'm going to make it easy for you," he said with a triumphant twinkle. Zoltán eyed him carefully. Whatever Andras was about to say, he had saved for precisely this moment. "If you agree to conduct, I will arrange for this concert to be dedicated to Mária."

Zoltán looked from one to the other, from his only child to his only friends. Did they know that Mária was in this room, siding with them, counseling him? Did they know how important they were to him?

"I'll be happy to conduct your concert, Andras. In fact, I'd be honored. But I want you to know I'm not doing this solely for Mária. I'm doing this for all of you." With a hesitant hand, he reached out toward Katalin. "Especially you, *kicsi szilva*."

Katalin flung her arms around him and kissed his cheek. "Do it for yourself, Papa," she said as their tears met and mingled. "Do it for yourself."

Over the next four months Zoltán continued his daytime job, but at night, instead of driving a cab, he pored over musical scores, studying the composer's notations concerning dynamics and tempi. Through Andras, he arranged meetings with professors at the Academy to discuss conducting techniques. He spent endless hours listening to recordings of those he considered to be the finest conductors, analyzing the differences, comparing the similarities. And every night before retiring, he stood in front of a mirror and practiced leading an orchestra with à baton.

As his skills sharpened and his confidence grew, his mood brightened. His appetite increased. He was easier to talk to, more pleasant to be with. And he began taking an active interest in Katalin's life, a change that had both a positive and negative effect, for the closer attention he paid, the more difficult it became for Katalin to slip away unnoticed to play with Tibor.

On the night before the Academy concert, Katalin suspected rehearsals would run late. Afterward, Zoltán and Andras were scheduled to meet to review the program. When Tibor said he and the troupe were going to Tata, Katalin gladly signed on.

It was a disappointing outing. Farah accompanied them. As she did whenever she danced with the group, she turned a simple performance into a jousting match. She'd flaunt herself in front of Tibor, exceeding all limits of taste. She'd deliberately position herself in front of Katalin so the audience had no view of her. Often, she knocked into the cimbalom, jarring it, pushing Katalin's hammers onto the wrong strings, so it sounded as if she struck the wrong notes. This time Katalin pushed back.

During a break she took Farah aside.

"I don't know what your problem is," she snapped, "but your vulgar antics have to stop. You're messing up the band."

"No," Farah countered, baring her teeth. "You're messing up the band. You're a *gorgio*. We don't need your kind."

"Either you're a worse bigot than any Magyar I've ever met or you're a jealous woman who thinks I'm after her man. Well, I'm not. Tibor and I are friends. That's all."

With an angry leer, Katalin spun on her heels, leaving Farah alone in the parking lot. Farah's black eyes blazed at the other woman's back.

Farah was twenty years old. Having been pledged to Tibor when she was ten, she should have been long married by now, with at least three children bearing his name. Instead, she remained promised but unwed, a disgrace for her parents, a humiliation for herself. Tradition demanded that gypsies marry young—fourteen was not an unlikely age for a bride— yet something was preventing Tibor from doing the honorable thing. She used to think she was cursed, that without realizing it she had committed a crime against someone who sought revenge by jinxing her marriage. Now she knew it was his curse that maintained the wedge between them.

Music was the hex. Though she didn't completely understand it, Farah supposed that he was so bewitched, he believed he could transcend the barriers that existed between their world and the world of the *gorgio*, rise above the circumstances of his birth and perform onstage, outside the restaurant circuit. Every gypsy knew that was absurd. Yet Tibor persisted, practicing, performing, reading, listening to recordings, struggling and striving to better himself.

Why he would want to be part of the white man's world, she didn't know, but one thing was clear: Until he saw that there was absolutely no chance for him to move beyond his tribal circle, either she would have to seek dissolution of their marriage contract or exercise an unholy patience. She had up to now found the fortitude to wait, until Katalin Gáspár had insinuated herself into their lives.

Now, all Tibor talked about was her. Her beauty. Her talent. Her zest. Her musical verve. He could hardly wait for the next opportunity to play with her. When they were onstage together, it was as though they were in bed. The looks that passed between them, the excitement each generated in the other, the climactic joy they clearly felt at the end of each set—it was enough to make any woman jealous. And Farah wasn't any woman. She was gypsy. Tibor was bound to marry her, but what she wanted was for him to love her.

Though Farah knew Katalin the woman wasn't her competition—

Katalin the musician was—it didn't erase her bitterness or her anger. Katalin wasn't the cause of Farah's unhappiness or the root of her problem, but it was easier to hate the Magyar woman than to challenge Tibor.

It was late when Katalin returned home. She had her key in the door when Judit appeared from the shadows.

"You have to come with me," she whispered, her eyes fired with fear.

"What's the matter?"

"They've taken Attila," she said, her voice straining from the effort to silence her hysteria.

"You mean they've arrested him?"

"I wish it were that simple." Judit kept looking from side to side, convinced that she had been followed. "Please, Katya. Kovács Magda sent a message asking to meet me at Attila's coffeehouse. You know the one."

Katalin nodded.

"I'm afraid to go alone."

"Could this be a trap?" Katalin asked, knowing all too well how often the AVO convinced one member of a family to act as bait by threatening to kill another member of the family. "Could she be setting you up?"

Judit considered the possibility. "Maybe. She does have reason to dislike me, but no, I don't think so."

"Okay, then. Let's go."

When Judit donned a blond wig and glasses, Katalin was alarmed— if Judit felt the need to disguise herself, she *was* in danger. Yet Katalin was also amused. She wondered what Judit would think if she knew that Katalin also wore disguises, that Katalin was also leading a double life.

When they reached the underground café, a greasy-haired, pock-marked man led them to a table in a corner. It was so dark, Katalin almost tripped over the chair. Within seconds after they were seated, Magda Kovács joined them.

Whether it was age, or stress, or simply the effects of bad lighting Katalin didn't know, but Madame Kovács looked older than Katalin had imagined. Though her blond hair was plaited in a youthful braid, the color was dulled by an injection of gray. Her skin was doughy, her body tone slack, her manner sluggish. Her blue eyes were a shade that should have conjured images of cornflowers and summer skies, but there was too much red from too little sleep and too many dark circles from too many worries for anyone to see anything in those eyes but a beleaguered soul.

"He's gone," she announced without preamble.

"Fő Street?" Judit named the prison in a tone laced with disgust.

Magda shook her head no. Her eyes teared, her fingers curled into a bellicose fist. "Two men broke into our apartment about eight o'clock tonight."

"Who were they?" Judit demanded.

"I don't know. Police. Soldiers. The AVO. I'm not sure. One was young, handsome, but hard. The other was older." She shuddered. "He was ugly, terribly, terribly ugly, but worse than that, he enjoyed doing ugly things."

Katalin watched Judit's face pale. She too felt ill in anticipation of what was to come.

"The younger man had brought a copy of Attila's latest play. He read a page from it, ripped it out, turned to another page, read it and ripped that one out as well. By the time he was finished, the floor was littered with Attila's words. He never raised his voice," Magda said, still amazed that a man playing the role of the aggressor would speak so softly and with such control. "He kept telling Attila he wasn't seeing things as they were, that his vision of Hungary was distorted, that he was deliberately shutting out the good that was being done." Magda's eyes widened and then clamped shut, as if she was reliving the scene she was about to relate. "He asked Attila to recant what he had written. Attila refused. The man said he knew that Attila was smuggling his plays to the West, that that was an act of treason, that he was betraying his country. Attila laughed." Again, Magda's eyes closed. Her head fell into her hands and for several moments she wept.

"What happened?" Judit begged Magda to continue. She had to know the rest of it.

Magda wiped her eyes and looked directly at Judit. "The other man, the ugly one, threw acid in Attila's face. Then he laughed. It was such a hideous sound. He was so delighted to have been the one to blind Attila."

"Blind? What do you mean?" Judit's hands began to tremble. Katalin took them and held them.

"He's blind, Judit. I tried to wash the acid from his eyes, but it was too late. They dragged him out of the apartment. I tried to follow, but the ugly one held a gun on me until they got Attila into a car. He turned to look out the window while the car sped away, but by then his face was burned and scarred and his eyes were gray and sightless."

Judit gasped for breath. She yanked free of Katalin and held on to the table for support. "Where did they take him?"

"I don't know. I don't even know if he's still alive."

"We'll stage a protest," Judit said, thinking aloud, refusing even to comment on Magda's last statement. "We'll demand that they produce him so that everyone can see what they did. We'll force them to release him."

Magda's voice was low, but chilling. "You won't do anything of the kind. In case you have forgotten, Attila is my husband. I'll decide what's to be done about him, not you."

Judit bristled, but remained silent out of respect for the truth.

Katalin watched as Magda's tired eyes turned steely with purpose. She had not come here out of kindness or the need to share her grief. She had not come to see if Judit had any knowledge of Attila's whereabouts. She had come because there was something she needed done and she intended to use Judit, just as Katalin was certain Attila had used her.

"I've been given twenty-four hours to get out of the country. Before I go, I have to fulfill a promise I made to Attila." She reached inside her bra and extracted a key, which she held up in front of Judit. "Since they will search me and my baggage, I can't carry anything out. This is a key to a locker in Keleti Station where Attila hid all his manuscripts. Get them to the West."

Again Katalin wondered if this was a setup. It sounded authentic, but so did most well-run scams. She kicked Judit under the table, hoping Judit understood. She did.

"I don't know what you're talking about," Judit said innocently. "How would I know how to smuggle anything out of the country?"

"Stop it!" Magda reached across the table and grabbed Judit's hand. "Don't pull this naive act on me. You've been ferrying Attila's works over the border for years."

"I did it for him," Judit said, needing to take credit for what she had done, expecting to be praised.

"And he paid you."

"What do you mean?" Judit's entire body was trembling.

"He paid you in the currency you demanded," Magda said, losing patience. "You wanted him, he gave himself to you. For services rendered." She glared at Judit, not caring about the pain she saw in the younger woman's eyes. "Just consider the past few months with him payment in advance." She slapped the key down in front of Judit. "Stop feeling sorry for yourself. You thought you were his mistress. If you understood Attila at all, you would have known that you were simply another toy, another diversion from the reality of life. He wasn't a good husband and he wasn't a loyal lover. But he's a brilliant writer and his work deserves to be heard and seen. You can arrange that. Now are you going to let your wounded pride stand in the way of doing the right thing, or are you going to take this key and do what you're supposed to do?"

Katalin hated being a witness to Judit's embarrassment. She hated seeing the sadness and rejection that had chalked themselves on her face. More than that, she hated seeing her capitulate to Magda's demands. Beyond having verbally degraded Judit, the woman was insisting that Judit do something very dangerous. Katalin wondered if, perhaps, Magda wanted Judit to be caught.

When Magda left, Judit and Katalin stared at each other.

"I'm sorry you had to listen to that," Judit said.

"I'm only sorry for you," Katalin said, sliding onto the bench where Judit sat, moving next to her friend. "I know you loved him, and in his own way maybe he loved you. It doesn't matter now. You have your memories and his plays."

"Magda's right about the importance of getting them published."

"Yes, she is." Katalin could see that Judit was preparing both of them for the decision she had already made.

"I did smuggle his other plays out, you know."

"Yes, I know."

"I haven't done any of that for awhile, though."

"Because you were threatened."

Judit nodded. She didn't bother to ask how Katalin knew. It was enough that she did and hadn't mentioned it before. Judit knew she would never mention it to anyone else.

"It will take some doing, but I can get the job done." She studied the key. "My only problem is getting the manuscripts from Keleti Station. I know they follow me. And if they don't, when they search Magda and come up empty, they will."

"I'll get the manuscripts from the locker." Katalin said it quietly, quickly, as if she feared that if she spoke louder or slower she would come to her senses and recant what she had just said.

"You?" Judit was incredulous.

"Let's just say I know my way around there. I'll go tomorrow morning, during the rush."

The next morning, Katalin did as she promised. Donning her gypsy garb, she shuffled into Keleti as she had so many times before. Losing herself in the crowd that always filled the massive East Station, she made her way to Attila's secret locker. She checked to be sure no one was watching before she opened it. Without looking to see what was in there, she swept the contents into a ragged carpetbag and headed for the ladies room. There, she changed clothes and shifted the manuscripts into a leather briefcase more suited to her outfit. A look in the mirror to assure herself she looked like every other office worker and out she went.

She was supposed to meet Judit in the back of the synagogue on the corner of Wesselényi and Dohány utca at noon. It was after one when Judit arrived, her skin the color of white ash, her eyes filled with such terror Katalin was certain she had been arrested and tortured.

"Where have you been?" Katalin said in a harsh, nervous whisper.

"Attila's friend Egon called me. He had been outside the Kovács' apartment when Attila was abducted. He followed the car." Judit collapsed into the pew alongside Katalin. "They transferred him to one of those trains."

Judit didn't have to explain. Soviet trains still shipped dissidents and other undesirables to labor camps deep inside the Soviet Union. There were never any trains coming the other way.

"At least you know he's alive," Katalin said, digging deep for a bright side.

"For now." Judit nodded, as if that bit of knowledge was enough to soothe her pain, but then the dam burst. Resting her arms on the pew in front of her, she fell onto them and sobbed. "Magda was telling the truth. He's blind. Egon said he was stumbling, groping around for something to hold onto. He said that his face was horribly burned by the acid."

Katalin draped an arm around her friend, knowing there was nothing she could say to console her.

"Egon knows someone inside the police station. His source said he thought that once they got Attila outside the country, they were going to kill him."

"I don't think so," Katalin said, suspecting that death would be a relief for what Attila was about to endure. "He's a well-known figure. People will notice he's missing and ask about him, just as they have every other time he's been arrested."

"Maybe, but who's going to notice they sent him to Siberia? They could murder him and claim he committed suicide."

"That's true, Judit, but if this is any comfort, remember: No matter what they do, as long as the world has access to his plays, they can't silence him."

Katalin took Judit's hand. Together, each in her own way, they prayed for Attila Kovács.

Despite his lapses in character, despite his idiosyncracies and self-indulgences, he had been a visionary, a prophet, the articulate voice of the masses. They had arrested him and beaten him and imprisoned him time and time again. Still, he had been courageous enough to continue challenging the system.

Though Katalin knew she was correct in saying that even if they snuffed out his life, they couldn't mute his message, she lowered her head and prayed for God's mercy on the soul of Attila Kovács. Somehow, Judit would get his plays into the right hands. Somehow, his words would find their way onto the stage and into the international press. Somehow, he would be heard.

For now, however, the voice of the man the people called "Freedom's Playwright" had been stilled.

23

*F*ranz Liszt was one of Hungary's most famous sons. Unique, complicated, he existed in a class by himself. There was Franz Liszt, and then, there were all other pianists. When he played, he had infused his performances with such sensual energy, such electric magnetism, that women swooned, tossing their jewels onstage instead of flowers. They fought over the green gloves he casually, deliberately, left on the piano. They plucked broken strings from the piano, took them home, and enshrined them as one would a religious relic.

The Franz Liszt Academy of Music, established by and named for this exceptional man, was housed in a magnificent art nouveau building. As befitted its founder, who was as stellar a teacher as he was a performer, the school's reputation for excellence had spread far beyond its boundaries. With musicians such as Béla Bartók, Zoltán Kodály, Ernö Dohnányi, and Leo Weiner inscribing their names on the Academy's list of distinguished faculty, the institution and its graduates was a source of tremendous pride for all Hungarians. Each year the Academy's anniversary concert filled every one of the twelve hundred seats in its auditorium.

This night, Katalin thought, glittered more than others she recalled.

Though some might have said it was wishful thinking, she honestly believed that the excitement was due to her father, that most ticketholders considered it a coup to be present at the conducting debut of Zoltán Gáspár. As she and Ilona and Judit mingled with the crowd in the small hall on the first floor, listening to their conversations, she knew the concertgoers were curious. No one had ever understood why Zoltán had abdicated his crown in the royal circle of international concert stars. There had been no newspaper coverage of his stay in Recsk (even now, no one spoke that terrible word), no press release announcing his retirement, no explanation whatsoever as to why Hungary's premier violinist had suddenly, mysteriously, quit the stage.

As curtain time grew nearer, the buzz about his return heightened. Katalin could feel it. As she studied the faces of those who would soon become her father's jury, she crossed her fingers and prayed all would go well. Drawing on her own experience, she calmed herself by recalling the axiom that stage fright was a reverse barometer of the quality of a performance: The more nervous a performer was, the better the performance. If that was true, Zoltán was going to be fantastic. Getting dressed, he had been a veritable wreck. He couldn't tie his tie. He forgot to zip his trousers. He mis-buttoned his shirt. He fretted that he would forget the music. When she had suggested that he keep the score on a stand in front of him, he harrumphed out of the room. Though he knew some conductors did, he considered them inferior and would not—even at the risk of error—cast his lot with them. By the time Andras picked him up to take him to the hall, Katalin didn't know who was closer to a breakdown—Zoltán or her.

Actually, the one verging on nervous collapse was Judit. She, too, was surveying the crowd, but not because she was interested in whether or not they were predisposed to enjoy the concert and not because she was being sociable. She was looking for tails, for police flunkies dressed in civilian clothes. She was certain that she was under surveillance. The last thing she wanted was to be arrested in front of her parents. That morning, when she told Katalin she thought it would be best if she concocted an excuse and stayed home, it had taken all Katalin's powers to convince her otherwise.

"They're watching you. You have to remain cool. You can't let on that you know anything about Attila's arrest. If you do, they'll invent some reason to take you in and interrogate you. We've got the manuscripts. When the time is right, you'll do what you have to do. For now, you have to pretend that his absence means nothing to you."

Aside from a tightness around her mouth and eyes, Katalin thought Judit looked wonderful. Though she had pulled her hair back into a low, fluffy ponytail and sashed it in a soft black bow, a crop of brown curls danced on her forehead, giving her a delicate turn-of-the-century look. By adorning one of the black ankle-length sheaths she wore when she performed with a frothy lace collar and cuffs, she added to the illusion of another time and place. With lipstick now scarce, she and Katalin had shared a red, Judit dashing her lips with color brilliant enough to belie the lackluster state of her soul.

Ilona also had dressed for the occasion. It was so rare to see her in anything other than sensible work clothes, Katalin was shocked when the doctor appeared in a décolleté floral print with her hair sprung from its usual chignon, exhuberant in its unfettered state. She had rouged her lips and shadowed her eyes and dabbed her skin with a subtle but sexy perfume. Because she was wearing high heels, her legs appeared longer and shaplier, her body leaner, more sensuous. In truth, she looked like another woman, like the woman Andras used to talk about on those days during a lesson when something would prompt him to share with Katalin an image from the past. Then, he would describe Ilona and Mária as young women. He would speak of their beauty and their bravery and the quality of each of their souls. He would speak of the strength of their friendship, only relating the happy times, never the bad.

Recalling Andras's remembrances provoked a tear and a wish that her mother could have been with them tonight. Katalin would have given anything to have Mária sitting between her and Ilona as Zoltán mounted the conductor's platform. Another tear formed as she realized she had given everything and, still, Mária had died.

They had started for their seats when, suddenly, Katalin spotted him. Again, he was staring at her. Again, she felt the pull of those seal brown eyes. She had seen him for only a moment three years before at Mária's funeral, but she recognized him immediately. She leaned over and whispered in Judit's ear, directing her to look at the officer standing by the eastern doors. Judit did. Katalin did. He was gone.

"Who is he?" Judit asked.

"I have no idea. I thought you might know."

"I make it my business to know as few military men or policemen as possible," Judit said. "It's bad for my health, you know."

Katalin grinned, grabbed her friend's arm and hurried to catch Ilona. The concert was about to begin. She'd worry about the officer later. Now, she had to focus on Zoltán.

Zoltán had forgotten what an Elysium the concert stage was. He had forgotten that when the orchestra birthed its music and glorious eruptions of sound swirled around you, you were transported out of reality into a place that transcended time. Then, there was no audience, no auditorium, no critics, no officials to please or displease. There was no past to revive or regret, no future to plan or pursue. There was only the imperative the music created.

His first offering was "Má Vlast"—My Country—a cycle of six symphonic poems composed by the founder of Czech music, Bedřich Smetana. Bohemian in flavor, nationalistic in tone, this was a piece that had always moved Zoltán. Like Kodály, Smetana based his compositions on the folk tunes of the peasantry. He enlarged them and enhanced them, but the Czech spirit remained at the core of whatever he did. Knowing that Smetana had been a friend of Liszt's, knowing that since the Prague Spring of '68, many Hungarians secretly felt ashamed at their government's alliance with the Soviets against the Czechs, Zoltán had decided that this was the perfect opening piece, a tribute to the man whose name adorned the facade of the Academy. More than that, it was a way of stirring his countrymen without angering their occupiers. Hungarians felt a kinship with the Czechs. The Soviets felt a kinship for no one. But since Smetana was not on the forbidden list—Zoltán believed it was an oversight by Kocsis—Zoltán could not be challenged on its selection.

The uproarious applause proved him correct. As he turned and faced the audience to take his bows, he felt a sense of joy he had believed he would never feel again. Andras has been so right. It didn't matter whether it was with a bow or a baton, his life was meant to include music. When he exited to give the stagehands time to position the piano, he went straight for Andras and hugged him.

"Thank you, my friend." His voice was garbled with emotion, but he knew he didn't have to say anything else. Andras understood.

"You were wonderful," Andras said, grabbing Zoltán by the arms and embracing him. "But remember, I'm on next and I'm the soloist. I don't want you hogging the stage the way you used to when we played together."

For a moment, each of them could see the red velvet music room. For a moment, they were young. Zoltán's Guarneri was tucked under his chin. Andras was seated at the mahogany Bösendorfer. And though the world was spewing death and destruction with the unstoppable flow of an Etna, those two young men had managed to find beauty through music.

"Just try to keep up." Grinning, Zoltán affectionately straightened Andras's tie.

"Just try and lose me," Andras shot back.

"Never," Zoltán said, his smile gone, his heart in his eyes. "Never."

• • •

Andras's Concerto No. 1 in E minor was brilliant. Ilona knew he had never played this or any other piece with such perfection. As she listened to her husband bring the Chopin to life and heard the orchestra paint a subtle background to his portrait, knowing it was the conductor who insisted upon flattering, not overwhelming the soloist, she thought that just for an instant she could see the heavenly cord that connected Andras with the balding, graying man on the podium. She blinked and the golden string became invisible, but she knew it was there. She knew that as surely as she was sitting between their daughters, those two men were knitted together with stitches too tight for war or death or injury or even personal jealousy to unravel.

The music swelled and ebbed, the melody growing more and more hypnotic. With each measure, Ilona felt herself sliding between the present and the past.

Watching Andras onstage, seeing the delicacy with which his fingers caressed the keys, listening to this flawless, haunting performance, it seemed inconceivable that this man had once been a commando who had risked his life to save others. To this day, she had never asked him whether or not he had killed anyone. Certainly, he had never volunteered it. Yet in her heart she knew. Face to face with a Nazi or a Nyilas, her quiet, elegant, cultured husband had undoubtedly become an instrument of vengeance.

What would he think if he knew what she was doing, she wondered. And had been doing for years? What would he think if he knew that she had involved their daughter in a hazardous form of espionage? Inside, she giggled. More than anything, he would be shocked. It wasn't that he didn't consider her courageous, it was simply that he had defined the borders of her bravery. In his mind, she was valiant within the walls of a hospital, within the realm of healing. He never thought of her in any other way. Which, she supposed, was why she had been able to keep her furtive activities from him all these years.

Now, however, Judit's dilemma could bring everything into the open. This matter of Attila Kovács's manuscripts was extremely sensitive. The regime of János Kádár would be unconcerned about the internal negative opinion that might be generated by Kovács's arrest, but Kádár and his henchmen could not afford to have the outside world hear the truth in Kovács's plays.

Ilona dared a peek at her daughter. She was very proud of Judit. Not only was she talented and bright and willing to step forward to declare herself—despite the danger—she had grown into a lovely young woman, albeit an unhappy one. Ilona had known about Judit's affair with Attila Kovács, but since Judit hadn't sought her approval, Ilona hadn't been forced to withhold it. She would have, though. She didn't question Kovács's brilliance. She had gone with María to see one of his plays and, also through María, had read much of his poetry. She believed in his philosophy of dissent. She agreed with his politics. She applauded his bravery. But she hadn't wanted him to break her daughter's heart. Worse, he had put Judit's life in danger and though Ilona pitied him for what the AVO had done and what the Soviets might do to him in Siberia, she could never forgive him for using her child.

Again, she glanced sideways. Tonight, with her hair back and her neck collared in lace, Judit looked very much like the woman for whom she was named. Once more, the past insisted upon asserting itself. Ilona remembered the day Judit was born. Andras had asked if she wanted to name their child Sarí, after her mother. Ilona had been adamant. Jews named their children after the dead, as a memorial. In 1949, Ilona still clung to the faint hope that by some miracle her parents had escaped the death camps and were alive.

"Maybe they found their way to Israel," she had said. "For all we know, they're living in Russia or Yugoslavia or maybe even in America."

Judit Strasser's death, on the other hand, was a fact witnessed by her own son. Because Ilona had adored her mother-in-law, she had delighted in the notion of her newborn daughter carrying on the name of such a remarkable woman. She had liked the idea of this tiny baby being graced with a name that, for Ilona, had always been associated with nobility. Over the years, she had noticed similarities between the baroness and her namesake: a strong will, a sense of humor, a preference for bright colors and textured fabrics, manual nimbleness and a love for needlework. Yet because she had loved the first Judit so genuinely, and because the pain of her gruesome death still lay heavily on Ilona's heart, she had never, in twenty-six years, called Judit by the diminutive, Jutka.

The original Judit had been an optimist. She had believed that goodness and right would always prevail. Ilona recalled that, once, during the darkest hours of that terrible time, when she had lapsed into a moment of panic and despair, Judit had put her arms around her and said, "I know it looks as if evil is going to triumph, but it won't. Ultimately, it never has. Evil has conquered and ruled. But sooner or later, the people have always risen up and demanded that evil be squashed. Protect yourself during this black night so that you can be here to see the sun shine tomorrow."

Ilona was still waiting for the night of Soviet occupation to end.

Each day, it was harder to believe the sun would ever shine, but Ilona kept the faith, protecting herself and her family as best she could. Three years ago, when Judit had been threatened outside the convent where Mária was buried, Ilona had notified Phil King. Through an intermediary, they had decided that rather than gamble on exposing an entire network of people and jeopardizing an international operation, they would simply put the machine in neutral, letting it idle until the pressure eased, or something so urgent materialized that the end justified whatever risks the means entailed.

This morning, Ilona had sent a message to Phil King.

The reception following the concert was as gala as anything in Kádár's Hungary. As the audience filed out of the concert hall, those who had been invited to attend the postperformance supper retreated to the hall on the first floor. When Katalin saw Zoltán, she almost burst into tears. Instead, she flung her arms around his neck and hugged him.

"You were so wonderful, Papa," she said. "I was so proud, so happy, so . . . so . . . I don't know what."

Despite the crowd gathering around them, father and daughter closed them out, insisting on this one private moment.

"Before you or Andras or Ilona say it, I'll say it for you. I should have done this years ago." He was beaming.

"None of that matters now," Katalin said, kissing both his cheeks.

"You matter," he said, pulling her nearer, turning serious. "I want you to be happy, cica. Tomorrow, we shall sit and have a long talk about how to do that."

"I'm fine, Papa. You just . . ."

"Excuse me." It was the officer with the seal brown eyes. "I don't mean to interrupt, but I had to offer my congratulations, Gáspár Zoltán." He clicked his heels and proffered a crisp bend at the waist in Zoltán's honor. "It was a pleasure to be part of the audience for this historic concert."

"Köszönöm szépen," Zoltán replied, accentuating his thank-you-very-much with an equally neat bow. "And you, sir, are?"

"Major Böhm László."

"Well, Major. May I introduce my daughter, Gáspár Katalin."

László Böhm turned toward Katalin with an eagerness that could not be concealed. He took her hand and raised it to his lips, stretching the moment, proceeding far more slowly than protocol allowed. The prolonged gesture unnerved Katalin. She felt as if every eye were on her, watching this man publicly ogle her. Yet a quick glance assured her no one was watching. Andras and Ilona had burst upon Zoltán like a thundercloud, enveloping him in their embrace. Judit had lost herself somewhere in the crowd. Everyone else was a stranger. How odd that this unknown man pressing his lips against her hand did not seem a stranger to her.

"I've always been a great admirer of your talents as well, Miss Gáspár."

His eyes traveled from her face to the curve of her neck, to the bareness of her chest, pausing on the graceful swell of flesh above her gown. Katalin had worn the black strapless she had bought for the Chickering. She knew her choice of raiment would raise eyebrows, but tonight was a special occasion; she had wanted to wear something in which she felt special. For modesty's sake she had cloaked her shoulders with a cape, but it had grown so warm in the small room that she had removed it. Judging by the looks she was receiving, many people were shocked. The major was not one of them.

"Finally being able to meet you instead of staring at you from afar, I can see that the only thing that exceeds your talent is your beauty." His eyes panned her body like an explorer reconnoitering new terrain. "You really are quite exquisite."

"That's very kind."

"It's not kind at all. It's honest." His eyes bored through her, past the facade of sociability. Though she tried to resist, that same magnetic hold she had felt in the graveyard, she felt now.

"Why were you at my mother's funeral?" she blurted, uncomfortable in the glare of his gaze.

"I was there out of respect for the magnificent Gáspár Mária." He smiled and his round face softened, making him look boyish and somewhat shy. "I had to go. I know it sounds presumptuous, but I felt a tremendous loss at her passing. As you can see, I'm an avid admirer of those in the arts. I'm quite envious of talent."

Katalin felt as if she were being drowned in a flood of flattery. Though she tried to remain afloat, the water level was rising. "I would think that to be a major at such a young age takes a great deal of talent," she said.

"I thank you for the compliment, but the military requires a different kind of skill. Especially in peacetime."

Katalin found it fascinating that he considered this a peace. She supposed that for someone trained to fight battles, it was. For the ordinary man and woman on the street, who felt oppressed by the ubiquitous presence of the Hungarian Army and the Soviet forces, it felt very different indeed. She was about to challenge him, but caught herself. That instinct—to confront and dispute—was something she had learned in America. It was something she might have done with Steven. But this wasn't New York and the man in front of her wasn't Steven.

A waiter came by with glasses of fruit brandy. *"Pálinkát?"*

"Plum, please," Katalin said, taking the glass handed her, watching as László did the same.

"Egészségére!" he said, as he touched his glass to hers with the same titillating delicacy as when his lips had touched her flesh. In spite of herself, she felt a twinge of excitement.

They sipped their brandy in silence, yet the messages conveyed over the tops of their glasses were louder than the din of the crowd.

"I would like very much to take you to dinner, Miss Gáspár. Would it offend you if I asked to see you as soon as this Saturday evening?"

It seemed impossible to believe that a simple request could create such a cyclonic response, but suddenly Katalin felt besieged by a storm of emotions. She was attracted to Major László Böhm, but along with that attraction had come feelings of guilt, of disloyalty, of betrayal. She was supposed to be in love with Steven Kardos. Love was supposed to be eternal. Why, she didn't know, but she looked down at her finger where a ring should have been. There was none. She looked inside her heart for assurances that Steven loved her. There were none. She searched her mind, trying to conjure an image of Steven's face, so desperate for proof of the continued rightness of their relationship she was willing to settle for a mere specter as evidence. None appeared. Steven's face had faded from her immediate memory, receding into that dark place called *long ago*, next to the bleaker spot called *never again*.

"No," she said in a cautious voice—testing, daring, waiting for Steven's voice to tell her not to do what she was about to do—"I wouldn't be offended at all."

"Then you'll accept my invitation?"

"Yes," she said, keeping her eyes firmly locked on his, refusing to look back. "I accept."

Steven Kardos never would have said, "I don't know when it happened. One day I turned around and everything was different." He was not a man who believed life simply evolved, smoothly shifting from one cycle to another with the imperceptible motion of a planetary revolution. For him, the world had jerked from one station to the next, catapulting him from one stage to the next, ready or not.

If asked, Steven could pinpoint the exact day on which each major change in his life had occurred. The day his parents were killed. The day he arrived in Woodridge, Kentucky. The day he landed in Vietnam. The day Katalin Gáspár disappeared.

Each date had marked the onset of an extended period of almost unbearable anguish. After each incident, like an eclipse, the world had turned black. Steven had hung on, riding out the darkness as best he could, clinging to his sanity, doing whatever was needed to make it to that moment when the sun shone again. Those who espoused the theory that we learn more from bad times than good, might have said that those bleaker periods of Steven's early life taught him the skills he would need to succeed later on, that the teeth of his character had been cut on those pitiable calamities. And yes, when he looked at it objectively, he supposed he was the better for having suffered and survived, but emotionally, Steven knew he was scarred.

Sublimation had become his weapon against stress. As a young boy, he had buried his frustrations in schoolwork for Nell Mahoney. In Vietnam, it was in learning as much as he could about soldiering and leading and keeping himself and his men alive. During the four years since Katalin had gone, he had done nothing but study and work for Owen Rhinehart. He didn't date. He had no friends other than those on the Senator's staff. He took no vacations. He had no leisure activities. The last thing he wanted was time to think about Katalin and what had gone wrong.

When she returned to Hungary, he had left his address with Zsuzsanna before heading to Georgetown. He wrote many times over the next several months, waiting to hear from her, calling New York once a week to be certain that Zsuzsanna hadn't forgotten to send him his mail or that the postal service hadn't chosen this time to renege on their "neither rain nor sleet nor snow . . ." pledge of efficiency. He had believed, as had everyone else, that she would write, and then after Mária had died and she had helped her father adjust, would return to him and the life she had begun in New York. But there were no letters, no postcards, no phone calls. She hadn't simply gone away. She had vanished.

Steven refused to accept her lack of communication. Despite her preoccupation with her mother and her concern for her father, Steven remained convinced that Katalin would have found the time to write. Believing that political stumbling blocks had been thrown in their path, Steven began to mail letters from different locations, hoping that postmarks from places other than New York would fool the censors. When, after a year and a half, that ruse had not produced so much as a card, he appealed to Senator Rhinehart to use his influence to find out whether

Katalin had tried to leave and her exit was mired in red tape, or if there was some other reason for her silence.

"According to the boys at our embassy, their Hungarian contacts say there's no reason you haven't heard from her other than the fact that she hasn't written," Owen had told him in his normal blunt manner. "They claim the days of censoring the mail are over. And besides, they said, kind old János Kádár would never stand in the way of true love, especially when the Romeo in this romance is a native son and the Juliet is one of Hungary's prize pianists."

Hadn't written. Pain marked Steven's face immediately. Rhinehart's manner turned gentle.

"They could be lying, you know. Commies are known for that."

Could be? Steven didn't know how to deal with the implications contained within those words. Could it be that once Katalin's feet touched her native soil, she decided she preferred it there, that the New World was indeed a strange and frightening world, and that her love for Steven wasn't enough to compensate for all she would be leaving behind? Could it be that she had never loved him at all? Could it be that what had been love to him had been nothing more than another perq from her Salzburg scholarship—just a brief but satisfying affair with someone from your past?

Each answer cut like a knife. He bled, but in private, refusing to discuss Katalin's absence with anyone, including Matthew. To compensate for his heartache, he worked even harder, authoring position papers for the Senator through which he was gaining a reputation as one of the brightest, most diligent legislative assistants on Capitol Hill. In June, he graduated summa cum laude from Georgetown University and went to work full-time. He was twenty-nine years old.

Later that year, Jimmy Carter was elected President of the United States. Shortly after his election, he appointed his old friend and fellow Southerner—and one of his biggest campaign contributors—Senator Owen Rhinehart, as Ambassador to the Court of St. James. The first person Rhinehart asked to accompany him to London was the honest young officer he had met in a bombed-out building in Saigon, the hardworking young man who, over the past four years, had been an inspiration to the more privileged members of Rhinehart's staff, Steven Kardos.

"I know this is short order, but I need you to be in London next week as part of the advance team I'm sending over to start setting things up," Rhinehart said, pleased at Steven's enthusiastic response to his appointment. "Can you do it?"

"Yes, sir." Steven's expression showed a sudden conflict. "I mean, of course I'm honored and would love to be able to do whatever you ask, but, well, before I knew, I had planned to spend the weekend in Lexington with my brother."

They both heard the period at the end of that sentence. Steven was not going to volunteer to cancel that visit. And Rhinehart wasn't going to ask him. It was just that sort of loyalty that had drawn him to Kardos in the first place.

"Enjoy your weekend, son," he said, touched by the love of this young man for his brother. "Whenever you get to London, it'll be fine with me. Just as long as you're there when I get there."

After Steven's discharge from the army, Matthew had quit the mines and moved to Lexington to set up an investment firm with Walter Perry. Steven had visited him during his first Christmas vacation from Georgetown. If Steven was surprised to hear that Matthew was going into business—and the investment business at that—he was stunned when Matthew had presented him with a check for fifty thousand dollars.

"Where did you get this kind of money?" he asked, holding the check by two fingers, staring at it as if it were contaminated with some fatal disease.

"The day you left for Fort Polk, I opened two investment accounts, one for you and one for me. I funded each of them with twenty-five hundred dollars." He smiled at the look of astonishment on Steven's face. "We did well."

"To say the least." Steven was impressed.

"I took the eleven hundred dollars you had given me and put it in a savings account, just like I promised I would. At the end of each year, I took whatever interest had accrued and invested that as well."

"What did you buy? Gold?"

"Better. Utilities, energy stocks, and anything I could find related to computers. They're the coming thing."

"I thought you spent your days shoveling coal. How did you become such a financial wizard?"

"I used to wrap my lunch in *The Wall Street Journal*." Matthew laughed, remembering how he had studied the market results by the light of his helmet. "You read, you learn. You do. You make mistakes. You learn some more."

Steven just listened as Matthew talked about meeting Walter and poring over highs and lows and Dow Jones averages.

"I can't believe this." He shook his head in amazement. "I can't believe that my brother, a man who has spent most of his life in the boondocks, is so tuned in to the happenings of the New York Stock Exchange."

"It's not where you live," Matthew said, "it's what you want to do and how well you do it. That's the great thing about this country. There are thousands of people getting rich who've never been to New York or Washington or Los Angeles."

Again, Steven just shook his head. "I'm not putting you down. You just took me by surprise. I didn't know."

That bothered Steven. It made him feel negligent, uncaring, disinterested, all those things his brother never was with him. Why hadn't he known what Matthew was up to? Because he had been too steeped in his own brew, too self-obsessed to see beyond his nose.

"You're really an impressive guy," Steven said, humbled by his brother's success.

"Me? All I did was make some money," Matthew said, as uncomfortable as always when the spotlight was on him. "You're the impressive one. A captain in the army. On scholarship at Georgetown. On the staff of a United States senator. One of these days, I expect to see you running for President."

Matthew grinned and raised his glass, toasting his younger brother. Steven's glass remained on the table. His mouth remained set.

"I've always had the advantages because you've always made the sacrifices." Steven's guilt had spilled onto his face, washing it a pale dun. "Whatever I've achieved, I couldn't have done without you. I'm embarrassed to think that you can't say the same thing. You've gotten where you are all by yourself."

Matthew put his drink on the table. He rested his arms on his knees and leaned forward.

"When Mama and Papa and Vera died, I became the elder. I did what the elder was supposed to do. I cared for the younger. I never minded my role and I never considered it a burden. I did the best I could, but I did it for myself. I love you, István, and your success is my success. We're brothers. And there's nothing more binding or more powerful than blood."

He reached across the table, grabbed Steven's hand and squeezed it. They were grown men, yet there was no embarrassment at the tears that fell.

Steven couldn't speak. He was lost in a swirl of memories. Suddenly, they were guarding the cave in the forest outside Budapest. They had been so frightened and vulnerable then. Life had loomed as a fragile construction, easily crushed, easily destroyed. Yet Steven remembered the confidence Matthew had displayed. It had been a sham, of course,

Steven knew that now; but then, it had taken Herculean courage not to give in to your fears, to sound brave even though, inside, every part of you was trembling. He thought about how Matthew had struggled with the language at Camp Kilmer, insisting that the authorities find János Vas, refusing to separate from Steven. If not for Matthew, they might have been sent to different homes, raised in different states. They might not have grown up as brothers. The thought was devastating.

"So tell me about this business you're going into," Steven said, wiping his eyes, shooing away all bad thoughts, focusing only on the good. "Isn't it a bit risky?"

Matthew shrugged his shoulders. "What have I got to lose?"

To Steven, it was the most uncharacteristic move he'd ever seen his brother make, the most uncharacteristic thing he'd ever heard him say. Matthew was innately conservative, careful, always questioning. When he'd had nothing, he acted as if he had everything to lose.

"Fifty thousand dollars, that's what!"

"So what's my alternative, staying in the mines? Working until I retire or die of black lung disease?" Matthew's face grayed. "I'd rather take my chances."

Steven lifted the check Matthew had given him from the table. "I'll take a chance on you too," he said, turning the check back to his brother.

"What are you doing? You need this for college."

"I've got the GI Bill, remember? I've got a Georgetown scholarship. And I've got a job. Besides, I've got that bank account you set up for me. I don't need this and if I do, you'll sell something off. I want to be your first customer."

A slow smile edged onto Matthew's lips. "This means a lot to me," he said.

"You mean a lot to me," Steven said.

Four years had passed since then. Perry & Kardos was prospering. This time, instead of a check, Matthew presented Steven an accounting of everything in his stock portfolio and its current face value. It was worth in excess of two hundred thousand dollars.

"Just keep doing whatever it is you do," Steven said, with honest amazement. "You've got the touch."

Matthew was pleased. "I did take the liberty of liquidating a few stocks. I know ambassador's aides don't make a lot of money. You might need some new clothes. You might want to travel while you're in Europe. I thought you might need a nest egg." He handed Steven an envelope. Inside was a check for twenty thousand dollars. "I'd suggest putting it into a bank with branches in the U.K. That way, if you need it, you have it," he said. Matthew eyed his brother before he continued. "Do you think you'll get back to Hungary?"

Steven shook his head. Too quickly for Matthew's liking. "Not unless Rhinehart has some reason to go there."

"What about on your own?"

Steven knew what Matthew was asking. "I have no reason to go there," he answered.

"I'm sure it's changed a lot in twenty years. Aren't you curious?"

"You have many good traits, Matthew. Subtlety is not one of them. I'm not going to try to see Katalin. I haven't heard a single word from her in four years. I can take a hint."

"How do you know she's hinting at anything?"

"Because Rhinehart checked it out. The people his people spoke to said there was only one reason I didn't hear from her. She didn't want to have anything to do with me."

"Uh-uh." Matthew shook his head and waved his hand, dismissing what Steven had said. "I don't care what bullshit is coming out of there these days. Reform or no reform, Hungary is still behind the Iron Curtain. You can't believe anything unless you see it and hear it firsthand."

Steven's temper boiled. "For Christ's sake, Matthew! It's over. It's done. I got the message."

"I think you're reading it all wrong."

"Oh really?" Steven said, raising his voice. "This is rejection. Pay attention. Some day this might happen to you."

Matthew leaned back on his couch, folded his hands behind his head and laughed. "It already has, brother dear," he said, grateful that enough time had passed that he could laugh about what had happened with Lucinda Crown. "That's why I know what it looks like and what it feels like. Rejection isn't usually this quiet. When a woman wants you out of her life, she tells you so. Loud and clear."

Steven's anger ebbed as his curiosity heightened. "Who? When? How come I never met her? Or did I? Are you talking about Sophie?"

Again, Matthew laughed. "For one, yes." He had never and would never tell anyone about Lucinda. "Every time I see her, she makes it perfectly clear that she wants nothing to do with me."

"I heard that," Steven said. "*Every time.* How often do you see her?"

The laugh faded to a mysterious smile. "Not very often. She does call whenever she plays one of the clubs in town. We go out to dinner. I catch her act. That's about it."

There was regret in Matthew's voice.

"At one time, you couldn't stand Sophie. What happened?"

"When I first met her," Matthew explained, "I thought she was a brash, obnoxious New York broad with a lot of attitude. Seeing her onstage, I guessed that her life was more of an act than her performance. Seeing her in the hospital, so weak and scared and vulnerable, confirmed it. There was another layer. Knowing that made me more interested."

"How interested are you?"

"Don't get excited. I'm not one for one-night stands. Besides, she's headed for Hollywood. I'm staying here." Matthew checked his watch. Steven had a flight to catch. "And you're going to London."

"That I am," Steven said, rising reluctantly. "I'm going to miss you, big brother."

"I'll miss you too, but we'll keep in touch." Matthew wrapped his arms around Steven, hugging him, holding him. "Just do well and have fun."

"I'll make you proud," Steven said, ever the little boy seeking approval.

"You always do," Matthew said, ever the elder, granting that approval without conditions. "You always do."

24

"The ambassador and his entourage have arrived. They're settling in to their private quarters even as we speak. Is everything set for dinner?"

Clarke Estridge had a way of speaking that annoyed the hell out of Steven. His nose was pinched, his lips barely moved, and his back teeth appeared to have been welded together. It was as if he didn't dare breathe properly in the presence of someone so far beneath his ancestors-who-came-over-on-the-Mayflower station.

"As far as I know," Steven said. "The pig is on the spit. The corn is husked. The coals are all fired up. And Mammy Yokum's got a deep-dish apple pie in the oven. It's going to be a real humdinger of a down-home American meal."

"You're not funny, Kardos."

"Neither am I a steward, a downstairs maid, his lordship's personal valet, or a chef. If you have questions about dinner, ask one of them." Without looking back, Steven strode down the long hall of the embassy, toward the offices where he felt more comfortable and more in control.

He and Estridge and the rest of Rhinehart's staff had been in London for a month, designating space, arranging a social calendar, hiring additional personnel—readying the embassy for the ambassador. Steven's brief was to familiarize himself with local politics and to bring himself up to date on what the United States's allies were saying about the U.S. and each other, as well as discerning where they stood on matters relating to the rest of the world. Although he had distinguished himself analyzing domestic issues, Rhinehart had expressed great confidence in Steven's ability to ferret out the issues he would have to deal with as America's ambassador to Great Britain. Steven had been working night and day so as not to prove the ambassador's judgment about him wrong.

Because there was so much to study and so little time in which to do it, Steven's desk was a mass of newspapers and file folders and hastily scribbled notes. 1976 had been a hectic year. The United States had celebrated its bicentennial. James Callaghan had succeeded Harold Wilson as Britain's Prime Minister. More than one hundred South African blacks had been slain in riots stemming from apartheid. An Israeli commando raid had freed one hundred hostages from Uganda's Entebbe Airport. The British ambassador to Ireland had been killed by a land mine. There were protests in Poland over high food costs. East Germany was cracking down on dissidents, disallowing emigration. The Soviets and the U.S. had signed a pact limiting the size of underground nuclear tests. Mao Tse-tung and Chou En-lai had died. Isabel Perón was overthrown in Argentina. Kurt Waldheim was elected for a second term as Secretary General of the United Nations.

And Clarke Estridge was worried about dinner.

Steven knew it was bad form to be late, but he had lost track of time. He was about to leave his office when a news bulletin came in over the UPI wire. The East Germans had imprisoned the leader of an underground printing press. Steven called Larry Wijtold, his contact at the news agency, for more information. During their conversation, mention was made of the disappearance of Attila Kovács several months before.

"Any connection?" Steven asked.

"Yes and no. There's no question, the Eastern Bloc's clamping down again. Not all the arrests are as public as this one, but take it from me, they're happening."

"What did they do with Kovács?"

"No one knows. This thing is being kept so quiet, I'm getting a headache from the intensity of the silence. As for a connection, I don't know that that incident directly relates to this one, but a pattern's emerging so it's worth watching."

"How strict are they about visits outside the Curtain?"

"In East Germany no one is leaving."

"And in Hungary?" Steven asked, annoyed that he was allowing his personal life to intrude on his job.

"To the casual observer, it appears as if Hungary is the most liberal country in the Warsaw Pact. They make you go through hell before they grant you a visa, but their figures show a liberal flow of visitor's passes to the West."

Steven felt a familiar knot in his gut. "And to the trained observer?"

"If you're a local yokel visiting a farm in Iowa or a distant relative in Cleveland, you get a pass. New York. Chicago. Washington, D.C. Los Angeles? Denied! Even Disneyland is questionable. And if you're a name who might be interviewed by Western press? Denied! Particularly if it's known that you once spoke to someone who spoke against the government." Wijtold sighed. Steven could almost see him shaking his head in frustration. "Kádár can feed his people whatever crap he wants. If they buy it, good for him, bad for them. A communist is a communist and a socialist state is still a prison."

While dressing, Steven couldn't stop thinking about what Larry had said. Maybe Matthew was right, he had misinterpreted signals. Katalin was certainly a name, especially having won the Chickering. If she came to New York, the press would be all over her. And her father was not exactly on the government's list of top ten favorites. It was entirely possible that she had applied for an exit visa and had been denied, that she had tried to get to him and couldn't, that she was being detained; that he wasn't being rejected.

After several minutes of mental calisthenics—thinking and rethinking, assessing and reassessing, trying to be rational about something that was purely emotional—possibility became probability, despair made way for a glimmer of hope and the grinding pain he had been feeling in his heart for four years eased, just a bit.

He was still feeling rather buoyant when he raced into Winfield House, the ambassador's official residence, and discovered that he had missed the receiving line. Composing himself, he slowed to a walk, paused beneath a crystal and ormolu chandelier to offer a polite nod to Thomas Jefferson, whose portrait dominated the elegant reception hall, and as nonchalantly as he could entered the yellow drawing room where cocktails were being served.

"Where were you?" Estridge seemed to pop out from behind the door. There was a triumphant gleam in his eye, as if he had caught Steven with lipstick stains on his collar.

"I was working," Steven said. "You ought to try it sometime, Estridge. You might like it."

"The ambassador was looking for you."

"Well, now he'll be able to find me."

Without dignifying his adversary with another second of his time, Steven spotted Rhinehart and took off in his direction.

"Anything I should know about?" Rhinehart said under his breath as he shook Steven's hand.

Steven appreciated Rhinehart's instinctive understanding that he hadn't been late deliberately or due to laggardness. "Another dissident arrest in East Germany."

Rhinehart nodded, accepting Steven's appraisal of the matter and his conclusion that it did not warrant immediate discussion. That settled, Rhinehart graciously introduced Steven to the dignitaries and celebrities in his immediate circle: the author Robert Ludlum; a member of the House of Lords and his Lady; two barristers, sans wigs and wives; the head of one of the largest banks in Zurich; and the American violinist Isaac Stern, who was scheduled to regale Rhinehart's guests after dinner with a private recital in the Garden Room.

Steven was pleased when Rhinehart asked him to escort the famed musician in to dinner. Though he would have liked to continue the conversation they had begun about life on the concert tour, once they were seated, they found themselves across from each other, separated by a silver epergne teeming with fresh roses, a British industrialist who looked as if he had imbibed one cocktail too many, and an empty seat belonging to a magnificent young woman whom Stern and everyone else at the table seemed to know. Only Steven was ignorant of her name and position.

Steven watched with admiration as she made her way along the long length of the enormous table centered in the state dining room, bestowing on each guest a compliment or a bon mot. Her long, near-black hair hung down her back like a luxurious shawl. Her skin, bared by the cut of her strapless red chiffon gown, was as white and luminous as the Royal Doulton china that graced each setting. Her face was thin and oval; her nose was small and retroussé. Large, deep-set hazel eyes stared out from beneath thin arched brows that sketched a look of perpetual innocence and surprise, a look that belied her aura of supreme confidence.

As she slid into the chair Steven held for her, she said simply, "I'm Cynthia Rhinehart."

Steven had heard about her. For the moment, however, all he remembered was that every male in Rhinehart's Washington office had lusted for her, each claiming she was one of the most beautiful women he had ever seen and that if she weren't the boss's daughter, he would have pounced on her. Aside from two professional lotharios who would never confess to failure, most admitted that their chances of even getting near her were very, very slim. She lived in Paris and came home only for occasional visits, then, only to the estate in Kentucky. And she was known to be rather snobbish about her acquaintances.

While she chatted with Stern and the industrialist to her left, Steven tried to recall what else he had heard. Cynthia was the younger of Rhinehart's two daughters. The older one, Claudia, was considered an authority on the breeding of thoroughbreds. Married to a Southern gentleman not unlike her father, with two young children, she ran Mayfair Farms, Rhinehart's Lexington stables. She rarely left Kentucky, except to inspect a particularly attractive brood mare, to attend horse auctions, or to accompany her animals to their races, where, more often than not, she was photographed alongside the jockey and his mount in the winner's circle.

Steven recalled seeing several of those photographs hanging in Rhinehart's office. He conjured Claudia's image, mentally holding it next to the flesh-and-blood presence of her younger sister. Though Claudia was attractive, it was in a fresh-faced way. He couldn't imagine Claudia wearing anything as daring as Cynthia's gown, nor anything as opulent as the diamond and ruby choker that glittered on Cynthia's neck.

"My father speaks of you as if you're the Second Coming. Are you as great as he thinks you are?"

She had caught him off guard—staring into her cleavage, in fact— and wondering why Rhinehart didn't have so much as a single snapshot of this dazzling daughter in his office.

"I didn't know he spoke that way about me," Steven said, quickly gathering his social graces. "I'm flattered."

"And I'm intrigued to meet someone who's involved in American politics and, at the same time, remains unassuming." She turned her hazel eyes to him, allowing a tease of a smile to flicker across her lips. "Frankly, I don't see the two together. To me, a modest politician is an oxymoron."

"And I thought it was called diplomacy," Steven said, offering her a full-fledged grin. Three seats down, he heard Clarke Estridge groan. Cynthia Rhinehart laughed.

"Touché." Within an instant, her entire aspect narrowed, becoming completely fixed on Steven Kardos. "Father said you were born in Hungary."

"I was."

"No wonder you have such a love for classical music," Isaac Stern couldn't help commenting. "It's a land that has produced extraordinary talent, including some exceptional violinists."

"Did you ever hear of Zoltán Gáspár?" Steven asked with an excited curiosity.

Stern smiled and nodded his head. "He was one of the greats. I never understood why he stopped performing." His smile waned. "How do you know Gáspár?"

"At one time, our two families were very close." Steven would have preferred to leave it at that, but Stern's silence asked for further explanation. "When my parents were killed in '56, my brother and I emigrated to the United States. I haven't seen Zoltán since."

Stern grimaced, as if Steven's words had poked a sore spot. "I was born in Russia. Fortunately, I came to the States as an infant." His eyes clouded, as if looking back and counting the horrors that might have befallen him had he stayed in his birthland, counting his blessings that he hadn't. "Gáspár and I are the same age, you know."

"No," Steven said, "I didn't know that."

"He debuted much younger than I did." Suddenly, Stern laughed. "Compared to him, I was an old man of fifteen when I took the stage with the San Francisco Symphony."

"Fifteen is hardly old," Steven said with a respectful nod. "And, if I might say so, the breadth of your talent has only increased with age."

"You can seat me near this gentleman any time, Cynthia," Stern said with a pleased chuckle. "Not only is he a music lover, but he's a charmer as well."

"That he is," Cynthia said, taking note of Steven's gloriously blue eyes and the thin black crescent that scarred his face. "How did this happen?" she asked, boldly directing a red-lacquered fingernail to the scar beneath his left eye, feeling Steven's skin flush at her touch.

"An accident in a coal mine."

"What were you doing in a coal mine?"

He couldn't tell whether she was fascinated or repulsed.

"I worked there." Anticipating her next question, Steven continued. "I grew up in Woodridge, Kentucky. It's a small mountain burg where everyone works the mines. You have to. Coal's the only game in town."

"What an exciting life you've led," Cynthia said, her interest in Steven growing obvious.

"I don't think I'd call it exciting." Steven was embarrassed. He hadn't meant to draw attention to himself, yet all around him people were listening to the story of his life.

"Escaping from Hungary. Working in coal mines. Coming out of Vietnam a hero." Cynthia recited the facts as if she were presenting a case. "If you wouldn't call that exciting, what would you call it?"

"Eventful." Steven acknowledged the laughter that greeted his comment with a shy smile. It was nice to be admired, but he was more than grateful when Estridge interrupted and the subject of Steven Kardos was finally dropped.

"Did I hear someone mention Zoltán Gáspár before?"

"I did." Isaac Stern turned toward the tall, attenuated blond with the round tortoise-shell glasses and lockjawed accent.

"Before I came to London, I was on holiday with a school chum who's posted at the embassy in Budapest." Steven went on alert. For the first time since he had met Estridge, he listened to every word the man said. "He had been to a concert at the Franz Liszt Music Academy. Evidently, it's a yearly thing," Estridge said, in that patronizing tone he used whenever he wanted you to know something he knew that only those in the know knew. "Anyway, this year, the big news was that Zoltán Gáspár was the conductor! With all due respect," he nodded to Isaac Stern, "I had never heard of Gáspár, but my friend told me that in Hungary he was positively revered."

"With good reason," Stern said, quietly but pointedly.

"Right." Estridge had been chided and knew it. Undaunted, he plodded on. "There does seem to be some mystery surrounding him, though. He was at the absolute pinnacle of his career and just stopped playing. No one seems to know why." Estridge turned to Steven. "You used to be a family friend, Kardos. Do you know anything about this?"

Steven stared at Estridge, hating him for reducing Zoltán's circumstance to common gossip, using this tidbit of information as a feather in his social cap. He looked at Stern and at Cynthia Rhinehart and the other people at his end of the table. They appeared genuinely interested. Steven struggled with his conscience. By revealing the truth, was he betraying a confidence? Zoltán had always been so private, so insistent that the matter of his imprisonment and its consequences remain relegated to the dark. Yet he had taken up the baton; he had come out of the darkness. Obviously, he had turned that corner.

"Zoltán didn't stop playing of his own accord." Steven hadn't realized how intense he sounded, but suddenly the entire room quieted. "In the early fifties, during Stalin's reign of terror, Zoltán Gáspár was dragged from his home in the middle of the night and imprisoned in a labor camp called Recsk. It was a torture chamber, a slaughterhouse, a living hell. Thousands of people died there, including my uncle. Zoltán survived, but barely. One of the savages in charge smashed Zoltán's hands with a billy club. His fingers were crushed. That's why he stopped playing!"

Stern was visibly stricken, reflexively sliding his own hands under the table. Cynthia gasped. Beyond that, nothing was said. Yet the character of the silence began to change, subtly but definitely. At first, a shocked, appalled stillness prevailed. Then, it became awkward. People had been moved by Zoltán's story—Steven could see that on their faces—but all too quickly their expressions began to register more discomfort than dismay.

Steven had forgotten his manners. No one liked being confronted with man's bestiality, especially in fancy dress. Torture was not an acceptable dinner-table topic. Pain did not go well with salmon *en croute*.

"Well," Estridge said to Steven with a nervous, self-conscious laugh, glancing down at Rhinehart and then up at Cynthia, assessing the damage to his own esteem. "You've certainly thrown a damper on the party."

"I'd like to be able to say I'm sorry," Steven said evenly, "but you asked me a question. I gave you the answer. And no matter how upsetting it is or how inappropriate for the occasion, I don't believe in apologizing for telling the truth."

"*Bravo!*" From the other end of the table, Owen Rhinehart gave physical evidence of his approval, applauding his young assistant with honest gusto.

"*Bravo!*" agreed Cynthia, resting her hand softly on Steven's arm.

Later, after dinner and after Stern's performance—which most felt had been heightened by Steven's revelation about Zoltán—Cynthia drew Steven aside.

"I know we've only just met and I know your schedule must be simply ghastly, but I wonder if you would do me the honor of escorting me to a dinner being given by the French ambassador." When Steven eyed her quizzically, she sensed what he was wondering immediately. "I know you're thinking that my father should be my escort to this sort of function, but he's already committed for that evening and since it's a private dinner, I can bring whomever I'd like. I'd like it to be you."

Her voice was low and throaty, sounding the way her perfume smelled, lush and sensuous and full of promise.

"It would be my pleasure, Miss Rhinehart," he said, finding it difficult to resist her.

"First of all," she said, moving closer, smothering him with the scent of gardenias and jasmine, "it's Cynthia. And secondly, Steven, let me assure you, the pleasure is all mine."

Owen Rhinehart's great-grandfather made his money farming tobacco in the rich soil around Lexington. Owen's grandfather increased the family fortune by mining bituminous coal in Hopkins County, deep in the Western Coal Fields. Owen's father, wanting to add his two cents, so to speak, to the millions already in the Rhinehart coffers, mined stone from quarries in Jefferson County, outside of Louisville. When it became Owen's turn to expand the empire, he decided the Rhineharts had more than enough money and not nearly enough power.

When he decided to take his first run for public office, it was suggested that he go for the state legislature. He was young, untried, and despite his family's holdings, unknown in the political arena. Because the Rhineharts employed people in every region of Kentucky, his advisers believed he had a built-in electorate. Owen refused to take any votes for granted. He took to the stump, wooing his constituents, courting them, cajoling them, promising them twice what was humanly possible to deliver. He gave speeches from the back of pickup trucks and in the bottom of mines. He kissed babies and shook hands and rang doorbells and attended ladies luncheons and Rotary dinners until he thought if he saw another piece of chicken he would be sick. But he did it because he wanted the power badly enough to do almost anything.

He was twenty-four years old when he was elected to the Kentucky House of Representatives. He was to serve a two-year term. While his advisers thought that was an auspicious beginning and talked of his running for the state senate when he was thirty, Owen simply smiled. That may have been their plan. It wasn't his. At twenty-six he ran for the State Senate. At thirty-two, he ran for the United States House of Representatives. At forty, he ran for the United States Senate, where he had remained until Jimmy Carter sent him to London.

Owen Rhinehart was a handsome man, tall and muscular, with an athlete's grace and a businessman's cunning. He had coal black hair and grass green eyes, a quick wit and an agile mind. His heart was somewhat smaller, open to those he loved, closed to those he didn't. He was focused, though some labeled him narrow, even stubborn. He was intelligent, but not an intellectual. Owen Rhinehart was not a pure man, nor did he feel it was an attribute to be so. Over the course of his life, he had been known to lie, to cheat, and, on occasion, to employ call girls. He had also been known to give hundred-dollar bills to beggars on the street or anonymously to pay for the upkeep of a homeless shelter or a badly needed clinic or a home for unwed mothers. To him, virtue without vice was like salt without pepper: It was all right to prefer one over the other, but he believed most things tasted better with a sprinkle of each.

The person who understood him best, accepting him with all his faults and peccadillos, was Cecilia Délon, the woman he had loved till death parted them. Of their two daughters, Cecilia had favored Claudia, while Owen, despite all his efforts to apportion his love impartially, had always adored Cynthia.

He could never help loving Cynthia the way he did then.

Just as he couldn't help hating her now.

Most people thought the rift had been caused by the fact that Cynthia hadn't been around the day Cecilia had been thrown from her horse, crushing her skull against a pile of rocks. Others said it was because no one could find her for the two days her mother lay dying in the hospital. Only Owen knew the real reason he had emotionally disowned his favorite child. It was where she was—and with whom—that Owen would never, could never, forgive.

For more than ten years, father and daughter didn't speak. They didn't argue in public—they were above that sort of thing. They simply covered their estrangement with distance. Cynthia went to school in Europe, vacationed in Europe and, after graduation, settled in Europe. She had returned home only for Claudia's wedding, the christenings of Claudia's two children, and when she had heard about Owen's appointment to the Court of St. James's.

Thinking back on that visit, Owen had to congratulate Cynthia. She had nerve and—though he loathed admitting it—tremendous style. She strode into his library like a general claiming conquered lands, wearing a chic Saint Laurent suit draped with a fur boa. She had closed the door, seated herself in a chair opposite his, and calmly announced her intention to be his hostess in London.

"Have you lost your mind?" he said.

"Not at all." She removed her gloves, finger by finger, infuriating him with her unflappable composure as she smoothed the black kid, placed the gloves on her knee, and, when she had stretched the moment to its ultimate limit, looked him squarely in the eye. "I lost my mother and you lost your wife, which means that you need a hostess. Claudia is otherwise engaged. Fortunately for you, I am available and more than qualified for the position. You would be foolish to turn me away."

"Now or then," he had said, meeting her double meaning with one of his own.

She hadn't expected that. She squirmed, but only slightly.

"I didn't come here to discuss the past. I came to make peace and to try and establish some sort of amiable future. Whether you like it or not, I am still your daughter."

Owen fumed. It had been ten years, yet his anger was as hot as it had been back then. "A daughter doesn't abandon her mother. Nor does she betray the love and devotion her mother showered on her by turning her back on her family and her family's values."

Cynthia had a dozen comebacks, but she swallowed all of them. She was on a mission and even if she choked on her words, she would not destroy her chances of accomplishing what she had set out to do. If obsequiousness was what he wanted, obsequiousness was what he was going to get. She rose from the chair, walked around the desk, and kneeled on the floor in front of her father, her hands clasped like a supplicant, her voice only slightly tinged with sarcasm.

"I think I've been banished from the kingdom long enough, sire. I'm here to beg your forgiveness and to offer myself in servitude."

Owen stared down at her. It would be so much easier if she were less stunning and more remorseful, less intriguing and truly repentant. But regret was not a word in Cynthia's vocabulary. Why should it be? Except for that one time, he had always encouraged her to do whatever she wanted; he had always given her whatever she wanted. Why should she expect anything less?

"I don't find any of this amusing," he said, sounding as if the burden of the past ten years had wearied him. "I don't know if I'll ever get over what you did."

"The statute of limitations on most crimes is limited to seven years," she said quietly as she arose. She took her time returning to her seat. "What you seem to forget, father dear, is that, thanks to you, I became a victim of this heinous thing you like to label as my crime. Thanks to you, I have to live with the consequences of my actions—and yours— for the rest of my life. So don't think you're the only one who suffered!"

He thought he noticed a tear in her eye. He thought he heard a catch in her voice.

"I'm very well aware of the fact that you weren't the only victim, Cynthia, and that you are not the only one who's had to live with the results of your sins."

Cynthia inhaled deeply. She leaned over the desk and looked deep into her father's eyes. "Can't it be over? Can't we be done with it? Can't you give me a chance to earn a place in your life again?" Her fingers curled into nervous fists. "I want to come to London with you. I want to do what mother trained me to do, to be a lady and a gracious hostess and a partner to a powerful man." She stared at Owen. "That is what you both trained me to be, you know."

Owen allowed a faint smile to peek out of his mouth. "I guess we did."

And so Owen had agreed, albeit reluctantly. Cynthia returned to Paris to close her apartment and met him the day he arrived in London. As mistress of Winfield House, she had proved herself invaluable. She was as advertised: glamorous, engaging, resourceful, vivacious, insightful, intelligent—a totally adept partner for a man who moved in circles of power and influence.

Yet despite her accomplishments, Owen remained suspicious. She had come to him because she wanted something, and this role as hostess of the manor was only part of the package. He didn't know the end to the means, but he knew she had a goal and he guessed he was part of it. What he didn't know was, what part did Steven Kardos play? At that first dinner, it was obvious that she had set her sights on that young man. She had pursued him with messianic zeal. Why? Owen asked himself. Some might have said simply, that she was falling in love with him. Most would have found that quite logical and would have been thrilled at the prospect of having someone like Kardos as a son-in-law. Owen would be, too, if the bride were anyone but Cynthia.

It wasn't that Owen thought Steven wasn't good enough for Cynthia. He didn't think Cynthia was good enough for Steven.

From the outset, it was apparent that László Böhm was determined to woo Katalin. When he came to pick her up at her apartment, he brought a lavish bouquet of red Bulgarian roses. He was charming and respectful to Zoltán, who was so delighted that Katalin was going out, he declared Major Böhm an exception to his customary hatred for anyone in an army uniform. They were chauffeured to Kodály's on Magyar utca in the back of a government car. When they reached the bottom of the stairs leading to the cellar restaurant, the owners greeted them effusively, fawning over Katalin as if she were visiting royalty. Clearly, if she was in the company of László Böhm, she was.

Their table was in the smaller of the two rooms, tucked in a corner to afford them as much privacy as possible. Katalin had never been to Kodály's. It was more pricey and more sophisticated than most Budapest restaurants. The tables were laid with fine linen and expensive glassware. The flowers were lush and fresh. The service was attentive. And the food was divine. After tossing back a shot of apricot brandy—a male, premeal custom from which women usually refrained—László ordered a selection of fine goose pâtés as starters. Katalin decided on *fogas*—a delicately flavored pike from Lake Balaton—in a green pepper and tomato sauce. László also chose *fogas*, but he preferred his with mushrooms and a sour cream sauce.

When they had finished most of the bottle of dry Szekszárd Red with the pâtés, László selected a *Badacsonyi kéknyelü* to accompany their dinner. When the captain had poured the smooth, light white wine into both their glasses, he offered them an old-fashioned Hungarian toast: "*Bort, buzát, békességet, szép asszony feleséget!*"—Wine, wheat, peace, and a beautiful woman for a wife! Katalin was embarrassed. László was amused.

From the other room, they could hear the gypsy violinist. He wasn't nearly as good as Tibor, Katalin thought. Without meaning to, she had let her attention wander away from László's description of his last trip to

Moscow, suddenly struck by the image of Tibor roaming from table to table playing tunes for tips in restaurants like this. She hated the very idea of it. Earlier, the violinist had tried to serenade them, but László had shooed him away. The notion of someone dismissing Tibor disturbed her. Talent like his should never be dismissed. It should be enjoyed and applauded and respected for the gift that it was. Here, in Hungary, because Tibor was a gypsy, he would never receive that applause and respect. It wouldn't be that way in the United States, she thought. Yes, America had its share of prejudice, and yes, certain avenues were narrowed for those of color, but in the creative fields the vistas seemed broader, the opportunities greater, the possibilities better. Somehow, she was going to find a way to showcase Tibor's extraordinary gift.

"Did you like New York?"

"New York?" Katalin had been so lost in her own thoughts, she hadn't realized László had finished his discourse and had steered the conversation elsewhere.

"Yes. I know you spent several years there."

"I liked it very much," Katalin said, wishing she could tell him what she really thought about the United States, knowing that she had to cap her enthusiasm. It wouldn't look good to rave about a country that was anathema to her government, particularly to one of her government's servants. Besides, how did she know this wasn't all a setup, that László wasn't looking to trap Judit through her, or find a way to discredit her for some twisted reason. He had been at Mária's funeral. He had been at Zoltán's conducting debut. Though his explanations about both appearances had sounded plausible, Katalin was a Hungarian, born during the reign of Stalin, raised on a diet of suspicion and distrust. Doubt had become instinctive, misgivings a habit. Now that she thought about it, this date had been rather sudden. He had interrupted her and Zoltán, insistent upon meeting and speaking with her. His attentions seemed suddenly convenient. Why would he be interested in her? He was an officer in the army. Zoltán was a listed dissident, as were all her relatives, alive or dead, and most of her known friends. And if he had been so interested, why hadn't he approached her before now, before Kovács's arrest and her father's return to the public eye? The more she thought about it, the more she wondered whether Major Böhm was truly a suitor, or one of Kádár's spies.

"Did you find it very different from Budapest?"

She weighed her words. "The two cities are worlds apart."

"Is one better than the other?" he probed.

"They're simply different." She kept her tone as light and noncommittal as his.

László moved his chair next to hers and took her hand. "I'm not spying on you," he whispered, placing his mouth close to her ear. "You don't have to be so cautious."

"I don't know what you mean." Her heart was pounding and not because he had read her thoughts. His nearness was more intoxicating than she wanted it to be.

"Katalin. I saw the change. I felt the shift. The minute I asked you about your stay in the West, you withdrew. I'm really just curious."

He didn't move his chair. He didn't let go of her hand. For several minutes, they sat in silence, each considering the other.

"The pace is faster in New York," she said finally, deciding to satisfy his curiosity without commenting on his observations. "They work hard and they play hard."

"It doesn't sound very gracious."

"It is what it is," she said, wondering how he could imply that such an adjective might accurately describe life in Budapest.

"Did you enjoy Juilliard?" She didn't miss his shift to a subject less political, less potentially incriminating.

"I loved it," she said, deciding that she couldn't be arrested for enjoying her work. "I had a marvelous tutor, which to a musician is the most important thing. It doesn't matter what country you study in, it's with whom you study."

László nodded in agreement. "I understand you won a major piano competition."

"The Chickering. Yes, I did."

"But you returned home."

"My mother was dying."

Again, László nodded. Katalin was uncomfortable with how much he knew about her.

"So the Yugoslav who came in second, Lauc Pedjá, took your place on the tour."

"I suppose he did." Katalin hadn't thought about that. Of course he did. Without her to fulfill her role as the winner of the Chickering, Pedjá reaped the benefits—ten-thousand-dollar check, recital at Carnegie Hall, all of it. She tried not to let it bother her, but disappointment and regret surfaced despite her efforts to keep her feelings contained.

"Are you sorry you came back?" László asked, responding to the sadness on her face.

"Of course not!" Her answer was too immediate, too defensive to have any credibility.

"I'm sorry," he said, quickly apologizing for upsetting her. "I didn't mean are you sorry you were with your mother at the end. I meant, do you miss New York?"

Katalin was annoyed with herself for revealing a private emotion to a man she hardly knew, irritated that something as petty as jealousy of Pedjá's fortune had caused her to lose her composure.

"Not at all," she said with as much conviction as she could muster. "Not at all!" She prayed she sounded convincing.

Since the rest of the evening progressed without incident or further questioning, she decided she had.

"I'd like to see you again," László said at the door to her apartment.

Katalin still harbored suspicions about this handsome man with the charismatic eyes. In spite of that, she said, "I'd like that as well."

László's mouth drew upward into a pleased smile. He took her hands in his, raised them and gently kissed her fingers. "Underneath this officer's uniform," he said, in a soft, beguiling voice, "is a simple man who thinks you're the most wonderful, most exciting, most beautiful woman he's ever met. In time, I hope you'll learn to ignore the uniform and trust the man."

For a year, László paid suit to Katalin with all the chivalry of a knight in King Arthur's court. Red roses arrived once a week. He called her every other night. He wined her and dined her in cozy, intimate restaurants where he could hold her hand and whisper adorations in her ear. Often, he came by the Academy, content just to sit outside her practice room and listen to her play. When she performed, he followed her—to Bucharest and Warsaw and Sofia and Prague—offering worshipful applause at the end of each concert. He brought her to state dinners, introducing her to his comrades and visiting dignitaries with undisguised pride. On Sundays, he included Zoltán in the elaborate plans he made for Katalin's enjoyment—picnics, and visits to charming country inns for sumptuous lunches. Everything he said, everything he did, was symptomatic of a man falling deeper and deeper in love.

Katalin was not blind to his condition. And she was not immune to his charm. Had she been totally innocent, her feelings for László would have matched his in both intensity and rapidity. But she was not innocent. She had loved before and the relationship had not ended naturally. In truth, it had not ended at all. There had been no devastating fight, no angry words, no parting salvos or insults. There hadn't even been any words of good-bye. Instead, there had been only a tortuous state of perpetual suspension.

Every day, for a year, there was László. László to ease her loneliness, to fill the vacuum that had been left by the lack of correspondence and encouragement. A woman like Katalin, so filled with passion and affection, was not meant to be alone forever. She wanted to be loyal. But it had been years, and she was feeling the strain of needing someone to love and someone to love her in return.

It was early September, 1976. László had taken her to Margitkert, a rustic nineteenth-century restaurant tucked away in the hills of Buda. Blessed with a warm night and a starry sky, they sat in the garden, in the shadows of a leafy trellis kiosk, watching paper lanterns sway back and forth on the thin wire that traced the square with soft, orange light. All the garden tables were filled. There was a family gathering, a business meeting, an office party, a group of tourists, and at the other end of the kiosk, another table for two. A gypsy band played in a corner. The prevailing mood was happy, as if everyone was celebrating the warm wane of summer. From inside, came the raucous sounds of a party in progress.

"I love you, Katalin," László said, pouring the last of the wine into her glass. "I think you've known that for a long time. I thought it was time for me to say it and for you to hear it."

He leaned forward and kissed her. His lips tasted fruity, like the two bottles of wine they had consumed. They had kissed before, many times, in many different places, with many different accompaniments. Yet somehow, this time felt new. Was it because László had declared himself? Katalin didn't know, but her heart was full, and he was very near. She, who had maintained a proper distance during most of this courtship, felt her constraints loosening, her grip on propriety slipping. She knew he had wanted her from that first meeting at the Academy. She wasn't certain when she had begun to dream about being in his arms and having him make love to her, but sitting beneath a full autumnal moon, feeling his desire for her escalate, she knew she would not be sleeping in her bed that night. She would not be sleeping alone.

His apartment was in the *Víziváros*, or Watertown, district. A wedge of streets between Castle Hill and the Danube, Watertown was once a seedy quarter housing fishermen and craftspeople. During the seventeenth century, at the height of the one-hundred-and-fifty-year Turkish occupation, the population seemed to vanish. When the area was rebuilt in the nineteenth century, the neighborhood was gentrified by nobler folk, who commissioned mansions and townhouses reached by narrow alleys and stone staircases rising from the main street up into the hillside.

László's house was small in comparison to most of the grander maisons, but wonderfully located at the southern end of Watertown, near "Kilometer Zero"—the stone from which all distances from Budapest are measured—and wonderfully decorated. Inside was a fine gathering of antiques, mostly Russian and German Biedermeier. Blue was the predominant color, ranging from royal to pale and all shades in between.

László explained that he preferred to think of himself as a child of the Blue Danube, rather than the son of the gray *Duna*. Blue-and-gold striped silk covered an elegant Russian settee and two matching armchairs. An Austrian secretaire of burl walnut and amboyna dominated one wall, a starkly modern painting by Vasarely the wall opposite. Several parquetry gueridons placed near the various seats held pieces from a vast collection of crystal animals. In the dining room, a satinwood breakfront housed a colorful assemblage of Herend china. If Katalin weren't feeling so romantic, she might have bristled at the unfairness of an army officer living amid such expensive furnishings while most Hungarians worked two and three jobs just to get by. But her mind was not focused on the inequities of socialism. Her mind was on László Böhm and the delicious way he was making her feel.

He showed her upstairs to his bedroom—an elegant lair that spoke volumes about László's admiration for gentility and beautiful things—and invited her to wait while he readied the room. Within minutes, the capri-blue room was bathed in the delicate yellow light of a dozen candles. Gently, he approached her. His hands held her face and drew her to him. She could feel his lips tremble as they touched hers. They stayed for only a moment. Then, he allowed his eyes to kiss her while his hands worshiped her face. A finger outlined her mouth. The back of his hand stroked her cheek. The tip of a fingernail followed her hairline from beneath one ear to the other. All the while, his eyes remained fixed on hers.

She felt herself slipping into a trancelike state where intelligence and wit were rendered powerless, becoming enfeebled, humble servants to the stronger rule of feelings and physical sensitivities. When his hands slid behind her neck and entangled themselves in her hair, she tilted her head back and closed her eyes, allowing sensation to wash over her and bathe her in a pool of anticipation. His tongue glanced against the skin on her neck, moving quickly to the soft flesh beneath her chin. His fingers laced through her silken hair. His body pressed against her. She shivered. She was fully clothed, and yet she felt naked and eager for him to cover her with his nakedness.

She never felt him unbutton the back of her dress. She never felt him undo her bra or remove her slip. Yet suddenly her flesh was exposed and he was caressing her, petting and fondling her breasts with his hands and his mouth, creating a heat so powerful her knees buckled. She backed away, finding refuge in a nearby chair. Their eyes remained locked as he began to undress. She undid her stockings, one at a time, moving them down the length of her leg with tantalizing slowness, watching as he responded to the temptation she was laying before him. When there was nothing more, she shimmied out of her garter belt, removing the last impediment to their joining.

He took her hand and led her to the wide canopied bed. Throwing back the coverlet, he invited her to lie with him atop the sheets. Feeling like a princess, she lay down on the grand bed, resting her head against feather-soft pillows, brushing her hand across the headboard of satin and silk. Despite the warmth of the night, the sheets were cool against her back. When László's hands returned to her flesh, they felt moist and hot against her skin. But it was nothing compared to the heat she felt within.

Katalin allowed it to sweep over her like a raging fire, wallowing in the rich eroticism of foreplay. She had forgotten how much she enjoyed sex, how much she liked being nuzzled, being handled, being rubbed and touched and kissed and held. She had only had one lover, and in the deeper recesses of her mind, she admitted that nothing could ever equal the way she had felt with him; but he was thousands of miles away, and whether she had wanted it to happen or not, prolonged distance had a way of cooling the fervor of love. For an instant, she permitted another confession—that she blamed Steven for their lack of contact, that she believed if he had wanted to reach her, he could have. Suddenly, miraculously, as if God knew she needed a sign, Katalin felt a release. It was as if by admitting her anger she had opened her eyes to the futility of holding on to a fantasy when there was someone in her reality who wanted her. The man holding her was loving her, and it was to him she responded, for him she bared herself, with him she would ride the waves of carnal passion.

László could feel her hunger. He rejoiced in it, reveled in it, luxuriated in it. Though he had dreamed of this one night for a hundred nights before, he suddenly braked, separating from her for a brief moment. It was hard for him to believe that she was really there. He had to blink to assure himself the magnificent creature next to him was not a mirage, not a phantom sent to tease and torment him. Illumined by the glow of bedside candles, her skin glistening with the dew of desire, she appeared far more ethereal in person than she ever had in his dreams. Pale yellow ghosts of light danced on her body, licking places he wanted to visit, gliding across vistas he wanted to explore. Her eyes were closed. Her mouth was pursed in a sensuous moue. Her breasts were lush and full and enticing. Unable to contain himself, he accepted their implicit invitation, lowering his mouth onto her, devouring her flesh and the essence that lived beyond the flesh, loving her and touching her, consuming so much of her he was certain he and she had become parts of the same whole.

To his delight, he felt her hands on him, moving from his back to where his virility pulsed in response to her touch. He felt her teeth on his lips, her tongue in his mouth, her hips pressed against his in a way that begged fulfillment. Not yet, he thought, needing more time to indulge himself in the glory of her. Not yet, he said to himself as he shifted his body nearer her sex, sliding his hands beneath her back, lifting her chest to his mouth so that once more he could feast on her and taste the ambrosia of her femininity.

She undulated beneath him, the sensuousness of her movements stimulating him beyond control. His nerves were raw, his muscles were tense. His body was strained to near breaking. He felt her hands pressing him toward union, her lips beseeching him to complete them. Yet something held him back. He looked down at her, wondering what and why.

Katalin felt him watching her. Her eyes opened. She stared into the face of the man who, for one entire year, had dedicated himself to making her happy. He had succeeded and something told her it was important for him to know that.

"I love you," she whispered, rewarded by the immediate smile that curled his lips.

She knew he wanted something more. Still, she hesitated, needing to be certain. But there was no time to think or to speak or to wonder about what might happen after. His arms wrapped around her, pulling her to within a breath of him. She felt him nearing her, she felt him filling her, taking her with him on a journey to a faraway nirvana. It was a place with no ground, no sky, no daylight, no night. It was a place of rising bliss and thunderous joy. It was a place where words had no meaning and feelings could never be wrong. It was a place where a man and a woman could meet in the paradisiacal otherworld called love.

When their passion was spent, they lay together in the golden afterglow of satisfaction. His lips sipped the sweat of fulfillment from her brow as his hand brushed a damp strand of hair from her face. He was gentle and caring, just as he had been moments before.

A thought intruded on Katalin's reverie. She knew what he had wanted her to say and why she had hesitated. From the first, a question had formed a wedge between them. It could never have been answered any other way but by making love, by stripping away all pretense and facade, leaving nothing but the uninhibited, unbridled, purely primitive core of the being.

"I love you," he said, planting a delicate kiss on her lips.

"I love you too," she said with even greater certainty, convinced that now she knew the man beneath the uniform. "And I trust you."

Nothing she could have said could have pleased László more.

"Enough to marry me?"

Katalin was stunned by his proposal. She hadn't thought about marriage. But why not? She loved him. He loved her. Zoltán liked him. He had already proved to what lengths he would go to make her happy. What more could she ask? And why should she even bother asking?

"Yes," she said, "I'll marry you."

Two months later, in the church where Mária had been laid to rest, Katalin Gáspár became the bride of Major László Böhm. Zoltán walked her down the aisle. Andras played the wedding march. And despite Judit's qualified congratulations—"You can never really trust anyone who pledges his allegiance to communists"—she stood up for Katalin as maid of honor. Since László's parents were dead, his senior officer served as best man. The reception, organized by Ilona, was small but lively, continuing until László and Katalin left for their honeymoon weekend at Lake Balaton.

As family and friends showered them with rice and the happy bride and groom left to begin their life together, only Judit mused about how different it all would have been if Katalin had received just one letter from Steven Kardos.

25

*G*azing out of the upstairs window of Winfield House was like peering
through the frame of a Constable landscape. Resplendent in its spring
finery, the rolling, undulating lawn and magnificently landscaped gardens
seemed to glow in the warm May sun. The sky was a gift of clear blue.
Lime and chestnut trees splashed the horizon with a leafy virescence. A
family of swans floated along Regent's Canal. It was a sight of such
incredible splendor, poets would have rushed to the pen and painters to
the brush to capture a day like this.

Unfortunately, the view was completely lost on Cynthia Rhinehart.
Her mind was elsewhere—in her bed, to be exact. Its emptiness was
beginning to wear on her. A lusty woman, Cynthia was not used to
having her needs unsatisfied. Since her arrival in London she had been
playing the celibate, and she was not happy in the role. For twelve long,
frustrating months, she had not had one lover, one one-night stand, one
lost weekend, one anything. She could hardly remember what it felt like
to be naked, let alone be ravished by the ministrations of a member of

the opposite sex. Knowing she was on trial, believing that her father had eyes watching her every move, she had restrained every natural impulse and had comported herself like a perfect lady.

Angrily, she turned away from the window. Just thinking about the sacrifices she had made propelled her toward the large mirror over the fireplace. Leaning over the mantel she examined her face carefully, checking for lines or blemishes, strange blotches or previously uncharted creases. To Cynthia, it was a certitude that abstinence damaged one's looks. After all, she reasoned, there was no such thing as an enchanting spinster or a seductive old maid; there was no one knocking down the cloister door to woo a monk or court a nun. Yet there she stood, a sexual hermitess, a prisoner of propriety, a victim of her own choices. A *perfect lady*.

When Cynthia had humbled herself before her father, it was because she had decided it was time to marry. It had taken years to formulate a profile of the man she wanted as her groom, but once she had, she was ready to find him and get on with her plan.

Because it was her nature to be thorough, before she had arrived in London—before she had flown to Lexington—she had acquired a full dossier on everyone in her father's inner circle. The name that stood out was Steven Kardos. Through her network of informers, Cynthia learned how much Owen respected Steven. She knew how they had met, where they had met, how Owen had sponsored Steven's scholarship and guided his rise through the ranks of his Washington organization. She knew how much Owen had come to rely on Steven's instincts and talents, how much he had come to depend on Steven's friendship and fealty. She knew that Steven was the heir-apparent. That alone would have been enough to center him in her aim, but when she met him, he overshadowed his own data. Plots, plans, schemes, and strategies be dashed. Cynthia was taken with the man.

Even now, she could remember how she had felt when she first looked at him. He was handsome to the point of making her ache in that private spot that only wanted to be touched by someone as splendid as he. His body was firm and virile; his face was planed and strong. His eyes were positively magnetic, so blue she wanted to immerse herself in their depths. Even the scar that blackened his cheek like a badge of courage touched off a rush of craving she hadn't experienced in a very long time.

In getting to know him better, she realized that part of his appeal was that he seemed completely oblivious of his impact. He was so comfortable in his body and his being that he didn't work at making an impression. He simply *was*. To Cynthia his most seductive quality was the fire in his soul. She felt it as surely as she felt her own fire burning whenever he looked at her or accidentally grazed her skin or spoke about something important. This was a man flaming with ambition and passion, a man who wanted to change the world. Since Cynthia wanted to rule the world, she was convinced they were made for each other. What she had been trying to do for the past year was to convince him of the same thing.

She had invited him to escort her to everything from state dinners to poetry readings to the finals at Wimbledon. If it provided her with an excuse to see him, she grabbed it. What she really wanted was to grab him, but despite an occasional flicker of interest, he had remained infuriatingly polite, respectful, and aloof.

Cynthia had never been faced with such forbearance. In all her twenty-eight years, Steven Kardos had been her only conscientious objector. She wasn't subtle and he wasn't stupid. He knew what she wanted. She thought he might have wanted it too. Still, he insisted on being noble. Why? Because he worked for her father? Clarke Estridge didn't share those feelings. All Cynthia would have to do is wink and he would drop his pants in a second, as would a dozen other staffers. Only Steven resisted. Which was too bad, because it was only Steven she wanted.

Though her patience was strained, Cynthia was not a woman easily dissuaded. Tonight's assignation had been planned for weeks. When she had discovered Owen was going to Edinburgh for a four-day conference, she immediately invited Steven to attend a small supper in the family's private dining room with friends of hers from Brussels, bankers with important connections throughout Europe and the Middle East.

Of course, there were no friends from Brussels. And, if she had her way, even the private dining room wouldn't be private enough.

Steven wasn't surprised to hear that Cynthia's guests had been forced to cancel at the last minute, or to find the table set for two. Neither was he surprised to see Cynthia in a dangerously low-cut, sinuously tight gown of black *mousseline de soie*. He wasn't as naive as Cynthia believed him to be. No matter how diaphanous it was, he could still feel a net being slipped over his head. She was pursuing him, and yes, he was enjoying the pursuit, but the why behind it had him perplexed.

Still, he resisted, reined in by pride and protocol. Cynthia was Owen's daughter and Steven owed that relationship a certain respect. Besides, he didn't want to be just another stud wearing the colors of Mayfair Farms. According to the legends that had grown up around Cynthia's life-style, it was not unreasonable to assume that her attraction was purely physical. She wanted his body—no ties, no strings, no commitments other than to an enjoyable sexual romp. Had she been anyone other than who she was, Steven would have been delighted to oblige. But her name was a string, her father was a tie, his job at the embassy was a commitment.

If she had arranged this evening as a personal showcase, she had done an admirable job. Drinks had been served in the Garden Room, a glorious space gleaming with gilded mirrors and exquisite antiques and intricately carved moldings and pale green eighteenth-century Chinese wallpaper installed when Walter Annenberg had held the title of ambassador. She had been charming, as usual, drawing him out about his work and his interests, discussing world events with surprising insight.

When they moved into the small dining room she continued to be the quintessential dinner companion. Breathtaking in her black halter-top gown with its plummeting neckline, she knew how to lean, how to sit, how to twist in her chair to show herself off to her best advantage. While many women might have relied solely on their beauty to attract, she allowed her intellect and her wit to surface, continuing their cocktail conversations, telling amusing anecdotes, delighting him with stories about her childhood and what life had been like on the other side of the Cumberland Plateau.

Halfway through dinner, as if a bell had sounded the second act of a play, the atmosphere changed, becoming charged with an energy that could only be defined as primal. He wasn't certain whether it was the sumptuous aroma of her perfume, the Veuve Cliquot champagne, or the nearness of her body, but his ears had closed to her words, allowing all his other senses to awaken. He became acutely aware of the whiteness of her skin, the gleam of her hair, the evenness of her teeth. He became fascinated by the way her lips moved when she spoke, the way her eyes danced when she smiled. He knew she was drawing him deeper into her web. He knew he should resist, but just then, he couldn't think of a single reason why.

Like an animal picking up a scent, Cynthia sensed the moment and rose from her chair. He followed suit. Without a word, she stepped forward and laced her arms around his neck. He complied, bending, nearing the lips that seemed to be calling him. Instead of pressing against his, they invited him to have a brandy. He didn't ask where and she didn't say. She simply led him down the hall and up the stairs. When they reached the door to her suite, she confronted him.

"I'm giving you advance warning," she said in a throaty voice. "I want you, Mr. Kardos, and if you take one step inside this room, I don't intend to let you out until I've devoured every inch of you."

He laughed. She smiled. He reached past her and opened the door. She locked it behind them.

The room was a cool, oyster-white refuge of tranquility. Louis XVI-style boiserie provided an elegant backdrop for comfortable furnishings upholstered in pale blue silks. A collection of botanical engravings in gilded frames hung alongside the fireplace and between two of the floor-to-ceiling windows. A crystal chandelier hovered overhead, a glittering chain of glass beads that caught the light and held it gently, tenderly, as one would hold a breath or a kiss. A decanter of brandy and two snifters waited for them on a silver tray placed on a cocktail table in front of the couch. Whoever had left the brandy had also dimmed the lights and filled the room with the delicate sounds of Bach's "Brandenburg" concertos.

Cynthia curled into one corner of the couch. Steven seated himself in the other. For a while they sipped their brandy in silence, reconnoitering, assessing, appraising, anticipating.

"When you were a teenager in Woodridge, did you ever play games like strip poker or twenty questions or spin the bottle?" Cynthia asked, interrupting the stillness.

"No," Steven answered, a curious smile tilting his mouth. "We didn't have time to play games in my neighborhood. I'm afraid I missed out on those particular experiences."

"What a shame." Cynthia refilled their glasses. "We have plenty of time now. How about if we make up for that horrible gap in your education?" She returned Steven's brandy to him, keeping her eyes fixed on his face. "What if we combine twenty questions and strip poker? I ask you a question. You answer. I strip something off. You ask me a question. I answer. You take something off."

"Sounds interesting." Steven took a long swig of his brandy. Something told him interesting was too mild an adjective to describe what was about to happen.

"Of course, since you have on many more clothes than I do, you have to take off two articles to my one. Fair?"

Steven laughed and shook his head. "Fair."

"I'll start." She snuggled farther into the corner of the couch, as if she knew the fun of this game was to keep a distance while creating a closeness. "Do you still see your friend Shadow?"

Steven was surprised she knew about him. Then he realized that she might have heard about Shadow through Estridge or Owen or any of a number of people who knew the two of them had roomed together while he was at Georgetown and Shadow was at George Washington University.

"He's in Chicago, working for Head Start. We write now and then."

Cynthia nodded, raised her legs onto the couch, lifted her gown to just below her knees and slipped off her shoes, tossing them behind the couch. "Your turn," she said.

"Were you always this gorgeous?"

"Yes."

Steven smiled as he, too, removed his shoes, and, adhering to the rules, his socks.

"Do you miss your brother?"

"Very much. He's the only family I have."

Cynthia unlatched her bracelet, dropping the diamond and sapphire cuff into a glittery pile on the silver tray before her.

"Do you miss your sister?"

"No. We can't stand each other."

Steven removed his jacket, folding it over the back of the couch. His bow tie followed.

"Were you happy when you became a citizen?"

"It was one of the proudest moments of my life."

She reached back to unhook her necklace. Steven was intrigued by the slow, enticing way she raised her arms, with how much time she took to do such a simple task, at how exciting it was to watch this woman at play. When the diamond choker clanked onto the tray next to the bracelet, it startled him.

"Your turn," she said, delighting in the gleam she saw building in his eyes.

"What did you do in Paris?"

The other questions she had answered with no hesitation. This one prompted a sip of brandy and a momentary pause.

"I shopped, attended every gala, every party, every opening, and bedded every man I could. I thought I was having fun. Now I know I was just looking for you."

Without taking his eyes from her face, Steven removed his studs and cuff links, leaving his shirt open. Cynthia stared at his chest, running her tongue along her lower lip.

"What do you want to be when you grow up?" she asked, her voice growing softer, wispier.

"President of the United States," he said, feeling her sensuality pulling at him like a powerful magnet. "Just like every other red-blooded American boy."

He thought his skin would burn watching her hands glide beneath her gown. One by one, she unhooked a stocking and rolled the silken fabric down her leg at a deliberately unhurried pace. When both hose lay in a heap alongside the couch, she reached up again, this time sliding a black lace garter belt off her hips.

"What do you want to be when you grow up?" he asked, finding it difficult to concentrate on anything other than the knowledge that beneath her dress she was completely naked.

"Your wife," she answered, pleased that there was no shock on his face, only desire. As he took off his shirt and cast aside his belt, she could feel him wanting her.

"Have you ever been in love?" She spoke and then closed her eyes, not wanting to see his face as he answered, "Yes."

When she opened her eyes, she was ecstatic to see that just then, it didn't matter that he had been in love. Nothing mattered except what was happening between them. She plucked the diamond clusters from her ears and threw them on the floor.

"Have you?" he asked, already unzipping his pants, stepping out of his boxer shorts, and returning to his seat on the couch.

"I thought so at the time," she said gasping at the sight of him. "It was nothing compared to the way I feel now."

"Your turn," he said, naked and more than ready to make love to the woman rising before him, preparing to remove her gown.

"Are you still in love with her?" She said it quickly and then, as if she regretted it, added, "Could you be in love with me?"

"Yes," he said, not clarifying which question he was answering.

She took two small steps and stood directly in front of him. She moistened her lips as she lowered one side of the halter top and then the other. Her eyes held his as she undid the zipper that ran down her side. She waited for a second that seemed interminable. When neither of them could stand another moment of separateness, she slid the clingy fabric down past her breasts, past her waist, past her hips. When, finally, she had stepped out of the limpid pool of black, she reached for his hand. She wanted to draw him up off the couch, but he pulled her down on him instead, guiding her toward the place they both needed to be. In a mad rush, they found each other.

They required no further arousal, no additional stroking or touching to fan the fires of their sexuality. Their two bodies were so hot and so eager that in an instant, they were joined in a blistering union. It wasn't sweet. It wasn't loving. It wasn't like any other first time. But it was explosive and extraordinary and something neither of them would ever forget.

"More," she said, still joined to him, unwilling to separate for even a second. "More," she repeated, biting his neck, gnawing at his lips, unable to gratify the monstrous desire she had for him, a hunger that had grown into a greedy, unquenchable desperation.

Gently, he disengaged himself from her. He stood, but her arms refused to leave his neck. He lifted her and her mouth covered his. As he carried her toward her bedroom, she squirmed in his arms, pressing against him with an eagerness that was irresistible. When they found her bed, they did as she wanted, making love again and again, exploring each other with a freedom and intensity and inventiveness that instead of sating and exhausting, energized and incited.

When morning came Steven started to go.

"Don't," she pleaded, reaching out after him, stopping him before he could leave her bed. "Stay with me."

"I can't be found here," he said, his eyes traveling from her tousled black hair to her small white breasts, wondering where his willpower had gone, where his mind had gone. "It wouldn't look right."

"I don't care about how things look." She took his hand and placed it between her legs. "All I care about is how things feel. And this feels very, very right."

Since Steven couldn't disagree, he stayed—for two days.

The afternoon Steven left, Cynthia remained in bed, rubbing her hand across the sheets where they had lain together, burying her nose in his pillow, breathing in his scent. She closed her eyes and envisioned his face. She pictured his body. She tried to recreate the sensations he had produced in her, tried to remember the responses he had to the sensations she had produced in him.

Though she was thoroughly exhausted, she refused sleep, preferring to spend the night dreaming of him, imagining how it would be when they married (after this weekend, there was no question that they would marry). To her, his prowess as a lover only confirmed her belief that she had indeed chosen the perfect partner.

The next morning, trying to keep to their agreement to maintain a public distance, she controlled the urge to call him, to see him, to beg him to return to her bed. By late afternoon, however, when he hadn't called her, she began to worry. She dialed the embassy and asked to be put through to his office. One of the secretaries—Cynthia never bothered to remember any of their names—politely informed her that Mr. Kardos had gone to Paris.

"When did he leave?" Cynthia asked, covering her disappointment, reminding herself that he worked for an ambassador and it wasn't unusual for attachés to take sudden trips.

"This afternoon."

"And when is he expected back?"

"I'm not sure."

"What do you mean you're not sure? It's your job to know these things."

"I'm sorry, Miss Rhinehart, but Mr. Kardos took a personal leave. He had said he might be gone a week. Maybe a few days more. Maybe a few days less."

Cynthia slammed the phone down. Personal leave. Paris. What had gone wrong? What could have happened in twenty-four hours that would prompt him to leave town?

"There's only one way to find out," Cynthia mumbled as she grabbed her purse and called for her car.

In less than half an hour Cynthia was standing inside Steven's flat. She had gone to the brick building in Hammersmith that housed many of the embassy staffers and convinced the superintendent that she was there on an emergency, that Steven had asked her to find something for him in his apartment. When the old bloke had looked unsure, she repeated her name, a clear reminder that she had the power to dismiss him if he were foolish enough to deny her.

Left alone, she rummaged through his drawers and rifled the pockets of his clothes. Since Cynthia rarely suffered from guilt, she felt no shame about invading his privacy. She only wished she knew what she was looking for. On his desk she found a photograph of a man, a very hand-some man, she thought, whom she assumed was Matthew, Steven's brother. Another photograph—this one older and quite yellowed—showed two adults, two young boys, and a very thin girl standing in front of a stone statue. Respectfully, she lifted the frame and looked at the faces of the people she assumed were Steven's parents. His mother had been a lovely-looking woman. His father had been a handsome man. She smiled when she looked at Steven's little-boy face. He had been so adorable then, the image prompted an instantaneous, reflexive thought about how adorable a child of Steven's would be. Her hand shook. Tiny beads of sweat formed on her brow. She returned the frame to its place on the desk, face down. It was a ridiculous thought and she chased it quickly away. There would be no little boys who looked like Steven or little girls who looked like her. Put quite simply, there would be no children.

She was about to leave when she realized she hadn't examined the contents of his wastebasket. Picking through it, she found a page from the morning newspaper. An article had been cut out. She folded the paper, stuffed it in her purse, and returned home. Safely inside her bedroom, she took her own copy of the paper, found the corresponding page, and studied the piece that had been removed:

IN CONCERT
KATALIN GÁSPÁR
THE PRINCESS OF THE PIANO RETURNS.

The advertisement went on to trumpet the reemergence of one of classical music's brightest stars. According to the article that accompanied the ad, this was the first time in five years the estimable Miss Gáspár had performed outside the Iron Curtain. The last time she had been seen was at the finals of the Chickering International Piano Competition. She had garnered first place, but because her mother was seriously ill, she had elected to forfeit her prizes and return to Hungary. Since then, for all intents and purposes she had disappeared.

"Well, well, well," Cynthia said aloud, examining the young woman in the advertisement, hoping the photograph was old or heavily retouched.

It didn't take a genius to figure out that this Gáspár was related to the Gáspár whom Steven had described as a family friend. It was possible that she was just that—a friend—and his visit to Paris was nothing more than a gesture based on old feelings for old times. It was also possible that this was the woman he had loved.

Whatever his reasons, Steven clearly intended to be in the audience when Katalin Gáspár took the stage. So did Cynthia.

Backstage at the *Salle Pleyel,* Katalin rested on a chaise longue in her dressing room, her eyes closed, her hands folded across her chest. Clothed in nothing but her underwear and a light robe, she lay quietly, attempting to blank her mind and enter the state of total absorption she needed to perform. Usually it was easy. She would breathe deeply and meditate on something pleasant—a peaceful scene, a poetic verse, an enjoyable memory. Tonight she was finding it difficult to let the music in. Her mind was jammed, her body was tight

This concert meant a great deal to her. If it went well, it could mean other concert dates in other European cities. It could mean recording contracts and increased prestige. This was the opportunity she had been waiting for for five years, the chance to resuscitate her stalled career, to breathe life into her dream of being an international star.

During these past years, barely a day had gone by without Katalin's sitting down at the piano. Often, when she had felt the loneliest, she had practiced with the same driving intensity she would have employed if she'd had a concert the very next day. As always, music was her succor, her sustenance, her escape from the harshness of her reality. Though

Andras was acting as her manager, arranging concert dates within the boundaries set by Kocsis's Ministry of Culture, Katalin's method of practice had not varied at all from the routine Paul Greco had established for her. She selected a piece and "read" it until she felt she knew the meaning behind every measure, the feeling within every section of the score. Then she worked out her fingering, the pedaling, the tempo, the dynamics. When a particular piece gave her trouble, she could almost hear Greco demanding that she work harder, that she look deeper, first into the soul of the composer and then into the soul of the pianist.

"Find the common ground," he used to say to her. "Find that place where both souls can meet and rejoice in the music."

Tonight, in addition to Liszt, the composer whose work had become her signature, Katalin was playing Debussy's "L'Isle Joyeuse." Claude Debussy was new for her and she had searched hard for his soul, but until a few days ago it had managed to elude her. After she and László had arrived in Paris, he rested while she took herself to the Louvre to spend time with the Watteau painting that had inspired the piece. Camping on one of the benches that lined the long hallway where the Watteau was displayed, she tried to climb inside Debussy's head and pinpoint precisely what had triggered the Frenchman's musical imagination.

The painting, called "The Embarkment for Cythère," depicted lovers crossing to Cytherea, the mythical island near which Aphrodite was fabled to have risen from the waves. The colors were soft, feathery, misty pastels that seemed to sit lightly on the canvas. Katalin suspected Debussy had delighted in the diffused colorations, because he had achieved the same sfumato by softening the edges of his chording. Within a single chord, he had created a world: a seeing, feeling, hearing world filled with delicacy and atmosphere. It was as if his notes, like Watteau's clouds, hovered in space like a constellation of sound, an airy contrast to the solid ground below.

But color and chording were surface. She was searching for spirit. Finally, after hours of staring and dreaming and thinking and placing herself in that Edenic setting, it came to her. The painting held a story within its frame, a poetic allegory that used the crossing to the island as a euphemism for an amorous adventure. This was not about courtship with a plan or a long-term relationship. This was about the exciting uncertainty of love, the joy of stolen moments, the thrill of taking a chance.

Katalin had smiled then, just as she smiled now. How many times had Sophie admonished her when she had fretted about what was going to happen with Steven. How many times had Sophie told her, "Just have fun," or "Just go with the flow." The smile faded. Katalin wasn't good at just having fun. She took things too seriously and she knew it. It was hard for her to think of her time with Steven as just an amorous adventure that had existed, run its course, and then had simply ceased to exist. According to her other, more existential confidante, Judit, it didn't matter how it had ended. It was, it had been wonderful and she had to be grateful for that.

"You have to treat your memories the same way you would treat precious jewels," she had said to Katalin. "You put them away in a safe place where no one can steal them or tamper with them so that when you're alone and you need to be reminded of something important, you have them to comfort you. For me, when I need to remember that I'm a desirable woman, I think about Attila. I'll never see him again, but I have my memories. It's not what I wanted, but it's enough."

It had taken Katalin years, but eventually she had relegated her heartache over Steven to the past. It surfaced now and then. When it did, she retrieved her memories, she luxuriated in them and treasured them and relived them. Sometimes she cried. Sometimes, as now, she called on them for courage, because in the blur of time, Steven had come to represent those years when life had been lyrical and exhilarating and she had felt confident and triumphant and deliciously free.

Her thoughts circled back to the concert ahead of her. Freedom was exactly what she had come to Paris to find. Musical freedom. Artistic freedom. The ability to play wherever and whatever she wanted, whenever she wanted. Almost from the day they were married, she had implored László to use his influence on Kocsis, to convince the boorish minister to allow her to travel outside the Bloc. Now that he had, Katalin felt pressured to prove herself—to the Western music critics, to Western audiences, to the international music community, and to László. Though he professed great pride in her career, he had trouble understanding her need to perform outside the Eastern Bloc. To him, playing fifty concerts a year in cities like Moscow and Leningrad and Leipzig and Dresden and Bratislava and Cracow should have been more than satisfying. The halls were large and grand. The audiences were knowledgeable and enthusiastic. Most of the time, because he had business in those cities, he was able to accompany her when she traveled. She was always well received and well reviewed. He couldn't fathom wanting more.

Katalin had tried to explain that musicians had to play and performers had to perform, that fifty concerts were not a lot, that it was the exposure to varied audiences that was important, not the location or the politics of those audiences. But, as she was beginning to learn, politics defined László in a way nothing else did. To be a communist, to be an officer in the army that protected a socialistic state, was something honorable and commendable, the work of a man concerned with good and welfare, not the banal concepts of profit and loss. On the rare occasions when he and Katalin discussed the differences between East and West, László decried capitalism, calling it the true oppressor, denouncing it as a system that needed an impoverished lower class to fuel the machine that fed the rich. Katalin had come to see that arguing with him about it was senseless. She didn't live in New York. She lived in Budapest, where his ideas were those of the majority. And her ideas were treason.

Lying on her chaise, still waiting for a sense of calm to descend, she wondered why he had agreed to this particular concert. Was it a concession? A way of proving a point? Another gift? In the year and a half they had been married, Katalin had discovered her husband was a generous man who enjoyed lavishing her with surprises. Some were small—bouquets of flowers, a special dinner out, an intimate uncorking of a vintage bottle of wine. Some were grand—a vacation on the Black Sea, an amber necklace from Poland, crystal goblets from Finland, a weekend at the spa at Karlsbad. Though she was delighted with his thoughtfulness, sometimes she felt he needed to shower her with presents because he found it easier to express his love for her with tangibles than with words.

László was a man who kept his emotions in check most of the time. In public, he rarely touched her; if they were at a dinner with politicos, he barely spoke to her, rarely revealed much about himself. Even in private he was restrained about how much he said. He told her he loved her. He told her he thought she was beautiful. But infrequently. It was only in bed that he wasn't afraid to be open and passionate. Whenever they made love—and it was often—László adored her, exalting her loveliness with his hands, glorifying her womanliness with his lips, giving physically what he couldn't give verbally. The problem was that Katalin enjoyed affection as much as she enjoyed sex. She liked hugging and kissing and holding hands and walking arm in arm, and though she encouraged László to reciprocate, he was incapable of such public displays. And so, Katalin believed, he compensated with gifts.

If that was what this concert was, Katalin decided, thankful that at last her body had begun to relax and her mind had begun to empty, she would accept it without questions and thank him with a gift of her own. She would give him a performance he could be proud of.

The audience offered Katalin a tumultuous welcome and Steven was abruptly transported to New York, to a box in Avery Fisher Hall where he had watched the same magnificent creature take the stage. Katalin was wearing a different gown from the one she had worn then, but it was black and it was strapless and, made of a fine silk, it draped her lean form like a tube of gossamer. Her hair was twisted and pinned into a style distinctly French, definitely chic. Still, a few tendrils had escaped, pirouetting on her shoulders like pixies dancing on a pearl. He had to fight to control the rush of emotions that flooded him when she bowed to the audience and he was able to gaze at her face, to see the green of her eyes, the luscious puff of her lips, the smooth velvet of her skin. As she took her seat, it was all he could do not to bound onstage.

Though the program listed Katalin's first offering as Schumann's Toccata in C major, describing the work as "bracing and energetic," Steven heard little of it. He was mesmerized by her presence. He watched her hands. He studied her face. He tried to remember the sound of her voice, the feel of her touch. Guiltily, the touch he recalled was Cynthia's—the memory of their two days together was fresh and hot; his time with Katalin was fuzzy and distant.

Katalin's Debussy better fit his mood. Poignant yet joyous, sensuous yet polite, the piece seemed to illustrate the contrapuntal state of his emotions as his feelings pushed against each other. One minute he was certain that fate had put the ad for this concert in front of him just at the point when he was seriously considering a future with another woman, warning him not to make a decision until after he had come to Paris. The next minute, he dismissed those thoughts as the immature reflections of someone who had always had trouble letting go. It had been five years. He was not the same. How could he think she was the same, that their feelings were the same, that nothing had changed except their ages.

Finally, in Katalin's Liszt, the Sonata in B minor he had heard her play before, he could hear her maturity as a musician, see her confidence as a performer. With the passage of time she had matured: What had been an exceptional talent had become an incomparable one. When the audience stormed to their feet to express their awe with a thunderous ovation, some tossing flowers, others shouting "Brava!" Steven rose with them, not just to applaud the woman onstage, but to acknowledge the woman who, despite time and distance and other distractions, still lived in his heart.

Katalin felt as if she had swallowed a July Fourth's worth of fire-crackers. Emotions rocketed. Feelings boomed. Her head reeled. Everything was light and color and sound and unbelievably intense sensation. Waves of riotous, uproarious applause surged toward her from the belly of the cavernous concert hall, bursting onstage, charging through her system like jolts of electricity, making her blood race and her temples pulse. She had been gifted with ovations before, showered with adulation and praise and shouts of undisguised worship, yet this felt gloriously, deliciously singular.

Looking at the faces of the hundreds who now stood at her feet, her own face burning with the flush of success, she knew she had done what she had set out to do. She had trained for this moment, prayed for this moment, longed for this moment for five interminable years. And now . . . now, perhaps, her horizons could stretch beyond the curtain of repression. Maybe now she could open the window of her talent on to a greater vista, a larger panorama. Those three brief years in New York had exposed her to the limitless possibility afforded by the free world, to the infinite store of opportunity available on the other side. Katalin had tasted that freedom and, with an insatiable craving as for a sweet or a drug, she had never lost her determination to taste it again.

As she stood to receive the admiration of her audience and to gather the bouquets they had strewn before her, a sea of friendly smiles and encouraging eyes stared at her, prompting a wild, crazy thought. What if she defected? What if she simply left the stage, walked out the side door, headed for the American Embassy and asked for asylum? She bowed low, covering the traitorous thoughts she knew must have been displayed on her features. The Americans would take her in. She could return to New York. To Zsuzsanna. To Sophie. To Paul Greco. To Steven.

The thought began to grow, sprouting like a weed after a healthy rain. Why not? she asked herself. Zoltán was settled into his new life. He would miss her and she would miss him, but now that he had made peace with his muse, surely he would understand her need to satisfy hers.

Smothering thoughts of László and what it would mean to leave him, stifling the pull of the life she had in Hungary, she bent down to retrieve yet another bouquet. As she did, a single blossom fell at her feet, crashing through her fantasy with a reminder of her reality. It was a wild rose tied with a pink ribbon. She straightened up quickly, searching the front rows for Tibor, knowing the flower had to have come from him. Unable to spot him, she turned to the side aisles, but with everyone standing, if he was there—and she knew he was—he was hidden by the mass of bodies. She didn't know how he had gotten out of Hungary or how he had made his way to Paris, but before she exited, she lifted the wild rose above her head, smiled and waved to the man she had come to think of as her invisible friend.

• • •

Backstage, László stood off to the side, watching as members of the musical world and the international press, as well as Paris society bedecked in couture, bejeweled in precious gems, fawned over his wife. In languages he didn't understand they congratulated her and praised her. Some, he knew, were offering her concert dates and record contracts and anything else they thought they could use to profit off her talent.

László's feelings were mixed. Katalin had been brilliant, there was no denying that. He was proud and impressed and completely over- whelmed by her ability. Moreover, he was gratified to call her his wife, to know that, first and foremost, she belonged to him. Yet he was uncom- fortable: jealous of the way men looked at her in that sleek, strapless dress she had insisted upon wearing; disconcerted by the way she appeared so at ease in the spotlight, so comfortable with the concept of fame. Though he was certain no one here thought so, he knew that to his comrades back in Budapest and his superiors in Moscow, her behavior would be viewed as unbecoming to the wife of a future member of the Politburo.

He was about to rescue her from the pool of flattery before she drowned, when, suddenly, he noticed Katalin's face had gone ashen. She was staring at a man coming toward her with a pace that quickened the closer he got to her. Before László knew what was happening, Katalin pulled away from the crowd and ran into the stranger's arms.

Katalin felt as if an angel had lifted her off the ground and trans- ported her to heaven. She saw his face, but didn't trust her eyes. She heard his voice, but was certain her ears were playing tricks. It couldn't be him. He was thousands of miles away in another place, another time, another world. Elongating seconds until they had been stretched so far they became minutes, she stayed where she was and studied the features of the mirage: the blue eyes, the scar, the planed cheeks, the strong build, the upper lip with the deep arch, the lower lip with the gentle swell. He looked familiar. The aura rang true. But still, she couldn't accept that he stood before her. It was only when he took her in his arms that she knew for certain.

"If I blink, will you be gone?" she said, whispering as if she was afraid someone would hear her, yet clinging to him as if she didn't care who saw or who knew how much it meant to her to see him again.

"I didn't come all this way to be gone in a blink," he replied, pressing her closer, wanting to feel the bond that had once joined them refastening.

Katalin's entire being was in a state of excitation. Just the feel of his body next to hers made her heart pound like a kettledrum, banging inside her chest until she thought it would burst. Though she sensed a dozen eyes staring at them, a dozen tongues questioning her behavior, she was loath to separate from Steven. She would have been content to remain in his arms forever, but wonder and curiosity won out. She had to look at him again, to assure herself that he wasn't a hallucination, that he wasn't a manifestation of a bizarre dream she had been having onstage, that she hadn't gone completely mad. When they did part, she felt a rush of desperation, a fear that now that they had left a space, someone or something would come between them.

"You were wonderful," Steven said, still holding her hands in his. "You look wonderful." He laughed at his own blithering. "I feel wonderful being here with you."

"Me too," Katalin admitted, her cheeks stained with a blush. "Where did you come from?" she asked, suddenly starved for news about what he was doing, where he was living, why he hadn't contacted her.

"London. I'm with the American Embassy there." Katalin nodded. He had answered only one of her questions. "I saw an ad in the paper for this concert and knew I had to be here." His eyes darkened and his grip on her hands tightened. "I had to see you, Katya, to touch you, to know if you were all right, to . . . to find out what had happened to you."

"Miss Gáspár. We need a picture." Before she could stop them, one man pulled her away from Steven while another urged her to smile as he snapped her photograph. When they were finished, she turned back to Steven and tried to continue their conversation, anxious to recapture the mood.

"Mama died," she said, anticipating the mournful shadow that passed over his eyes.

"I hope it was merciful."

"It wasn't."

Steven held her again, hating himself for using Mária's death as an excuse to hold her daughter, but his feelings disobeyed his will. He was helpless to control them.

"And then I had to take care of Papa." Katalin stepped back, suddenly frightened by the powerful surge of her own emotions. Love and anger, sadness and elation, all were beginning to eddy inside her. "He's taken up conducting." She smiled, her mouth edged with a touch of personal victory, Steven thought.

"Someone at the embassy was at his debut concert. He said Zoltán was wonderful."

"He was," she said. "I think he's finally happy."

"And you?" Confusion and shades of irritation edged his voice and outlined his face. "Are you happy in Budapest?"

Bewilderment visited her eyes as she contemplated his question. She had never really had the option of considering whether or not she was happy. It was a state of mind that never seemed prominent enough or lasted long enough to require examination. In the years since she had returned, she had simply responded to events, bouncing from one to the other like a soccer ball being kicked about a field. Some events were more pleasant than others. Some of her responses had been more enjoyable than others. But happy? At best, it was a moot point.

"Now or then?" she said quietly, yet not without a tinge of resentment. If he wanted to know why she had stayed, she wanted to know why he hadn't questioned the delay in her return to the States.

"Both," Steven said, unsure as to how he felt about the sudden stiffness in her pose, the darkening of her voice.

"Then, I was frantic. I wanted to come back to you. You don't know how much I wanted to come back to you. But," she said, choking back the ghost of heartbreak, swallowing a reincarnated hurt, "I couldn't leave Papa. Later, when he was settled, I applied for a visa, but was denied. They never even allowed me to play outside the Iron Curtain until now."

Steven rubbed his hands across his eyes in frustration and grief and disgust.

"Two dozen. Three dozen. Four dozen letters." He shook his head. "I wrote and I wrote and I checked my mailbox every day for the letters I was sure you had written. I mailed letters from ten different states! I never got so much as a postcard."

"I wrote," she said, finding an odd contentment in the sight of his pain, recalling those two censored letters and finally understanding what had happened, that his silence hadn't been of his own doing. "You know I wrote," she said, hating the fact that they were both defending themselves against something beyond themselves. "I loved you. How could I not?"

Steven stared at her, letting her words sluice over him, giving himself time to understand the enormity of what had happened to them. "They've robbed us of so many years." He sighed and took her hands in his, raising them to his lips, resting them there for a moment before propriety demanded he drop them. "And now?" he asked, moving forward, needing one more answer to one more question. "Are you happy now?"

Katalin's face took on a strange aspect, but before she could respond, more reporters and photographers interrupted, bombarding her with questions about her future. Steven wanted to shout at them, to chase them away, to make them disappear. He hadn't finished catching up on the past or finding out about the present or offering suggestions for a future.

Just then, a dark-haired, dark-eyed man in the uniform of the Hungarian Army approached Katalin, took her in his arms, kissed her, and adroitly spirited her away. They talked briefly then returned to Steven. Katalin looked uncomfortable. The army officer was smiling as he stuck out his hand.

"I understand you're an old friend of Katalin's. I'm Böhm László," he said in Hungarian.

"Nice to meet you," Steven said in English, shaking the man's hand, disliking the look in his eye and the hollow, ominous feeling he had in the pit of his stomach.

"I'm Katalin's husband."

A thick curtain of awkwardness descended. Steven looked from László to Katalin for confirmation of what this stranger had just said. He waited for Katalin to deny the blasphemy that had fouled the air. Instead, Katalin simply nodded as, again, László embraced her.

It was a move that annoyed her. He had never done it before, despite her entreaties that he be more demonstrative, despite her need for him to show more affection for her. Why now? Now when she was struggling with the indescribable anguish she saw contorting Steven's face, now when she wished he would leave and allow her the privacy she needed to explain herself to Steven. But László stood firm.

"I understand you were born in Hungary." There was a trace of derision in his tone, the implicit criticism from one who stayed to one who left.

"I emigrated in '56. After my parents were killed," Steven said sharply, knowing he was reacting to the uniform, knowing, too, that he was reacting to the intimacy between this man and Katalin. "I'm an American citizen now."

Pride and defiance underlined his words. His fists had clenched. His jaw had tightened. His body was so rigid he almost didn't feel the arm that slinked around his waist or the lips that grazed against his cheek.

"Hello, darling," Cynthia Rhinehart oozed, as if she had been by his side all evening. "I've been looking all over for you." Without waiting for an answer, she turned to Katalin and took both of Katalin's hands in hers. "You were simply divine, my dear. Never have I heard anything quite so exquisite. Wasn't she exquisite, sweetheart?"

If Steven weren't in such excruciating pain, he would have laughed. Cynthia's performance was nearly as professional as Katalin's.

"And you are?" she asked, reaching for László's hand, tossing her gleaming dark mane onto her back, making certain the uptight military man with the fabulous eyes and the scowling mouth didn't miss a decoration on her uniform: not her black, one-shoulder, Madame Grès Grecian-styled gown, or her enormous ruby and diamond brooch, or her ruby and diamond bracelet, or her long, ruby red nails.

"László Böhm," he said, dazzled in spite of himself. "Katalin's husband."

"You must be so proud." She smiled for a millisecond, then dismissed the major as a general would dismiss a private, and turned to Steven. "I hate to drag you away from your friends, darling, but we do have a party to attend."

"Right." Steven wanted to punch László for stealing Katalin, scream at Katalin for breaking his heart, and kiss Cynthia for saving his ego. All he could do was nod and say, "It was good to see you again, Katalin. You were special."

After he and Cynthia left, Katalin's insides collapsed. She knew he hadn't been referring to her music. He had been talking about them, what they had been to each other, what they could have been, what they should have been. She was certain she would never forget the look on his face when László introduced himself as her husband. She had hurt him terribly and she knew it. Only God knew how much she had hurt herself. She wanted to run after him and beg his forgiveness and try to explain, but László was standing next to her. There were reporters and photographers and impresarios crowding around her. She was basking in the warmth of her success, surrounded by her celebrity and her husband.

So why, she wondered, did she feel so cold and so very alone?

Two days later, before a justice of the peace in Paris's City Hall, Cynthia Rhinehart and Steven Kardos became husband and wife. Cynthia wasn't certain that Steven had been honest when he had pledged to forsake all others, but then again, Cynthia had never placed a high priority on honesty. To her, the most important thing was getting what she wanted. She had. And she didn't care how.

IV

Variations

1977–1983

26

London, November 1977

*A*cross from their bed, a sudden downdraft propelled a puff of
gray smoke through the nineteenth-century brass-edged firescreen into the
eggshell blue room. As if to affirm that an outside force had been responsible for the cloud of soot, a gust of cold, damp air rushed through the
lone open window, pushed past the striped silk draperies and slapped
Cynthia's bare shoulders with an icy chill. Without taking her eyes off
the newspaper she was reading, she reached for her quilted satin bedjacket
and slid her arms into the loose, lace-trimmed sleeves. Still reading, she
groped about on her nightstand, located her coffee, and lifted the delicate
china cup to her lips, grimacing as the tepid brew painted her tongue
with an acrid aftertaste. Issuing a grunt of mild disgust, she returned the
cup to its saucer and her attention to the article before her.

In the six months they had been married, the Kardoses had established several family traditions. Monday nights, unless it was a matter of
state, they dined alone. Wednesday afternoons, they had tea with Owen.
Whenever possible, they declared a quiet night. Steven listened to classi-

cal music and read a novel. Cynthia indulged in beauty treatments—
bubble baths and steams and facials and massages. Sunday mornings,
they had breakfast in bed, usually following a languorous but intensely
satisfying session of lovemaking. Afterward, they piled stacks of newspapers on the bed and spent the better part of the day going through them.
While Steven digested every single word of the *London Times, The Herald
International,* and *The New York Times,* Cynthia perused *The Washington Post* and then skimmed a week's worth of *The Herald Leader,* the
Lexington daily. This particular morning, she had found the same item
in both papers, an item which had her extremely excited.

"This is such good news!" she exclaimed with a huge smile. "I can't
believe what a stroke of luck this is!"

"What is?" Steven asked, his response perfunctory, his interest
casual. He was certain that Cynthia's bulletin was just a bit of gossip
about an old schoolmate. If he had learned anything about his new wife,
it was that Cynthia loved gossip. Not because she cared about the people
involved or because she enjoyed frittering away a few hours with harmless
small talk. Rather, it was because Cynthia was a woman who stored
information away for later use.

"Hale Preston dropped dead last Wednesday."

"And that's good news?" Hale Preston was the congressman from
Cynthia's home district. Nearly seventy, he had served in the House of
Representatives for twenty years and was much beloved by his constituents.

"Not for him, of course, but for us it's fabulous!" Cynthia turned
toward her husband, hooked her hand around the back of his neck and
pulled his mouth to hers for a quick, hard kiss. "Don't you see? Dear,
sweet Uncle Hale's demise creates a blank on the ballot, a perfectly timed,
positively propitious, absolutely divine blank."

"How considerate of him," Steven said, recognizing that she hadn't
heard what he said, let alone the facetious way he'd said it. Judging by
the distracted look on her face, it was clear that she didn't care a whit if
her naked delight over this man's passing—not just any man, mind you,
but an old family friend—appeared ghoulish or inappropriate. As complicated as Cynthia was, that was how basic she was. Despite the many
twists and turns of her personality, she had a one-track, fast-track mind.
Goals took precedence over sentiment; getting to the finish line first was
the bottom line to everything she did. This death had provided an opportunity. Why waste time and energy on nonproductive emotions like sympathy or remorse or sincere condolence?

Though it wasn't his way, oddly enough Steven understood, and in
this case respected that single-minded calculation. He wasn't naive about
the political process. He knew there was no magic wand to spirit him

into the House of Representatives on the wings of a wish. If he wanted it—and he did—he was going to have to go after it.

"If Hale had died last year," Cynthia said, still figuring, still conjuring, "the governor would have appointed someone to finish out his term."

"And that someone would have become an instant incumbent," Steven said, completing her thought. "Since he wouldn't have been in office long enough to do anything either way, he would have been extremely difficult to remove."

Cynthia nodded and twisted her lips, looking as if she had just sucked a lemon. "Especially because the voting public is lazy. They love incumbents because they don't have to work too hard to be informed," she said sarcastically. "If he hasn't done anything criminal, he's done a good job." She sighed and rolled her eyes as if the task of dealing with the great unwashed American public was simply too tedious and too distasteful to discuss. "However," she said, back to business, "since it's less than a year before the election, my guess is the governor will leave the seat vacant."

"I agree," Steven said, his thoughts running along the same track as his wife's. "Why should the governor risk criticism when he can avoid the issue completely?"

"Exactly!" Cynthia's hazel eyes glowed so, they looked as if they had been shot with electricity. "It's just the opportunity we've been waiting for. The party will need a candidate. And you, my precious, are just the man they need."

"Says who?"

Cynthia scrambled onto her knees and took Steven's face in her hands. She fixed on his eyes and for a long moment peered inside, plumbing the depths of his commitment, assessing the strength of his resolution to succeed. They were about to embark on the Ulyssean journey that was the purpose of their union; it was their destiny, and in order to fulfill it, they had to be as one. She looked deeper, searching for the molten core of his ambition. When she could feel the orange heat of determination radiating from within his soul, she smiled and kissed him firmly on the mouth. "Says me."

"That makes two of us," Steven said, admiring the sinuous curves of her body as she climbed out of bed, slid her feet into maribou-trimmed mules, and replaced her bedjacket with a proper robe. "A clear consensus."

Cynthia dismissed his sarcasm with a wave of her hand. "The Republicans are going to run that stiff, Albert Thornbridge. The man is a born loser if I've ever met one, and believe me, I have known a great many losers in my time. We're going to win this election in a walk."

"Is that before or after I'm crowned Emperor of Oz?" Steven crossed his arms and stared at her as she bent over and ran a brush through her long, dark hair. His mouth was set in a bemused half-smile.

"Make fun if you must," she said, swinging her hair back, brushing harder.

"I'm not making fun, but really, Cynthia. It's naive to think the Democrats are frantically beating the bushes trying to find someone to run against Thornbridge. Their list of possible candidates must be a block long. Preston wasn't a youngster, and you of all people know that party policy demands they give the shot to someone who's been in the organization for a while, someone who's paid his dues."

"I do so love your idealism, darling," she said, leaning forward toward the mirror atop her dressing table, giving her skin a quick once-over, "but let me give you your first lesson in real life." Satisfied that during the night nothing had sneaked in and ravaged her porcelain finish, she completed her personal inventory and gave Steven her full attention. "The powers that be don't care about some local-yokel and his nickel-dime dues. They care about dollars. Cash dollars. In politics the Golden Rule is this: The one who has the gold, rules."

Steven wanted to disagree, but he couldn't. To him, government represented a chance to do something worthwhile, something that would benefit the people and improve the quality of their lives. He believed that to most involved in the system it was just that; that in spite of the abuses and the occasional revelations of corruption, most members of Congress believed in their mission of goodwill. But, to get to Capitol Hill, one had to climb—over others as well as up. The question was whether he was willing to do that, whether he was aggressive enough to keep his eyes straight ahead without too many sideward glances. The answer was, yes, within reason, he was. Because, to him, the end justified the means.

"Where are you going?" he asked, coming out of his fog, watching Cynthia trot toward her sitting room. "We have to talk about this."

"To get my phone book. I'm going to place a little wake-up call to Wendell Vaughn. He's the party chairman and over the years, he has pocketed many, many Rhinehart dollars." She disappeared into the other room. A second later, she poked her head through the door and grinned at him. "If I were you, darling, I'd start packing. We'll have plenty of time to talk on the plane back to Kentucky!"

Steven found Owen in the family sitting room, studying the dozens of photographs that lined the bottom shelf of the bookcases flanking the rose-marble fireplace. There were pictures of him with reigning heads of state, politicians, royalty, film and television personalities, society swells. There were several photographs of Claudia and her husband and children, several of Owen and his grandchildren, and two of Cecilia—one in her wedding gown, one a portrait taken only weeks before she died. The sole picture of Cynthia was the one she'd had taken of herself and Steven in Paris, on the day they were married. It was that picture Owen held in his hands when Steven entered the room.

"Smartest thing that filly ever did was to hitch up with you," Owen said, without turning around. He replaced the picture on the shelf. As he did, he appeared drawn to the likeness of his late wife. His eyes lingered on her portrait for a few seconds.

It amazed Steven that after all these years, Owen still evidenced such tremendous pain over the loss of his wife. Once or twice Steven had asked Cynthia about Cecilia's accident. She had refused to discuss it.

With obvious reluctance, Owen let go of the picture. When he turned and faced his son-in-law, though he forced his mouth to smile, his eyes retained a tinge of sadness. "I don't know how clever you were for agreeing to marry her, however."

With a cynical laugh he invited Steven in, beckoning him to take a seat. Steven settled on the large celery green sofa that sat along the far wall of the room. In front of him a brass-legged, glass-topped cocktail table held an antique sterling silver coffee service, a plate of sweet rolls, and two settings of bone china, heirloom flatware, and linen. Owen eased himself into a club chair upholstered in a gold-and-white paisley-patterned silk damask.

"When are you leaving?"

"Tomorrow morning." Steven had taken on the task of pouring the coffee. Owen took milk and two sugars. Steven drank his black. "I don't know what Cynthia said to Wendell Vaughn, but whatever it was, he agreed to my candidacy." Though he had had several days to absorb the news, Steven was still in shock. "Can you believe I'm going to be running for Congress?"

Owen took his cup from Steven. He stirred the coffee several times before tasting it.

"I believe it and I approve of it," he said, a slow smile building. "You're good people, Steven. You'll make a fine congressman."

Steven wondered how much input Owen had had in Vaughn's decision. "Your support means a great deal to me. I . . . ."

Despite Owen's ego, he was embarrassed by compliments and expressions of emotion. Instead of allowing an awkward situation to develop, he cut Steven off. "I've offered Cynthia the house in Lexington."

"I know." Cynthia had been shocked, convinced that the only reason her father had done such a thing was because he cared about Steven. It couldn't have been because he cared about her. "Thank you. That's very generous, Owen."

"Generous my butt! It's selfish on the one hand and politic on the other. The house has been standing empty and I don't like that. Also, there's the question of residency. I know you're officially listed as living with your brother, and that's fortunate since it's in the right district. But if you're going to carry the Rhinehart flag, you have to live on Rhinehart land."

In spite of himself, Steven bucked. He was his own man, running on his own name, with his own agenda. He didn't want to be thought of as carrying anyone else's flag, even his wife's.

Owen must have sensed he hit a nerve, because the instant Steven's eyes went dark, he reached out and patted the younger man's hand. "I didn't mean that the way it sounded, Steven. I know how independent you are. It's one of the qualities I respect most about you. But everyone needs a leg up. I had my ancestors. You have me. It's not a sin, boy, to use whatever you can to get out of the gate, nor is it a crime." He watched for signs of softening and understanding. The last thing he wanted was to create discord between them. "I'll tell you something else, if you don't use what's available to you, someone else will use it against you."

"You're right. I overreacted, I guess. I'm sorry. I don't mean to behave like a spoiled, ungrateful brat."

"You don't have it in you to be a brat, Steven," Owen said with genuine liking. Suddenly, he chuckled. "Cynthia's another story, however. She was born spoiled. Or haven't you figured that out by now?"

Steven smiled. "She is a bit on the determined side."

"What a nice way of putting it. In my neck of the woods, they call it pigheaded. But since you're the one living with her, you can call it whatever you like."

Steven laughed. He enjoyed these moments with Owen. Over the years they had forged a unique friendship. They were not, despite the efforts of people like Clarke Estridge wishing to label them thus, a pseudo-sublimated father-son. Thanks to Matthew, Steven had no need for a father figure. And to those astute enough to notice, it should have been clear that Owen derived little pleasure from parenting. Theirs was a symbiotic friendship. Steven benefited from Owen's political knowledge and experience. Owen found inspiration in Steven's drive and integrity. Their connection was a fierce loyalty to the idea of democracy and an intellectual trust, a belief that a question honestly asked would be honestly answered. Because they shared a vision of a world dedicated to freedom and peaceful coexistence, even between enemies, and because they were willing to commit their lives to working toward that end, they had created a bond that continued to strengthen—despite the fact that Owen frequently disappointed Steven with what Steven considered abuses of the system, and Steven had disappointed Owen with what Owen considered his ill-advised marriage to Cynthia.

"Was running for Congress your idea or hers?" Owen asked.

"It was a mutual decision."

"Want some advice?"

"From you, yes."

"Surround yourself with good people, Steven. People you trust. Who think the way you think. Who want what you want. It's tough enough fighting the system. Fighting with your staff is hell."

Steven hadn't gotten that far, but now that Owen mentioned it, he realized that, subconsciously, he already had several names on his list.

"Another thing. Don't waver. Voters are allowed to be undecided. Not candidates. If you take a position, die with it if you must, but don't waffle."

"Will you be able to make a campaign appearance on my behalf?"

Owen smiled. "I love you for asking, son, but let's take a wait and see on that. You may find that I'm the last one you want speaking out for you. But," he said, spotting disappointment, "if you need me, I'm there. How's that?"

"Good enough."

Owen nodded, glad they had cleared that up. Then he stared into his cup, as if he were looking for fortune-telling tea leaves in the remains of his coffee.

"Do you love Cynthia?"

"Yes." Steven thought he answered immediately, but he had hesitated for a second. Owen had heard the pause as clearly as if it had been a cannon blast.

"My last bit of advice is a warning." He put down his cup and looked Steven squarely in the eye. "My daughter is a beautiful woman, Steven. I grant you that. And I'm certain she's quite expert at plying her feminine charms. But take it from me, she's a viper. Make love to her with your eyes open, boy, 'cause if you don't, one of these days she's gonna cut your balls off."

Mayfair Farms sprawled over three thousand acres of prime bluegrass. It boarded five hundred horses, including twelve stallions and two hundred mares. Aside from the stables and the dozen other structures dedicated to the care and breeding of thoroughbreds, there were several houses on the property: a large red-brick Federal-style home built as a wedding present for Claudia and her husband, Billy Fieldston; an old farmhouse that Cecilia had converted into a spacious guesthouse; and, sitting high on a rise, Mayfair House, a stately white Classical Revival mansion.

Having grown up in Kentucky, Steven had heard all about the fairy-tale homes at the end of mile-long, tree-lined drives. He had seen pictures of Kentucky's royalty frolicking on the lawns of estates that had names instead of street addresses and garages with more square footage than most houses in Woodridge. On those rare occasions when he and Matthew had driven to Lexington, they had made a game of speculating about who lived in those invisible palaces marked by intimidating roadside gates and fences. Never, in his wildest dreams, did Steven ever expect to be riding up one of those drives in a chauffeured limousine driven by a man who called him "Sir."

While it was true that he had been residing in Winfield House for the past several months, an august home if ever he saw one, and was therefore not a virgin when it came to grandeur, he had thought of Winfield as government property. This house was private property, and his first sight of it literally took his breath away. Massive in structure yet inviting by design, it was truly spectacular. Four thickly fluted Ionic columns supported a roofline that extended over a veranda skirting the entire front of the house. Large windows shuttered in black maintained a sense of architectural symmetry while creating an illusion of lightness and openness, appearing to cut the density of the building so that its enormous size didn't overwhelm the eye.

Owen had told Steven that the original decoration had been done by his wife, and that although over the years he had employed interior designers to refresh and refurbish, the vision remained Cecilia's. And what an elegant vision it was. Exquisite French antiques rubbed gilded shoulders with sumptuous fabrics and sophisticated furnishings and hand-loomed rugs and prize pieces of art. Words like *Aubusson* and *ormolu* and *bureau plat* and *Régence*, which once had as much impact on Steven's life as algebra equations, were suddenly gaining in meaning. He walked on, sat in, would dine from, and sleep on treasures that defied his imagination.

For the first few days following their arrival, while Cynthia attended to the business of settling in and arranging a dinner for Steven to meet state party officials, Steven continued to explore his new environment. The particulars of decor had never been part of his consciousness. Here, as he had done at Winfield House, he found himself examining every object, every bowl, every box, every bibelot; appreciating, studying, memorizing, trying to learn and retain. He ran his fingers across finely polished woods and luxurious fabrics. He stood in front of each painting until it no longer felt like a stranger. He examined the craftsmanship of the furniture maker, the artistry of the painter. He observed details like the inlaid leaf design that bordered the highly polished, mahogany-stained floors; the sponge work on the foyer's terra-cotta-colored walls that created the look of an Italian villa; the silk grass cloth that upholstered the walls of the living room, adding texture as well as color to the high-ceilinged space.

Most of all, he tried to make himself comfortable within his new surroundings. Despite its obvious appeal, Steven found that difficult. It wasn't his home. Owen owned the deed to Mayfair Farms, and Owen's wife still reigned as chatelaine, even if only in spirit. If that wasn't enough to make him feel irrelevant, Claudia ran the horse farm, her husband oversaw the care of the land, and Cynthia had declared the main house as her domain. Though there were servants aplenty, one to tend to each of his needs, his greatest need appeared to be defining his own territory within the Rhinehart kingdom.

After careful consideration of his options, he decided that for the time being he would have to satisfy himself by simply taking dominion over himself and his fledgling political career. To that end, he closeted himself in Owen's library, studying issues and developing a platform. By the night of their dinner, he felt nervous, but focused and prepared.

Tired of waiting for Cynthia, impatient for the evening to begin, Steven descended the long staircase and strolled into the sitting room where Cynthia planned to serve cocktails and hors d'oeuvres.

As he made his way to the couch, Steven smiled at the Alfred Maurer painting that hung over the couch. Steven's favorite, it was a large portrait of a turn-of-the-century woman wearing a white taffeta dress tied with a black ribbon belt, a white feather boa, and a straw hat decorated with a stuffed bird. The artist had caught his subject sneaking a smoke. Instead of looking chagrined, she bared her teeth and spread her lush red lips in a waggish, conventions-be-damned smile. Steven wondered whether Cecilia had befriended "Jeanne" because she represented who Cecilia was, or who Cecilia wanted to be.

Moving a cushion aside Steven sat beneath her, folded his hands behind his head, leaned back, closed his eyes, and attempted to relax.

"Bored already?"

Steven's eyes popped open as if they were on a spring. Without a second's hesitation he bounded to his feet, wrapped his arms around his brother, and hugged him with a ferocity that required no further explanation.

"I'm glad to see you too," Matthew said, grinning, relieved to find that age and distance and marriage to an heiress hadn't diminished Steven's fraternal feelings. "Let me look at you." He stepped back and eyed his younger brother carefully, trying not to linger on the new custom-tailored tuxedo and the gold studs that gleamed from his pleated silk shirt, studying instead the man within the clothes. "Still handsome as hell. No wonder the Princess Rhinehart fell head over heels for you."

"Ah, but you're wrong," said a throaty voice laced with a bit of tease. "I didn't marry him for his face, although it is quite a face. I married him because he's great in bed."

Both men turned toward Cynthia, who posed imperiously in the doorway. Matthew gaped. Steven laughed, shook his head at her boldness, and then gave his wife an appreciative nod. Her near-black hair was pulled back into a low chignon, calling attention to her hazel eyes, which at that moment danced with mischief and flirtation. Clothed all in ivory, wearing a cashmere sweater and a long charmeuse skirt the color of the pearls she wore at her ears and neck, she was the personification of the word *thoroughbred*.

"Welcome to Mayfair Farms, dear brother-in-law," she said, still framed in the entry. "And in case you're interested, you're also handsome as hell." Coming from Cynthia, it sounded like a royal pronouncement. As if to verify her sincerity, she walked toward Matthew and kissed him on both cheeks.

"You're rather spectacular yourself," Matthew said with obvious admiration.

"As charming as he is good-looking," she said to no one in particular. "I like that."

Cynthia linked her arm through his and led him toward the couch. She claimed one of the corners and invited Matthew to sit in the adjacent chair. By patting the seat next to her she announced where she wished Steven to sit. Deciding he preferred to select his own place, Steven ignored the curious arch of her eyebrow and occupied the other chair, the one facing his brother. Without any awkward pause Cynthia exchanged pleasantries with Matthew, asking if he had any trouble finding the house, how the weather had been in Lexington lately, how his business was coming along, and why he had declined to bring someone as his date for the evening.

"I'm unavoidably unattached."

"What a shame. And me, so out of touch with what's happening here in Lexington. Why, I'm certain there are hundreds of women out there simply pining for a man like you."

Inside, Steven smiled. Cynthia was trying to impress Matthew by playing the coquette. He knew because her accent had deepened, growing more lyrical, more Southern-belle than it usually was.

"If they are," Matthew said with an unpretentious chuckle, enjoying the attention, "they're being real quiet about it."

"Perhaps my sister, Claudia, knows someone." Cynthia patted Matthew's knee with a reassuring hand. "We'll have to ask her when she arrives."

"Well, then, ask away, because I have arrived."

Claudia Fieldston was as tall as Cynthia, but her frame was larger, more reminiscent of Owen's than of the Délon side of the family. Her hair, thick and Rhinehart-black, was cut for ease of care and therefore displayed little style or chic. Her dress was expensive—clearly of good cloth and cut—but there, too, she fell short. Fashioned with a jewel neckline and short sleeves, the velvet top was too spare, the taffeta skirt a touch too full to be anything other than Queen Motherish. Even the elaborate bib of diamonds and sapphires did little to lighten the stolid I'd-rather-be-safe-than-vogue image.

Her husband, Billy—William IV—was a blond-haired, blue-eyed, florid-faced Southerner who could barely wait for the introductions to be completed before wrapping his hand around a Jack Daniels's. Thin, with an attenuated face and undistinguished features, he struck Steven as the type who believed that being the scion of one of Kentucky's oldest families was accomplishment enough.

Claudia, on the other hand, was delightful. After she and Cynthia exchanged brief, socially correct but emotionally vapid greetings, she turned her attention to Steven.

"I'm so glad to finally meet you," she said, warmly grasping his hand and giving him a generous smile. "Daddy thinks you're wonderful. If even half of what he said is true, either you've got a blind spot a mile wide or Cynthia has pulled off a minor miracle."

Steven laughed, finding himself immediately drawn to his new sister-in-law. Clearly, Claudia knew that Cynthia had not portrayed the sisters as close. Instead of sounding bitter or angry or vindictive or defensive, Claudia had chosen honesty, as if she felt freed by Cynthia's description of their relationship to express herself without restraint.

"Your father has some flattering things to say about you," he said, returning the compliment. "He told me that if I spent a day with you,

I'd learn everything I ever wanted to know about breeding and caring for champions. He says you're the best. My gut tells me he's right and that he wasn't just talking about the horses."

Claudia blushed, and suddenly the pink of her cheeks combined with the green of her eyes and the ebony of her hair to give her a momentary brush with true beauty. She must have seen it in his eyes, because the blush deepened and she moved quickly to change the subject.

"I want to volunteer here and now to help you in whatever way I can. I know people on both sides of the fence, Steven, those with the money to fund the campaign and those with the votes to win the election. All you have to do is ask."

"I'm asking," he said, gratified by her offer.

"Done."

"Champagne, Miss Claudia?" Jefferson, the butler and majordomo of the household staff, proffered a silver tray with several crystal flutes and a highball glass. Claudia helped herself to one of the flutes. "The Jack Daniels's is for you, Mr. Steven. I only gave you one finger's worth. Have to remain sharp tonight, you know."

"Thanks, Jefferson." Steven smiled and watched as the elderly black man moved away to serve Matthew and several of the other guests who had arrived while he and Claudia had been engrossed in their conversation. "He's really terrific," he said, his eyes still fixed on the tall, elegant butler. "I like him a lot."

"Me too," Claudia said. "Jefferson and Ruby have been at Mayfair forever. They're practically family."

Then why is he so cold to Cynthia, Steven wondered, keeping his thoughts to himself. During the several days since Steven's arrival, he had noticed a distance between Cynthia and Jefferson. Though Ruby had made more of a fuss over Cynthia's return, she, too, had been quick to take her leave. Something wasn't right. Even from his limited dealings with Jefferson, Steven found him to be someone who exuded geniality and self-assurance. It was evident that he took pride in his work. In Steven's uneducated opinion, Jefferson was as professional as they came, which was why he found his aloofness with Cynthia so surprising. She was the mistress of the house. He had known her all her life, served her family all his life. True, she had been gone for many years, and her estrangement from her father was well-known, but still.

While he might have wanted to probe the issue with Claudia, he had no time. Wendell Vaughn, his wife, and his contingent of party dons had arrived. For the next hour, Steven charmed the women, attempted to convince the men that he was capable of delivering the election, and fervently wished that Jefferson had been a finger more generous with the Jack Daniels's.

• • •

Three days later, Steven held a press conference in his newly inaugurated campaign headquarters, a converted storefront Matthew had found in downtown Lexington. Before a gaggle of reporters hungry for the fresh meat of an unknown, he announced his candidacy. Half a second elapsed between the last word of his speech and the first question from the floor.

"Albert Thornbridge says you're a carpetbagger, that you're no more a Lexingtonian than you are a native Kentuckian."

"He's right about the fact that I wasn't born in Kentucky, nor was I raised in Lexington. As everyone knows, I was born in Budapest, Hungary. I came to Woodridge, Kentucky, when I was nine. I'm now thirty-one. I'm not a native, but after twenty-two years, I'm close."

Two reporters smiled. The others were too busying writing in small notepads or waving their hands in the air trying to get his attention.

"How about Thornbridge's claims that you're an opportunist and that you're simply trying to trade on your father-in-law's name?"

"I'm a man who believes in realities. Hale Preston's passing has cost the state of Kentucky a valuable public servant. While surely we mourn that loss, the reality is that the House of Representatives has a vacant seat that must be filled. Albert Thornbridge wants to fill it. So do I. Why does that make him a viable candidate and me an opportunist?" He paused, giving everyone time to think about what he had said and to record it accurately. "The other reality is that, yes, I am married to Owen Rhinehart's daughter. But the name on the ballot will be Kardos. K-A-R-D-O-S. And for those unfamiliar with Hungarian, the *s* is pronounced *sh. Kardosh.*"

"You do realize, Mr. *Kardosh*, that despite the longtime Democratic hold on this seat, you're the dark horse?"

"Seattle Slew wasn't given much of a chance either," Steven rebutted, invoking the name of the colt who that year had surprised everyone by winning the Triple Crown.

For nearly an hour, Steven fielded questions with the skill of a shortstop. He deflected jabs aimed at his political inexperience with admission of the same, tossing the ball back with the rejoinder, "Everybody's a first-timer at something sometime in his life." He blocked comments pertaining to his youth by reminding his audience of his years in the mines, his years in Vietnam, and his years in Washington. He introduced his wife and his brother, put an arm around each and smiled at photographers eager for photo opportunities. He joked about his accent and his formidable native tongue, quoting an old Hungarian saying: "Hungarian is not so much a language as it is a disease of the throat."

And when one reporter, a man with a lupine face and a taunting, confrontational tone accused him of being nothing more than a dilettante
looking for a hobby, Steven dropped his good-guy mask.

"I resent that comment, sir. I am not dabbling in politics nor do I
consider serving the American people a hobby. At the risk of retelling
the same tale too many times, let me remind you that I am a man who
has viewed freedom from both sides of the curtain. I have been both a
political have and a political have-not and in case you're curious, it's
much better to have. I am running for the House of Representatives
because I believe in the democratic system of government and because I
feel obligated to give something back to the land that took me in." He
paused, his eyes fixed on the reporter who had triggered this diatribe. "If
you knew anything about me or my brother or any of the hundreds of
thousands of people who beg to enter this country every year, you would
know that once a victim of communism, forever a champion of freedom."

His voice rose above the strained silence in the room, filling the air
with the haunting sound of heartfelt emotion. He would not be baited.
Steven was willing to be accommodating to the press, he was even willing
to submit to a certain amount of grilling, but if attacked, he would fight
back.

He did not intend to be taken lightly and he wanted the media to
know it. He did not intend to lose the election. He wanted them to know
that, too.

Over the next several months, Steven and Cynthia worked together
to form an organization. Though Cynthia wasn't wildly enthusiastic over
Steven's insistence that Matthew share the campaign manager's job with
the man she suggested, she acquiesced. Though Steven loathed the tri-
weekly social get-togethers with people designated by Cynthia as prime
contributors, he acquiesced. When she studied the meteoric rise of Perry
& Kardos and ran a secret Dun & Bradstreet financial check on both
partners, she didn't raise any objections to Walter Perry coming on board
as manager of campaign finances. She never said anything about Claudia's visible and active participation in his campaign. But she did question
Steven's hiring of his friend Shadow Jackson.

"And what exactly is he going to contribute? He doesn't have a dime
to his name, nor is he the most eloquent speaker I've ever heard."

Steven had expected this particular barrage and was ready with his
defense. "But he does understand a large segment of my prospective
constituency."

Cynthia had grumbled, harping on the possibility of a backlash on the part of wealthy white supporters, but eventually she relented. Having run one of her secret background checks on Shadow months before, she already knew that during his tenure at Head Start, Mr. James Jackson had begun to build a reputation in Washington as someone who was able to speak to blacks and for blacks. No matter how she felt about him personally, she had to admit that in the end he could prove to be more asset than liability.

All in all, Cynthia and Steven worked well together. She found him a dazzling candidate, exceeding even her most ambitious dreams. He spoke brilliantly, bringing both humor and passion to his orations. He touched the souls of the most common man as easily as he won the hearts of the most elegant ladies. He never took a bad photograph. He never delivered a boring speech. He raised money and consciousness with the same gentle hand. Yet, as late as August, he was still slightly behind in the polls.

Reading over the most recent press releases, he felt as if he were being used for target practice by Albert Thornbridge's supporters. Despite all the time he had spent on issues and definitions of policy, Thornbridge's people continued to pound away at the same tired irrelevancies: his age, his inexperience, and the charge that he was a pawn in Rhinehart's quest for political immortality.

While Wendell Vaughn and Samuel Rutherford, cochairmen of Steven's election committee, suggested they initiate a smear campaign against Thornbridge, digging into some of the rumors they had heard about his spurious business deals and his fascination with fourteen-year-old girls, Matthew came up with the idea of moving their campaign beyond the usual groups of support, going after the undecideds or the politically disenfranchised. At first Cynthia opposed the notion, inventing scenarios that forecast nothing but doom. Naturally, Vaughn and Rutherford, the men whose reputed expertise she was protecting, agreed with her grim prognoses.

"I think it's precisely the right move," Steven said, siding with his brother. "We're only a few percentage points behind. We know who's solidly in our camp and Matthew's suggestion is not going to push them away. It's the blue-collar workers and the minorities that need to believe we're behind them. If we can convince them we are, they'll get behind us and Thornbridge won't stand a chance."

"Politics is a funny business," Rutherford said with a patronizing look that insinuated Steven was too innocent to offer opinions. "By courting one group, you risk offending another. Sometimes, the prudent thing to do is to make a choice."

"I did." Steven saw Cynthia tilt her head toward Rutherford. He understood she meant it as a signal to temper his remarks. Steven noted her concern but continued. "I chose to run to represent this district and everyone in it. That's what I intend to do."

"That's a noble sentiment, my boy, and I do appreciate your desire to be supportive of your brother's ideas, but I think changing course is a mistake."

"I don't." Steven's voice held a stubborn edge.

Rutherford stood, his face flushed with indignation. "If you're going to take the counsel of an inexperienced naïf over that of a seasoned politician, I don't see how I can possibly continue as your campaign manager."

He paused, waiting for a sign of contrition or apology. When there was none, he stormed from the room, leaving Vaughn bewildered and Cynthia weighing her next move. She could take Steven aside, do her best to pacify him, and urge him to reinstate Rutherford. She might even appeal to Matthew to explain to Steven how important it was not to give the press anything negative to report. But she was beginning to know the man she married. For some time, she had sensed Steven's disaffection with Rutherford's methods. She knew he found catering to the aristocracy personally distasteful and politically dishonest. She also knew that Steven's instincts were keen. His sense of loyalty was fierce, but rarely did he let his allegiances cloud his judgment. It took less than a minute for her to make her own choice.

She turned to Matthew, and, as if an invisible scepter had been passed from one man to the other, said, "What can I do to help?"

Following Matthew's recommendation, she organized a picnic on the grounds of Mayfair for underprivileged children, putting Claudia in charge of the day, knowing that her sister was eminently capable of introducing the children to the horses. At a luncheon for Lexington's working women, she waved the banner of the women's movement, applauding the emergence of women as an effective political action group.

Meanwhile, Steven and Shadow attended Sunday services at the black churches in the area, delivering sermons to the men and women who worked the farms and the factories and who rarely were given more than a passing nod by high-tone politicians. They went on a house-to-house campaign, meeting with the poor, talking, listening, trying to form a list of priorities.

When Matthew proposed that Steven return to the mountains and enlist the support of the miners, even Steven questioned the sagacity of such a move. Not only was the region completely outside his district, but that past March many of the miners had come off a sixteen-week strike demanding safer conditions and better pay. Though the owners had approved a pact to raise wages, the strike had gone on so long that the union's funds were low and there was growing dissension among its members.

"You're not looking for votes," Matthew said. "You're looking to give and to receive moral support. You grew up there. You still have family there. What better way to illustrate your natural link to this state and its people than to visit the mines." Matthew's mouth lifted in a sly grin. "One thing's for sure. You won't run into Thornbridge. He isn't going to go anywhere near there at a time like this. He can't. He isn't one of them. You are."

It was early September when Matthew and Steven drove up into the Appalachians and scaled the heights of the Cumberland Plateau. Green, in all its shadings, dominated the scenery. Now and then a cloud eclipsed the sun, casting a lavender shadow, veiling patches of the mountain with motile shapes that changed at the whim of the wind.

"I had forgotten how beautiful this was," Steven said, his eyes panning the expanse of hills.

"Whenever I visit János and Rosza, I take the long way just so I can remind myself of the more positive aspects of life in Woodridge."

Matthew was peering out the window, so Steven couldn't see his face, but his voice carried the residue of an existence marked by loneliness and hardship.

"Things are better for you now, aren't they, Mátyás?"

Matthew turned. Rarely did he and Steven use their given names. When they did, it signaled concern.

"Yes, things are better." He paused, lowering his voice and raising the window between the front and back seats so the driver wouldn't hear what he was about to say. "You don't have to worry about me. Mátyás the coal miner is well on his way to becoming a millionaire." He chuckled, filling the car with a prideful sound. "Hell, since you're invested in everything I'm invested in, you're on your way to becoming both a millionaire and a United States congressman!" He leaned over and squeezed Steven's hand. "We're living the life America promises in its ads. What more could anyone want?"

"How about someone to share it all with?"

"It would be nice."

"Anyone on the horizon?"

"Do you see anyone out there?" Matthew said, splaying his hand, tracing the line of the ridge. For an instant, a flash of memory placed him in the Crown cabin atop one of those distant ridges. He saw Lucinda as she was then, passionate and caring and beautiful and loving. The light shifted. The memory faded. "Neither do I."

"Maybe the woman of your dreams isn't in Kentucky. Maybe she's a city girl," Steven said, alluding to their old friend, the new queen of the comedy clubs, Sophie Warsaw/Wisnewski.

"Did you marry the woman of your dreams?" Matthew asked, gingerly but pointedly.

Steven's forehead furrowed. He wasn't about to give a flip retort. Unconsciously, his hand slid into his pocket and began to play with his keyring. Though he no longer wore Katalin's key around his neck—he no longer harbored any illusions about their having a relationship—he couldn't bear to throw the key away. It had become a symbol of his eventual return to Hungary. He didn't know when and he didn't know why, but someday he would return. Because he was so certain of that, he kept the key with him at all times, as if that, and that alone, would grant him admission to his homeland.

"No. I didn't marry the girl who dominated my childhood dreams," he said, still smarting from the sight of László with his arm around Katalin, still feeling the sting of the words, *I'm Katalin's husband.* "She was a fantasy and fantasies rarely work in the real world. The woman I married is very real and quite perfect for me. She's gorgeous and clever and cultured and scintillating and very, very sexy."

Not once had Steven mentioned the word *love.* Its absence clanged like a bell. Matthew heard it and said nothing. A shadow of uneasiness darkened his eyes.

"You don't like her very much, do you?" Steven asked, misinterpreting Matthew's reaction.

Matthew's gut response was, *no.* Instead he said, "She's your wife. You love her, I love her."

"In the beginning, I thought you two were going to be great pals. What happened?"

There was no way Matthew would ever tell Steven about the contretemps he and Cynthia had had. It had occurred two months before, just before the meeting which had precipitated Rutherford's leaving the team. Steven had been off giving a speech. Matthew had gone back to his office at Perry & Kardos. Cynthia had followed him. After five minutes of meaningless small talk, Cynthia got to the point.

"I'd like you to resign as Steven's campaign chairman."

"Why?"

"It gets very crowded with two men in the driver's seat. Rutherford is experienced at this sort of thing. You're darling, Matthew, but face it, you're an amateur."

"And since I don't always agree with Rutherford or you, you'd rather I disappear. Is that it?"

Cynthia hadn't read Matthew correctly. Quickly, she regrouped.

"It's just that I'm very concerned about the precariousness of politics," she said. "This is Steven's first race. I want to be certain he makes the right moves."

"Well you see, that's where we differ. I'm more concerned about people," Matthew rejoined. "And about whether or not Steven does the right thing."

Cynthia's back had stiffened. The smile had vanished from her mouth. In its place was a tight, thin line that quivered from her attempt to control her temper.

"You're his brother," she said. "Isn't that title enough? Must you be his campaign manager as well?"

"I'm a multifaceted type of guy, Cynthia. I can walk and chew gum at the same time and I can handle more than one job. I like being Steven's campaign manager and I love being his brother. So I think I'll just hang in there."

"Fine," she said, her face flushed with anger. "Just remember one thing. He's only going to have one wife. And I'm it!"

Even now, Matthew could feel the stiff breeze she had created when she stormed out of his office. They had been cordial to each other since, but little more.

"How many relatives meet one day and dive into a hotly contested political race the next?" he said in answer to his brother's question. He grinned at Steven, hoping his face didn't disclose the truth. "It's an unusual scenario. We're all a bit on edge. Give it some time. We'll be fine."

That settled, they spent the rest of the ride going over the day's agenda. Their first stop was private and personal. Bill Mahoney had died and both men wanted to pay their respects to Nell. Then, it was on to Woodridge. The plan was to arrive an hour before the five o'clock whistle so that Steven and Caleb Crown could have a reunion, part of which was open to the press. Crown had jumped at the chance. He viewed it as an opportunity to remind his disgruntled workers that he had been the one to present the soon-to-be-elected congressman with his prize money when he had been a mere teen and won the national citizenship essay contest. During the strike, Crown's reputation had taken a beating. Though he had capitulated on the wage increase, going along with his fellow mine-owners, he had been slow to improve working conditions.

He had promised everything. According to the miners, to date he had delivered nothing.

When they had been formulating this day, it had surprised Steven that Matthew did not intend to join him at this meeting with Crown.

"You worked for him for years," Steven had said, repeating himself now in the car. "Why wouldn't you want to come back and show him what a success you've become?"

"The last thing Crown wants to see is what a success I've become." As always, Matthew kept silent about his involvement with Lucinda. Despite her protests to the contrary, after Lucinda left town Crown's attitude toward Matthew had taken a chilly turn, making him certain that somehow his name had been mentioned as the possible father of Lucinda's aborted child. But even if that weren't the case, Crown had another reason to dislike him. "In the beginning of my investment career I bought a load of Crown stock. When I began to sense that the future was in oil and not in coal, I dumped it, depressing his bottom line." Matthew's eyes glinted with a curious hint of triumph. "No, Caleb Crown is not a member of my fan club. Nor I of his. While you two catch up, I'm going to visit with Aunt Rosza. I'll meet you at the entrance to the mine at five."

At four-thirty, in the middle of what had proved to be a very congenial meeting, there was a violent explosion. It rocked the building, filling the air with an instantaneous heat. When the alarm rang, Caleb Crown raced to the control panel that monitored the tunnels within the mine to see where the problem was. Steven stripped off his jacket and tie and jumped into a pair of overalls and a helmet he knew he'd find in the front office closet. The press reloaded their cameras, recharged their flashbulbs, and called in to their papers to alert their editors to a breaking story.

"It's on the B level of Crown #1," Caleb shouted, pressing panic buttons connected to both the police and the fire departments. "It's a methane explosion and it's bad!"

Needing no further information, Steven charged out of the building and ran toward the mine, with Crown and the press corps close on his heels. Dozens of men and women streamed out of the colliery, heading for the elevator. Steven caught the first cage down. Workers had handed every man an oxygen tank and mask. With his face covered, no one noticed him, nor did he look to identify any of them. All he could think of was his uncle. János, he knew, had returned to the mines. With the new wage increase, the money was better for those who took the risk of working below the ground than for those who opted for the safety of above-ground jobs.

As the stultifying blackness closed in around him, he shut his mind to any intrusive memories and steeled himself for the task ahead. Extricating men from a fiery mine was like reaching into the mouth of a volcano. The heat alone was enough to terrify the hardiest of souls. Aside from the fear of asphyxiation was the dread of collapsing timbers. As the flames spread, wood that supported the shafts gave way, forcing cave-ins and avalanches of stone and coal and wood and boiling water.

The cage opened and disgorged a team of anxious men. Steven followed the others, mindless of the danger. Soon, firemen trained to deal with explosions such as these would pour into the corridors and set about containing the blaze. For now, however, the first priority was finding as many men as they could and sparing them the horror of the inferno.

B-6 was where the explosion had occurred. Though men would later try to enter the shaft, it was presumed that anyone trapped there was dead. Steven followed the others to the adjacent corridors, galloping as quickly as the circumstances allowed, hoping to save as many as they could.

"*Hang in! We're coming! Keep down! Cover your faces!*"

By the time Steven wended his way through the maze of tunnels leading to B-6, men were already being carried out. Some were unconscious. Others were burned almost beyond recognition. The ones who could walk hung on to the men lugging the injured. The fire roared, creating a fierce, carnivorous sound. Flames reached out from the belly of the mine like a snake's tongue threatening to swallow everyone in its path.

In a corner of the tunnel, Steven found a stack of bodies. They lay as they had fallen, too frightened and too weak to disentangle themselves from the pile. Frantically, Steven and several other men sifted the living from the dead, closing their ears to the shrieks of pain, listening instead for the nearly indistinct moans coming from those who were fading and needed the most immediate attention. One voice, so low it was barely audible above the clamor, pierced Steven's soul and paralyzed him.

"*Segítség,*" the voice repeated in a language only Steven could understand. "Help." It grew fainter with every utterance.

Steven's hands shook as he turned the blackened face toward him and wiped the man's cheek with his sleeve. His helmet had been knocked off in the blast. His hair was singed, his scalp was burned. Black scratches mapped his cheeks. His lower lip was cut and bleeding. Yet Steven knew he had found his uncle.

"János!"

The mouth was too enfeebled to speak. The eyes wanted to speak, but all they could do was weep. Quickly, Steven pulled János from the pile, took off his own oxygen mask and held it to the older man's face until his lungs were filled with clean air and the color of his skin pinked. Immediately, Steven was assaulted by the high concentration of toxic gases. He retrieved the mask. Procedure dictated that he remain strong enough to complete the rescue. He was about to hoist János onto his shoulders, when János pointed to the other side of the corridor, where a man was pinned beneath a burning timber.

"Please, István," he pleaded, hysteria building as he watched the flames lick at the body beneath the fiery block of wood. "It's Ernie."

Steven propped János against a wall where he thought he would be safe and carefully approached his cousin. A quick inspection revealed that the timber that had fallen on top of Ernie was a joist that had been pried loose from its supports by the fire. By chance, it had fallen in such a way that it was wedged against yet another flaming joist. Within minutes, either beam could burn down enough to bring the ceiling crashing onto all of them. Ernie was screaming, howling in agony, begging for someone to save him. "Stay calm," Steven said, bending down so he could be heard over the din. "It's me. István." Ernie stared into Steven's eyes. His face tensed. They both knew why. He started to plead, but Steven cut him off. "Listen carefully. I'm going to come around behind you and pull you out. Make your body as limp as you can. Do you understand?" Ernie nodded his head, his eyes riveted on the burning rafters.

Steven slid his hands behind the other man's back. For support, he linked them across Ernie's chest. Slowly, as if he were playing a life-and-death version of pick-up sticks, he pulled Ernie out from beneath the enflamed poles.

"Can you walk?" Ernie's left leg was red and blistered. His shirt was torn. His chest was a mass of angry blotches oozing pus. His arm looked broken. Despite all that, Ernie the soldier nodded yes. "Good," Steven said. "Let me get your father, then I'll be back for you."

The fire was expanding, flooding the tunnel with noxious fumes and scorching heat. Crackling sounds were followed by the thud of crashing timbers. Racing against the inevitable, men were cradling other men, hauling them, carrying them, doing whatever they could to clear the area. Steven warned about the ceiling, shouting as loudly as he could, directing everyone to get out as quickly as possible. Meantime, he secured János in his arms. Ernie rested the bulk of his weight against Steven's back and held on to his arm as they struggled toward the cage.

"I owe you," Ernie said, his voice garbled with sobs of fear and relief and embarrassment and gratitude.

"Forget it," Steven yelled, listening to the increased thunder of the blast, knowing that the louder it got, the closer it was. "Let's just get the hell out of here."

"I owe you," Ernie repeated, saying it over and over and over, as if the act of verbalizing his debt to Steven was the only way he could stay alive long enough to reach the surface.

When the door of the elevator opened, miners and rescuers tumbled out looking like bits of charcoal. Blackened, broken, reeking of smoke, they fell to the ground heaving and gasping, desperately trying to replace the hot, fetid air of the mine with fresh, unsullied oxygen. Steven was one of the last ones out. As he staggered into the ebbing daylight, Matthew and Rosza ran to him. Rosza saw János and Ernie and nearly collapsed. Matthew took János from Steven, instructed Rosza to help Ernie, and led them to where medics were tending to the injured. Steven crumpled to the ground, his lungs seared, his face and body still radiating heat.

Later, he wouldn't remember the flashbulbs popping, nor would he recall answering any questions or telling any stories. Yet the next morning, on the front pages of newspapers all across the country, there was a picture of Steven stumbling off the elevator with János in his arms and Ernie by his side. The accompanying articles told of Steven's escape from Hungary, his flight to America, and his resettlement in Kentucky. They told about the garage apartment at János and Rosza's house, spoke of his unwavering sense of loyalty and family, particularly his exceptional closeness with his brother. There were quotes from Caleb Crown about Steven's bravery, about how he had rushed into the mine, risking his own life to save others. There were kudos from miners who were in the tunnel with him and remembered him shouting instructions, pitching in, doing his share. But the most surprising statement came from none other than Ernie Vas:

> "He saved my life and I'm not sure I deserved it. I wasn't very nice to him growing up. In fact, the scar on his left cheek was 'cause of me. Believe me. Anyone else would've left me to die in that mine. But Steven isn't like anyone else. Thank God."

Though no one wanted to pin it on any one thing or any one person, in November, when Thornbridge was defeated by a landslide vote, more than one person was heard to say that the most junior member of the House of Representatives—though charming and able and well qualified for the post—had Ernie Vas to thank for his victory.

That may have been true, but on that bitterly cold day in January, when Steven entered the House of Representatives for the first time as a member of that august body, how he got there seemed less important than the fact that he was there. Dizzied by a rush of feelings, Steven strode down the aisle as slowly as a bride, savoring the walk, lingering over each step, branding each moment on his memory. As he took his seat and ran his hands across the wooden desktop where so many congressmen had sat before him, he was besieged by a swirl of emotion. Incidents and images from his past collided with hopes and dreams for his future. Visions of his parents mingled with the pride he had seen in his brother's face on election day when Matthew had taken the microphone in Kardos headquarters and officially announced Steven the winner. Voices from long ago rarely allowed to surface—the voices of Vera and Katalin—called out to him in spectral whispers, saying what he thought they might have said if they knew, if they were there to acknowledge the fulfillment of a promise made in another place, in another time, in another language. His head filled with the excited voices of Zsuzsanna and Sophie and Paul Greco and Owen, all of whom had called to congratulate him; with the grateful voices of János and Rosza when he and Matthew had presented them with a trust fund that would keep János out of the mine forever and when Steven had offered Ernie a job as his chauffeur/bodyguard; with the joyful tone in Cynthia's voice as she had hugged and kissed him and then later, celebrated their victory in her own special way.

The oddest echo, however, repeated words from twenty-three years before. Steven, then István, had sat in the Gáspár living room mesmerized by Miklós Gáspár's description of liberty's package. Miklós had spoken of the choices in a free society. Miklós had exhorted them to fight for their liberty, to defend themselves against the tyranny that raged in their streets and threatened to annihilate them. It was because of those words that Steven was here. That day, Miklós Gáspár had planted the seeds of inspiration in a nine-year-old boy. He had sown a future dedicated to the preservation of those rights that had been denied István and Miklós. Steven shuddered. Miklós had painted the dream for Steven, but never realized it for himself. Perhaps, Steven thought, that was why he was sitting in the House of Representatives of the United States of America. Perhaps he was meant to realize Miklós's dream for him.

Moved by the awesome concept of destiny, he paid strict attention while the Clerk of the House called the roll. It seemed interminable, but finally, he heard it. Ringing throughout the hall was the name Steven Kardos.

"Here!" He shouted his response and thrust his hand into the air, unashamed by his enthusiasm or the bemused looks of his colleagues. "And," he muttered silently to himself as the Clerk called the next name and then the next, "damn glad of it!"

•   •   •

In the visitors' gallery, Cynthia Kardos watched as her husband took his place and recorded his presence. She was delighted to watch him claim his seat, but not so overcome with wifely pride that she forgot the anger that had enraged her when Steven appointed Matthew district manager of the Kardos offices in Lexington and Shadow Jackson his senior legislative assistant in Washington; or her disappointment when, instead of acceding to her wishes to buy a five-acre estate in Virginia, Steven had opted for an elegant but modest townhouse in Georgetown that fit his budget rather than her inheritance.

She loved Steven—as much as she could love anyone—but love was not the emotion that fueled Cynthia. Long ago, she had set a goal for herself. Steven was her conduit, her means to achieving the end she desired. It was simple, really. All he had to do was follow her plan, a plan that required nothing of him other than to use his social skills, his intelligence, his political instincts, and his extraordinary good looks. When he had gained the prestige and power he wanted, she would extract the revenge she wanted. She would prod Steven to turn on Owen and ruin him. Just as Owen had turned and tried to ruin her.

27

Budapest, 1979

H appiness, Katalin decided, like music, was a matter of interpretation. To one who was sick, a painfree day was cause for celebration. To one who was citybound, an afternoon at Lake Balaton felt like a gift. To one plagued by routine and sameness, any break from the everyday could prod a smile.

Once, it had been how well she was playing that prompted the high. Now, it was where she was performing. Kádár had finally relented and eased travel restrictions for certain categories of citizens. Fortunately, those like Katalin with enough talent to make the motherland look good, qualified. Katalin looked forward to her trips outside the Eastern Bloc. Though she couldn't discuss this with anyone but Judit—least of all, László—she had begun to feel like a divided soul: One part of her was pure Magyar, the other part longed to live somewhere else, somewhere where she would be free of limits and stipulations and censorship and regulations. Yes, things were easing, but a chain with slack was still a chain.

"Last week, when I was in Brussels, I played at the Palais des Beaux Arts," Katalin told Judit one afternoon over coffee and pastry at Angelika, a tiny *cukrászda* near Katalin's house in Watertown. "You can't imagine how beautiful it was. All the women were elegantly dressed. The men wore formal attire. The mood was gay. The hall was magnificent. The audience loved the music. I loved the audience!"

"Just like dear old Budapest." Katalin was used to Judit's cynicism. Her comments had grown more outspoken with each passing year. Having endured the trauma of Attila's capture and the strain of her own surveillance, she no longer made any attempt to hide her dissidence. *They* had brought it out in the open. Why not leave it there for all to see and hear?

"The audiences here may be humble, but they're enthusiastic," Katalin said defensively.

Judit nibbled on her chestnut cake, refusing to give any quarter. "Since when does László approve of you giving concerts in enemy territory?"

"Since he discovered the West compensates musicians better than the East." Katalin laughed at her own joke, then caught herself. She had spoken without thinking, but she had never been guarded with Judit. She supposed she should feel disloyal, but what she had said was the truth. When Marxism catapulted the skilled worker upward, it suppressed the salaries of professionals and technicians. Doctors, lawyers, musicians, engineers, teachers—all were forced to survive on salaries so low it was difficult to make ends meet. Performing in Hungary fed her soul, but little else.

"He's such a loyal communist, I'm surprised he doesn't donate your earnings to the Party." Judit eyed her friend, gauging how much further she could push. "Having been to your home however, I know he doesn't."

"You're being bitchy, Judit. László's a good man. So he likes the finer things. What's wrong with that?"

"Nothing, if you're a capitalist!"

Judit had disliked László from the first and had said so, many times. Though she tried not to attack him personally, she was not shy about her distrust of him. "Stalin used to say, 'Those who are not with us are against us.' Now Kádár says, 'Those who are not against us, are with us.' My problem is that I don't know where László stands. Is he with us or against us?"

Katalin dismissed Judit's animosity as phobic, based on fear of the uniform he wore rather than knowledge of the person he was. Since Judit couldn't back up any of her suspicions with fact, relying on nothing more than feelings or rumors, Katalin refused to take her misgivings seriously. She assured Judit she was wrong and let it go at that. For the sake of their friendship, Judit changed the subject. That didn't mean she'd changed her mind.

"How are things with Emke?" Katalin asked, moving on.

"He's a swine." Judit crinkled her nose and shivered, underscoring her point. "If I didn't need the job so badly, I'd shoot the pig, I swear I would." Suddenly, Judit leaned forward. A mischievous smirk colored her face. "Sándor's been getting a little full of himself," she said. "You know, strutting around as if he were an Archduke. We were in Crakow, on the last leg of a three-week tour. After each concert, instead of pointing to me so that I could receive my meager applause, he simply took his bows and made his grand exit, leaving me to scramble after him. Since this was the last concert, I decided to teach him a little lesson. I helped him into his jacket beforehand, just as I always do. He mentioned that the suit felt a little tight. I told him he was still bloated from the kielbasa he had devoured at lunch. Since I also knew he made a habit of quaffing several beers in his dressing room before he sang, I figured he wouldn't question me. He didn't."

"When the performance ended and he went to take his bow, he bent down very low." Katalin had started to giggle. She knew exactly what Judit had done. "No one could hear the jacket and pants ripping over the sound of the applause, but he felt it. Out of the corner of my eye, I saw him twitching his head, signaling me to leave the piano so I could position myself behind him and literally cover his ass as he walked offstage. Not a chance. I sat there with my hands in my lap like the obedient serf, giving the maestro his due. He continued to stand center stage. The audience was confused. They had applauded enough. He had been good, but really! I continued to sit. Finally, when the back rows began filing out, Emke realized he couldn't stand there anymore. He turned to leave and the people in the front rows were treated to a full view of his rear view. They began to laugh and to spread the word that the great Emke Sándor had split his seams. I loved it!"

"You're terrible!"

"Not at all." Judit pretended offense. "His weight fluctuates so much, he has tuxedoes in three sizes. I simply helped him to the smaller one. No harm was done except to his already overblown ego." She chuckled at the memory. "In this life, you get your jollies wherever you can." Her eyes twinkled as she said, "Where do you get yours?"

Katalin knew Judit had hoped to catch her off guard so that she might reveal some delicious little secret. Katalin had a secret and, oddly enough, it was the answer to Judit's question. Katalin took her pleasure as she had for years now—playing with Tibor's band.

"From my music," she said, telling the truth, but not completely.

Judit groaned. "Why did I know you'd say that?"

"Because you know me better than anyone else."

Judit put down her coffee and stared at Katalin. "I do, don't I?" she said, then added reflectively, "But what I see is different from what I used to see."

Katalin was taken aback. "Good or bad?"

Judit considered the question with judicial sobriety. "Good," she pronounced. "You've become a lot stronger, Katya. Feisty, even. I've actually heard you say things that are in clear opposition to government policy." She grinned and gasped and clutched her chest. "That's not the Katalin Gáspár I grew up with. Uh-uh. That Katalin was a good little girl who only spoke when spoken to and only said what was expected of her." Judit leaned across the table and whispered with conspiratorial glee, "It must be those years you spent in the decadent West."

Katalin laughed. Of course that was true. One bred in oppression couldn't spend time in a free country without being changed by the experience. What was pleasing was that Judit had noticed the change and had cast such a positive light on it. At home, if she challenged the status quo as she often did, László rebuked her, accusing her of having opinions spawned by the subtle brainwashing of Western advertising.

"Those years did have an effect."

Katalin was alluding to something, Judit knew. "Don't tell me. You've decided to march on Parliament singlehandedly."

"Nothing quite that extreme." Katalin should have known Judit wouldn't take her seriously, at least not at first.

"So? What?"

"*Samizdat*." She said it quietly. It wasn't something people spoke about loudly.

"What about it?"

"You're involved, aren't you?"

Judit nodded, but she was only confirming what Katalin already knew. With Judit's history of dissidence, it was a given that she would be involved in the secret publication and distribution of newspapers and magazines. It was through *samizdat* that the opposition was able to spread their word throughout a society deprived of a free press. It was through *samizdat* that democracy had a voice.

In Hungary, *samizdat* flourished. There were even rumors that there were special publications with a distribution restricted to Party secretaries and branches, laughingly called "State *samizdat*." Usually, they were translations from the Western press, but often, they were foreign books disallowed the general public.

Naturally, the largest proliferation of *samizdat* was produced by an underground core of dissidents. One, a journal called *Beszélö—The Talker*—, was more than a hundred pages thick and, though published irregularly, boasted an enormous following. There was very little fiction in *Beszélö*. Most of the articles were penned by sociologists, economists, and historians. What dignified and distinguished this publication from most others was that on the title page, the names and telephone numbers of the editors were conspicuously displayed. The purpose of such a madly courageous act was to let the authorities see how many prominent people—mostly intellectuals with a worldwide reputation—stood on the opposing side. Though it was doubtful that the government would be foolish enough to arrest these international celebrities—the last thing they wanted was to attract that kind of attention—prosecution, or worse, was always possible. The case of Attila Kovács proved that. Ordinary people, even those who didn't read the truly intellectual journals, considered the editors of publications like *Beszélö* heroes. "Because," as one of Judit's cohorts said, "they dare not to be faceless."

"I'd like to be involved," Katalin said in a tone that brooked no argument.

Judit's face registered surprise. "You have changed."

Katalin looked embarrassed. "It's time I added my voice to the protests. It's not right to let others do it for me."

Judit squeezed her friend's hand, welcoming her to a club with a rapidly increasing membership. "What do you want to do?"

"I could help in the distribution."

"In Budapest, the distribution is pretty efficient."

"I'm sure it is," Katalin said, automatically dropping her voice, "but you need to get *samizdat* to the people in the country, outside of Budapest. I give concerts in Szeged and Debrecen and Pécs and the other big cities. I could spread the word." As Vadrósza, she also performed in small towns like Siófok and Hollókö and Salgó. "How do I start?"

Judit reached over and hugged Katalin. "Go to the Komjádi swimming pool. You know, the one in Óbuda where the Olympic swimmers train." Katalin nodded. "Pick up whatever you think you can distribute and then do it!"

"Sounds simple enough."

Judit's face betrayed concern. "It's not simple, Katya. The government frowns on *samizdat*. They can get nasty."

"I'll be fine. You don't have to worry about me."

"That would be a first!" Though Judit punctuated her comment with a sardonic harrumph, she detected a determination in her friend that made her proud and nervous at the same time. Katalin had never been a risk taker. What's more, she had always been far too trusting to suit Judit. The fact that she had volunteered for something like this was honorable and brave, but would she think to watch her back? "What about László? He wouldn't approve, you know."

Katalin smiled. He wouldn't approve of her playing with Tibor either. "Probably not, but I didn't marry him because I agreed with his politics. I married him because I loved him. And besides," she said, honestly excited about what she was about to do, "what he doesn't know, won't hurt him. Or me."

Katalin rubbed her dark makeup over her face, blending it in to her hairline with her fingers. It was early, just past six, so she had the Keleti restroom to herself. Before she kohled her eyes, she reached into the open suitcase on the tile floor and pulled out a raucous floral-print blouse and a flounced cotton skirt of red and orange. They looked odd among her other clothes, most of which were conservative pastels or sedate blacks, yet the juxtaposition seemed particularly apt, especially today.

Normally, Katalin changed into a costume, went with Tibor for a four-hour gig, and returned home. Once in a while, when László was out of town, they looped two jobs together. Katalin stayed in whatever tourist accommodations were available. The gypsies camped out. This time was different for several reasons: She was going to be gone for several days and she was going to be a guest at a wedding—Tibor's wedding.

She had been stunned when he had told her about it, more so because he had appeared dazed by the prospect. He had called and asked if she would meet him in a coffeeshop near the apartment. Though she hadn't donned her gypsy garb, she had covered her hair with a hat and her eyes with sunglasses. When they were seated and had been served, Tibor made his announcement.

"I have to tell you something," Tibor had said. "And then I want to ask you something."

Katalin looked at him. His jaw was rigid and set. She was afraid he was going to tell her she had been discovered.

"Farah and I are getting married."

He caught Katalin completely unprepared. She knew how Farah felt about Tibor—it was hardly a secret—but it had always been her impression that Tibor didn't return Farah's fondness.

"I had no idea." For Tibor's sake she would have preferred to seem more delighted, but try as she might, she couldn't seem to conjure any real enthusiasm.

"Farah and I have been pledged since we were children. Our marriage is years overdue." Katalin wished she could see his eyes, to know whether he was in pain or had come to terms with his fate, but he had lowered them, concentrating on a coffee spill and refusing to let her see his face. "I've shamed her long enough. The *kumpania* has decided it's time for me to make good on my father's pledge."

His voice was heavy with the burdens of custom. Katalin wanted to protest, to decry a practice that bound people together with gold coins instead of love, but she hesitated. Despite the time they spent together and the intense joy they shared when they created music, theirs was a friendship hampered by traditional racial distance. Most of the time they managed to bridge the chasm, yet certain boundaries remained uncrossed. Neither had been to the other's home. Neither had met the other's family. Neither had suggested that they see each other outside of the context of the band. Nonetheless, an unspoken affection existed between them. He had come to Paris to show support for her. She had obliged his requests to play with the band whenever she could. Despite societal limitations, they cared about each other.

"Is this what you want, Tibor?" she asked, loath to probe beyond what he was offering, yet unable to control herself. "Do you love Farah?"

The corners of his eyes crinkled as a sarcastic laugh escaped his lips. "No," he said. "But what I want and whom I love is irrelevant."

"Why?" She tried, but couldn't disguise her indignation.

"I know the *gorgio* likes to think of us as lawless heathens, but my people have rules just as your people have rules. Family is important to the gypsies. It's the core of our existence. I have to marry."

"Fine, but you should be able to marry someone you love, not someone picked for you."

"That would be nice, but even in your world, people don't always marry their true loves. Sometimes they marry the one who's acceptable, the one who best fits their lives."

Katalin squirmed in her seat. She didn't know whether Tibor had aimed that arrow directly at her, but she felt the sting of his words. László matched Tibor's description. He was acceptable. He fit her life. She loved him, yet often, her dreams insisted upon reminding her that another man's name was etched on the inner walls of her heart.

"I'd like you to come to the wedding." He paused. She started to answer, but he held up his hand. He wasn't finished with his invitation. "It might not be pleasant for you. Gypsies aren't always gracious to outsiders."

"I learned that the first time I walked into your apartment." They both laughed at the memory of the outrage that had masked the faces of his clan, the rude way they had treated her. Since then, of course, she had become an accepted member of the group. "I'm a veteran. They won't bother me. All that matters is that you want me there."

"I do."

"Then I'd be honored."

It must have been ordained for her to attend this wedding because even László cooperated. He was in Bucharest for the week attending a conference. As a precaution, Katalin had quietly surveyed those close to her, readying a list of unsuspicious excuses for her absence in case László phoned and she wasn't there to receive his call. He would believe dinner with her father, Judit, or the Strassers. He would believe a night at the Gellért Baths or the Opera Ház. He would even believe that she had been practicing and didn't hear the telephone. Actually, Katalin thought she had little to worry about. Because the telephone system in Hungary was so poor, László, like everyone else, maintained a why-bother attitude about long-distance calls. Rarely did he try, because rarely would he succeed.

As she knotted the kerchief at the back of her neck and surveyed her costume, she thought about what Tibor had told her.

"You're my only friend in the white world, Katalin," he had said. "You're important to me. My family understands that. They've mingled with the *gaje*. They know that there are exceptions to every rule. You're my exception."

Katalin had laughed. "I have a Jewish friend who always says the two most infuriating phrases in the world are: 'Some of my best friends are Jewish' and 'But you're different.' "

"I didn't mean to insult you." Tibor rushed to apologize.

"You didn't. It's just the way things are. When individuals from warring groups find they like each other, it's a shock and it makes us defensive. You were brought up to suspect every white person you meet. I was brought up to suspect every gypsy. It's what our parents were taught, what our teachers were taught. It was supposed to be true and absolute. No exceptions." She smiled and patted his hand. "Yet, here we are."

Tibor nodded his head, his white teeth gleaming in a satisfied smile. "Good for us!" he said.

"Good for us."

By the time Katalin left the station, it was seven o'clock. Tibor's battered black Trabant was parked on a side street, away from the curious eyes that crowded Keleti Station. Katalin tossed her bag into the back seat and climbed into the car. Though they were heading for Debrecen and the ride was a long one, she had opted for her gypsy clothes; a white woman and a gypsy man were far too conspicuous for police to resist. Katalin feared that somewhere along their route they would be stopped and interrogated. She couldn't afford for that to happen.

"What's in the knapsack?" Tibor asked, helping to remove the bulky carryall from her shoulder.

"*Samizdat.* I promised a friend I would distribute it. I thought that when we got to Debrecen, I would parcel it out to the various newsstands and hand out the rest to whomever I can."

Keeping pace with his fellow drivers, Tibor swerved in and out of lanes and careened down boulevards at breakneck speeds. At first, Katalin thought he was concentrating so hard he hadn't heard her answer, but then he shook his head and said, "Dressed like that, the only way you'll be able to give those journals away is by leaving them on a table at the *Cigány piac.* No one takes anything from gypsies except maybe at the market."

"I forgot," she said, feeling guilty and stupid for not considering the obvious.

Katalin was well aware of the lowly status of gypsies, but, she supposed, because the prejudice against them didn't directly impact her existence, because she wasn't the butt of the scorn, she didn't really see it or feel it. Only victims of bigotry could be so keenly sensitized to the subtle everyday slights against them. They recognized their foes even when disguised as friends. They knew the pitfalls to avoid, the buzz words that would incite an attack, the real meaning behind certain facial expressions and lightly veiled verbal affronts. Katalin was white. She was in the majority. Though she sympathized, and because while in costume she had been treated to the same snubs accorded Tibor and his friends and was able to claim a certain amount of empathy, she recognized that her understanding was superficial.

"We have plenty of time before the performance. If you want, you can get back into your Magyar clothes and visit every newsstand in town."

"Don't worry about it." It embarrassed her to acknowledge, even to herself, that in order to complete a simple task, she would have to remove all vestiges of the *cigány.* "I'll figure it out."

After that they rode in silence, Katalin deep in thought, Tibor struggling with the sputtering, ramshackle fiberglass machine laughingly called a car. They traveled southeast from Budapest, along one of the many routes leading to the *puszta.* The day was beautifully clear, allowing both of them to lose themselves in the scenery. At Szolnok they crossed the mighty Tisza River, which curved and funneled its way across a stretch of more than four hundred miles. The Tisza, once a powerful curving snake of a river, had long been considered the great divide separating western Hungary from the Great Plain. Though the bends had been tamed and the break was no longer as obvious as it once had been, Katalin always felt the change in atmosphere from the sophisticated, hurry-scurry pace of the more industrialized west to the bucolic, mellow tempo of the Plain.

As they approached Debrecen and its domed and turreted skyline reshaped the horizon, Katalin's calm was disturbed. She looked beyond the landscape trying to see into the Szabolcs hinterland where Tibor would take a bride. Though she could see nothing but sky and sun, the commotion inside her grew. Was it fear of losing a friend to an alien world? Jealousy about losing him to Farah? Or both?

They came from the banks of the Indus River, taking their name from an area in northwest India then referred to as "Little Egypt," a band of brown-skinned, black-eyed people with an eternal wanderlust, who began a migration that would grow and spread and eventually cover the globe—north to Pakistan and Iran, south to Syria and Egypt, and, by the fifteenth century, throughout Western Europe.

Surrounded by mystery, suffused with folklore. Admired for their musical ability, shunned for their thievery. Disdained for their slovenliness, envied for their unfettered life-style. The Gitanos of Spain, the Gypsies of England, the Rudari of Romania, the Walachians, Lováris, and the Musicians of Hungary, the Tsiganes of France, the Jat from Iran, the Banjara and the Sansi of India, the Lowara and Kalderash—whatever tribe they belonged to, whatever country they settled in, they shared a common ancestry, a common language and a common determination to maintain their ways at any cost. They were gypsies, "the last happy grasshoppers in a world of ants." They were *Rom*.

Katalin was *gadjé*. Tibor was worried that she might need both a guide and a friend during the days ahead; so, when the band had finished its last number of the performance and the room had emptied, Tibor took Katalin's arm and led her toward the back.

Standing in a corner was a young girl with the café-au-lait skin of the Musicians. Wearing a low-cut fuchsia blouse festooned with garlands of beads and a long three-tiered cotton skirt splashed in shades of red and rose, she watched the gypsy man and the false gypsy woman approach. Her dark, almond-shaped eyes boldly surveyed every inch of Katalin, assessing, questioning, passing judgment.

"This is my sister Paprika," Tibor said, casting a warning glance meant to temper the actions of the fiery girl he claimed as kin.

"Mama says that when I was an infant, I cried so much my face was always bright red. My father said it was because she ate too much paprika during her pregnancy." She offered the explanation with a blasé shrug of her shoulders. "I think she should be grateful I was so difficult," the young gypsy continued. "If not for me, she might have had more children." She blew out a puff of air and shook her head as if her mother's efforts had exhausted her. "Ten is enough!"

"Nice to meet you, Paprika." Katalin extended her hand, liking the young woman's unabashed candor and easy humor. Tibor's sister grasped it firmly. When she smiled, Katalin noticed that her teeth were large and white and surprisingly even. Gypsy smiles often exposed neglected mouths with blank spaces or yellowed enamel or golden caps covering rotting teeth.

"Paprika is going to take care of you for the next few days," Tibor said. "It's custom that the groom remain isolated until the marriage. Because I won't be around, Paprika will introduce you to everyone. She's there to remind everyone you are my guest and my friend." In a rare display of playfulness, he pinched his sister's cheek and tugged at one of the braids that hung about her ears. "She's young, but she's wily. The perfect escort to a gypsy wedding."

That night, while Tibor went on ahead, Paprika stayed behind, bunking in with Katalin at a hostel on the outskirts of Debrecen. Though the plan was to leave first thing in the morning, Katalin asked Paprika to delay their departure for a couple of hours.

"There's something I have to do in town," she said, hiking her knapsack onto her shoulders. "I'll finish up as quickly as I can."

"Come to Petőfi Square when you're ready. I'll be waiting."

Katalin was relieved. She had expected an argument, questions, suspicion. Katalin was nervous enough. Having to justify her behavior to a stranger would only have added to the tension. It never dawned on her that Paprika required no explanation because she already knew where Katalin was going and what she was going to do. During the night while Katalin slept, Paprika had searched her bags. This blond-haired, green-eyed woman might have bewitched Tibor with her music and her beauty, but Paprika wasn't so easily captivated.

For Katalin, the next two hours proved to be a test of nerves. To weed out the newsstands that would be receptive from those that might provoke a call to the police was dicey. Before she approached anyone, she browsed through the stocks of newspapers and magazines. In some stores, week-old issues of The International Herald Tribune peeked out from underneath Népszabadság, the Party daily. In some there were papers from West Germany or France. If she didn't see any capitalist newspapers, she looked for pornography. A shop that stocked those magazines, which to the Party were as foul as the Western press, might handle samizdat.

By the time she had given out her last five journals, she was sweating and her head was pounding from the strain. Taking a moment, she leaned against the wall of a building, closed her eyes, and inhaled slowly and deeply, trying to regain some semblance of calm. When the spasm passed and her mind cleared, she continued on her way. As she walked, she pictured Judit's smile when she told her what she had accomplished. Though she didn't want to, she imagined how László's face would look if he knew what she had done. It disturbed her to think that once again she had gone against him, that she had created yet another secret, another reason to lie to her husband. But those concerns faded when she saw her own features in a store window as she headed down Vörös Hadsereg útja toward Petőfi Square. On her face, she saw satisfaction and pride.

In New York, Katalin had marched against Vietnam. But that had been America's war. This was hers. Though she hadn't paraded down a main thoroughfare surrounded by hundreds of flag-waving, slogan-chanting supporters, she felt she had accomplished the same thing. She had protested the actions and policies of her government. She had said, "I think what you're doing is wrong," in the only way open to her.

Smiling now, she congratulated her reflection on a job well done. If she had looked behind her, she might have seen the stern visage of the man who had traced her steps throughout Debrecen, the man who had followed her from Budapest. But Katalin was not a woman who looked back. She was too intent on looking forward. Which was exactly what Judit had feared.

With Paprika pointing the way, Katalin steered Tibor's Trabant north of Debrecen, toward Szabolcs-Szatmár county, an area derided by most Magyars as the "black country." Leaving the dark, alluvial steppes where the csikós roamed, they entered a region that seemed locked into another time. Historically isolated by swamps, Szabolcs had long ago fallen out of step with progress elsewhere. Beyond the drab industrialized town of Nyíregyháza was a purely agrarian society; private vehicles were a rarity on the unpaved roads frequented instead by horse-drawn carts.

By the time they reached the outskirts of Mátészalka, a shabby village of low yellow houses and dilapidated estates, an uneasy sense of separation and isolation had attached itself to Katalin. Nothing looked familiar. Everything was hazy and vague, like scenes drawn in a centuries-old watercolor. A farmer shuffled along the dirt paths, leading a cow by a rope or poking some goats with a stick to keep them in line. Round-faced, red-cheeked, babushkaed women toting baskets filled with vegetables or herbs, juggled babies and packages as they trudged toward the ramshackle structures that served as their homes. A man beating a drum that hung across his chest shouted news of a pig about to be slaughtered and sold.

Paprika instructed Katalin not to drive into the town, but rather to turn up a steep hill off to the left. Halfway there, they were greeted with hoots and hollers and excited screams and whoops. The sight of a car had created a furor. Barefoot children with soot-caked legs and dirt-smudged faces raced after the Trabant, giggling and shouting in a strange language Katalin assumed was *Romany*, the Sanskrit-derived tongue of the gypsies. Paprika leaned out the window and waved to the ragtag horde, answering their heckling with gibes of her own. Dogs and chickens joined the procession, causing Katalin to brake and clutch and jerk the car until finally she reached the top of the hill and stopped in a sputtering climax of steam and whining gears.

The next curiosity was Katalin herself. As she and Paprika got out of the car, inquisitive adult faces eyed her warily. But they kept their distance. The children, however, buzzed around Katalin as if she were a hive. They touched her clothes and tugged at her hair. They pointed and grinned at her. One or two spat at her. Several kicked dirt onto her shoes. One scruffy little urchin tried to steal her wedding band off her finger. The experience was unnerving. Frightened, she wanted nothing more than to jump back into the Trabant and drive away as fast as the car would go, but she stood her ground. No matter how terrifying this mobbing was, it wasn't enough to make her desert Tibor. She needed to prove herself to all who were watching—including Paprika.

Finally, after what seemed an eternity, Paprika dispersed the swarm of filthy youth with one sentence.

"You could have done that right away," Katalin said, brushing dirt from her shoes and straightening her clothes, not bothering to disguise her anger.

"You should be glad I didn't." Katalin glared at her, but Paprika wasn't at all cowed. "Some of my people don't like my brother's friendship with you. There are many who feel that if not for you, he would have married Farah sooner and spared her and her family disgrace. I wanted them to see what you were made of." Paprika winked. "You were brave. You didn't shrink away. You're a friend. I knew it. And now they know it."

Katalin sighed and acknowledged the compliment.

"Are there any other tests I should know about? Do I have to walk over hot coals or drink sheep's blood?"

Paprika laughed. "Nothing as simple as that." Katalin's eyes widened. "You have to deal with Farah's jealousy of you and the hostility of her family."

Katalin's eyes flamed with offense. "I'm Tibor's friend. We share a passion for music and a liking for each other. I'm here as his guest and not his lover. Whatever his reasons for not jumping the broom sooner, they're his and his alone."

Paprika scrunched her features into an arrangement of earnestness. Tibor had instructed her to explain things to Katalin. She didn't like Farah any more than Katalin did, but she understood her better.

"Farah has suffered great shame at her continued maidenhood. She has been badgered and teased and humiliated. At some campfires, she was a laughingstock. She needed to place blame. You were convenient."

Funny, Katalin thought, how different a story could sound when told from another perspective.

"I didn't know," Katalin said to Paprika with honest sympathy. "If that's so, I'm glad for Farah that she's finally going to wed her groom. And," she said with a certain amount of relief, "I'm glad for me. When Tibor is her husband, she can stop hating me and we can all live happily ever after."

Paprika nodded and smiled, but in her heart she doubted that was possible. As long as Farah was Farah and Tibor insisted upon keeping Katalin as a friend, there could be no happily ever after.

She didn't know what she had imagined, but the hilltop gypsy community of Báthordomb, with its red-roofed buildings, surprised her. For despite terrible decay and disrepair, and though animals ran loose through its streets, it had the look of a town.

Paprika took her through the village to the far end of the community. Parked at the edge of a green were several metal trailers, the kind used by most modern-day traveling gypsies. After World War II, Hungary, as well as most other European countries, had passed laws that prohibited wandering and required the gypsies to settle. Paprika said these trailers belonged to the Tar family and had been used to transport them here for the wedding.

"I thought Tibor said his family lived in apartments in Budapest."

"We do," Paprika said, "but without these, how would we make the pilgrimage to Saintes Maries de la Mer?"

Each year in May gypsies from all over the world converged on the small town of Saintes Maries de la Mer on the Île de la Camargue at the mouth of the Rhone River in southern France to celebrate the feast of Sarah. By tradition, this feast celebrated the arrival in A.D. 42 of two Biblical "sisters" of the Virgin Mary: Saint Mary Jacobe and Saint Mary Salome, mother of the Saints John and James. According to legend, they drifted all the way from the Holy Land in a small boat without oars or sails. With them came the dusky Egyptian servant girl Sarah, now called "Black Sarah" and hailed by the gypsies as their patron saint.

"And those?" Katalin pointed to another trio of caravans, the lavishly, garishly decorated wooden boxes called *vardos*.

"Those are for the wedding," Paprika said with evident pride. "My parents are staying in one of them. Tibor is in the other. And that one," she said, indicating an especially elaborate, gilded and stenciled barrel-top *vardo*, "is the one Tibor will bring his bride to."

Katalin hated being so ignorant about the customs of someone she called friend, but she was and so she asked, "Will they live there?"

Paprika shook her head. "The final part of the marriage ceremony is when the groom collects his bride from her parents' house and walks her to the house he's supposed to be building for them. Since Tibor lives in Budapest, this trailer is symbolic of that home."

"It's beautiful," Katalin said, walking closer, admiring the teal green color of the wood, the gilded leaves and flowers that decorated the panels flanking the door, the horses and stags depicted on the sides. A cut-glass bouquet sprouted in one of the windows, an equally delicate bird was etched in the glass of another. Beneath the wagon, everything—wheels, axle, undercarriage—was brushed with gold and then finely stenciled in cordovan and black. When Paprika opened the door, Katalin's eyes bulged at the opulent interior. Yards of shirred red satin fabric covered the ceiling. At the far end, a vividly enameled wooden cabinet with gilded trim and hand-carved moldings boasted a wondrously golden horse caught in its race across a meadow, its tail and mane brushed back by the wind, its powerful legs challenging the forces of nature. Along the side wall, another cabinet, smaller and stockier, was covered by a silken cloth embroidered with the flowers and birds favored by the peasants of the region. Leaning against that bureau was a stack of down-filled *dunhas*, layered one on top of the other like flaky pastry leaves, making a soft, cushy bed fit for the deflowering of a bride. Two brass lanterns guarded the door. Richly patterned rugs blanketed the floor. Next to a couch built into yet another carved and gilded niche, a candle and a bible rested atop an octagonal table of wood and brass inlay, while underneath, in a hand-woven basket, a mass of rose petals gifted the cabin with a soft, provocative scent.

"Come," Paprika said, dragging Katalin back toward the center of town, "they're about to bargain for the bride."

By the time they arrived, the two sides had set up camp: the groom's father and his advisers on one side of the street, the bride's father and his coterie on the other, with a huge audience of imbibing observers ringing all of them.

"This is really just a show," Paprika whispered to Katalin. "In Tibor and Farah's case, everything was decided a long time ago." She pursed her lips and furrowed her forehead in a studied scowl. "Papa will have to arrange my marriage soon, or I'll be considered too old to fetch a good price."

Katalin stared at Paprika. She couldn't have been more than fifteen.

"Many girls are brides at fourteen," Paprika said, reading Katalin's thoughts. "Now you know why Tibor's delay is so shameful. She's twenty. He's twenty-four. They should have had four children by now."

Katalin gulped. She was twenty-nine and childless. Before she could dwell on that, Paprika nudged her, urging her to watch.

Lajos, Tibor's father, made the initial approach, which was favorably received. As Lajos returned to his camp, his delegation pressed around him, paying him court as attendants would a king. Meanwhile, Gyula, Farah's father, conferred with his advisers, debating the offer loudly enough for everyone to hear. After an acceptable amount of time, several of his emissaries walked the twenty paces to the other side to announce how many gold pieces Gyula would accept as the price for Farah. Lajos's men shook their heads, clucked their tongues, and feigned great dismay. With broad gestures and exaggerated flattery, they cajoled the bride's father as a prelude to a counteroffer. It was Gyula's turn to pretend dismay, to reiterate the blessings his daughter would bring to the union, playing up the way she danced, playing down the way she looked.

When Katalin questioned that, Paprika explained that to the gypsies, when one selected one's daughter-in-law, it was customary to do it "with the ears and not with the eyes," meaning that more consideration should be given to a girl's reputation than to her looks.

Just as the negotiation was reaching a frenzied peak, one of the groom's sponsors produced a special bottle of brandy wrapped in a bright silken kerchief and tied with a string of gold pieces. As the two fathers drank from the *pliashka*, the crowd cheered, the roar growing louder as the two men embraced.

"This is the most important part of the ceremony," Paprika said between her own exultations. "To the Rom, the drinking from the *pliashka* is what makes the union valid and binding. Though the marriage is between Farah and Tibor, the contract is between my father and Gyula."

Just then, Lajos's side began to bargain all over again. Lajos insisted that he had spent more than he had planned and that now—blessed be the bride and her father as well—he and his family would not be able to put on a feast worthy of one of their own. It wasn't that the bride was not worth every single piece of gold they had agreed upon. It was that her high price had left them too impoverished to pay for the kind of lavish celebration that would do honor to their new in-laws.

Keeping with tradition, Gyula protested and huffed and puffed, but did as he was expected to do. He returned part of the bride's price, which, according to custom, was handed over to Tibor's mother so she could buy Farah's wedding costume. The moment the exchange was completed and the cheers had abated, Farah was brought out from her parents' house and led into the center of the crowd. Her hands were wrapped in cloth. Paprika had already told Katalin that Farah's hands had been smeared with henna. The stain from the dye was a sign of piety.

Katalin watched intently as another woman, this one older, walked forward. Wearing a long skirt, a white blouse, and the traditional head-covering of a married woman—a scarf tied at the back of the neck—she proceeded toward Farah with slow, deliberate steps. This was Tekla, Tibor's mother. With everyone watching, she solemnly hung a string of gold pieces around Farah's neck, thereby warning other men that this woman was spoken for.

Instantly, the gathering became a festival. Hoards of food were brought out onto tables that stretched nearly an entire block. Wine seemed to flow as freely as the Tisza. As darkness began to envelop the enclave, the houses closest to the street turned on all their lights. Torches were lit. Katalin felt as if Báthordomb had been magically transformed into a wonderful carnival. Paprika dragged her around as if she were on a leash, introducing her—calling her Vadrósza to protect her real identity—filling her plate with roast goose stuffed with currants and apples, cucumbers in brine with a touch of dill, beans reddened with paprika, mashed chick-peas with sesame oil, and cabbage leaves stuffed with chopped meat and rice. She filled Katalin's glass with *pálinká* and laughed as Katalin tossed it back, sputtering as the brandy stung her throat.

"I see you're having a good time." It was the first time Katalin and Farah had spoken since her arrival in Báthordomb. She looked almost beautiful in her long braid and golden necklace. The brilliance of her turquoise blouse seemed to spotlight the intriguing darkness of her eyes and the fullness of her lips, which she had stained berry-red. The cloths had been removed from Farah's hands and she gestured wildly, as if to show everyone how dark the dye had made her flesh. "Has Paprika treated you well?"

"Yes," Katalin said, smiling at the young girl who had become a friend. "I don't know what the proper salutation is, but I wish you and Tibor much happiness."

Though Farah nodded and smiled and appeared to accept Katalin's felicitations, her mouth was slanted with doubt, her eyes narrowed with disbelief.

"This is wonderful," Katalin said, drawing her hand into an arc that described the banquet. "It's a shame Tibor can't be here." Katalin wished she could talk to him, see him, know that all was well.

"The groom is not allowed to be present for this part of the celebration, only the bride. You'll see him tomorrow, when he comes for me."

Katalin heard the undertone of possession, but chose to ignore it. She refused to nip at Farah's bait, no matter how often it was dangled in front of her nose.

"As long as you're here," Farah said, turning a little too sweet to suit Katalin, "why not let my aunt *dukker* for you?"

Katalin turned to Paprika for translation. "*Dukker* means to tell fortunes."

"Ludu is the best," Farah said, motioning to Paprika to take Katalin to the small house on the corner of the next block. "Don't you want to know what the future has in store for you?"

Katalin felt suddenly uncomfortable, pressured into something she wasn't certain she wanted to do. But, she told herself, fortune-telling was part of the gypsy culture. She was at a gypsy wedding. She had eaten their food, partaken of their drink, watched their ceremonies. Why not submit to their magic?

"Sure," she said, not sure at all. "Let's go meet Aunt Ludu."

Ludu's house was at the edge of Báthordomb. When Paprika and Katalin rapped at the door, a husky voice called them into the back. Wending their way through an unlighted hallway over a squeaking floor made more treacherous by an occasional missing plank, they followed the voice to the kitchen. There, seated behind a wooden table, surrounded by a half-dozen scrawny cats, was an enormous woman with pendulous breasts, ham-hock arms, and a neck so fat the flesh trembled as she breathed. The room reeked of stale food and animal excretions. Dirty dishes languished in a sink half-filled with greasy water. Candles burned on a windowsill and atop an ancient icebox. A teapot simmered on the stove behind the table. Ludu perched on a spindly wooden chair. She had tied a string of golden coins across her forehead, back around her matron's scarf.

Without any warning, she pounded the table in two places, bringing a massive fist down near the chairs where the two women were to sit. When they had obeyed she turned to Katalin. Her hooded black eyes, puffed from a dependency on *pálinká* and salt, wandered over Katalin's face and form, absorbing the details of the woman's appearance into her own psychic system.

"You've come for *dukkerin?*"

The woman's stale breath, the rankness of her body stench, and the other malodorous smells infesting the air around them were almost more than Katalin could bear. Unable to speak, she simply nodded her head.

"And you?" Ludu turned toward Paprika, who seemed almost to tremble beneath the gaze of the fortune-teller.

"Farah says you're a true Wise Woman." Paprika's voice wavered between terror and respect. Ludu was pleased by both.

"I am *shuvani,*" she bellowed, as if daring the spirits to challenge her. Her voice resonated throughout the room, chasing the cats and rattling the teacups that waited in front of her to be filled with the leaves of fortune. When she had allowed enough time for the spirits to settle, her voice softened. Her rheumy black eyes reached out and pulled Paprika closer. "What do you wish to know, little one?"

"When will I marry?" Paprika asked timorously.

Katalin stifled a smile. She would have bet on that being Paprika's question. With intense fascination, she watched as Ludu prepared the answer. Reaching behind her for the teapot, she poured water into one cup, filling it halfway. She returned the pot to the stove and then balanced a teaspoon on the edge of another, empty cup. Carefully, almost magically, she dripped tea into the bowl of the spoon—one drop at a time. The spoon wobbled after two drops, but remained on the edge. Paprika sat at the edge of her chair. Two more drops, the balance was broken and the spoon toppled into the cup.

"Four years until you will be a bride," Ludu said, patting Paprika's hand, knowing the anxious maiden had wanted a different reading. "Let's see what the leaves say."

Pushing the pale blue cup toward Paprika—gypsies never used white china; white was for mourning and brought bad luck—she ordered her to take three sips of the tea, rotate the cup three times using the left hand and then tip it upside down onto the saucer. Paprika did as she was told. Ludu took the emptied cup and stared into it for what seemed like a long time. When she looked up, she smiled.

"Fortune smiles on you," she said, pointing to a clump of tea leaves. "See the triangle?" Paprika nodded, while Katalin watched. "It's a sign of good luck and because it's near the handle, which represents you, it's your *kushti bok.*"

Paprika's mouth spread into a delighted grin. Ludu basked in the praise of the youngster for several minutes before turning her attention to Katalin.

"And now, green-eyed one. Let's see what the leaves say about you."

She repeated the process, leaving out the balancing act of the spoon.

When Katalin had completed all the steps, Ludu pulled the emptied cup toward her and looked in. She appeared to need extra strength to lift her head so she could face Katalin.

"Yours is not so rosy."

Throughout Paprika's reading, Katalin had tried to assess the level of her belief in fortune-telling. Her initial reaction was to dismiss it as chicanery. Most people she knew didn't view crystal balls or tarot cards or dice as implements of divination, but as ruses used by the gypsies to fleece and swindle. Then why, she wondered, was she distressed by what Ludu found in her cup?

Ludu showed her the leaves, as if Katalin understood their meanings.

"See these broken lines?" Katalin nodded. "These are broken promises. Someone has lied to you, green-eyed one, or betrayed you." She paused, letting Katalin wonder. "Here." Ludu moved on to another cluster of wet brown leaves. "The table means you will be called to a reunion of some sort." Her eyes actually looked kind as if she knew Katalin needed to hear something positive. "A gathering of old friends perhaps."

Again, Katalin nodded without comment. Her attention had already shifted to the third clump of leaves.

"This is the one I don't like," Ludu said, shaking her head, causing the bag of flesh beneath her chin to flap back and forth like a piece of wet laundry. "I see a vulture here."

Katalin looked. She wanted to deny it, to laugh at Ludu and tell her she was nothing but a charlatan, but the remains of the tea did look like a black bird with large wings and a tiny head.

"This vile, ugly thing is a sign of cruelty and oppression. It could mean nothing more than our beloved government. It could mean the possibility of a theft. I don't know, but be on guard, musical lady. Be on guard."

A chill ran through Katalin like an electrical jolt. It was quick, but every nerve cell in her body felt it.

"What about the cards?" Paprika asked, not wanting Katalin to leave with such a dreary reading.

Ludu looked from one to the other. Suddenly, a gas bubble rumbled through her body, exiting in a loud, foul-smelling belch. Afterward, she smiled, as if that effluvium had been the reason behind the bad fortune and now that her body was relieved of the pressure, things would go better for her *gorgio* visitor. She reached down under the table and pulled up a black velvet sack, which she dumped on the table before her. Paprika's eyes brightened as she heard the jangle of gems. Katalin's interest also peaked.

Ludu ordered Paprika to clear the table and bring her a stick of kindling from the bin alongside the stove. When she had the thin branch in hand, she turned on the stove, burned the tip of the thin stick, and blew out the flame, leaving a charred, black end. Using it like a pencil, she drew a large circle on the wooden tabletop. Then, she drew two lines across the center of the circle at what appeared to be one-third intervals.

"This is the present," she said, pointing to the section closest to Katalin. "This is the near future," she said, indicating the center section, "and this is the far future." She handed Katalin the sack. "There are twelve jewels in this bag, one for each sign of the zodiac. Shake them up and spill them out over the circle."

Katalin's palms were moist and she felt her fingers tremble slightly as she took the velvet bag from Ludu. She shook it, listening to the sound of delicate stones clicking against each other. Holding her breath, she turned the sack over and watched as colored crystals spilled onto the table. Her heart pounded and she laughed at herself for worrying about whether she had done it correctly.

Ludu leaned over the circle, pushing aside those gems that had fallen outside the charcoal line. She also eliminated those that floated inside each section. Clearly, it was proximity to the center lines that mattered. When there were only three stones left, she picked up the golden piece of amber that signified the present and faced Katalin.

"This is the stone of Scorpio." Her voice deepened as she tightened her grip around the amber and attempted to transfuse her body with its message. "It asks that you be cautious, that you not do anything reckless or foolhardy."

Katalin smiled. She was sitting in the kitchen of a gypsy having her fortune told, she had spent that morning distributing illegal publications, and she intended to keep all of this secret from her husband. The stones were right. She should exercise more caution.

Ludu picked up the second stone, a clear, cornflower blue sapphire. "For those born under Virgo's sign, this jewel usually brings happiness and love." Ludu saw Katalin hold her breath. "When it's thrown in the circle, it divines that a wrong done in the past will catch up to you. Sometime within the next six months, you will have to pay a price for something you did and shouldn't have."

Katalin couldn't help but run a quick tally of every little sin or lie or hateful thought she had ever had. The truth was she wasn't someone who committed horrible wrongs. But *dukkerin* didn't deal with earthly laws and human truths. It dealt with magic and the spirits and whatever offended them. Droplets of sweat lined her forehead and beaded her neck as she waited for Ludu to interpret the final stone.

The huge woman lifted a cloudy white opal off the table. She reached for Katalin's hand, placed the milky stone in the palm and closed Katalin's fingers around it.

"This is death, isn't it?" Katalin asked, seeing her answer in Ludu's fathomless eyes.

"For Romani, opals mean death, not necessarily for you, but certainly for someone close to you." Katalin dropped the opal on the table. Ludu pushed it aside and leaned onto her corpulent arms so that her broad face was close to Katalin's. "This stone fell into the sector of your far future, my friend. I wouldn't worry about it. Death will come to all of us. It is the future for everyone."

Though Katalin recognized that Ludu's words were meant to ease the shock of the stones' message, her own personal history—the violent deaths of Béla and Margit Kardos, the early loss of her mother, the constant threat of disaster and reprisal inherent in oppression—tended to make the interpretation seem ominous. Though she tried to appear unperturbed as she and Paprika left, her insides were frozen with fear and her eyes were moist with concern about everyone she loved, anyone she would hate to lose.

She was too intent on what she was feeling to focus on the shadowy figure of a young woman skulking in the back door of Ludu's house.

"Was her future bleak?" Farah asked her aunt, dropping a handful of coins into the fat woman's lap.

Ludu ignored the coins. "I am *shuvani*," she said, her lips quivering with angry indignation. "I don't invent fortunes. The leaves fell into their own pattern. She spilled the stones."

"I don't care who did what. Was her future bleak?" Farah asked again.

"As bleak as it gets."

By late afternoon the next day, every citizen of Báthordomb was at the green, anxious for the wedding festivities to resume. Long tables had been set up under the trees—one for the men, one for the women and children—all laden with food, though without fresh flowers, which the Rom believed should be left as part of nature, not cut or ripped from their roots. To them, cut flowers represented premature death. This was a celebration of the perpetuation of life.

While a group of women organized the feast, the younger married men worked the roasting spits, some turning whole piglets and flanks of beef, others feeding the voracious fire with wooden planks and aromatic herbs. The younger boys were charged with the task of grinding enough coffee for the entire camp.

At Farah's mother's house, a small gathering of women prepared the bride. First, they symbolically unplaited her braid. Then, they slipped a white satin shiftlike dress over one of magenta silk. A headdress of white silk flowers was pinned to her hair, holding a sheer veil to cover her face while a trim of silver threads cascaded onto her shoulders. As each member of her family kissed her, Farah wept. Tradition called for a tearful bride. Farah had waited too long for this day to forsake even the smallest custom.

When all was in readiness, the Rom converged. The men proceeded toward the banquet first, walking in groups of three and four, slowly and with great ceremony. The older, more important men arrived first. The others followed at a short distance.

Katalin, who had spent the morning brooding over Ludu's predictions, was still a bit woebegone when Paprika came to fetch her.

"Come! It's time," Paprika said, her dark eyes snapping with excitement. When Katalin appeared to be dragging, Paprika stood in the doorway of the room where Katalin had spent the night. "You can't let the future become too big in your mind. If you do," she said, sounding so much wiser than her years, "you'll cast such a large shadow on the present, you'll blind yourself to possible changes."

"I thought one's fate was predetermined." Katalin's voice remained level, but clouds of gloom dimmed her eyes.

Paprika closed the door behind her. It wouldn't serve her well to be overheard minimizing the talents of a *shuvani*.

"Ludu speaks with the broad tongue of the fortune-teller. Hear what she says, heed what she says, but then, do what you have to do."

"I can't change the stars," Katalin said.

"Stars don't move, Katalin, but the earth does. We do have some control over what happens to us. We just have to keep our eyes and ears open so we don't miss our chance."

Feeling slightly mollified but not completely convinced, Katalin begged a smile onto her lips. Paprika's brother was getting married today. It was unfair of Katalin to burden this child with something as weighty as the future of a stranger.

"My eyes and ears are open!" she declared, her face covered with a happy mask. "Come. We have a wedding to go to!"

By the time they found a place at the women's table, Tibor's five brothers were handing out silken kerchiefs, or *diklos*, to the men to be wound around the neck after the fashion of the Rom. In return, the men handed them a cash donation to help set up the new household and, as the gypsies said, "give a push to the wheel of the new wagon." Once that was done and the money was counted, the sum announced to the throng—providing another reason to down yet another drink—the two families set about entertaining.

Lajos and his sons brought violins to the chin and filled the air with the flamboyant melodies and rich, freewheeling rhythms of the Musicians. Paprika sprang to her feet and joined her two older sisters in the center of the crowd to dance the *chingerdyi*. They clapped their hands and smacked their ankles, scuffing their shoes on the hard earth in a rhythmic pattern. Not a face in the assemblage, including Katalin's, was minus an exultant smile. The Tars had invited the Devil to this feast; his spirit had gladly accepted.

Farah's kin were of the Walachian tribe. While several sang gypsy folk tunes, women began to rap their knuckles on the tables. Some tapped spoons. Men stamped their feet and clicked their tongues. This, as Paprika explained, slightly out of breath from her own performance, was traditional gypsy music. Though the music her father and brothers made was Hungarian gypsy music, the table songs were Rom.

Suddenly, Farah's father and brothers, eager to put on a display of their own, leapt to their feet wielding wooden poles and sticks. Drums and horns and spoons and knuckles provided the rhythm as one dancer armed with a stick tried to whack the legs of other dancers, all of them jumping and whirling in the dirt, accompanied by the clapping and hooting of the audience.

When everyone was near exhaustion, they started back to the center of town, Tibor's family leading the way. Their first stop was to collect the groom. As Tibor climbed down the steps of the *vardo*, his blue-black hair slicked back, his handsome brown face set in a look of solemn acceptance, his eyes searched the crowd. When he found Katalin, she smiled and he nodded. It was the only communication allowed them, yet for each it was enough.

Tibor took his place at the head of the procession and they moved toward Farah's house. Band music flared. Walking alongside Tibor was a bearer of a long pole bedecked with wedding presents of bolts of cloth, pillowcases, and shirts. Accompanied by loud, frenzied noises, the throng approached the house. The bride's family had formed a human barricade, waving sticks and axes and shovels at those who tried to pass. Only when Lajos again bargained for the bride and paid a toll of beer and brandy, did the in-laws remove the barricade.

Then Tibor ascended four wooden steps to a porch bedecked with crepe-paper flowers. With deliberate movements, he walked to the door and rapped loudly. In keeping with gypsy custom, when she emerged, Farah was crying, sobbing actually, proudly allowing a veil of tears to wash her face. Despite the concluding of a contract between the parents, despite the two days of celebration, the bride still had to surrender to her new husband—and to gypsies, submission was never an easy task.

Walking side by side, not touching, not talking, Tibor led his bride to his house. When they were only several paces away, she stopped, he continued. The entire village had gathered behind Farah to watch as Tibor stood alongside the teal green *vardo* and tossed candy to the crowd. One of his brothers carried a mirror before the bride so she could watch her face as she slowly made the transition from maiden to wife. Mounting the steps, she took her place at the door of Tibor's home. Tekla, Paprika, Tibor's five brothers, and two other sisters flocked to the trailer and handed Farah a loaf of bread, a symbol of their support, and smashed a cup—to break with the past. Then, Tibor's mother fed Farah sweets. Tomorrow morning, when the bloodstained bridal sheet was displayed, she would knot a kerchief on Farah's head. From then on, Farah could never appear without it.

As Farah walked inside the trailer, she turned, waiting for her groom. He also turned, but away from her, toward Katalin. She stood at the far edge of the crowd, so far back he could barely see her. He couldn't wave or shout or motion in any way, but still, it would have meant a great deal to him to make contact, even if only for a second. Though he willed her to look at him, screaming at her with the silent but powerful voice of intense concentration, she didn't respond. She was frozen in a pose of fear, her body tensed, her eyes fixed on the hulking, menacing form of Ludu, the fortune-teller. He felt Farah's hand drawing him in. He felt Katalin's need drawing him out. As had been true for most of his life, Tibor, for that horrible moment, felt conflicted, trapped between the pull of ancient custom and the lure of current loyalties. As had been true for most of his life, custom won.

With only half a heart, he retreated into the *vardo* to consummate his future, leaving Katalin on the outskirts of this strange, unfamiliar world to wrestle with hers.

28

$\mathcal{J}$t happened six months to the day after Katalin's sojourn to Báthor-domb. It was the end of the work day. Ilona was standing on a street corner near Shalom Hospital. The light was red. She was waiting for it to turn green so she could cross. She looked down at her watch, debating whether or not she had time to stop at the florist on the way home. She heard the trolley. It was a ubiquitous sound in Budapest, the rumbling of the electric car as it screeched along the metal tracks, but she paid it no heed. She even felt the bulk of the person who stepped behind her and pushed her in front of the speeding trolley. Within seconds of being hit, she heard and felt nothing else.

By the time Zoltán and Katalin arrived at the hospital, Ilona was in surgery. Andras, in shock, sat in a chair outside the hallway leading to the operating theaters. His hands were folded and hanging between his legs; his back was curved in an arc of despair. Zoltán approached him carefully, unwilling to startle or disturb him.

"Andras," he whispered as he took the seat next to his friend, swallowing his own tears, his own desperation at the thought of losing Ilona.

The thin man turned. He said nothing. After a while, his eyes appeared to focus on Zoltán's mouth as he tried to listen to the words of comfort and support being offered him. Now and then his head bobbed, indicating comprehension. Zoltán refused to press for more. He had sat in Andras's chair. He knew that every corpuscle in that man's body was concentrated in prayer, in begging whatever Omnipotence would listen to heal his beloved and not take her from him. Zoltán knew Andras believed that to waste so much as a puff of air on ordinary conversation was to risk angering God or whatever force it was that controlled the spin of the universe, bringing down on Ilona the wrath of an irate deity.

Judit was as stormy as Andras was placid. It was all Katalin could do to control the tornado of emotion raging from Ilona's daughter. Up and down the corridor she stomped, flapping her hands at her sides, flagellating herself as if hoping that by doing so she could rid her body of its rancor.

"It's my fault," she said, wringing her hands, ignoring the hot tears that coursed down her cheeks.

"It was an accident," Katalin said, trying to soothe her, "a horrible, terrible accident. No one's to blame."

Judit stopped and glared at Katalin. "How can you be so damned naive? They did this to punish me!" When she saw that Katalin still didn't understand, she gripped Katalin's arms and held her close so she could explain without everyone in the hospital overhearing. "Mama regained consciousness for a few minutes before they took her up to surgery. She said she was pushed."

"She'd been seriously hurt," Katalin reminded Judit, adopting an attitude of incredulity she did not feel. That someone had shoved Ilona in front of a moving trolley was not out of the realm of possibility. Still, Katalin preferred to believe otherwise. "She might have been delirious."

"She said she was pushed." Judit's teeth were clenched, her voice was flat.

"Okay, it was deliberate." Katalin didn't want to argue with Judit. "But Ilona's been using the underground for years. So have you. They've never bothered either of you before. Why now?"

"Because they warned me and I didn't listen. They told me that if I continued to mule, if I continued to consort with criminals against the state, if I continued to print and distribute samizdat, they would get me." She wiped her tears with the back of her hand and shrugged her shoulders in a gesture of helplessness; the government could view her repeated acts of defiance as wrong, but she could not stop herself from doing what she believed was right. "Last month, when I was with Emke, I ferried copies of Beszélő. They must have spotted a few of the articles in the American press." She gulped for air; her body spasmed as if the oxygen had been tainted with poison. When she stilled, she appeared drained of energy. Her voice was quiet, muted by defeat. "Kádár's busy putting on a show. He's running around wearing the mask of a reformer. My people were afraid outsiders were actually beginning to believe him. We couldn't let that happen." Her eyes filled again, spilling over onto a face etched with agony. "So this happened."

Convulsed, her body racked with sobs, she collapsed into Katalin's arms. Katalin held her and stroked her, unable to find anything consoling to say. She was haunted by the unreasonable, irrational, totally absurd thought that perhaps Ilona's accident was the fulfillment of part of Ludu's fortune, that this was the result of her wrongs, not just Judit's, that this was punishment for her sins, her crimes, her lack of obedience. Though she wanted to claim the curse as her own and thereby remove the onus for this horrible accident from Judit, she couldn't. She couldn't tell anyone where she had been or with whom. It was just as Mária used to tell her: "Lies and secrets beget lies and secrets."

It was nearly eight o'clock when László arrived.

"I just heard," he said, his face grim as he bent down to speak to Andras. "Any word from the doctors?"

"Not yet." Zoltán answered. Andras was incapable of response, polite or otherwise. "A nurse told us it would be hours before we know anything."

László squeezed his eyelids as if in pain and shook his head. He rose slowly, nearly tiptoeing over to Katalin, who had come to greet him. "How bad is it?"

"The wheels of the trolley severed her leg, just below the knee." Katalin couldn't say the words without grabbing hold of herself, touching and squeezing her own flesh as if to be certain her limbs were intact, her body was whole. "Thank goodness it happened so close to the hospital."

"Why do you say that? What difference does it make?"

"There were other medical people around. They knew what to do. While two doctors and a nurse tended Ilona, someone wrapped her leg in a coat and raced it inside where it was preserved. They're going to try and reattach it."

"I hope it works," László said, putting his arm around Katalin. "It would be a terrible thing to have a woman like Ilona out of commission."

"Leg or no leg, Ilona would never be out of commission." Katalin said with unmistakable pride. "That's what makes her so remarkable!"

She was about to tell him about Ilona's assertion that someone had pushed her, but held her tongue. Though she hated to admit it, she was reticent to confide such things in László. It was, as Judit contended, the uniform. Despite their closeness, Katalin found it almost impossible to confide in him; he wore the uniform of those in power, of those who may have ordered this so-called accident.

Judit, who had been standing outside the doors to the operating theaters, returned to the waiting area, her face ravaged with guilt and anguish. László approached her cautiously. He was not unaware of Judit's animosity toward him.

"I'm so sorry about this," he said gently, softly, sincerely. "My prayers are with her."

Judit was tempted to remind him that communists didn't pray, but she resisted the impulse. Instead, she nodded and allowed him to squeeze her hand in a display of sympathy. Knowing how restrained László was, it was an eloquent gesture. Though she had to force herself, she was as dignified in the receipt as he was in the giving.

"Have you eaten?" he asked. "Has your father or Zoltán?"

"No one has any appetite for food."

"I understand," he said, motioning for Katalin to take his place with her friend. "But I think I'll go out and get some food anyway. You're all going to need your strength. This is going to be a long night."

László was right. The night was interminable. Twelve long, harrowing hours after Ilona had been wheeled into the operating room, a young man with tightly curled hair and round metal spectacles came into the waiting room and headed straight for Andras.

"Ilona's going to be all right," he said, kneeling so he could speak to Andras without looking down on him, patting Andras's knee as if he were the elder and Andras the younger. "She's going to need a great deal of rehabilitation, and in all probability she will lose most of the mobility in that leg; but she's in one piece, body and spirit. She's going to be fine, Andras, just fine."

Andras dropped his head into his hands and wept. The doctor soothed the quaking man, holding him while he vented his emotions. Judit ran to her father.

"Is she really going to be okay?" Judit leaned over and confronted the messenger with tear-stained eyes. "Don't lie to us or tell us what you think we want to hear. We want the truth."

His face was square, strong-jawed, high-browed, dragged down a bit by fatigue, but a kind, inviting visage nonetheless. Dark brown eyes peered at her through rounds of glass. His mouth, full-lipped and wide, pursed as he considered his response.

"I always tell the truth." He paused, waiting for Judit to question him further or believe him. "First of all, I don't think it helps anyone— doctor, patient, or relative—to practice deception, no matter how well-meaning. And secondly, according to my mother, I'm a terrible liar."

Judit stared at him. She saw the twinkle in his eyes. She saw the lift in his upper lip. How could he be so casual at a time like this? Andras looked up. Instead of scowling in concert with his daughter, he smiled.

"That's true, Gábor, you are." Andras patted the young man's cheeks with his hands, calmer, steadier, less frantic now. "Judit, this is Weiss Gábor. According to Mama, he's the best surgeon at Shalom."

"Only at Shalom?" Gábor Weiss said with mock astonishment, making the smile on Andras's face broader and brighter. "How about the best in Budapest? The best in Hungary? The best in all the world?" He clucked his tongue and shook his head. "As soon as Ilona regains consciousness, she and I are going to have it out. I will not have my reputation narrowed by the likes of her!"

He stood and then, quite gently, bent down to help Andras to his feet. From being the comic, he was once again the healer.

"Come. I'll take you to see her. You can only look through a window in the recovery room for now, but it might make you feel better." Andras nodded and gulped and allowed a fresh supply of tears to wash his face. "How about you?" Gábor turned to Judit and held out his hand. "Would you like to see your mother?"

Judit's lower lip trembled. She looked confused, disoriented. Fearing she might faint, Gábor left Andras and went to her. Without asking permission, he pressed his fingers against her wrist. Observant eyes scanned her face. It was a cursory examination and a quick diagnosis, but he was certain that what he was looking at was abject fear.

"You can't see anything. Her leg is completely bandaged, Judit." His voice was a whisper, his words were directed to her and her alone. "Her hair is covered by a surgical cap and she has tubes coming out of her mouth and nose, but she's fine. She's sedated, which means she's feeling no pain."

Judit stared at him. Her dark eyes had locked onto his as if they were a lifeline and to look away would mean severing the cord. He understood. Without further comment, he took her hand, led her to her father and then escorted both of them down the hall to where Ilona lay.

As Katalin watched them, she felt László's arm slip around her waist.

"You look like you could use some rest. Would you like me to take you home?"

Katalin leaned against him. "I can't. You go. I'm going to stay."

"Then I'll stay with you."

Katalin offered him a fatigued smile. "That's sweet, but you have to be at work. Why not go home, rest, do what you have to do at the office, and then come back later tonight."

again so he could whisper in her ear and avoid being overheard. "As Hazalah I learned that if you're going to persist in defying the law, you must always look right, left, straight ahead, and most important, over your shoulder. When you live in a police state, safety is something you can never take for granted."

Ilona's recovery was protracted and painful. As her days in the hospital became weeks, her immediate circle altered the patterns of their lives to accommodate her confinement. Andras visited in the morning before going to the Academy and returned after his last class. Judit, too, was at the hospital every day, every minute she could spare. Her time away was spent rehearsing for recitals. Since they had been booked months in advance and since she knew that cancellations ruined a musician's reputation, she fulfilled her obligations, but refused any new assignments that would take her out of town. Zoltán and Katalin viewed themselves as the second team, providing backup for Judit and Andras, spelling them when fatigue overwhelmed them or their lives demanded that they be somewhere other than at Ilona's side. Even László appeared several times a week, sometimes reading to Ilona, other times chatting about nothing in particular, sometimes simply standing by while others visited, willingly receding into the background while family and lifelong friends crowded the foreground.

Judit's feelings for Gábor sneaked up on her. Since Attila, she had erected a stone shelter around her emotions, allowing no one entry, permitting visits to very few. She supposed that three months of watching Gábor care for her mother as well as her father had softened her heart. He treated her mother's wounds without stepping on her pride. He tended her father's need for consolation without making him seem weak. And, miracle of miracles, he tolerated her constant barrage of questions and occasional frustrated outbursts without dismissing her or making her feel foolish and unimportant. This was a gentle man, a man with a heightened sensitivity to pain—both sentimental and physical.

One night after Ilona had fallen off to sleep, Judit wearily left her room and headed for the lounge, seeking a quiet place to rest. She was too exhausted to start the trek across town. What she needed, she felt, was a minute to herself, a respite from the strain of nursing. She hadn't realized she had drifted off until she felt someone shaking her and heard a voice entreating her to waken. When she opened her eyes, it was Gábor standing over her. He was clucking his tongue and shaking his head.

"What's wrong?" she asked, startled awake.

"Judging from the drooping eyelids and the ashen pallor of the skin, I would say that what you need is a Jewish transfusion."

Her smile was spontaneous. "A Jewish transfusion?"

"Yes. Immediately!" He held out his hand and helped her to her feet.

"And what, may I ask, is that?"

He didn't answer. Instead, he rushed her to the elevator, down to the lobby, and out of the hospital, around one corner and across two streets until they came to a small *cukrászda*. Waving to a large woman Judit assumed was the owner, he commandeered a table in the back, held up two fingers to a waiter who also seemed to know him, and helped her into her chair. Before she had a chance to speak, two cups of coffee and two plates bearing a sugary mound of golden dumplings were placed before them.

"Coffeecake," he said simply, answering the question she had posed before he spirited her from the hospital. "Not just any coffeecake, mind you, but *aranygaluska!*" He eyed the sweet dumpling with a look that bordered on the sensual. Noting that she appeared as eager as he to indulge in the warm yeast cake, he picked up his fork, cut a piece, and lifted it off the plate, hesitating before tempting his mouth with its nearness. "*Jó étvágyat!*" he said.

"Bon appetit!" she replied, matching his smile with her own.

When every last puff of dough and every granule of sugar had been scraped off the plate and savored, and the second cup of coffee had been poured, Judit thanked Gábor for his culinary first aid.

"You're a nice man," she said honestly.

"I like you, too."

Judit blushed and that surprised her. She had always believed she had better control of her emotions. The last thing she wanted was to seem as if she were flirting with him. She scrambled to find something to distract him, to take his eyes from her face where she was certain they could read what she was feeling inside.

"Tell me a little about yourself," she said. "Were you born in Budapest? Did you train here?" *Are you married? Engaged? Involved?*

"I was born right here in Shalom Hospital in June 1942." He said it matter-of-factly, but no Jew ever talked about that time without a shadow darkening his eyes. "My father was a doctor. He was also Hazalah, same as yours. Unfortunately, he was captured by the Nazis and died on the march to Hegyeshalom."

Judit's body shook.

"My mother and I survived by hiding in the basement of an abandoned store on the outskirts of Óbuda."

"My parents hid in a closet in the Gáspár apartment."

"I know."

It interested Judit that one or both of her parents had discussed with this relative stranger a subject that had rarely been open to her. As Gábor outlined the rigors of his early childhood, she listened intently. He told of foraging food from garbage cans, of trying to keep warm in a building without heat, of trying to keep clean with only a sink and a toilet to service their needs. He spoke of trying to escape, of the futile efforts to find relatives and friends who might have been able to take them in. When she saw the ghosts in Gábor's eyes and heard the echoes in his voice, she shuddered at a sight that was all too familiar. She had been witness to similar specters from her parents and other survivors.

Suddenly, a realization struck. Gábor was presenting her with frightening tableaux. Yes, she felt revulsion at the thought of what he had gone through. Yes, she was intellectually appalled by the horrors man had visited upon his fellow man. But she felt no visceral response to his words, no physical familiarity with the pain he was talking about. Her parents had tried to tell her, they had fought to explain their lack of discussion with her, but until now she hadn't fully understood. Those who hadn't experienced the living nightmare of that unspeakable era were incapable of fathoming the atrocities suffered by those who had. No matter how keen one's intellect or how compassionate one's soul, there could be no true understanding for those who had not lived the horror.

"Despite the best efforts of the Arrowcross and the Nazis, we made it," Gábor said, his tone tinged with fatigue, as if reliving the past had exhausted him.

"Where is your mother now?"

"Probably in her office." He laughed because it was nearly midnight and he would have bet every forint in his meager bank account on her being at her desk. "It's hard to sleep when one carries the burden of centuries on one's shoulders."

Judit looked confused.

"My mother runs the school system within the Jewish community. She holds the title of superintendent, but those who work for her call her Queen Eszter." He laughed again. It was a sound filled with love and respect. "Not to her face, of course."

Judit knew of Eszter Weiss. Every Jew in Budapest knew her. Tireless, fearless, undaunted by bureaucracy, communism, anti-Semitism, or any other ideological roadblock, she had set for herself the task of making certain that every boy and girl born into the Jewish community knew his heritage. "Knowledge breeds pride," was one of her favorite slogans.

When Judit had attended religious school, Eszter had been her teacher. Thinking back, Judit smiled. A formidable woman, she deplored inattentiveness, refused to accept any excuse other than abject tragedy for absenteeism and found it impossible to comprehend the fact that there were children in her classroom who lacked her enthusiasm for the study of things Judaic.

"I can see by your face that you've met my mom." Gábor chuckled. "Scared you to death, did she?"

"Nothing scares me, but I will admit, I learned my Hebrew." Judit smiled at the memories. "She's quite a lady."

"So are you."

"You hardly know me."

"Thanks to your mother, my mother, and Phil King, I know a lot about you."

At the mention of King's name, Judit's entire body went on alert. Gábor noticed and acted quickly to reassure her.

"My mother took receipt of the Torah from Prague," he said quietly. "Some of the medicines you ferried were sent to help my surgical patients. You saved their lives, Judit. Though they don't know you or what you risked on their behalf, they're grateful for your courage. And so am I."

Judit withered in the warmth of his compliment. She wasn't used to praise or admiration, especially from young men.

"Someone once told me, 'In the battle between the oppressed and the oppressor, we're either soldiers or victims,' " she said, quoting Attila. "I chose to be a soldier."

A slow, appreciative grin played on Gábor's mouth. "If all Hungarian soldiers were as beautiful and as clever as you, we wouldn't have to worry about how to defeat the Soviets. We could simply bewitch them."

"Are you flirting with me?" Judit asked, shocking both of them with her bluntness.

"Yes." Gábor leaned closer to her, the grin widening. "Want to make something of it?"

Judit studied his face. She saw no guile, no male artifice, no macho intent to ravish and conquer. Instead, there was respect. In his dark eyes she saw attraction and even a bit of awe.

"Yes," she said, astonished at how special she felt. "Yes, I do."

Katalin knew she was being foolish, but Ilona's accident had shaken her to her core. Inside that tiny part of her brain that allowed irrational behavior, she had decided that perhaps if she did something exceptionally good or extraordinarily meritorious, she could reverse the curse of Ludu's stones. When first she had conceived this idea, it had seemed so obvious and so right that she scolded herself for not thinking of it sooner. It wasn't until she had begun to implement her plan that second thoughts arose. It had taken weeks to convince both parties that their efforts wouldn't be in vain. Now that the day of reckoning had arrived, she had to convince herself of the very same thing.

She had set this up very carefully. She and Zoltán sat in the back of one of the small recital halls at the Academy. The stage was dim, almost dark. In the center, a tall three-panel screen concealed the identity of the performer. Initially, Zoltán had rejected the notion of such a thing. How would he judge fingering or bow strokes or stance or emotional intensity? A performer's appearance was important, he claimed. She agreed, but defended her request with inferences that for the audition, this performer required a certain dispensation.

"It's more important to hear him than to see him," she had said.

Making the assumption that all these elaborate preparations were to hide the fact that his mystery performer was physically disabled in some way, Zoltán had agreed to the hearing. What he found most fascinating was Katalin's nervousness. It appeared to be very important to her that he take this person on as a student. Once, he might have viewed this as another attempt to entice him back into the world of the violin, but he was content with his role as a conductor and she knew that. She also knew that several months ago he had said he would be willing to tutor someone in his instrument if he deemed the talent outstanding. So who was this auditioner and where had Katalin met him?

Within ten minutes, Zoltán didn't care about anything other than the music being produced behind that screen. It was exquisite! His heart pounded as he listened to an excerpt from the intricate "Carmen Fantasy" by Pablo de Sarasate. Though the piece was meant to be played with the accompaniment of an orchestra, Zoltán felt no absence of sound. Whoever was playing clearly felt a kinship with the rhythms. Via lush vibrato and lightning-quick fingering, the essence of the character permeated the air as if Carmen herself had been in that hall just moments before, branding the space with her scent. Zoltán could feel the spice and spunk of her personality, the fire of romance.

In the next selection, the first movement of the Concerto No. 5 by Belgian composer Henri Vieuxtemps, Zoltán heard some hesitation. Once or twice the staccato was too quick, the double stops awkwardly done. But in the final offering, the Bach C-major Sonata, composer and musician became one. Zoltán closed his eyes and let the harmonic complexity of the music hold him in its thrall. Each angular leap, each vertiginous slide, each impassioned spiral charged his body with enchantment.

Inside that dark crypt where he kept his feelings, ghosts from his past cried out to him, luring him backward to that time when he had created the music, when his hands had coaxed both tears and laughter from the strings of a violin. As Bach's notes swirled within his brain, he could feel the strings beneath his fingers, the sweet wood of his Guarneri pressed against his chin. Even his body moved, bending with the changing tempi, swaying as if the bow were in his hand, as if he were the creator rather than the listener.

Suddenly the music stopped. Zoltán's fantasy dissolved. He felt Katalin tense beside him. He could almost feel the anxiety of the performer behind the screen. He knew he was expected to speak, but he remained mute, savoring the lingering echo of something magnificent.

"Papa." Katalin couldn't stand the suspense another moment.

"Show yourself." Zoltán's voice boomed toward the stage. His eyes fixed on a circle of light into which a young, thin, brown man stepped. "A gypsy."

There was no disguising the disgust in his voice. Katalin's worst fears had been realized. She had made a fool of Tibor and trapped her father.

"Forget what he is," she whispered, a frantic edge haunting her voice. "Remember how he played. I watched you. You were impressed, Papa. You were struck by his talent, you know you were."

"He's a gypsy." Katalin couldn't tell whether it was revulsion or amazement that resounded in Zoltán's voice, but neither would stop her from pressing her cause.

"So what? Since when are you so bigoted that you can't accept talent, whatever the source? All my life I heard you preach about how horrible anti-Semitism was, how only the ignorant and the weak allowed themselves to hate others for no reason. Tibor is a gypsy. He's also one of the most brilliant violinists I've ever heard."

"And where did you hear him?"

"Here and there. In restaurants. Once at an outdoor festival in Pécs. What difference does it make? He's good. You could make him great!"

Zoltán said nothing. As Katalin continued to plead her case, he stared at the young man who stood with the violin hanging at his side. Though he tried to prevent it, images of his first audition with Madame Vásáry paraded across his memory. He had been a poor, farm-bred child with dirt beneath his fingers and the smell of horses clinging to his clothes. He was no more appealing to the likes of Madame than this gypsy boy was to him. What if she had turned him away simply because he wasn't properly dressed or of a station more suited to her own? Still.

A gypsy had no chance to play in an orchestra. Racial prejudices ran too deep for him to hold out any hope to this young man for breaking down barriers. Why train him if the young man couldn't put it to use? he asked himself, attempting to build a defense for rejection. Because he has the gift! And who would understand better than Zoltán the sin of wasting such a gift?

"Come here!"

Tibor's legs shook as he left the stage and headed up the aisle. As he struggled to put one foot in front of the other, he tried to remember why he had ever agreed to put himself in such a humiliating position. What had Katalin said to convince him to do such a thing? What madness had gripped him that would make him think that the great Zoltán Gáspár could ever entertain the thought of tutoring a gypsy? It was ridiculous! Absurd! A waste of time! When at last he reached the row where Zoltán and Katalin sat, he could hardly breathe.

"Why would you want to be tutored when you and I both know you'll never win a seat in an orchestra?"

The question hit Tibor like a roundhouse punch. Needing time to recover, he lowered his eyes, gathering strength. When he looked at Zoltán again, his voice was soft and respectful, but clear and strong.

"The violin is my life. My blood is filled with music. I wake up with sound in my head. I go to sleep with rhythms in my heart. The fact that my skin is brown and my eyes are black and my laws are those of my *kumpania* doesn't make me less of a violinist than someone with white skin and blue eyes. The violin can't tell the difference between the hands of a gypsy and the hands of a *gorgio*. It cares only how its strings are plucked and stroked and caressed. I love it and it loves me. All I want is to learn as much about it as I can. Where that takes me, I don't know, but right now the learning is what's important. If playing with an orchestra becomes important, I will find one that will accept me," he said, looking directly into Zoltán's eyes. "It doesn't matter whether it's here in Hungary or somewhere else. The music is what matters."

Zoltán stared at the young man called Tibor. He felt the ghost of Madame Vásáry pushing him, challenging him to be exceptional. He heard his father's voice urging him to work harder, to use what God had given him. He heard the awestruck *Bravos!* and the wild applause of appreciative audiences. He heard the pride in Mária's voice when she spoke of his abilities. He heard Ferenc Kassak's laughter as he crushed Zoltán's hands.

"When I met my tutor for the first time," he said quietly, still overcome by his reminiscences, "I was too young to express my feelings as eloquently as you just did, but that's exactly how I felt. The music is what matters." From the corner of his eye, he saw his daughter's mouth flicker in a cautious but grateful smile. "Obviously Orpheus is color blind. He's given you an extraordinary gift and if you're willing to share it, I'm willing to nurse it."

Tibor was dumbstruck. A lifetime of rejection had deafened him to the sound of acceptance.

"Tibor," Katalin said, gently poking her friend in the ribs. "He said yes! Papa's going to tutor you. I told you he would."

Tibor blinked. Shock faded. Embarrassment took its place.

"I'm so grateful," he said, reaching out to shake Zoltán's hand, pulling it back in case Zoltán was queasy about touching gypsies. "I'll pay you whatever you ask. I'll do whatever you ask. I'm . . . I'm . . . I'm happy! Unbelievably happy!" Unable to maintain his composure a moment longer, he allowed a joyous smile to possess his face.

"Our lessons will be at my apartment. Wednesday afternoons at two o'clock."

"Fine. Wonderful. Whatever you say."

Katalin leaned over and kissed Zoltán's cheek. "Thank you, Papa."

Zoltán patted her arm, grumbled a good-bye to Tibor and left the auditorium, still wrestling with himself. Despite his misgivings about teaching a gypsy, Zoltán was secretly pleased at the young man's awed delight and honestly looked forward to molding his talent. He was not pleased at the apparent friendship between Tibor and Katalin, however. No matter how casual she tried to make it sound, she had known him longer and better than her words implied. While Zoltán wondered about the truth of their relationship, he knew that if life had taught him anything, it was that ignorance can offer protection. He understood her desire to spare him difficult moments or shield him from sticky situations. He also understood that she was an adult and was entitled to privacy, even secrecy.

Knowing that, he swallowed his impulses and decided to honor her wishes. He would keep his questions to himself . . . for now.

Tibor Tar was born in a caravan on the outskirts of Pécs. Instead of a cradle, he slept in the crook of a horse collar, tended by his mother and the women of her tribe, the Lovári. While normally a bride joined the tribe of her husband, Tekla's mother had died very young, leaving a large motherless brood. As the eldest, Tekla bore the responsibility for raising them and for ten years, until the last of her siblings was wed, the Tars remained in Pécs. Lajos set aside his violin to earn a living digging coal in the Mecsek Mountains. His two older sons apprenticed with a gypsy blacksmith. The older girls learned *dukkerin* and dancing, while the youngest of them, Tibor included, learned to beg.

When he wasn't panhandling, he stayed at home, learning about horses at the knee of his maternal grandfather. Though the Lavári swore that gypsies no longer practiced horse trading, Tibor couldn't recall hearing stories about anything else. His grandfather, Dénesh, who believed the old gypsy saying, "A gypsy without a horse is no genuine gypsy," loved nothing more than teaching his grandsons the art of the trick.

He showed them how to train the good horses and disguise the bad, how to cajole and bargain and how to clinch the sale with oaths only a gypsy would take: "May my life dissolve if this horse is not a wonderful beast," "May the Lord strike dead this child if the horse is not a prized animal." Tibor loved most when Dénesh would take off his hat, hold it just below his chin, and swear, "If what I've said isn't all true, may my two eyes drop in this hat."

When Tibor was ten years old, Lajos moved his family north to Budapest, introducing them to his people, the Musicians. They were a more sophisticated sort, prizing artistry over haggling, performing over debunking. Lighter-skinned, accustomed to city life, they often appeared more Magyar than Rom. Though most gypsies abhorred the notion of assimilation, some, like Lajos—horrified by the hundreds of thousands of gypsies exterminated by the Nazis—had altered their way of thinking. Lajos taught his children the ways of their ancestors, but instructed them in the ways of the *gaje* as well. Following the lead of other Musicians, he moved them into apartments and out of the caravans. He exposed them to the church and demanded they attend school, encouraging them to read the history of Hungary, much of which Lajos believed also belonged to the gypsies.

"We came in 1415," he was fond of saying. "We're not exactly newcomers."

Yet every Sunday was spent passing on the oral tradition of the Rom through the *Swatura*. A group of rambling stories that chronicled the travels of the Rom throughout the world, the tales were more than simple amusements or parables. They were the history of a people without a nation, without institutions, without books of their own to pass on the wisdom of their heritage. There were *Swatura* dealing with magic, superstition, fortune-telling, and supernatural phenomena. They were called *Darane Swatura* and were told for pure enjoyment. Others served as lessons through which parents taught children linguistics or elements of a trade or descriptions of how to handle specific emergencies. They were also the memories of a centuries-old travelogue, with scenes from many minds, told in many tongues.

One of the other things taught by the *Swatura* were perceptions: the various customs, weaknesses, and character of the *gaje*, and their superstitions about the gypsy.

Having been inculcated with all this lore as a boy, Tibor supposed it shouldn't have surprised him when, after a year of coming to Zoltán's apartment without incident, he was told that there had been a number of thefts in the building and he had been accused.

Zoltán had not delivered this news easily. His face had mirrored his discomfort and his voice had been shaded with apology and embarrassment.

"Do you think I robbed your neighbors?" Tibor asked, dreading the answer.

"I didn't want to," Zoltán said. "For months, when each theft was reported, I told myself it was someone from the street, or that the object had been misplaced or lost." Zoltán shifted his weight from one foot to another. His eyes wandered, as if the sight of Tibor was as unsettling as the glare of an August sun. "But then, Mária's gold cross was missing. It had been given to her by the sisters at the convent where she was raised. It was her prized possession. I kept it on a lace doily on top of the dresser. It's gone, Tibor. Tell me where it's gone."

Though his insides stormed with a mix of rage and defensiveness, Tibor showed only unruffled concern. "I don't know, Zoltán. I honestly don't know." Zoltán sat. Tibor remained standing. "I didn't steal from your neighbors and I certainly wouldn't steal from you."

"That's what Katalin said. She said gypsies don't steal from their friends." He paused and then looked squarely at the young man he thought he had come to know. "Is that true, Tibor? And if so, am I a friend?"

"I know it's hard to believe, but we do have our own sense of honor. I am not a thief, but even if I were, you are my friend, Zoltán. According to my laws, that's a sacred trust."

Zoltán looked tired, as if all the discussion and debate leading up to this had dragged the heart out of him. In truth, it had. Finding Mária's cross missing, calling Katalin, having to confess to her and László that his neighbors were complaining about his inviting a gypsy into the building, blaming him and Tibor for their losses—it had taken a terrible toll. Katalin had reacted as he expected she would, defending Tibor, refusing even to think of him as anything other than completely innocent and wrongly accused. László, on the other hand, had been offended. He hadn't known about Tibor or his wife's involvement with him.

"Those people are an abomination," he railed, stunned by revelation that "this lowlife" had been introduced to Zoltán by none other than his wife. "What were you thinking?" he had demanded, first of Katalin, then of Zoltán.

"That he was an incredible violinist who could benefit from Papa's teaching." Katalin stood her ground, a fact that had served to further infuriate László.

"And you," he said, pointing a finger at Zoltán. "Are you so desperate for money that you would stoop to training animals?"

"Tibor is not an animal," Zoltán said, seeing a side of László he had never seen before, a side he did not like. "Besides, I didn't adopt him. I'm simply tutoring him."

"I don't see how you can bear to be in the same room with a gypsy."

László had continued his diatribe against gypsies for some time, enumerating all the standard prejudices against them, listing incident upon incident of swindling and thievery. If he hadn't sounded exactly like most other Hungarians, Zoltán could have argued more forcefully, but László had a lot of company in his beliefs. Zoltán knew this because before meeting Tibor he had been one of them.

"I believe you, Tibor," he said now, "but—"

"But no one else will." Tibor nodded, his head bobbing with the weight of his associations. He bent down, picked up his violin case, and turned toward the door. "I thank you for all you've done and all you've tried to do for me. I only care that you and Katalin know I wouldn't hurt either of you." He twisted the doorknob. His heart twisted at the same time.

Zoltán felt the young man's pain. He knew what it was like to be punished for something he didn't do.

"Our lessons will continue," he said quietly, firmly, "but we'll meet in my office at the Academy instead of here in my home. Next week. Same day. Same time. New place."

Tibor looked at Zoltán. "Bless you," he said in a voice breaking with emotion. Except for Katalin, no one in the white world had ever shown him such friendship, such trust. Though he knew Zoltán had offered both freely, Tibor felt indebted.

Standing outside Zoltán's door, still shaking with the sting of his accusations coupled with the shock of Zoltán's dismissal of those charges, he silently proclaimed his tutor a *"Romane gaje"* and pledged eternal loyalty. This declaration of friendship was something no gypsy took lightly. Nor should any *gaje*.

Though Tibor's face was a portrait of composure, his manner belied his calm. Farah moved to greet him, but he pushed by her, heading toward their bedroom with a look of purpose that frightened her. Without

responding to her questions or reacting to the shrill rise in her voice, he
opened drawers, savaging through them like a man on a hunt. Dissatisfied, he ransacked the closets, tossing skirts and blouses and shawls onto
the floor in a frenzy of exploration. He toppled chairs. He stripped their
bed. He slashed open the mattress and pillows. Still unsuccessful, he
moved his rampage into the kitchen, emptying cabinets of pots and pans,
throwing them without aim, careless about where they fell or whom they
hit.

"What are you doing?" Farah's voice was a shriek. "What are you
looking for?"

Dropping to his knees, he opened the doors of the cabinet beneath
the sink and reached inside, groping about, tapping pipes, touching walls,
poking inside every crevice.

"Stop it!" Farah said. She was screaming at him, her hands beating
on his back. "You're destroying our house!"

He reached back and with one swipe of his arm swept her off him.
Slowly, he extricated himself from the cabinet and clambered to his feet.

"No," he said, grabbing Farah's wrist, his black eyes fired with an
anger so red it looked as though Satan had possessed his soul. "You're
destroying our house."

Without removing his eyes from her face, he raised his free hand.
In it, he held a golden cross the size of his fist. Dangling it in front of
her, he dared her to look away.

"Why?" he demanded. His fingers tightened his grip on her wrist.
"Why did you do it?"

Instead of answering, she turned her head away in a huff of defiance.
Still holding Mária's cross, he took her chin in his hand and forced her
face in alignment with his.

"He's one of the greatest violinists of our time. Do you understand
that? He was the best and he thought enough of me to tutor me, to teach
me—"

"No!" she shouted, interrupting his praise of Zoltán Gáspár. "He
was putting the carrot before your nose, tempting you to forsake your
people, to forsake me. I had to show you. I had to prove to you that no
matter how chummy you think you are with the gorgio, they are not
chummy with you. You are gypsy and if you don't want to remember
that, I wanted you to see that they never forget it!"

Furious, Tibor shoved her away from him, indifferent to her cry as
she tripped over one of the pots and hit the floor. With clenched fists
and emotions so close to the surface he feared they would erupt in a
burst of violence, he began to pace, hoping the movement would cap
his anger before he did something he would regret, although at that

moment he didn't think it was possible to regret anything more than marrying Farah.

She scrambled to her feet, inching backward out of his way. Her dark eyes followed him like a mouse being stalked by a cat. She studied his movements, on guard for the minutest sign of change. Her body was taut, attentive, alert, ready to fight him or bed him, however his rage chose to manifest itself.

When, finally, he faced her again, though she wanted to believe the tempest had passed, the set of his jaw told her it was simply a break in the clouds.

"I've been playing the violin since I was five years old. It's as important to me as the air that I breathe or the food that I eat. It has always brought me joy even when life insisted upon bringing me pain. Though it fills my pockets, I don't care about the money I earn with my music. I only care about the music." He paused, giving her time to absorb what he had said. "I'm good, Farah. Zoltán was going to make me better." He shook his head, as if he was struggling to find words simple enough and clear enough to make her understand. "Why would you want to ruin that for me? Why would you think my lessons with Zoltán were a danger? I've been playing in *gaje* restaurants and fairs all my life. What difference would it make if I played in a concert hall?"

"When you play in the restaurants, you play as a gypsy. You dress as a gypsy, you stand with gypsies, you play the music of gypsies. In their halls, Tibor, you can't be gypsy. You have to be one of them and to be one of them means to deny being one of us."

"I would never deny who I am!" His eyes flamed and his fist pounded the top of a table in refutation.

She laughed without mirth. Her eyes filled with doubt and challenge. Her only gesture was a flick of her hand.

Though he could dismiss her disdain with ease, Tibor found it difficult to ignore what she said next. It was what gypsies always said to one they believed was torn between two worlds:

"With one behind you cannot sit on two horses."

29

Washington, D.C., 1982

*W*ashington was a city that ran on power. Now, in his second term, Steven's political muscle was increasing every day. By disregarding his freshman status and boldly speaking out on issues dear to him and those he represented, he had become a respected member of the House in a very short period of time. It helped that the press loved him. Because he had what media folk labeled charisma, they sought him out, often at the expense of more senior members of Congress, to whom he was becoming a burr. In the minds of the warhorses, he was still a parvenu. While some of them waited eagerly for his rocket to fizzle, others, his contemporaries, had taken to inviting him to speak to their constituencies at important fundraisers. As one congressman put it, "Kardos has a voice that opens wallets and picks pockets."

In addition to his own talents, Steven was blessed with a clever and efficient staff. Matthew, who had turned over the management of Perry & Kardos to Walter, ran the district office and came to Washington frequently to confer with his brother.

Shadow had grown with his job. He had assembled an enviable cadre of bright, energetic young people, well-balanced between the truly experienced and the merely enthusiastic. By working overtime, he and his crew had made contact with important politicos on and off the Hill, had figured out which lobbyists to court, which to avoid, which interest groups enflamed the public, which enraged the administration. They prepared position papers and press releases, wrote speeches and answered mail. They were, as Steven repeatedly told them, "the tail that wagged the dog."

One of the most valuable members of Steven's team didn't work in either office. Cynthia Kardos was most effective at home. As a hostess in a town where entertaining was often a means of maneuvering, she was without peer. The moment Steven was elected to Congress, she hired Mark Hampton to decorate the Georgetown townhouse, instructing him to create an atmosphere conducive to the cultivation of power. The Kardos home in Georgetown was exquisite and, thanks to Cynthia's remarkable social skills, quickly became a den for America's political lions.

Twice a month, Cynthia hosted dinner parties. Sometimes they were small, twelve people comfortably seated in the blue-and-white dining room. Sometimes, the number increased and tables were set throughout the main floor of the elegant residence. Occasionally, when another congressional wife was catering a gala evening that Cynthia felt needed dilution, she threw a lavish cocktail party designed to snatch the other woman's glory.

This evening, Cynthia was giving a black-tie dinner for fifty in honor of Steven's thirty-fifth birthday. In addition to the requisite family, staff, and friends, she had invited a number of Steven's colleagues, several top-ranking Democrats, and a smattering of Republicans. As a surprise for Steven, she had hired Sophie Warsaw to entertain.

Because the weather had refused to cooperate, Cynthia had scuttled her plans to serve cocktails on the terrace, setting up in the garden room instead. Her most recent addition to the building, it was a large, airy room with four skylights and three sets of French doors overlooking the small but carefully tended garden at the rear of the house. Huge ficus trees in white planters brought the feeling of green inside, augmenting the florals that upholstered the furniture and the flower-filled vases that luxuriated on tabletops. Overhead, a massive crystal chandelier became a firmament, its lights twinkling in concert with the candles Cynthia had placed around the room.

As always, Cynthia was ravishing. Her long, narrow-skirted evening dress was a simple affair. Designed by Galanos of the richest black silk jersey, it conveyed a regal femininity through broad, lushly draped shoulders and a straight yet modest neckline. The back was pure Galanos drama. Inset with a panel of patterned lace, tied with a large satin bow whose sash trailed to the crook of her knees, it was the quintessence of sophisticated design, a silhouette that demanded minimal embellishment. Cynthia's raven-toned hair had been swept up and slicked back; her eyes had been kohled and dusted with black; her cheeks lightly, almost invisibly, blushed. Her lips bore the only color, a ripe, luscious, strawberry-red. Except for a pair of spectacular diamond earrings with large emerald drops, her person was bare of jewelry; she wore no accessory except the one she believed truly set her apart—her husband.

She loved to watch him as he moved among the mighty. While once he had shown signs of insecurity and intimidation in this type of setting, time had made him more comfortable with himself. While Steven had always had charm, under her tutelage—or so she liked to think—he had learned to channel his magnetism into an effective tool of persuasion. As she watched him now, smiling at the plain-Jane wife of the chairman of the Foreign Affairs Committee (of which Steven was a member), laughing with her supremely serious, odiously dull husband, she marveled at how far Steven had come, and how fast.

While many might have given some of the credit for that meteoric rise to Matthew, Cynthia was loathe to give her brother-in-law anything more than the time of day. Spotting him in the entry introducing his date to Claudia and Billy, she experienced the same flush of anxiety she always felt when he was near. Matthew Kardos provoked uncontrollable responses in Cynthia. She knew he detested her as much as she detested him, but Cynthia was used to people disliking her. This was something else, something more.

At first she'd thought that he wanted to split her and Steven up so Steven could be reunited with that Hungarian piano player; but Matthew had never done anything to discredit Cynthia, despite the fact that she had tried her damnedest to discredit him. Then she decided it was a matter of basic competition. He wanted to be Steven's unchallenged adviser, the only voice whispering in the king's ear. Yet when she made a viable suggestion he not only implemented it, but he applauded it. He was generous with his compliments about evenings like this, understanding the effort and the effect of such flawless entertaining. Never did he step on her toes or ignore her position. Just that morning, he had called to ask if she could set another place for someone who could be important to Steven.

So what was it that raised bumps on her skin and churned her stomach? Just then, Matthew turned. His eyes caught hers and held

564 / DORIS MORTMAN

them. Suddenly, as the force of his gaze pierced her, she understood. He frightened her because he saw through her.

And Cynthia could not afford to be exposed.

Though it was rude to leave one's guests, Steven took advantage of the interlude between dinner and dessert to sneak away with Owen, Matthew, Shadow, and Sam Otis. Needing privacy, he led them upstairs to the study on the second floor.

"I'm sorry to take you away from your party," Sam said. "I know it's an imposition, Steven, but I needed to speak to you tonight."

Sam Otis was a young and gritty man. A son of Appalachia, newly elected as president of the United Mineworker's Union, he burned with commitment. Hardened by his own years in the belly of the earth, as well as by the deaths of his father and uncles from black lung disease, he refused to countenance debate on safety measures or economic compensation for those who did humanity's dirty work. Owen had brought Steven and Sam Otis together several years before because he was confident that, sooner or later, Otis would prove to be politically beneficial.

"I always have time for one of my own," Steven said, offering the four men a brandy. "What's on your mind?"

"You." Otis cracked a smile. He wasn't handsome by anyone's definition, but at least when his mouth curved upward his angry mask softened into something more appealing. "Tomorrow I have a meeting with the Speaker of the House. With your approval, I'm going to place your name in nomination for the chairmanship of the Democratic Congressional Campaign Committee."

Shadow let go with an admiring whoop. Matthew smiled at his brother's expression of shock. Owen nodded his head, offering his support of the nomination.

"You must be kidding," Steven said, truly surprised.

"I have many good points," Sam said, his mountain drawl stretching his words, "but I don't think telling jokes is one of them. This is for real."

Steven took a second to absorb what Otis had proposed. Chairmanship of the D-Triple-C was a position that required a great deal of work, but wielded an even greater amount of influence. Charged with the task of raising money for Congressional races throughout the country, the chairman was also empowered to allot the funds raised. If a particular race was hotly contested and in danger of being lost to the other party, the campaign was juiced with additional money. If, on the other hand, a candidate appeared to have little or no chance of victory, funding would be kept to a minimum.

It was a job that would require extra staffing, as well as a large increase in the amount of time Steven spent traveling. In an odd way, he would welcome that. Though he hated to admit it, the seams of his marriage were beginning to fray. More and more, he and Cynthia were leading separate lives together. When they were at home, the surface seemed the same, but the substance of their relationship had changed.

Cynthia rarely returned to Kentucky. Her life was completely centered in Washington. It was where her friends were, her interests, her shops, her home, her power base. Though Steven spent most of his week in the capital, his job demanded that he maintain a visible presence in both places, and so he did.

"I don't have the seniority for a post like that, Sam," Steven said, nervous that they were all getting ahead of themselves. "Why waste a nomination on me?"

"Because the last chairman had no sympathy for the unions. He fought us every chance he got, looking to paint us as the reason for the country's current financial woes." Otis shook his head. His thin face tightened as he clamped his teeth together and pressed his lips into a hostile line. "It's corporate waste and government inefficiency that's put us in this hole," he said, thumping a clenched fist on the antique table before him, showing no regard for its two-hundred-year history. "The party owes us. And I'm here to collect."

Steven's brow furrowed. Words like owe and collect made him edgy. "I appreciate your faith, Sam, but I have to be honest. I can't promise full support for a guy simply because he's union. The party can't afford to throw money away on a loser."

"I'm not asking you for a rubber stamp. All I want is a fair eye."

"That I can promise."

Sam extended his hand, grasped Steven's firmly and laughed. "Anyone who promises more is a liar."

"Here! Here!"

Owen raised his glass, heartily toasted his son-in-law, and took a hefty swig of his brandy. When he turned to thank Owen for the toast, Steven noticed that despite the older man's enthusiasm, his hand was shaking and his complexion was pale. Steven also realized that Owen had been out of breath after climbing the stairs. In the morning, he intended to speak to Owen about the state of his health.

"Are there any other nominations?" Matthew asked.

Otis opened his mouth and chugged his brandy. "A couple. But the lead horse is Douglas from Arkansas."

"I know Douglas," Shadow said with a disapproving nod. "Comes from a family of slave traders. Votes yes on major civil rights issues, but fudges on some of the less publicized bills."

"That's true, but Fenton Douglas had made a name for himself by championing several important causes," Steven said, immediately weighing his chances against someone with Douglas's record. "I can understand why he worries you, though. He represents a right-to-work state."

"Making support for a union candidate unlikely," Matthew added, following Steven's lead and rising so they could return to the party.

"That's not hard to believe when you consider who his wife is," Sam muttered.

"Who's his wife?" Matthew asked, holding open the door.

Sam looked from one brother to the other. "Someone I'll bet you guys knew in your past lives. Lucinda Crown."

"A friend of mine just had a baby. She was in labor for thirty-six hours. Whew! I can't imagine doing something I *like* for thirty-six hours."

Sophie stared into the faces of the guests in the front row, stoking their laughter by parading before them in a vibrant orange strapless dress, turquoise opera-length gloves and orange high heels with large turquoise polka dots. Her hair, teased and spiked, was a reasonable shade of reddish blond streaked here and there with an unreal shade of turquoise blue.

"I can't imagine our First Lady in labor, can you?" Sophie shook her head and pursed her lips, making it clear that it was simply unthinkable. "She was probably the only woman in history to have an immaculate delivery." She paused and shook her head. "Please! You can bet that at birth her kid came out washed and scrubbed, each strand of hair lacquered in place, and a designer label already sewn on its butt!"

The laughter crossed party lines.

"Don't get me wrong. I like the Reagans well enough. Sometimes I think someone should remind Nancy America is not a monarchy, and I've never liked men in brown suits, but hey, Ron's okay in my book. How could he not be? The man is crazy about polls." She fluffed her hair and preened, giving everyone time to catch her double entendre. "Actually, it surprises me that he and the Soviets don't get along. They have so much in common. Reagan does something he's afraid the people won't like, he takes a poll. Solidarity does something the Soviets don't like, they take a Pole."

Back and forth she strode, riding the waves of the applause. Every now and then she zeroed in on the audience: senators, congressmen, the rich, the famous, the powerful. These were the people who governed, the people who decided the fate of millions; yet just then, she, Sophie Wisnewski, had them laughing.

She watched their reactions carefully. By now she had a finely tuned internal meter that told her how many political jokes to do, how many ethnic jokes, women-versus-men jokes, rich-versus-poor. Over the years, she had worked up a large and varied repertoire, but since her trademark was her Polish jokes, when her audience was loose she rapid-fired them.

"The average age of a Polish soldier is fifty-two. Why? Because the army gets them right out of high school."

"The birth rate among animals is rising? Do what the Warsaw Zoo did. Shoot the storks!"

"My aunt and uncle decided to have only three children. They heard that one in every four children born is a Chinese."

"Then there's the Polish housewife who had an accident while ironing the curtains. She fell out of the window."

By the time she finished, women who made librarians seem raucous were mopping mascara from beneath their eyes and normally dignified men were slapping their thighs.

"You were simply fabulous," Cynthia cooed afterward, silently congratulating herself. "You were the perfect birthday gift for Steven."

"Had I known," Sophie said, aware she shouldn't bite the hand that was signing her check but reacting as she always did when people like Cynthia attempted to dismiss her as hired help, "I would've scotch-taped my sides, papered my rump, and shoved a bow in my mouth."

Cynthia chuckled, but Sophie's sarcasm hadn't escaped her. "I'd love to have you join us for dessert. Do you think you could?"

"Gee, that would be special!"

"Wonderful." Having secured her star's presence for a while longer, Cynthia scouted for one of her waiters. "Let me have someone . . ."

"I'll take care of Miss Warsaw." Matthew sauntered over to the two women, smiled politely at his hostess, and kissed Sophie on the cheek. He felt her flush beneath his lips. "You were great!" he said, admiration coloring his voice.

"Did you think so? Really?"

"Honest and truly." Why he cared for this woman he'd never know, but he did. For years, they had been ships passing in the night. They saw each other three, four, sometimes five times a year. Occasionally they had dinner together. Often they spent a day together. Never had they spent the night.

"Come," he said, taking Sophie's arm, gently drawing her near him. "I know some people who are dying to meet you."

"What a fabulous idea," Cynthia said, eager to move on to her other guests. "Introduce Sophie around. I'm sure she has a ton of fans."

"Your father, for one."

As Matthew steered Sophie into the drawing room, toward the table where Owen, Claudia, and Billy sat, he shot Cynthia a look that turned her smile to stone.

Matthew made the introductions, noting how Sophie paused at each guest's chair, charming each one with her wit, flattering with her attention. At Owen's chair, she really turned it on, playing to him while deliberately excluding the woman on his left.

"As ambassador, did you have to make life-and-death decisions, like whether or not we send troops to fend off communism in Newark?"

Owen laughed. "Not quite."

"Too bad," she said, her expression one of mock dismay. "Newark's on the brink, you know."

He laughed again, prompting three more quips. She would have preferred talking to Owen for the rest of the evening, but Matthew took her arm and moved her along.

"I'd like you to meet Janet Royce. Janet's a lawyer who lobbies for women's rights."

"I'm a big fan of yours, Miss Warsaw."

The woman extended her hand. She was blond, unbelievably gorgeous, and openly interested in the handsome, well-to-do Mr. Kardos. Sophie had to fight to get out a proper, "Thank you."

"Here," Matthew said, offering Sophie a seat. "Join us."

"I'd love too, but I can't. I'm simply exhausted. I think I'm going to say good night. You'll excuse me, won't you?"

Matthew followed her toward the door. "Are you all right?"

"Are you two an item?" Sophie asked, more upset than she cared to admit.

"What does that mean?"

It took every ounce of courage Sophie possessed to ask this question. "Are you in love with her?"

Matthew trained his hazel eyes on her face, disallowing her to look away or hide behind a smart remark. "I'm in love with you, but since you've made it abundantly clear that you are unavailable to me as anything other than a friend, I've decided to seek romantic alternatives."

For a woman who had a wisecrack for everything, it amazed Sophie that she couldn't find anything funny to say as she stood and watched helplessly as Matthew took his place alongside the beautiful and brilliant and noble Ms. Royce.

The next morning, Owen Rhinehart was found dead in his hotel room. The coroner's office listed the cause of death as a heart attack and released the body so it could be shipped to Lexington for burial.

The day of the funeral, Cynthia rose early. Tossing on a pair of jeans and a sweater, she went to the stable, saddled a horse, and for two hours rode as hard and as fast as she could. She galloped the vast expanse of Rhinehart land, flying as if the steed beneath her were indeed the winged horse Pegasus. Racing through the open fields, her black hair floating on the wind like a cape, she seemed oblivious to the chill that clung to that April morning.

She had forgotten how much she loved riding, how wonderful it felt when the muscles of an exceptional beast rippled between her legs. The sensation of speed, the notion of running wild, the feeling of being one with nature and the gods—nothing else she had ever done in her life had equaled the thrill she got when she saddled up and left civilization behind.

She couldn't remember the first time she had mounted a horse. Sometimes she felt as if she had been born, swaddled, and placed immediately atop one of her mother's English saddles. But today, as the sun began to rise and its yellow rays sliced into the light gray fog that lifted off the green, Cynthia began to feel as if a ghost rode beside her—Cecilia, sitting high in the saddle the way she always had, her hands controlling the reins with her usual gentle grace. Her mother had been an elegant equestrienne who rode with exquisite control. Everyone knew that, which was why when she went to jump that stone wall and toppled her horse, smashing her head against the wall, there was an investigation. No one could believe it was Cecilia's fault. And it wasn't. In fact, her horse hadn't been properly saddled. The groom who had readied the animal had neglected to secure the straps properly. When she signaled the jump, the saddle slipped. In trying to keep her balance, Cecilia must have jerked on the reins, confusing the horse, killing them both.

Chased by the mirage of her mother, Cynthia had come to the

Rhinehart family plot. Set high on a bluff at the edge of the property, it was a square piece of land shaded by large old trees and protected by a hand-worked metal fence. Here rested the remains of all the Rhineharts, each grave marked by a headstone inscribed with lines from a favorite poem, a custom started by Owen's great-grandfather Ulrich.

Cynthia dismounted and tied her horse to a nearby tree. Unconsciously, she ran her fingers through her hair and slapped the dust from her jeans, fixing herself before entering the sanctity of the burial green. The gate squealed as she opened it and rattled when she closed it behind her. She stood there for a moment, surveying her ancestors, reading the verse chosen by those who comprised her heritage. They had been an educated lot, opting for lines from Shakespeare and Donne, Homer and Goethe, Byron and Keats, Whitman and Emerson, Longfellow and Thoreau. The earlier tombstones were simple rectangles. As the generations increased and the family fortune multiplied, the memorials had become more ornate, more heavily carved. Several appeared to be more sculpture than sepulcher.

Only the one that marked the final resting place of Cecilia Délon Rhinehart, a large, thick slab of black marble, loomed as a stark statement of eternal, unremitting mourning. Cynthia approached it slowly, careful not to slip on the loose dirt that lay around the open hole into which her father's coffin would be placed later that day. While every other grave was a single one, Owen and Cecilia had decided early in their marriage to be buried together, with one headstone, one line of verse carved after death to define the essence of their lives.

They had selected a line penned by the Elizabethan courtier, Sir Philip Sidney.

Cynthia ran her hand across the words that had been carved deep into the soul of the block:

MY TRUE LOVE HATH MY HEART AND I HAVE HIS.

Lowering her eyes, she stared at the letters that spelled her mother's name. Tears formed.

"I didn't mean it, you know," she said, venting the grief she had held back the day her mother had been interred here, releasing the sorrow she had buried inside her heart on that day and had kept submerged until this moment. "How was I to know that you would fall and hit your head? How could I possibly have known that you would die? You were so young, so perfect, so invincible. I thought you'd never die."

Her shoulders shook and her body trembled, quaking as if she could hear her mother crying out for her, demanding to know where she had been, why she hadn't come to the hospital, why she hadn't been there to say good-bye. Crossing her arms over her chest, Cynthia grabbed herself, trying to halt the tremors.

"I loved you and no matter what he says: Never, ever, did I intend to disgrace or dishonor you."

Her eyes shifted to the freshly dug grave. Later, she would be dressed in clothes of mourning; her face would be set in a pose of grief; her words would express a sense of loss. Now, she intended to be honest and say what she felt.

"I'm truly sorry that you're dead, Daddy," she said, wiping her eyes with the sleeve of her sweater. "More than anyone, I wanted you to live. Not because I loved you. Because I wanted to bury you alive. I wanted to make you pay for what you did to me."

She stared down into the chasm, speaking beyond the void that would soon be filled, to the void in her heart that would never be filled.

"I used to love you. More than anyone, including Maman. You used to love me too. Maybe that was the problem. We loved each other too much. We were too close. There was no room for error, no space for one honest mistake."

Though she fought it, her eyes flowed with heated tears.

"Yes! I messed up," she shouted at the morning sky, then down to the broken earth. "No! I wasn't around when my mother needed me, when you needed me. But your retaliation was exceptionally cruel. You stretched the limits of vengeance, Daddy, and I hate you for what you did to me. I'll always hate you." Her voice wavered as furious sobs racked her body. "But as virulent as my hatred is, Daddy, it could never be a match for yours."

She leaned down and scooped up a large handful of dirt, sifting it through her fingers until she found several small rocks. Raising her hand, she hurled them at the place on the black marble where Owen's name would be inscribed.

"Don't you dare rest in peace, you bastard! Don't you dare!"

The sun was high in the sky as more than four hundred people crowded onto the hill where Owen Rhinehart joined with his ancestors and his beloved Cecilia. Lending support to his grieving family and loyal staff were the men and women who catalogued the various chapters of his life: the mayor of Lexington and the governor of Kentucky, ex-President Carter and Vice-President Bush, the British ambassador and the Speaker of the House. Here, too, were the grooms and trainers who managed his stables, the overseers who ran his farms, and the foremen who operated his factories, as well as the comic Sophie Warsaw, two dozen members of the Senate, and a dozen retired elder statesmen. Those who had been touched by Owen Rhinehart gathered to pay their last respects and say good-bye to the gentleman from Kentucky.

Later after the service, when many had returned to the house for luncheon, one of those mourners sought out Matthew Kardos. She found him in a quiet corner of the veranda. When she approached him, she could tell that he thought he recognized her, but wasn't sure. Clearly, past images of who he thought she might be had clashed with the present reality and confused him.

"Your first instinct was correct," she said in that slow, soft drawl he had always said belonged on a pillow. "It's Lucinda."

Though fifteen years had changed her, he couldn't say they had been unkind. Her skin was still as pale and velvet soft as a fresh gardenia, but her hair, once the light brown of a walnut shell, was streaked now with strands of ash-blond. Her frame had widened, her breasts had surrendered to the tug of gravity, but, he noted with delight, she still had terrific legs. Without any further hesitation, he swept her in his arms and hugged her.

"God, it's good to see you," he said, enjoying the smile that graced her mouth and lit her eyes.

"Let me just tell you something," Lucinda said, tilting her head and eyeing him blatantly. "You are still one fine piece of manhood, Matthew Kardos. Real fine. How come no one's nabbed you yet?"

"After you . . . well . . ." He shrugged his shoulders as if to say, *No one else could measure up.*

She laughed. "I'll tell you one thing that's changed. Now you fling the bull with the best of them. Back then, well, back then you were the most honest person I'd ever known. What you said, you meant."

"And if I said I've thought about you often over the years?"

"I'd believe it, because you've not been totally absent from my thoughts either."

"I recently discovered you're married to Fenton Douglas."

Lucinda nodded. Matthew tried to dissect the gesture and determine whether she was happy or not, madly in love or merely content. He needn't have bothered. Lucinda told him what he wanted to know.

"I met Fenton the way all Southern girls meet their husbands, at one of those darned dances designed to showcase available female flesh. He was bright and charming enough. Handsome, too, in a tall, thin, aristocratic way. Of course as far as my folks were concerned, it was his pedigree that made him the perfect catch. Fenton comes from an old Southern family that made its money raising cotton." She threw her head back and laughed as if she were reciting an amusing piece of fiction instead of relating the facts of her life. "Hell, we live on a plantation just outside of West Memphis that makes Tara look like a toolshed. We've got four children." Matthew looked impressed. Again, Lucinda chuckled. "After three girls I was beginning to panic, but finally I birthed a male child. The Douglas name is safe for at least one more generation."

"You sound happy."

"I suppose I am." She took a long look at Matthew, as if deciding whether or not to say what was on her mind. With a slow smile lifting her lips, she raised her hand and caressed his cheek. "I love Fenton, but there's no passion, Matthew. Not like there was with us. I'm not saying that's good or bad. I'm just saying what is."

Matthew took her hand from his cheek and brought it to his lips. She had been his first love and though seeing her again had not rekindled that heated passion, inside he felt a comfortable warmth.

"There's only one question I need answered."

She held up her hand. "I know. But this is not the place. I'm going to be staying on in Kentucky for the next few days, visiting my parents. If you're free, we could meet for lunch."

"Any time," he said, keeping his eyes fixed on her face, wondering why her gaze had wandered, watching to see who was listening. "Lucinda, you will tell me what I want to know."

She faced him squarely. Her voice dropped to a whisper, but Matthew was certain he detected an undercurrent of urgency.

"I'll tell you exactly what you want to know," she promised, "as well as several things I think you need to know."

April 20, 1982, was an eventful day. That morning, Steven received word that he had been appointed Chairman of the Democratic Congressional Campaign Committee. The call from the Speaker of the House was followed by one from Sam Otis and one from the number-two Democrat in the House, the majority whip. So as not to antagonize that faction of the party that was not particularly pro-union, and in recognition of his effectiveness in rallying his fellow Democrats behind important causes, Fenton Douglas had been made deputy whip of the House, a decision that pleased Steven. His appointment was controversial enough. The last thing he wanted to do was alienate anyone, let alone a fellow Southerner. One never knew when he would have to call on that alliance.

At noon that day, Matthew had an enlightening lunch with Lucinda Douglas.

And at three, the entire Rhinehart clan gathered in the drawing room at Mayfair Farms for the reading of Owen's will.

Much of it was standard. He bequeathed the house in Frankfort, its contents, and its surrounding acreage to the state of Kentucky to be used as a museum and park, named in memory of Cecilia Délon Rhinehart. He left the business of Mayfair Farms to Claudia and her husband, Billy, generously added to the trusts established during his lifetime for his grandchildren, and made numerous bequests to charity. Because he was aware of Billy's love for them, Owen left his English hunt paintings for his son-in-law. He gifted Steven, whom he called "as near to a son as I could have wanted," with most of his jewelry: a dozen pairs of cuff links, two fob watches—one English, one French—several sets of formal studs, several antique wristwatches, and his gold and onyx ring; as well as Steven's favorite painting, Maurer's "Jeanne."

During the reading of this first section of the will there were nods and smiles and other gestures indicating that those present had expected Owen to do much as he had done. It was during the reading of the second section that the atmosphere became charged with tension.

"To Jefferson and Ruby, who have been loyal friends, above and beyond any sense of duty I know of, I bequeath the house on Mayfair Farms in which they currently reside, together with all of its contents, to sit on one acre of land that they will own free and clear. In addition, as my way of compensating for all they sacrificed in the name of the Rhineharts, I bequeath to them the sum of one million dollars outright and unconditionally with my eternal thanks. May God Bless."

Owen's lawyer, Dallas Crawford, coughed and tried several times to clear his throat. While a servant was summoned and told to bring a glass of water, Cynthia counted the seconds anxiously, as if somehow the paper on which the will had been written were capable of self-destructing; as if it only had so much life in it and the longer the servant took, the more remote her chances were of making claim to her rightful share of her father's estate.

When Crawford had recovered, he replaced his glasses and retrieved the papers before him, clearing his throat several times more before continuing.

"I leave equally to my daughters the bulk of my estate."

Claudia smiled. Cynthia felt her insides roller-coaster. He hadn't disowned her as she had suspected he might. Maybe he had loved her after all. If not that, perhaps she could comfort herself by believing that he felt some guilt about what he had done.

"I hereby grant my daughter Claudia receive her inheritance outright and without conditions. In the event of her death, the monies shall pass on to her issue. If they have not yet gained maturity, the monies shall be placed in trust until they have reached the age of twenty-one, at which point they will receive their inheritance in increments as set forth in the codicil attached to this document and to be read to Claudia and her husband, William, in private.

"My daughter Cynthia's share shall not be given to her outright and without conditions. Instead, it is to be placed in trust for life. The interest from such bequest shall be paid to her annually, with the right to apply principal to manage her life-style only with the approval of the executors of this trust, her sister, Claudia Fieldston, and her husband, Steven Kardos. In the event of a divorce or the death of Steven Kardos, control of the trust shall revert exclusively to my eldest daughter, Claudia.

"I know that I have put you in an awkward position, Claudia, and for that I apologize, but throughout your life, you've been burdened with the perpetual awkwardness of being my daughter, Cecilia's firstborn, and Cynthia's sister. You have always handled your position with grace and character. I am certain that in this situation you will do the same. Though I never told you often enough, I love you dearly. You make me proud.

"By birth, Cynthia, you are entitled to share in the estate of your parents. I have granted you your entitlement. I have not given you anything that once belonged to your mother because you forfeited that right at the time of her death. I find it amusing that the only legal terminology available for the mechanism I have elected as a control on your enjoyment of your entitlement is the phrase 'trust fund.' I never trusted you in life. In death, I feel the same."

Cynthia turned toward Claudia, her face contorted with rage.

"Are you happy now?" she said, spitting her words through gritted teeth. Her hands had gripped the arms of her chair so tightly her knuckles were white. "You finally got what you wanted, didn't you, Claudia? The old man put you first. You got the gold star, the pat on the head. And," she said, staring at her older sister with a hostility that frightened those around her, "to make everything perfect, you get to haunt me for the rest of my natural life. Well, don't count on it, my darling sibling. I intend to contest this will. I'll fight it every way I can, and do you know why? Not because of the money. God knows, interest on fifty million dollars is more than enough to keep me in fresh pantyhose. No. I'm going to contest this because I don't want you in my life. I don't want to have to call you or write you or see you ever again!"

Saying that, Cynthia stormed from the room like a hurricane. Steven caught up to her on the veranda.

"You were out of line, Cynthia. There was no reason for that kind of tirade. You know Claudia is never going to deny you anything."

"And how about you, my dear husband? Are you going to deny me? Are you going to get high on the power my father invested in you and use it as a way of controlling me?" She was pacing, racing without destination, her face contorted with a fury that erased all rationality.

"What are you talking about?" Steven said, letting his anger show. He didn't want to antagonize her further, but he didn't like the direction of the conversation.

"Money makes a wonderful weapon."

"I didn't think I needed a weapon against you."

Cynthia threw her head back and laughed. It contained no mirth, no joy, only irony and hatred.

"That's because you never had it and so you don't know how to use it. Look how effective it is," she said, gesticulating wildly. "My father's body is decomposing eight feet below ground and still, he manages to humiliate me thoroughly. Don't tell me money isn't powerful." She was still fuming. It was clear by the tightness in her jaw and the fire in her eyes.

"I'm not your father, Cynthia. I have no reason to deny you anything or to use this against you. In fact, the way I see it, there's no reason for us to be having this argument. It's demeaning for both of us. When you've calmed down, I'll be inside."

He strode past her knowing that she was not going to calm down until she got what she believed she deserved. *But*, he wondered, *had Owen already given her exactly what she deserved?*

When he returned to the drawing room, the reading was over.

"Is she all right?" Claudia asked, noticeably rattled.

"What do you think?"

"Stupid question."

"Why does she hate you?" he asked, having decided that if Owen's will had provided him with anything, it was the right to push beyond previously closed barriers. "I know it has to do with your mother's accident and her death. What happened?"

Claudia struggled with her conscience. She could have told him everything. After Cynthia's outburst, her sister deserved to have her secrets exposed. But Claudia was a woman who respected the boundary of family, the obligations blood placed on one member to protect the other, even when it was undeserved. She did, however, feel that Steven was owed an answer, so she gave him what she could.

"When Maman fell, Cynthia was nowhere to be found. For two days she remained missing."

"I know that, Claudia," Steven said, not yet satisfied. "Why does she hate you?"

Her eyes darkened with the gray cloud of continuous guilt. The lines of her face deepened as her mouth confessed the sin that had separated sister from sister. "I told my father where she was."

Matthew wasn't present at the reading of Owen's will, nor was his name mentioned in a single clause, yet the terms of that document had presented him with a dilemma of conscience. When he learned from Steven of the strings attached to the purses Owen had bequeathed and the language used to distribute what appeared to be tremendous largesse, Matthew found himself mired in a conundrum.

He was an honorable man, one who did not give his word lightly. He had promised Lucinda not to repeat what she had told him. Not only would it compromise the subject of the story, but Lucinda as well. Because she had been honest in answering the question he wanted answered—she had loved him, the child had been his, she had lied to protect him, and yes, she had suffered a miscarriage and tremendous regret about leaving him—he felt he owed her the confidence she had requested.

At the time of their lunch, he had found the content of her revelation unsettling. After lengthy consideration, he had decided it was not worth risking an incident. He had felt perfectly comfortable with the notion of filing the information away in a drawer marked interesting but not newsworthy. His conversation with Steven opened the drawer.

From the start, Matthew had sensed that Lucinda's tale was only part of a larger story. He had stifled his investigative instincts because there had seemed to be no purpose indulging them. It was different now. Owen's will had added new pieces to the puzzle. A picture was developing and Matthew didn't like what he saw. Though Lucinda had sworn that she was the only one privy to the information she had given him, Matthew now viewed that as naive and due to the obvious need to protect herself.

For weeks, he wrestled with the issue of truth and its consequences. Did he honor his word to Lucinda and leave well enough alone? Did he poke around in forbidden corners looking for skeletons that might or might not exist? Did he tell what little he knew and hazard invoking the wrath of those involved? The one thing he knew for certain was that he could not do nothing. In the meantime, his decision was to remain silent while at the same time slowly and secretively seeking the pieces that would complete the puzzle.

If his suspicions were confirmed and the tale played out the way he thought it might, those few snippets handed him over a Cobb salad and a glass of wine held an awesome power. Like a gun with one bullet, by itself it might not seem terrifying, but properly aimed it was capable of blowing away everything in its path—including Steven.

30

Budapest, 1982

László Böhm's mother worshiped God. His father worshiped communism. Before the war, Ernö Böhm boxed light bulbs. He was an ordinary man doing an ordinary job. His wife, Livia, was an ordinary woman who worked in an ordinary neighborhood beauty salon. Each morning, they left their apartment at six-thirty to be at work by seven. Each night, they returned home at six, ate, read the newspapers, talked, made love now and then, and were asleep by ten.

After church on Sundays, they would stroll the streets of Buda, looking at the stately villas and grand homes that housed the wealthy, or windowshop in Pest, fantasizing about what they would buy if only they could. While his poverty upset Ernö, Livia, a pretty young woman with a gentle, accepting soul, was a staunch Catholic who viewed everything—both plenty and poverty—as a test of faith.

World War II was the best thing that ever happened to Ernö Böhm. From the moment he donned the brown uniform of the Hungarian Army, he knew it fit him as nothing had ever fit before. Being a soldier afforded power and prestige, respect, and even a certain reverence. He strode down a street and people stepped aside. He spoke and people listened. He walked into a restaurant and was given a table without waiting. Though he, like every other sane man conscripted into a wartime fighting force, feared death, he was delighted to have a chance to prove himself. Unlike in the factory, in the army his efforts were not only noticed, but rewarded. He was promoted, gaining the rank of lieutenant; he was awarded medals for bravery and citations for honor in the heat of battle. When the war ended and his army buddies went back to the factories, Ernö stayed in uniform.

In 1944, a year before the Germans fled from Hungary, Livia gave birth to her only child, László. The delivery had been difficult. The doctor had been careless about the placenta, neglecting to check whether or not it had been delivered in one piece. It had not. A portion remained attached to the uterine wall. Though Livia continued to experience excruciating pain, she was told to bear it, that it was nothing, that it was simply the body readjusting. There was no one for her to talk to, to ask whether or not this constant agony was normal. Ernö was away. Because of the advancing Russians, her family couldn't visit her. Under the Nazi occupation of Budapest, her friends had problems of their own. Livia took her baby home alone and, for his sake, tried to suffer in silence, but within a matter of days she was back in the hospital. A hysterectomy was performed, leaving Livia both physically and spiritually weakened. She had wanted a large family with lots of children. She had wanted to propagate the earth the way the Bible said she must. Now she was barren, unable to carry out the Lord's wishes. In her fragile state of mind, she believed she had failed.

For László, who grew up hearing little but his mother's prayers and his father's politics, the problem was not sorting out which philosophy was correct—he was too young for that—but rather what he could do about the disintegrating state of his parents' marriage. They fought constantly. Though he understood little of what they said, one thing was clear: Since one was arguing on the side of religion and the other was arguing on the side of politics, their differences were completely irreconcilable.

In 1948, officially called "The Year of Change," the communists seized church schools, jailed Cardinal Mindszenty for espionage, and effectively eliminated the practice of religion from Hungarian life. Ernö applauded the moves. Livia ran away. All four-year-old László remembered was waking up one morning to find his mother's rosary on his pillow along with a note:

I'll always love you, but I can't live in a land without God.
May He bless you and keep you.

László never knew where she had gone until fifteen years later, when he received word that she had died of stomach cancer. The Mother Superior of the Austrian convent Livia had joined sent him a package containing Sister Celeste's rosary, an icon of the order's patron saint that she had kept by her bedside for inspiration and strength, a snapshot of him as a little boy, and a stack of letters. Once a month for fifteen years, Livia had written to her son. Since contact with the outside world was forbidden, she never mailed the letters, but had requested that they be given to him upon her death. László was nineteen when he received the package.

He held the box of letters in his hands and stared at them, trying, as he had for fifteen years, to understand why his mother had preferred God to him, trying to stem the tide of resentment that filled him whenever he thought about her abandoning him, leaving him in the care of an emotionally distant father, an aged, illiterate grandmother, and an indifferent, coldly regimented system. He stared at the picture of himself, willing his mind to search his heart for whatever he had felt then, but when she left him, his heart had emptied of all feeling for her. Without a single qualm, he struck a match, tossed it into the box, and burned her letters without ever reading them.

László was thirty-eight now. Katalin and Zoltán were his only family. Career was his only creed. His father was gone, having died in a car accident in 1970. At the time of his death, Ernö Böhm was, according to his own definitions, an important man. He was a proven servant of the people, having performed many tasks that, although unpleasant, had been deemed necessary by the Party. He had introduced his son to men with the power and influence to further László's career. He had taught László allegiance and service. He had seen his son rise in the ranks of the military and gain acceptance in the eyes of the Party. He died a happy man.

One of the significant differences between father and son was that throughout his life Ernö had retained a blind veneration of communism. He had been quite content to accept without challenge, to obey without question. In other words, he was satisfied to remain a soldier. László was more of a pragmatist. While he was profoundly committed to the philosophical core of Marxism, László had opened his eyes to things his father had chosen to avoid. Whatever the ideology of the ruling system, control was the common denominator. Power begot privilege. Influence was exerted to gain comfort. Rank was used for advantage.

In the aftermath of the 1956 Uprising, Kádár's Hungary had gone from complete totalitarianism to an economic structure that accommodated limited reform. Times had changed since Ernö had joined the Party in the forties. It was the eighties. A private sector was emerging. Forint millionaires were being created. By practicing their own peculiar brand of "goulash communism," Hungary was becoming the most affluent country in the socialist bloc—"the happiest barracks in the camp," as jokesters were fond of saying. Though government spokesmen never openly acknowledged any of those advances, government officials were not beyond reaping the benefits of the new "market socialism."

László was an extremely intelligent man. In his current role as commercial liaison between the Hungarian government and foreign businessmen, he walked a political tightrope, balancing the need to attract a wide range of trading partners with the narrowing demands of collectivism and centralization. As a major agricultural nation in a region plagued by constant shortages, Hungary had much to sell. Aside from produce, the country was also a supplier of such desirable exports as machine tools, medical instruments, sources of energy, and the highly regarded Ikarus bus. The problem was that when Kádár opened the door to reform, he created expectation without permitting open-ended importation. Moonlighting became a way of life. A black market for luxury goods was born. Expectations grew, rising faster and higher than the economy could reasonably provide for. Those like László who understood how to manipulate the system to their advantage and were in a position with enough power to direct their fates, lived very well; while most worked two and three jobs and, despite a few added comforts, struggled to get by.

In a country that boasted rule by committee rather than by individuals, László stood out because he possessed three characteristics most of his comrades lacked: personality, an inclination toward diligence that sometimes bordered on the obsessive, and an acute sense of political savvy. Hungary was in a state of flux. Within the government and among the populace there was a generation gap: Older members of the Party clung to the original tenets of Marxism, as Ernö had; younger, more progressive men seemed to understand that even within a system as logical as socialism, there had to be adjustments.

László juggled both sides of the Hungarian political coin with expert precision. He was charming with the reformers and conservative with the hard-liners, plying the former with frequent opportunities for financial profit, catering to the latter with occasional illustrations of a familiarity with the techniques of control. He completed business transactions with the same ease and thoroughness he used when doing favors for his friends on the Central Committee. He knew how to separate those who belonged in his home with their wives for an evening of music and elegant dining, from those who were more comfortable in a borozó, or wine bar, stag. He understood the dichotomous standard that would not countenance his driving anything more ostentatious than a Lada, but would envy and applaud an apartment lavishly furnished with expensive antiques and impressive art. Ernö had believed that ambition and communism didn't mix. László knew that they mixed very well indeed.

The balance was a delicate one. For years László had trod a carefully planned path, keeping his aspirations in check, placing one foot in front of the other with deliberate precision. Though progress was never swift in the climb up the socialist ladder, he had felt himself moving in a consistently forward direction. Recently there had been no movement, and that he found troublesome. When he was summoned to the office of the Minister of Commerce, he didn't know whether to be pleased or nervous.

Károly Molnár was a man who believed in economy to the extreme. Small and thin, with sharp features and a rapidly receding hairline, he spoke bluntly. An accountant by training, he viewed his life as a series of debits and credits. On the plus side, he believed in rewarding a job well done. On the minus side, he believed just as strongly in punishing anyone who had upset his bottom line.

When László entered his office, he saluted and took the seat offered without even attempting to read his superior's face. Having once been told by Molnár that "excessive expression is a waste of muscular activity," László opted to conserve his own facial strength. Besides, he reminded himself, he would know soon enough the exact purpose of this meeting. Molnár would not waste any time on meaningless preamble.

"We're sending you to New York," Molnár said, verifying László's prediction. "Officially, you will be attached to the Hungarian Mission to the United Nations. That way, you will have full diplomatic status and full diplomatic privilege."

László bobbed his head in acceptance. Molnár was doing his best to make this appear to be a major promotion, but László recognized it for the ploy that it was. This was the first step in a plan to remove László from the political scene as well as to discredit him. Though he allowed no change of mien, inside he was seething.

"You've done a superb job opening markets throughout Eastern Europe for Hungarian products. What we'd like you to do in New York is to explore market possibilities there. Naturally, we expect you to exercise the utmost discretion."

Again, László nodded. He admired Molnár's phrasing. *Market possibilities.* Though for more than a dozen years Hungary had done its own economic dance, it was still considered a Soviet satellite and was therefore a low priority for Western investors. László knew he'd be lucky if he could get in the door of America's financial community, let alone close any significant deals. *Utmost discretion,* another clever turn of phrase.

As a Warsaw Pact nation, Molnár knew it wouldn't look right to the Soviets for Hungary to appear to be openly courting Western trade. Making László the courtier placed him on a diplomatic tightrope.

"Since your job will entail entertaining government officials as well as high-ranking members of the American corporate sector, and since it would not be wise for you to be seen with any of them in public, we've rented a spacious apartment for you and Mrs. Böhm, furnished in what my aides assure me is American elegance." He smiled. It was so quick, it looked more like a twitch. "It even has a large piano so your wife can keep up with her music."

"Thank you, sir."

Molnár paused. A ragged bit of cuticle on his left thumb had grabbed his attention. Annoyed, he lifted his finger to his mouth and gnawed at the offensive piece of skin until it had been removed. Satisfied that his body was no longer marred by imperfection, he picked up the threads of his conversation with László.

"She's a valuable asset, Major Böhm. While we all appreciate and applaud her talent, affording her the respect a concert pianist deserves, in America," he said with a sneer, "they don't understand culture, they only understand celebrity. If she strikes their fancy"—he paused as if to express his disgust at what he was about to say—"well . . . celebrity can be useful. Though we might find that sort of thing offensive," he went on, "while in New York I suggest you accede to the customs of the land. From what I understand, even their shrewdest, sharpest businessmen are attracted to celebrities." He paused, weighing his words. "Let your wife's star shine, Böhm. Not too much to turn her head, or yours. Just enough to suit our purposes."

Later, after they had reviewed all the details and he had left Molnár's office, László continued to fume. He didn't like anything about his new assignment, including Katalin's role. Knowing she was being watched, that she was being tested, that his control of her was being observed and tested as well, upset him. While Katalin had proved herself a good wife—a woman who understood the importance of appearing manageable and compliant when in the company of her husband—nonetheless, she had an independent streak that had, on occasion, worried László. It was difficult enough to regulate Katalin's activities in Budapest. In New York, where she had prior experience, friends, family, and a following, he feared that supervision would be impossible, especially over an extended period of time.

It won't be extended, he told himself. Bitter but determined, László decided that while he might not have had a choice about accepting this assignment, he could, and would, limit its duration. While Molnár sat in his office congratulating himself on László's exile, László began formulating his return.

When László brought her the news Katalin found herself swirling in a whirlwind of emotion. For years she had dreamed of nothing more than the chance to see Zsuzsanna and Sophie and Pedjá and Matthew and Paul Greco and . . . others. Yet now the ties of family and friendship were a powerful leash that tugged at her and tempted her to stay.

Because they had shared some secrets and respected those they couldn't share, her friendship with Judit had matured into something so strong it was almost inviolate. In less than a month, Judit was going to be married. She had asked Katalin to stand up for her. How could she not?

Though Mária's death had put a wedge of grief between them, she and Zoltán had found their way back to each other. Now that he was conducting, he was a changed man, a happier man, a more self-sufficient man. Yet Katalin still felt the bonds of promise. She had vowed to watch over him and to take care of him. Could she do that thousands of miles away?

She had goaded Tibor into his tutorial program with Zoltán. While they both knew that artistically he was benefiting, the rewards remained intangible while the penalties continued to mount. He was fighting prejudice from those at the Academy who resented his presence, fighting it at home from a wife who resented his absence. Katalin was his only neutral zone. Was it fair to leave him stranded?

And how about Ilona and Andras? Ilona's accident had been disabling. Most times, she rode in a wheelchair. Occasionally, she struggled with a cane. Despite the logic that proved otherwise, Katalin felt partly responsible for her disfigurement. Could she remove her support from Andras and Ilona when they needed her?

Katalin laughed at herself as she wiped tears from her eyes. The truth was they didn't need her. None of them did. Ilona was mending, slowly but surely. She was back at the hospital. As she'd told Katalin the last time they visited, "I don't need my legs to diagnose a patient. As long as my brain works, I work."

Judit had Gábor, a man who loved her and cared for her and would surely be able to fill whatever void Katalin's leaving created. "I finally found someone who puts me first," Judit had said when she had told Katalin of her wedding plans. "I'm the most important person in his life. Can you imagine that?"

Whether she liked it or not, Tibor had a wife and a family and a band that had once played very well without her and surely could do so now.

If there were any reason to stay, it was Zoltán, but instead of protesting her going, he encouraged her.

"You'll be with Zsuzsanna. You'll speak to that teacher, that Greco. He'll put you back onstage where you belong." He had taken her face in his hands and kissed both her cheeks. "Ah, Katya, my *kicsi szilva*. I will miss you. You know that. But you won't be gone forever. László is too Hungarian to stay in New York for very long. You'll be back sooner than you think." Tenderly, he wiped the single tear that had escaped from eyes straining to remain bright. "You don't have to worry about me, Katya. I'm healthy. I'm content. I have my music. I have Andras and Ilona, Judit and Gábor. I've made new friends among the members of my orchestra. Go, *edesem*. Enjoy yourself. I'll be fine."

It was then she had realized that she was, for all of them, a desirable part of their lives, but nonessential to their existence. There was only one person who had verbalized his need for her and it was with that person that she boarded a plane bound for New York, almost ten years from the time she had boarded a plane going the other way.

Zsuzsanna had aged, but not in the way of those who allowed themselves to gray or slow their pace. At sixty-seven, her spirit was as youthful and vibrant as it had been when she was a girl. It was true that she had tiny puffs beneath her eyes and a chin line that had seen firmer days. Her body was rounder, her clothes a size bigger, a sixteenth of an inch looser. At the roots, her hair was pure silver, but since she believed the advertisements that said blonds had more fun, she stayed blonde and continued to have a very good time. Her lovers were older, her liaisons less frequent, her memories more passionate than her reality; but despite time's best efforts, she was still the reigning queen of New York's Hungarian-Americans, still the lusty chatelaine of a Magyar inn on 74th Street called Csárda.

When she received Katalin's telegram, Zsuzsanna became so excited she feared she would have a heart attack. Her godchild, that special creature who filled the desert of her childlessness, her Katalin, was coming back! Yet just as she was bathing in the exquisite joy of her return, Zsuzsanna was slapped by the excruciating pain that had ravaged her when she had waved good-bye to Katalin so many years before.

There wasn't much she missed about her native land—she managed to perpetuate most of Hungary's best traditions in her restaurant—but she had never truly reconciled herself to her separation from her brother, Mária, and their beautiful daughter. She had been in the United States for more than twenty-five years, yet missing them was a constant, like being a victim to a chronic disease that persisted as a low-grade, ever-present malady. She always felt as if she were waiting for that one precise, universal moment when all the stars and planets would be properly aligned and she and Zoltán would be reunited. She was still waiting.

Zsuzsanna had less trouble dealing with the absence of her parents and her other brothers—Sándor, Imre, Tomás, Miklós. She accepted them as dead, departed, gone, beyond her grasp physically and spiritually. On their birthdays and the anniversaries of their deaths she participated in a ritual of her own design. The only exception was Miklós. In deference to Zoltán's insistence that Miklós was alive, Zsuzsanna venerated him only on the day of his birth. On those days of remembrance she went to church, lit a candle, said a prayer, and then returned to her apartment where she spent the day among scrapbooks and photographs and memories, bringing to life again images of what they had been like, recollecting special times they had spent together.

Zsuzsanna's ghosts didn't haunt her the way Zoltán and Katalin did. For years, she had been visited by a dream in which she stood at Kennedy Airport with bouquets of flowers in her arms, tossing one blossom after another at the feet of her brother as he took his first steps on American soil. The dream changed when Katalin left. Zsuzsanna saw her flying off into a blue infinity, never landing, never arriving, never being anywhere but in that plane flying away from New York, away from Zsuzsanna, away from Steven.

So much had happened. Mária had died. Sophie had become a big star. Steven had married a high-tone heiress from Kentucky and was now a United States congressman. Matthew was wealthy beyond imagination, still single, still taking care of his brother. And Katalin had married. A major in the Hungarian Army. A communist. A man with ambitions of sitting on the Politburo. Zsuzsanna wanted to spit. It seemed unthinkable that her Katya could fall for a man so tied to the government that had mangled her father and killed her uncles and chased hundreds of thousands of her people over the border and still managed to repress those who remained.

"Give him a chance." That's what Paul Greco had told her. "Don't jump to conclusions."

Easy for Greco to say. He was an American. He had never heard the sound of bullets piercing a neighbor's flesh or the rumble of a tank climbing the hill to one's home. He couldn't possibly understand.

Besides, if the truth were known, he wouldn't have cared if Katalin came to New York with Attila the Hun so long as he could see her and talk to her and hear her play.

Zsuzsanna and Greco had ceased to be lovers years ago, but they had remained close friends. He came to Csárda at least once a week, and often on a quiet Sunday he and Zsuzsanna would open a bottle of wine, turn on the radio, and spend the afternoon listening to opera. Frequently they spoke of Katalin. Since Zsuzsanna had received no letters for the first few years, they could only conjecture about what had happened to her. None of their thoughts was comforting. When Steven had come to town and told Zsuzsanna he had met Katalin's husband, her dismay took a quantum leap. First, there was the clear and obvious fact that Katalin had broken Steven's heart. Then, there was his sudden marriage to a woman Zsuzsanna liked almost as much as she imagined she would like Katalin's husband. But the real problem, as Zsuzsanna saw it, was that marriage to a Hungarian officer was tantamount to taking a vow to remain in Hungary.

"You never know," Greco had said, two weeks before Katalin's scheduled arrival.

"I always thought I was the most foolish optimist God ever created," Zsuzsanna said with a wistful laugh. "I was wrong. You are."

A satisfied smile leapt onto Greco's mouth as he reached into his pocket, took out a telegram, and waved it in front of Zsuzsanna's face.

"I got this telegram a month ago. Katalin wanted me to see if I could arrange some concert dates for her," he said with undisguised glee. "I did."

"You did? How? Programs are set. Soloists have been contracted years in advance." Zsuzsanna felt as if her heart were pushing through her skin. "What did you say? What did you promise?"

Greco held her glass of wine to her lips and made her drink.

"Zsa-zsa," he said, stroking her cheek with gentle, honest affection, "Katalin's a story. It's the return of the Princess of the Piano, the beautiful heroine forced to leave to be by her mother's side, held prisoner in the evil land of Soviet domination, back in the United States after ten years. The American press eats that sort of thing up and every manager of every major concert hall in this country knows it. She'll fill the house, and so, if they have to reschedule someone or add an extra concert, they will. Katalin Gáspár is money."

An unwelcome doubt shadowed Zsuzsanna's eyes. "What if she's not as good as she used to be?"

Greco nodded. He had expected the question. He had already asked it and answered it. "She's performed throughout Eastern Europe and from the few reviews I could find, she hasn't lost her touch. Besides, I know Katalin. She can't be away from the piano for more than two days without having an anxiety attack. I'm certain she's been playing."

Zsuzsanna dismissed his pat assurances with a wave of her hand. "What if she's not as good as she used to be?" she demanded again, verbalizing the fear that perhaps circumstances had diminished her ability.

"I've taken a sabbatical from Juilliard," Greco said quietly.

"Why?"

"You know how deeply I feel about music." Zsuzsanna nodded. "Katalin's gift is rare. I had given her my word that if she entrusted it to me, I would help her rise to the pinnacle. I want to finish what I started."

Zsuzsanna bit her lip to keep from crying.

"By the time she makes her comeback appearance," he said, to himself as well as to Zsuzsanna, "she'll be better than she used to be!"

"Promise?"

"Have I ever lied to you?"

Zsuzsanna's entire body quaked with laughter. "At least a thousand times, but you always did it with such charm, I could never get angry with you."

Greco smiled and then, unexpectedly, turned serious. "I hope Katalin's charming when she lies to her husband."

"What are you talking about?"

"In her telegram, she specifically asked me not to respond. She said to set everything up and that she would speak to me when she arrived." His dark eyebrows knotted in concern. "I got the impression that she didn't want the Major to know what she was doing until it was too late to stop her."

Zsuzsanna's first thought was: If Katalin was keeping secrets from her husband, then perhaps love was not blind after all. Perhaps this marriage was not a forever thing; perhaps if all went well, the vows tying Katalin to Hungary would loosen, maybe even become undone. Warming as that prospect was, her second thought caused a shiver to ice its way through her bloodstream. Zsuzsanna read the papers. She read between the lines in the occasional letters she and her friends received from Hungary. Twenty-five years had changed nothing. Army was army. Police were police. Communism was communism. She had never met László Böhm, but she feared him nonetheless.

Sophie Warsaw had come a long way. After years on the road, doing one-night stands in places like Pocatello, Idaho, Evansville, Indiana, and

592 / D O R I S   M O R T M A N

twelve-foot chaise. Six Regency chairs upholstered in magenta silk provided spots of color. A collection of eight ebony mother-of-pearl-inlaid
Chinese tables sat before sofas and between chairs, bearing golden boxes
and black ceramic bowls and Baccarat crystal candlesticks with ivory
tapers that flickered as if in anticipation of the evening ahead.

Whenever Sophie surveyed this room, she acknowledged its magnificence while at the same time laughed at herself—at the incongruity of
someone as bizarre as she reigning over something as sophisticated as this.

Tonight, tears mingled with laughter. When the door opened and
she saw Katalin standing there, she cried. Instantly, the two women fell
into an embrace, hugging each other, shedding tears of reunion, squealing with delight in their togetherness. A pointed cough served as a
reminder that someone else was present.

"Oh, I'm so sorry." Katalin took László's hand, encouraging him to
come forward and meet her friend. "Sophie, this is my husband, László.
László, this is the famous Sophie Warsaw."

Katalin giggled. She loved the fact that Sophie was a star. She also
loved watching Sophie react to László's gallantry. With great style, he
bowed low at the waist, lifted Sophie's hand to his lips, and kissed it.
She actually blushed.

"Gee, that was nice," she said, admiring the handsome dark-eyed
man who stood before her. When he smiled, he was glorious, Sophie
thought. Lucky Katalin.

"It's a pleasure to meet you," he said, speaking slowly and enunciating each word, clearly nervous that his English would betray him and
make him look foolish.

"Likewise." Sophie couldn't stop studying this man who had married
her favorite little *galushka*. Judging by the way he kept fingering his jacket
and craning his neck away from his collar, Sophie guessed that he wasn't
used to formal attire. *Probably isn't much call for a tuxedo inside a tank*,
she thought, stifling her urge to quip out of respect for Katalin. Something told her Major László Böhm would not find her repertoire of jokes
about Eastern European military types amusing. Later, maybe she could
test his sense of humor by mentioning Solidarity. Though true Sovieto-
philes rarely found the activities of the upstart Polish union riotously
funny—pardon the pun—one could never tell.

"Champagne?"

"Absolutely!" Sophie plucked three glasses from the silver tray offered
by the waiter, handed one to Katalin, one to László, and kept one for
herself. "To friendship," she said raising her glass.

"Is Zsuzsanna here?" Katalin asked, after they had completed their
toast.

"No one is here yet," Sophie answered. "But within the hour, my darling, everyone who is anyone will be here."

And they were. Pinchas Zukerman, Beverly Sills, Joan Rivers, Placido Domingo, Barbara Walters, Zubin Mehta, Paul Simon, Bette Midler, Tony Curtis, Billy Crystal, David Dubal, Harrison Ford, Oscar de la Renta, Henry Kissinger, Peter Jennings, Jane Pauley, Bill Buckley, George Lucas, Itzhak Perlman, Georg Stolti, and dozens of other notables milled about the gorgeous surround.

For Katalin, the next several hours were the most exhilarating, most exhausting she had ever spent.

Then Pedjá arrived. He and Katalin embraced amid a shower of applause as the assemblage expressed their pleasure at seeing those two reunited. The Prince of Darkness and the Princess of the Piano. They had created a sensation in a placid and civilized world. Thanks to them, the Chickering Competition had become an event in the ten years since their celebrated rivalry, no longer the private domain of longhairs.

"Katalin, my pet," Pedjá oozed as he moved forward to greet his former schoolmate and competitor. He kissed the air next to her cheek. "You look wonderful! What a treat it is to have you back! Isn't it a treat?" he asked the crowd.

"You haven't changed," Katalin said, speaking softly through a smile, turning toward him. "You're the same self-centered, publicity-hungry, pompous ass you were when I left ten years ago."

Pedjá surprised her by flushing pink at her accusations.

"I am, aren't I?" he confessed, allowing himself a momentary laugh at his own expense. "Well, as someone brilliant and famous once said, we don't change, we simply become more of what we are."

"If that's true, Pedjá, you can relax. You've reached the pinnacle. You couldn't possibly be more of what you already are." Katalin shook her head and laughed.

"May I say something on a more serious note?" Sincerity was rare for Pedjá, but Katalin had seen it before so she recognized it now and nodded. "You did understand about my taking the prize money and concert dates, didn't you?"

"I left. They needed a winner." She patted Pedjá's cheek. "If I had to cede my crown to anyone, I'm glad it went to a friend."

"And an extraordinary talent," he said, raising an arm in a grand arc, tossing his head back in a maestro-like gesture that brushed his blond mane against his satin collar. "Don't forget that."

"How could I?" Katalin said. "You keep reminding me and everyone else."

He laughed, but it had a false ring to it. The sincerity of seconds ago was gone, safely hidden away behind the bravura that was Pedjá Lauc's style.

"Well, Katy my girl," he said, already eager to move on, "I hate to kiss and run, but it's time for me to work the room. Catch you later."

Amused, she watched as he shook hands and bussed cheeks and slapped backs, playing the role of the star. Actually, Katalin realized with a start, he didn't have to play the role. He was a star. Over the past ten years, Pedjá, capitalizing on the momentum of the Chickering tour, had become a popular fixture on the concert circuit, drawing large crowds—including an inordinate number of young women—wherever he played. Watching him parade about like a prized peacock—still arrogant, still garbed solely in the color of midnight, still hopelessly blond, and getting away with it—should have intimidated Katalin. Instead, it inspired her. If Pedjá Lauc could maintain such a stellar glow, with her talent and her willingness to work, she was certain she could capture a bit of the American limelight for herself.

If she needed any confirmation of that, it came when Paul Greco arrived.

"This city has been weeping since you left," he said, kissing Katalin, then turning to the man who stood at her side. "Major Böhm, you have no idea what a good deed you've done returning Katalin to these shores, even if only for a brief stay." He knew he had to play to László and so he did. "She wowed the hell out of this town and that's not an easy thing to do."

"She vows the hell out of every place," László said, unable to pronounce the *w*, liking the sound of the word nonetheless.

Greco laughed. Score a point for the soldier in the tuxedo. "That she does." He paused and then dove in. "If you wouldn't mind, there are cities in this country that would love to be blessed with an appearance by your wife."

László heard the way Greco phrased the question. He liked the subtle request for permission. It showed respect for his role as Katalin's husband. "It's up to Katalin," he said. Having been accorded his due, he could afford to be generous.

Katalin couldn't believe her ears. "Do you mean it?" she asked, feeling a sudden, powerful rush of emotion for László.

"While I work, you play. I'll make our government happy. You'll make America happy." He had anticipated both the question and Katalin's response. As Katalin kissed his cheek, inside László was delighted at the opportunity to make use of his wife's talents. With her celebrity offering him increased visibility, he felt certain he would be able to establish profitable contacts quickly. The brighter her star shone, the faster he could complete his business. And the sooner they could leave America.

• • •

Matthew was struck by how stunning Katalin was. In a room filled with supremely elegant, gloriously jeweled, party-hardened women, Katalin was distinguished by simplicity and softness. Swathed in an off-the-shoulder ivory silk gown, her hair pulled back into a low arrangement of braids held together by an ivory silk bow, she appeared sophisticated, but not in a studied, citified way. Somehow, she had managed to retain an aura of innocence, an air of intensely appealing guilelessness.

He fought it, but the comparison between Katalin and Cynthia demanded to be made. Though he couldn't stand her, Matthew knew that Cynthia would have walked into this party and seized the attention of everyone there. She was that striking. She would have held the room captive with her intelligence and her form of caustic wit, but only for a while. Cynthia was like a too-bright light that shone incessantly in one's eyes, making one want to close out the source of such glaring brilliance. Katalin's light was far more delicate, but no less powerful. If only . . .

For Zsuzsanna, who had spoken to Katalin several times in the two days since the Böhms's arrival, it was her nephew-in-law who demanded her attention. Zsuzsanna had come to this soireé wanting to hate László Böhm: for all the right reasons—his military and political affiliations—and the singularly wrong reason—that he was married to Katalin instead of Steven. Now, standing in Sophie's apartment next to Steven's brother, watching László deal with the new faces being thrust before him and Katalin, to whom he appeared truly devoted, she could see he was going to make disliking him difficult. Handsome, he was. Poised as well. And despite his halting English, he sounded as if he was possessed of a facile, intelligent mind.

Then, when the crowd had parted and she and Katalin had embraced, Zsuzsanna was also—despite herself—impressed with the warm way he greeted her.

"I am so happy to meet one of Katalin's family." He shook her hand, kissed it, and held on to it as he said, "It's an honor to meet the sister of the great Gáspár Zoltán."

Sophie, nearby, said to Matthew, "He sure knows how to push all the right buttons, doesn't he? Zsuzsanna looks like she's in a trance."

"Don't be so sure," Matthew said, eyeing László as he continued to woo his wife's aunt. Zsuzsanna was as good an actress as she was an innkeeper. There was no telling what was going on inside that blond head of hers.

"Well, then you must be the one in a trance."

"I beg your pardon?"

or you think I'm naive. You can talk all you want to whomever you want. It's still nothing but talk. Economic reform doesn't work without political reform. It's as simple as that."

"Are you making demands on the Hungarian government?"

Matthew laughed. "I'm in no position to make demands on anyone. I am in a position, however, to say no to you, which is precisely what I'm doing. You can make a thousand contacts. You can tell your tale to every bigwig from here to Washington and beyond. But you'll have to meet them through someone else."

"How petty," László snapped. "You're saying no to me simply because I married the woman your brother loved."

It took every ounce of Matthew's control not to strangle the man before him. "You're wrong, Major," he said in a derisive tone that conveyed all that he felt. "I'm saying no because beneath that fancy suit and that fancy talk is a Soviet-trained soldier who happily salutes the men who killed my parents!"

As Matthew spun on his heels and headed for the bar, László chided himself. He should have anticipated Kardos's response; certainly, he understood it. He had baited Matthew, yet it wasn't the outburst that surprised him. It was the intensity of the anger, still so strong after so many years. He had miscalculated. Rather than compound his error, László's military mind reclassified Matthew and Steven immediately: from harmless, possibly useful allies, to dangerous, possibly harmful enemies. And as decent and cooperative as László was with his allies, his enemies saw a different side—a different side indeed.

The last guest had gone. Sophie and Matthew were alone in the living room. Matthew removed his bow tie, stuffed it into his pocket, took off his jacket, and made a place for himself on the thick cushions of the couch that faced the wall of windows. Sophie had kicked off her shoes and seated herself beside him. Cross-legged, hugging a cushion, she studied him.

Even with only the residual light from the front hall and a few candles giving off the last of their flames, he looked magnificent. His hazel eyes were studying the cityscape before him. They were intelligent eyes, capable of enjoying the sweep without glossing over a single detail of the reality. Looking at his profile, he appeared a vision of strength, even now while he was relaxed. Why was it she found it so hard to lean on that strength? she wondered. He had offered it to her often enough, yet she had always pushed it away as if she didn't need it, when in truth she did. Sophie had been with a lot of men. Matthew was the only man to whom she had ever felt a connection. He was also the only man with whom she felt uneasy.

She had thought about it. She had practiced saying it: "I love you. I've always loved you. I want and need you. Please say you want and need me." In her heart, she knew he wouldn't reject her. She knew how he felt. He had said so in a dozen different ways. Then again, the problem had never been with Matthew. The problem had always been her.

"So," she said, turning off her private mode, switching to the safer, more public persona. "What did you think of Major Paprikash?"

"I don't like him," Matthew said simply.

"Why not? He's great-looking. He knows how to use a knife and fork. He didn't pull out an Uzi and shoot anyone. What more do you want?"

"I would've been happier if she had married a house painter, a plumber, a cab driver. Anything but a man from the military."

"Let's be honest, coal-mining man. You wanted her to marry Steven. There's no way you'd ever be happy with anyone else."

"True." He picked up his brandy. He swirled it around in the goblet before lifting it to his lips and sipping it. "Just so you know I'm fair, I don't like Cynthia any better than I do László."

"Cynthia! Now there's a piece of work." Sophie guffawed. "You can bet that is not red polish on those fancy fingernails of hers, my dear. That is fresh, type-O, human blood. It's a wonder Steven can live with her. He can't possibly be happy with her."

Matthew laughed in agreement, but before Sophie could continue with her monologue, he took her hand and pressed it against her mouth. "Halt! I don't want to talk about Steven or Cynthia or Katalin or László or who's happy with whom. I want to talk about what would make *me* happy. And that's you."

Sophie pulled her hand away. Matthew took it again and held it firmly.

"No you don't. You are not running away this time. Whether you like it or not, the time has come to talk about us."

"There is no us."

"Oh, but there is and you know it."

Inside her head, the nightmare began again. His words tangled with images and feelings and pain that wouldn't die. The Spanish taunts of her attackers. Her father's bludgeoned body. His voice screaming obscenities at her. Her brothers looking away from her. Her mother crying.

Matthew drew her to within a breath of him. "I love you, Sophie, and you love me. Why can't you admit it? More important, why can't you accept it and enjoy it?"

31

New York, December 1983

*K*atalin couldn't remember the last time she had been this nervous before a performance. Every nerve ending in her body was abuzz, as if each had been jolted by a live wire, charred and singed with the fire of anticipation. This evening would be a clear, inescapable turning point.

While she paced her dressing room, massaging and stretching her fingers, shaking her arms so she could stay loose, hundreds of people were filing into the Kennedy Center for the Performing Arts for this concert benefiting world hunger. Every seat had been sold. Tonight, Katalin would share the bill with a number of major American stars, but the audience would consist of even greater celebrities. The President and the First Lady of the United States. Senators. Ambassadors. Musicians. Foreign dignitaries. Hollywood luminaries. New York socialites. Texas oil barons. Wall Street tycoons. Congressmen.

Congressmen. As the word passed through her consciousness she felt her throat constrict, her palms grow sweaty, her heart thump rapidly. Seeking refuge in the comfort of a large chair, she lifted her feet onto a matching ottoman, focused on a spot on the ceiling, and breathed deeply. It was foolish of her to think she could get through the night without thinking about him. For days after she had heard that Congressman and Mrs. Kardos would indeed be attending, that in fact he was one of the organizers of this event, Katalin had suffered an attack of nerves that had left her nearly paralyzed. During her practice sessions, the thought of him sitting in the audience, watching her, judging her, perhaps still hating her for what he perceived as her betrayal of him, had immobilized her hands, freezing them above the keys.

Even now, she imagined him in the front row, his wife's arm possessively linked through his, his interest in his wife's chit-chat greater than in the performance, his love for the woman at his side greater than it had ever been for the woman at the piano.

Her mind fast-forwarded to their meeting at the après-concert reception. Of course he would come over to her. He'd have to. The press would demand it: Hungarian pianist being greeted by Hungarian émigré. He'd shake her hand and offer her a patented smile, the one he used in obligatory photographs. She'd thank him for attending, accept his congratulations, shake hands with his wife, and move on, as if they were strangers, as if they had never shared anything more than a nationality.

Immersed in her fears, she never heard the door to her dressing room open. Lips dusted her cheek, a gentle hand swept a stray lock of hair off her neck. A dream was beginning. When she opened her eyes, she was confronted with a completely different reality.

"I didn't mean to upset you," László said, reacting to the startled look on her face. "I came to wish you good luck."

Katalin answered his smile with one of her own, begging the tempest inside her to still.

"You look smashing," she said after a brief but satisfying appraisal of her husband. No matter how many items she might have inscribed on a list of László's flaws, physical appearance was not among them. He was a devastatingly handsome man. In a tuxedo, his dark hair and dark eyes intensified by the sharp black and white, he was positively cinematic.

László's gaze shifted from his wife's face to her gown, which hung on a brass hook on the wall next to her dressing table. A slim, spare column of shimmering gold lamé, even on the hanger it was elegantly simple. Yet when she had first brought it home, he had objected to it and had not been shy about saying so. Investing it with more symbolism than it deserved, he claimed it transmitted treasonous messages. She was Hungarian. Her land did not adhere to the customs, tenets, or fashion trends of America. Her people were more humble, more serious than that gown implied. To wear something that garish was almost traitorous.

It was so gold, so glittery, so *glitzy*—he nearly spat the word she had taught him—it could only be viewed as an insult to the Hungarian people. Katalin had protested that it was a dress, a costume, a gown selected to compliment a formal event and nothing more. It had been a bitter argument. They had not discussed any aspect of this evening since.

"You're going to look quite beautiful yourself," László said, cloaking the words *I'm sorry* in his compliment.

"I hope so," Katalin said, accepting his unspoken apology. "Are you sitting with Greco and Aunt Zsuzsanna?" she asked, guessing he wasn't, hoping she was wrong.

"No. I'm in a box with the Hungarian delegation."

"How nice," she said, fussing over his bow tie so that her eyes were averted from his and he wouldn't see her disappointment.

Early on, Katalin had realized that László was not going to allow any ties to develop between him and any of Katalin's American friends. There would be no roots established here, no relationships, no connections. Though he was polite, even charming, his prevailing climate was chilly and everyone felt it.

László couldn't stand Sophie, nor she him. When they were in the same room, she insisted upon using her humor as a weapon. Though she never insulted him directly, she poked fun at the system to which he paid allegiance, rattling off one anti-Soviet joke after another, mocking his affiliation until it was all he could do not to strangle her.

László and Zsuzsanna danced around each other. They had never warred, but each harbored so many suspicions that the best they could do was an undeclared peace. As for Greco, not only didn't László like him, he didn't trust him. Greco determined her practice schedule. He arranged her concert dates. He organized her time and dictated the terms of her contracts. To László, Greco wasn't a friend, but a Machiavellian puppeteer who, by pulling the strings of her career, intended to undermine László's influence and wrest control of Katalin's soul.

Greco knew what László thought about him; it only confirmed what Greco thought about László: He was an ego-consumed philistine, a man who placed deliberate restraints on the woman he was supposed to love, a man so absorbed in his own pursuits he would never understand the truth. Greco took his lead from Katalin. He was not the one engineering her emergence or challenging László's authority. László was being challenged by his wife, but his stubborn machismo had so thoroughly blinded him to all needs save his own, he blamed the influence of others, rather than Katalin's growing self-reliance and increased personal strength.

As he rose to leave and Katalin kissed him good-bye, promising to see him after the concert, she shuddered at the thought of what he would say if he knew what she had done. After that horrible night, after Sophie's party when he had turned her out of his bed, cruelly punishing her for enjoying her return to New York, coldly reminding her that to him, she was his wife first and foremost, her own person only when he said so, she had made a silent vow to protect herself.

When she and Greco had negotiated her record contract, she had acted on that vow. Knowing that the standard procedure was for her royalties to be paid to her agent, who would subtract his fee and then pass the remaining monies on to her, she made a private arrangement with Greco. He was to take his percentage off the top. An additional ten percent was to be sent to Walter Perry, who, having been instructed to do so by Matthew, would place the money in a numbered account and invest it. The remaining royalties would be mailed directly to Katalin along with her fees for concert appearances, to be deposited, as all her income was, in a joint bank account.

She knew she was being secretive and disloyal and technically unfaithful to her marriage vows, but the woman who had promised to love, honor, and obey László Böhm no longer existed. As a bride, she had carried certain expectations down the aisle with her. Few of them had been met. Childless, living in László's home with furnishings of László's choosing, submerging her career to his, she often felt more like an accessory than a wife. The snags had been there all along, but it wasn't until the Böhms had come to New York that the fabric of their relationship began to unravel and Katalin was compelled to deal with the truth of who László was, who she was—and what their marriage was not.

He was a military man, a devout communist, a singularly directed politician with his sights focused on a Politburo seat. She had hoped that during their stay here the hardness would soften, that exposed to the clear and obvious benefits of liberty his eyes would open. Her hopes were quickly dashed. László had no peripheral vision. He did not want to see another way or hear about divergent philosophies or admit to alternative possibilities. He was on a train following a track without a switch, and Katalin was convinced that even if he saw that the train was going to crash into a brick wall, László was too rigid and too intractable to jump off. He was going to ride it to the end, no matter what that end was.

She, on the other hand, had lived in the opposing camp and had come away converted. She suspected that soon László was going to take her back to Hungary. She hated herself for dreading that day, because Budapest was where her father and Judit and Andras and Ilona and Tibor were, but she couldn't help it. Here, she was certain she could feel her essence growing, sprouting like a flower given water and sunlight and tender loving care. There, she believed her creativity would wither in the darkness that existed behind the gloomy curtain of oppression.

Often over the past few months the thought returned that had flashed through her mind that night onstage in Paris. What if she defected? It would be easy. Just walk into a government office and ask for asylum. She knew she would be protected, that she wouldn't have to worry about escaping or being tailed by AVO or being interrogated by sadistic officials. But she would have to worry about the safety of her father. No matter how many times she considered the idea, or how many plans she concocted to spare Zoltán, she knew with absolute certainty that he would pay for her perfidy. She couldn't allow that to happen. When László returned, she would return. But this time she would have a way out.

She had opened that private investment account as a safety net, as an answer to the questions that haunted her sleep: What if I go back and I can't bear it? What if László and I begin to fight more often and it becomes intolerable? What if things take a terrible turn and the horror of 1956 returns?

"Ten minutes, Miss Gáspár."

Katalin jumped when the stage manager rapped on her door. She hadn't realized what time it was. She had to dress. She had to fix her makeup. She had to scrub everything from her mind except the music. A quick swipe of blush, a dash of mascara, a dusting of glitter on her bare shoulders and collarbones.

"If the music is divine, everything else will fall into place," she said as she rouged her lips with a burnished red. Forget the secret bank accounts and blot out the nightmares, she told herself as she slipped out of her robe and into the sliver of gold lamé. Forget Steven and László and Greco. Concentrate on the one man who is most important this evening—Ludwig van Beethoven.

Steven thought he had prepared himself for the sight of her, but there was no way to arm himself against the torrent of feeling that assaulted him when Katalin walked out onstage. It had been years since Paris, a lifetime it seemed, and yet as she made her way to the piano, stopping to offer respect to President and Mrs. Reagan, turning toward the opposite box and nodding her head gracefully at the contingent of her countrymen, smiling at the audience that had greeted her with such incredible enthusiasm, he felt as if time had been erased, as if his emotional slate had been wiped clean of the anger and heartbreak she had caused and was ready to be filled again.

She took her seat, and in spite of himself he saw the six-year-old girl whose music had created images of elephants in outlandish clothes cavorting in the woods. She closed her eyes and lowered her head, readying herself for her performance, and he saw the frightened little girl who had sneaked through an embattled city with him to place flowers on his parents' grave. She cued Leonard Bernstein, and he saw the young woman at the cimbalom at Csárda, garbed in gypsy finery, smiling at the *primás*. And when her hands struck the keys and her body quivered, he saw the naked beauty who had lain with him and trembled in the dark until she learned that she didn't have to fear the shadows; that his love would keep her safe.

But he had not kept her safe. For a long time after Paris, he had avoided New York and Zsuzsanna. He had wanted nothing to do with anything that would remind him of Katalin and the promises she had broken. Yet something inside him continued to nag. A year ago, shortly after Katalin and László had arrived, he was in New York to speak at a fund-raiser. On impulse, he stopped in at Csárda, where he and Zsuzsanna had a very long talk. She told him what Katalin had told her, about the year preceding Mária's death and the dreadfully lonely time following it. She told him of Zoltán's depression, of Katalin's devotion. She repeated what Katalin had told him in Paris, that she had received no word from him at all, that for all she knew, he had forgotten her. He softened. But still, he said to Zsuzsanna, she had married someone else, she had found someone else to chase the darkness.

Then Zsuzsanna gave him her sense of László.

"He's done nothing I can point to that would confirm my suspicions, but in here," she said, thumping her fist against her heart, "I know he's not what he seems. There's an edge to him, István, a sharp, cutting edge."

"Do you think he would hurt her?" Steven had asked.

Zsuzsanna had shrugged her shoulders. "I think he loves her, but I know he's army."

Zsuzsanna's words had upset Steven then and they upset him now as his eyes panned the auditorium, traveling to the box where László Böhm sat flanked by several high-ranking members of the Hungarian government. Though his eyes were gazing with pride on the woman who bore his name, László's entire mien said that it was rather those men whose investment of confidence mattered, those men whose approval defined the difference between content and discontent. Steven felt his heart sink as he admitted the truth of Katalin's situation: in a land where power was absolute, there was little room for love.

Leonard Bernstein's baton lunged forward and a powerful chord heralded the arrival of the "Emperor" Concerto. With the grace of a diver bounding off a board, Katalin's hands arched and soared into the air, remaining suspended for one magical, infinitesimal moment before rapidly descending into a pool of sound. Like spider's legs, her fingers skipped over the keys, delivering the opening cadenza with astounding brilliance. Another explosive chord, another startling cadenza and she and the orchestra became one.

The "Emperor" roared throughout the hall. As Katalin opened herself to the spirit of Beethoven, a cathedral silence prevailed and the audience surrendered to the hypnotic majesty of the man who had continued to hold music in his head long after his ears had ceased to hear. They heard his rage and their blood raced. They felt his pain and his desolation and their eyes teared. His anxiety unnerved them. His silences frightened them. His pathos pained them.

Yet this was the power of music: to give sound to our emotions, to translate sentiment into something palpable. Poetry and literature spoke of feeling. Art depicted mood. But only music gave it life, only music gave it definition. Each creation, each opus became a confessional in which composers revealed themselves, converting their emotional essence into sound. Beethoven introduced us to anger. Haydn taught us capriciousness, Rachmaninoff melancholy. Wagner was demonic. Bach was pious. Schumann was mad, and because his genius was able to record his fight for sanity, we heard what isolation and the edge of lunacy sounded like. Liszt was lusty and vigorous and insisted that we confront his overwhelming sexuality as well as our own. Chopin was a poet, and without him we never would have understood what night was, what perfume was, what romance was.

This night, there was no perfume, no humor, no lunacy. This night, the sounds were of conflict and resolution, struggle and victory. Translating the score into a language uniquely her own, Katalin allowed herself to become the vehicle for Beethoven's expression. In a powerfully eloquent voice, the hero of the concerto spanned the centuries to wage his existential fight for survival. He fought the forces of nature, the demands of God, the frailty of humanity, the lure of that side of man that remains animal. By summoning superhuman powers, he vanquished all that threatened to destroy him and emerged victorious, his final words echoing the joy of self-illumination.

Finally, Katalin's hands fell to her lap. Bernstein's arms collapsed at his sides. And the audience rose to its feet, shouting its approval in one awestruck voice. That voice called Katalin back time and time again, forcing an encore.

László beamed when she returned to the piano, curtsied to him and those around him, and, as a tribute, played one of Liszt's "Hungarian

Rhapsodies." Again, the voice demanded that she return. This time, László was confused. She curtsied to the President and then played a piece László had never heard before. It was short and lyrical, more like a song than a concert piece, yet the Americans seemed to love it. The woman who served as interpreter for several in the delegation told him it was composed by Edward MacDowell and was part of a series called *Ten Woodland Sketches*. The name of that particular sketch was "To a Wild Rose."

"You were brilliant!" Greco said, grabbing Katalin backstage, kissing each cheek, patting each arm as if trying to assure himself she was truly of the flesh and not a heavenly spirit.

"I felt it, Paul," she said, laughing and crying at the same time. "I felt as if my soul were pouring out of my body onto those keys. I felt as if my father were sitting on my right hand, my mother on my left, you on my shoulder." Katalin was shaking. "*Jésuz Mária!* What an extraordinary feeling!"

Before she had a chance to say or do anything more, the entire orchestra swallowed her in their midst, showering her with praise and congratulations. Suddenly, the maestro parted the vast sea of musicians. Taking Katalin's hands in his, he brought them to his lips and kissed them.

"Take care of these," he said. "They are a gift from God."

Flashbulbs popped, filling the air with thousands of incandescent dots. Reporters muscled their way to Katalin's side, tossing questions at her. Men with cameras on their shoulders aimed their lenses at her face while assistants shoved microphones under her chin. Whatever she said was recorded. Wherever she looked, she was photographed. Many of the other stars who had appeared earlier that evening came over to shake Katalin's hand and bask in the spotlight that seemed exclusively pointed at her. Bookers descended on Greco, badgering him about Katalin's appearing on this morning show or that afternoon talk fest or this nighttime magazine or that celebrity tell-all. A lone wolf, overhearing someone mention Katalin's aunt, cornered Zsuzsanna for an inside scoop on the private life of her talented niece. Once it was discovered that László was "the husband," he, too, was bombarded by the press.

Off to the side, Sophie Warsaw stood watching with a full heart as Katalin was anointed by the media, and the gates of irrefutable international stardom were opened. It seemed forever since Katalin had walked into Csárda, so gawky and odd-looking, so trusting and yet so scared.

Looking at Katalin now, arrayed in her strapless pour of molten lamé, her face flushed with success, her mouth caught in a smile that was at once pleased with herself yet at the same time befuddled by the attention being lavished upon her, Sophie felt a twinge.

Jealousy? Perhaps, but not of Katalin's burgeoning fame. Sophie was not one of those who believed that fame was a room with limited capacity; that one could only get in when someone else dropped out. What Sophie envied was Katalin's clear sense of what it was that made her unique, her unerring faith in her ability to make music. Knowing the reach of her talent, the depth of it, the power of it, acknowledging the very fact of it, was something quite special indeed; knowing *who you are*, in a way Sophie knew she did not.

Then, she saw him. He was on the other side of the stage, sipping a glass of champagne, deep in conversation with some politico she didn't recognize. They hadn't seen or spoken to each other since that lamentable night in her apartment. Afterward, she had spent weeks alternately hating him for leaving her, hating herself for losing him.

Mustering every ounce of confidence she possessed, she made her way through the crowd. When she was several feet away, he turned, saw her, eyed her quizzically and turned back to his companion. He hadn't encouraged her, nor had he discouraged her. Though she felt certain she was going to make a total fool out of herself, she stayed the course. The man he had been talking to had moved away. He was alone. She headed straight for him, taking one step at a time, proceeding as carefully as her three-inch heels would allow. The last thing she wanted to do was trip over her own feet and fall flat on her face before she ever had a chance to say a word.

He felt her approaching. She could tell by the way his head tilted slightly to the side, as if listening for her footsteps. That little movement meant the world to her.

Then, she was at his side, and paralysis struck.

"Okay," she said before he could greet her, her eyes wide, her jaw tight. "I have something to say and I don't want you to interrupt. I'm sorry about that night. About what I did and what I said. I'm more than sorry, in fact. I'm mortified. I mean, how could I?" The words came in a rush, pouring like water from an unstopped dam. "I do love you. You know I do. And God knows, I want you to make love to me, but, well . . ." She wrestled with her embarrassment, but the outburst continued. "I can't remember if I loved you from the first, which I think I did, or it was when you showed up at the hospital with that soppy look on your face and those bedraggled flowers in your hand and you picked me up and put me in your lap so I wouldn't have to sit in that wheelchair."

A slow, small grin ellipsed Matthew's mouth as he remembered that day. It continued to cling to his lips as he looked directly into Sophie's frightened eyes. "It's been years since then. I've told you how I've felt a thousand times."

"I know, but don't you get it? I'm not healthy. I mean, look at me." She raised her hands, pointing to her spiked hair—streaked with red and green in honor of the holidays—and the green glass Christmas trees that dangled from her ears. "Isn't it obvious that I've got some deep-seated problem and I hide from reality rather than face it? Isn't it clear to you by now that behind this wacko facade is an insecure, blithering basketcase and beneath all this I-can-take-'em-or-leave-'em bullshit, I'm terrified of men?"

Matthew took her by the arm and steered her toward a small hallway, away from prying eyes and ears.

"All men or just me?"

"Especially you."

"Why?"

"Because the others never meant anything to me. If they fucked me and left me it was okay."

A volcanic rage was building in Matthew. "No, Sophie. That's not okay. Why would you think it was?"

Tears welled in her eyes, glistening like clear raindrops against the bluest sky. "Because when I was thirteen years old, three guys raped me and humiliated me. They took my virginity and along with it my pride." He went to hold her, to comfort her, but she shook him off. "When my father tried to stop them, they crushed his spine with a lead pipe and he spent the rest of his miserable life in a wheelchair, cursing me and blaming me and making me believe he was right." She struggled not to give in to the sobs that begged to be released. "After that, after what they did to me and what he said to me . . . don't you see? It was easy to believe I didn't deserve any better, that I wasn't worth loving, that I was only good for one thing."

She looked away, afraid to see the disapproval and disgust she was certain had gathered in his eyes. He did disapprove and he was disgusted, but not with her. Placing a finger beneath her chin, he guided her head back to face him.

"Why didn't you ever tell me this before?"

She tried to laugh, but the effort only increased the flow of her tears. Before she answered, she searched his features for the minutest sign of mockery or rejection. When she felt safe, she responded in a small voice, "Because I still don't believe I deserve someone like you."

His arms slid around her waist. Gently, he drew her to him. "You may be right," he said, smiling as his lips glanced hers, "but I'm willing to put it to a test. What do you say?"

"Multiple choice?" she asked as he kissed her again and her body trembled with relief and joy.

"No way," he said, delighting in his own sense of fulfillment. "Fill in the blank."

"Miss Gáspár. Could we get a picture of you and Congressman Kardos?"

It was happening just as she'd predicted. The concert had been over for more than an hour and still they hadn't spoken a single word. Everyone had greeted her, save the one person she wanted to see. He was walking toward her now, trailed by an army of photographers and reporters.

"You were spectacular tonight," he said taking her hand in his, holding it. "I'm honored to be in your company." He leaned forward, kissed both her cheeks, turned and smiled for the cameras.

She cooperated, but as he spoke to the press about how he had known her as a child, she examined his eyes and read his body language, looking for something else, something beyond this sham of a meeting. For a minute, when he spoke of the times he had spent with her family and how grateful he was for their kindness after his parents were killed, she thought she spotted a glimmer of the man she had known as István. It flashed, it was gone; and the stranger, the suave, smooth Congressman Kardos returned.

Their entire reunion took less than six minutes. They had no conversation; they answered questions. They stood together, but faced a barrage of cameras instead of each other. When the Hungarian delegation interrupted so they could bid Katalin good night, Steven excused himself. When she next looked for him, he was standing with his back to her, deep in conversation with a group of diplomats. She had never felt so awful.

Cynthia missed nothing. She had felt Steven's body tense as Katalin had walked onstage. She had sensed that while Katalin played, he had disappeared into a private place, a sanctum where he kept memories he refused to share, recollections of experiences either too painful or too wonderful to risk bringing to the surface. After the performance, he had led the ovation, leaping to his feet, shouting *Brava!*, clapping his hands in a frenzied display of awe and admiration.

She accepted that Katalin was part of Steven's past. She acknowledged that Katalin and Steven had once been romantically involved. She conceded that Katalin was an extraordinary pianist and that her performance had been without parallel. She, too, had risen to her feet and had honestly and enthusiastically accorded the musical genius her due. But, past connections and present glories aside, she was not about to risk Katalin Gáspár's becoming part of Steven's future.

As much as Cynthia disliked owning up to mistakes, if pressed she would admit that since Owen's death she had been on an emotional roller coaster. Angered by the financial handcuffs he had snapped onto her wrists, frustrated by the fact that he had died before she had a chance to extract the revenge she so desperately sought, Cynthia had spent the last dozen months fighting personal demons and the terms of that accursed will. She had been obsessed.

Tonight, charting Steven's reactions, it struck her that perhaps her obsession—and the distance it had created between them—had left him vulnerable to another woman's charms. For all she knew, he was already involved. He wouldn't be the only one. In Washington affairs were as commonplace as monuments. She would hate it if he were fooling around, but she could live with it. Another congressman's wife, an officeworker, a staffer, a Hollywood celebrity—Steven would have everything to lose and nothing to gain except a moment or two of illicit satisfaction. What she could not live with was the one who could affect his heart.

Throughout the reception, Cynthia kept one eye on Katalin, the other on her husband. Yet nothing she had anticipated had come to pass. She had expected Steven to race to Katalin's side. He didn't. She had expected them to embrace and huddle in a corner and engage in private conversation. They didn't. She watched for whispers or stolen touches; she was alert for passed messages or meaningful glances. Instead, they said hello, greeted the press together, and parted company. It was almost too good to be true.

In the course of her own reconnaisance, she had noticed that László Böhm also had his eyes trained on Steven and Katalin. Curious as to whether or not he had expected something more than had occurred, Cynthia took advantage of the opportunity to renew her acquaintance with the major.

"We can't go on meeting like this," she said, extending a carefully manicured hand.

László couldn't help staring. As always, Cynthia demanded attention. Sheathed in a low-cut, long-sleeved, body-hugging sliver of mid-night blue velvet, her neck banded with a collar of antique pearls and diamonds, her hair coaxed into a sleekly combed twist, she looked like a John Singer Sargent portrait.

"You are as beautiful as I remember you." László took her hand, bowed low, grazed her flesh with his lips, and then looked straight into her eyes. "Perhaps more so."

As she accepted his compliment and they exchanged the requisite small talk, the thought did flash through Cynthia's mind that this was a very good-looking man with a commanding aura and a seething sexuality. She had felt it years before in Paris; she felt it now. What was it, she wondered as she allowed herself a brief but sensuous fantasy, that created magnetism such as his?

Hoping to draw him out, she asked him to explain the purpose of his current mission, pumping him a bit about his future ambitions. Not a loquacious man, he disposed of her questions in a matter of minutes. Shifting direction, trying to move onto a more personal plane, she played the hunch that he—like she—loathed being an appendage to a celebrity. There, she hit home. As she had suspected, he resented being ignored and dismissed. On this point, he was willing to commiserate.

Attempting to sink her probe deeper, she remarked, as casually as she could, "We'll probably be seeing a great deal of each other."

"That would be delightful, but what makes you say that?" László asked, his attention split between her and their respective mates.

"Oh, I don't know; I guess because they knew each other as children and seem to have this eternal affinity and, well, also, they have so many people in common, it's only natural that we'll all find ourselves in the same places at the same time."

"I wouldn't count on that," he said in a clipped tone. "Katalin and I will not be in the United States much longer. We're going home very soon."

"I'm sorry to hear that," Cynthia said, immediately crossing Katalin off her list of potential problems. "I had heard that your wife intended to stay and continue her concert tour." She had heard no such thing. Clearly, neither had he.

László's mouth curved in a facsimile of a smile, but his eyes were dark and hard. "My wife will be coming with me," he said. "Good evening, Mrs. Kardos. It was a pleasure."

"Likewise," Cynthia said, bidding him adieu.

As she watched him march away in a controlled fury, Cynthia con-cluded that her first impression of László Böhm had been correct. His lure, his appeal was the same thing that always attracted and excited her—power. This man coveted power—and was determined to have it.

What's more, Cynthia realized with a mix of respect and fear, when he got it, he wouldn't hesitate to use it.

"Here, darling, put these on." Zsuzsanna was carrying Katalin's coat and waving a pair of gold opera-length gloves in front of her.

"Here," she said, pressing the gloves into Katalin's hands. "It's cold outside. We wouldn't want those precious fingers to get frostbite, would we?" she said, looking to László for confirmation of her concerns.

Zsuzsanna was acting strangely. Katalin was about to remind her aunt that they were going from the concert hall into a limousine and probably wouldn't be out in the cold for more than a minute or two, when something told her to be quiet and do as Zsuzsanna said. Separating the gloves, she slid one onto her left hand. When she took the other one, she was certain Zsuzsanna held her breath. Carefully, she inserted her hand into the long tube. As her fingers reached the palm of the glove, she felt a piece of paper taped to the fabric.

"You know what," she said to László, Zsuzsanna, and Greco, all of whom were waiting to leave, "if you wouldn't mind, I'd like to use the ladies room. I'll only be a moment."

Leaving her coat and her purse with Zsuzsanna, Katalin headed for the powder room. She nodded to the women seated at the mirror repairing their makeup and retired to one of the stalls. In case anyone was watching, she lifted her skirt and seated herself on the toilet. Quickly, she stripped off the right glove and retrieved the note. Her fingers trembled as she read it:

I must see you. Please. Csárda.
Wednesday at noon. István.

She closed her eyes and pressed the note to her chest, straining to stem the tears of joy she felt rising from her heart. It had been an act, a front, an elaborate game of charades.

Knowing that László and the others were waiting for her, she stood, dropped the note into the toilet, and flushed, waiting to be certain that it was gone. Though she wanted to dance out of the ladies room, she left as calmly as she had entered.

Her entourage waited outside the door.

"Is everything all right?" Zsuzsanna asked.

"Everything's fine," Katalin said, winking at her aunt as László helped her with her coat. "Just fine."

• • •

It was like an out-of-body experience with everything moving in slow motion. He was sitting at the bar, his face shadowed and profiled. She entered. He heard the door and turned. She paused, suddenly unsure. He slid off the stool. She started for him, he for her. They wanted to fly, but gravity's invisible brakes restrained them. As she moved toward him, she felt hot tears on her face, felt her heart pounding. His arms closed around her, his lips pressed against hers, and instantly the composition of the atmosphere changed. The air became lighter, the oxygen level lower. She swooned. He held her closer, his hands caressing her face, his eyes exploring her soul. Time lost its substance. There was no such thing as minutes or seconds or any other means of counting its passage. Their embrace became an unmeasurable moment, an interlude of renewal and reunion, a joining of two rent asunder by the forces of fate. They clung to each other until wholeness was restored.

"I couldn't stand not being with you," he said, stroking her as if she were porcelain. "I saw you on that stage and I knew. No matter what I told myself, no matter how I thought I felt, it was a lie. The only truth is that I love you. I always have. I always will."

"I thought I'd never feel this way again," Katalin said, weeping, smiling, unable to keep from touching his face, his hair, his lips.

Years became minutes as they celebrated their closeness, talking, touching, splicing together frames of separate memories and individual experiences to make a shared whole. The clock ticked, but they had no awareness, no sense of ephemerality.

Steven was caught in the same maelstrom of emotion as Katalin, but while she was able to mute her intellect, he was not. Though his body longed to lose itself in the fantasy of her flesh, his brain insisted upon flashing reality in front of his eyes.

"Katya, we have a problem."

Katalin felt as if she had been pushed into a freezing pool of water. She recoiled from the cold slap of fact, pulling back and away from him.

"Don't . . . I . . . ," he stammered, fearing he had hurt her.

"I'm all right." She proffered a reassuring smile and took a seat. "It's just, I can't think when I'm so close to you."

"I didn't mean . . ."

She held up her hand. "But you're right."

Steven took a seat and then her hand. "I've thought this through a thousand times since I slipped Zsuzsanna that note and I still don't have a solution."

"Do you love her?"

"No." It embarrassed him to answer so quickly. It said little for his character that he had married and continued to stay married to someone for reasons other than love. "She came along at a time when I was feeling very lonely, very down. Cynthia's beautiful and exciting and exceedingly determined." He debated continuing, then concluded that honesty was essential. They had eliminated it in the past, which was why they were in this current fix. "She pursued me. I resisted for a while, but then, when I saw you in Paris and László announced that you were his wife . . . I no longer had a reason to resist."

"Have you been happy?"

"We have a great deal in common," he said, answering without answering, deliberately neglecting to list the three ties that bound them together: sex, politics, power. "And you? Do you love László? Are you happy?"

An ironic smile accompanied Katalin's response. "It sounds like such a simple question. Am I happy? I don't know about you, István, but for me it depends on the alternative. Happy with László was better than being alone and frightened. It's not the same feeling I have sitting here with you, being able to touch you and look at you and not hide how I feel about you. But when I was in Budapest and I was emotionally stranded, he was my lifeline, my only chance at anything even approaching happiness. I didn't have many choices." She traced the line of his cheek with a shaky hand. "I'm not sure I have any more now than I did then."

"I don't accept that we're not a choice," he insisted, smothering the outcries of logic and reason and reality. "I love you, Katya. I need you in my life." He leaned forward and kissed her. They were silent. When he spoke, his voice was soft, but laced with determination. "I don't want you to be a mistress or a sometime thing. I want you to be my wife and there's only one way that's going to happen. I know it won't be easy, but I'm prepared to get a divorce. It won't be pleasant, but it shouldn't be complicated. We have no children."

"Why not?" Recently, Katalin had thought a great deal about that subject.

"When Cynthia was a young girl, she had an accident. She's unable to bear children."

"I'm sorry."

"Me too," he said, focusing for the moment on something he usually kept suppressed. "How about you?"

"While we've never really tried to have children, we've never not tried either. I guess our timing's been off."

people as they could. "But then again, I don't know of a man on the Hill that squeaks. We're keeping an eye on him."

"Who's the number-four man?" Cynthia asked, referring to the person who traditionally held the title of chairman of the Democratic Policy Committee.

"Arth from Wisconsin," Steven said and nodded thoughtfully. "He's young, aggressive, good on domestic issues, but still learning the ins and outs of haggling foreign policy. He's well-liked by the unions, but not in their pocket."

"Are you two engaged or what?" Cynthia said. "Should I worry?"

Steven and Shadow laughed. Matthew was deep in thought.

"You know, Steven," he said, still thinking things through. "You could be the big winner in this fracas."

"How so?"

"As chairman of the D-Triple-C, you raised more money than any of your predecessors. More important, despite Reagan's Teflon popularity, the party retained control of both houses. Even your enemies have acknowledged that in some key states, your appearances made the difference."

"I hear you," Shadow said, "and I like what I hear, but there's a whole load of bodies to climb over on the way to the top."

"True, but with so many people jockeying for position, it's more than possible that some of them are going to be thrown."

"Why not look to push a few of them?" Cynthia said, daring Matthew, knowing how they differed on these matters.

"Because you never know who's going to push back."

The others didn't react. They accepted Matthew's comment as relevant only to the conversation at hand. Cynthia knew otherwise. That was a warning.

"Let's keep our heads clear and our hands clean," Steven was saying. "This whole matter of succession is going to play out like a game of dominoes. If they really do topple the leader, the result will depend on how many fall and who's left standing in the end."

László had decided it was time to go home. World events were putting tremendous pressure on Hungary. Kádár was getting old. His hold was slipping. From what László had heard, the jockeying for his successor had begun. Kocsis had been replaced as minister of culture by the outspoken Imre Pozsgay. The name of Károly Grósz kept coming up. Talk of reform was more frequent and more insistent; significantly, *samizdat* was no longer the only forum for such talk.

Since it was apparent that Molnár would block László's return every way he could, László decided simply to circumvent him. While he was at it, he intended to extract revenge for his banishment by disgracing and unseating the minister.

Molnár was a greedy man. Throughout his tenure as minister of commerce, factory foremen had found it beneficial to pay a forgiveness fee so that occasional lapses in production or missed delivery dates or runs of less than acceptable merchandise would be overlooked or forgotten.

Though Molnár extorted more than most, he was not the only government official to find a way to supplement his share of the common good. It was a club to which they all belonged, but within the very limited, very exclusive membership there existed the natural competition among thieves.

László's plan was to play off the various rivalries. Using soldiers he had used for other "special chores," he essentially opened Molnár's books for a public accounting. First, he made certain that Molnár's peers were apprised of the full extent of the minister's acquisitions. László knew that Molnár's land purchases in Switzerland and his country home in Salzburg and his shares in a South African diamond mine would raise a few prominent and powerful eyebrows. He made certain another group knew of Molnár's growing collection of Old Masters. Yet a third group was casually informed about his mistress. Then, he sent word to several trusted comrades on Kádár's staff that he was worried about a workers' revolt. He claimed to have gotten hold of some samizdat in which there were rumblings about workers growing angry at the pressure placed on them by foremen who had to meet either unreasonable production quotas or meet the equally unreasonable payoff schedule demanded by Molnár.

One by one, László planted the seeds of Molnár's destruction and his own resurrection. He tended them and watered them and then sat back to wait for his seeds to take root.

For months, every newspaper in the country regurgitated the details of the involvement between the Greek, the Speaker, and the wife. Several congressmen formed a defense team and attempted to calm the storm that was building. They pointed fingers at possible conflicts-of-interest on the Republican side and other questionable matters of ethics. Though much of what they found and revealed had merit, their man had been caught. The Speaker was going to have to resign for the good of the party and for the sake of his family's name.

Less than two months later, Otto Hildebrand, citing poor health, also resigned from the House. Insiders said the only thing making old

Otto ill was the thought that some of his stock dealings would be made public.

Suddenly the talk all centered around Fenton Douglas and Eben Arth. For the moment, they appeared the inevitable one and two. Beneath them, the scrambling for position was intense. The floor of the House was besieged by a spate of orators eager to grab the spotlight and establish a national presence. Between the ever-present media and the overeager politicians, the Capitol steps became the site of a daily feeding frenzy.

Throughout, Steven stuck to his promise to keep his head clear and his hands clean. Though he avoided commenting on the political scene, he was extremely vocal about things that mattered. He decried Reagan's appearance at Bitburg, condemning the visit to the military cemetery as an insult to those who had died at the hands of the Nazis buried there. He upheld the notion of sanctions against the government of South Africa. He participated in the Live-Aid concert for African famine relief. He deplored the use of terrorism to dictate foreign policy. And he became the voice of the homeless, pleading with his colleagues to open their eyes to the plight of "those who sleep on the streets of the Land of Opportunity" and to enact legislation to help them.

Cynthia was busy looking for a different sort of opportunity. In late October, just after Hildebrand retired, she found it in a place her husband would have thought quite unlikely as a source of ruination for a man's career, but one that she had always found to be a font of valuable, otherwise unattainable information—the beauty salon.

Because it was the toniest salon in the capital and because Cynthia's personal maintenance program was so extensive—color every month, a manicure every week, a pedicure once a month, a facial every five weeks, a cut every six weeks, conditioning treatments every ten days, a shampoo and blowout according to the dictates of her social calendar—at one time or another Cynthia was bound to run into most, if not all, Congressional wives.

That particular Wednesday she was there for a pedicure, a manicure, and a facial. La Femme was a large, elegant salon, decorated in varying shades of pink, with lush displays of flowers, and walls of mirror, and soft music piped in from hidden speakers.

The front room where all the cuts and sets and blowouts were done was an open and lively meetingplace. The back room, where the colorists and treatment specialists worked, was quieter, more sybaritic. Cynthia was sequestered in a curtained cubicle near the rear. She was lying on a recliner, her eyes closed, her hands and feet freshly polished, her face recuperating from a rugged cleansing beneath a hot terrycloth towel. In the cubicle next to her, Lucinda Douglas was having her hair frosted.

Cynthia rarely paid any attention to Lucinda, and might not have that day either if not for Hilda Clement.

Hilda, wife of one of Tennessee's representatives, had a drinking problem. It wasn't serious. She didn't fall down at inappropriate times or make a total fool of herself, but she wasn't known for her discretion, nor for her dulcet tones. She stopped by Lucinda's chair and in her ear-splitting Grand Ole Opry voice announced, "Don't forget to pack a hat, Lucinda. You wouldn't want Raoul's gorgeous color job to turn orange in that hot South American sun, now would you? See you in Cartagena!"

With a loud ta-ta and a laugh more equine than human, Hilda was gone. Cynthia was annoyed at having had her solitude disturbed. She had wanted to relax and nap. Now she was awake and more alert than she wanted to be. Seconds later, she was sitting upright in her chair.

"If you're going to be in tropical sun, Lucinda, we really should darken the formula and follow your color with a deep, deep conditioning. Otherwise, darling," Raoul said, "you're going to frizz."

Lucinda must have agreed because the next thing Cynthia heard was Raoul telling his assistant to prepare a special conditioner.

"I must admit, I'm fainting from the thought of you vacationing with Madame Hilda," Raoul said, clearly aghast. "How are you going to stand it?"

Lucinda laughed. She meant for her voice to be low and their conversation to be limited to the two of them, but the curtain between cubicles was very sheer.

"She's kidding. She's not going with us, Raoul. It's just Fenton and me and the children. You know, a little sun, a little fun on the beach at Cartagena. You know."

He might not have known, but Cynthia knew very well what had happened. As soon as she could get out of there, she was going to check it out. And if she found what she was certain she'd find, Lucinda was not going to be holidaying in Colombia. She was going to be back in Arkansas . . . permanently.

It took her two days to get what she wanted. When she had it, she confronted Matthew with irrefutable evidence that four months before, while the Speaker was still at his job, Fenton Douglas had requisitioned an Air Force plane to fly him and three other congressmen to Colombia. It was supposed to be an expedition to investigate the feasibility of increasing Colombia's oil production. Though the other representatives had signed their names to the requisition form, thereby insuring the Speaker's approval, none was going with Douglas. It was to be a family vacation courtesy of the American taxpayers.

"Either you make it public or I will."

"There's no need to go to that extreme. If I confront him, he'll turn down whatever appointment is offered. If we make it public, he'll be destroyed."

"So what?"

"Why ruin the guy?"

"Why not? What do you care about Fenton Douglas?"

Matthew felt pressed to answer that question, if only to himself. Was he resisting because he truly felt it was unnecessary to flay the man in public? Was he protecting Lucinda?

"And what about the others," he asked, still debating the matter in his own head, "the ones who signed the form?"

"They're irrelevant. Nothing will happen to them. They'll claim they thought the trip was genuine, that Douglas told them at the last minute it was cancelled. Everyone will believe them and they'll be off the hook."

Cynthia circled Matthew's desk. When she was next to his chair, she perched herself on his desk, crossed her legs, and leaned down so that her face was only inches from his.

"I don't care about them," she said as if she were speaking to a child. "But Douglas is in the way."

She straightened up and stared down at him, her manner deliberately patronizing.

"I know how honorable you are, Matthew. It's one of your most attractive traits. But personally, I think it's foolish to believe that after a private conversation with you, Fenton is simply going to decline the chance of a lifetime." She leaned forward again, her eyes hard again. "No politician is going to turn down a position of power unless he's got a gun to his head."

She lifted the file off his desk, waved it in front of his face and glowered.

"Here!" she said slapping it on the desk. "Here's the gun. Are you going to use it or not?"

"I'm going to think about it."

"You do that," she said as she slid off his desk, pinched his cheek, and strode out of his office.

Matthew shook his head as she slammed the door behind her. "Why do I have the feeling I just pulled the pin on a grenade?" he asked the space where minutes before she had sat.

Because he knew he had.

•   •   •

Minutes after Cynthia left Matthew's office, she hired a private messenger and addressed a package to Ben Bradlee at *The Washington Post*. The next morning, Fenton Douglas's political obituary appeared on the front page. Two weeks later, Eben Arth was elected Speaker of the House. Steven Kardos was elected Democratic Whip.

That same day, László Böhm received notice that Molnár had been ousted. László was being named minister of commerce and was to return home immediately.

With only two days to pack, Katalin didn't have much time to get in touch with Steven. Over the past months, they had managed a phone call now and then, using Zsuzsanna and Csárda as cover. Since Steven's relationship with Zsuzsanna was known, if her number appeared on a phone bill, there would be no questions. Nor were there any questions when Katalin went to visit her aunt. Since László and Zsuzsanna didn't get along, he preferred that Katalin see her on her own.

This visit would be her last. Greco was there. He was emotional, but practical. He reported that her investment fund was indeed doing well and that *when* she returned, she would have more than enough to get herself settled. She instructed him to continue to find bookings for her, but to concentrate on Western Europe. Though she was certain that he would be able to reach her by ordinary post, she gave him Phil King's phone number just in case. Judit and Ilona had retired from the underground, but others had taken their place.

After Greco left, Katalin and Zsuzsanna waited for Steven's call. While they did, they talked.

"It's not forever, my pet," Zsuzsanna said, stroking her godchild's arm, praying she had spoken the truth. "Steven will find a way to get you and your papa out of there." She sighed and smiled and cried at the same time. "If God is good, He'll let me dance with my brother Zoltán at your wedding. Ah! To see you and István married, to be with Zoltán again! I would die a happy woman."

Katalin hugged her, wishing she had some words of comfort for Zsuzsanna. Unfortunately, she had few for herself.

"You have to have hope," Zsuzsanna continued, trying to distract Katalin. "Look at Sophie and Mátyás." Again, she sighed. "It took forever, but they've found each other."

Katalin smiled. "They have, haven't they."

Sophie had told her what had happened between her and Matthew. She had told her about that awful night in New York and that miraculous evening in Washington when he had proved to her that she was capable of accepting love, that love could be something kind and gentle and still have passion and heat, that someone could honestly and truly love her. Katalin had never been jealous of Sophie. She was now.

The silence was growing more and more disturbing. Each minute that passed was an opportunity lost. Soon, Katalin would have to go. In a few hours, she was leaving for Budapest.

"He'll call. He's never disappointed you before. He knows you're going. Something must have held him up."

Katalin was getting frantic. "I don't want to go back, Aunt Zsuzsanna."

"It'll be all right." Zsuzsanna would have given anything if she could have kept Katalin here, out of Hungary, away from László. "It won't be for long. Steven will think of something."

The phone rang. Katalin grabbed it.

"Katya?"

She heard his voice and tears flooded her eyes.

"Don't cry," he said, hating the fact that he wasn't there, that he couldn't hold her. "I love you. Don't ever forget that."

"I love you, too." A grinding pain had invaded her chest, twisting her heart until it felt like it would break.

"This is only temporary, Katalin. Do you understand?"

She nodded. He couldn't hear her, but she couldn't speak.

"I know how to reach you and I will. If you need me, you know how to reach me, don't you?"

"Yes. The embassy. Clarke Estridge."

"Greco's going to tell me where he's booked you. We'll be together sooner than you think. I love you."

Neither could bear to say good-bye so they simply hung up the phone. Afterward, Katalin wept. When she could cry no more, she dried her eyes, but her heart continued to ache.

"He loves you."

"Maybe love isn't the most important thing in his life. Maybe this is." Katalin picked up the newspapers on the bar. Zsuzsanna had saved them because every one had pictures and articles about the new Democratic whip, the new political superstar, Steven Kardos. "He's on the rise, Aunt Zsuzsanna. He's an important man. I can't compete with this."

"To István, love comes before everything."

"Don't be so sure," Katalin said with a tinge of resignation. "I'm married to a man on the rise, so I know. They can't help it. It's as though they get caught in a machine and even if they wanted to, they can't get out."

"You can't compare Steven to László."

"Why not? They both believe in their political systems. They both want to be officials in their governments. They both want to make their mark on the world they live in. They both understand that to effect change one needs power and they're both working very hard to get that power firmly in their grasp." One lonely tear dribbled down her cheek. "They both claim to want me, but if push came to shove, I wonder who would do what."

Later, after Katalin had gone, Zsuzsanna thought about what Katalin had said. Though much of it rang true, truer than Zsuzsanna might have wished, she didn't have to wonder what either man would do. Steven would give up everything to have Katalin. László would give up nothing.

V

Coda

1985–1988

32

Vienna, December 31, 1985

New Year's Eve in Vienna was an extravaganza—a festival of
music and elegance, a celebration of the city's glorious past, a joyous
welcome to its immediate future. There were gala concerts, the annual
performance of *Die Fledermaus* at the Staatsoper, the Emperor's Ball at
the Hofburg Winter Palace, and dozens of auxiliary balls at hotels and
palaces throughout the city. Fireworks lit the midnight sky and a Tyrolean
band oompahed at 2:00 A.M. On New Year's morning, the Vienna Philharmonic awakened its citizens with its traditional concert of Strauss
waltzes. All day the music continued. And on New Year's night the
Vienna Symphony performed Beethoven's Ninth Symphony in the Konz-
erthaus, hundreds of voices joining together to celebrate the "Ode to
Joy."

For Katalin, this was an evening of firsts: It was her first performance
in the Great Gallery of Schönbrunn Palace and her first New Year's Eve
in Vienna; for the first time László had not accompanied her abroad for
a concert; and for the first time since she'd left New York—over a year
ago, she was going to see Steven.

Their correspondence had been spotty, but they had managed to funnel occasional letters to each other via Clarke Estridge, who had been promoted and sent to Budapest to assist the ambassador, and via Paul Greco. Though the intensity of their love had not waned, the status of their relationship had not changed either. What Katalin had told Zsuzsanna that day in Csárda had proved correct: The Machine Politic was like a conveyor belt, moving steadily forward with no stops, no exits. Both of the men in her life were strapped to that belt, while she was left standing on the side, connected to each, yet without any means of controlling her fate.

László, having attained the post of Minister of Commerce, had set his sights even higher: chairman of the Council of Ministers, the man who served as Hungary's head of government or premier. Steven, now chairman of the Foreign Affairs Committee as well as Democratic whip, wielded power and influence that extended far beyond the House. His proven magnetism in the media and at the polls had led to a number of attractive offers: Would he consider the prestigious Intelligence Committee? Could he be persuaded to run for the Senate? His letters brimmed with possibilities. Never did he mention Cynthia.

Katalin smoothed the folds of her white gown. Strapless, as always, a simple drape of silk to which she had added only one decoration: a tricolor ribbon of red, white, and green that slanted across the bodice. Here in the summer palace of the rulers of the Austro-Hungarian Empire, it felt appropriate to wear her national colors to remind those in her audience that they were, in some way, related. Suddenly, she heard her name. She stretched her fingers, shook her arms, and straightened her shoulders.

Two elaborately costumed guards opened the doors to the Great Gallery. Katalin's first view of it caused her to gasp. It was a dazzling space of white and gold with an extraordinary ceiling fresco by Guglielmi, a startling number of gilded candelabra, and a line of breathtaking golden chandeliers. A third liveried, bewigged guard offered her his arm and with great ceremony escorted her past rows of formally attired guests seated on golden ballroom chairs to the small stage set up in the middle of the grand hall. She accepted their greeting, wondering as she took her place at the gold and white Steinway grand, *Is he here?*

Katalin scolded herself. She had to chase Steven from her mind. Concentrate on the music. Only the music. For tonight, she had selected three of Vienna's favorite composers, and from their works those jewel-like pieces they called "Fantasies." The first was Brahms's "Seven Fantasies," a collection of intimate moments so intensely personal that his own indications on the scores begged for them to be played in a chamber, to be heard quietly before a small audience.

As she often did when she played Brahms, she wondered about this man who composed such lush, sensuous, romantic music and yet had not only never married, but was reported to have been impotent with women other than those for hire. Who was he, this handsome, soulful man of supreme intelligence and superior education? This complicated man forever burdened by the awesome challenge of following Beethoven? For most, the answer lay in his mightier works, in the passionate lyricism with which he built monuments to his talent. Yet every now and then, as in this smaller work of fantasy and unfulfilled dreams, Katalin was certain she heard the sound of a lonely man weeping.

Her second offering was Mozart's Fantasia in D minor, a piece that opened with a series of languorous arpeggios and closed with a brisk, surprising allegretto in D major. To play this work in this place, where Mozart himself had been brought as a small boy to play for the Empress Maria Theresa, gave her a private, secret pleasure.

Katalin had saved the Schubert, the most demanding of her selections, for last. She knew how much the Viennese adored the tragic Schubert. The Fantasia in C major, known as the "Wanderer," was the most virtuosic work of Schubert's piano music. So technically taxing was it that the composer himself during one performance had encountered such trouble that he rose to his feet in a fit of frustration and shouted to the audience that perhaps the devil could play this piece, but he could not. This night, however, there were no devils dancing on Katalin's fingers, only angels guiding her hands through a performance that earned her a standing ovation. But as she took her bows she had a single thought: *Where was Steven?*

He had not come.

At ten o'clock, the black Mercedes turned off the main boulevard of Kärntnerring onto the narrow street that fronted the Imperial Hotel. Katalin's guard, an eager young man named Rezsö, jumped out of the front seat and opened the back door for her. As the doorman ushered her inside the hotel, the guard dismissed the car and raced after his charge. Keeping a respectful distance, he followed Katalin to the elevator and then to her room. Unlocking the door, he went in first, looked around, and then allowed her to enter. Katalin resented his presence, but said nothing. He was László's idea. When László and the other fourteen ministers had been summoned to Moscow, he had decided that since she was already contracted to play this concert, he would agree to her fulfilling her obligation as long as she was "protected." It was a nice word, but she knew better. He had no reason to expect that she might defect, but he also took no chances. This man was not here to keep others away. He was here to keep her in. For three days, she had been trying to figure out how to get rid of him.

Closing the door behind her, she looked to see if the red message light was blinking on her phone. It was not. She looked to see if there was a note anywhere. There was none. There was a bottle of champagne cooling in an ice bucket, a gift from László, but she had little interest in drinking a toast by herself. Dejected and confused, she began to undress. It was when she opened the closet that she found what she had been looking for. There, hanging beneath a fur-trimmed cape of white satin, was the most magnificent ballgown she had ever seen, made of satin so white and shimmery it looked as if it had been fashioned of crushed pearls. Dangling from the hanger was a white ribbon attached to a corsage of white roses. When Katalin went to lift the delicate spray, she spotted a note tucked between the flowers:

At ten-forty-five, a car will be waiting downstairs for Frau Hofbauer. The driver will be looking for a vision in white. So will I.

A broad smile wreathed her mouth. She wanted to dance around the room and shout with joy. He hadn't forgotten! They were going to spend the evening together! If she could get rid of her baby-sitter. But how? She was certain that László's instructions were to stay by her side no matter what. Thinking about László gave her an idea. Closing the closet, she went to the door to her room and invited Rezsö inside.

"It's New Year's Eve," she said, handing him the bottle of champagne. "I thought we'd share a toast."

Pleased and surprised, Rezsö popped the cork and poured the bubbly ecru liquid into the two crystal flutes provided by the hotel.

"To a wonderful '86," Katalin said, clinking her glass with his, keeping her eye on the clock behind him.

At first, he was uncomfortable having a drink with her, but he was young, which was László's mistake and her good fortune. Had he been older and more experienced, he never would have entered her room. But, as László bemoaned often enough, Hungary's youth didn't have the same zeal he and his comrades had had when they joined the army.

When he had finished the first glass, she refilled it. When he had finished that one as well, she said, "I know you have a job to do, Rezsö, but I feel terrible about the thought of you sitting outside my door while the entire city of Vienna is partying and I'm sleeping. Why not take the night off?"

He shook his head, but she thought she saw a flicker of excitement in his eyes. "No. I couldn't. I have my orders."

"Major Böhm wouldn't like it," she said in her most compassionate, understanding tone. "He told you to stay with me."

"Yes, ma'am."

"I know that, but he wanted you to protect me and I'm fine here. Really. My concert exhausted me and all I want to do is climb into that bed and sleep. No one is going to bother me." She sipped her champagne, encouraging him to do the same. "Do you have friends in Vienna?"

"I know a few people here, yes."

"So, why not join them?"

"I can't."

"I won't tell the Major if you won't," she said, patting his arm and giving him her warmest, friendliest smile. "In fact, here." She gave the bottle of champagne to him. "Offer your friends a drink."

"That's so kind of you, Madame Böhm," he said, blushing, shuffling, eager to go, eager to please, afraid to go, afraid to displease. "If you think it's all right . . ."

"Good night, Rezsö," she said firmly, steering him toward the door. "Have a wonderful time tonight and sleep late tomorrow. I don't intend to budge until afternoon, if at all."

By the time he had left, she had less than twenty minutes to get ready. A quick shower, a quick maquillage, and voilà, she stood before the mirror looking like a snow princess from the north. As she spun around, sneaking glances at herself, she smiled, wondering if Steven had ordered a troika instead of a car. There was one last piece to her costume. On a shelf above the gown was a hatbox. In it was a headpiece of white fox. When she lifted it out of the box, she saw it was little more than a fur band attached to a dark wig. Pinning up her own hair, she slipped it on, fluffing the soft bangs that shaded her forehead, securing the chignon that rested at the nape of her neck. Again, she smiled. With this on, she could go out in public and remain anonymous. If Steven were recognized, from afar she could easily be taken for the brunette Mrs. Kardos.

After attaching her corsage to her purse, she went to the phone and told the operator not to put any calls through to her room until she notified them otherwise.

"I'm quite exhausted," she said, "and I don't wish to be awakened."

Then, she hung the DO NOT DISTURB sign on the doorknob outside her room and went to meet Steven.

•　　•　　•

He was in the car. She slid in beside him, the door closed, she was in his arms, and all that was corporeal and material and tangible evaporated into an intoxicating mist of emotion. There was no reality to her sensations, no nerve endings to feel cold or heat or pain or pressure. It was as if they had stepped inside an illusion, leaving time and truth behind. They were no longer two individuals. They were a single, inseparable presence.

Inside the Imperial Ballroom at the Hofburg, hundreds of elegantly dressed couples swirled by them, waltzing to the strains of a century past. Men in white-tie and tails, women lavishly gowned, a surround that was majestic and glorious—yet, they saw nothing except each other. Outside, as the old year yielded to the new, the heavens filled with color and sound and flashes of light. All around them, voices shouted greetings and hopes for a better time. For them, this night was the best time, the only time they might have.

When suddenly Steven spirited her toward the car, she feared they had been discovered, that the dream might be over.

"What's wrong? Where are we going?"

"Someplace very special."

The ride out of Vienna became a pause in the fantasy, a gap during which Katalin reminisced about the last time she had visited the Wachau.

"I was on my way to Salzburg," she said, recalling the train ride with Andras. "I was very young and very nervous. I was also very confused. Everyone I loved wanted something different. Some wanted me to win. Some wanted me to lose."

"What did you want?" Steven asked, moved that she was reliving a part of her life with him. He honestly believed that Katalin was his destiny. He believed that the fates had selected her for him. Yet for unfathomable reasons, those same fates had cruelly deprived him of so many years and so many shared memories, so that now, he listened greedily, filling himself with as much of her as he could.

"I'm not sure. I knew I wanted to play well. I always want to play well. It wasn't that. It was the prize that frightened me." She peered out at the darkened landscape, wishing it would prod her memory and allow her to touch her feelings then, but that was impossible. The past was blocked with the intensity of what she was feeling now. "If I hadn't won that competition, I never would have found you again."

The silence that descended pulsed with agitated anticipation. It was as if an enormous vise were pushing the vast expanse of time into a narrow crevasse. They had to hurry. They had to use these hours before they became moments, before the time disappeared and the oneness was broken.

When the driver veered off route 3 onto a narrow winding road, Katalin's heart began to race. Out of the darkness, there was light. At the top of a hill, they came to a stone gate with two black wrought-iron lanterns beckoning them inside.

"Where are we?"

"Welcome to Schloss Dürnstein," Steven said. "I thought a princess deserved a stay in a castle."

"But all the hotels in this area are closed for the winter."

"That's right. They are. So is this one."

"So, how . . ."

"Here and there, I've made a few friends."

Without saying more, he led her inside. Only the wall sconces were lit, and dimly so, making the rooms on the main floor appear like stage settings from a play recently closed. Toward the back, leading out to a garden, was a narrow cocktail bar with high vaulted ceilings and cozy seating groups. There were two comfortable drawing rooms, each with an imposing porcelain stove typical of nineteenth-century Austria, and an array of richly upholstered furniture comfortably mixing styles from the Baroque, Biedermeier, and Empire.

A young man bowed and offered her his arm, leading her down the steps into a dining room distinguished by stone walls and grand arches and Romanesque coves, tiled floors spread with Oriental rugs, and leaded windows that overlooked the Wachau gorge. While during the season there would have been twenty tables in the room, tonight there was only one. The gentleman seated Katalin and then Steven. He lit the candles, opened the wine, and discreetly disappeared.

When Steven had assured himself the wine was sufficiently chilled, he poured some for her and then for himself.

"Legend has it that around 1860, two growers here in Dürnstein found the vine for this *Neuburger* grape floating down the Danube like a piece of driftwood. They retrieved it from the river and planted it near here." He raised his glass and tilted it toward her. "It survived and so shall we."

Katalin wanted to cry for loving him so much, but by bringing her here he had escorted her deeper into the illusion, further into the folds of the dream. There could be no sadness here, no regrets, no dwelling on what might have been or what could not be. This was a space to be filled with fantasy.

They dined on a light supper of rainbow trout and parslied potatoes and then retired to their room. There, too, Steven had waved a wand, creating a phantasmagoria. In the midst of antique treasures and flickering candles and vases bursting with the pink roses he knew she adored, Katalin's imagination indulged itself. She fancied it a room in their house, hers and Steven's, a room where they had been before and would be again. She moved about in it easily, enjoying the feel of the silk upholstery that covered the chairs, the smell of polish on the exquisite woodwork of the gilded Empire bed and adjoining nightstands; she even delighted in the sting of the cold, wintery air that whistled through a break in the velvet draped windows. Nothing seemed strange or unfamiliar: not the huge white porcelain stove that heated the room, nor the bottle of wine that rested on a table before a gilded love seat, nor the cupboard in which she found nightclothes and a wardrobe for the next day.

She watched as Steven untied the drapes and closed out the world, leaving them alone in a yellow haze of candlelight and expectation. She felt as if she would burst with wanting, but she was so utterly bewitched, she was helpless to do anything except follow his lead. He poured more wine. They drank in silence, staring at each other. They needed no words to communicate how they felt.

Steven put his glass on the table. He took Katalin's glass away as well. When his hands first touched her skin they were cold and moist. She shivered. Slowly, they warmed and glided smoothly from the top of her neck down across the curve of her shoulders. His fingers closed around her arms and he pulled her to him. When their lips met, a sob caught in Katalin's throat.

"I love you."

She heard him say it, but more important, in her heart she knew he meant it. Every touch told her that, every embrace, every kiss begged her to believe that those words were an inviolable vow.

His lips fired the body beneath them as they traveled from her mouth to the swell of her breasts. His tongue traced the sinuous line of her form, tasting satin and flesh. As he unzipped her dress, lowering the gown to her waist, he pressed his face against her, nuzzling the softness, savoring the sweetness, breathing in the perfume that mingled with the scent of her growing passion.

Inside, waves of emotion crashed against the walls of Katalin's being, causing her to tremble from the powerful nearness of him. Her head felt light, fuzzy, as if she had imbibed too much wine, but she knew it wasn't the grape that was filling her with these symptoms of frenzy. Unable to restrain herself, she tore at his jacket and his tie, ripping them from him and tossing them on the floor. She removed his shirt and immediately pressed against him, rubbing against him, luxuriating in the sensation of his naked flesh against hers. Her hands slid down his body, moving with undeniable purpose. Her lips sought his, cleaving to him with the desperation of someone needing sanctuary.

He, too, had passed beyond the borders of control. While he had wanted their joining to be romantic and sensuous, they were too hungry for leisure. They wanted to feast upon each other, to devour each other, to ravage each other. Unable to stand it a moment longer, they fell on the bed in a frantic tangle of arms and legs. Though they tried to slow themselves their desire was stronger than their rein. They joined and for one burning, searing, explosive moment, the world stopped and allowed them to rejoice in the glory of their own private universe.

Afterward, Steven wrapped her in her cape, folding the fur-lined satin around her nakedness. He wished he could paint her the way she looked now, but he did not possess the talent to do justice to her beauty. Instead, raised on one elbow, he gratified himself with a private viewing. He studied her, memorizing her, carefully recording the way contentment softened the green of her eyes, the way her silken hair surrounded her face like a halo of burnished gold, the way a drop of moisture from his lips still clung to hers, glistening diamond-like in the candlelight.

"Your concert was brilliant," he said, leaning down to kiss her neck.

"I didn't know you were there."

His hands wandered beneath the cape, caressing her.

"I was."

His lips nibbled on her earlobe.

"Did anyone see you?" She was trying to concentrate, but her body had begun to move on its own.

"I don't think so, but a part of me wishes someone had."

"How can you say that?" she asked, quivering beneath the probe of his fingers.

"Then this game of hide and seek would be over," he said as he lifted her on top of him and covered them both with the cape, "and we could begin to live the rest of our lives the way we're meant to."

As he filled her again and again, she felt herself surrendering to the erotic rhythms of volcanic passion. But for one second, one brief instant of sanity, in that moment before reality disappeared in the frisson created by their union, intuition spoke, and despite her efforts to shut it out, she listened.

The game was not going to be over any time soon. Instead, it was going to become complicated. And deadly.

"I'm pregnant," Katalin said abruptly. She was on the floor playing with Sarí, Judit and Gábor's two-year-old daughter and Katalin's godchild.

"Mazeltov!" Judit squealed as she hugged her friend. "Sarí needs a playmate. So will whatever this one is," she said patting her bulging belly. "It's so perfect. I mean we grew up best friends and now our children will . . ."

"I don't know who the father is."

"I think it's time for Sarí to take a nap." Without another word, Judit scooped her daughter into her arms and hustled her out of the room.

Katalin watched through the doorway as Judit cajoled the little girl into bed. Sarí was a miniature Judit, all brown bouncy curls and huge brown eyes. Her personality was Judit's as well. Though she had been born when Katalin and László had been in New York, it had taken no time for Katalin to forge a friendship with the toddler. She played with her and giggled with her and lavished her with affection and let her do what she had always let Judit do—get away with anything and everything.

Fortunately for Sarí, she had inherited none of her mother's congenital insecurity. Although she was too young for anyone to know for sure, it appeared as if she had been gifted with her father's unwavering confidence and his easygoing insouciance. Everyday inconsequential things that Judit labeled "dire" caused Gábor merely to shrug, "so what?" If dinner was overcooked or traffic was impossibly jammed or Sarí didn't finish her noodles, Judit fretted. Gábor took it all in stride, saving his emotional energy for those situations he felt deserved the expense. And so, it seemed, did his daughter. Just before, Katalin had been helping Sarí build a tower of blocks. When it got too high and tumbled, she simply said, "Again." There were no hysterics, no tantrums of frustration, just a decision to have another go at the project.

Yet Sarí was as spunky and stubborn as her mother. When Judit reprimanded Sarí, she'd stare back with a look of angelic innocence and then, the instant Judit's back was turned, do precisely what she wanted. While Katalin admitted that in a child that sort of willfulness could be troublesome, she knew what a wonderful trait it was in an adult, especially if it translated into qualities like dedication and purpose, as it had in Judit.

After Sarí was born Judit had accommodated her new life-style the same way she did everything—with total commitment. The focus of her world became her family and the Jewish community. Instead of accompanying Hungary's finest singers and soloists, Judit taught music at the Jewish High School of Budapest. Instead of running off copies of politically oriented *samizdat*, she used those same two days a week to take meals to the old and the infirm. And on the Sabbath, instead of ferrying for the underground, she played organ in the synagogue.

Now, watching Judit tuck a blanket around Sarí and lean down to plant a kiss on the child's head, Katalin pressed her hand to her abdomen and wondered what changes would occur in her life, what accommodations she would have to make, which traits her baby would inherit—and from whom.

"Okay," Judit said. "Don't make me guess. Who, other than László, could have fathered my future godchild, as if I didn't know?"

"István." She said his name and her eyes brimmed with tears. The two months since she had left him in Vienna had been the most difficult months of her life. "I spent some time with him when I was in Austria," she said, a mix of love and pain coloring her cheeks.

It hurt and frustrated Judit to see Katalin like this. Judit prided herself on being able to find solutions for problems. Good, bad, or otherwise, experience had taught her that with a little flexibility, most things could be taken care of. Over the past year, she and Katalin had spent countless hours discussing this triangle of emotion. They had worked out dozens of plans. None worked, because when two people in love are married to two other people to whom they feel an obligation—morally if not emotionally—there are fewer options. When one of those couples lives behind the Iron Curtain, there are none.

"And when did you and László sleep together?"

Katalin shuddered. She knew Judit had to ask the question, but hearing it made her feel ashamed of her infidelity, not to one, but to both. "István and I spent New Year's Eve and New Year's Day together. I got home on the second. So did László. He missed me."

Judit nodded. According to Katalin, the major was an amorous man. "Have you told him?"

"No. He's in Pécs and won't be home until later. Besides, I needed to speak to you first." The tears had become a deluge. "I don't know what to do. Do I tell István?"

"No! Yes!" Judit threw her hands in the air. "I don't know." Even in her enlarged state, Judit did her best thinking on her feet. Lumbering up off the couch, she paced the perimeter of her living room, rearranging knickknacks Sarí had disarranged during her play. "You can't tell István because there's nothing he can do except get upset and frantic and that doesn't solve anything or help anyone. You have to tell László because he's your husband and he's going to assume, quite naturally, I might add, that he is the father." She weighed her next words carefully. "I hate to tell you this, Katya, but you're going to have to forget about the matter of this baby's paternity. You're going to have to assume it's László's child and go on from there."

"I can't stand the idea of not knowing whose baby this is." Steven had confessed that night that he would love to have a child. What if . . . ?

Judit put her arm around her friend's shoulder. "You do know whose baby this is. It's your baby, Katya," she said, "the baby you've always wanted."

Katalin pondered that for a moment. As always, Judit had narrowed the matter to a more manageable size. "I hope László's happy about it."

Judit wasn't certain he would be. The few chances she had had to observe László around children, he had been stiff, almost afraid. When she had mentioned it to Gábor, he had reminded her that many men felt strange cavorting with other people's children. He also had reminded her that according to Katalin, László's own childhood had been a disaster.

Maybe he didn't know how to act with children, Judit thought, trying to be optimistic. Maybe with his own, he would be different.

"Well," Judit said with a sudden giggle, "I know someone who will be happy. Your father!"

Katalin left Judit's apartment and headed straight for the Academy. The closer she came, the more excited she got. Judit was right. Zoltán would be thrilled. She hoped his enthusiasm would be contagious.

Since he was finishing a lesson with one of his violin students, Katalin waited outside his office. As she listened through the door, she smiled thinking about what a wonderful pedagogue her father was. Though he was concerned about all his students and had produced major changes in most, Tibor was his miracle. Tibor had been good when she had beseeched Zoltán to take him on, but his talent had been raw. Recently, she had heard Tibor play. The change was extraordinary. So was Tibor's tale of transformation.

According to Tibor, Zoltán had treated him like a complete novice, discounting his years of playing in gypsy orchestras.

"That was fiddling," Zoltán had said, as Madame Vásáry had once said to him. "Now, you're going to learn to play the violin."

One of his primary objectives was to instill in Tibor a sense of taste about music. To that end, he introduced him to opera, symphonic, and chamber music. He gave him pieces from different eras to study simultaneously, training his ear as well as his fingers. He provided him with books on history and art so that he would understand what had influenced the composers of a particular day. He commanded him to attend performances and practice sessions at the Academy so that he could hear how the violin sounded in concert with other instruments.

It wasn't Zoltán's way to concentrate on purely technical problems. He, better than most, understood the importance of artistic interpretation.

He never put Tibor on an "empty strings" diet of scales or exercises. He dealt with technological problems by solving them in relation to a certain musical image, by working on a phrase, or by striving to create a sound.

Another task was to break down Tibor's notion of music, of the violin itself. Tibor was intimidated by the concept of performing classical works and by Zoltán. He was extremely conscious of Zoltán's place in the violin legacy, of the burden of responsibility it was to be one of the master's disciples. Zoltán combated that by working Tibor so hard he had no time to think about the teacher, he was too busy complying with the teacher's demands.

"The worst thing he did to me and the best thing he did for me," Tibor had said when describing his relationship with Zoltán to Katalin, "was having me sit in on one of his master classes."

Zoltán's master classes were like small recitals. A group of students gathered in one of the smaller halls. At random, or so it seemed, Zoltán would select a violinist and demand that he or she play a particular piece. Sometimes he requested that it be played in its entirety. More often, he demanded the rondo or the allegro, a phrase from this movement, the development section from that movement. The day Tibor attended, Zoltán started the class by commanding each of several pupils to attempt one of Paganini's "Caprices," Zoltán's signature piece.

The first three students struggled. Zoltán's comments were pointed, but kindly put. The fourth student, however, incurred the wrath of the maestro by standing before the class in an ungainly, awkward stance meant to imitate Paganini's way of playing: right foot forward, beating time with his left, bent over at the waist, elbow tucked close to the body, all the bowing done from the wrist.

"And what may I ask are you doing?" Zoltán's voice had boomed through the recital hall. Tibor had noticed several students physically tremble in its wake.

"I didn't want simply to play Paganini," the young man had said with dramatic affectation. "I wanted to be Paganini. I thought if I could make myself feel the way he felt, I could stretch my reach and possibly attain his extraordinary left-hand facility."

Silence followed—the silence, Tibor noted, that precedes the storm.

"The reason Paganini's hand stretched the way it did," Zoltán said, enunciating his words as if speaking to a simpleton, "was because he suffered from Ehlers-Danlos Syndrome, meaning that he had abnormal connective tissue. In addition, there is no way you could ever know how he felt unless you carried with you the collection of physical ailments that afflicted him." Zoltán paused like a hunter holding a spear over his intended kill. "Paganini had measles at four, scarlet fever at five, and pneumonia at fourteen. He had chronic colitis, a persistent cough, sensitive skin, and excessive perspiration. He wore flannel underwear all the time. He had insomnia. He had bad eyes and wore blue glasses. He had hemorrhoids, rectal stenosis, and rheumatism. He had an abcess in his jaw, trouble with his prostate, syphilis, and tuberculosis of the larynx. He lost all his teeth and took so many laxatives they almost killed him." Zoltán glared at the withering boy. "I would suggest that you find your own way of interpreting Paganini. It's safer."

It was right after that scathing contretemps that Zoltán had invited Tibor to play for the class. Tibor heard the gasp and the whispered asides that accompanied his walk to the stage. He heard the snickers when he raised his violin and tucked it under his chin. Panicked, he looked to Zoltán, whose eyes were fixed on Tibor as if they contained a beam that could project confidence across a room. *Play,* they said. *Just play.*

Tibor complied, and within minutes a stunned hush canopied the hall. Whereas the students had expected a vulgar gypsy version of a sacred classic, what they heard was beautiful music; not an impressive piece meant to simply dazzle with technical hurdles, but an artistic display of the elegance and grace and melodiousness of Italian music played on a violin.

Zoltán had planned this to expose Tibor to the other students and, more important, to expose them to him. He wanted them to do what Katalin had made Zoltán himself do, rise above their prejudice and accept the talent without judging the source. Tibor's talent won their respect, if not their affection.

Now, the door to Zoltán's office opened and a bedraggled young girl shuffled out. As she passed Katalin and recognized her, she tried to smile, but her efforts seemed to exhaust her. Katalin was laughing as she closed the door behind her.

"You are a tyrant!" she said, walking toward her father with open arms, noting as she always did the instantaneous joy that enveloped him when he saw her, and realizing, not for the first time, that for all her fantasies of leaving Budapest for Steven that she could never leave her father behind and risk his being hurt on her account. Nor could she simply demand that he uproot himself. After years of grinding personal misery, Zoltán was conducting, teaching, meeting people. If she demanded that he come with her and if he agreed, she had asked herself, what would he do in New York? He'd have to start all over again—new language, new surroundings, new people. Then, she had concluded she couldn't do it to him. Now, she simply couldn't do it . . . period.

"I'm not a tyrant," he said, patting her cheek, helping her into a chair. "An onorous son of a bitch, yes, but not a tyrant." He sank down into the swivel chair behind his desk, resting his hands on his stomach. "To what do I owe the pleasure of this visit?"

"I have wonderful news."

Zoltán couldn't imagine what it was. Other than that period after the traumatic night at the Strassers when everyone had ganged up on Zoltán and Katalin had revealed her feelings for Steven, she and Zoltán had never discussed him again. She didn't mention him. Zoltán didn't ask, but that didn't mean he didn't know.

Zsuzsanna had written Zoltán several times since Katalin and László had returned—though it appeared as if the government had finally stopped screening his mail, Zsuzsanna, unwilling to risk reprisals, had sent her letters through Estridge at the American embassy. In each letter, she had tried to explain the way it was between István and Katalin, the way it was meant to be. Her words had echoed the words of Mária, when she, too, had spoken to Zoltán of their daughter's love for Béla and Margit's child. Often, he had wondered what he would do if she ever decided to leave László and leave Hungary. Was this the moment he was going to have to come up with an answer?

"You are going to be a grandfather!"

"What?" This was completely unexpected. He had never wanted to pry. He had simply assumed that either Katalin and László had decided not to have children or that nature had decided it for them.

"I'm pregnant. Due in October." His features still registered shock. "Are you happy?"

His face flushed red as he bounded out of his chair to hug her. "Happy? That's a puny word for the way I feel! I am delirious! Ecstatic! Delighted! What else would I be?"

Katalin felt his arms wrap around her, and for the first time she, too, felt happy about the new life inside her.

"How did László take the news?"

"I'm going to tell him tonight."

Zoltán was grinning from ear to ear, "He may be the father, but there's no way he's going to be happier than I am."

Katalin smiled, and, appreciating the irony of Zoltán's comment, agreed. "No way."

László and Katalin no longer lived in Watertown. Within a month following their return, László had purchased a villa in the exclusive *Rózsadomb* section of Buda. On Rose Hill, top Party *funcionárusok* lived alongside well-to-do reformers, forint millionaires rubbed shoulders with wealthy film directors, nationalists shared the same street as actors and writers like György Konrád, whose apartment was the hive around which foreign journalists buzzed.

Whether it was because he suspected that Katalin had never felt any sense of real belonging in the Watertown house, or because he knew he had given her a rough time in New York, or because he wanted to create a project that would bring them closer together—László invited Katalin to take charge of the decoration of their new abode. Katalin accepted the task the way it was given. László's home was important to him. For him to grant her domain over its furnishing was a grand trust.

Since they already owned so many fine antiques, Katalin's main concerns became color and texture and infusing their surroundings with a sense of warmth and sociability she felt had been missing in Watertown. Knowing how much László loved blue, she used a great deal of it. If it wasn't the primary color of a room, she used it for accents. She even created a "blue" collection, gathering vases and bowls and porcelains and glass, pieces that ranged from rare finds to flea-market bargains. In the course of her searching, she found herself attracted to Bohemian ruby glass, richly colored glassware from the mid- to late-nineteenth century etched with Rococo scroll motifs and forest scenes. Soon, alongside László's blues were Katalin's reds.

Her first major purchase was a Steinway grand. Because the villa was blessed with so much precious space, Katalin was able to have her very own practice room. With an eye to pleasing both László and herself, Katalin created a Victorian music room. Making the piano the centerpiece, she surrounded it with the elaborately layered draperies, intricately patterned rugs, gilded mirrors, and the numerous tea tables that distinguished most music rooms of that bygone era. Instead of paint, she upholstered the walls with a lush caramel velvet. Instead of the requisite love seats and the bevy of occasional chairs, she installed banquettes in all four corners of the room. Tufted, festooned with dozens of throw pillows and skirted with a thick layer of fringe, they became an invitation for guests to sit and relax as their hostess entertained them.

But the most beautiful room, the place she had chosen for her disclosure of her pregnancy, was László's library. Paneled in richly carved walnut, with intricate moldings and mirrored doors and a stretch of bookshelves fronted with exquisitely crafted paned glass, the library housed László's collection of fine art and a store of lushly upholstered furniture. On a table that sat before one of the larger couches, Katalin laid two place settings and a bowl of fresh flowers. She had set candles on either side of the table, on the windowsills, and along the ledge of the bookcase wall, delighting in the way the flames were reflected in the glass. Several of the larger, more important paintings had their own awning lights. She lit these as well. A fire burned in the marble hearth that centered the room. She had stared into it so long she began to believe it was taunting her with its crackling laugh and those long orange fingers that seemed to reach beyond the grate to point at her.

It would have been so much easier if her marriage had continued to disintegrate in the months following their return to Budapest, if the bickering and sniping that had marked their relationship in New York had mushroomed into something so intolerable that both of them would have sought a dissolution. But that was not the case. If anything, since he had attained the Ministry and was beginning to feel comfortable in the shoes of power, László's irritability had calmed. For once, he seemed at peace within his world.

It had taken years for Katalin to understand that László was not a man who would ever enjoy total contentment. He didn't confide much about his feelings, but clearly his driving ambition stemmed from his need to cloak himself in visible forms of esteem. His father had revered titles, so it wasn't unnatural for László to seek them. His father had worshiped those in power, so it wasn't unusual to find a son who wanted to be one of those idols. László might be physically adoring of her, proud of her achievements and devoted in his way, but no one had ever taught him how to express his feelings or to accept that expression from others. When his mother abandoned him, she left no one in her stead who could show him what caring was. His father, the soldier, only understood commands. His grandmother, old and of a brittle, acrid nature, had taken exception to having to care for someone so young at a time in her life when she should have been free of such tedious obligations. Though he never said anything, László felt her resentment keenly. At some unspecified moment, Katalin thought, he must have vowed never to allow anyone to bear responsibility for his needs again.

As much as he was able, Katalin believed László trusted her. She had betrayed that trust, and on that level she sorely regretted her actions. Though she wasn't about to confess her transgression, what she was going to do was spiritually to renew her marital vows, to make a new commitment to love and honor the man who had taken her as a wife and was going to be the father of her child.

The logs snapped. A downdraft pushed a gray cloud into the room, which loomed in front of her like a fire-breathing chimera. She closed her eyes and shook her head. Steven could not be allowed in this room. Her feelings for him could not live in László's home. It wasn't right. She pressed her hands against her ears, shutting out the voice of her heart, listening only to the voice of reason. She had spent one night with

Steven. The possibility of his being the father was remote. She had made love to her husband before and after that one night—several times before and several times after. The probability was that László had created this child. Even if he hadn't, legally the baby was his. And morally it was his.

Which was why she had stopped by the embassy late that afternoon and handed Estridge a letter to be forwarded to Steven. Her last letter.

> *My darling István,*
> *Sometimes people get lost in their own fantasies. I often think that's what happened to us. You were the boy who went away. I was the girl you left behind. Given the history that surrounded us, incidents that should have faded into a distant memory became so exaggerated they created a romance. They wrote a story for us in which we were the main characters. We had roles to play and speeches to give and actions to follow. And we did. I don't know if we ever truly loved each other or if it was simply a matter of being in love with the idea of loving each other.*
> *Since I returned from Vienna, things have changed. I see how wrong we are. My life is here, in Budapest, with László. Your life is there, in Washington, with Cynthia. You're an important man in your government. I have my music. We each have our families. But if we're honest, really honest, what we never had was each other. I know we said we would try to work things out, but recently, the risks have gotten greater. Since I'm not comfortable in a bed of lies and I'm not good at games of chance, Viszontlátásra. Good-bye.*

"This is nice," László said as he bent down to kiss Katalin good evening. "I'm sorry I'm so late."

"It's all right," she said, chasing her ghosts with a smile for her husband. "I have a big pot of *palócleves* simmering on the stove."

"Sounds wonderful!" László loved *palócleves*, a mix of mutton, French beans, potatoes, and sour cream, seasoned with paprika, garlic, and caraway seeds. It was the perfect meal for a cold, raw, wintery night.

"A little wine, a loaf of bread, a bowl of soup. And then," she said, rising off the couch and playfully pecking at his cheek, "I have a surprise."

"Really. What?"

"If I tell you, it won't be a surprise. Go change while I get our supper."

By the time László returned in a pair of slacks and a sweater, Katalin had everything laid out and had turned on the phonograph, filling the room with Chopin's poetry. She wanted everything to be perfect.

After they had eaten and Katalin had cleared away the dishes, László waited for her on the couch. He had added some fresh logs to the fire and changed the music from Chopin to Rachmaninoff. Leaning back, stretching out, letting his eyes drink in the beauty of his surroundings, he allowed a smile to grace his lips. He felt good.

That afternoon, he had quelled a protest by residents of several communities in the outlying sections of Pécs who objected to government plans to bury nuclear waste in an area near them. Several towns south of Bonyhád had been exempted when surveys disclosed seven springs and an earthquake fault within a mile of the prospective site, but that news only served to make the towns still considered eligible even more nervous. Though he had made promises he doubted he could keep, by quieting the protesters he had given the industry time to consider alternative solutions.

Tonight, he had arrived home to find his wife looking exceptionally beautiful. The moodiness and fatigue that had marked her manner for months was gone. He had worried that her concert schedule was putting too great a strain on her, but he knew better than to suggest that she cut back. There were many things about Katalin he didn't understand—her intense loyalty to anyone she deemed family or friend, her lack of discrimination against those who deserved to be discriminated against, and of course, her affection for all things Western—but one thing he knew for certain. To her, music was like oxygen. She could not live without it. Which was why he concluded that her surprise was career-related and why he was so unprepared for what he was about to hear.

Katalin snuggled next to him. "What do we need to make this picture complete?" she asked.

"What picture?"

"This," she said, sweeping her hand around the room. "Our home, our life together. What do we need to make it better?"

László knotted his brows quizzically. "I don't think we need anything," he said, cupping her chin in his hand, wondering what it was that had put this fizz in her. "I think its quite splendid just the way it is."

"I have something to make it even more splendid." She kissed him and pointed to her belly. "Right here." He looked at her as if she were mad. "We are going to have a baby. Isn't that incredible?"

So many emotions washed over his face so quickly that Katalin couldn't keep track of them, let alone understand what had prompted them. In a flash she saw astonishment, confusion, anger, nervousness, apprehension, shock. When each had completed its play on his facial screen, she was left with a man at a loss.

"László. Say something."

"I didn't expect this," he said.

"Neither did I. After all these years, I had given up hope of our ever having a child. It's like a miracle." Tears of joy and wonder and gratitude crossed over her smile, falling into a puddle on her lap. "We're going to be parents, László. Can you imagine that?"

He appeared dazed. "I'm not sure I can." And concerned. "I'm not sure I want to."

Katalin's heart pounded inside her chest. "What do you mean?"

"Just what I said. We've established a life for ourselves. A complicated life that requires time and travel and constant attention. I don't think we have room for a child."

Katalin wondered if his grandmother had said those things about him, if he was repeating things he had overheard.

"We have plenty of room," she said, moving closer to him, willing the warmth of her body to melt the coldness left by his past. "Both in our home and in our hearts. We'll probably have to make some changes, but I think they're worth it."

She held her breath and waited for a response. A word. A gesture. An expression of hope. After several minutes of staring into the fire, László disentangled himself from her and rose from the couch. His eyes appeared vacant, as if his mind was far away from her, far away from this room.

"I'm sorry," he said, his voice more an echo than an original sound. "I'm tired. You took me by surprise. We'll talk about this tomorrow."

He leaned over to kiss her, but the effort was half-hearted and unsettling. When he left, Katalin found herself in the same spot she was before he came in—alone, with only the fire for company.

Suddenly, she felt very attached to the incipient stirrings within her.

"Don't worry," she said to the spirit of her unborn child. "You're not real to him yet. He doesn't understand how wonderful it's going to be. When you're here, he'll love you." *I hope.*

33

Budapest, October 1986

On October 1, 1986, Katalin was delivered of an eight-pound, four-ounce baby girl. Crowned with soft red fuzz and gifted with light-green eyes, she was the image of her mother, a fact Katalin viewed as both a blessing and a relief. Throughout her pregnancy, she had blocked all thoughts about Steven and his possible paternity. In the delivery room, however, it was difficult not to feel a certain panic about resemblances, especially because, despite daily efforts to include him in her plans and warm him to the idea of fatherhood, László had remained aloof and detached. Even now, presented with this precious bundle, he appeared hesitant and unsure about what he was supposed to do and how he was supposed to feel.

"You make a very adorable pair," Katalin cooed as she watched the nurse place the baby in László's arms.

"She's very pretty," he said after a while, but in a tone a stranger would use.

"She needs a name."

"Pick one you like."

He looked very awkward and uncomfortable with the baby in his arms, but Katalin noticed that every now and then he sneaked a peek at her. That was encouraging.

"Would you like to name her for your mother?"

László handed Katalin the baby. "No."

"Or your father?"

"No."

She could see he was struggling with a fit of rage. It was at times like this that she wished he talked more so she could understand him better.

"Would you mind if I named her for my mother?"

"No. That would be fine."

Katalin had the feeling he couldn't have cared less.

"How about Márta?"

He nodded his head and mumbled "wonderful" several times, obviously grateful this tedious chore was over, then said rather abruptly:

"I have to leave now. I have to go to work. I'll be back later."

He returned later that night with a large bouquet of flowers and came twice the next day, but his stays were short and strained. Though Katalin wished he would stay longer, she was never at a loss for visitors, nor was Márta at a loss for admirers. Zoltán was there as often as hospital regulations permitted. As she knew he would be, he was beside himself with joy that Katalin had named the baby for Mária. So were Ilona and Andras and Judit. They all agreed that it was Mária's spirit that had given Katalin this child, and so it was only right that the baby be named for her. Gábor came by several times, always with drawings Sarí had done as a welcome for her new friend. People Katalin didn't even know sent cards and flowers and tokens of congratulations. Already, Márta had dozens of stuffed animals for her crib and toys for her playpen. For Katalin it was such a happy time, she didn't think anything, including László's slow acceptance of his new role, could upset her.

She was wrong. It was in the evening of the third day, during a visit with Judit and Gábor, that a doctor, accompanied by a nurse carrying a syringe and a small bottle, walked into Katalin's room wearing frighteningly grim expressions.

Katalin looked from one to the other. "What's happened?" Katalin asked, her body swimming in a sudden sweat, her mind racing through an index of infant illnesses. "Is Márta all right?"

"She's gone." Katalin, Judit and Gábor gasped in unison. The doctor, realizing they thought the baby had died, rushed to explain. "Someone took her."

"Gone? Took her?" Katalin was growing hysterical. Judit ran to her side, holding her, trying to calm her, trying to calm herself.

"You have to be clearer, doctor," Gábor said, barking at his colleague. "What exactly happened to Madame Böhm's baby?"

"She's been kidnapped. We think the gypsies took her." Still unable to mask his own puzzlement, he opened his hand. In his palm were six gold coins. "We found these in the baby's crib."

"No!" Katalin shouted. "No!" She was crying and screaming and wringing her hands. Her body was convulsed. The nurse filled the syringe and attempted to sedate Katalin, but Katalin pushed the woman's hand away. "Stop! Don't! I need to be alert." Cowering in the middle of the bed, she struggled to gulp back her tears. She closed her eyes and took deep breaths, attempting to control her hysteria, barely succeeding.

Suddenly, László burst into the room. He went right to Katalin. "They called and told me," he said, his face a map of anguish and distress. "I can't believe this has happened."

"You have to do something," Katalin said, her control slipping again. She flung herself at him, clutching at his jacket, every muscle in her body pleading with him to end this gruesome nightmare.

"I called the police," he said, smoothing her hair, kissing her hands, holding her, doing anything he could to quiet her. "They're headed for Esztergom."

"Please. Hurry. Go with them!" Katalin couldn't bear the thought of her infant being taken anywhere near the squalid gypsy slum in Esztergom. "That place is awful. It's filthy and disgusting. She'll get sick there. She'll die there."

"No, she won't," László said in a soft, reassuring voice. "I'll find her and bring her back. I promise." He took her face in his hands and gently kissed her lips. "Don't worry," he whispered. "Everything's going to be fine."

Katalin nodded numbly. She wanted to believe him and so she did. Shortly after László left, Gábor, unable to fathom such a lapse in hospital security, went with the doctor and the nurse to investigate. Judit stayed with Katalin.

"László and the police will find Márta," she said. "What you need to do now is to try to relax."

Katalin shook her head. Before Judit could argue, Katalin turned and rifled through the drawer of her bedstand. Taking out a piece of paper and a pencil, she wrote down an address and a telephone number and handed the paper to Judit. Out of instinct, she lowered her voice so the women in the other beds couldn't hear her.

"Get Tibor here as quickly as you can. If it was the gypsies who took my Márta, he'll know how to find her."

He and his band had been playing at Mátyáspince, a restaurant on Március Tér. By the time Judit tracked him down, it was close to midnight.

"It's not possible," he said, taken aback by Katalin's bedraggled appearance. Her eyes were bulging and her skin had an eerie cast, as if she had been possessed by demons. "Show me the coins."

Her hand was shaking as she dropped the six pieces of gold into his palm.

"They're gypsy coins, Tibor. I know. I've seen enough of them." Her throat was raspy from her fight to keep her voice low.

"Yes, they are."

"Why?" Rampaging fear and suspicion caused her body to tremble.

"I don't know why." He took her hand and squeezed it. "But I have an idea where Márta is."

"You do?" Katalin nearly collapsed. "I knew you would. Go get her, Tibor. Please, before something happens to her." She tried not to, but tears filled with terror dropped from her eyes. "She's so little, so innocent."

"I know." He wiped the tears from her eyes, hating whomever had done this to her. "It's going to take some time to get to her though, so please, be patient and trust me."

"I do. You know I do."

He thought about that a lot as he left the hospital. She did trust him. She always had. She had risked a great deal on his behalf: playing with his band, masquerading as Vadrósza, arranging his audition with Zoltán, defending him to everyone—including her husband—against those wrongful accusations of theft. He had never really had a chance to repay her for her continuous unwavering faith in him. He had that chance now and although he knew the consequences of what he was about to do, he did it just the same.

Knowing that if he retrieved Márta he would need someone to care for her on the ride back to Budapest, he asked Judit if she would go with him. While he went to Katalin's room, Judit raced home to tell Gábor what she was about to do and to pack some blankets and formula and diapers and whatever else she thought they might need. When Tibor came out of the hospital, Judit was waiting in the car.

They had both agreed that his Trabant would never survive the journey, so they used Judit's Lada instead. Because it was late and there would be few police out on the roads, Tibor drove. It took them nearly four hours to reach the Romanian border. Since all the other crossings were closed at night, Tibor had been forced to take a longer, more round-about route, circling down toward Gyula, a pass that was open twenty-four hours. After enduring the mandatory search of the car and giving the Romanian guard the expected bribe, he and Judit headed for Mera, a small village outside of Cluj, the capital of Transylvania.

"Why do you think she's in that particular village?" Judit said, refusing to give in to the nervousness she felt about being in Romania—a country that loathed Hungarians and wasn't too fond of Jews—and about being brought into a gypsy camp.

"It's a hunch. Before I left the hospital, I called around and checked out a few places where Márta might have been taken. She wasn't in any of them. By process of elimination, I came up with Mera or Satu Mare."

Once or twice along the way, especially after dawn had begun its ascent, they encountered a gypsy with a wagon or leading a horse along a dirt road. When Tibor stopped and, hoping for information, asked which tribe he belonged to, invariably the man denied he was gypsy. One told him he was Abyssinian.

"Why would he do that?" Judit asked. "He can see you're gypsy. Why hide it?"

"It's habit," Tibor explained. "If you think it's hard on us in Hungary, in Romania gypsies are the lowest form of creature."

By the time they arrived in Mera, home to a tribe of Musicians, it was nearly eight o'clock. Like Báthordomb, Mera was a scrapheap of a town built atop a steep hill. Barnyard animals cackled and oinked and brayed at Judit and Tibor as their car climbed the steep, dusty streets. Tibor paid no attention to the pointed fingers or the questions being hurled at him. He concentrated on finding a specific house. When he did, he parked the car.

"I think it's best if you stay here."

Judit surveyed the scene. Gypsies had swarmed around the car. They were pressing their noses against the windows, talking about her in a language she didn't understand, laughing and screwing their faces into expressions that looked menacing.

"I don't agree," she said, sliding across the seat and exiting on Tibor's side of the car, too unnerved even to open her door. "Whatever's in there, can't be as bad as what's out here."

Tibor chuckled and took Judit's hand. He remembered the first time Katalin had come among his people. She, too, had been frightened. But she had grown to understand the gypsies—as much as any *gorgio* could—and they had come to understand her. Which was why this situation with Márta angered him so. All that effort at bridging cultural gaps, all that time taken to build and generate trust—it was lost now, on both sides.

Leading Judit up the steps and onto the porch of a house that looked as if a huff and a puff would surely blow it down, he prayed that Paprika had been able to get word to the leader of this village and had persuaded him to cooperate.

When Tibor rapped on the door, it opened and a wizened old man stared at the gypsy and his white companion. His name was Imre Almási and he was the head of this community. Nothing went on here that he did not know about.

He and Tibor conversed for a bit in what Judit assumed was Rom. Almási pointed to another house and nodded to several young men who immediately took off in that direction. Tibor and Judit followed, but at a slower pace. Whatever Almási had said, Tibor no longer felt the need to rush. As they walked, he appeared to be planning his next move. Judging by the look on his face, whoever was holed up in that house was in for some serious trouble.

Despite her anxieties, Judit was gaining tremendous respect for Katalin's friend. Though she didn't understand the reasons for the relationship or how it had come into being, she was beginning to understand why Katalin liked Tibor so much. While she had held her tongue during the long ride here, if they found Márta and she was all right, and if his temper had calmed, on the ride back she intended to satisfy her curiosity.

Tibor flung open the door. He strode into the house and headed up the stairs to a rear bedroom. Judit followed closely behind, as did most of the citizens of Mera. Squatting in the center of a large mattress, a swaddled infant sleeping in her lap, was a young gypsy woman. Though Judit had no idea who she was, Tibor knew her. And she knew him.

"Give me the child."

Not a muscle moved. Not an eyelash fluttered. The woman's face was a portrait of defiance.

"Now!" Tibor demanded.

She bared her teeth in an angry snarl and growled her objection to his command, but she complied nonetheless. Tibor took Márta and handed her over to Judit, who anxiously examined the infant.

"She's fine," the gypsy said, spitting at Tibor's feet. "I didn't harm a hair on her precious little head."

"You'd better hope so," he said, his body a mass of contained rage. "If she has suffered at your hand, you shall suffer at mine!"

"Why did you do this?" Judit said, disgusted and uncomprehending. "How could you take another woman's child?"

"She took my husband," Farah flung the words from her mouth as if they were flames. "It was only fair that I take something from her."

"You're sick," Judit said to Farah, clutching Márta to her breast.

"Get me out of here," she said to Tibor, "before I do something I shouldn't."

Without another look at Farah, Tibor steered Judit out of the room, motioned for Almási's young men to come in, and proceeded down the stairs. In Almási's house Judit sponge-bathed Márta, changed her, fed her, and nestled her in a makeshift crib offered her by the gypsy women. It was a large basket stuffed with a fluffy down pillow. Judit spread one of Sarí's blankets over it, placed Márta on it, and thanked the women for their kindness. In the car, they found another basket, this one stuffed with a loaf of Romanian corn-meal bread, some cheese, some cold *mititei* sausages and a drink for the journey home.

"Who was she?" Judit asked, an hour into the ride.

Without blinking, Tibor answered. "My wife, Farah."

He had caught Judit in midswallow. She was so surprised by his answer, she choked on her own saliva.

"Why would she do something like this?" Judit said, unable to accept Farah's answer.

He was about to say, *Because she hates my relationship with Katalin, with Zoltán, with all non-gypsies,* but something told him there was more to it than jealousy.

"I don't know, but the why doesn't matter. What she did was wrong and she's going to have to pay."

"According to our laws or yours?" Judit asked.

"Ours, which in many ways are worse than yours."

His tone was so ominous, it caused Judit to shiver.

"You knew right away she had taken the baby, didn't you?"

Tibor nodded. "The coins were the same as those my mother had hung around her neck on our wedding day."

Again, Judit felt a chill. "How did you know where she had gone?"

"I checked with her family and mine. When they said they hadn't seen her, I realized she must have fled Hungary to avoid the police, and me. Romania would be a natural choice, but then I had to figure out whom she would have trusted enough to hide her. I remembered we used to have a couple in our band who came from Mera. Farah had liked them and they had gotten on with her."

He paused. There was something else, something he wasn't telling her.

"Did this other couple know Katalin? Do they have anything to do with Katalin's baby being taken?"

"Yes and no."

He struggled with his conscience—what to say, how much to reveal. He glanced over at the woman on his right. Having given birth to a baby boy less than four months before, she now had two small children at home, a husband, a job, obligations, and yet she had agreed to go with him in an instant. She would do anything for Katalin, that much was clear. He hoped that included keeping her mouth shut.

"They knew Vadrósza," he said, quietly. "When Farah came to them and said that Vadrósza had given her the baby for safekeeping, they believed her. And because of their affection for Vadrósza, they were more than willing to protect the child."

She heard him, but at first she couldn't believe what she had heard. When she had asked, *"Did this other couple know Katalin?"* he had answered, *"They knew Vadrósza."* Was he telling her they were one and the same?

For the next hour or so, Tibor recounted his meeting with Katalin, during that dark time when Mária lay dying in the hospital. He told Judit how Katalin was when she played with his band, how she was when, quite naturally, she became one of them, when she became Vadrósza.

"The people love her," he said with affection and admiration. "Wherever we play, they wait for her, as if she carries with her some sort of religious message. She's so vivacious, so energetic, and so full of the Magyar spirit, they've come to think of her as someone more than mortal. Especially in the *puszta*. There, they've decided she's the child of Czinka Panna."

Judit's eyebrows arched and an amused laugh escaped her lips. She knew the story of Czinka Panna. A legend in Hungary since the eighteenth century, when the gypsies, known then as Romanichals, were beginning to emerge from their pariah state, she was believed to be the granddaughter of the famed gypsy minstrel Michael Barna. According to this oft-told tale of the *puszta*, she fell in love with one of Hungary's national heroes, Prince Rákóczi.

Though born of the despised gypsy race, her fiddling set her apart and made her a symbol of Hungarian national spirit and aspirations. Unlike most gypsies, Czinka Panna had married her Magyar and settled down with him. When spring came, however, and she saw the Romanichals in the distance, she left her home, her husband, and her children, to wander with her tribe. Only when the mists of autumn rose from the plain did she return.

Czinka Panna became synonymous with the enjoyment of gypsy music, and though Judit had never heard Katalin play cimbalom, it was easy to imagine her friend playing the music of the Cigany with such fervor that all those who listened were immediately bewitched.

Tibor confirmed her suspicions when he said, "When we're in the countryside, things are different from in the city. Magyar peasants may scorn us and treat us badly if they meet us on a dirt road or in a store, but when Magyars feel the need to purge themselves with music, they come to us. They drink and they dance and they become wild with ecstasy." Tibor paused to see if Judit was listening. She was rapt. "There's a Hungarian proverb which says that if you give a Hungarian peasant a glass of water and a gypsy, he will become completely and hopelessly drunk. Vadrósza makes them drunk."

"Perhaps the next time Vadrósza plays with your band, you'll invite me to come along," Judit said seriously.

"I don't know if she'll ever play with us again after this."

Judit looked back over the seat. Márta was sleeping peacefully in her woven crib. Then she looked at Tibor. He had risked a lot going after this child.

"She'll play," Judit said, patting his arm, speaking to him as one friend to another. "Believe me, Tibor, Vadrósza will play again."

"We're very grateful to you," László said to Tibor.

Zoltán stood opposite László on the other side of Katalin's bed, hovering over mother and child. His face was tear-stained, but he was smiling. Judit, exhausted, sat in a chair, Gábor standing behind her. At the foot of the bed, Tibor watched Katalin cuddle her baby, cooing to her, dripping tears onto her, delighting in every movement and sound that she made. Though László had offered him a monetary reward, he had turned it down. This was reward enough.

"I have to go," Tibor said.

"Why?" Katalin's voice was edged with tension. She hadn't thought about it before, but suddenly she feared that he was going to be blamed for Márta's kidnapping, that he would be charged with another crime he hadn't committed. Tibor looked into her eyes and understood.

"Don't worry. I'm all right. I have some business to take care of in Báthordomb."

Off to the side, Judit twitched in her seat. Katalin stole a glance at her. Judit's eyes said to let him go without any further questions.

Tibor said his good-byes and prepared to leave, but Zoltán followed him out into the hall.

"I'll never forget this, Tibor."

"I would do anything for you or Katalin."

"If you hadn't proved that before," Zoltán said, reaching out and hugging Tibor, "you proved it now."

Tibor blushed and quickly turned to go.

"Go do whatever it is you have to do," Zoltán called after him, "but remember, you have a lesson on Wednesday."

Tibor was too emotional to let Zoltán see his face, but he raised his hand, waved, and yelled back, "I'll be there."

Beyond the town of Báthordomb, on the field where Tibor and Farah had been wed, the flames of a campfire spit sparks into the graying dusk. A brisk autumnal wind gusted bunches of withered leaves. This evening no small children played in the field. No women suckled babies or shepherded stock or performed the chores they did at the end of the day. They were at home, peeking out from behind curtained windows, spying on the solemn gathering taking place on the hilltop green.

In a wide circle, on an assortment of improvised chairs, sat a small group of elders known as the *krisatora*. They wore no judicial robes, no powdered wigs, no symbols of the court, yet their faces bore testimony to the solemn duty of judgment. One man sat on a wooden packing crate, another on a metal bucket, a third on a chair with no back. Still the collective spirit was one of dignity and respect for the law of the *Kris*. It was this law that prevented the Rom from descending into savagery, this law which made them a people instead of a herd of wild animals.

Tibor stood to the side of the court surrounded by members of his family. His mother, Tekla, held year-old Jaroka, Tibor's youngest son. His sister Paprika held the hand of his four-year-old daughter, Rosza. Tibor's eldest child, six-year-old Csoka, stood alongside his father, his black eyes staring at the group of men charged with the task of deciding his mother's fate.

Around the campfire the elders smoked quietly, allowing a somber, reflective mood to close around them like an invisible tent. Glasses were distributed. Bottles of red wine were passed. There was some small conversation, but it was meaningless, except as a means of enabling the men to make the transition from spoon-maker or musician or factory worker or blacksmith to jurist. When the mood felt right, one of the men mumbled a few words in a low voice. He poured part of his wine onto the ground in a gesture deliberately void of excessive drama. He was offering a libation to *Mule*, the Ancestor Spirits, inviting them to sit amidst the circle and witness the proceedings that were about to take place.

Normally at a meeting of the *Kris*, a man chosen to act as the tribe's plaintiff would enter the circle and, after paying homage to the assembled Rom, would present either some unresolved questions for the court's consideration or list a number of complaints or *bayura* that needed investigation. This evening, there was only one case on the docket. Lajos Tar, his head bowed by shame and personal anguish, stepped into the circle, his wide-brimmed hat in his hands.

"It is with great humiliation that I stand before you tonight. I am here to announce a defiance of our laws and to accuse one of my family with the crime."

Farah's mother howled, her sorrowful keen filling the night with a woeful dirge. Gyula and his sons held her and attempted to quiet her. Lajos continued.

"The wife of my son Tibor kidnapped the child of a *gorgio*. Though the crime would be severe no matter which child she abducted, this was the kin of a *Romane Gaje*."

In the assembly that stood outside the circle, gasps and whispers abounded. Everyone knew how sacred the bond was between a gypsy and a *Romane Gaje*. Though their reasons were more practical than moral, since gypsies needed friends in the world of the *gaje*, it was a tie that commanded the respect of all gypsies, a bond that was never to be broken.

"She has brought shame to my son and his children, shame to my wife and my children, shame to her parents and shame to her people. My heart is filled with sadness, but I am gypsy and I know the law." The silence grew thick with apprehension. No one moved. No one spoke. No one dared breathe. "*Banishment!*" Lajos shouted, ignoring the plaintive cries of Farah's family and the swooning of the crowd. "*Banishment!*"

Tibor closed his eyes as his father invoked the plea for the ultimate penalty of Gypsy law. Tibor had known from the moment he held those coins in his hand that any action he took would lead to this. He had known that by going after Márta and returning Katalin's child to her, he would be removing his children's mother from them. Pained, he looked at them now. Tekla had pressed the baby's face against her bosom, comforting him, sheltering him from the sight of his grandfather begging for the exile of his daughter-in-law. Rosza had buried her face against Paprika, who had taken Tibor's hand in a show of support. Only Csoka continued to watch the proceedings.

Tibor had explained to him what Farah had done, about the disgrace that she had brought to their family and to their tribe. Despite his age, Csoka understood the gravity of her crime. Because gypsy children were victimized by bigotry almost from the day they were born, the reasons for that bigotry were explained to them at a very tender age. Csoka knew that one of the standard, violent denouncements against gypsies was that in addition to swiping chickens from other men's coops, they stole Christian children from their beds. It pained Csoka to think that his own mother had put a smile on the faces of those *gorgios* who liked to sit around and say "I told you so."

The man who had poured the wine upon the ground stood and

clapped his hands. Two young men of the *kumpania* brought Farah into the center of the circle and then walked away, leaving her alone, unescorted, unprotected. The light from the fire played on her face, alternating dark, mournful shadows with slashes of white heat. Without taking a step toward her, Tibor confronted her with his eyes, refusing to look away or defend himself against the hatred oozing from every pore of her being. Her jaw worked as she gritted her teeth. Her hands were clenched at her sides, her fingers balled into truculent fists. Her onyx eyes narrowed and blazed with an anger that threatened revenge more powerfully than any words ever could.

The *krisatori* commanded that Farah stand before him. She moved with leaden feet, slow to accept what she knew was coming.

"Do you wish to offer a defense?" he asked.

Farah shook her head. She could not say what she wanted to say, so she said what they expected to hear. "What I did was indefensible."

These men of the *kumpania*, in their scruffy vests and dusty pants and knotted *diklos*, were as stern and unbending as the most magisterial men on the bench. Their verdicts were final. The Rom had no police force, no prisons, no executioners to enforce their judgments, but tradition demanded that they be accepted as valid and binding by the convicted as well as his kinsmen. What the elders said, the gypsies obeyed.

The spokesman emptied the rest of his wine into the dust. The dark red mixed with the dirt, looking like blood that had been spilt.

"You have dishonored the Rom," he said in a voice that allowed no debate, no challenge to its authority. "You have committed a crime that could invite the strong arm of the *gaje* law to punish our people for something you did on your own."

The wind whistled behind the *krisatori* like a chorus in a classical tragedy. A whirl of dust blew into the fire, smothering the flames, changing brilliantly colored sparks to black ribbons of smoke. The leader raised his hands, allowing his arms to describe the circle in which he stood as well as the larger circle of gypsies behind him. When he spoke it was not as an ordinary gypsy man, or even as one appointed a judge. When he spoke, it was as the voice of many generations.

"You are banished from the *kumpania*. You will shun all places where the Rom gather and they will shun you. From this day, you are no longer one of us. You are no longer Rom. This we have decided."

Farah's body lurched forward as if she had been stabbed. She grabbed at her chest and stumbled to regain her ground. No one assisted her. Tekla and Paprika led Farah's children toward the village. Farah cried for her baby and called out to Rosza, but Tekla and Paprika continued on their way without looking back.

"Csoka!" Farah screamed after him, but he refused to stop. "Csoka!" She begged him to come with her, but he never lost step with Tekla and the others. Though she had expected this verdict, indeed had known from the first that this would be her end, watching her small son walk away from her, with his back so rigid and unyielding, was by far the sharpest blow of all.

One by one the *kumpania* dispersed, walking by her as if she didn't exist, because for them she longer did. Tibor was the last. He knew he couldn't speak to her, but even if he could have, he didn't know what he would have said. He just looked at her, watching as legions of emotion battled on her face. Fear and defiance and anger and an ungodly hurt campaigned against each other. To her credit, she fought to maintain her dignity. She would not permit him to see the extent of her desolation.

"You think you're rid of me," Farah shouted, straining against the urge to throw herself at him and claw out his heart. "You'll never be rid of me."

It was not without great pain that Tibor turned from the woman he had married, the woman with whom he had sired three children. He was almost to the edge of the field when he heard her invoke the *armaya*, boosting her fists into the air and shouting so those who had judged her could hear her curse: "May I redden the earth with my blood, if I don't avenge this expulsion. Those who were responsible will pay for what they did, and pay dearly."

As for the people in the village, Farah's curse fell on deaf ears. Because they knew she would not challenge the law, they ignored her malediction. The only one who took it seriously was Tibor. Her hex was not aimed at the children of Rom. And though she didn't name her enemy, Tibor knew exactly whose face was targeted in the sight of her gun.

For months, Katalin refused to leave her daughter's side. On those occasions when she absolutely had to go out—to attend a political function with László or to perform before visiting dignitaries on behalf of the Hungarian government—she accepted help from Ilona or Judit or Zoltán, but no one else. She knew her obsessiveness was not helping her efforts to prove to László that a child was a blessing and not a burden, but for a long while it was beyond her ability to change.

After nearly ten months of uneventful confinement, she received a formal invitation to perform with the London Philharmonic. Judit was adamant that she accept.

"You can't hide forever," she said. "That was a one-time incident by some crazy who's been tried, convicted, and banished. You have to forget it or you're going to drive yourself nuts and smother Márta."

"I don't want to do that," Katalin admitted.

"Besides, it's time you got back to your music. You're not the same without it," Judit said. "And I think it would please László to have things return to what he thinks is normal."

"He's not one who takes well to disruption, that's true."

"Disruption. What a strange way to describe fatherhood."

"Don't start." The last thing Katalin wanted was to. debate her husband with Judit. "He didn't plan this child. She was thrust upon him."

Judit had expected this. Katalin refused to countenance any comment about László's lack of paternal instincts. She deluded herself by calling it loyalty. Judit knew it was guilt.

"Plan or not, Márta is hardly a burden. She's an adorable little girl. He should be doting on her."

As Gábor doted on his children. "He's adjusting . . . slowly."

"If he moved any slower, he'd be at a dead halt," Judit said.

Katalin busied herself refilling Judit's coffee cup and then her own.

"Well, I think you may be right about accepting this concert," she said brightly, ending one discussion by starting another. "I think it would be good for me and good for Márta."

"It would be great!"

"Whom could I get to stay with her?"

"Mama Judit will get you a nurse from the hospital. That's what I do."

"I could handle that," Katalin said, processing the idea, coming to a conclusion, and making a decision all in a matter of seconds. "A nurse would be good. Performing again would be good. I'll tell László tonight. Tomorrow I'll arrange everything else."

Katalin didn't have to bother making any arrangements because László wouldn't hear of her performing outside Hungary.

"You wanted a baby? You wanted to be a mother. Be one!" he said, speaking to her more sharply than she ever remembered.

"I am," she said, angered by his implied criticism. "And a damn good one at that!"

"Then how can you leave Márta in a stranger's care while you go off to London?"

"Stop making it sound as if I'm going to a party. I'd be performing in a concert. That's what I do. I'm a concert pianist. Or have you forgotten that?"

"That's what you *were*. Now you are a mother and a wife. It's time you remembered that!"

An hour later she was still shaking, still staggered by the realization that he had forbidden her to play. Moreover, he had forbidden her to leave the country.

How dare he! She paced her bedroom, a prisoner married to her jailer. How dare he make being a mother and a pianist mutually exclusive! Every woman in Hungary combined motherhood and a job. It was the communist way! Why was he, the great defender of the socialistic system, insisting that she be different?

"Because his mother abandoned him, that's why," Katalin muttered, thoroughly fed up with the consequences of László's youth.

She had spent years trying to compensate for the damage Livia had done to her son's psyche. She had tiptoed around anything she thought might resurrect the pain László's mother had caused him, but she was growing weary from the effort. Besides, her priorities were different now; she was different. She had a child to worry about. And she had her own happiness to consider.

Though she would never have admitted it to anyone, not even Judit, she had little love left for László. And she was certain he had little left for her. He wanted to possess her, that was obvious. He was passionate about her, that too, was obvious. But he didn't love her. Katalin often wondered if he ever had. If he had, she was always a distant second to his ambition. She was his wife, but communism was his mistress and on her he lavished all his attention and all his talent. Even now, when reformers were becoming more vocal, László continued to preach the Party line, closing his ears to all talk of change.

Yet change was occurring all around him. In 1985, Konstantin Chernenko had died and Mikhail Gorbachev became the new Soviet leader, the youngest ever. Since Gorbachev's ascendency, though his public stance on human rights had remained the same, professional listeners claimed they heard signs of softening. In April of '86, the accident at Chernobyl released deadly radiation into the atmosphere and a plague of terror throughout Eastern Europe. Hungarian farmers compelled to destroy tainted crops and Hungarian citizens facing food shortages and financial deficits from the loss of those crops suddenly became environmentalists. When the government announced a joint venture with Czechoslovakia to build a dam at Nagymaros to harness the Danube so it could be tapped for energy, protests abounded. László was outraged.

Any softening of the Party line, any tolerance of dissidence, outraged him. As László saw it, this new patience in Hungary had not come about because men like him had undergone a conversion, but because the regime was in desperate need of loans from Western banks. They were subjugating socialistic principle to the capitalistic dollar. They were selling out, becoming traitors to their own cause.

Because Katalin counted herself among the ranks of the reformers, by definition she had always known that László believed her to be a traitor. She had assumed that he had kept those thoughts to himself. The day after their argument she found out how wrong she was. She had decided that she would not be bullied about something as personal and as important as her career. In an act of total defiance, she went for a visa. Immigration denied her application.

"How could you do that to me?" she demanded of László that night.

"I don't know what you're talking about." It infuriated her that he continued to eat his dinner while she reported what had happened to her.

"You told them not to issue me a visa, didn't you?"

"I did no such thing."

"Is my name on their list of oppositionists?"

"I don't know. Should it be?"

"As a matter of fact, yes!" she said, pounding her fist on the table for emphasis. "Absolutely!"

László put down his fork and stared at her. His eyes narrowed, intensifying the heat of his anger, but Katalin was on a tear. Her face was flushed and her voice bordered on the shrill. Despite those signs of indiscipline, her speech remained clear and concise, her message blunt and directed.

"I am opposed to a system that refuses to let me ply my trade. I am opposed to a system that would rather keep me prisoner than allow me to bring music to those who want to listen, no matter where they are. It's music. It's not politics. I don't want to participate in arms talks or military meetings or economic summits. I don't want to argue philosophy. I want to play the piano and I am opposed to anyone and anything that won't let me do that!"

Instead of immediately answering her charge, László raised his napkin to his lips, blotted them, replaced the napkin on the table and rose from his chair, taking his time, acting as if they had been discussing nothing more important than whether to have dessert now or later.

"Everything is political, Katalin. Even music."

Having said that, he left the room. Minutes later, she heard him leave the house. When the door closed, it sounded as if the original had been replaced by one with bars and a lock. In a way, it had.

Days grew into weeks, which turned into months. Yet the passage of time had done nothing to quell Katalin's fury. Like a seedling, it had taken root in that argument, spreading, flourishing, becoming something almost beyond control. In order to sublimate her rage, Katalin practiced endlessly. Because habit demanded that she establish a goal, she set about mastering the Beethoven sonata cycle. As was her wont, she didn't simply study them, she immersed herself in them: thirty-two sonatas composed for the piano, each one a landmark of the form, each a technical challenge, each an emotional purgation. Again, her obsessive dedication proved her salvation.

Between Márta and Beethoven, Katalin was able to retain a certain equilibrium. Mother and daughter strolled past the shops along Váci utca with Judit and her two children; they went ice skating on the frozen boat basin in City Park; they visited museums and parks and baked cookies. Because of Márta, Katalin shopped for food and prepared meals and executed the ordinary chores of everyday life. Without Márta, she might have withdrawn from life, retreating solely into her music. Yet when she needed it, the music was there, just as it had always been there. She used it to make her happy, to accompany her when she cried. She used it as a release for her anger, as a sedative for her nerves. She used it as a substitute for a marriage, as a vehicle for reassembling broken dreams. Eventually, she intended to use it as her ticket to freedom.

Throughout this difficult period, Zoltán had proved a limitless source of support. He visited at least twice a week, more often if László was out of town. Though at first he asked no questions, when Katalin's mood became increasingly somber he demanded that she tell him what was going on inside the Böhm household. Initially, she toyed with the notion of sugarcoating her circumstances, but if she wanted to leave Hungary—and the longer the ban against her travel privileges remained intact, the more emigration loomed as her only alternative—she needed to know if Zoltán would come with her.

"I don't want you to answer me right away, Papa," she said, leaning against the side of the pool at the Gellért Baths, holding onto Márta, who was splashing about. "I don't know how I'm going to do it, or when, or even who's going to help me, but this can't continue. If an opportunity presents itself, I'd like to take it. But I won't go without you."

Zoltán lay back and floated a bit while he mulled over what she said. He loved the baths, especially here in the maze of marble tunnels beneath the Gellért Hotel. Nothing was more relaxing or restorative than a few hours inside the cavernous Edwardian bathing hall with its golden light and steamy atmosphere, its potted palms and towering columns.

Though the Gellért was no longer the queen of Budapest the way it had been in the thirties when the Duke and Duchess of Windsor had gamboled here, even in its faded state it remained a mecca for those who enjoyed the sybaritic pleasure of warm water, lively chatter, and a sense of history. Here, during the second century, the Romans soothed their ills, bringing their aches and pains to the minerals that bubbled up from the earth below.

If only the waters could cure the aches and pains of the heart, Zoltán thought as he looked at the sadness in his daughter's eyes. "Can't István help?"

"No." She said it quickly, confirming his suspicion that despite her silence a torch still burned. "He's a congressman now. It could compromise his position to do something for a citizen of an Iron Curtain country."

Zoltán nodded his acceptance of her explanation. Why wouldn't he? Katalin had never confided in him anything about her assignation with Steven or about the letter she had written ending their relationship. She hadn't wanted Márta at the center of any controversy, and so she had simply eliminated the possibility. Having done so, however, she wouldn't feel comfortable asking Steven for his help in getting away from László.

"I might be able to ask his friend Clarke Estridge for help, but I need a plan and I need everything to be in order."

"Thirty years ago, Zsuzsanna asked me to come with her."

"I remember," Katalin said, shivering in the warm water at the memory of the dank, raw cold of that deserted vestry. "You said you had to be here when Miklós returned. Papa," she said, patting his arm gently, "Uncle Miklós isn't coming back to us." She paused. The wound wasn't new, yet the pain remained fresh. "It's only you and me and Márta and Aunt Zsuzsanna. She's dying to see you again, Papa. And I know what it would mean for you to see her."

He nodded. He tried to imagine how his sister looked now. All he could see was how she had looked then, pleading with him to go with her and Mihai, pulling the strings of their attachment until he thought he would choke from the strain of loving her and letting go.

"Over the years, there have been many political prisoners who have returned from the camps. Either they were released or they escaped and entered the country with falsified papers. I went to see each and every one of them. I spoke to them. I asked about Miklós. I asked if anyone had seen him or heard of him. None had." He shook his head, as if he had just been told of his brother's death. "You're right, Katya. He's not coming back. If you find a way, I'll go with you."

Katalin threw her arms around him, nearly drowning the three of them.

"You and that precious child are all I have, Katya," he said. "When you were in New York, I learned that I could live without you. I also learned I didn't like it."

Several weeks later, Zoltán visited the house on Rose Hill. He came carrying a suitcase and wearing an enormous smile.

"I have three surprises for you," he said to Katalin, taking her by the hand and leading her to her music room.

He was positively bubbly. She began to wonder if one of those surprises wasn't about Madame Anna Kovalik, the piano pedagogue at the Academy he had taken to dinner and the opera several times. She hated herself for the fillip of anxiety she felt. If Zoltán had become attached to someone, he might not be so eager to leave. Immediately, she chided herself for her selfishness and demanded her mood elevate enough to match his.

"What's in that bag?" she asked, curiosity taking over.

"Patience, my child." He opened the suitcase, but only a trifle, not enough for her to see inside. He reached in and grabbed on to something. "This is my first surprise." He pulled his hand out of the suitcase and waved a baton in front of her. "I have been appointed head conductor of the Budapest Symphony Orchestra."

Katalin was in shock. For at least two minutes, she stared at him in disbelief. Then, she exploded with joy, leaping up from her seat, hugging him, kissing him, congratulating him on his new appointment. He laughed along with her and then encouraged her to take her seat.

"Surprise number two." Again, he reached into the suitcase. This time, a sheet of paper and a glossy photograph filled his hand. "As a thank-you for saving my granddaughter and as a reward for his work and his exceptional talent, my first act as conductor was to invite Tar Tibor to join the violin section."

This time, Katalin was too emotional to shout or leap or do anything except stare at her father and thank God for him. For him to do this was to risk losing something he had just gained. She knew he must have had to fight long and hard for Tibor. That he did so would have been enough for her. That he prevailed was nothing short of a miracle.

"For surprise number three, I need my Márta here."

Without asking any questions, Katalin went to fetch her little girl. It only took a matter of moments. Márta's favorite person in the entire world was Papa Zoltán. She squealed as he lifted her up off the ground and spun her around like a gyro. They played for a while and then he asked her to join her mommy on the banquette. He told her he had a surprise for both of them in the suitcase. Márta scampered into Katalin's lap, her eyes wide with anticipation as if Zoltán were about to pull an entire circus out of that one small bag.

"You're now going to see something your Mama has never seen," he said, speaking to Márta.

He turned around, putting his back to them. When he faced them again, he was holding his Guarneri. Katalin gasped and then bit her lip, fearful that he was under a spell and if she spoke it would be broken. He raised the violin and tucked it under his chin. Slowly, he began to play. Katalin held her breath as the fingers of his left hand pressed against the bridge and the fingers of the right led the bow over the four strings of his violin. Slowly, seductively, the sounds of Tchaikovsky's "Andante Cantabile" filled the room. She could barely see him through her tears. How many years had she spent listening to recordings of her father, the famous Zoltán Gáspár? How many times had she played her version of his interpretation of Paganini's "Caprices?" To hear him and see him at the same time filled her with an emotion so powerful, it could only be described as religious. She was grateful and astounded and awestruck at the sight of him. Though she could tell that he lacked the technical fire he had possessed as a youth and that his fingering and phrasing were labored, he was playing the violin. *He was playing the violin!*

When he finished, she and Márta applauded until their hands were red. He smiled, but not without caution. He was concerned about what she would say, about how he had done.

"This is the most wonderful moment of my life," she said with reverence. "I've never heard such beautiful music! I never thought I'd see this or hear you except on those recordings I know you know I stole." His smile broadened. "How? How did you get your fingers to do what they did?"

She pulled him onto the banquette with her and took his hands in hers, studying them, noticing for the first time that his fingers looked different, straighter, less mangled.

"I didn't do much," he said quietly. "It was Gábor. One day, while you and László were in New York, he asked me if I had ever considered having my hands operated on. I never had. He told me it wasn't a complicated procedure and that he thought I should do it. He didn't promise me anything. And I didn't expect anything." His voice stumbled over a lump in his throat. "His hands have magic in them, Katya. Look what they did for my hands."

He held them up. They still looked crooked, but it was not how they looked that mattered. It was what they could do. He wiggled his fingers. Márta, thinking it was a game, followed suit.

"Why didn't you tell me when I came home?"

"I wanted to tell you in my own time and in my own way."

She reached over and hugged him very close. "And it was a beautiful way indeed. I loved every last note."

"I'm glad."

"Do you want to perform again?"

"Want to? Yes. Intend to, no." He shook his head and chuckled as Márta began to play a secretive childlike game with his fingers. "I'd love to perform again. No one should know better than you the thrill of standing before an audience and entrancing them with your music. But I have standards and my playing doesn't come up to those standards."

"Does that bother you?"

"It might, except that I'm so grateful to be able to make any sounds at all, I'm content to count my blessings and be done with it. From now on, my performing will be done on the conductor's podium. I'll save my violin playing for very small, very special audiences." He kissed Márta on the tip of her nose and Katalin on each of her cheeks. "I leave the larger audiences to you."

His words taunted her for days. Unwittingly, he had hit upon the one thing she had not been able to compensate for—performing. She had Márta. She had her music. She had Zoltán and Andras and Ilona and Judit and Gábor. She had even learned to accept the compromised state of her marriage and function within it. But she had never found a way to fill the emptiness created by a lack of performing. By cutting off her access to the concert stage, László had excised a part of her being. It was as if there were a gaping hole at her very core.

Katalin knew of only one way to plug that depression. It had always been a risk before. Now with a child and with the strain that existed between her and László, the risk was increased, but she had only so much restraint.

Three days later, with László in Sofia on business and Márta safely ensconced at Judit's, Vadrósza returned to the *puszta*. Like her spiritual ancestor, Czinka Panna, a legend was beginning to grow up around her. In the countryside, where the thieving hand of socialism dug the deepest and life was the most difficult, the peasants had begun to regard Vadrósza as a spirit who would appear only to those who believed.

Despite the winds of change, these were hard times in Hungary. Inflation was becoming an insatiable beast. Radiation had sullied the earth and the air and the waters. Politicians spoke about imposing income taxes and sales taxes and about economic austerity. On the Great Plain, where economic austerity had always been a way of life, in the region where her father had been born and his music was first played, hundreds of people gathered. They brought blankets or makeshift chairs or sat on the bare ground. They stood. They climbed trees and sat on limbs. In the Hortobágy where medieval tales of cities in the clouds and phantom forests and a huge lake cloaked in a gray mist abounded, the masses waited for Vadrósza.

Anticipation mounted when Tibor and his band set up the instruments and took their places. There was a quick buzz of conversation and then a sudden, expectant silence. Enthusiasm turned to frenzy as Vadrósza walked to the cimbalom. A roar of welcome greeted her. She smiled and acknowledged the enormous crowd, most of whom were waving and grinning and shouting to her. Then, cueing the audience, she looked to Tibor. He was the *primás*. When they were quiet and he was ready, she would play.

Within minutes, the air crackled with the heat of a gypsy *csárdás*. Katalin's hands cavorted over the metal strings of the cimbalom. Long dangling earrings bounded off her neck and golden chains rattled against her chest as her body swayed with the passionate rhythms of the Rom. Hundreds of people clapped and stomped and cheered. They had been transported to that magical place where sound controlled emotion the way the moon ruled the tides.

Powerful waves of sensation tugged at everyone, including Katalin. Feelings rose and crashed, ebbed and then rose again. For Katalin, this was the summit, the emotional climax, the reason she performed—to experience that special moment when the music filled her and excited her and completed her. That moment when she became who these hundreds of people believed she was—the gypsy spirit of the *puszta*, Vadrósza.

34

Washington, D.C., February 1988

Colton Garvey was a nasty man, but because he was a man with a mission, he believed he had God on his side and the right to do whatever he wanted. With big-time Texas money in his bank account and a good-old-boy political network that stretched all across the South, Garvey was a power to be reckoned with. Though others with his resources would have engraved their names on a ballot, Garvey wanted no part of elected office. He preferred the behind-the-scenes action, the back-room juggling that was the real Washington. Why put yourself in the spotlight where you're accountable to the electorate, when backstage you can wield more power than almost any official and be accountable to no one?

Garvey's office was exactly what Steven had expected: leather furniture, an enormous oak desk, a collection of guns in a glass wall case, an array of photographs attesting to his far-flung connections, and, hidden somewhere amidst the drapery and the crown moldings, a camera. Waiting for Steven were several other guests, also precisely what he had expected—members of Garvey's special cadre of bootlickers. On Capitol

Hill they were known as the Tailors, because they were experts at altering the facts. One didn't ignore them, but given the choice, one avoided having any contact with them.

"And to what do I owe the pleasure," Steven said, shaking Garvey's hand, nodding to the boys, wishing he had worn his flack jacket instead of his navy blue pinstripe.

"I thought we might have a discussion about your future."

One thing about Garvey, Steven thought, he came right to the point. "And since when does my future concern you?"

"Since you seem to be on the road to being the most popular man in the U.S. of A." He laughed, but it was a hollow sound that came from the front of his mouth, not his gut. "If I see your picture on the front page of one more newspaper or see your face on one more TV news program, well, to be honest, Kardos, I'm gonna be ill."

The boys laughed. Steven smiled, but if he had had a weapon in his pocket, he would have cocked the trigger.

"I will say, your covers for *Time* and *Newsweek* were mighty attractive." He laced his fingers together, tossed his feet up onto his desk, leaned back in his chair, and rested his hands on his lean, four-mile-a-morning abdomen. "You're a handsome guy. The ladies love you."

Again the boys laughed. Steven didn't. "Okay, Colton, let's cut to the chase. What's this all about?"

The feet came off the desk, the chair came to an upright position, and the smile left Garvey's face.

"You're becoming a pain in my ass, Kardos. That's what this is all about. You stand up on the floor of the House and whatever you say is front-page news. You give a speech at some rubber chicken dinner and I have to see it repeated on the news while I eat my dinner." He sucked air through his teeth, as if some bit of food still remained between his incisors and his bicuspids. "I have a candidate to elect, Kardos, and even though I don't think your guy has a shot at the White House, the polls are beginning to say that the one smart thing the Dems did was to toss your name out there as a possibility for State. The minute you were added to the stew, the ticket became a lot tastier. Suddenly, there was slippage in the crossovers and the undecideds. We asked people why and guess what they said?"

"I haven't the foggiest," Steven said, delighted to hear that he was having the desired impact.

"The public thinks you've got all the answers."

"Maybe I do," Steven said. By now he had guessed where this meeting was headed. He just didn't know how Garvey was going to do it.

"Well, you see, that's what worries me. The last thing I want is you making your candidate look better than he is because that makes my job more difficult."

"Hard work never hurt anyone, Colton."

"I know that, but I'm the kind of guy who likes things to be neat. Know what I mean? I don't like complications. When things get bollixed up, I get itchy. And when I get itchy, I know you're going to find this hard to believe, I get ornery. And when I get ornery, sometimes I just start swinging. Now, you're a helluva nice guy and I respect you. In fact I wish you were on our side, but you're not. And so . . ."

"You'd like me to lower my profile."

"Hell yes! As a matter of fact, I would." Garvey nodded and thrust his index finger in Steven's direction, shaking it, emphasizing his point. "It's not a big deal, really. I just want you to try and restrain yourself whenever the urge comes to criticize the administration or to challenge something my candidate says."

"What if I don't give a damn what you want?"

"Now, now. Don't be that way, Steven. I don't want to hurt you."

"But you would if you had to and you wouldn't think twice about it."

"Damn right!" He grinned and pounded his desk. He liked a man who understood what's what.

Suddenly, a thought that had been hovering in Steven's subconscious moved forward. Clearly, Garvey had dredged up something he planned to use as a tool to persuade Steven to do as he wished. What it was, what sort of damage it would inflict, Steven didn't know. If he had to hazard a guess, it was formidable enough to make his life uncomfortable but not potent enough to completely demolish his career. If his assessment was correct, he had two choices. He could capitulate to Garvey's demands, muzzle himself, and avoid a complete dismantling of his power base; or he could turn this entire situation around and use Garvey's overeagerness to silence him to his advantage. Though he hadn't meant to, Colton Garvey was about to do Steven the biggest favor of his life.

Vienna had changed Steven's life. Being together with Katalin had proved to him that they could no longer be apart. While he understood that both of them had obligations and responsibilities and ties that wouldn't come undone easily, they had shrunk in significance. The single important thing to Steven was that he find a way for them to be together.

For months he had searched for a way to get to Katalin. Then Katalin's letter had arrived. Though at first sight it had upset him, further reflection had only confirmed his initial opinion. He knew she intended it to be a good-bye and had tried to make it sound like a finalization of something that she felt had never been, but he refused to read it that way. He knew Katalin better than that. All he had to do was think about Vienna, to remember how right she had felt in his arms and he knew that her letter was a phony. It wasn't a good-bye, it was a loving release, Katalin's way of letting him go so he could live his life without guilt or encumbrance, so he could continue to climb the political ladder without feeling he had to look back. What she didn't understand—what he had to make her understand—was that until they were together, he would always be looking back.

Not a day went by that he didn't think about her, that he didn't concoct a plan that would untangle them from the present and free them for the future he believed they had always been meant to have. The glitch in all of his plans was always the same—she couldn't get out of Hungary, he couldn't get in. Until now.

"Tell the boys to leave," Steven said in a clipped, authoritative tone. "And shut off your peeping eye. I'm about to make you one of those offers you've heard so much about."

"The kind you can't refuse?" Garvey said, intrigued yet unsettled. This was his show. When had Steven taken control of the floor?

"Exactly," Steven said, noting the gleam in Garvey's eye, hoping he wasn't about to deal with a marked deck.

Garvey waved his hand and the Tailors excused themselves.

When they were alone, and Garvey had switched off the camera, Steven said, "How would you like it if I got out of your way altogether?"

"What does that mean?"

"I tell the party to stop hinting that I would be their Secretary of State, I resign my Congressional seat, and you make me ambassador to Hungary."

Garvey was so stunned he laughed. "You're kidding, right? You're telling me you'd willingly vacate your power base as Whip of the House to be an ambassador?"

"That's what I said."

"Have you lost it, Kardos? Going from Whip to ambassador is a staircase down. Why the hell would you want to do that?"

"The why doesn't matter, and frankly, I don't know why you would give a damn. I should think you'd be delighted. Out of sight, out of mind, out of the paper. You couldn't get a better deal if you'd thought of it yourself."

"That's why I don't trust it. What are you up to?"

"Absolutely nothing." Steven lifted his hands above the desk, as if to show Garvey there was nothing up his sleeve. "If I were you I'd take this deal and I'd be happy about it."

"You're not me." Garvey squinted at Steven, wishing he could see inside the man's head. "I'm not happy with things that don't make sense."

"It makes a lot of sense, Colton. You want me to keep my mouth shut for political reasons. I want to be ambassador to Hungary for personal reasons. Believe me, Colton, it's a good deal all around. Now, are you going to take it or leave it?"

Garvey reached into his pocket, pulled out his hankie, and waved it like a flag of surrender. "I don't get it, but you're right. I can't refuse it." He stuck out his hand, anxious to conclude the deal before he woke up and found it was all a dream.

"Before we finalize this little transaction, there's one lingering bit of business to take care of."

Garvey's hand fell onto the desk. "I knew there was a catch."

"And I know you. You didn't come to this meeting empty-handed, Colton. You've got something stuffed in your back pocket and I want to know what it is. What exactly do you think you have on me?"

Colton Garvey's modus operandi was to find the smallest needle in the largest haystack and stick you with it wherever it would hurt the most. Steven couldn't imagine which haystack Garvey had been rolling around in.

"I have nothing on you," he said, his voice tinged with disappointment.

"Then what made you think you could twist my arm?"

Garvey leaned across his desk. His thin lips disappeared as his mouth spread in a wicked grin.

"I've got stuff on your wife that'd make your hair curl."

Steven met Matthew at Matthew's apartment. He didn't want anyone around when they discussed what had transpired in Garvey's office. He laid it out simply, without artifice or a lot of defensive color. He told Matthew what he had done and why.

"I'm sorry I did this without discussing it with you, but the opportunity presented itself and I grabbed it."

Steven had expected Matthew to be astonished with the news of his resignation, astonished and disappointed. His face registered neither of those responses. Instead, he laughed.

"You really are a romantic, aren't you?"

"You're taking this awfully well. I come in here and tell you I just committed political suicide and you think it's romantic?"

"How else would you describe it?" Matthew still had a smile on his lips. "Relax, baby brother, I understand and, surprise, surprise, I applaud you. I only hope it works out the way you want."

"Me too." It was Steven's turn to smile. "I have no idea what I'm going to do once I get there, but at least Katalin and I will be on the same soil. Somehow, we'll work it out from there."

"And what about Cynthia?"

"Then pack your bags, brother dear. It looks like we're going home to Budapest!"

"Budapest?" Cynthia stared at him as if he had lost his mind. "Are you mad? I'm not leaving Washington to go live in Budapest!" Cynthia threw down the book she had been reading in disgust. "And why would you agree to something like that? Why would you want to give up your position as Whip to become an ambassador?"

"I didn't say I wanted to. I said I had to."

Since Steven couldn't tell her the whole truth, he had decided to tell her half the truth; that the opposition wanted him out of the way and, twisting the tale, that they had made him the proverbial offer.

Cynthia steepled her hands, touching fingertips together. Tapping them against each other, she considered her husband. He should have been devastated at losing his position. If not that, he should have been angry or disappointed or a dozen other things rather than calm and collected.

"Does this have anything to do with your favorite Hungarian dish, the scrumptious Katalin Gáspár?"

Steven would have liked nothing more than to respond, Yes! but the worst thing he could do for Katalin would be to put her in Cynthia's mouth.

"Absolutely nothing. I didn't pick the place. I didn't pick the position. I didn't do anything except agree to agree."

"How could you?"

"Colton Garvey gave me very little choice in the matter."

Steven took off his jacket and draped it over a chair. A maid knocked on the door and brought him the coffee he had requested. His head was pounding from too much scotch, not enough to eat, and too many lies and secrets.

"Garvey? What does that slime have to do with this?" Cynthia, like everyone else in Washington, knew Garvey's reputation. He made the careers of a few by ruining many. She also knew that she had an awful lot of ghosts rattling around in her closet.

"Everything. He's the one who made me the offer and he's the one who explained the reasons I wouldn't want to refuse."

"And what might those reasons be?"

There was something perverse in watching Cynthia squirm. It was a comment on the current state of their marriage that Steven was enjoying revealing these bits of information one by one. Long ago, he had concluded that he had never loved Cynthia, but there had been passion, respect, mutual admiration, and shared goals. Over the past few years, Cynthia had chipped away at each of those bricks until, now, the foundation of their union was as fragile as a house of cards.

"Let's just say that you had one too many lovers." He said it slowly, keeping his eyes fixed on her face. There was a blink, a nearly imperceptible blink, and then nothing. If someone had confronted him about instances of errant behavior in his past, he could not have covered it as well.

"One never has too many lovers," Cynthia said pointedly. "Especially when one's needs are not being satisfied at home."

"I agree."

Steven noted another blink, this time accompanied by a quick downturn of her lips. He had surprised her with that comment, just as he knew he would. Since Cynthia rarely looked at herself through clear, untinted glasses, she rarely saw the whole picture. She saw scenes in which she was wronged, clips in which she had been denied, but not those occasions when she had been the offender, when she had been the one to inflict pain. In her drama, she was the only one entitled to extracurricular activities. It would never dawn on her that he would find her lacking.

"If that's the way you feel, then why should I bother going with you?" Deference, even in the guise of petulance, was unusual for Cynthia. She appeared uncomfortable in the role.

"The way I feel has nothing to do with it." Steven refused to play her game. He was not going to comfort her by complimenting her on her sexuality or reassure her by swearing he had never strayed from her perfectly feathered nest. He needed her to believe that they were in this predicament because of her. "If I go and you stay, it invites questions. The press will ask and Garvey will be only too happy to answer. Trust me, Cynthia. You don't want him to do that."

"How do I know that going with you will make me happier than staying here?"

"You don't, but let me tell you." He approached the chaise where she sat glowering at him, rested his hands on the tufted arms and leaned over her until he was only inches away, "Life is a series of choices, my darling. Everyone is faced with them. Everyone has to decide what to do with them. What's happened here is that you've made more bad choices than good. So, on this go-around, you have no choice at all."

Within hours of landing, Steven and Matthew left the embassy on Szabadság tér. It was a bittersweet journey they took, strolling around

Liberation Square, along Münnich Ferenc Avenue toward Kossuth Lajos tér, the square that housed the Parliament, the place in which their parents had been shot. As they entered the large plaza, they half-expected to be greeted by the sight of thousands of people crammed together on the cobblestones, by the sounds of gunfire from rooftops and cannons on the noses of Soviet tanks. Instead, the square was empty. Except for a few birds fluttering about the statues of Kossuth and Rákóczi, the air was quiet.

The brothers walked in silence, each lost in his own assortment of memories. Matthew's eyes remained riveted on the ground, as if he feared that by looking up he might stumble on the bullet-torn bodies of Béla and Margit. It had been thirty-one years, yet he could see their blood staining the gray stones, turning from red to brown as the blood dried and their lives slipped away. He could still see those gruesome black machines with guns mounted on turrets and huge red stars painted on the sides, facing into the square. From the rooftops of adjacent buildings, AVO with rifles and machine guns pointed down into the crowd. He saw people running in all directions. He saw bodies being trampled and bodies being dragged. Worst of all, with the twenty-twenty vision of hindsight, what he saw most clearly was that on that day, in that place, at that time, no one had stood a chance.

Steven heard more than he saw. He heard cries of pain and screams of terror. He heard the explosive pop of guns and the sirens of ambulances that raced into the square and within seconds were rendered helpless. He heard the alarm ringing in Katalin's voice when she had found them and tried to get them to go with her. He heard his shoes clomping against the rock-hard ground as he raced to reach his parents before death claimed them. He heard his heart pounding in his chest as he neared the spot where he had last seen them. And he heard the horrifying silence of their lifeless bodies as they lay sprawled at his feet.

Standing here now, an adult with experience and knowledge he hadn't had when he'd stood here as a child, Steven knew that entering this square had been like crossing the Rubicon. For a thousand years, the Hungarians had suffered oppression at one hand and then another: the Romans, the Turks, the Austrians, the Germans, the Soviets. History should have taught them that when they raised their arms in rebellion and pointed guns at their enemies in defense of freedom, there would be no turning back, that blood would be shed and lives would be lost. Perhaps his parents had known all that, but at nine years of age, when he and his brother and his sister, Vera, had marched into this square, Steven had honestly believed that freedom was possible. What struck him now was that all these years later, with all his experience and knowledge and insight, he still believed that freedom for Hungary was possible.

Matthew turned toward Steven, his eyes asking a question. Steven answered it with a quick nod. Slowly, the two men exited the square, turning toward Széchenyi rakpart. At the quay, their pace slowed to a funereal gait, slowing even more as they reached the tiny patch of grass that covered the grave where they had buried their mother and father. Wordlessly, they bowed their heads, mumbled a hasty, halting prayer and crossed themselves.

Afterward, they found a bench near the river. As the Danube rolled by, they looked across to the Buda Hills.

"It's beautiful, isn't it?" Steven said, his eyes taking in the fairyland turrets and towers of Matthias Church and the Fishermen's Bastion; the massive Royal Palace, which occupied the southern spur of Castle Hill; the imposing block of dolomite known as Gellért Hill; and on the southeast point of Gellért Hill, towering over the skyline, a forty-six-foot female figure with arms aloft bearing a palm branch, known as the Liberation Memorial in commemoration of the victory of the Soviet Army over the Germans in the Second World War.

"How do you feel about being back here?" Matthew asked, noticing that an eerie calm had befallen his younger brother.

Steven's eyes misted as he turned toward Matthew and said, "Like it was meant to be."

On the night of the gala at the home of the American ambassador, tensions in the Böhm household were running unusually high. Three weeks before, when the invitation had arrived, Katalin had assumed that László would reject it. Instead, he astounded her by insisting that they attend.

"I'm an important man in Budapest," he told her. "If I weren't there, it might look as if I hadn't been invited and that would not serve my image."

It always amused Katalin when László spoke of image. That was such a Western concept, and yet it seemed as if those in the upper strata of Eastern European socialism thought about little else.

"I hope you're not planning to wear one of those scandalous gowns," he said as he knotted his tie and adjusted the jacket of his dress uniform.

"I most certainly am." As if to make her point, Katalin went to her closet, pulled out the gold lamé gown she had worn at the Kennedy Center and laid it on the bed. She could have chosen a more modest black or a less garish ivory. Because László had challenged her, she had selected the gold.

"The entire Minister's Council is going to be there, as well most of the members of the Politburo. Can't you be a bit more discreet?"

"No, I don't think so," she said, busying herself at her dressing table. "After all, I, too, have an image to uphold."

He left the room grumbling. She knew that he had swallowed a retort, just as she had gulped down words she would have liked to have said. It wasn't what either of them would have chosen, but despite their best intentions, this was what their marriage had become: an emotional warren of cautious speeches and angry silences, of smothered feelings and formalized gestures.

It was when she went to apply her lipstick that she noticed her hand was shaking. She supposed she had been waiting for some visible sign of the cyclone that was roaring inside her. Whether she wanted to or not, she was going to see Steven again and it was going to be difficult. Nothing had changed, yet everything had changed. They had loved each other and lost each other. They had found each other again, and again circumstances had forced them apart. Though she wished they wouldn't, words from that letter she had mailed to Steven insisted upon repeating themselves:

I don't know if we ever truly loved each other . . . things have changed . . . I'm not comfortable in a bed of lies . . . Viszontlátásra.

She had thought she would never see him again. In less than an hour, she would be on a receiving line, standing in front of him, shaking his hand. What would he say?

Steven and Cynthia's residence was an umber-colored building on Úri utca, the longest street in the elegant Castle District. Because the changeover had been so hurried, expediency dictated that instead of searching for another house, they simply moved into the one vacated by Steven's predecessor. Steven, knowing the history of the area as well as the status connected to many of the Baroque structures, was delighted. Cynthia, disgruntled at having to be in Budapest in the first place, appeared determined to be dissatisfied with most aspects of her new location. She loathed the furnishings, despised the colorations, found the shopping inconvenient, her staff inefficient. Everything else fell into a category labeled—bourgeois.

Knowing, however, that one's reputation as a hostess was made or lost on first impressions, she had set aside her list of grievances long enough to arrange this evening's gala. Differences of language and customs aside, she had corraled her staff and organized a spectacle more in keeping with Beverly Hills than the Buda Hills. Guests were discharged from their cars and ushered into an elegantly contrived courtyard awash with early spring blossoms and bathed in the faint sounds of a string quartet. Inside the mansion, liveried waiters accepted coats and dispensed graceful flutes of champagne. Silver trays laden with exquisite hors d'oeuvres were passed by handsome young men in white-tie and tails. The lighting was dim, the music was Haydn.

In the crook of a sinuous staircase, in a foyer replete with a series of gilt-framed nineteenth-century prints depicting the history of Buda, an inlaid marble floor, several multilight sconces, and an astonishing Austrian crystal chandelier, the ambassador and his lady stood. Katalin caught a glimpse of Cynthia as she entered and immediately felt uncomfortable. Cynthia wasn't receiving, she was reigning over the assembled crowd. Gowned in a diaphanous cloud of pale blue chiffon, a suite of sapphires and diamonds adding to the illusion of royalty, she shook hands and offered polite but impersonal smiles to all who passed her on their way to the salon. If ever a woman had wanted to make a distinction between West and East, have and have-not, Cynthia had done it, and without brandishing a sword or painting a picture or drawing lines of demarcation.

As Katalin and László neared their host and hostess, Katalin's nervous system clicked into high gear causing palpitations, flutters, and sweaty palms. She wanted to turn and run, but it was too late. They were being announced.

"Major and Madame Böhm László."

"Well, well," Cynthia oozed. "What a delight to see you both again. It's been so long. When was it? Oh, yes. At that concert in Washington? Of course. How could I forget? You wore that same dress. Well," she said, stepping back and surveying Katalin as a school mistress would a child, "it looks just as sweet on you now as it did then."

If Katalin had a knife, she could have cut that woman's tongue out. Instead, she offered Cynthia the same saccharine smile Cynthia had proffered her and moved on to Steven. Holding her by the arms, he kissed her on both cheeks, allowing his lips to linger a second longer than they should have.

"It's wonderful to see you."

"Congratulations on your appointment." She couldn't possibly verbalize how she felt about seeing him again, so she covered it with formalities. "How are you enjoying our city?"

Steven sensed her discomfort. He wasn't exactly at ease himself. Nor was he pleased with Katalin's characterization of Budapest as *our* city, as if it belonged to her and László, as if he didn't belong here at all. "It feels very strange being back, but yes, I am enjoying it."

Katalin nodded and started to move away from the line. He caught her.

"Why haven't you been performing?" he asked. Greco had told him she had cancelled two years' commitments with no explanation.

"I have been," she said, wishing he hadn't asked that, hoping he wouldn't pursue it.

"Not in the West."

"Katalin's taken a sabbatical from the concert tour," László said. "She's a mother now. Her place is with her child."

"A child?" Steven's eyebrows arched. Was that the risk she had spoken of in her letter, was that the change? "How nice for you both. Boy? Girl?"

"A beautiful little girl," Katalin said, unable to keep a proud smile from her lips. "Her name is Márta."

Cynthia was finding this conversation almost as interesting as Steven was. As she always did when Steven and Katalin were in the same room, she worried about them. Knowing that Katalin had a child, she worried less.

"How old is she?" Cynthia asked.

"One and a half."

"It's no wonder you're not performing," Cynthia said, a thought nibbling at her subconscious. "If what they say about the terrible twos is true, you must walk around in a constant state of exhaustion."

"Márta is hardly a hardship."

"But she is a handful," László added, "which is why we felt it was better for Katalin to back away from her concert schedule. Less stress, you know."

Katalin was annoyed at that. First, because Márta was not a handful. Second, because he wouldn't know if she were. And third, because *we* had not made the decision to cancel her tour. He had.

The next guests were announced. Katalin and László moved into the center of the hall. Katalin was relieved.

"I must go speak to Grósz."

László left her and headed for Károly Grósz, the new Prime Minister. She was about to look for the salon when she was embraced by Matthew.

"I'm so happy to see you I have no words," she said, begging herself not to cry.

"The feeling is mutual." He hugged her again, maintaining a hold on her hands when they separated.

"Is Sophie here?"

Matthew shook his head. "She's filming another special. She sends her love and promises to try to get here soon."

Katalin nodded. She didn't know what to do, but this might be the only time she had Matthew to herself. Pulling him close to her, she said, "Is my fund all right? I heard about the stock market crash. Was I wiped out?" Out of reflex, she looked back to see whether or not László had been watching or was near enough to listen. He was too involved in his own politicking to care what she was doing.

Matthew also looked over his shoulder at László, then spoke quickly to Katalin. "Fortunately, Walter and I had decided long before that nose-dive to divest of everything except the real blue chips. We went into high-yield bonds, which is where we put you. Don't worry, you're doing just fine. As a matter of fact, you're doing more than fine. Since you, uh, disappeared again," he said, noting that she looked away rather than tell him anything with her eyes, "your records have been selling like mad. Why do you ask?"

"No reason. I just wanted to know, that's all."

Matthew wished she were less transparent. It would be safer.

"Okay, but if you need any advice, on anything, you know you can always come to me. Remember, I spent my formative years in this burg and one thing I learned was how to keep a secret."

"I'll keep that in mind," she said, patting his cheek and flashing him a grateful smile. "Now, tell me about you and Sophie."

"For that, you need a drink," he said, linking her arm through his and leading her toward a pale yellow salon. "Follow me."

Zoltán cried when he saw Steven and Matthew. He tried not to, but his emotions bubbled so quickly, they rushed to the surface before he could stop them.

"I can't believe it," he mumbled as he hugged one and then the other. "Mátyás and *fiatal* István."

"Please, Zoltán," Steven said, wrapping an arm around his old friend, "I'm the ambassador. It doesn't sound right for you to be calling me young István. I'm supposed to be dignified and worldly."

Zoltán laughed. "You're right. Forgive me, Your Excellency."

"That's better," Steven said. "Much better."

"You look like Margit," Zoltán said, addressing Steven, then turning to Matthew. "And you, like your papa, Béla." He sighed, but his breath quivered. "They would be so proud of the two of you."

"I have regards from Zsuzsanna," Steven said.

Again, Zoltán's eyes teared. "Katalin's told me how you boys keep in touch with her and take care of her. I'm grateful."

"She's a terrific lady."

Matthew agreed with his brother. "She'd love to see you again, Zoltán."

"I know. Me too. Maybe, someday."

"She can't come here," Matthew said. Having linked Zoltán's comments with Katalin's concern for her private fund, he said this to confirm or deny his suspicions that father and daughter were concocting a plan.

"I know that too." He appeared uncomfortable, as if he were in a police station being grilled about things he couldn't discuss.

"Now that you're conducting, will you be traveling outside of Hungary?"

Zoltán laughed. "Not a chance! Even after all these years, I'm still on their list of unreliable citizens."

"Is Katalin on that list?" Steven asked.

Though he didn't mean to, Zoltán glanced to his side, where László was caucusing with Grósz and Pozsgay.

"Yes."

Steven didn't like the look in Zoltán's eyes. Neither did Matthew. He was beginning to sense an escape in the planning.

"Maybe we can help." Without knowing what Matthew knew, Steven had intuited trouble.

Zoltán took his time before answering. He weighed pluses and minuses, risks and benefits, dangers and rewards. He looked at László and then at Katalin. He thought about Márta and Zsuzsanna.

"Maybe you can," he said, still struggling, still juggling pros and cons. "We're not ready yet."

"When you are?" Steven asked, his chest flooded with hope.

Zoltán looked from one brother to the other, drawing from each as much support and caring as they were willing to give. An unexpected calm enfolded him. Suddenly, he didn't feel terrified at the thought of leaving Hungary and resettling in the United States. Suddenly, he realized he wouldn't be alone.

"I'll let you know."

László was amazed at how well things were going. To put it mildly, he had not been looking forward to this evening. It had loomed as little more than a reunion of Katalin and those two conquering heroes, the Kardos boys. It was that, certainly. Katalin, Zoltán, the Strassers, the Weisses, and Steven and Matthew were reveling in their reunion. Even now, Katalin was laughing with a black man she called Shadow. László cringed. What was it about her that made her do things like that? That gypsy Tibor. This man. Had she no pride? No sense of who she was, who they were?

Quickly, he looked to see if his comrades were as distressed at Katalin's choice of companion as he was. Obviously not. Most were paying attention to nothing but the food on their plates and the wine in their goblets. László supposed he shouldn't complain. During cocktails, an association he had thought would be a liability had been revealed to be an asset.

When he had introduced Grósz to Steven, Steven had surprised him by offering his cooperation in establishing a more favorable trade package between the two nations. He had told Grósz he had great confidence in László and, at László's convenience, would be delighted to set up a series of meetings to get things moving. When Steven had walked away, Grósz had been effusive in his praise.

Pozsgay also had been impressed with László's connections. He had found Steven affable and cooperative. He had been particularly pleased with Steven's suggestion about a cultural exchange program, involving both performers and students. The way Pozsgay explained the idea to László, they would set up a series of concerts with Hungary sending musicians and singers to the United States, and the U.S. sending comparable performers to Hungary. Also, they would arrange scholarship programs to Juilliard and the Curtis Institute in Philadelphia and the Peabody School of Music in Baltimore, and alternately, programs at the Franz Liszt Academy and the Music Conservatories in Debrecen and Szeged.

Just moments before, he had overheard Steven and Ilona Strasser talking about the main synagogue on Doháni utca. Prolonged neglect had caused its Byzantine-Moorish architecture to crack. The roof was near to caving in. Most of the restoration was being funded by the Hungarian-Jewish diaspora, spearheaded by the American actor Tony Curtis, whose family had emigrated in the twenties. Steven vowed to try to raise the rest of the funds.

László had to congratulate the new ambassador. In one night, to use an American idiom, he had covered all his bases. In one night, he had managed to ingratiate himself with just about everyone. László didn't like Steven, but he had to respect him. The man understood what it was to be a diplomat, what it was to be in a position of leadership. He understood power and influence and how to use both to achieve a particular end. But if Steven thought he had dazzled László with his performance, he had not.

László was not a naïf. He understood the American political hierarchy well enough to know that Steven's post was a comedown. Something had happened to knock the charismatic congressman off his lofty perch.

Though László would have loved to know what that something was, in reality it didn't matter. Steven had been banished to Budapest. If he ever intended to step onto the political ladder again, he had to do something extraordinary, he had to make a name for himself all over again.

When László had come to New York, Steven had been on the rise, with the reins of power firmly in his grasp. László had been the one in the uncomfortable position of having to give in order to get. Now, situations had reversed themselves. László was up. Steven was down.

And while he was, László intended to use him every way he could.

It was late by the time Steven had a chance to speak to Judit alone. Most of the guests had already gone, including Katalin and László. Cynthia, having decided that everyone of any importance had left, claimed a headache and retreated to her bedroom. Gábor had gone to help Ilona and Andras to their car.

"I like Gábor," Steven said, noting with a surprising twinge of jealousy the love in Judit's eyes as she watched her husband care for her mother.

"I'm glad." Judit faced him with an expression that went from polite to presumptuous in the blink of an eye. "I don't like Cynthia."

He laughed. "Katalin was right. She once told me you were still saying things you shouldn't to people you shouldn't."

"Why shouldn't I tell you how I feel?" Judit asked with absolutely no hint of apology. "I was always honest with you. Why lie now?"

"You have a point." He felt as if he had dice in his hand. For several seconds, he rolled them about before deciding to give them a toss. "As long as you're being so honest, tell me about Katalin and László."

"What do you want to know?"

"Is she happy?"

"*Are you?*"

"No. Now what?"

"You have to answer that one, not me."

"I have to see her," Steven said, appealing to Judit for help. "We have to talk."

"László keeps a pretty careful watch on her."

"Doesn't he go out of town on business?"

"Occasionally."

"Do you know when he does?"

Judit smiled. She had liked Steven when he was nine. She liked him even more now.

"Yes," she said, standing on her toes to kiss his cheek. "And so will you."

Summers in Budapest were always sticky, but that July the humidity had reached a new level of discomfort. Like so many others, Katalin couldn't wait to escape to the country. The Böhm retreat was a villa in a small resort town called Leányfalu. On the west bank, just past Szentendre, it was part of a region north of Budapest, where the flow of the Danube shifted from west-east to north-south, an area called the Danube Bend.

Whereas László favored the larger Rose Hill residence, Katalin and Márta preferred the house at Leányfalu. It was a comfortable place that invited the kind of easy relaxation that seemed to go along with summer. They were near enough to the Baroque art colony of Szentendre to be able to stroll about the tiny streets crammed with artist's studios and galleries and quaint restaurants, yet far enough away to avoid the crowds of tourists that flooded the historic town. They were near the water, the beaches, a campground, and the ferry to Pocsmegyer on Szentendre Island.

The bright, marigold yellow, two-bedroom house was situated on a hill overlooking a magnificent stretch of river. Behind them was the Pilas range, before them, the large island that divided the Danube in two along the last leg of its journey to Budapest. It was an Edenic place where everything was lush and green, every vista a painting in need of a canvas. The house itself wasn't large but it was roomy, with wide windows that provided a frame for the scenic outdoors, a low, broad hearth that in winter created a cozy den, and wrap-around gardens that in summer were a panoply of color. It also had a small apartment above the garage that could be used for guests. Zoltán had stayed several times, and once when Gábor had been at a medical conference and László had been at one of his infernal meetings, Judit and the children had spent a weekend. Though they didn't take advantage of it as often as Katalin would have liked, it was there.

The gardens were special. Katalin and Márta tended them, Katalin planting and caring for the flowers, Márta digging and disturbing the dirt. This particular morning, Katalin was out in the back cutting roses. Márta was her mother's helper, carrying a basket in which Katalin laid the delicate blossoms. When the basket was full, they went inside and Katalin arranged the roses in vases that decorated every vacant tabletop. Naturally, they saved the prettiest roses for the nightstand next to Márta's bed. While

Katalin still preferred pink blossoms, Márta, like her Aunt Judit, favored red.

Having completed their chores, mother and daughter washed up and retired to the living room for another of their daily rituals. Every day, both here in Leányfalu and on Rose Hill, Katalin seated Márta on a bench next to her and played the piano, her aim simply to introduce Márta to the piano and to the joys of making music.

The door was open. As Steven peeked in, he could hardly believe his eyes and ears. Katalin was entertaining her daughter with the same piece she and Mária had performed the first time he had ever heard Katalin play. Again, it was the whimsical score about Babar, the elephant. Again, the narrator told the story of King Babar and Queen Celeste. And again, Katalin's hands brought the animals and their fanciful jungle to life. When she had finished, Steven rapped on the door and poked his head inside.

"I was in the neighborhood," he said with a guilty smile. "I thought I'd stop in and pay a visit."

Judit had called him the week before to say that László was scheduled to attend a meeting of the Warsaw Pact in Prague the following week and that Katalin was going to their country home.

For a moment, Katalin was frozen on her bench. She was shocked to see him, but in a sense, she wasn't at all surprised. She had known he would come. From the instant she heard he had been appointed ambassador to Hungary, she had known. She didn't know where or how or under what guise or pretense, but she had known.

"Are you alone?" Katalin asked as she approached the door. She looked past him to the driveway. There was no car.

"Ernie and Shadow dropped me off at the bottom of the hill. They're going to tour Szentendre and while they're at it, they're going to speak to the people at the Margit Kovács Museum about a group of American ceramicists who would like to study her work."

"Who are you?"

Márta tugged at Steven's trousers with great impatience. He looked down into her face and his heart stopped. She was one of the most beautiful little girls he had ever seen. Her eyes were almond-shaped and green, but paler than Katalin's, while her hair was a shade darker. Probably because she had been out in the sun, her cheeks and her arms were pink, making her look even more delicate in her ruffled sundress and sandals. When he smiled at her, she smiled back, and he felt as if the sun that had pinked her skin had warmed his heart.

"I'm an old friend of your Mama's," he said. It was at times like these when he was grateful that he and Matthew had never let their Hungarian lapse. "My name is Kardos István."

With great solemnity, Márta held out her hand. "I'm Böhm Márta."

"How do you do," Steven said, truly bewitched.

She curtsied politely.

"Come in," Katalin said, finding it increasingly uncomfortable to be standing at the door. "Sit. I have some coffee in the kitchen."

Márta showed him to the couch. Once he was seated, she ran to a huge box in the corner of the room and brought every one of her toys and books over to him for his inspection. When she asked him to read *The Prince and His Magic Horse* Steven gladly obliged. It had been one of his favorites when he was her age. By the time Katalin returned, Márta had snuggled between Steven's chest and arm and had fallen asleep.

"That used to happen to me in the House," Steven whispered as he lifted the sleeping child into his arms and followed Katalin to Márta's room. "I'd start to speak and everyone would nod off."

Katalin pulled back the covers. Steven lay Márta down and pulled the cotton blanket up, under her chin. He didn't know why he did it, but he leaned down and kissed her.

"She's wonderful," he said to Katalin when they had returned to the living room and were enjoying their coffee. "She must make you very happy."

"She does." Katalin looked away. She was finding it impossible to discuss Márta with him, to see Márta with him. They had gotten on so quickly, so easily. László barely spoke to the child. "She's the most important thing in my life."

Steven asked her to tell him about Márta, what she was like, what made her laugh, what made her cry. He wanted to know her favorite color, her favorite story, which foods she liked and which she didn't. As Katalin went on, the pain in her heart worsened. If someone tested László on these questions, she wasn't certain he would know any of the answers.

"Is Márta the risk you spoke of in your letter?" Steven asked after watching Katalin as she described her child. Only a blind man would have missed the intensity of her love for Márta. "Is she the reason you broke it off between us?"

Katalin's insides became a symphony of percussive sounds.

"Yes," she said, surprised to hear defensiveness in her voice. She didn't have to defend herself to him, or to anyone for that matter. "Once I had a child, the entire focus of my world shifted to her."

At the embassy, when László had mentioned Márta, he had referred to her as Katalin's child. Just now, Katalin had said "I" instead of "we." Steven was beginning to draw the natural conclusion that László was not about to be nominated for father of the century. Add to that Matthew's suspicion that Katalin and Zoltán were planning to leave Hungary and

Judit's contention that Katalin was not a happily married woman, and he concluded that the decision he had reached in Garvey's office had been perspicacious and right.

"I understand that," he said gently, begging the question. "What I don't understand is why you stopped loving me." He heard her breath catch in her throat. He saw her eyes blink. "I never stopped loving you."

"Don't," she said, shaking her head. "I can't. It's too complicated."

"You're wrong," he said, putting his cup on the table in front of him and leaning close to Katalin. "We've loved each other since we were children. We've never stopped."

"Life isn't that simple," she protested. "You make it sound very lovely, but it's too idyllic. It has nothing to do with the real world. In the real world, our lives have always been very complicated."

"Things are getting easier every day."

"What do you mean?"

"For all intents and purposes, I'm out of public life and my marriage is over."

"I'm sorry . . ."

Steven held up his hand. "This is not something that requires a requiem. It was a loveless marriage to begin with. Now, it's a mutual liability." He was certain he noticed a flicker of satisfaction in Katalin's eyes. "And you? Are you and László the Romeo and Juliet of the Magyars?"

The question stung more than she would have liked. Ever since that night when she had told László of her pregnancy, Katalin had honored her vows to be a better wife. She had been loving and attentive and aggressive about making their marriage a more solid union. She had actually convinced herself that it was, until recently, but being with Steven, a man for whom her love was real and intense, she knew that her life with László was a sham. Love shouldn't be an effort or a trial. It should be a joy.

"Hardly." As Katalin said it, the tension left her face. The old saw was true: Confession was good for the soul.

"You don't love him?"

She had been fighting the answer to that question for so long, it surprised her to hear how quickly it came to her lips. "No, I don't."

"Delighted to hear that. Do you love me?"

"Yes."

Instantly, simultaneously, they grinned at each other as if they had just come upon a wondrous treasure.

"Then why don't we do something about it?" Steven asked.

"I would, but I don't know what to do." Katalin's face had darkened. "I have Márta and my father to consider."

"You could come to the Embassy and request asylum."

"I thought about that. If I did, László would be humiliated and he would lash out against everyone I care about. Judit, Ilona, Andras, and most especially Tibor." She shook her head. "I can't take that chance."

"Why do you think it would be any different if you left the country?"

"I would be gone. He could say whatever he wanted. He could make it appear as if I defected because of Zoltán." She held her hands up in confusion and frustration. "Oh, I don't know. I just know that I'm afraid to shove this in his face. You don't know him, Steven. He'll shove back."

"Can you hang in a little longer?"

Tears filled Katalin's eyes, but a smile filled her face. "If I know we're really going to be together, I can hang in as long as I have to."

"Good." Steven's mind was racing. "First order of business for me is to clear things up with Cynthia. When she returns from Paris, I'm going to ask her for a divorce."

"Will she fight it?"

"Probably, but Matthew and Shadow are searching for something. When they find it, the battle will be over."

"What if they don't find whatever it is?"

Steven kissed her. "Then your bridegroom will be bloodied but unbowed."

"What about László?" The thought of confronting him terrified her. What if he demanded custody of Márta?

"It would be easier if you could divorce him before we get you out of here." He sensed her trepidation and understood it, but what he had just said was true. It would be easier. Then again, nothing had ever been easy for them. Why should he expect it to be different now?

"Okay. What then?"

"I don't know right now, but we'll figure it out. I promise."

"I'm nervous."

Steven folded her into his arms and held her. "I won't let anything happen to you or Zoltán or that precious little bundle in the next room."

"I never stopped loving you," Katalin said, "no matter how it looked."

Steven had been waiting for that. Despite his facade of confidence, he was still a man who needed to know that the woman he loved, loved him.

"When I got that letter," he said quietly, "I was furious with you for writing it, but then I realized you were right. We had been living a fantasy. We hadn't ever really committed ourselves to being together. We talked about it. We thought about it. But all along, we were busy putting us off so that we could protect other things. We kept worrying about what we had to lose." He held her face in his hands and stared deep into her eyes. "I don't care anymore, Katya. I don't want to live without you." His lips touched hers. "You're the one with the greater risk. It's up to you."

Katalin traced the planes of his face with the side of her hand. It seemed so foolish to debate or discuss something that had been preordained. They were destined, she believed that, but he was right: They had bartered their future for other things, she for her music, he for his political life. They had used excuses like borders and visas and barbed-wire fences, but those excuses didn't work anymore. They had blown too many chances. They had angered the gods. What she saw in his eyes and what she heard in his voice was what she felt in her heart: Their future was now. If they didn't grab it this time, if they didn't seize the moment, it would be gone and it would never come again.

Katalin returned his kiss and answered his question. "I'm willing to risk everything rather than lose you."

35

Leányfalu, August 1988

Katalin had rehearsed this scene so often, she was certain she spoke her lines in her sleep. This morning, knowing László was coming to the country, she had accompanied each chore with a performance. As she dusted and swept and polished and washed, she went over her speech, imagining what he would say, what his responses would be, how she would respond in turn. Because she didn't want Márta as an audience for this particular drama, she had arranged for her to spend the day at the beach with the family of one of her playmates. She had called Zoltán to tell him what was happening, just in case things didn't go well and she needed to get word to Steven. Then she had called Judit, and without telling her why, asked her to check on Zoltán later that day. She hung up relieved and grateful to have a friend who would agree to something simply because it was asked of her.

She had just finished setting the table for lunch when László's car came up the drive. Katalin's insides rioted. A sheer veil of sweat covered her skin. She had believed she was ready for this, that she had fortified herself adequately for the task ahead. But he walked in the door and she knew—no amount of preparation or rehearsal would ever have been enough.

He greeted her pleasantly enough, kissing her cheek, asking how her week had been, how the weather had held up, whether she had gone to the beach or simply languished in her garden or at her piano. Eventually, he asked about Márta. Katalin answered all his questions in an even conversational tone as she placed the food on the table. While she picked at her meal, he ate heartily, making her realize that without thinking she had made him his favorite lunch: cold apple soup and *puszta* salad, slices of sausage in a vinaigrette sauce. When he finished, she planned to ask him for a divorce. Was she fattening the pig for slaughter, she wondered, or feeding him comfort food so he would consider her request more kindly? Whatever her purpose, the time had come. He had finished his coffee and had settled himself in an armchair by one of the front windows.

"László," Katalin said, taking a seat opposite him. "We have to talk."

"About what?"

His feet were propped on an ottoman. His fingers were laced and planted on his abdomen. His chin was tilted upward, causing his eyes to appear as if they were looking down at her. Katalin had always called this pose "the Emperor." It was the one he adopted whenever he wanted to diminish the person speaking to him. Though she resented his using it with her, she refused to bow before it. It did make her wonder, however, if somehow he had gleaned the subject of this discussion. Though she didn't think it was possible, if by chance he did know, any preamble would only make her look foolish and weak. Suddenly, she reconsidered her script. Editing quickly, she decided to go right to the heart of the matter.

"I'm not happy in our marriage, László," she said, careful to strain all negative emotion from her voice. "And I haven't been for quite some time. We're not as close as we used to be, not as caring about each other as we once were. I don't know exactly when things began to change or even why, but in the past several years, I've felt as if we've been drifting on opposing currents."

There was no movement on László's face, no change of expression, no physical acknowledgment that he was responding in any way to what she was saying.

"I want a divorce," Katalin said flatly, accustomed to his depriving her of external clues to his internal reactions.

"Absolutely not!" His response was quiet, but definite. His face remained an unreadable block of granite.

Be honest with him, her mind said, again rewriting her original script. "I love another man, László. I think you know that. I think you've always known that. István and I have loved each other since we were children. We want to be together. I don't want to hurt you, but I can't help it. I need to be free, László. Please, let me go."

"Not a chance."

Katalin felt a red rage beginning in her gut. At the same time, she felt an icy shiver of fear slither up her spine. "Are you denying me because you love me or because you want to own me?"

László laughed. It was a disagreeable sound, like the grinding of gears. "Feelings have nothing to do with it, Katalin. They never have. It's always been a matter of image and status. You had a name. Your parents had recognizable names. You had status. I courted you because of it, married you because of it, and I will never divorce you because of it. You're an accessory. Nothing more, nothing less."

She had anticipated anger. This was worse. This hurt more than anger. This made all the years they had spent together a lie.

Forget it, she told herself. *Don't let your ego or your pride get in the way of what you have to do.*

"You've got your Ministry," she said, refusing to acknowledge his degredation of her. "You've got your power platform. You don't need me. Why not let me go?"

"Because the political winds are swirling, dear Katalin. Grósz is vulnerable. Gorbachev doesn't like him. The Politburo doesn't like him. Even the people don't like him. It's only a matter of time before he's out." He removed his feet from the ottoman, set them on the floor, and leaned forward to address her at close range. "And I am the key man. I'm the one in position to take his place. Within a few months, I could be Prime Minister. The Party bosses have always been very impressed that my wife is an international concert star. Whether I like it or not, or whether you like it, you add a definite stature, and if you think I'm going to let you mess things up for me, you're mad!"

"You're wrong. The Party doesn't care about wives," Katalin said, speaking from years of experience. "They barely notice the existence of women. A divorce wouldn't put a dent in your ambitions and you know it!"

"Unfortunately, Katalin, we disagree on that and in the case of a disagreement, my opinion is the only one that counts."

"That's not true," Katalin said, frustration and anger building. "I count. My feelings count and I'm telling you I don't want to stay married to you. I want to be with Steven."

László simply stared at her. He appeared incredulous, as if she were truly demented. "Certainly, darling. I understand now. You want to leave me for the American ambassador. Why would I object to something as sensible as that?" His voice shifted from sarcasm to rage in the time it took for the patronizing smile to leave his lips. "What kind of fool do you take me for?"

"I'll leave the country," Katalin said, persisting, despite the obvious futility. "I'll put off marrying Steven until you're elevated to Prime Minister." She heard the edge of desperation in her voice, but was helpless to remove it. "I won't ask for any money or any property. I'll arrange generous visits with Márta."

Again László laughed. This time, something in the tone and something in his eyes slowed the flow of Katalin's blood.

"Why should I care about a child who's not mine?"

She heard him, but she couldn't believe what she heard. He didn't repeat himself, but he didn't have to. His words reverberated, boomeranging off walls, crashing against her consciousness like enormous brass cymbals. Her head grew light and began to spin. Thousands of blue and yellow sparks exploded before her eyes. Her heart thumped against the wall of her chest.

"What are you saying?" She barely eked out the words.

A triumphant smile wreathed his mouth like a victory trophy. "Oh, did I forget to tell you? I had a terrible case of scarlet fever as a child. It wasn't treated properly and left me sterile. I can't have children."

Katalin was in a state of shock. She kept shaking her head back and forth in a spasm of disbelief. "Then . . ."

"I knew from the start that Márta wasn't my child. I suspected that Kardos was the father, but until now I didn't know for sure, nor did I much care."

"But," Katalin said, still reeling from the double-edged sword that had named Steven as Márta's father and revealed the horror of László's deception, "you were so concerned when she was stolen. You called the police. You went with them."

"Unfortunately, we went in the wrong direction." He clucked his tongue in a most taunting manner.

A bilious, acrid taste filled Katalin's mouth as the truth assaulted her.

"You knew where she was?"

"Of course," he said, his voice becoming an infuriating jeer. "I paid to have her stolen. Gypsies work cheap. Especially gypsies with a grudge against the *gorgio*."

As each dosage of reality took effect, Katalin became anesthetized to the pain. Numbed, she pressed him. She knew there was more. She may as well hear it all.

"How did you know Farah had a grudge against me?"

László rose from his chair and encircled the couch where she sat, walking around her, dizzying her with his route.

"From time to time, my darling wife, I've had you followed." He leaned over, his face as near to her as a breath. "You've led such an interesting life. Not only are you Gáspár Katalin, the Princess of the Piano, but you're the gypsy Vadrósza, the Princess of the Great Plain." His lips curled in an expression of disgust. "I couldn't understand your defense of that smarmy violinist. I couldn't understand how you could have suggested that your father tutor him in your home. So I put a tail on you." Again, he looked as if he were going to be ill. "You went to Báthordomb. To a wedding at that pigsty of a place. You slept with them and ate with them. Have you no pride? No sense of right and wrong?"

"Just because you're a narrow-minded, color-blind bigot doesn't mean I have to be," Katalin asserted, rising to her feet, allowing the flush of outrage to rouge her cheeks. "There's nothing wrong with my friendship with Tibor."

"Everything's wrong with it," László insisted, shouting for the first time. "The fact that you don't see that is precisely what's wrong with you."

"What did you use to threaten Farah?" she asked, seeing László with frightening clarity, despising what she saw.

László stroked his chin with his fingers, encouraging a satisfied grin. "Several things. First, I reminded her about the thefts in your father's building. Once I knew who she was and how she felt about you, it wasn't hard to figure out that she had been the thief. Knowing how gypsies are treated in jail, I threatened prison." His brown eyes blackened at the memory of his discussion with the gypsy. "The wench didn't flinch. She was as feisty and ornery as any gypsy I've ever dealt with."

For once, Katalin wished Farah were there. She would have applauded her bravery.

"I then felt it necessary to inform her that several members of her family were suspected of crimes against the state. Serious crimes," he said, shaking his head with mock concern. "I told her I was afraid that, any day, charges might be brought against them."

Katalin knew the charges would have been trumped up and the punishments would have been unconscionably severe. She was growing to loathe this man.

"I'm surprised she didn't tell Tibor." She hadn't meant to give voice to her thoughts, to allow László to know what she was thinking or feeling, but she had.

"Another difference of opinion. I would have been surprised if she had. I had warned her it would be a mistake to confide in her mate. I pointed out that he, being such a good friend of yours, would most likely have told you of our plan."

In a minute, Katalin thought.

"If you had known, I would have known that Farah had broken the rules. I would have been obliged to discipline her."

"By punishing Tibor." Katalin wondered if he would have ordered Tibor killed. The thought iced her veins.

"Or her children."

"László, I want a divorce!" Katalin couldn't stand the thought of living with him another moment. "You can't make me stay with you."

"That's where you're wrong, Katalin. I can. And I will. In fact, for the time being, you and Márta are going to stay right here in Leányfalu. Until you get over this crankiness, I don't want you in Budapest."

"Are you saying what I think you're saying?" Katalin was dumbstruck. "Are Márta and I going to be prisoners in our own home?"

"Why be so negative?" he said, his voice dripping with condescension. "It's a beastly summer. It's much nicer here in Leányfalu than it is in the city. Márta has friends here. Why make it unpleasant for yourself?"

"Because prison is unpleasant!" Her teeth were so tightly gritted, her jawbone felt as if it might crack from the pressure.

"Don't think of it as a prison, Katalin. Think of it as an extended stay in the country."

"I don't want to think about it at all!"

With that, she stormed the door. He beat her to it and blocked her way. His fingers closed around her arm like a vise.

"Don't push me, Katalin. I'm going to install guards in the guest cottage. They'll give you as much privacy as good security allows, but they're highly trained. I wouldn't test them."

Katalin heard the threat. Rather than being cowed, it only increased her determination to be free of him.

"What about my father? Isn't he going to be curious about where I am?"

"I will allow Zoltán to visit once a week, but don't ask him to do anything that could get him into trouble."

Another warning. Another reason to hate him.

"I have things to do. Important things. I can't afford to have a disobedient wife running around Budapest," he said, defining her immediate future. "When you rid yourself of this ill humor and are ready to resume your role as Mrs. Böhm, you'll be able to return to Rose Hill. Until then, you don't leave Leányfalu."

Katalin stood mute. She said nothing, because just then there was nothing to say. This had started out as a request for a divorce. She had never been naive enough to believe it would be simple, but in her wildest dreams she never would have imagined it would turn out like this.

She retreated because she needed to think. She needed to plan, to figure out a way to escape. She didn't know how or when, but she and Márta and Zoltán were leaving. Katalin had told Steven she was willing to fight to marry the man she loved. She had meant it. She still did. But first, she had to fight for her freedom.

Steven found Cynthia in the sitting room adjoining their bedroom, lounging on a tufted chaise. Her feet were bare, her toes glistening with freshly applied nail enamel. Her long, carefully sculpted fingernails were damp as well, having just been painted with a rich red shade that matched the rosy chintz covering the walls and draping the windows of this ultra-feminine room. Her knees were raised, forming a stand for the July issue of *Paris Vogue*. She perused a page, licked the skin of her index finger, and slid it across the glossy paper, turning to the next display of the latest Parisian fashions. When he walked in, she didn't look up, but she did acknowledge his presence.

"Did I tell you that while I was in Paris I bought an apartment in the Marais," she said, licking the pad of her finger, curving the paper up, and then pressing it down when it had completed its turn.

"Did I tell you I want a divorce," he said in precisely the same tone.

Cynthia didn't look up. She took a moment. Then, she closed the magazine, pushed it off her lap, and rested her hands on her thighs. Clearly, they were about to have a discussion. That was fine. It didn't mean she had to smudge her manicure.

"I don't want to give you one," she said, as if her reply should have been obvious.

"We don't love each other, Cynthia. We don't have children. We don't need each other for financial support. Why remain married?"

"Speak for yourself, darling. I'm still quite mad for you."

She was. It had taken her a long time to realize that fact, but within the past several years it had become an inescapable truth. Though she had resented it when Steven had taken control of his own political fate, his ability to use his power and influence as effectively as he had became intoxicating. She had watched him grow in his role of mover-and-shaker—she claimed a certain amount of credit for that growth—but, much to her surprise, his independence became even more of a turn-on than his dependence had been.

Also, it was not as if Cynthia hadn't scoured the marketplace looking for a replacement for Steven. What she had discovered during her sexual safari was that there were few men—and she had "interviewed" many—with Steven's combination of intelligence and passion and dedication and strength, and yes, integrity. If only she had realized all this before she had initiated that whole damned Fenton Douglas fiasco. She had destroyed Douglas, but in doing so, she had destroyed her marriage.

"Don't make this difficult, Cynthia," Steven said, straddling a silken tabouret. "Just give me what I want and we'll part friends."

It hurt her that he could say this with such ease, that he could negotiate her away without a tinge of regret or a hint of rancor. She was at least worth a smidgeon of anger.

"I don't want to be your friend," she said. "I need you."

"What for?" Steven was growing exasperated. She was pleased. Any reaction was better than no reaction at all.

"I told you. I love you. I know I haven't always done the right thing, but I don't want to lose you."

Steven studied her carefully, searching for sarcasm or anger or whatever was hidden behind the sincerity he was faced with. Since he couldn't unearth anything, he opted to meet honesty with honesty.

"You lost me a long time ago, Cynthia."

"Nothing's ever lost until it's gone. As long as you're here, I stand a chance of winning you back."

Steven shook his head. He hadn't expected this. A certain amount of fencing, yes, but a concrete roadblock? Never.

"No," he said as gently as he could. "There is no chance. I'm in love with Katalin. I intend to marry her."

It was Cynthia's turn to shake her head. "There is no way László Böhm is going to let his status symbol off his hook." She rose from the chaise and crossed over to her dressing table. "There's no way I'm letting you off my hook either."

Without any further explanation, she bent down, reached beneath the ruffled skirt on her vanity, and extracted a manila envelope that had been taped to its bottom. She raised her hand and waved it like a flag, but there was no capitulation in her attitude, no surrender in her voice.

"In here," she said, opening the envelope with the same seductive slowness she often used when undressing, "I have photographs of your visit to Katalin's quaint little cottage at Leányfalu."

She pulled out a stack of pictures and tossed them on the floor in front of him. Steven at the door talking to Katalin. Steven greeting Márta. Steven reading Márta a story. Steven tucking Márta into her bed. Steven and Katalin locked in an embrace.

"Good for you," Steven said without granting her the satisfaction of looking at her ill-gotten snapshots, surprised that he wasn't surprised she had had him followed. "So what."

"So nothing, until you link those photographs with this." Still protecting her nails, she shook the envelope, letting the remaining piece of paper fall into her hand. "This is a copy of László Böhm's medical records." Steven's eyebrows came together in a doubtful scowl. "There's a good side and a bad side to the state of the Hungarian economy," she said, as if she were giving a lesson on inflation to a four-year-old. "The bad side is that file clerks barely make enough to feed themselves, let alone a family. The good side is, it doesn't take much to bribe them."

A smug, proud smile danced on her lips.

"And what does that paper say?" Steven said, knowing in his gut that whatever she was holding was the trump card.

"It says: Congratulations, Steven Kardos, you're the father of a baby girl!"

"What the hell are you talking about?"

"You. Katalin. Márta."

"Whatever game you're playing, Cynthia, I'm not having a good time."

"Ah," she said, stalking him, leering at him. "But you did. When you were in Vienna. Remember?" She paused. She wanted him to absorb every last word of this conversation. "Katalin was there as well. Nine months after that coincidence, there was another coincidence. A baby was born."

"Why is that a coincidence?" Steven asked, trying to control the commotion inside him. "Katalin's married. I don't believe that either of them has ever taken a vow of celibacy. It would be only natural for her and her husband to have sex."

"That's true. But it would not be natural for her and her husband to have a child."

"And why is that?"

"Because according to László's military medical record, he's sterile and has been since he was seven years old."

Steven felt as if a concrete wall had fallen on him. His head throbbed with the impact of what Cynthia had just said. *Márta was his, his and Katalin's.*

"Then László knows Márta isn't his. He's a prideful man, Cynthia. He'll give her a divorce. Just as you will."

Cynthia shook her head. Her jaw was set and her eyes had turned to hard, cold glass. "You try to divorce me and I'll ruin her. If you think I used the press to damage Fenton Douglas, wait and see what I do to your precious Katalin."

"What purpose would it serve? You'd smear all of us in the process,"

Steven said, scraping around for an argument that might induce her not to follow through on her threat. If only Matthew and Shadow had produced that evidence.

"That's not quite true, my precious. I don't ever have to mention you or me. I simply leak the news that the famous Katalin Gáspár has a child and that her husband is sterile. Even the dumbest cluck out there can put those two facts together and come up with a juicy scandal."

Steven stood and faced her, glowering at her, hating her. "Do you think that by threatening me with this I'm going to love you?"

"You'll get over it," she said blithely. "It'll take time, but eventually, you'll get over it."

"Never!"

She didn't like the rage she saw in his eyes, nor the way he clenched his fists as he stormed from the room. Then again, she hadn't expected him to thank her for this. It was a calculated risk. She had taken it and even though at the moment it didn't look good, she came from thoroughbred stock. She would ride it out.

Zoltán had about an hour before he was supposed to meet László at Gerbeaud's. He had never shared pastry and coffee with his son-in-law before so this date concerned him. More so because he hadn't heard from Katalin in three days. When she had called to tell him she was going to ask László for a divorce, he had warned her about her husband's temper. She had told him not to worry. He had worried anyway. He was even more distressed now.

While a trip to a cemetery was not his usual way of calming nerves, that morning Zoltán had made a pilgrimage to the Farkasréti graveyard. The month before, on July 7, the remains of Béla Bartók had been returned from the United States and reinterred in this small burial ground in Buda's XI district. As he stood looking at Bartók's grave, he tipped his hat to the man resting there. He was the greatest Hungarian composer of the twentieth century, a man who had combined the asymmetrical phrasing and irregular meters of modern music with the lilting, spirited quality of Magyar folk tunes, creating a sound uniquely his own. But that was not why Zoltán had chosen to visit his grave.

It was Bartók's strength of character that Zoltán found most inspiring. In 1940, Bartók had left Hungary for New York. He didn't go quietly. He told all who would listen that he was fleeing a "regime of thieves and murderers." Five years later, at the age of sixty-four, he died. After the war, many of his admirers, Zoltán included, sought to memorialize him, but Bartók didn't forgive easily. His will forbade the erection of monuments in his honor so long as there was a single street in Hungary named after Hitler or Mussolini.

Zoltán wondered about the correctness of his decision to remain in this land of thieves and murderers. How different things would be if he had agreed to go with Zsuzsanna and Mihai. For once in their lives, he and his family might have experienced freedom. Mária might have become an international film star. He might have found his way back to music sooner than he did. Katalin's career wouldn't have had as many stops and starts as it had, impeded as it seemed to be by the whims and caprices of those who controlled the Iron Curtain. Would she have married Steven if they had grown up together? Who could say. One thing was certain, however—she never would have married the likes of László Böhm.

For years, Zoltán refused to question his decision to stay. He had believed Miklós would return. He had believed that right would triumph over wrong. He had also believed that this was his country and if anyone was going to leave, it should be the Soviets, not the Hungarians. Yet they were still here and he was still here, and unless something extraordinary happened, he feared that when he, like Bartók, was lying in a cemetery, nothing would have changed.

He took the subway and got off at Vörösmarty tér. As he left the underground and came onto the square, the sunlight blinded him. He blinked, closed his eyes, and rummaged through his pockets searching for his dark glasses. The warmth felt good on his face, and for a moment he let it caress him. He loved this part of Budapest, this bustling square with its white, marble-topped tea tables and cane-backed chairs, its tourists and its shoppers, its lively atmosphere and elegant look.

Vörösmarty was at the end of Váci utca, the long, winding pedestrian street that boasted most of the city's finest shops. Even with his eyes closed, he could hear the sounds of life: of babies squealing in their strollers and teenagers giggling and female shoppers oohing over a dress in a window and young lovers cooing. He opened his eyes and allowed them to travel down the utca. Tall, three-light streetlamps from another time alluded to the history of the promenade, its importance in the nineteenth century as a showcase for those who were fashionable and rich and could afford to spend their noontime hours walking leisurely among the shops.

Huge white wooden planters spotted the street with greenery. Mimes and street clowns entertained for forints. Countrywomen in heavy peasant garb—kerchiefs and long flower-patterned skirts—waved embroideries at those passing by them, trying to persuade someone to buy their wares. A group of young musicians with long hair and black workers' caps had set up by the Hermes fountain, charging the air with the electric sounds of rock and roll. He was standing by another statue, this one commemorating Mihály Vörösmarty, one of Hungary's greatest poets. On one side of him was a trio of university students loudly protesting Grósz's latest vacillation. On the other, several men of his generation stood shaking their heads as a flock of young girls in short skirts and skimpy tops strutted by. It was then that he saw László approach in the company of a rather unattractive young man. László said something to the homely blond, pointed to an empty table in front of Gerbeaud's marble entrance, and walked inside. For reasons he didn't understand then, Zoltán opted to avoid this young man, circumventing his table and covering his face as he went to meet László.

He found his son-in-law in the front salon, at a window table. László rose when he approached, shaking Zoltán's hand and offering him a seat. While they waited for someone to take their order, László stubbed out one cigarette and lit another, all the while chatting away about such ordinary things as the Academy and the orchestra and Zoltán's health. A porky waitress in a brown skirt and a brown-and-white striped blouse wiped off the green marble tabletop, emptied László's ashtray, and took their order: two *kavés*, two *tortas*.

Someone from the next table—Zoltán assumed by his ill-fitting suit that he was a politician and not one of the wealthier businessmen with whom László usually consorted—asked László to come over. While he was gone, Zoltán looked around the elegant room, enjoying the dark nineteenth-century wooden window frames, the green silk upholstered walls, the golden chandeliers, and the exquisitely carved ceiling. It was a room designed for elegant people and certainly, if Hungary had an upper class—which it did—it was they who surrounded him. Zoltán knew why László was here—for pastry and a chance to relax and see and be seen. But why was *he* here, he wondered. When László took his seat and their snacks were served, he got his answer.

"I wanted to speak to you about Katalin," László said.

"What about her?"

"She's asked for a divorce."

"I'm aware," Zoltán said, keeping his eyes trained on his coffee instead of his companion.

"Surely, you realize that's impossible."

Zoltán met László's gaze. "Why?"

"Because Katalin is my wife, 'til death do us part."

"You don't love her, László," Zoltán said, understanding that this meeting was intended as a warning of some kind.

"Whether I do or don't is none of your concern."

"I beg to differ. My daughter and granddaughter are very much my concern. Where are they?"

"Happily and safely ensconced at Leányfalu." László lit yet another cigarette. "I've told Katalin that you are free to visit once a week."

If I were free to visit, why limit me to once a week? Zoltán thought, realizing immediately that, in essence, Katalin and Márta were under house arrest.

"That's very generous of you, László. What if Katalin wants to visit me?"

László ground the butt of his cigarette into the ashtray, looked out the window, and motioned to his aide. "Let's not play word games, Zoltán. They're tiresome."

"So is oppression. For any reason. Against anyone. My daughter wants a divorce, László. Give it to her."

"Don't tell me what to do, Zoltán."

"Or what?"

Again, László chose not to answer. Instead, he smiled at the blond in the baggy suit.

"I'd like you to meet my assistant, Kassak Péter." László paused, waiting for a reaction from Zoltán. When there was none, he embellished his introduction. "I believe you know his father, Ferenc."

Claiming total mastery of his emotions, Zoltán managed to look the man in the eye and say, "Of course I knew him. He was the animal who smashed my fingers and ruined my career." The young Kassak's face reddened. He hadn't expected such a frontal assault. Neither had László. Quickly, he looked around to see who had heard what Zoltán had said.

"Are you following in your father's illustrious footsteps, Péter?" Zoltán continued, "Or has the Kassak family evolved?"

Without waiting for an answer, Zoltán rose, pushed back his chair and prepared to leave. Before he did, he looked at Péter and then at László.

"They say a man is known by the company he keeps. From where I stand, that doesn't say much for either of you."

The letter took Ilona by surprise. When she opened it, she noticed immediately there was no signature and no return address. The author described himself as an internist at one of the hospitals where Ilona was on staff. He named several colleagues and a number of cases both he and Ilona had worked on as a way of verifying his credentials. He went on to say how kind she had been to him when he had come on to her service as an intern, how much he had always respected her work, and how much he had admired her courage in dealing with the results of her accident. It was that accident that had prompted the writing of this anonymous letter.

I was treating a man who was dying of cancer. When he was nearing the end, he asked me to summon a priest, which I did. Several minutes later, the man became delirious. He thought I was the priest and asked me to hear his confession. I tried to tell him I was his doctor and that he should keep his sins to himself until the priest arrived, but he didn't seem to understand. He began to unburden himself. Since he was AVO, I don't have to tell you that his list of sins was long and horrible. As he droned on, often succumbing to his delirium, moving off the point, meandering about, rattling off nonsense, I became almost hypnotized and, I'm ashamed to say, almost disinterested in his purgation. Then, he mumbled your name. He said, "Dr. Strasser," "trolley." I shook him and asked him to repeat what he had said. With some careful prodding, I got him to string a few sentences together in a reasonably comprehensible way. He had been ordered to push you in front of a trolley. He muttered something about an underground system of supply and about your daughter, Judit. He used the words, "ferrying" and "samizdat." I know your daughter's work, Dr. Strasser. It's been a source of inspiration to me and others like me who don't know how to translate their hopes and dreams into words or brave acts. Because I'm afraid of reprisals against my family, I've left off my name. I hope you understand. I don't know if this will make things better or worse for you, but as a way of thanking your daughter for what she's doing and a way of thanking you for all you've done, I have the name of the man who ordered your so-called accident—Böhm László.

Ilona was stunned. She read the letter over and over again, wanting to dismiss its contents. She couldn't do it. Too much of it rang true. Then she waited for a sense of acceptance to overwhelm her, a belief that what was written was absolute fact, but she couldn't do that either. There was an accusation, but no proof; a charge, but no witnesses; a confession, but no corroboration. László? Judit had disliked him from the start. She had always believed he was evil, going on and on about how phony he was, how superficial his act was, but Ilona had never paid her much mind. Until now.

She debated whether or not to discuss this with Andras or Judit. Her first instinct said, of course, they deserved to know, and besides, she wanted their thoughts on the matter. Considering it, however, she realized that both of them would react with a fury she might not be able to control once it was unleashed. Then, there were Zoltán and Katalin to consider. No, the claims in this letter needed further investigation, and it needed to be done by a clearer, cooler head than her daughter or her husband would have been able to provide.

Ilona would show this to them later. Now, she intended to bring it to Steven.

For the fourth time since he'd entered his apartment, Zoltán picked up the telephone, only to replace it a second later. He didn't know why he bothered. He had heard the click the first time. Obviously, while he and László had been lingering over a cup of espresso, László's crew had tapped his phone and, he assumed, planted a series of bugs.

Since he couldn't talk to anyone about his contretemps with László, he paced the living room, letting the debate rage within himself. How was he going to extricate Katalin and Márta from the house in Leányfalu? Knowing László, guards had been installed in the small guesthouse adjacent to the cottage. Zoltán would need a brigade to get past them. But he couldn't stand by and do nothing. He had to do something. He had to get to Steven, but how? If there was a tap, there would surely be a tail. If he went to the embassy, László would know before he got inside the door. He needed someone to go for him. Tibor! He would do it. No. László hated Tibor. If Tibor fronted for Zoltán, László would surely arrest him on some charge or other. Maybe someone from the orchestra would take a note to Estridge, who would forward it to Steven. No. He couldn't ask a stranger to risk getting involved in this.

Zoltán's frustration was mounting. Outside, the sun was setting, but he didn't bother to turn on any lights. Instead, he sat in a chair watching the skies over Budapest darken into the charcoal gray of early evening. His heart was heavy with the burden of guilt over wrong decisions and misplayed cards. He hated knowing that his daughter and his beloved Márta needed him; he hated feeling unable to help them.

At first, he ignored the knock at the door. It was light. He dismissed it as someone next door. But it continued. Slowly, he raised himself up out of the chair. He switched on a lamp and went to the door.

"Who's there?"

There was no voice, just another rap of knuckles.

716 / DORIS MORTMAN

"Who do you want?"

"Gáspár Zoltán."

The man didn't sound like the police. Carefully, Zoltán unlatched the door. When he opened it, the face that greeted him belonged to an old man. Zoltán squinted, trying to get a better view of his features, but the hall was almost as dark as Zoltán's apartment. Yet something about this white-haired, stooped man looked familiar.

"Do I know you?" he asked.

The man nodded his head and smiled. It was then that Zoltán knew.

"Miklós! Is it really you?"

"Yes, Zoltán. It's really me. Finally, I've come home."

The two men collapsed in each other's arms, clinging to each other with a ferocity born of gratitude and fear. Still keeping an arm wrapped around Miklós's shoulders, Zoltán ushered him inside. As he turned on the overhead lights, he remembered the hidden microphones. The last thing he wanted László Böhm to hear was that Miklós had returned. He tapped Miklós on the shoulder and held his finger to his lips, warning his brother to be still. Then, he went to the phonograph, placed a record on the turntable and upped the volume.

When Zoltán turned to Miklós, the elderly man was shaking his head, a look of sadness appearing like a caul over his face.

"I've been gone thirty-two years," he said. "I survived a Soviet labor camp, exile, an escape, and months of hiding and running just so I could come home. How depressing to know that after all this time, nothing's changed."

"That's not quite true," Zoltán said, unable to look at Miklós without weeping in amazement. "There have been many changes. Some good, some bad." The noise from the phonograph was annoying him. Zoltán looked around, trying to figure out how he was going to talk to Miklós without talking to László at the same time. "You know what, my long lost brother? You look like you could use a soak."

Miklós's eyes brightened. "The baths! What a wonderful idea! This creaking old body is screaming for a dip in the waters." He chuckled. "And if you've a tail, it's hard to blend in with the background unless you're naked. You go first. I'll meet you at the Gellért."

"I'll be the bald guy in the corner," Zoltán said.

Miklós nodded, biting back his own tears. "Don't worry, Zoltán. I'll find you."

When the security guard at the entrance buzzed Steven's office and said that Miklós Gáspár was in the lobby and wanted to see him, Steven thought it was a cruel joke. Even now, looking at him face-to-face, Steven had a hard time believing the truth.

"So this is where they hid Cardinal Mindszenty," Miklós said, walking around Steven's office, running his fingers along the smoothly polished surface of Steven's desk, and the painted tiles that decorated the enormous hearth.

This office was, as Miklós said, the room in which the Cardinal, a political prisoner of the communists, had lived for fifteen years. Jailed in 1949, he was released in 1956 during those five glorious days of freedom. When the Soviet tanks rolled into Budapest, he took refuge in the American Legation, now the U.S. Embassy, where he stayed until he was allowed to leave Hungary in 1971.

"They say that Mindszenty was convinced that the Soviets had planted a microphone in that fireplace," Steven said. "According to embassy legend, the Cardinal was constantly poking around in the chimney with broomsticks and the like, looking for spies or listening devices."

"Should I do the same?" Miklós asked.

"No need. I swept it this morning." They both laughed as Steven helped the man who had been his inspiration into a chair.

It bothered Steven to see Miklós's weakened physical state. He was thin and his skin appeared sallow. His fingers, afflicted with arthritis, were gnarled and bent. Though he claimed to be in good health, he was stooped and walked with a limp. Steven guessed that both conditions had been caused by repeated beatings and other forms of labor-farm brutality. Yet in his eyes, Steven saw the same bright flame he remembered seeing thirty-two years before. The Soviets might have caged Miklós's person, but they never succeeded in taking custody of his mind.

"And where is Mátyás?" he asked. "Is he in Budapest also? Will I get to see him?"

"Mátyás is out of town." Steven said. "I can hardly wait to tell him the incredible news that you're still alive."

"Might I say the same about you." Miklós leaned back and appraised the man he had known as a boy. It had been too many long hard years for Miklós to see absolute resemblances between youth and age, but he did recall the unbelievable blue of István's eyes. He had always felt they were his signature feature, the one thing that would never change. He noticed a black scar curved like a scimitar near his left eye. He wondered how many other scars István bore that couldn't be seen. "Your escape couldn't have been easy," Miklós said.

"It wasn't. We lost my sister, Vera."

Miklós's bushy white eyebrows drooped as he tried to conjure a face to go with the name. "She was thin, as I recall, sickly."

Steven's eyes darkened. His posture grew rigid and he started to wring his hands.

"Zoltán doesn't think László will ever grant Katalin's request for a divorce. Do you agree?" Miklós asked.

"Unfortunately, I do."

"Then how do we get her away from him?"

Steven smiled. Miklós was back less than forty-eight hours and already he had volunteered for a battle. Once a fighter, always a fighter, Steven thought.

"I don't know yet," Steven said with a distracted air. He was thinking as he was speaking. "But there's more to it than rescuing Katalin and Márta from Leányfalu. Not only do we have to get them away from him, but we have to make sure we can keep him away from them."

"Do you have anything on him?"

"I was given a letter just the other day that accused him of something, but it's an unsupported claim. It's a second-hand report of a death-bed confession. Though I'd like to hang the bastard with it, it's not enough. We need more."

Miklós nodded and patted Steven's knee in a gesture of encouragement. "I leave that end of it to you, István, but I want to be in on the escape plans. If anyone can tell you how to break out of a prison, I can."

Steven embraced the elderly man next to him. "I'm glad you're back, Miklós. We missed you. And we need you."

"Well, you know what they say," Miklós said, clasping hands with Steven as if taking a pledge. "Timing is everything."

36

September 1988

In Cleveland, Ohio, a woman carried her dinner to the table and turned on her television, clicking channels until she came to *World News Tonight*. It was a part of a daily ritual. Five nights a week, she came home from her job as an editor at the Hungarian language newspaper and ate dinner with Peter Jennings. Tonight, he was introducing a report on a visit made to Moscow by several Hungarian dignitaries. The woman raised the sound. With Red Square behind him, a young man with closely cropped hair, round tortoiseshell glasses and a camel's-hair overcoat, described a meeting between Gorbachev and a high-ranking Hungarian official:

> *"In Moscow today, there seemed to be an echo of the cry raised at this summer's Democratic convention: Where is Grósz? Yesterday, when several top Hungarian political figures arrived in Moscow, Prime Minister Károly Grósz was conspicuously absent, fanning the flames of rumors that discontent with Grósz and his*

*regime is widespread and growing. The claim is that Grósz, who
succeeded János Kádár, can't decide which side his bread is but-
tered on. He seems to be working overtime trying to court the
West and still please his superiors in the Soviet Union. It's precisely this vacillation that's provoked the tremendous debate currently raging between the conservatives and the reformers. While
that would not be unusual or significant in the United States,
in a nation known for imprisoning its opposition or silencing
them with tanks and guns, the fact that there is any debate at
all is something those of us in the West should pay attention to.
Certainly, they're listening here in Moscow.*

*"The big question, both here and in Budapest, is what hap-
pens if Grósz goes? Does the government remain in the tight
grip of the communists, or does it respond to the pressure being
mounted by the reformers? Today, László Böhm, the man considered by many to be the conservative most likely to succeed
Grósz, spent nearly an hour in a private meeting with President
Gorbachev. Afterward, the two men claimed that they had discussed matters pertaining to commerce and Gorbachev's scheduled visit to Budapest in October. Insiders claim they discussed
the feasibility of ousting Grósz and putting Böhm in charge.
With Böhm's hard-line record, there's no doubt his appointment
would greatly please those currently in power. And greatly displease those who aren't."*

László Böhm. The woman raced to the phone. With trembling fingers, she dialed the number of the one man who could help her, a man
who had become a close friend since she had emigrated from Hungary
in the seventies and settled in Cleveland. He was the retired head of the
electricians' union and a renowned union spokesman, Mihai Pal.

"Mihai? It's Kovács Magda."

"Magda. Good to hear from you," Mihai said, wiping some scraps
of dinner from his mouth. Normally, he would have asked if he could
have called back after he and his wife, Klara, had finished eating, but
Magda sounded upset. Very upset.

"I saw him. He was on the news. They said he's going to be the
next Prime Minister of Hungary." She was frantic. She switched from
Hungarian to English and back again. The words were coming so fast,
Mihai had to listen closely to understand her.

"Who was on the news?" Mihai asked, trying to calm her.

"You can't let them do that. You have political friends, don't you?
One of them's the ambassador, right?"

"Yes, that's right." Mihai had been so proud when Steven had been appointed to the post. He had sent him a telegram and had received a long, wonderful letter in return. In it, Steven had promised to call when he returned to the States. Now, Magda was asking him to call Steven. "What do you want me to do?"

"I don't know, but you have to do something. You have to convince your friends to do something. László Böhm cannot be head of the government!"

"Why not, Magda?" Mihai said. "What do you know about László Böhm?"

"He's the man who blinded Attila."

Katalin was at the piano when he arrived, lost in the andante con moto of Beethoven's "Appassionata." Since László never announced his visits beforehand, Katalin never prepared for them, though she wouldn't even if he did. He walked in. She kept right on playing. She had seen him. She chose to ignore him. He stood by her bench waiting for her to stop. When she didn't, he slammed his hands over hers.

"Don't do that," she said, wrenching her hands free, pushing the bench back and standing. She wouldn't permit him to look down on her.

"Then don't challenge me." László disliked encountering a battle every time he visited. He would have preferred that Katalin be more docile, more accepting of her situation. Clearly, that was not to be.

"I want to know when Márta and I are going to get out of here."

"Actually, that's why I came to see you."

Katalin couldn't stop the smile that burst onto her face. "You're letting us go?"

"I'm letting you perform for Mikhail Gorbachev."

"What?" The smile faded. Suspicion replaced it.

"Gorbachev is coming to Budapest. I've arranged a concert in his honor and you are the star." László folded his arms across his chest. A satisfied smile curled his lips. "You should be flattered. He asked for you."

"And you bartered me away like a pig at a county fair, didn't you?"

"You're supposed to be a concert pianist. I thought you would be delighted to play for someone of Gorbachev's stature."

"I would be if this concert were of my choosing, but it's not. You dangled me in front of his nose as a favor. You used me yet again and I hate it!"

The planes on László's face became sharper. His eyes darkened until they were almost black. Katalin refused to back off. She glared at him.

"Throughout this sham of a marriage, you used my name and talent to further your cause and you used my income to stuff your pockets. Well, I'm not going to let you use me now. I won't play at your special concert. Get another one of your prisoners to perform."

László was at her side in three strides. His hand gripped her arm so tightly she could feel the blood stop at his fingers.

"You're going to perform, Katalin, or I'm going to have to hurt someone. Do you understand?"

"Of course I understand. You're a bully," she said, her face still flushed with defiance. "You can only feel important when you're brow-beating others. But you know what? You're a dying breed, László. The reformers are getting stronger and stronger. Most of your comrades have smelled the change that's coming. They're beginning to make noises that sound an awful lot like capitulation. Not you, though. You're still old-time, hard-line László. Well, there's another revolution coming, Major Böhm, and when it hits, they're going to get you."

"You'd love that, wouldn't you," he said, pushing her away from him with such force she fell to the floor.

"You bet I would," she said, refusing to wince or scramble to her feet.

"Unfortunately for you, until this revolution of which you so fondly speak arrives, I'm in charge and you will play at that concert, Katalin. You have one month to prepare."

Long after the door slammed, Katalin remained on the floor, refusing to get up until she was certain that László's evil aura had dissipated. Each day, her hatred for him intensified. Not only because of the things he did, but also because of the way he made her feel. She hated feeling cut off from everyone and everything. She hated placing the burden of communication between herself and Steven on her father. She hated the fact that her uncle, her dear Uncle Miklós, had come back from the dead and she couldn't see him. And she hated the fact that she was separated from Steven without any immediate hope of reconciliation.

The other problem was that being alone opened the door to intro-spection. She spent hours examining her life and her choices, particularly her selection of László as her husband. What had she seen in him? If she asked it once, she asked it a thousand times. Yet each time, the answer was different. She had been lonely. He had been attentive. He had been gallant and respectful and passionate. Too, she remembered convincing herself that beneath the staid, controlled surface he presented to the world, a window of vulnerability existed, a window through which she would be able to find his heart and then his soul. For years she searched, often thinking she was nearing her goal and that he would become the full, complete person she wanted him to be. Now she knew the truth. Her quest had been hopeless from the start. László's mother had broken his heart and communism had killed his soul. She hadn't married a man, she had wed an emotionless cyborg fueled by an ambition to control the world around him.

If she had wanted to be more compassionate, she might have said he was doing all this because he had been so hurt and so frightened when he was a child, that the way he fought fear and avoided pain was by regulating events, that he was as helpless to change himself as she was to change him. But Katalin had spent years being compassionate and sympathetic about his needs. She had spent years trying to understand and accept the eccentricities of his behavior. No more. Now, she cared only about what happened to her and Márta and her family. She couldn't care less what happened to him.

"I have good news and bad news that could be great news," Matthew said as he entered Steven's office and closed the door behind him.

"Would you mind translating that?"

Matthew held up his right hand. "I have here the documentation we've been waiting for. You may now file for divorce from the estimable Madame Kardos. A moment of silence." He bowed his head and then held up his left hand. "I have here notes from a conversation I just had with—are you ready—Mihai Pal." Steven's eyes widened. He leaned forward, eager to hear what Mihai had to say. "A woman in Cleveland saw László's face on TV and fingered him as the man who blinded Attila Kovács."

"How does she know?"

"She was there," Matthew said, enjoying every moment of this revelation. "Her name is Magda Kovács. She was Attila's wife."

Steven pounded his desk and let go a triumphant howl.

"You wanted something to hang Böhm on. Here's your noose, baby brother."

"This, plus that letter to Ilona. It could be enough." He thought it over. "I need the Kovács woman. I need a signed affidavit."

"Taken care of. I've told Mihai to take her to Washington. The boys at State will depose her. They'll send us the paperwork. She's also said she would come here to testify against him if needed."

"Kovács has become a martyr," Steven said. "These are touchy times. The last thing the Soviets want is to replace Grósz with the man who blinded one of Hungary's most revered writers."

"It's things like that that start revolutions," Matthew said.

"The question is when do we fire the shot?"

Steven's secretary came in and handed him a piece of paper. "I thought you might want to see this," she said.

Steven read it quickly, but judging by the expression on his face, its contents were very engaging.

"It's a press release," Steven said. "On October twenty-third, there's going to be a concert at the Opera House honoring Soviet President Gorbachev. The Budapest Symphony will be conducted by Zoltán Gáspár and the soloist will be his daughter, the premiere pianist, Katalin Gáspár. The man responsible for this noble effort?"

"Let me guess," Matthew said. "Major László Böhm."

"Give that man a cigar," Steven said to his secretary, "and while you're at it, get Mr. Jackson and Mr. Vas in here, please."

"Are we about to plan our own revolution?" Matthew asked, taking a seat.

"Sort of." He swiveled his chair around so that he faced the window that looked out on Szabadság tér. He watched with detached amusement as a group of Soviet soldiers strutted about to the cacophonous music of a trumpet and a drum. They were having another one of their never-ending wreath-laying ceremonies. "Once we put together the armature of our coup, we'll call in Zoltán and Miklós so they can help us flesh it out."

"How is Miklós doing?"

Until they could ascertain whether or not Miklós's name was on a wanted list, Steven had suggested that Miklós stay in a suite of rooms in the Embassy. Each day, he and Zoltán met somewhere that allowed them to spend time together without attracting undue attention to either. Steven had decided that although Zoltán believed he was being followed, there was nothing László could do about his visiting the Embassy. Everyone knew Zoltán was friendly with Steven and Matthew and so his visits couldn't be questioned without raising questions about László. Besides, Miklós was practically unrecognizable, making it possible for the brothers to visit often, sometimes with Steven and Matthew, sometimes on their own. Several times, Steven had arranged for a car to take Miklós to the Strassers' or the Weisses' for dinner. Zoltán arrived after Miklós and left before him.

"So far, so good." Steven responded quickly because he wanted to move on.

Matthew nodded. He, too, was anxious to begin formulating a plan. "We have a lot of people to consider," he said.

"I know. It won't be easy, but it has to be done. And soon."

"How soon?" Matthew asked the question, but he had already anticipated the answer.

"One month," Steven said, circling the date on his desk calendar. "The night of the concert."

It was so rare that Steven and Cynthia dined together that when she entered the dining room and found him waiting, she was surprised, and nervous. A quick glance said he was relatively relaxed. His shoulders were not in that stiff-backed, military posture he adopted when he was angry, nor had his eyes darkened and narrowed as they did just before an explosion of temper. In fact, she thought, as she took her seat, he looked splendidly handsome. Perhaps he had used this brief separation to rethink his options and had concluded—properly so—that she was a much more valuable mate than that Hungarian woman.

Perhaps he had missed her. Despite their other differences, their bed had always proved a common denominator, a ground on which they could meet and agree—exquisitely, if she did say so herself. After the Douglas debacle he had vacated her bed, moving into another suite of rooms in the townhouse. She had refused to accept that decision as final. She treated it as a fit of pique, a temporary situation that would reverse itself with time and persistence. To that end, in Washington and here— until he locked his door against her—she had frequently insinuated herself into his bed, finding compelling ways of reminding him what they were when they were together, what he would be missing if he insisted upon their being apart.

Not that Cynthia evaluated herself solely in terms of her desirability as a sex object. She was too much of a feminist for that. To use such a narrow scale of judgment, one that didn't include intelligence or wit or savvy or substance, would be insulting and degrading. It was simply that in her experience, sex had always proved to be a fairly accurate barometer of compatibility. Those who had nothing in common had no passion. Those who shared surface interests shared good times, but rarely a memorable moment. They, on the other hand, had the capacity to create thunder, to shift the universe when their bodies fused in cataclysmic oneness. Who in their right minds could give that up forever?

Comforted by that thought, Cynthia lifted her napkin off the table, fluttered it slightly, and then laid it across her lap. The butler brought a bottle of wine for her approval. Steven drank the local grape. She drank only those wines she had imported from France.

"Wouldn't you like some Meursault, darling?"

"Thank you, no," Steven said. "I'm quite content with this."

As ambassador, Steven thought it rude not to drink the wines produced in Hungary, especially since he considered them first rate.

"It's so nice to see you across the table." Her mouth curved in an arc of loving sincerity. "I've missed that."

Steven returned her smile, but his had a different shading. "That's too bad, because you're going to have to get used to it."

Cynthia nearly spilled her wine. Her insides began to jump. She had to will her hand to set the glass down without toppling it.

"Excuse me?"

From beneath the table, Steven pulled a file folder. From that he extracted several photographs, which he tossed over to her. They were snapshots of the same person at various stages in his life. Cynthia looked at them with little interest. She couldn't imagine what they had to do with her.

"I think you can see it in the shape of the eyes," Steven said, holding up a picture of young man in his early twenties. He looked at Cynthia and then back at the photo. "The chin is the same as well."

"What are you talking about?" Beads of sweat traced her hairline, moving down the back of her neck and staining the collar of her satin blouse.

"This is your son, Cynthia. Yours and Benjamin's."

The glass shattered as she grabbed the photographs from Steven's hand. The wine ran like a loose stream across the table. Steven held on to several pictures. Cynthia clutched the others, looking at one, then another, then another. Her eyes were wide with a mix of fear and astonishment and discovery.

"Benjamin was a stable boy," Steven said, telling the story Cynthia had wished would never be told. "He was Jefferson and Ruby's oldest son. You and he were the same age, nineteen. Benjamin was handsome and he worshiped you."

Cynthia refused to look at him, but tears filled her eyes as she looked at Benjamin's child and remembered the boy's father.

"You and he had a rather torrid affair, from what I understand, meeting whenever you could. Your favorite rendezvous was a small cabin on the outskirts of Mayfair that had belonged to one of your mother's grooms. He had been let go and had not yet been replaced, leaving the cabin conveniently vacant. The day of your mother's accident, you and Benjamin went to the cabin early. He wasn't around when Cecilia came to the stable for her horse. The other boy wasn't as good as Benjamin. He forgot to check the straps."

Cynthia's head moved from side to side. Her tears collected in a pool on the table. Still, she refused to look at Steven. She couldn't. Her field of vision was too crowded with scenes of the past.

"After Cecilia's fall, no one could find you. For two days, while your mother lay dying in a hospital, you and Benjamin remained in that cabin. Claudia, desperate to find you, went on a search. She covered every inch of Mayfair, several times over. It was after Cecilia died that she remembered seeing a light on in a cabin that was supposed to be empty. She tried to get to you before Owen did, but he had suspected that she knew where you were and he followed her."

Cynthia recoiled at the memory of Owen bursting into that cabin, shouting obscenities at her and Benjamin, tearing at everything in his path. He was mad from grief, blaming the two of them for Cecilia's death, unwilling to listen to any explanation, any apology, any expressions of remorse. She trembled as she remembered how Owen had refused to let her stand by him during the funeral, how he had demanded that she be allowed by the grave only after he had gone, how he had sworn never to forgive her for taking his Cecilia from him.

"Benjamin was shattered, wasn't he, Cynthia? He felt responsible for your mother's death. If he had mounted the saddle, she wouldn't have fallen and died. Isn't that how he felt, Cynthia?"

Cynthia nodded and then cupped her head in her hands.

"The day after the funeral, Benjamin got stinking drunk, climbed into his truck, tear-assed around Lexington and ran himself into a tree. He died instantly."

Cynthia gasped, reacting just as she had when she heard the news for the first time.

"You never went to his funeral though, did you?"

Cynthia didn't respond. She held her breath, waiting for the other shoe to drop.

"You thought if you didn't go, no one would know about you and Benjamin, that it would be over and done with as if it never happened, that it would simply become another skeleton in a closet already crowded with skeletons."

Cynthia's tears had stopped. For the moment, her face was blank, void of expression, as if she was too emotionally exhausted to mount even the slightest response.

"But you were pregnant and the child was definitely Benjamin's. Since the last thing Owen wanted was a scandal, he shipped you off to Switzerland where you had the baby, this baby."

He took one of the photos from his stack and pushed it toward her. It had been taken two days after the birth. Cynthia was holding the baby, snuggling it to her, looking down at the sleeping infant and caressing its cheek.

"You gave him away."

Cynthia looked at the photo and put it down. She didn't need to

Katalin walked down the path toward the river, trailing after Márta, who was scampering ahead of them, a breeze caused Katalin to draw her sweater tighter around her body.

"István and Mátyás have come up with a plan," Zoltán said, keeping his head facing forward so his voice couldn't travel to the guard following several yards behind. "They're working on the details now."

Katalin nodded. "Did you get in touch with Tibor?"

"Yes. He'll be at the market, behind one of the flower stands."

"Good." Katalin was pleased. She had worked out her own plans for Márta's safety. Tibor was crucial to those plans.

"I have a letter from István."

Zoltán dug the envelope out of his pocket and gave it to Katalin. It surprised him that the guards, who searched him before and after each visit, allowed him to bring Katalin mail. He supposed it was because László didn't care whether Katalin and her beloved wrote to each other. As long as she had agreed to what he wanted and she remained under his control, he could afford to be generous.

Katalin opened the envelope and read the note. Neither she nor Steven knew when or if László would decide to revert to type and confiscate their letters, so they kept them brief.

> *Katya,*
>
> *The pictures of our daughter were wonderful. They've made a big difference. She's beautiful, like her mother.*
>
> *I love you.*
>
> *István.*

"I'm glad the photographs were helpful."

On one of Zoltán's visits, he and Katalin snapped two rolls of film, posing Márta here and there along the property line, making certain that they had covered most of the area surrounding the house. The guards had taken them to a shop in Szentendre, had them developed, studied them, and seeing nothing but a little girl hamming it up for a camera, returned them to Zoltán. He gave them to Steven so that Ernie Vas and Shadow could examine them.

"István said that Ernie has already been out here going over the routes in and out."

Katalin smiled. Ernie must be thrilled to be doing something so military in nature. He was a bit odd, she had to admit, but she liked him. More than that, she knew he would die protecting Steven.

"Katya, I have something to tell you."

Katalin turned toward her father. She didn't like the sound of his voice, or the look on his face.

"I'm not going with you."

Katalin stopped dead in her tracks. "What do you mean? You have to. I need you with me. Márta needs you."

"Hush." He held his finger to his lips and put his arm around her, comforting her. "Listen to me. I wanted to go, you know I did. You and Márta and István, you're my family. There's nothing I want more in this world than to see you two married and living happily ever after with your child, that beautiful little girl. But then, Miklós returned. Katya, I'm his family too, and he has no one else. I can't leave him alone now. You understand that."

Katalin had been expecting this because she did understand. "It's just that I'm frightened for you both," she said. "I'd feel so much better if Uncle Miklós came with us. Then I'd be able to take care of you both. Ask him to come. Please, Papa. Ask him to come."

"I did, but it's too much for him right now. He's just returned, Katya. When you see him you'll know. He's weak. He needs time to recuperate. To take part in another escape? It's too much. Maybe later."

What Katalin feared is that there would be no later. What if something went wrong? Katalin kept her eyes forward. She didn't want anyone to see the worry or the pain she felt. Zoltán saw.

"István promised that László will be taken care of and I believe him. He won't be a threat to me or to Miklós."

Katalin took Zoltán's arm. She would kill László with her own hands if he harmed either of these men, though she knew it would never come to that. Steven would never allow it.

"Things are changing, Katalin. Last week there was a student rally in Szeged. Thirty-five thousand people protested the building of the dam. No one was arrested. Just this morning in the newspaper there was a letter to the editor objecting to Ceauşescu's treatment of the ethnic Hungarians living in Romania. When have they ever printed a letter to the editor! Katya, things are happening."

"You don't know what's happening, Papa. Don't invest your life in false hopes."

"I'm not. If things take a turn, István will get us out of here. If not, we'll visit. Visas are being issued to those who can show proof that they're visiting relatives in the United States. You're a relative. Miklós and I will visit you. You'll visit us. Please, Katya. Say you understand."

She couldn't speak. Her heart was too full. Instead, she threw her arms around her father.

"I'll miss you, Papa."

"You won't have to miss me, *dragam*. You'll see."

At the bottom of the hill, they turned onto the road that led from

Leányfalu to Szentendre. There, filling a wide bend in the road was a market teeming with merchandise. Flowers, vegetables, jars of jam and honey, racks of clothing and peasant embroideries, baked goods, butchered meat, an array of sausages, tanks of fish, boxes of fruit, trolleys loaded with pig carcasses, and of course, masses of cherry-red and yellow paprika pods, strung into wreaths or hanging like garlands. Anything and everything was there, all on trestle tables, all for a bartered price.

Márta ran to the first *langós* stand she found. Zoltán watched the peasant vendor sling a lump of pale dough into a caldron of hot fat. It wriggled and writhed until it dimpled and turned golden in color. Márta liked hers sprinkled with powdered sugar, Zoltán preferred his plain. But Katalin had no stomach now for treats. She was looking for Tibor. When she found him, she left grandfather and child to explore the market while she headed for the flower stand. To her relief, the guard, assuming quite correctly that she wouldn't bolt without her daughter, followed Márta and Zoltán, leaving her free to talk with Tibor.

"I've been worried about you," he said, playing with a bouquet of late summer blossoms.

"And I about you. How are you? How are your children?"

"We're all well. But it's your child we're talking about now."

Katalin nodded, reaching over to examine some purple and red anemones.

"I need to know she's safe before anything else takes place."

"When I returned her to you, I told you then I was one of her caretakers. I meant it." Tibor squeezed her hand quickly, before anyone could witness such a breach of behavior. "My brother and his wife will do what you asked. They will care for Márta as if she were their own."

"I know that, Tibor."

Over Katalin's shoulder, Tibor noticed her guard approaching. "Here, lady. Your flowers."

He handed her a bunch of wild roses, bright pink with a pale center. She looked at them and then at him. Who at this bustling market would ever believe that she was going to entrust her daughter to the care of this gypsy? But she was. She would trust him with her life.

"Thank you," she said, proffering a quick smile. "For everything."

She started to go. The guard then went to track down Zoltán and Márta.

"Don't thank me now," Tibor said. "After. There'll be plenty of time for that."

After. She nodded and waved, but they both knew that afterward, they might never see each other again.

37

Budapest, October 1988

At seven o'clock in the morning, Katalin ran to the guesthouse. Racing up the stairs, she pounded on the door of the guard's room.

"My daughter's ill," she said when he asked what the problem was. "She has a fever and chills and she's coughing. I need a doctor."

"Can't you give her something?" He looked worried, unsure about what to do.

"I tried, but it's not working. That's why I need a doctor," she said, pleading.

"I'll have to call the Major."

"I don't care whom you call. I need someone out here to look at my child!"

He debated about what to do. Katalin tapped her foot on the ground with obvious impatience.

"Why don't you call Dr. Strasser?" she suggested. "You know who she is, don't you?" He nodded. "She's old and lame. She's not going to run off with Márta or beat you up. She will simply examine Márta, give her medication, and stay with her while I go into Budapest for the concert."

"I don't . . ."

"Just call the Major."

While the guard went to the phone, Katalin returned to Márta's room.

"How are you feeling, sweetheart?"

Márta looked at Katalin and grinned. Then she coughed, hacking loudly. When she had coughed so much her throat hurt, she stopped and whispered in Katalin's ear. "How was that?"

Katalin kissed her cheek and hugged her close. "That was wonderful. Now don't forget, no smiling."

Márta nodded and put on her most serious face. The guard knocked on the door of the room. Katalin tiptoed to meet him, walking into the hall and closing the door behind her.

"The Major said he would call Dr. Strasser and take care of the arrangements."

Katalin's stomach lurched at the thought. She hoped László wouldn't do anything that would ruin this end of the plan. They had considered most contingencies, but most wasn't necessarily all.

László arrived at his office at eight o'clock. Already, he had someone waiting. According to his secretary, Ambassador Steven Kardos was in his office.

No surprise there. László had been expecting a visit from the honorable Ambassador. László had thought that once Steven heard that Katalin was confined to Leányfalu, he would have trampled down his door, wailed about his love for the fair Madame Böhm, and begged for her freedom. Actually, László had been looking forward to it.

"Ambassador Kardos," he said, sticking out his hand "what a delightful surprise. To what do I owe the pleasure of such an early morning visit? You did get your tickets for the concert this evening, didn't you?" He walked around behind his large desk and stood before his high-back chair, knowing that the setting exuded power and position. "Do you need a few more perhaps?"

"I received my tickets, Major, and I have a sufficient amount, thank you. But I did not come to discuss the concert."

Steven sat in the chair in front of László's desk and began to rummage around in his attaché case. Protocol insisted that he wait until asked to be seated or until László took a seat. This was a deliberate affront. Steven meant it that way. And that's exactly the way László took it.

"I thought you might like to know what papers I am presenting to Soviet President Gorbachev, Prime Minister Grósz, and the international press."

László, having been given little choice, took his seat and glowered at Steven, who was arranging papers on the desk.

"This is a letter sent to Dr. Ilona Strasser naming you as the man who issued the order to have her pushed in front of a trolley, thereby severing her leg and causing a lifetime disability."

Steven took a copy of the letter, turned it around and placed it in front of László for his perusal.

"This is a copy of an affidavit given by Mrs. Magda Kovács to the FBI in Washington and sworn to in front of witnesses. It states, unequivocally, that you were responsible for the blinding and imprisonment of the playwright, Attila Kovács."

Steven put that piece of paper in front of László.

"I also have a video of Mrs. Kovács making her accusation and giving her personal account of the crime. In it, she was shown photographs of you as you look today, and as you looked in 1975 when she alleges you coldbloodedly ordered acid to be thrown in her husband's face by your accomplice. She provided positive identification."

Steven held up one last piece of paper. "As corroboration, I have a signed statement from a gentleman who lived with Attila Kovács in Dudinka for all of the five years following Attila's arrival there until the time of his death. The story Attila told his fellow prisoner duplicates exactly the one his wife told to our FBI agents in Washington. Of course, Attila was unable to give an eye-witness account, nor was he able to name the names of his two attackers, but because the two stories were identical, down to a description of the gold signet ring you wear on your hand, the one with the woman of the liberation monument in the center, his story becomes admissible evidence."

László's hands were under the table. Without thinking, his left hand covered his right, the one with the ring on it. It had been given to his father, Ernö, by the Soviets in recognition for his helpfulness during the tedious process of liberating Budapest from the Germans. Ernö had given it to László when he had graduated from the Military Academy.

"The way I see it," Steven said, keeping his eyes fixed on László's face, "You're in a whole lot of trouble, Major."

"I deny it all."

"You can deny it to me all you want. I'm not the one who's going to arrest you, although I will confess I would enjoy the task. Frankly, I couldn't care less what happens to you. My concern is simply that you divorce Katalin and let her and my daughter go." He said the last words with deliberate emphasis. László tried not to, but he flinched. What annoyed Steven was that László hadn't flinched because he loved Márta and had believed himself her father; this was instead, embarrassment that he couldn't father any child; Márta or otherwise, and that some other man had a real claim to the child others thought was his. "I would guess that you might have to go to some lengths to deny all this to Gorby and Grósz, however."

"If you think they'll take your word over mine, you're—how do they say in your country—" László said smugly, "off base."

Steven laughed and shook his head. "I don't think so. I have concrete evidence and an unimpeachable witness. Besides, while you've been playing media star and jailing innocent women and children, the Cold War has been thawing. All of a sudden, the bad guys are running around trying to look like good guys. I know it's getting confusing, but I think you ought to pay attention." Steven clucked his tongue, giving László a look of pity. "They don't want any bad publicity and take it from me, László, this is bad publicity, especially the part about blinding Freedom's Playwright." Steven whistled. "Whew! This is going to make them look mean, László, and these days, they don't like to look mean."

"I thought you said there were two men in the room with Kovács."

"That's true. Both Magda and Attila claim there was someone with you."

László leaned back against his throne and chuckled. Though he tried to cover it, Steven heard the nervous edge.

"I know who that someone was. Do you?"

"No, but I knew before I walked in here that you were going to tell me." Steven folded his arms across his chest, crossed his legs, leaned back, and prepared to listen to László's alibi.

"Kassak Ferenc. Surely you know who that is."

Miklós had told Steven that. In fact, he and Miklós and Zoltán had spent quite some time talking about the frightening irony of Kassak being László's sidekick.

"He's the man who mangled your father-in-law's hands at Recsk. Just for the record," Steven said, with clear revulsion in his voice, "the fact that you married Katalin and still chummed with that man testifies to your lack of character."

"I would hardly call a lowlife such as Kassak a chum, but speaking of testifying," László said with insufferable arrogance, "you've given me a wonderful idea. If anyone would be foolish enough to bring charges against me, which I doubt, I'll subpoena Zoltán and have him testify on my behalf. Surely he'd be delighted to tell a courtroom what a feral beast Kassak is."

László laughed. It was a slightly hysterical cackle. If Steven could have, he would have leapt over the desk and choked him.

"Think of it! Gáspár Zoltán, a man I would guess hates my guts, being forced to defend me. You have to love it, don't you, Kardos?"

"I don't love it and if I were you, I wouldn't count on it, Major." Steven stood, collected his papers, put them back in his case, and slammed it shut. "I would count on doing some jail time, however. If you have a spare hour or two before the concert, I suggest you go shopping for long underwear. According to my source, it gets very cold in Dudinka."

Steven spun on his heel and, with an annoyingly confident gait, strode out of László's office. Because he was checking his watch to see if he was going to be on time for his next appointment, he never noticed the young man in the hallway, the one who had been listening at the door of the side entrance to László's office, the young man named Péter Kassak.

It was only nine o'clock in the morning. The Opera Ház was as still as a church. While the other gypsies went about their business in the basement, Farah explored the house. First, she strolled about the lobby, trying to imagine what it must have been like when the Opera Ház had first been built, when Hungary had a nobility and an upper class that came to evenings here in fancy dress. She dragged her feet along the floor, letting her worn-down soles scrape where elegant heels once trod, progressing toward one of the two grand white marble staircases that led to the circle level. Step by step, she made her way up to the promenade, her eyes drinking in the lavish decorations, the arched and frescoed ceiling, the eight red marble columns that defined the clerestory, the half-dozen brass chandeliers with fat milk-white globes covering the electric light bulbs, the series of paintings that dotted the walls, the black diamond-shaped insets in the marble floor.

Farah pushed open one of the doors leading into the auditorium. She walked toward the stage and then looked back and up. In the rear of the horseshoe-shaped hall was the box of honor. Gilded, extremely ornate, it was the place where Soviet President Gorbachev would be, the place where László Böhm would be. Farah squinted, narrowing her eyes, zooming in on the seat she thought would be his. How she hated him!

László Böhm was the man responsible for her banishment. He was the one who had caused her to lose her husband and her children and her very people. He was the one who had damned her to walk among those who didn't want her, the one who had damned her to be shunned forever by those she loved. She glared at the box, recalling the day of the *Kris*. Inside her head a voice had screamed at her, urging her to tell the *krisatori* why she had kidnapped the baby, that she had been threatened, that she had been forced to do it, that she hadn't meant to bring disgrace and dishonor to the *kumpania*. But she had held her tongue. He had warned her. Any mention of his name and one of her children might have an accident, or Tibor or her parents might find themselves in jail, or in a camp.

"Böhm!" Farah shouted his name now, letting it bounce off the ceiling and reverberate against the walls of the elegant auditorium. She thrust her arms into the air above her head, exhorting the spirit world to help her punish this man who had punished her for eternity. "Böhm!" Her body quaked from the violence of her outburst. She grabbed a chair for support and waited for the spasm to pass.

Still breathing heavily, but calmer, she turned toward the stage. There, in the center, directly opposite one enemy, her other enemy would sit. The famous Katalin Gáspár. The infamous Vadrósza. Whatever name she used, Farah hated her. It was her fault. All of it! If she hadn't come to that courtyard, none of this would have happened. Tibor would have been content to make music with a gypsy band. He would have been content with life the way he was supposed to live it, with her and their children and their people. He wouldn't have let his dreams run wild.

She bewitched him, Farah thought as she mounted the stage and stood by the piano where Katalin would sit. She cast a spell over him. It had to be. Otherwise, Tibor would have loved Farah. He would have been happy with her. He would have defended her instead of turning her in.

Farah shook her head, wishing she could scramble her brains so that when they settled she could make sense of all that had happened. Her husband had turned her in to the *Kris!* He should have stood by her side and pleaded her case, no matter what she had done. He should have explained what a horrible man László Böhm was and how persuasive he could be. But Tibor never even heard her side of the story. She had hinted that there was more to it than jealous revenge, that without additional provocation she wouldn't have taken another woman's baby. But he wouldn't listen. He had recounted her other sins, the thefts, the lies, the taunts and barbs she had tossed at Katalin over the years.

Farah pulled at her hair. It pained her to realize that she had built a case against herself. Worse, she had done such a masterful job of it that, now, she stood alone. Tibor had the tribe, his family, their children, Katalin, and his damned music. László had power and position and Katalin and his child and whatever else he wanted. She, Farah, had nothing. She had no family, no friends, no home. But tonight, she would avenge herself.

For two years she had tramped all over Hungary and Romania, begging in the streets, sleeping in doorways or vacant lean-tos or outside under the stars. Eventually, she had found her way back to Esztergom where her family lived. For weeks, she hovered at the outskirts of the gypsy community, not daring to enter, not able to stay away. One day, she summoned the courage to go to the garage where her father worked. She tried to get him to speak to her. He ignored her, but she came again and again and again. He looked past her or through her or around her. She pleaded with him to listen to the truth about what happened. She had decided that nothing László Böhm could do to her could be worse than the agony of alienation, not even death.

She told her father about László's threats, his warnings about reprisals for disobedience. She told him how she had feared for him, for her mother, for her husband, and most of all, for her children. She begged him to do something, to go to the elders and speak to them about rescinding the decree of the *krisatori* of Báthordomb.

One afternoon, without turning around to face her, he said, "They have agreed to convene a special council to hear you. Come to the concert ground on Prímás sziget. Eight o'clock."

Nine men were waiting for her at the kiosk on Bandleader Island. One by one, they climbed the wooden steps and entered the wooden structure, turning their backs on her as she moved toward the center. She had expected someone to address her, but she was greeted with complete silence. It was she who was supposed to speak. They were there to listen. She told them how one *gorgio* had forced her to bring dishonor on the gypsies, how another had masqueraded as a gypsy, using the clan for her own purposes without giving anything back. She regaled them with her tales of injustice and unfairness, ticking off each of László's ugly threats, each of his wicked lies. She told them why she hadn't confessed all this to the *krisatori*, how terrified she had been that László would seek revenge on her children. She beseeched them to understand and forgive, to see that it was Katalin who had disgraced the gypsies with her pretense, László who had dishonored the gypsies with his manipulation.

It had taken less than an hour for them to reach a decision. They could not commute the sentence of Tibor's tribe. To them, she was dead. The tribe into which she had been born, the Walachia, was willing to allow her to exist as an outcast, one who lives on the fringe of their world, but only if she could prove what she had just claimed. If she couldn't, she would be banished forever.

Several weeks later, she spotted a number of posters announcing Katalin's concert. Immediately, she asked for people. They gave her a small army, but even among her own troops she was shunned. They would not speak to her. The would not share their food with her. They would not lie with her. But they would be with her tonight when she did what had to be done.

Once again, her eyes went from the stage to the gilded box. Her heart raced as she thought about what she was going to do. She was nervous, and so she laughed. The sound echoed, growing more shrill with each reverberation.

"What is that *gorgio* expression," she asked the spirits she felt had gathered around her. "What is it they say about situations like this?" She raised her arms again and waved her fingers toward her face, begging the answer to come to her. "Ah yes," she said aloud, her laugh becoming desperate and sinister. "I'm going to kill two birds with one stone."

At ten o'clock, Steven presented his credentials at the Soviet Embassy and requested an emergency meeting with the Soviet ambassador. When he was ushered in to his counterpart's office, the florid-faced man appeared confused. It was unusual for them to call on each other. It was almost unheard of to do so without prior notice.

"I have some information that is of importance to you and your government," Steven said. He was offered a seat next to the translator. "I'm aware that your President has been meeting with a man named László Böhm. Though I realize I have no business questioning with whom your President seeks counsel, the word is that Mr. Gorbachev and Major Böhm have become quite close."

"They have been having a series of discussions. What of it?"

Thankfully, his tone was more curious than combative. For Steven, that was his go-ahead.

"With all that's going on in the world today, Mr. Ambassador, I think a man should know whom he's getting into bed with, don't you?"

At eleven o'clock, Gábor's car stopped in front of the cottage at Leányfalu. The guard opened the door and bent to help Dr. Strasser from the passenger seat. Ilona moved slowly, awkwardly. Gábor busied the guard with questions about when his mother-in-law could be picked up and how they were going to get medication if they needed something other than what was in Ilona's black bag. The guard answered as best he could, all the while inspecting Ilona's medical kit, her overnight bag, and her purse.

Meanwhile, at the back of the cottage, a switch was being made.

"You go with Aunt Judit," Katalin said, disallowing her tears as she kissed her daughter's cheeks and handed her out the window to Judit. "Mama will see you later tonight."

"I love you, Mama." Márta scrambled out of Judit's arms and hugged Sarí, who was then hoisted up and through the window. "I left you my dolly," Márta said.

"I left you mine," Sarí whispered, giggling nervously. Quickly, Katalin helped her into Márta's terry-cloth bathrobe, pulling the hood up over the child's hair.

"Gábor and I will follow the wagon until they meet Matthew. When I know she's with him, we'll head back to Budapest."

"How can I ever thank you?"

Judit kissed her finger and touched it to Katalin's nose. "You just did," she said, refusing to give full vent to her feelings. "As for you," she said, pulling Sarí to the window for one last kiss, "remember what we talked about."

"I'm doing this for Márta because she's my friend."

"Right!" With that, Judit lifted Márta into her arms and the two of them headed for the bushes. From there, they would double back down the road, where they would meet Gábor. At the market, they would give Márta to Tibor's brother, who would get her out of town in a *vardo*. Matthew would meet them at Esztergom, take Márta, and head for the border. With his diplomatic papers and the ones he had made for Márta, they should have no trouble passing through to Austria.

Sarí watched her mother and Márta disappear into the trees. Katalin nodded and the little girl wriggled down under the covers. She was to pretend to be Márta and to be sick. Grandma was going to pretend to take care of her and Katalin was going to make believe she was her mother. When they heard footsteps approaching, Katalin took her place on the bed, positioned herself so that Sarí's form was clearly visible but not her face, leaned over, and kissed her godchild for luck.

The play had begun.

It was noon. Ernie Vas had finally made it into an officer's uniform. It belonged to an officer of the Hungarian security police and not the United States Army, but Ernie didn't care. It looked good. It felt good. And it was just what he needed to fool the man who was exiting the police station and heading for this car. As the young man approached, Ernie rehearsed his lines. Though he had been studying Hungarian for years—his way of thanking Steven for saving his life and his way of apologizing to both brothers for all the razzing he had given them for their accents—this was the first time he was going to use it with a native.

"Don't rush," he said, holding up a hand. "I've got the next watch. And you, you lucky beast, have the night off."

Before the man could ask, Ernie produced his orders, forged to a fare-thee-well by Shadow Jackson, right down to a precise replica of László Böhm's signature.

"What happened?"

"Madame Böhm is coming into town for the concert. Her daughter is ill and someone's there watching her. I guess the Major decided this was as good a night as any to give you a break."

"I could use it."

"I'll bet," Ernie said. "All I need are the keys and I'll be on my way."

The officer reached into his pocket, handed Ernie the keys, and turned to go. "Do you know how to get there?"

"I have a map," Ernie said, knowing it wouldn't sound good for him to say that he had been scouting the area for weeks. "It looks easy enough."

"It is. Take care. See you tomorrow."

Ernie nodded and waved. "Later, baby," he mumbled under his breath as he climbed into the Lada. "Much, much later."

It was one o'clock when Matthew met Tibor's brother and sister-in-law on the other side of Esztergom. After he had greeted Márta and made her comfortable in the front seat of his car, he offered his thanks and his assurances that so far, all was well.

"Tibor's children were taken to Mera last night," Matthew said. "We've received word that they're safe and welcome to stay until Tibor collects them."

Since they had no way of knowing whether or not László would be arrested, there had to be a plan to protect everyone who might find himself in his murderous path.

"And Tibor?"

"He's going to be onstage. It's risky, but I think we've got him covered," Matthew said honestly. "When Katalin moves, they all move. Tibor will be taken to the Embassy, along with Katalin's father and uncle. They'll be safe there."

"I hope so," the gypsy said.

"So do I," Matthew answered, looking at the little girl in the car, thinking about what her parents must go through before they saw her tonight. "So do I."

At two o'clock, Steven prepared himself to present the same documents to Károly Grósz as he had to the Soviet ambassador. Since the Soviets had no grounds on which to arrest or to condemn Böhm, all Steven had hoped to accomplish with the ambassador was an immediate and open distancing of the Soviet powers from László. Upon leaving, although the ambassador had appeared concerned and had promised to relay the information to President Gorbachev as quickly as possible, Steven realized he wouldn't know the results of that interview until later.

With Grósz, the emphasis had to be entirely different. Steven not only had to convince the Prime Minister that László was a threat to his position, he had to persuade him that László was a dangerous man who should be arrested. The sooner, the better. It was not going to be easy. Steven couldn't reveal the plans involving Katalin because that could place her in jeopardy. He couldn't push, because he couldn't risk Grósz feeling resentful of Steven's interference. Though in private they had an easy, comfortable relationship, in public they remained adversaries. There was also the possibility that Grósz was deliberately blind to László's maneuvering. László was intimidating. Who knew what he had on Grósz?

When Steven entered Grósz's office, he blanked his mind of negatives. Instead, he focused on his mission: to prosecute László Böhm and to prove him guilty, not only of the crimes he actually committed, but also of potential treason against Grósz. He intended to use every ounce of his persuasiveness, every bit of gossip, every hint of scandal he had ever heard about László, every slimy insinuation, accusation, or allegation. He needed everything he could get his hands on. Getting Grósz to listen was one thing. Getting him to act in time was another.

In Leányfalu, at precisely two o'clock, Ernie pulled up in front of Katalin's house and parked alongside the other police car. After presenting himself and his papers to the guard, he began the hustle.

"The Major doesn't want her to be late," he said looking at his wrist as if he and László had synchronized watches. "This concert is important. Madame Böhm still has to rehearse. Drive carefully, but move it!"

"She's saying good-bye to her daughter."

"How is she? What's her name? Márta?" The other guard nodded. "The Major said there's someone here taking care of her."

The guard nodded again. "Dr. Strasser. The kid has a bad cold. No problem, though. She slept most of the day."

"Good," Ernie said. "I could use an easy night."

"I'm ready." Katalin had a garment bag and a small duffle with her.

Ernie helped Katalin into the back of the car while the policeman slid into the driver's seat. Once they were gone, Ernie went in to check on Ilona and Sarí. In half an hour, when he was certain they wouldn't be seen, they would be on the road to Budapest.

At three o'clock, Gábor Weiss went to the garage that repaired Shalom's ambulances. Because it was in the Jewish section of town and staffed by men who attended the same synagogue as the Weisses, it wasn't difficult to talk the head mechanic into lending him an ambulance scheduled to be delivered to the hospital the next day.

"I have an aunt who's taken a bad turn," Gábor said. "She lives in Kaposvár and refuses to go to the hospital there. She's too ill to travel in a car and I can't get anyone to transport her up. If you agree, I'll rent this from you. Tomorrow, when I deliver her to Shalom, I'll deliver the ambulance as well."

József liked Gábor. He had operated on József's father and had done a good job. And he could use the money. The hospital wasn't expecting the ambulance until tomorrow. What would the harm be? he figured.

What, indeed.

At four o'clock, while the orchestra was on a break, Katalin did her preconcert test of the performance piano and readied herself for the general rehearsal. Running scales, she felt for the responsiveness of the hammers and the tightness of the strings. She listened to the sound and the resonance, checking to be certain there was no tinniness, only deep, pure honest tones. As she worked, she became conscious of someone watching her. Without stopping or removing her fingers from the keys, she searched the empty auditorium. Something caught her eye. It was a glimmer of light coming from a booth. At first she thought it was one of the stagehands testing the spotlight. A second glance told her the location was in the adjoining booth and it was not a light, but a reflection. She continued to play. Two minutes later, she checked again. It was gone. She looked again. There was nothing but darkness.

It could have been her imagination.

At five o'clock, Steven knocked on the door to Cynthia's sitting room. When she bade him enter, he found her lounging on her favorite chaise, her legs peeking out from beneath a pale pink peignoir. Her eyes followed him as he walked toward her. Grabbing the chair from her dressing table, he pulled it alongside the chaise and seated himself.

"I received the papers today," he said, referring to the divorce papers Dallas Crawford had filed on Cynthia's behalf. "Thank you for being so prompt and so understanding."

"Never let it be said that I stood in the way of true love." Cynthia had wanted to sound sarcastic. Instead, she sounded sad and uncharacteristically vulnerable.

"I never meant to hurt you," Steven said. He meant it and because it was an honest sentiment, Cynthia believed him. "Despite everything, Katalin and I could never escape each other."

"You didn't want to escape from her, Steven. If you had, I might have stood a chance."

Steven reached over and took her hand in his. "Maybe it was a bond that was knotted too tightly when we were children. Maybe it was because fate continued to bring us together. Whatever it was, Cynthia, my loving Katalin didn't stop me from caring for you." When she looked skeptical, he raised her hand to his lips and kissed it. "I did care. You know I did."

She pulled her hand away and used it to wipe away a traitorous tear. "That's what makes this so painful. You did care. I know that. I even think that for a brief time you loved me, but I killed it, just as I always do." She laughed, but it was so close to a sob, it was hard to differentiate. "When it comes to love, I have a black thumb. Look what I did to my mother and my father. Look what I did to Claudia. All she ever wanted to do was protect me and love me and I've succeeded in making her hate me, just like Owen did."

"He didn't hate you, Cynthia," Steven said gently. "He wanted to, but he didn't. He loved you with all his heart. He just couldn't forgive you."

Cynthia dropped her head into her hands. She didn't want Steven to see her this way. She had always been so proud, so strong, so controlled. Suddenly, a disobedient sob escaped her lips. If she had been less proud, less strong, less controlled, she could have held on to him.

"And," she said, looking into his eyes, "look what I did to Benjamin. I not only destroyed the love he had for me, I killed him."

"Cynthia . . ."

"I did," she insisted, "It was all my fault. If you doubt me, just look into Jefferson's eyes or Ruby's. Just watch them when I'm around. Ask them if they understand why their son got drunk and ran his car into a pole." She sighed and shook her head from side to side, grieving over a death that had occurred years ago. She wiped her eyes with her sleeve. "Do they know? About the baby, I mean."

"I don't think so," Steven said. "You can ask Dallas. He's the one who's been forwarding the support money. My guess is that in wanting to spare you and himself the embarrassment of an illegitimate child, Owen simply disposed of the matter via adoption. Telling Jefferson and Ruby would have complicated things."

"But it would have been the right thing to do," Cynthia said, reading Steven's mind.

"Yes. It would have." Steven eyed her carefully. "You've never asked me about the child. Aren't you curious about him?"

"Very much so." Cynthia's tone surprised him. It was filled with concern and caring. "When you first brought it up, I was too angry to ask and too frightened to listen. I'm neither of those things right now, so tell me what you know."

Steven smiled. "His name is the one you gave him in the hospital."

"Benjamin." She didn't say it as much as it rode through her lips on a heavy sigh.

"Benjamin Grässe. He's twenty-two years old and a first-year law student in Zurich. He's seeing a lovely young woman, also a law student, whom he plans to wed as soon as they've finished school."

"Does he know about me?"

"He knows he was adopted. Obviously, he knows he's of mixed blood. But no, he doesn't know about you."

"Do you know where he lives?"

"Yes."

"What do you think would happen if I went to see him?"

This was unexpected. Cynthia's whole demeanor was unexpected. He didn't regret divorcing her for Katalin, but seeing her this way made him regret that he had never found this side of her before.

"I don't know, but it's certainly worth a visit." He looked at her, saw her trepidation about introducing herself to her own child, and suddenly he saw Márta's face. He, too, had a child whom he had yet to claim as a parent. "He's your son. You should know who he is. And he should know you."

Cynthia stared at him. It was said with such kindness, with such wishes for her success, that she nearly cried.

"How could I allow myself to lose you?" she said, reaching out, taking his face in her hands and bringing his lips to hers for a brief farewell kiss. When she released him, she held up her hands. "Don't," she said. "I can't bear sitting through another recitation of my sins and foibles. Nor can my shaky emotions handle another nice word from your mouth. We're divorcing. We're supposed to dislike each other intensely."

"I don't, you know."

"Then you're a jerk," she said, laughing, glad that the gloom that had been hovering over them had retreated to a corner. "I'm a rather detestable being."

"Only when you want to be," Steven said, laughing with her.

"I'm also rather stunning when I want to be," she said, miserable that this marriage was ending, at the same time eternally grateful that it was ending this way. "If you'll be so kind as to clear out of here, I'll begin my toilette."

"You're going to the concert?" He had hoped that she would—he didn't want anything to alert László that something might be up—but he had thought it was so far out of the realm of possibility, he had decided not to ask.

"I'm still your wife, Ambassador Kardos," she said, rising from the chaise, flinging her dark mane behind her, and tightening the sash on her peignoir. "And, in case you've forgotten, I never turn down jewelry, furs, champagne, box seats, or an opportunity to make an entrance."

Even, she reflected bitterly, when that entrance signals my exit.

At six o'clock, Zoltán entered Katalin's dressing room. She was waiting for him. They had planned on this time to say good-bye.

"Why aren't you wearing your strapless dress?" he asked, eyeing her red peasant skirt, her white blouse, and the silken shawl that girdled her hips.

"Because I wanted Mama to be with us tonight," she said, hugging him, needing to let him know how much she loved him.

When they separated, she appraised him, holding his hand and turning him about so she could see the entire picture. In his white-tie and tails he cut a dashing figure.

"You look wonderful, Papa." His response was a deep, formal bow. "I've waited a lifetime for us to perform together."

"Me too," he said, patting her hand, his head bobbing in agreement. "But this won't be the last time. You'll be back. I'll visit the United

States." Suddenly, he laughed. "Maybe your friend Greco can arrange a concert for us."

"I'll get him on it the minute I see him," she said.

They were avoiding the subject. Katalin was the first to broach it.

"Do you know what to do?" she asked, keeping her voice low. "Does Uncle Miklós know? And Tibor?"

Zoltán put his arm around her shoulder and walked her to a chair. He made her sit. He took another chair and sat across from her.

"Andras will be waiting in a taxi outside to take us to the Embassy. Each of us knows where to meet him. Each of us knows that Estridge will be in a car on the other side of the Opera Ház, just in case. We'll be fine, *edesem*. We'll all be fine."

"I don't like leaving you." She had promised herself she wouldn't make it harder on him than it already was, but she couldn't help it.

"You have to create another life for yourself, Katya, a life with István and Márta, a life filled with music and love and children and freedom. This is what your Mama wanted for you." He pressed his lips together as he conjured Mária's face. "On her deathbed, she made me swear that I would help you and István be together." He lifted his eyes toward the ceiling. "I said I would and I am," he declared to the beyond. When he looked at Katalin again, she was smiling, just as he hoped she would. "I would have come with you, but I can't leave Miklós now."

"I understand, Papa. Really, I do."

"I do need you to promise me something, though."

"Anything."

"Talk your Aunt Zsuzsanna into a visit." At the mention of her name, his lips wobbled and his smile quivered. "Tell her about Miklós. Tell her how much it would mean to the two of us if . . ."

"She'll be here," Katalin said. "And so will we."

"Good!" he said, standing, helping Katalin to her feet. "We will have dozens of family reunions and lots of happy times, but first, *kicsi szliva*, there is the music."

Katalin smiled as she walked him to the door. She had always been her father's daughter, but, she realized, never more than tonight. Despite all that was at stake, despite all the risk and the danger, she had no time to focus on it or think about it or deal with it. It had to be held in abeyance, because as Zoltán had said, *first, there was the music.*

It was the story of both their lives.

At seven o'clock, Ernie and Shadow showed their papers to the Hungarian security guards and ran through their own last-minute check.

Shadow had been through the building three times already, but it only takes five minutes to create a disaster. They inspected the fuse boxes, the entrances and exits, seating plans and stage diagrams. They went over the musical program and their own program. They clocked in with every member of their team. They scanned the seats where Steven and Cynthia and Miklós would be sitting, looking for explosives. They used a bomb detector to sweep the stage. Everything seemed to be in order, except for one thing.

While Ernie examined the piano, Shadow wanted to visit the two lighting booths. Katalin had called him earlier to report a strange sighting. He had calmed her then, assuring her it was nothing, but he didn't believe in *nothings*. To him, everything was *something*. And before his people walked into that auditorium, he was going to know exactly what that something was.

By seven forty-five, most of the seats were filled. László was pacing in the lobby. He had expected Gorbachev and his entourage to make a late entrance, but with only fifteen minutes before the start of the concert, there had been no sign of any of them, not even the Soviet ambassador, and he came to everything.

Imre Pozsgay and his group had appeared quite a while ago. László had hated being forced to explain the delayed arrival of his honored guests. He felt as if they had him on the defensive, which was not at all where he had planned to be. After a brief conversation, they had congratulated him on a successful evening, milled about with several other reformers, and eventually went inside to take their seats.

Five minutes later, Judit Weiss had passed him, literally. She had never liked him, that much he knew, but to snub him publicly was galling. Then again, he reminded himself, she had never been known for obedience or manners. He did find it curious that she had been alone. It took a minute before he realized that Gábor was probably on call or still in surgery. But why hadn't Andras escorted her? he wondered. With Ilona out at Leányfalu, he was probably babysitting the children.

When the American ambassador and his wife made their appearance, all heads turned, including László's. Cynthia carried herself like an empress, her sable coat and French perfume eliciting oohs and aahs from those still in the lobby and those looking down from the balcony above. László could see the diamonds at her throat and at her ears. He could only imagine the stir she would create when she took her place and removed her coat. Hungarians weren't used to Western style, particularly wealthy Western style.

As she wafted by him, László suffered a momentary pang of envy. Steven had Katalin in love with him and this exquisite creature on his arm. László was not a man who ever felt the need to make an emotional connection with a female—a sexual connection was all he required, all he wanted—but the few times when Katalin had reached him, those times when, due to her dogged perseverance, she had penetrated his thick, protective walls and made him care, he had to admit, it had been pleasant.

He watched them ascend the staircase. They moved like royalty. It grated on him that people actually stepped aside as they went by. Who were they to be accorded that kind of respect when they had shown him none? Surely, his enemies had noticed that Steven had ignored him. Surely, they would make much out of the fact that the American ambassador had passed by the Hungarian minister of commerce without so much as a one-word greeting. He wanted to make Steven pay for his slight, but he couldn't, not yet.

After Steven had left his office, László had spent the rest of the day sniffing out where Steven had been, whom he had seen, and what, if anything, his snitches could tell him about what had been said. So far, there had been no repercussions. Grósz hadn't called or come storming into his office. There had been no messages from any other Party officials. And there had been no calls from the Soviets.

And no Soviets here at the concert, he reminded himself, allowing a flash of panic to charge through his body. Quickly, he regrouped and made the decision to take his seat. He was beginning to look foolish standing by himself. As he mounted the steps and headed for the circle level, he concluded that their tardiness was most likely a matter of security. He didn't know why he hadn't thought of it before. Gorbachev's people probably didn't enter any public place until everyone was seated.

The moment he entered the gilded box of honor, he felt better. Hundreds of eyes turned toward him. He saw dislike in some, disinterest in others, but in most, he was certain he read respect. To them, he tilted his head in a modest bow. Then, he took his seat, ignoring the empty seats around him, hoping it looked as if there was no reason for concern, that his guests were expected to be late. Suddenly, the chairs around him filled. Next to him was the head of the Hungarian Secret Police. Surrounding him were members of that elite group.

"What's going on?" László said, refusing to allow concern to appear on his face.

"President Gorbachev left for Moscow at four o'clock this afternoon. He sent his tickets to Prime Minister Grósz, who sent the tickets to us. Didn't anyone tell you?"

László didn't answer. He couldn't. Fear had clogged his throat like thick phlegm, filling it so full that he could hardly breathe. Suddenly, his ears clogged with the sound of applause. Zoltán Gáspár had taken the stage. The concert had begun.

In the booth alongside the giant spotlight, someone watched the concert with special interest. Someone who didn't know one concerto from another, or consider it important to do so. There was only one moment that made a difference. It was that second between the end of a piece and the beginning of the applause, that infinitesimal window of silence that this particular someone was waiting for. Because it was then that the gun would be fired.

The Kodály and the Brahms were completed. There had been a brief intermission and now that everyone had been seated, including some stragglers, Zoltán stepped off his podium and walked to the microphone.

"It is always a great pleasure for a conductor to introduce a soloist of such enormous stature. For me, this is an exceptional pleasure because, tonight, the soloist is my daughter and this is the first time we have performed together."

The audience burst into applause. The Magyars were an emotional people who laughed as easily as they cried. They were also a people who treasured their talents. Having two such extraordinary artists from the same family on the same stage was special indeed, evoking an outpouring of appreciation that rocked the hall with its enthusiasm. When quiet had been restored, Zoltán continued his introduction.

"Making this evening even more special, especially for Katalin and me, is that another member of our family is with us tonight."

László's heart began to thump. His eyes scanned the darkness. He didn't know whom he was looking for, but something told him this relative, whoever it might be, was important to him.

"Thirty-two years ago, almost to this day, my brother Gáspár Miklós disappeared."

The silence thickened. Many could not believe that Zoltán had used this platform to mention the event that had changed their lives, that cataclysmic week the Hungarians called an uprising and the Soviets insisted upon calling a counter-revolution. They could not believe that Zoltán had raised the forbidden name of one of the leaders of that insurgency. It was like talking about Imre Nagy or László Rajk. It wasn't done. It wasn't safe. Just that afternoon, a peaceful rally organized to commemorate the occasion had been broken up by police, the same police sitting in the box of honor with László Böhm.

"Gáspár Miklós has returned," Zoltán said, noting with pleasure the gasps that flickered throughout the hall like fireflies. "He is here tonight and it is to him that my daughter and I dedicate the performance of the Concerto Number One by Franz Liszt."

Zoltán raised his hand toward the box where the American ambassador was seated. Slowly, a stooped, elderly gentlemen with hoary white hair and fire-intense eyes stood. Dumbstruck, the audience simply stared. When they realized the import of Miklós's return—where he had been, who had held him, the courage and fortitude it had taken to survive, the grit it had required to come back—they took to their feet and before the police and members of the Council of Ministers and ranking officials of the Party, they welcomed Miklós home.

László rubbed his temples with his fingers, trying to soothe the blinding pain that gripped his head like a vise. *So that was Kardos's unimpeachable witness.* Above the shouting and clapping and foot stomping, he heard the mumbling of the Police Chief and his cohorts. László wanted to laugh in their faces. He had warned them. He had tried to tell them. Go back to the old ways. Govern. Rule. Dominate. But no one would listen. They had capitulated and because they had, they had lost control. If they weren't careful, they would lose the country.

The armed spectator watched. Katalin completed the first movement of the Liszt. There was stillness. The trigger cocked. But there was no applause. Instead, the music began again. The gun fell to the person's side. It didn't matter how long it took, soon it would come.

The end of the music. The end of a life.

They came from the bowels of the building, up through the grand lobby, behind the massive stage, into the corridors, and through the doors. They moved silently, spreading throughout the hall like an infectious plague. The audience was too entranced with Katalin's performance to notice the force that was gathering behind it. She was close to the end of the third movement when the first sound was heard.

"Vadrósza!"

It was soft, a whisper, a hint.

"Vadrósza!"

It grew, increasing in volume like a gentle snow that suddenly becomes a storm.

"Vadrósza!"

They filled the auditorium, chanting, stamping their feet, demanding that the orchestra cease and heed their call. The orchestra complied. Zoltán turned and watched as the aisles filled and the boxes overflowed with gypsies. People in the audience recoiled. László, who thought he had seen the worst of this nightmare, felt himself gasping for air. Tibor rested his violin on his lap and shook his head in despair. His black eyes scanned the horde that had invaded the Opera Ház, looking for her. She was there somewhere, leading this pack of wolves. *What the hell did she want?*

Steven's eyebrows knitted together in a tight line of concern. How could this have happened? Everything had been planned to the minute. They couldn't afford any disruptions. His eyes flew to László. Was he the one responsible for this? If so, how much else did he know? Steven couldn't decide whether he was pleased or worried that László appeared as confused and unsettled by this commotion as he was. If this wasn't Böhm's handiwork, whose was it? And who was Vadrósza?

"What's going on?" Cynthia's voice rang with alarm. Instinctively, she had removed her earrings, tossed them in her purse and tightened her coat over her body.

"I don't know, but you're leaving. Now!"

Before they had left their house, Steven had told Cynthia his plans— it would have been unfair not to—and had given her the option of attending or not. He had been gratified when she had agreed. Now, he was sorry he had dragged her into this. Whatever their problems had been, she did not deserve to be caught in any of his crossfire. Without listening to her protests, Steven summoned the aide closest to him.

"Get Mrs. Kardos out of here and to the airport as quickly as possible." A private plane was waiting to take her to Paris.

As she rose to go, her exit accompanied by the rising chorus of "Vadrósza!" Steven caught her arm and pulled her face down to his. "Be happy," he said, as he kissed her good-bye.

She lingered. She didn't want to leave him, now or ever. Steven's aide tugged at her. She was wasting precious time. The melee was growing. "You too," she said, as she followed the young man out. "Be safe."

"Vadrósza! Vadrósza!"

A crowd of gypsies had gathered in front of the stage, clapping their hands in Katalin's face. She had known from the start that this moment would come, this moment of public confession and disclosure. As she shifted position on her bench, turning toward the audience, her eyes rose to the box of honor. László leaned on the railing and glared at her, just as he had when she had first come onstage. She thought he seemed more hysterical now, more frightened. Oddly enough, Katalin understood. He did not suffer humiliation well. For his comrades to know that his wife consorted with gypsies, for strangers to think he had approved of such ignominy, this would be the ultimate disgrace, the final blow to his staggering pride.

Katalin's eyes traveled from László to Steven. He looked confused, as well he might be, but supportive and loving, as she knew he would be. Knowing he was there, Miklós alongside him, that Zoltán and Tibor were behind her, she stood, commanding silence. Slowly, with a deliberate pace designed to show no fear, she approached the microphone.

Looking out into the audience and speaking in a cool, clear voice, she said, "For those of you who don't know, Vadrósza is a musician. She plays cymbalom with a band of gypsies that performs throughout the countryside, in parks and in restaurants, in fields and from the back of trucks. She has done so for years, with great pride and great humility, grateful that they would permit her to play with them."

Katalin paused, staring down at those who had wanted her to deny her connection to them, staring directly into the eyes of Farah Tar, who had elbowed her way to the front, needing to witness Katalin's downfall and her own vindication firsthand.

"I am Vadrósza," Katalin declared, ignoring the shocked gasps and confused mumbles and whispered asides that rippled throughout the audience, ignoring the look of disappointment on Farah's face. "These gypsies came here to scandalize me, to embarrass and shame me, but it is they who should be ashamed. They should be ashamed to admit that their intention was to use your bigotry against them to hurt me. They believed that if you knew I had cast my lot with them, you would shun me, as you shun them."

So many faces. So many different reactions.

"I am a woman obsessed with music," she said. "I love it. I breathe it. I need it to exist. Because of that, I don't care where it comes from or who plays it or listens to it. To me, music transcends everything." She turned her head toward Tibor. A quick smile from her, an understanding nod from him. He rose and the crowd fidgeted. "Let me show you what the gypsies taught me," Katalin said, returning to the piano. "Let me show you who Vadrósza is."

Her fingers descended onto the keyboard swiftly and decisively. Tibor's bow swept across the strings of his violin. Within seconds, the lightning-fast rhythms of the *csárdás* bolted from the stage into every corner of the gilded hall, charging the air with an electricity that fired the souls of everyone there. With deliberate ceremony, Zoltán raised a violin to his chin and began to play. Several other violinists followed his lead. Two of the clarinetists joined in, three cellists, a bass, a flute, and then more. The magic of *cigányzene* permeated the atmosphere. Soon, reluctant hands left their laps and clapped in time to the gypsy music. Feet heavy with skepticism tapped against the floor.

Katalin heard the din and smiled, knowing that the *duende* had come. She felt his presence as surely as she felt the ivory beneath her fingers. She let his spirit enter through the soles of her feet, rushing upward until it filled her blood and dizzied her head. It was no wonder she never heard the first shot.

When the second one was fired, everyone heard it. Bodies fell to the floor. People screamed. The lights went out, heightening the level of agitation.

"Katalin!" Zoltán rushed to his daughter's side and grabbed her hand. "Let's go! Now!"

With Tibor's help, he pulled Katalin to her feet. Hurrying, climbing over others, frantically trying to escape, they left the stage. Because the extinguishing of the lights had been part of the plan, Tibor had come prepared. Leading the way, his flashlight making a path through the warren of hallways and opera sets, the three of them circled around to the front of the house. Steven had guessed correctly, that if László had posted guards to block Katalin's exit, they would have been positioned near her dressing room, adjacent to the rear doors. Instead, Steven had them walk out the front, buried in a mass of bodies.

Directly in front of the building, just outside the grand arcade, an ambulance and a taxicab waited. Zoltán hugged Katalin and helped her into the ambulance. The door closed, the siren wailed, the flashing light atop its roof began to blink, and the vehicle sped into the midst of traffic, heading for the airport. Zoltán couldn't afford to watch his daughter leave, just as they hadn't been able to spend a moment on a good-bye. As he climbed into the taxi next to Andras and watched Tibor jump in the back where Miklós was, he decided it was just as well. Better to think about the next time they would see each other, better to think about hello than good-bye.

Inside the Opera Ház, confusion reigned. The lights had been restored, but calm had not. People couldn't get out fast enough. Stair-

ways were jammed. Aisles were blocked. Doorways were plastered with
bodies trying to escape what they thought was the start of a coup. They
needn't have panicked. It wasn't a coup. It was simply the settling of
a score.

At the same time as László was being led out of the auditorium by
the head of the Secret Police, the would-be assassin sat cowering against
the wall of the small booth, his body bent in an arc of agony.

"It's a good thing Katalin called me," Shadow said. "And it's a good
thing that your reflexes are so fast."

Ernie had grabbed the gunman's arm just as he was about to fire,
diverting his aim so that both shots had hit the ceiling and not a
person.

"Thank goodness you found the top of that cartridge box in here
this afternoon," Ernie said, "If you hadn't, someone would have been
history."

Shadow watched the ugly old man on the floor writhe in pain.

"That someone was probably going to be László, but after him, who
knows. It could have been Miklós and Zoltán and Katalin. All in one
round." Shadow looked at his watch. If everything had worked, they were
gone by now, on their way to their safe havens. "Do you know who he
is?" he asked Ernie.

"Damn right I do," Ernie said, legs apart, arms akimbo, eyes glued
to his prisoner.

Just then, Ferenc Kassak looked up, his left hand supporting the
remnants of his right. His eyes flamed with hatred.

"That's why I broke his fucking hand," Ernie said, matching the old
man's ire. "What goes around, comes around!"

The American Air Force helicopter lifted off its pad at Ferihegy
Airport. As it turned west, Steven took Katalin's hand. She was still
shaking.

"It's over, Katya," he said. "Estridge notified the pilot that everyone's
safe. Your father and uncle and Tibor are in the Embassy and will stay
there until we know it's okay for them to leave. László's being detained
at Fő Street. The word is he's going to be held over for trial. Matthew
and Márta are waiting for us in Austria. In a short while we'll all be
together. It's over."

Katalin allowed him to wipe the tears that dampened her cheeks.
She loved him so ferociously it was impossible to have any regrets. But
in her heart, in that tiny space that even love couldn't fill, was the

knowledge that she had left family and friends behind, that despite the rumors and the compromises and the promises, barbed wire still defined the borders that separated them, oppressors still governed the land they lived in, and freedom still remained a dream. Much as she wanted to agree with Steven, she couldn't. Because it wasn't over. Not yet.

VI

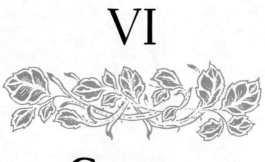

Encore

1989

38

Budapest, October 23, 1989

The mighty organ of the Matthias Church asserted itself, announcing to all who would listen that a ceremony of joy was about to begin. Shafts of morning sunlight sliced through the stained-glass windows, trembling as waves of sound filled the Gothic structure atop the Buda Hills. As each member of the wedding party entered, a chapter in the history of the couple exchanging vows unfolded.

Ilona had insisted upon navigating the aisle with only Andras's arm and a cane for support. For her, this was not only a celebration of marriage, but a fitting memorial for two women whom she had loved and lost. Ilona's step was slow and unsteady, yet as she moved toward the altar, she felt infused with an energy that could only have come from the spirit. She smiled. Mária was on her right. Margit was on her left. How happy they would be if only they knew what was taking place this day.

Andras helped Ilona into the chair at the top of the altar steps. He took his place behind his wife and with a full heart watched as his son-in-law, Gábor, strode down the center aisle of the ancient church, a child on either side. The awesome majesty of Matthias had subdued his grandchildren, Sarí and Endre. Andras had to stifle a smile as he watched them strain to stay in step while at the same time satisfy their curiosity about the ornately decorated walls and the intimidating statuary.

He looked at Ilona and then back at Gábor. It must have been God who had brought this young man to them, placing him at Shalom so he could befriend Ilona, so that when she was pushed into the path of a speeding trolley, he would be there to save her. A familiar wave of nausea washed over Andras as he thought about what could have happened. What had happened was dreadful enough. He recalled the weeks of recuperation, the months of therapy, her first step. She had stumbled and fallen to the floor. When Andras had started for Ilona, Gábor had raised his hand, signaling that Andras should stay back and let Ilona fend for herself. Time after time, her leg would give out, sending her sprawling to the floor; but her will prevailed, and eventually she learned to function within the confines of her disability. Andras knew he had Gábor to thank for that.

This same young man had performed another miracle. What a shock when Zoltán, with a mischievous glint, had asked Andras to play their favorite Mozart piece and had accompanied him on the violin. To this day, Andras could not think about it without his heart rising into his throat.

The third in Gábor's trilogy of blessings had been the way he had changed Judit's life, and for that, Andras was also eternally grateful. Gábor adored Judit, and because he wasn't shy about it, constantly reaffirming both his love for her as well as his admiration, he provided her with balance and a sense of security. For most of her life, Judit had believed that everyone was demanding that she prove herself. With Gábor, she had learned that she had nothing to prove. She merely had to be.

As Gábor, Sarí, and Endre joined the Strassers, Zsuzsanna and Miklós began the joyful journey down the center of the nave. For Zsuzsanna, because this was her second trip to Hungary in a year, this felt like a movement in a symphony of feeling. Returning to Hungary continued to be a trauma. After so many years in the United States, harboring anger at what had made her leave and anger at that which kept her separated from those of her blood, it was difficult to walk the streets of Budapest without enduring torrents of highs and lows. Remembering who had lived there, what had happened here, seeing people she had known when they were young, asking about others and being told they had never grown to be old—it made her forget those dreams that had not been realized and be grateful for those that had been.

Like being united with not one, but *two* of her brothers. Their initial reunion—at Christmas last year—had reduced her to a quivering mass of tears. She could not listen to Miklós's account of his imprisonment without having her hands on him, touching him, reassuring herself that those barbarian jailers had not maimed him or harmed him in an irreparable way. Despite Zoltán's assurances that Miklós was in relative good health, both mentally and physically, she had insisted upon playing psychologist with him, quizzing him, asking questions, trying to discern what, if any, mental damage he might have suffered. He was changed—how could he not be?—but in the end, she was satisfied that his soul had remained intact. Miklós was who he had always been—a reformer, a fighter, a man who knew that freedom was an instinct, not a theory.

And Zoltán! Head conductor of the Budapest Symphony Orchestra! Playing the violin again! A grandfather! It made her head swim. As she glanced over at Miklós, she saw that he, too, was overwhelmed by the emotion of the day. Her arm was linked through his, just as her blood was linked with his. Needing to feel the reality of his presence, she pulled him closer. He turned and smiled. In his eyes she saw tears that mirrored her own.

They stood on the right of the altar, clinging to each other as the groom and his best man began their march. Zsuzsanna could hardly believe that these two marvelously handsome men were the two small boys who had accompanied her and Mihai on their escape to Andau. In a way, she supposed little had changed. The bravery they had demonstrated then had evidenced itself many times over the course of their lives, as had their closeness. Few shared the kind of fraternal loyalty that these men had. Then again, few had been bound together by the tragedy and hardship that forged them. Still, who could have guessed that Mátyás would become the financial whiz that he was? And István? He had resigned his post as ambassador and moved to New York with Katalin and Márta, so she could pursue her career and he could run for the Senate in 1990.

Zsuzsanna had thanked God a thousand times for that fateful day when Steven and Shadow had walked into Csárda. She had known then that Steven and Katalin were destined to be together, and she had been right. What she hadn't known, but what had given her equal pleasure, was that Matthew and her darling Sophie had found each other as well. Just four months ago, Zsuzsanna had stood up for them, watching with a mother's pride as Sophie Wisnewski and Mátyás Kardos were united in marriage. Today, that bride was one of the matrons of honor for this bride.

As Sophie turned the corner and graced the aisle, her hair teased, spiked, and streaked hot red, Matthew caught her eye, and winked, and grinned at his wife. Only Sophie would think that a red suit fringed from collar to hem was appropriate fare for a matron of honor. Only Sophie could carry it off.

When she approached the altar, Steven stepped to the side, making room for his new sister-in-law and then, moments later, for Katalin's other matron of honor, Judit. He smiled at Ernie and Shadow and a nervous Paprika followed, they, too, taking their places. It was when Márta stood at the top of the aisle, however, that Steven thought his heart would burst.

He and Katalin had explained things to Márta in a simple way, that the man she had thought was her daddy wasn't really, that Steven was and would be forever, that he loved her and her mommy and would love and protect them forever. Though Márta hadn't quite understood the logistics, she had been thrilled by the basics. László had never allowed a connection to form between him and Márta, so there was no cord to sever. If Steven harbored any concern about his standing with his daughter, it was allayed when he extended his hand to help her up the steps and she asked, in her sweet baby-girl voice, "Did I do okay, Daddy?" When he picked her up, held her in his arms, and answered, "You did fine," she said, "Good, because I love you and I like doing okay for you."

The pipes of the organ swelled, rejoicing in the appearance of the bride and her father. Katalin wore a simple white suit and a hat with a short veil. She carried Mária's Bible, which had been covered with a spray of white roses. One pink wild rose peeked out from the lush bouquet. Tibor had taken his children and gone to Yugoslavia, where he had secured a job with an orchestra. Paprika had given Katalin the blossom with Tibor's love. Katalin had accepted it with pride.

As Zoltán escorted her toward her groom, he marveled at his daughter's beauty and at her courage. She had willed this day. She had been determined to marry the man she loved here in Hungary where they had met and first known each other, here in the same church where she had said good-bye to her mother and had christened her daughter. While it was true that she had wed László here, to her that had been a horrid mistake that needed to be corrected by the rightness of what was taking place here today.

Zoltán hadn't thought the Church would allow Katalin and Steven to marry, but since Steven had been married in a civil ceremony and Katalin's marriage—owing to the fact that László had never informed her of his sterility—had been annulled, the priest had found no reason to deny Katalin's request to be married in the sight of God.

Though standard procedure called for the father of the bride to hand over his daughter to her future husband, Katalin had cast aside tradition. In keeping with her desire to have this ceremony reflect the unique spirituality of this day, Zoltán and she mounted the steps and took their places, she to Steven's right, Zoltán to her right. When all were assembled, a garland of bright red roses was unfolded, starting at one end with Ilona, ending at the opposite end with Shadow. As each member of the wedding party took hold of the floral rope, each was linked with the next, all were linked with the bride and groom.

Katalin and Steven had not come to this moment without the love of each and every person standing with them. Nor were they taking vows as youngsters with eyes blinded by the glare of their hopes for the future. They shared a past. They shared a child. They shared memories of pain and loss as well as memories of joy and rediscovery. But most of all, they had shared themselves with everyone here. This morning, they were not being joined merely as husband and wife, but they and Márta were being united as a family. They would take their vows surrounded by those whom they considered part of that family.

At noon, the bells from Matthias Church and every other church in Budapest tolled. Memorial plaques were unveiled at sites of significant battles. Wreaths were laid. Patriotic poems were read. And tens of thousands of people thronged Parliament Square to mark the thirty-third anniversary of the uprising against Soviet oppression and to declare Hungary a republic.

In the center of the square, Steven and Katalin, Matthew and Sophie, Zoltán and Zsuzsanna, Judit and Gábor, Andras and Ilona, and the children gathered to share in the momentous occasion. On their arms were bands of red, white, and green. Many around them wore the same bands. Many carried flags with the communist hammer and sickle rent from the middle, as the insurgents had done in '56. Some yelled, "Russians go home!" Some shouted, "Gorby! Gorby!" Others wept for the time and the lives lost between that day so many years before and now. Others wept for joy.

Katalin glanced at Márta perched on Steven's shoulders and saw herself and Judit at six years old, riding their fathers' shoulders, chanting slogans they didn't fully understand, waving flags because they had thought it was fun. Their parents hadn't come to sing or to have a good time. They had believed democracy was at hand. Katalin hadn't known then what democracy was.

She looked at Matthew, his visage stern, his face reflecting the pain of the second day they had gathered in this same square—the day his parents had been shot down for no reason, the day everyone's hopes had died for no reason other than the voracious appetite of the Russian Bear for power and territorial gain.

She looked from Matthew to Steven and thought about Vera. Poor, frail Vera. She had never known anything other than discomfort and fear. Throughout her short life, she had been protected from the weather and overexertion and stress and too much cake and too little milk and anything else the Kardoses had thought would tax her heart. In the end, there was no protection strong enough to save her from events so completely beyond her control that they changed the course of history—and in doing so, forever altered her life. She had tried to run, just as she had tried to live, using every scintilla of strength and fortitude she possessed, but in the end her first taste of freedom had been her last. Over the years, Katalin had thought about Vera often. She had missed her. On this day, she missed her more than ever.

When Katalin looked at her father and Zsuzsanna, she felt glad for them, knowing how happy they were to be reunited at last. She studied their faces. There, among lines etched by age, were tears formed by memories of those they had lost. Mária, their parents, their brothers, their friends and neighbors. Yet, there was a brightness in those tears as they lifted their faces toward the balcony where Prime Minister Imre Nagy had stood thirty-three years earlier, inspiring a nation of rebels to follow their cause. Standing on that balcony now, with a portrait of Nagy behind him, was their brother Miklós, the boy who once took Zoltán out to the Hortobágy in search of the Fata Morgana, the young man who could quote philosophy while riding bareback on one of György's horses, the leader who had fired a nation to fight for what they believed. As he stepped up to the microphone to speak, Katalin watched Zoltán and Zsuzsanna embrace.

"Thirty-three years ago today, we stood in this square and pleaded for democracy. We begged our oppressors to grant us the right to be free and independent. They denied us, and in doing so they thought that they had silenced us, that they had defeated us. Yet here we are," he said, describing the immenseness of the crowd with a sweep of his arm. "On this day of national reconciliation, I remember and pay tribute to those who died in that rebellion thirty-three years ago. I remember and pay tribute to those who paid the price for their courage over those days, in foreign prisons and frozen labor camps. I honor those I never knew, but who continued the fight in their own way over all these long years of enforced silence and lonely struggle. And I honor all of you who stand before me now, those true and faithful Hungarians who never forgot the week in 1956 that became the wellspring of the democracy we declare today. Let freedom ring!"

Katalin felt Steven's arm slide around her waist. She leaned in against him, needing to feel his flesh against hers. Neither of them could find their voices to say what was in their hearts. For herself, Katalin felt no need to speak. She had Steven, they had their daughter, they had their family around them, and they had lived to see this glorious, miraculous day.

As Katalin drank in the sights and sounds of it, she knew there was no need for words. Uncle Miklós had said it all—*Let freedom ring!*